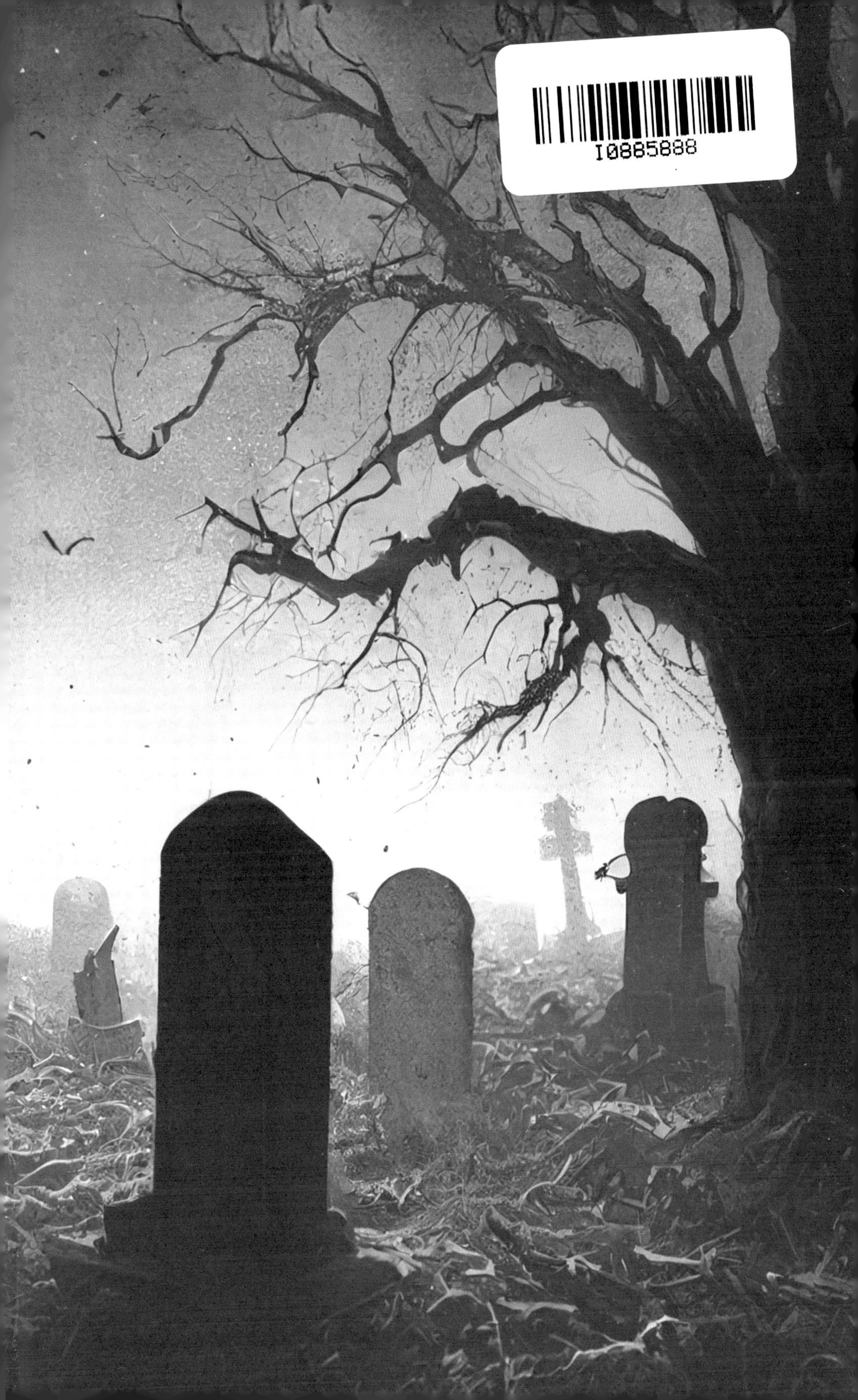

THE CLASSIC
EDGAR ALLAN POE
COLLECTION

THE CLASSIC
EDGAR ALLAN POE
COLLECTION

SIRIUS

SIRIUS

This edition published in 2025 by Sirius Publishing, a division of
Arcturus Publishing Limited,
26/27 Bickels Yard, 151–153 Bermondsey Street,
London SE1 3HA

Cover design: Peter Ridley
Cover illustration: Riptaid

ISBN: 978-1-3988-6099-5
AD005937US

Printed in China

CONTENTS

INTRODUCTION

Edgar Allan Poe was born in Boston, Massachusetts, in 1809 to a family of traveling actors. Only a year after he was born, his father abandoned him, and soon after his mother died. The newly orphaned Poe was informally adopted by two prominent Virginian tobacconists, John and Frances Allan. His relationship with his new father was a strained one, but John Allan's financial assets were able to provide the young Poe with an education and a head-start to his literary career. Moving from place to place, Poe never put down roots as a child. In 1815, the family moved from their house in Richmond to England and then to Scotland.

Poe soon began to show his intellectual gifts. He attended a grammar school in Irvine, Scotland for a year before returning to his family in London, where he joined a boarding school until 1817. There, he demonstrated his talents for languages. By the time he was 11, the family would be moving again, this time back to Richmond, Virginia. In 1826, he attended the newly founded University of Virginia. These early educational influences would show through in his later writings. His characters frequently use Latin and Ancient Greek while the complexity of prose that set him apart from his peers owed much to these early years.

At the University of Virginia, though, he found himself surrounded by Southern gentlemen. Though fairly well off, his adopted father was unable to provide Edgar with the same level of financial support as his classmates. Frustrated by the situation, Poe took what money he had and gambled it, hoping to earn the wealth required to be accepted into these social circles. It did not achieve what he had hoped it would.

Instead, saddled with significant debts, his father withdrew his support for the young man.

It was at this challenging time in 1827 that Poe published his first book, *Tamerlane and Other Poems*. Lacking both connections and finances, he was forced to enlist in the military. In 1830, he was admitted to West Point, the most prestigious officer training institution in the country. His temperament was entirely unsuited to the profession and just a year later he was dismissed.

By this time, Poe had obtained a modicum of literary success. He had a sonnet in the popular *Saturday Evening Post* published, and a new edition of poetry followed. In 1832, his first short stories appeared— "Metzengerstein" and "Bon-Bon." In these tales, he took the themes of metempsychosis, the return of human souls to animal bodies, and the idea of a deal with the devil, and put a new spin on old ideas.

Poe viewed his fellow writers as banal, commercial and populist. Unwilling to compromise his principles, he nevertheless yearned for fame. From an editorial position at the *Southern Literary Messenger*, which Poe took up in 1835, he was able to bring his sensational writings to a wider audience. One of these was "Berenice," a controversial story involving premature burial that led to a wave of complaints from horrified readers. Despite the controversy, Poe's unique style continued to draw readers in.

His marriage to his 13-year-old cousin Virginia Clemm in 1836 provided him with the inspiration for many of the female characters that fill his writing. The women of Poe's tales are often ill, pale and beautiful, and mirror the suffering his young wife was undergoing in her battle against tuberculosis. She was diagnosed with the disease in 1842.

It was one poem that would change Poe's fortunes: "The Raven". Published in 1845, he was asked to give recitations and toured America giving lectures on poetry. Today, it remains one of the most haunting and powerful pieces of American literature. With fame came rivals. Critics accused him of plagiarism and described him as a drunk. When his wife Virginia died in 1847, he soon moved on and married his childhood sweetheart, Elmira Royston, much to her family's consternation.

His success was short-lived. In October 1849, Edgar Allan Poe died in Baltimore. He was found delirious on the streets before being taken to the Washington Medical College but was unable to explain how he arrived in his condition. Local newspapers reported the cause of his death as "cerebral inflammation," a phrase often used at the time to hide alcoholism. Mystery continues to surround the circumstances of his death today. It is not clear why he was in Baltimore, as he lived in Richmond, and theories ranging from heart disease to syphilis, and even electoral fraud, have been put forward to explain his death.

This collection contains a selection of his writings ranging from his macabre stories to his otherworldly poetry. In "The Tell-Tale Heart," Poe wrote one of the true classics of Gothic fiction as an unnamed narrator tells the story of a murder he committed. "The Murders of the Rue Morgue" tells an entirely different type of story, establishing the detective story in the process, as C. Auguste Dupin attempts to solve the appalling murders of two women. His one and only novel, *The Narrative of Arthur Gordon Pym of Nantucket*, told what seems at first a conventional maritime adventure that becomes stranger and more horrifying as the tale progresses.

While Poe died young, his writing lived on. Consisting of countless short stories, numerous poems, non-fiction essays and a single complete novel. It took time for the memory of the writer to recover from the unscrupulous reputation he had developed in the United States. In Europe, however, Charles Baudelaire devoted himself to translating Poe's stories into French. His new audience appreciated his writing more than his American contemporaries had, and his influence spread quickly. Science fiction, horror, and mystery writers, including Jules Verne, Arthur Conan Doyle, and H. P. Lovecraft turned to Poe for their inspiration. They found outlandishness, fantasy, the macabre, and the scientific united all in a singular style, utterly different from the literary fashions of the time. Unappreciated in his life, Poe became a literary giant in the afterlife.

TALES

CONTENTS

MS. FOUND IN A BOTTLE

Qui n'a plus qu'un moment à vivre
N'a plus rien à dissimuler.[1]
Quinault, *Atys*

OF MY COUNTRY and of my family I have little to say. Ill-usage and length of years have driven me from the one, and estranged me from the other. Hereditary wealth afforded me an education of no common order, and a contemplative turn of mind enabled me to methodize the stores which early study diligently garnered up. Beyond all things, the works of the German moralists gave me great delight; not from my ill-advised admiration of their eloquent madness, but from the ease with which my habits of rigid thoughts enabled me to detect their falsities. I have often been reproached with the aridity of my genius; a deficiency of imagination has been imputed to me as a crime; and the Pyrrhonism of my opinions has at all times rendered me notorious. Indeed, a strong relish for physical philosophy has, I fear, tinctured my mind with a very common error of this age—I mean the habit of referring occurrences, even the least susceptible of such reference, to the principles of that science. Upon the whole, no person could be less liable than myself to be led away from the severe precincts of truth by the *ignes fatui* of superstition. I have thought proper to premise this much, lest the incredible tale I have to tell should be considered rather the raving of a crude imagination, than the positive experience of a mind to which the reveries of fancy have been a dead letter and a nullity.

After many years spent in foreign travel, I sailed in the year 18—, from

1 He who has but a moment to live has no longer anything to dissemble.

the port of Batavia, in the rich and populous island of Java, on a voyage to the Archipelago Islands. I went as passenger—having no other inducement than a kind of nervous restlessness which haunted me as a fiend.

Our vessel was a beautiful ship of about four hundred tons, copper-fastened, and built at Bombay of Malabar teak. She was freighted with cotton-wool and oil, from the Lachadive Islands. We had also on board coir, jaggeree, ghee, cocoanuts, and a few cases of opium. The stowage was clumsily done, and the vessel consequently crank.

We got under way with a mere breath of wind, and for many days stood along the eastern coast of Java, without any other incident to beguile the monotony of our course than the occasional meeting with some of the small grabs of the Archipelago to which we were bound.

One evening, leaning over the taffrail, I observed a very singular isolated cloud, to the N. W. It was remarkable, as well from its color as from its being the first we had seen since our departure from Batavia. I watched it attentively until sunset, when it spread all at once to the eastward and westward, girting the horizon with a narrow strip of vapor, and looking like a long line of low beach. My notice was soon afterward attracted by the dusky-red appearance of the moon, and the peculiar character of the sea. The latter was undergoing a rapid change, and the water seemed more than usually transparent. Although I could distinctly see the bottom, yet, heaving the lead, I found the ship in fifteen fathoms. The air now became intolerably hot, and was loaded with spiral exhalations similar to those arising from heated iron. As night came on, every breath of wind died away, and a more entire calm it is impossible to conceive. The flame of a candle burned upon the poop without the least perceptible motion, and a long hair, held between the finger and thumb, hung without the possibility of detecting a vibration. However, as the captain said he could perceive no indication of danger, and as we were drifting in bodily to shore, he ordered the sails to be furled, and the anchor let go. No watch was set, and the crew, consisting principally of Malays, stretched themselves deliberately upon deck. I went below—not without a full presentiment of evil. Indeed, every appearance warranted me in apprehending a simoom. I told the captain of my fears; but he paid no attention to what I said, and left me without deigning to give a reply. My uneasiness, however, prevented me from sleeping, and about midnight I went upon deck. As I placed my foot upon the upper step of the companion-ladder, I was startled by a loud, humming noise, like that occasioned by the rapid revolution of a mill-wheel, and before I could ascertain its meaning, I found the ship quivering to its center. In the next instant a wilderness of foam hurled us upon our beam-ends, and, rushing over us fore and aft, swept the entire decks from stem to stern.

The extreme fury of the blast proved, in a great measure, the salvation of the ship. Although completely water-logged, yet, as her masts had gone by the board, she rose, after a minute, heavily from the sea, and, staggering awhile beneath the immense pressure of the tempest, finally righted.

By what miracle I escaped destruction, it is impossible to say. Stunned by the shock of the water, I found myself, upon recovery, jammed in between the stern-post and rudder. With great difficulty I regained my feet, and looking dizzily around, was at first struck with the idea of our being among breakers; so terrific, beyond the wildest imagination, was the whirlpool of mountainous and foaming ocean within which we were engulfed. After a while I heard the voice of an old Swede, who had shipped with us at the moment of leaving port. I hallooed to him with all my strength, and presently he came reeling aft. We soon discovered that we were the sole survivors of the accident. All on deck, with the exception of ourselves, had been swept overboard; the captain and mates must have perished while they slept, for the cabins were deluged with water. Without assistance we could expect to do little for the security of the ship, and our exertions were at first paralysed by the momentary expectation of going down. Our cable had, of course, parted like pack-thread, at the first breath of the hurricane, or we should have been instantaneously overwhelmed. We scudded with frightful velocity before the sea, and the water made clear breaches over us. The framework of our stern was shattered excessively, and, in almost every respect, we had received considerable injury; but to our extreme joy we found the pumps unchoked, and that we had made no great shifting of our ballast. The main fury of the blast had already blown over, and we apprehended little danger from the violence of the wind; but we looked forward to its total cessation with dismay; well believing, that in our shattered condition, we should inevitably perish in the tremendous swell which would ensue. But this very just apprehension seemed by no means likely to be soon verified. For five entire days and nights—during which our only substance was a small quantity of jaggeree, procured with great difficulty from the forecastle—the hulk flew at a rate defying computation, before rapidly succeeding flaws of wind, which, without equaling the first violence of the simoom, were still more terrific than any tempest I had before encountered. Our course for the first four days was, with trifling variations, S.E. and by S.; and we must have run down the coast of New Holland. On the fifth day the cold became extreme, although the wind had hauled round a point more to the northward. The sun arose with a sickly yellow luster, and clambered a very few degrees above the horizon—emitting no decisive light. There were no clouds apparent, yet the wind was upon the increase, and blew with a fitful and unsteady fury. About noon, as nearly as we could guess, our attention was again arrested by the appearance of the sun. It gave out no light properly so called, but a dull and sullen glow without reflection, as if all its rays were polarized. Just before sinking within the turgid sea, its central fires suddenly went out, as if hurriedly extinguished by some unaccountable power. It was a dim, silver-like rim, alone, as it rushed down the unfathomable ocean.

We waited in vain for the arrival of the sixth day—that day to me has not yet arrived—to the Swede never did arrive. Thenceforward we were enshrouded in pitchy darkness, so that we could not have seen an object at twenty paces from the ship. Eternal night continued to envelop us, all unrelieved by the phosphoric sea-brilliancy to which we had been accustomed in the tropics. We observed, too, that, although the tempest continued to rage with unabated violence, there was no longer to be discovered the usual appearance of surf, or foam, which had hitherto attended us. All around were horror, and thick gloom, and a black sweltering desert of ebony. Superstitious terror crept by degrees into the spirit of the old Swede, and my own soul was wrapt in silent wonder. We neglected all care of the ship, as worse than useless, and securing ourselves as well as possible, to the stump of the mizzen-mast, looked out bitterly into the world of ocean. We had no means of calculating time, nor could we form any guess of our situation. We were, however, well aware of having made farther to the southward than any previous navigators, and felt great amazement at not meeting with the usual impediments of ice. In the meantime every moment threatened to be our last—every mountainous billow hurried to overwhelm us. The swell surpassed anything I had imagined possible, and that we were not instantly buried is a miracle. My companion spoke of the lightness of our cargo, and reminded me of the excellent qualities of our ship; but I could not help feeling the utter hopelessness of hope itself, and prepared myself gloomily for that death which I thought nothing could defer beyond an hour, as, with every knot of way the ship made the swelling of the black stupendous seas became more dismally appalling. At times we gasped for breath at an elevation beyond the albatross—at times became dizzy with the velocity of our descent into some watery hell, where the air grew stagnant, and no sound disturbed the slumbers of the kraken.

We were at the bottom of one of these abysses, when a quick scream from my companion broke fearfully upon the night. "See! see!" cried he, shrieking in my ears, "Almighty God! see! see!" As he spoke I became aware of a dull sullen glare of red light which streamed down the sides of the vast chasm where we lay, and threw a fitful brilliancy upon our deck. Casting my eyes upward, I beheld a spectacle which froze the current of my blood. At a terrific height directly above us, and upon the very verge of the precipitous descent, hovered a gigantic ship, of perhaps four thousand tons. Although up-reared upon the summit of a wave more than a hundred times her own altitude, her apparent size still exceeded that of any ship of the line or East Indiaman in existence. Her huge hull was of a deep dingy black, unrelieved by any of the customary carvings of a ship. A single row of brass cannon protruded from her open ports, and dashed from the polished surfaces the fires of innumerable battle-lanterns which swung to and fro about her rigging. But what mainly inspired us with horror and astonishment was that she bore up under a press of sail in the very teeth of that supernatural sea, and of that ungovernable hurricane. When we first discovered her, her bows were alone to be seen, as she rose slowly from the dim and horrible gulf beyond her. For a moment of intense terror she paused upon the giddy pinnacle as if in contemplation of her own sublimity, then trembled, and tottered, and—came down.

At this instant, I know not what sudden self-possession came over my spirit. Staggering as far aft as I could, I awaited fearlessly the ruin that was to overwhelm. Our own vessel was at length ceasing from her struggles, and sinking with her head to the sea. The shock of the descending mass struck her, consequently, in that portion of her frame which was nearly under water, and the inevitable result was to hurl me, with irresistible violence, upon the rigging of the stranger.

As I fell, the ship hove in stays, and went about; and to the confusion ensuing I attributed my escape from the notice of the crew. With little difficulty I made my way, unperceived, to the main hatchway, which was partially open, and soon found an opportunity of secreting myself in the hold. Why I did so I can hardly tell. An indefinite sense of awe, which at first sight of the navigators of the ship had taken hold of my mind, was perhaps the principle of my concealment. I was unwilling to trust myself with a race of people who had offered, to the cursory glance I had taken, so many points of vague novelty, doubt, and apprehension. I therefore thought proper to contrive a hiding-place in the hold. This I did by removing a small portion of the shifting-boards, in such a manner as to afford me a convenient retreat between the huge timbers of the ship.

I had scarcely completed my work, when a footstep in the hold forced me to make use of it. A man passed by my place of concealment with a feeble and unsteady gait. I could not see his face, but had an opportunity of observing his general appearance. There was about it an evidence of great age and infirmity. His knees tottered beneath a load of years, and his entire frame quivered under the burthen. He muttered to himself, in a low broken tone, some words of a language which I could not understand, and groped in a corner among a pile of singular-looking instruments, and decayed charts of navigation. His manner was a wild mixture of the peevishness of second childhood, and the solemn dignity of a god. He at length went on deck, and I saw him no more.

• • •

A feeling, for which I have no name, has taken possession of my soul—a sensation which will admit of no analysis, to which the lessons of bygone times are inadequate, and for which I fear futurity itself will offer me no key. To a mind constituted like my own, the latter consideration is an evil. I shall never—I know that I shall never—be satisfied with regard to the nature of my conceptions. Yet it is not wonderful that these conceptions are indefinite, since they have their origin in sources so utterly novel. A new sense—a new entity is added to my soul.

• • •

It is long since I first trod the deck of this terrible ship, and the rays of my destiny are, I think, gathering to a focus. Incomprehensible men! Wrapped up in meditations of a kind which I cannot divine, they pass me by unnoticed. Concealment is utter folly on my part, for the people will not see. It is but just now that I passed directly before the eyes of the mate; it was no long while ago that I ventured into the captain's own private cabin, and took thence the materials with which I write, and have written. I shall from time to time continue this journal. It is true that I may not find an opportunity of transmitting it to the world, but I will not fail to make the endeavor. At the last moment I will enclose the MS. in a bottle, and cast it within the sea.

• • •

An incident has occurred which has given me new room for meditation. Are such things the operation of ungoverned chance? I had ventured upon deck and thrown myself down, without attracting any notice, among a pile of ratlin-stuff and old sails, in the bottom of the yawl. While musing upon the singularity of my fate, I unwittingly daubed with a tar-brush the edges of a neatly-folded studding-sail which lay near me on a barrel. The studding-sail is now bent upon the ship, and the thoughtless touches of the brush are spread out into the word *Discovery*.

I have made my observations lately upon the structure of the vessel. Although well armed, she is not, I think, a ship of war. Her rigging, build, and general equipment, all negative a supposition of this kind. What she is not, I can easily perceive; what she is, I fear it is impossible to say. I know not how it is, but in scrutinizing her strange model and singular cast of spars, her huge size and overgrown suits of canvas, her severely simple bow and antiquated stern, there will occasionally flash across my mind a sensation of familiar things, and there is always mixed up with such indistinct shadows of recollection, an unaccountable memory of old foreign chronicles and ages long ago . . .

• • •

I have been looking at the timbers of the ship. She is built of a material to which I am a stranger. There is a peculiar character about the wood which strikes me as rendering it unfit for the purpose to which it has been applied. I mean its extreme porousness, considered independently of the worm-eaten condition which is a consequence of navigation in these seas, and apart from the rottenness attendant upon age. It will appear perhaps an observation somewhat overcurious, but this would have every characteristic of Spanish oak, if Spanish oak were distended by any unnatural means.

In reading the above sentence, a curious apothegm of an old weather-beaten Dutch navigator comes full upon my recollection. "It is as sure," he was wont to say, when any doubt was entertained of his veracity, "as sure as there is a sea where the ship itself will grow in bulk like the living body of the seaman."

• • •

About an hour ago, I made bold to trust myself among a group of the crew. They paid me no manner of attention, and, although I stood in the very midst of them all, seemed utterly unconscious of my presence. Like the one I had at first seen in the hold, they all bore about them the marks of a hoary old age. Their knees trembled with infirmity; their shoulders were bent double with decrepitude; their shriveled skins rattled in the wind; their voices were low, tremulous, and broken; their eyes glistened with the rheum of years; and their gray hairs streamed terribly in the tempest. Around them, on every part of the deck, lay scattered mathematical instruments of the most quaint and obsolete construction.

• • •

I mentioned, some time ago, the bending of a studding-sail. From that period, the ship, being thrown dead off the wind, has continued her terrific course due south, with every rag of canvas packed upon her, from her truck to her lower-studding-sail booms, and rolling every moment her top-gallant yard-arms into the most appalling hell of water which it can enter into the mind of man to imagine. I have just left the deck, where I found it impossible to maintain a footing, although the crew seemed to experience little inconvenience. It appears to me a miracle of miracles that our enormous bulk is not swallowed up at once and for ever. We are surely doomed to hover continually upon the brink of eternity, without taking a final plunge into the abyss. From billows a thousand times more stupendous than any I have ever seen, we glide away with the facility of the arrowy sea-gull; and the colossal waters rear their heads above us like demons of the deep, but like demons confined to simple threats, and forbidden to destroy. I am led to attribute these frequent escapes to the only natural cause which can account for such effect. I must suppose the ship to be within the influence of some strong current, or impetuous undertow.

• • •

I have seen the captain face to face, and in his own cabin—but, as I expected, he paid me no attention. Although in his appearance there is, to a casual observer, nothing which might bespeak him more or less than man, still, a feeling of irrepressible reverence and awe mingled with the sensation of wonder with which I regarded him. In stature, he is nearly my own height; that is, about five feet eight inches. He is of a well-knit and compact frame of body, neither robust nor remarkable otherwise. But it is the singularity of the expression which reigns upon the face—it is the intense, the wonderful, the thrilling evidence of old age so utter, so extreme, which excites within my spirit a sense—a sentiment ineffable. His forehead, although little wrinkled, seems to bear upon it the stamp of a myriad of years. His gray hairs are records of the past, and his grayer eyes are sybils of the future. The cabin floor was thickly strewn with strange, iron-clasped folios, and moldering instruments of science, and obsolete long-forgotten charts. His head was bowed down upon his hands, and he pored, with a fiery, unquiet eye, over a paper which I took to be a commission, and which, at all events, bore the signature of a monarch. He muttered to himself—as did the first seaman whom I saw in the hold—some low peevish syllables of a foreign tongue; and although the speaker was close at my elbow, his voice seemed to reach my ears from the distance of a mile.

• • •

The ship and all in it are imbued with the spirit of Eld. The crew glide to and fro like the ghosts of buried centuries; their eyes have an eager and uneasy meaning; and when their figures fall athwart my path in the wild glare of the battle-lanterns, I feel as I have never felt before, although I have been all my life a dealer in antiquities, and have imbibed the shadows of fallen columns at Balbec, and Tadmor, and Persepolis, until my very soul has become a ruin.

• • •

When I look around me, I feel ashamed of my former apprehensions. If I trembled at the blast which has hitherto attended us, shall I not stand aghast at a warring of wind and ocean, to convey any idea of which, the words tornado and simoom are trivial and ineffective? All in the immediate vicinity of the ship is the blackness of eternal night, and a chaos of foamless water; but, about a league on either side of us, may be seen, indistinctly and at intervals, stupendous ramparts of ice, towering away into the desolate sky, and looking like the walls of the universe.

• • •

As I imagined, the ship proves to be in a current—if that appellation can properly be given to a tide which, howling and shrieking by the white ice, thunders on to the southward with a velocity like the headlong dashing of a cataract.

• • •

To conceive the horror of my sensations is, I presume, utterly impossible; yet a curiosity to penetrate the mysteries of these awful regions predominates even over my despair, and will reconcile me to the most hideous aspect of death. It is evident that we are hurrying onward to some exciting knowledge—some never-to-be-imparted secret, whose attainment is destruction. Perhaps this current leads us to the southern pole itself. It must be confessed that a supposition apparently so wild has every probability in its favor.

• • •

The crew pace the deck with unquiet and tremulous step; but there is upon their countenance and expression more of the eagerness of hope than of the apathy of despair.

In the meantime the wind is still in our poop, and, as we carry a crowd of canvas, the ship is at times lifted bodily from out the sea! Oh, horror upon horror!—the ice opens suddenly to the right, and to the left, and we are whirling dizzily, in immense concentric circles, round and round the borders of a gigantic amphitheater, the summit of whose walls is lost in the darkness and the distance. But little time will be left me to ponder upon my destiny! The circles rapidly grow small—we are plunging madly within the grasp of the whirlpool—and amid a roaring, and bellowing, and thundering of ocean and of tempest, the ship is quivering—oh God! and——going down!

Note.—*The MS. Found in a Bottle* was originally published in 1831, and it was not until many years afterward that I became acquainted with the maps of Mercator, in which the ocean is represented as rushing, by four mouths, into the (northern) Polar Gulf, to be absorbed into the bowels of the earth; the Pole itself being represented by a black rock, towering to a prodigious height.

BERENICE

Dicebant mihi sodales si sepulchrum amicae visitarem curas meas aliquantulum fore levatas.[1]

Ebn Zaiat

MISERY IS MANIFOLD. The wretchedness of earth is multiform. Overreaching the wide horizon as the rainbow, its hues are as various as the hues of that arch,—as distinct too, yet as intimately blended. Overreaching the wide horizon as the rainbow! How is it that from beauty I have derived a type of unloveliness?—from the covenant of peace a simile of sorrow? But as, in ethics, evil is a consequence of good, so, in fact, out of joy is sorrow born. Either the memory of past bliss is the anguish of to-day, or the agonies which are have their origin in the ecstasies which might have been.

My baptismal name is Egæus; that of my family I will not mention. Yet there are no towers in the land more time-honored than my gloomy, gray, hereditary halls. Our line has been called a race of visionaries; and in many striking particulars—in the character of the family mansion—in the frescoes of the chief saloon—in the tapestries of the dormitories—in the chiseling of some buttresses in the armoury—but more especially in the gallery of antique paintings—in the fashion of the library chamber—and, lastly, in the very peculiar nature of the library's contents, there is more than sufficient evidence to warrant the belief.

The recollections of my earliest years are connected with that chamber, and with its volumes—of which latter I will say no more. Here

1 My companions told me I might find some little alleviation of my misery, in visiting the grave of my beloved.

died my mother. Herein was I born. But it is mere idleness to say that I had not lived before—that the soul has no previous existence. You deny it?—let us not argue the matter. Convinced myself, I seek not to convince. There is, however, a remembrance of aerial forms—of spiritual and meaning eyes—of sounds, musical yet sad—a remembrance which will not be excluded; a memory like a shadow, vague, variable, indefinite, unsteady; and like a shadow, too, in the impossibility of my getting rid of it while the sunlight of my reason shall exist.

In that chamber was I born. Thus awaking from the long night of what seemed, but was not, nonentity, at once into the very regions of fairy-land—into a palace of imagination—into the wild dominions of monastic thought and erudition—it is not singular that I gazed around me with a startled and ardent eye—that I loitered away my boyhood in books, and dissipated my youth in reverie; but it is singular that as years rolled away, and the noon of manhood found me still in the mansion of my fathers—it is wonderful what stagnation there fell upon the springs of my life—wonderful how total an inversion took place in the character of my commonest thought. The realities of the world affected me as visions, and as visions only, while the wild ideas of the land of dreams became, in turn,—not the material of my every-day existence—but in very deed that existence utterly and solely in itself.

Berenice and I were cousins, and we grew up together in my paternal halls. Yet differently we grew—I ill of health, and buried in gloom—she agile, graceful, and overflowing with energy; hers the ramble on the hill-side—mine the studies of the cloister—I living within my own heart, and addicted body and soul to the most intense and painful meditation—she roaming carelessly through life with no thought of the shadows in her path, or the silent flight of the raven-winged hours. Berenice!—I call upon her name—Berenice!—and from the gray ruins of memory a thousand tumultuous recollections are startled at the sound! Ah! vividly is her image before me now, as in the early days of her light-heartedness and joy! Oh! gorgeous yet fantastic beauty! Oh! sylph amid the shrubberies of Arnheim! Oh! Naiad among its fountains!—and then—then all is mystery and terror, and a tale which should not be told. Disease—a fatal disease—fell like the simoom upon her frame, and, even while I gazed upon her, the spirit of change swept over her, pervading her mind, her habits, and her character, and, in a manner the most subtle and terrible, disturbing even the identity of her person! Alas! the destroyer came and went, and the victim—where was she? I knew her not—or knew her no longer as Berenice.

Among the numerous train of maladies superinduced by that fatal and primary one which effected a revolution of so horrible a kind in the moral and physical being of my cousin, may be mentioned as the most distressing and obstinate in its nature, a species of epilepsy not unfrequently terminating in *trance* itself—trance very nearly resembling positive dissolution, and from which her manner of recovery was, in most instances, startlingly abrupt. In the meantime my own disease—for I have been told that I should call it by no other appellation—my own disease, then, grew rapidly upon me, and assumed finally a monomaniac character of a novel and extraordinary form—hourly and momently gaining vigor—and at length obtaining over me the most incomprehensible ascendency. This monomania, if I must so term it, consisted in a morbid irritability of those properties of the mind in metaphysical science termed the *attentive*. It is more than probable that I am not understood; but I fear, indeed, that it is in no manner possible to convey to the mind of the merely general reader, an adequate idea of that nervous *intensity of interest* with which, in my case, the powers of meditation (not to speak technically) busied and buried themselves, in the contemplation of even the most ordinary objects of the universe.

To muse for long unwearied hours with my attention riveted to some frivolous device on the margin, or in the typography of a book; to become absorbed for the better part of a summer's day, in a quaint shadow falling aslant upon the tapestry, or upon the door; to lose myself for an entire night in watching the steady flame of a lamp, or the embers of a fire; to dream away whole days over the perfume of a flower; to repeat monotonously some common word, until the sound, by dint of frequent repetition, ceased to convey any idea whatever to the mind; to lose all sense of motion or physical existence, by means of absolute bodily quiescence long and obstinately persevered in;—such were a few of the most common and least pernicious vagaries induced by a condition of the mental faculties, not, indeed, altogether unparalleled, but certainly bidding defiance to anything like analysis or explanation.

Yet let me not be misapprehended.—The undue, earnest, and morbid attention thus excited by objects in their own nature frivolous, must not be confounded in character with that ruminating propensity common to all mankind, and more especially indulged in by persons of ardent imagination. It was not even, as might be at first supposed, an extreme condition, or exaggeration of such propensity, but primarily and essentially distinct and different. In the one instance, the dreamer, or enthusiast, being interested by an object usually *not* frivolous, imperceptibly loses sight of this object in a wilderness of deductions and suggestions issuing therefrom, until, at the conclusion of a day-dream *often replete with luxury*, he finds the *incitamentum* or first cause of his musings entirely vanished and forgotten. In my case the primary object was *invariably frivolous*, although assuming, through the medium of my distempered vision, a refracted and unreal importance. Few deductions, if any, were made; and those few pertinaciously returning in upon the original object as a center. The meditations were *never* pleasurable; and, at the termination of the reverie, the first cause, so far from being out of sight, had attained that supernaturally exaggerated interest which was the prevailing feature of the disease. In a word, the powers of mind more particularly exercised were, with me, as I have said before, the *attentive*, and are, with the day-dreamer, the *speculative*.

My books, at this epoch, if they did not exactly serve to irritate the disorder, partook, it will be perceived, largely, in their imaginative and inconsequential nature, of the characteristic qualities of the disorder itself. I well remember, among others, the treatise of the noble Italian Cœlius Secundus Curio, *De Amplitudine Beati Regni Dei*; St Austin's great work, *The City of God*; and Tertullian, *De Carne Christi*, in which the paradoxical sentence, "*Mortuus est Dei filius; credibile est quia ineptum est: et sepultus resurrexit; certum est quia impossibile est*,"[1] occupied my undivided time, for many weeks of laborious and fruitless investigation.

Thus it will appear that, shaken from its balance only by trivial things, my reason bore resemblance to that ocean-crag spoken of by Ptolemy Hephestion, which, steadily resisting the attacks of human violence, and the fiercer fury of the waters and the winds, trembled only to the touch of the flower called Asphodel. And although, to a careless thinker, it might appear a matter beyond doubt, that the alteration produced by

1 "The son of God is dead; that is believable because it is foolish: and the buried is resurrected; that is certain because it is impossible."

her unhappy malady, in the *moral* condition of Berenice, would afford me many objects for the exercise of that intense and abnormal meditation whose nature I have been at some trouble in explaining, yet such was not in any degree the case. In the lucid intervals of my infirmity, her calamity, indeed, gave me pain, and, taking deeply to heart that total wreck of her fair and gentle life, I did not fail to ponder frequently and bitterly upon the wonder-working means by which so strange a revolution had been so suddenly brought to pass. But these reflections partook not of the idiosyncrasy of my disease, and were such as would have occurred, under similar circumstances, to the ordinary mass of mankind. True to its own character, my disorder reveled in the less important but more startling changes wrought in the *physical* frame of Berenice—in the singular and most appalling distortion of her personal identity.

During the brightest days of her unparalleled beauty, most surely I had never loved her. In the strange anomaly of my existence, feelings with me *had never been* of the heart, and my passions *always were* of the mind. Through the gray of the early morning—among the trellised shadows of the forest at noonday—and in the silence of my library at night, she had flitted by my eyes, and I had seen her—not as the living and breathing Berenice, but as the Berenice of a dream—not as a being of the earth, earthy, but as the abstraction of such a being—not as a thing to admire, but to analyze—not as an object of love, but as the theme of the most abstruse although desultory speculation. And *now*—now I shuddered in her presence, and grew pale at her approach; yet bitterly lamenting her fallen and desolate condition, I called to mind that she had loved me long, and, in an evil moment, I spoke to her of marriage.

And at length the period of our nuptials was approaching, when, upon an afternoon in the winter of the year,—one of those unseasonably warm, calm, and misty days which are the nurse of the beautiful Halcyon[1]—I sat (and sat, as I thought, alone) in the inner apartment of the library. But uplifting my eyes I saw that Berenice stood before me.

Was it my own excited imagination—or the misty influence of the atmosphere—or the uncertain twilight of the chamber—or the gray

1 For as Jove, during the winter season, gives twice seven days of warmth, men have called this element and temperate time the nurse of the beautiful Halcyon.—Simonides.

draperies which fell around her figure—that caused in it so vacillating and indistinct an outline? I could not tell. She spoke no word, and I—not for worlds could I have uttered a syllable. An icy chill ran through my frame; a sense of insufferable anxiety oppressed me; a consuming curiosity pervaded my soul; and sinking back upon the chair, I remained for some time breathless and motionless, with my eyes riveted upon her person. Alas! its emaciation was excessive, and not one vestige of the former being lurked in any single line of the contour. My burning glances at length fell upon the face.

The forehead was high, and very pale, and singularly placid; and the once jetty hair fell partially over it, and overshadowed the hollow temples with innumerable ringlets now of a vivid yellow, and jarring discordantly, in their fantastic character, with the reigning melancholy of the countenance. The eyes were lifeless, and lusterless, and seemingly pupilless, and I shrank involuntarily from their glassy stare to the contemplation of the thin and shrunken lips. They parted; and in a smile of peculiar meaning, *the teeth* of the changed Berenice disclosed themselves slowly to my view. Would to God that I had never beheld them, or that, having done so, I had died!

• • •

The shutting of a door disturbed me, and, looking up, I found that my cousin had departed from the chamber. But from the disordered chamber of my brain, had not, alas! departed, and would not be driven away, the white and ghastly *spectrum* of the teeth. Not a speck on their surface—not a shade on their enamel—not an indenture in their edges—but what that period of her smile had sufficed to brand in upon my memory. I saw them now even more unequivocally than I beheld them *then*. The teeth!—the teeth!—they were here, and there, and everywhere, and visibly and palpably before me; long, narrow, and excessively white, with the pale lips writhing about them, as in the very moment of their first terrible development. Then came the full fury of my monomania, and I struggled in vain against its strange and irresistible influence. In the multiplied objects of the external world I had no thoughts but for the teeth. For these I longed with a frenzied desire. All other matters and all different interests became absorbed in their single contemplation. They—they alone were present to the mental eye, and they, in their sole individuality, became the essence of my mental life. I held them in every light. I turned them in every attitude. I surveyed their characteristics. I dwelt upon their peculiarities. I pondered upon their conformation. I mused upon the alteration in their nature. I shuddered as I assigned to them in imagination a sensitive and sentient power, and even when unassisted by the lips, a capability of moral expression. Of Mad'selle Sallé it has been well said, "*que tous ses pas étaient des sentiments,*" and of Berenice I more seriously believed *que toutes ses dents étaient des idées. Des idées!*—ah here was the idiotic thought that destroyed me! *Des idées!*—ah therefore it was that I coveted them so madly! I felt that their possession could alone ever restore me to peace, in giving me back to reason.

And the evening closed in upon me thus—and then the darkness came, and tarried, and went—and the day again dawned—and the mists of a second night were now gathering around—and still I sat motionless in that solitary room; and still I sat buried in meditation, and still the *phantasma* of the teeth maintained its terrible ascendency as, with the most vivid and hideous distinctness, it floated about amid the changing lights and shadows of the chamber. At length there broke in upon my dreams a cry as of horror and dismay; and thereunto, after a pause, succeeded the sound of troubled voices, intermingled with many low moanings of sorrow, or of pain. I arose from my seat and, throwing open one of the doors of the library, saw standing out in the ante-chamber a servant maiden, all in tears, who told me that Berenice was—no more. She had been seized with epilepsy in the early morning, and now, at the closing in of the night, the grave was ready for its tenant, and all the preparations for the burial were completed.

• • •

I found myself sitting in the library, and again sitting there alone. It seemed that I had newly awakened from a confused and exciting dream. I knew that it was now midnight, and I was well aware that since the setting of the sun Berenice had been interred. But of that dreary period which intervened I had no positive—at least no definite comprehension. Yet its memory was replete with horror—horror more horrible from being vague, and terror more terrible from ambiguity. It was a fearful page in the record of my existence, written all over with dim, and hideous, and unintelligible recollections. I strived to decipher them, but in vain; while ever and anon, like the spirit of a departed sound, the shrill and piercing shriek of a female voice seemed to be ringing in my ears. I had done a deed—what was it? I asked myself the question aloud, and the whispering echoes of the chamber answered me, "What was it?"

On the table beside me burned a lamp, and near it lay a little box. It was of no remarkable character, and I had seen it frequently before, for it was the property of the family physician; but how came it there, upon my table, and why did I shudder in regarding it? These things were in no manner to be accounted for, and my eyes at length dropped to the open pages of a book, and to a sentence underscored therein. The words were the singular but simple ones of the poet Ebn Zaiat, "*Dicebant mihi sodales si sepulchrum amicae visitarem curas meas aliquantulum fore levatas.*" Why then, as I perused them, did the hairs of my head erect themselves on end, and the blood of my body become congealed within my veins?

There came a light tap at the library door, and pale as the tenant of a tomb, a menial entered upon tiptoe. His looks were wild with terror, and he spoke to me in a voice tremulous, husky, and very low. What said he?—some broken sentences I heard. He told me of a wild cry disturbing the silence of the night—of the gathering together of the household—of a search in the direction of the sound;—and then his tones grew thrillingly distinct as he whispered me of a violated grave—of a disfigured body enshrouded, yet still breathing, still palpitating, *still alive*!

He pointed to my garments;—they were muddy and clotted with gore. I spoke not, and he took me gently by the hand;—it was indented with the impress of human nails. He directed my attention to some object against the wall;—I looked at it for some minutes;—it was a spade. With a shriek I bounded to the table, and grasped the box that lay upon it. But I could not force it open; and in my tremor it slipped from my hands, and fell heavily, and burst into pieces; and from it, with a rattling sound, there rolled out some instruments of dental surgery, intermingled with thirty-two small, white and ivory-looking substances that were scattered to and fro about the floor.

MORELLA

Αυτο καθ΄ αυτο μεθ΄ αυτου, μονο ειδες αιει ου.
Itself, by itself, solely ONE everlastingly, and single.
Plato, *Sympos*

WITH A FEELING of deep yet most singular affection I regarded my friend Morella. Thrown by accident into her society many years ago, my soul, from our first meeting, burned with fires it had never before known; but the fires were not of Eros, and bitter and tormenting to my spirit was the gradual conviction that I could no more define their unusual meaning, or regulate their vague intensity. Yet we met; and fate bound us together at the altar; and I never spoke of passion, nor thought of love. She, however, shunned society, and attaching herself to me alone, rendered me happy. It is a happiness to wonder;—it is a happiness to dream.

Morella's erudition was profound. As I hope to live, her talents were of no common order—her powers of mind were gigantic. I felt this, and in many matters, became her pupil. I soon, however, found that perhaps on account of her Presburg education, she placed before me a number of those mystical writings which are usually considered the mere dross of the early German literature. These, for what reason I could not imagine, were her favorite and constant study—and that, in process of time they became my own, should be attributed to the simple but effectual influence of habit and example.

In all this, if I err not, my reason had little to do. My convictions, or I forget myself, were in no manner acted upon by the ideal, nor was any tincture of the mysticism which I read, to be discovered, unless I am greatly mistaken, either in my deeds or in my thoughts. Persuaded of this, I abandoned myself implicitly to the guidance of my wife, and entered with an unflinching heart into the intricacies of her studies. And then—then, when poring over forbidden pages, I felt a forbidden spirit enkindling within me—would Morella place her cold hand upon my own, and rake up from the ashes of a dead philosophy some low, singular words, whose strange meaning burned themselves in upon my memory. And then, hour after hour, would I linger by her side, and dwell upon the music of her voice—until, at length, its melody was tainted with terror,—and there fell a shadow upon my soul—and I grew pale, and shuddered inwardly at those too unearthly tones. And thus, joy suddenly faded into horror, and the most beautiful became the most hideous, as Hinnon became Ge-Henna.

It is unnecessary to state the exact character of those disquisitions which, growing out of the volumes I have mentioned, formed, for so long a time, almost the sole conversation of Morella and myself. By the learned in what might be termed theological morality they will be readily conceived, and by the unlearned they would, at all events, be little understood. The wild Pantheism of Fichte; the modified of Pythagoreans; and, above all, the doctrines of Identity as urged by Schelling, were generally the points of discussion presenting the most of beauty to the imaginative Morella. That identity which is termed personal, Mr. Locke, I think, truly defines to consist in the saneness of a rational being. And since by person we understand an intelligent essence having reason, and since there is a consciousness which always accompanies thinking, it is this which makes us all to be that which we call ourselves—thereby distinguishing us from other beings that think, and giving us our personal identity. But the *principium individuationis*—the notion of identity *which at death is or is not lost for ever*—was to me, at all times, a consideration of intense interest; not more from the perplexing and exciting nature of its consequences than from the marked and agitated manner in which Morella mentioned them.

But, indeed, the time had now arrived when the mystery of my wife's manner oppressed me as a spell. I could no longer bear the touch of her wan fingers, nor the low tone of her musical language, nor the luster of her melancholy eyes. And she knew all this, but did not upbraid; she seemed conscious of my weakness or folly, and, smiling, called it Fate. She seemed, also, conscious of a cause, to me unknown, for the gradual alienation of my regard; but she gave no hint or token of its nature. Yet was she woman, and pined away daily. In time, the crimson spot settled steadily upon the cheek, and the blue veins upon the pale forehead became prominent; and, one instant, my nature melted into pity, but, in the next, I met the glance of her meaning eyes, and then my soul sickened and became giddy with the giddiness of one who gazes downward into some dreary and unfathomable abyss.

Shall I then say that I longed with an earnest and consuming desire for the moment of Morella's decease? I did; but the fragile spirit clung to its tenement of clay for many days—for many weeks and irksome months—until my tortured nerves obtained the mastery over my mind, and I grew furious through delay, and, with the heart of a fiend, cursed the days, and the hours, and the bitter moments, which seemed to lengthen and lengthen as her gentle life declined—like shadows in the dying of the day.

But one autumnal evening, when the winds lay still in heaven, Morella called me to her bedside. There was a dim mist over all the earth, and a warm glow upon the waters, and, amid the rich October leaves of the forest, a rainbow from the firmament had surely fallen.

"It is a day of days," she said as I approached, "a day of all days either to live or die. It is a fair day for the sons of earth and life—ah, more fair for the daughters of heaven and death!"

I kissed her forehead, and she continued:

"I am dying, yet shall I live."

"Morella!"

"The days have never been when thou couldst love me—but her whom in life thou didst abhor, in death thou shalt adore."

"Morella!"

"I repeat that I am dying. But within me is a pledge of that affection—ah, how little!—which thou didst feel for me, Morella. And when my spirit departs shall the child live—thy child and mine, Morella's. But thy days shall be days of sorrow—that sorrow which is the most lasting of impressions, as the cypress is the most enduring of trees. For the hours of thy happiness are over; and joy is not gathered twice in a life, as the roses of Pæstum twice in a year. Thou shalt no longer, then, play the Teian with time, but being ignorant of the myrtle and the vine, thou shalt bear about with thee thy shroud on the earth as do the Moslemin at Mecca."

"Morella!" I cried, "Morella! how knowest thou this?"—but she turned away her face upon the pillow, and, a slight tremor coming over her limbs, she thus died, and I heard her voice no more.

Yet, as she had foretold, her child—to which in dying she had given birth, which breathed not until the mother breathed no more—her child, a daughter, lived. And she grew strangely in stature and intellect, and was the perfect resemblance of her who had departed, and I loved her with a love more fervent than I had believed it possible to feel for any denizen of earth.

But, ere long, the heaven of this pure affection became darkened, and gloom, and horror, and grief, swept over it in clouds. I said the child grew strangely in stature and intelligence. Strange, indeed, was her rapid increase in bodily size—but terrible, oh! terrible were the tumultuous thoughts which crowded upon me while watching the development of her mental being! Could it be otherwise, when I daily discovered in the conceptions of the child the adult powers and faculties of the woman?—when the lessons of experience fell from the lips of infancy? and when the wisdom or the passions of maturity I found hourly gleaming from its full and speculative eye? When, I say, all this became evident to my appalled senses—when I could no longer hide it from my soul, nor throw it off from those perceptions which trembled to receive it—is it to be wondered at that suspicions, of a nature fearful and exciting, crept in upon my spirit, or that my thoughts fell back aghast upon the wild tales and thrilling theories of the entombed Morella? I snatched from the scrutiny of the world a being whom destiny compelled me to adore, and in the rigorous seclusion of my home, watched with agonizing anxiety over all which concerned the beloved.

And, as years rolled away, and I gazed, day after day, upon her holy, and mild, and eloquent face, and pored over her maturing form, day after day I discovered new points of resemblance in the child to her mother, the melancholy and the dead. And, hourly, grew darker these shadows of similitude, and more full, and more definite, and more perplexing, and more hideously terrible in their aspect. For that her smile was like her mother's I could bear; but then I shuddered at its too perfect identity—that her eyes were like Morella's I could endure; but then they too often looked down into the depths of my soul with Morella's own intense and bewildering meaning. And in the contour of the high forehead, and in the ringlets of the silken hair, and in the wan fingers which buried themselves therein, and in the sad musical tones of her speech, and above all—oh! above all—in the phrases and expressions of the dead on the lips of the loved and the living, I found food for consuming thought and horror—for a worm that would not die.

Thus passed away two lustra of her life, and, as yet, my daughter remained nameless upon the earth. "My child," and "my love," were the designations usually prompted by a father's affection, and the rigid seclusion of her days precluded all other intercourse. Morella's name died with her at her death. Of the mother I had never spoken to the daughter;—it was impossible to speak. Indeed, during the brief period of her existence, the latter had received no impressions from the outer world, save such as might have been afforded by the narrow limits of her privacy. But at length the ceremony of baptism presented to my mind, in its unnerved and agitated condition, a present deliverance from the terrors of my destiny. And at the baptismal font I hesitated for a name. And many titles of the wise and beautiful, of old and modern times, of my own and foreign lands, came thronging to my lips, with many, many fair titles of the gentle, and the happy, and the good. What prompted me, then, to disturb the memory of the buried dead? What demon urged me to breathe that sound, which, in its very recollection, was wont to make ebb the purple blood in torrents from the temples to the heart? What fiend spoke from the recesses of my soul, when, amid those dim aisles, and in the silence of the night, I whispered within the ears of the holy man the syllables—Morella? What more than fiend convulsed the features of the child, and overspread them with hues of death, as starting at that scarcely audible sound, she turned her glassy eyes from the earth to heaven, and, falling prostrate on the black slabs of our ancestral vault, responded—"I am here!"

Distinct, coldly, calmly distinct, fell those few simple sounds within my ear, and thence like molten lead, rolled hissingly into my brain. Years—years may pass away, but the memory of that epoch—never! Nor was I indeed ignorant of the flowers and the vine—but the hemlock and the cypress overshadowed me night and day. And I kept no reckoning of time or place, and the stars of my fate faded from heaven, and therefore the earth grew dark, and its figures passed by me, like flitting shadows, and among them all I beheld only—Morella. The winds of the firmament breathed but one sound within my ears and the ripples upon the sea murmured evermore—Morella. But she died; and with my own hands I bore her to the tomb; and I laughed with a long and bitter laugh as I found no traces of the first, in the charnel where I laid the second—Morella.

SOME PASSAGES IN THE LIFE OF A LION (LIONIZING)

. . . all people went
Upon their ten toes in wild wonderment.
Bishop Hall's *Satires*

I AM—THAT is to say I was—a great man; but I am neither the author of Junius nor the man in the mask; for my name, I believe, is Robert Jones, and I was born somewhere in the city of Fum-Fudge.

The first action of my life was the taking hold of my nose with both hands. My mother saw this and called me a genius:—my father wept for joy and presented me with a treatise on Nosology. This I mastered before I was breeched.

I now began to feel my way in the science; and soon came to understand that, provided a man had a nose sufficiently conspicuous, he might, by merely following it, arrive at a Lionship. But my attention was not confined to theories alone. Every morning I gave my proboscis a couple of pulls and swallowed a half-dozen of drams.

When I came of age my father asked me, one day, if I would step with him into his study.

"My son," said he, when we were seated, "what is the chief end of your existence?"

"My father," I answered, "it is the study of Nosology."

"And what, Robert," he inquired, "is Nosology?"

"Sir," I said, "it is the Science of Noses."

"And can you tell me," he demanded, "what is the meaning of a nose?"

"A nose, my father," I replied, greatly softened, "has been variously defined by about a thousand different authors." [Here I pulled out my watch.] "It is now noon or thereabouts—We shall have time enough to get through with them all before midnight. To commence then:— The nose, according to Bartholinus, is that protuberance—that bump—that excrescence—that——"

—"Will do, Robert," interrupted the good old gentleman. "I am thunderstruck at the extent of your information—I am positively—upon my soul." [Here he closed his eyes and placed his hand upon his heart.] "Come here." [Here he took me by the arm.] "Your education may now be considered as finished—it is high time you should scuffle for yourself—and you cannot do a better thing than merely follow your nose—so—so—so—" [Here he kicked me downstairs and out of the door.]—"so get out of my house and God bless you!"

As I felt within me the divine afflatus, I considered this accident rather fortunate than otherwise. I resolved to be guided by the paternal advice. I determined to follow my nose. I gave it a pull or two upon the spot, and wrote a pamphlet on Nosology forthwith.

All Fum-Fudge was in an uproar.

"Wonderful genius!" said the *Quarterly*.

"Superb physiologist!" said the *Westminster*.

"Clever fellow!" said the *Foreign*.

"Fine writer!" said the *Edinburgh*.

"Profound thinker!" said the *Dublin*.

"Great man!" said Bentley.

"Divine soul!" said Fraser.

"One of us!" said Blackwood.

"Who can he be?" said Mrs. Bas-Bleu.

"What can he be?" said big Miss Bas-Bleu.

"Where can he be?" said little Miss Bas-Bleu.—But I paid these people no attention whatever—I just stepped into the shop of an artist.

The Duchess of Bless-my-soul was sitting for her portrait; the Marquis of So-and-So was holding the Duchess' poodle; the Earl of This-and-

That was flirting with her salts; and his Royal Highness of Touch-me-Not was leaning upon the back of her chair.

I approached the artist and turned up my nose.

"Oh, beautiful!" sighed her Grace.

"Oh, my!" lisped the Marquis.

"Oh, shocking!" groaned the Earl.

"Oh, abominable!" growled his Royal Highness.

"What will you take for it?" asked the artist.

"For his nose!" shouted her Grace.

"A thousand pounds," said I, sitting down.

"A thousand pounds?" inquired the artist, musingly.

"A thousand pounds," said I.

"Beautiful!" said he, entranced.

"A thousand pounds," said I.

"Do you warrant it?" he asked, turning the nose to the light.

"I do," said I, blowing it well.

"Is it quite original?" he inquired, touching it with reverence.

"Humph!" said I, twisting it to one side.

"Has no copy been taken?" he demanded, surveying it through a microscope.

"None," said I, turning it up.

"Admirable!" he ejaculated, thrown quite off his guard by the beauty of the manœuvre.

"A thousand pounds," said I.

"A thousand pounds?" said he.

"Precisely," said I.

"A thousand pounds?" said he.

"Just so," said I.

"You shall have them," said he, "what a piece of *virtù*!"—So he drew me a check upon the spot, and took a sketch of my nose. I engaged rooms in Jermyn Street, and sent her Majesty the ninety-ninth edition of the "Nosology" with a portrait of the proboscis. That sad little rake, the Prince of Wales, invited me to dinner.

We were all lions and *recherchés*.

There was a modern Platonist. He quoted Porphyry, Iamblicus, Plotinus, Proclus, Hierocles, Maximus Tyrius, and Syrianus.

There was a human-perfectibility man. He quoted Turgot, Price,

Priestley, Condorcet, De Staël, and the Ambitious Student in Ill Health.

There was Sir Positive Paradox. He observed that all fools were philosophers, and that all philosophers were fools.

There was Æstheticus Ethix. He spoke of fire, unity, and atoms; bi-part and pre-existent soul; affinity and discord; primitive intelligence and homoömeria.

There was Theologos Theology. He talked of Eusebius and Arianus; heresy and the Council of Nice; Puseyism and consubstantialism; Homoousios and Homoouioisios.

There was Fricassée from the Rocher de Cancale. He mentioned Muriton of red tongue; cauliflowers with *velouté* sauce; veal *à la* St Menehoult; marinade *à la* St Florentin; and orange jellies *en mosaïques*.

There was Bibulus O'Bumper. He touched upon Latour and Markbrünen; upon Mousseux and Chambertin; upon Richebourg and St George; upon Haubrion, Léonville, and Médoc; upon Barac and Preignac; upon Grâve, and upon St Péray. He shook his head at Clos de Vougeot, and told, with his eyes shut, the difference between Sherry and Amontillado.

There was Signor Tintontintino from Florence. He discoursed of Cimabue, Arpino, Carpaccio, and Argostino—of the gloom of Caravaggio, of the amenity of Albano, of the colors of Titian, of the frows of Rubens, and of the waggeries of Jan Steen.

There was the President of the Fum-Fudge University. He was of opinion that the moon was called Bendis in Thrace, Bubastis in Egypt, Dian in Rome, and Artemis in Greece.

There was a Grand Turk from Stamboul. He could not help thinking that the angels were horses, cocks, and bulls; that somebody in the sixth heaven had seventy thousand heads; and that the earth was supported by a sky-blue cow with an incalculable number of green horns.

There was Delphinus Polyglott. He told us what had become of the eighty-three lost tragedies of Æschylus; of the fifty-four orations of Isæus; of the three hundred and ninety-one speeches of Lysias; of the hundred and eighty treatises of Theophrastus; of the eighth book of the Conic Sections of Apollonius; of Pindar's hymns and dithyrambics; and of the five and forty tragedies of Homer Junior.

There was Ferdinand Fitz-Fossillus Feltspar. He informed us all about internal fires and tertiary formations; about aeriforms, fluidiforms, and solidiforms; about quartz and marl; about schist and schorl; about gypsum and trap; about talc and calc; about blende and horn-blende; about mica-slate and pudding-stone; about cyanite and lepidolite; about hæmatite and tremolite; about antimony and chalcedony; about manganese and whatever you please.

There was myself. I spoke of myself;—of myself, of myself, of myself;—of Nosology, of my pamphlet, and of myself. I turned up my nose and spoke of myself.

"Marvelous clever man!" said the Prince.

"Superb!" said his guests; and next morning her Grace of Bless-my-soul paid me a visit.

"Will you go to Almack's, pretty creature?" she said, tapping me under the chin.

"Upon honor," said I.

"Nose and all?" she asked.

"As I live," I replied.

"Here then is a card, my life. Shall I say you will be there?"

"Dear Duchess, with all my heart."

"Pshaw, no!—but with all your nose?"

"Every bit of it, my love," said I:—so I gave it a twist or two, and found myself at Almack's.

The rooms were crowded to suffocation.

"He is coming!" said somebody on the staircase.

"He is coming!" said somebody farther up.

"He is coming!" said somebody farther still.

"He is come!" exclaimed the Duchess—"he is come, the little love!"—and seizing me firmly by both hands, she kissed me thrice upon the nose.

A marked sensation immediately ensued.

"*Diavolo!*" cried Count Capricornutti.

"*Dios guarda!*" muttered Don Stiletto.

"*Mille tonnerres!*" ejaculated the Prince de Grenouille.

"*Tausend Teufel!*" growled the Elector of Bluddennuff.

It was not to be borne. I grew angry. I turned short upon Bluddennuff.

"Sir!" said I to him, "you are a baboon."

"Sir," he replied, after a pause, "Donner und Blitzen!"

This was all that could be desired. We exchanged cards. At Chalk

Farm, the next morning, I shot off his nose—and then called upon my friends.

"*Bête!*" said the first.

"Fool!" said the second.

"Dolt!" said the third.

"Ass!" said the fourth.

"Ninny!" said the fifth.

"Noodle!" said the sixth.

"Be off!" said the seventh.

At all this I felt mortified, and so called upon my father.

"Father," I asked, "what is the chief end of my existence?"

"My son," he replied, "it is still the study of Nosology; but in hitting the Elector upon the nose you have overshot your mark. You have a fine nose, it is true; but then Bluddennuff has none. You are damned, and he has become the hero of the day. I grant you that in Fum-Fudge the greatness of a lion is in proportion to the size of his proboscis—but, Good Heavens! there is no competing with a lion who has no proboscis at all."

THE ASSIGNATION

Stay for me there! I will not fail
To meet thee in that hollow vale.
Henry King, Bishop of Chichester,
Exequy on the death of his wife

ILL-FATED AND MYSTERIOUS man!—bewildered in the brilliancy of thine own imagination, and fallen in the flames of thine own youth! Again in fancy I behold thee! Once more thy form hath risen before me!—not—oh, not as thou art—in the cold valley and shadow—but as thou *shouldst be*—squandering away a life of magnificent meditation in that city of dim visions, thine own Venice which is a star-beloved Elysium of the sea, and the wide windows of whose Palladian palaces look down with a deep and bitter meaning upon the secrets of her silent waters. Yes! I repeat it—as thou *shouldst be*. There are surely other worlds than this—other thoughts than the thoughts of the multitude—other speculations than the speculations of the sophist. Who then shall call thy conduct into question? who blame thee for thy visionary hours, or denounce those occupations as a wasting away of life, which were but the overflowings of thine everlasting energies?

It was at Venice, beneath the covered archway there called the Ponte di Sospiri, that I met for the third or fourth time the person of whom I speak. It is with a confused recollection that I bring to mind the circumstances of that meeting. Yet I remember—ah! how should I forget?—the deep midnight, the Bridge of Sighs, the beauty of woman, and the Genius of Romance that stalked up and down the narrow canal.

It was a night of unusual gloom. The great clock of the Piazza had sounded the fifth hour of the Italian evening. The square of the

Campanile lay silent and deserted, and the lights in the old Ducal Palace were dying fast away. I was returning home from the Piazetta, by way of the Grand Canal. But as my gondola arrived opposite the mouth of the canal San Marco, a female voice from its recesses broke suddenly upon the night, in one wild, hysterical, and long-continued shriek. Startled at the sound, I sprang upon my feet: while the gondolier, letting slip his single oar, lost it in the pitchy darkness beyond a chance of recovery, and we were consequently left to the guidance of the current which here sets from the greater into the smaller channel. Like some huge and sable-feathered condor, we were slowly drifting down toward the Bridge of Sighs, when a thousand flambeaux flashing from the windows, and down the staircases of the Ducal Palace, turned all at once that deep gloom into a livid and preternatural day.

A child, slipping from the arms of its own mother, had fallen from an upper window of the lofty structure into the deep and dim canal. The quiet waters had closed placidly over their victim; and, although my own gondola was the only one in sight, many a stout swimmer, already in the stream, was seeking in vain upon the surface, the treasure which was to be found, alas! only within the abyss. Upon the broad black marble flagstones at the entrance of the palace, and a few steps above the water, stood a figure which none who then saw can have ever since forgotten. It was the Marchesa Aphrodite—the adoration of all Venice—the gayest of the gay—the most lovely where all were beautiful—but still the young wife of the old and intriguing Mentoni, and the mother of that fair child, her first and only one, who now deep beneath the murky water, was thinking in bitterness of heart upon her sweet caresses, and exhausting its little life in struggles to call upon her name.

She stood alone. Her small, bare, and silvery feet gleamed in the black mirror of marble beneath her. Her hair, not as yet more than half loosened for the night from its ball-room array, clustered, amid a shower of diamonds, round and round her classical head, in curls like those of the young hyacinth. A snowy-white and gauze-like drapery seemed to be nearly the sole covering to her delicate form; but the midsummer and midnight air was hot, sullen, and still, and no motion in the statue-like form itself stirred even the folds of that raiment of very vapor which hung around it as the heavy marble hangs around the Niobe. Yet—strange to say!—her large lustrous eyes were not turned downward upon that grave wherein her brightest hope lay buried—but riveted in a widely different direction! The prison of the Old Republic is, I think, the stateliest building in all Venice—but how *could* that lady gaze so fixedly upon it, when beneath her lay stifling her only child? Yon dark, gloomy niche, too, yawns right opposite her chamber window—what, then, could there be in its shadows—in its architecture—in its ivy-wreathed and solemn cornices—that the Marchesa di Mentoni had not wondered at a thousand times before? Nonsense!—Who does not remember that, at such a time as this, the eye, like a shattered mirror, multiplies the images of its sorrow, and sees in innumerable far-off places the woe which is close at hand?

Many steps above the Marchesa, and within the arch of the water-gate, stood, in full dress, the Satyr-like figure of Mentoni himself. He was occasionally occupied in thrumming a guitar, and seemed ennuyé to the very death, as at intervals he gave directions for the recovery of his child. Stupefied and aghast, I had myself no power to move from the upright position I had assumed upon first hearing the shriek, and must have presented to the eyes of the agitated group a spectral and ominous appearance, as with pale countenance and rigid limbs, I floated down among them in that funereal gondola.

All efforts proved in vain. Many of the most energetic in the search were relaxing their exertions, and yielding to a gloomy sorrow. There seemed but little hope for the child (how much less than for the mother!); but now, from the interior of that dark niche which has been already mentioned as forming a part of the Old Republican prison, and as fronting the lattice of the Marchesa, a figure muffled in a cloak stepped out within reach of the light, and, pausing a moment upon the verge of the giddy descent, plunged headlong into the canal. As, in an instant afterward, he stood with the still living and breathing child within his grasp, upon the marble flagstones by the side of the Marchesa, his cloak, heavy with the drenching water, became unfastened, and, falling in folds about his feet, discovered to the wonder-stricken spectators the graceful person of a very young man, with the sound of whose name the greater part of Europe was then ringing.

No word spoke the deliverer. But the Marchesa! She will now receive her child—she will press it to her heart—she will cling to its little form, and smother it with her caresses. Alas! *another's* arms have taken it from her stranger—*another's* arms have taken it away, and borne it afar off, unnoticed, into the palace! And the Marchesa! Her lip—her beautiful lip trembles: tears are gathering in her eyes—those eyes which, like Pliny's acanthus, are "soft and almost liquid." Yes! tears are gathering in those eyes—and see! the entire woman thrills throughout the soul, and the statue has started into life! The pallor of the marble countenance, the swelling of the marble bosom, the very purity of the marble feet, we behold suddenly flushed over with a tide of ungovernable crimson; and a slight shudder quivers about her delicate frame, as a gentle air at Napoli about the rich silver lilies in the grass.

Why should that lady blush! To this demand there is no answer—except that, having left, in the eager haste and terror of a mother's heart, the privacy of her own *boudoir*, she has neglected to enthral her tiny feet in their slippers, and utterly forgotten to throw over her Venetian shoulders that drapery which is their due. What other possible reason could there have been for her so blushing?—for the glance of those wild appealing eyes?—for the unusual tumult of that throbbing bosom?—for the convulsive pressure of that trembling hand?—that hand which fell, as Mentoni turned into the palace, accidentally, upon the hand of the stranger. What reason could there have been for the low—the singularly low tone of those unmeaning words which the lady uttered hurriedly in bidding him adieu? "Thou hast conquered—" she said, or the murmurs of the water deceived me—"thou hast conquered—one hour after sunrise—we shall meet—so let it be!"

• • •

The tumult had subsided, the lights had died away within the palace, and the stranger, whom I now recognized, stood alone upon the flags. He shook with inconceivable agitation, and his eye glanced around in search of a gondola. I could not do less than offer him the service of my own; and he accepted the civility. Having obtained an oar at the water-gate, we proceeded together to his residence, while he rapidly recovered his self-possession, and spoke of our former slight acquaintance in terms of great apparent cordiality.

There are some subjects upon which I take pleasure in being minute. The person of the stranger—let me call him by this title, who to all the world was still a stranger—the person of the stranger is one of these subjects. In height he might have been below rather than above the medium size: although there were moments of intense passion when his frame actually *expanded* and belied the assertion. The light, almost slender symmetry of his figure, promised more of that ready activity which he evinced at the Bridge of Sighs, than of that Herculean strength which he has been known to wield without an effort, upon occasions of more dangerous emergency. With the mouth and chin of a deity—singular, wild, full, liquid eyes, whose shadows varied from pure hazel to intense and brilliant jet—and a profusion of curling, black hair, from which a forehead of unusual breadth gleamed forth at intervals all light and ivory—his were features than which I have seen none more classically regular, except, perhaps, the marble ones of the Emperor Commodus. Yet his countenance was, nevertheless, one of those which all men have seen at some period of their lives, and have never afterward seen again. It had no peculiar—it had no settled predominant expression to be fastened upon the memory; a countenance seen and instantly forgotten—but forgotten with a vague and never-ceasing desire of recalling it to mind. Not that the spirit of each rapid passion failed, at any time, to throw its own distinct image upon the mirror of that face—but that the mirror, mirror-like, retained no vestige of the passion, when the passion had departed.

Upon leaving him on the night of our adventure, he solicited me, in what I thought an urgent manner, to call upon him *very* early the next morning. Shortly after sunrise, I found myself accordingly at his Palazzo, one of those huge structures of gloomy, yet fantastic pomp, which tower above the waters of the Grand Canal in the vicinity of the Rialto. I was shown up a broad winding staircase of mosaics, into an apartment whose unparalleled splendor burst through the opening door with an actual glare, making me blind and dizzy with luxuriousness.

I knew my acquaintance to be wealthy. Report had spoken of his possessions in terms which I had even ventured to call terms of ridiculous exaggeration. But as I gazed about me, I could not bring myself to believe that the wealth of any subject in Europe could have supplied the princely magnificence which burned and blazed around.

Although, as I say, the sun had arisen, yet the room was still brilliantly lighted up. I judge from this circumstance, as well as from an air of exhaustion in the countenance of my friend, that he had not retired to bed during the whole of the preceding night. In the architecture and embellishments of the chamber, the evident design had been to dazzle and astound. Little attention had been paid to the *decora* of what is technically called *keeping*, or to the proprieties of nationality. The eye wandered from object to object, and rested upon none— neither the *grotesques* of the Greek painters, nor the sculptures of the best Italian days, nor the huge carvings of untutored Egypt. Rich draperies in every part of the room trembled to the vibration of low, melancholy music, whose origin was not to be discovered. The senses were oppressed by mingled and conflicting perfumes, reeking up from strange convolute censers, together with multitudinous flaring and flickering tongues of emerald and violet fire. The rays of the newly risen sun poured in upon the whole, through windows formed each of a single pane of crimson-tinted glass. Glancing to and fro, in a thousand reflections, from curtains which rolled from their cornices like cataracts of molten silver, the beams of natural glory mingled at length fitfully with the artificial light, and lay weltering in subdued masses upon a carpet of rich, liquid-looking cloth of Chili gold.

"Ha! ha! ha!—ha! ha! ha!"—laughed the proprietor, motioning me to a seat as I entered the room, and throwing himself back at full length upon an ottoman. "I see," said he, perceiving that I could not immediately reconcile myself to the *bienséance* of so singular a welcome—"I see you are astonished at my apartment—at my statues—my pictures—my originality of conception in architecture and upholstery—absolutely drunk, eh? with my magnificence? But pardon me, my dear sir," (here his tone of voice dropped to the very spirit of cordiality) "pardon me for my uncharitable laughter. You appeared so *utterly* astonished. Besides, some things are so completely ludicrous that a man *must* laugh or die. To die laughing must be the most glorious of all glorious deaths! Sir Thomas More—a very fine man was Sir Thomas More—Sir Thomas More died laughing, you remember. Also in the *Absurdities* of Ravisius Textor, there is a long list of characters who came to the same magnificent end. Do you know, however," continued he musingly, "that at Sparta (which is now Palæochori)—at Sparta, I say, to the west of the citadel, among a chaos of scarcely visible ruins, is a kind of *socle*, upon which are still legible the letters ΛΑΞΜ. They are undoubtedly part of ΓΕΛΑΞΜΑ. Now at Sparta were a thousand temples and shrines to a thousand different divinities. How exceedingly strange that the altar of Laughter should have survived all the others! But in the present instance," he resumed, with a singular alteration of voice and manner, "I have no right to be merry at your expense. You might well have been amazed. Europe cannot produce anything so fine as this, my little regal cabinet. My other apartments are by no means of the same order; mere ultras of fashionable insipidity. This is better than fashion, is it not? Yet this has but to be seen to become the rage—that is, with those who could afford it at the cost of their entire patrimony. I have guarded, however, against any such profanation. With one exception you are the only human being besides myself and my *valet*, who has been admitted within the mysteries of these imperial precincts, since they have been bedizened as you see!"

I bowed in acknowledgment; for the overpowering sense of splendor and perfume, and music, together with the unexpected eccentricity of his address and manner, prevented me from expressing, in words, my appreciation of what I might have construed into a compliment.

"Here," he resumed, arising and leaning on my arm as he sauntered around the apartment,—"here are paintings from the Greeks to Cimabue, and from Cimabue to the present hour. Many are chosen, as you see, with little deference to the opinions of *Virtû*. They are all, however, fitting tapestry for a chamber such as this. Here too, are some *chefs d'œuvre* of the unknown great—and here unfinished designs by men, celebrated in their day, whose very names the perspicacity of the academies has left to silence and to me. What think you," said he, turning abruptly as he spoke—"what think you of this Madonna della Pietà?"

"It is Guido's own!" I said with all the enthusiasm of my nature, for I had been poring intently over its surpassing loveliness. "It is Guido's own!—how *could* you have obtained it?—she is undoubtedly in painting what the Venus is in sculpture."

"Ha!" said he thoughtfully, "the Venus—the beautiful Venus?—the Venus of the Medici?—she of the diminutive head and the gilded hair? Part of the left arm" (here his voice dropped so as to be heard with difficulty) "and all the right are restorations, and in the coquetry of that right arm lies, I think, the quintessence of all affectation. Give *me* the Canova! The Apollo, too!—is a copy—there can be no doubt of it—blind fool that I am, who cannot behold the boasted inspiration of the Apollo! I cannot help—pity me!—I cannot help preferring the Antinous. Was it not Socrates who said that the statuary found his statue in the block of marble? Then Michael Angelo was by no means original in his couplet—

> "Non ha l'ottimo artista alcun concetto
> Che un marmo solo in se non circonscriva."[1]

It has been, or should be remarked, that, in the manner of the true gentleman, we are always aware of a difference from the bearing of the vulgar, without being at once precisely able to determine in what such difference consists. Allowing the remark to have applied in its full force to the outward demeanor of my acquaintance, I felt it, on that eventful morning, still more fully applicable to his moral temperament and character. Nor can I better define that peculiarity of spirit which seemed to place him so essentially apart from all other human beings, than by calling it a *habit* of intense and continual thought, pervading even his most trivial actions—intruding upon his moments of dalliance—and interweaving itself with his very flashes of merriment—like adders which writhe from out the eyes of the grinning masks in the cornices around the temples of Persepolis.

I could not help, however, repeatedly observing, through the mingled tone of levity and solemnity with which he rapidly descanted upon matters of little importance, a certain air of trepidation—a degree of nervous unction in action and in speech—an unquiet excitability of manner which appeared to me at all times unaccountable, and upon some occasions even filled me with alarm. Frequently, too, pausing in the middle of a sentence whose commencement he had apparently forgotten, he seemed to be listening in the deepest attention, as if either in momentary expectation of a visitor, or to sounds which must have had existence in his imagination alone.

It was during one of these reveries or pauses of apparent abstraction,

1 "The best of artists has no conception that the marble alone does not contain within itself."

that, in turning over a page of the poet and scholar Politian's beautiful tragedy *The Orfeo* (the first native Italian tragedy) which lay near me upon an ottoman, I discovered a passage underlined in pencil. It was a passage toward the end of the third act—a passage of the most heart-stirring excitement—a passage which, although tainted with impurity, no man shall read without a thrill of novel emotion—no woman without a sigh. The whole page was blotted with fresh tears, and, upon the opposite interleaf, were the following English lines, written in a hand so very different from the peculiar characters of my acquaintance, that I had some difficulty in recognizing it as his own.

Thou wast that all to me, love,
   or which my soul did pine—
A green isle in the sea, love,
   fountain and a shrine,
All wreathed with fairy fruits and flowers,
   And all the flowers were mine.

Ah, dream too bright to last!
   Ah, starry Hope! that didst arise
But to be overcast!
   A voice from out the Future cries,
"On! on!"—but o'er the Past
   Dim gulf!) my spirit hovering lies
Mute, motionless, aghast!

For alas! alas! with me
   he light of life is o'er.
"No more—no more—no more"
(Such language holds the solemn sea
   To the sands upon the shore)
Shall bloom the thunder-blasted tree,
   Or the stricken eagle soar!

Now all my days are trances,
   And all my nightly dreams
Are where thy grey eye glances,

And where thy footstep gleams—
In what ethereal dances,
By what Italian streams.

Alas! for that accursed time
hey bore thee o'er the billow,
From Love to titled age and crime,
And an unholy pillow—
From me, and from our misty clime,
here weeps the silver willow!

That these lines were written in English—a language with which I had not believed their author acquainted—afforded me little matter for surprise. I was too well aware of the extent of his acquirements, and of the singular pleasure he took in concealing them from observation, to be astonished at any similar discovery; but the place of date, I must confess, occasioned me no little amazement. It had been originally written *London*, and afterward carefully overscored—not, however, so effectually as to conceal the word from a scrutinizing eye. I say this occasioned me no little amazement; for I well remember that, in a former conversation with my friend, I particularly inquired if he had at any time met in London the Marchesa di Mentoni (who for some years previous to her marriage had resided in that city), when his answer, if I mistake not, gave me to understand that he had never visited the metropolis of Great Britain. I might as well here mention, that I have more than once heard (without of course giving credit to a report involving so many improbabilities), that the person of whom I speak was not only by birth, but in education, an *Englishman*.

• • •

"There is one painting," said he, without being aware of my notice of the tragedy—"there is still one painting which you have not seen." And throwing aside a drapery, he discovered a full-length portrait of the Marchesa Aphrodite.

Human art could have done no more in the delineation of her superhuman beauty. The same ethereal figure which stood before me the preceding night upon the steps of the Ducal Palace, stood before me once again. But in the expression of the countenance, which was beaming all over with smiles, there still lurked (incomprehensible anomaly!) that fitful stain of melancholy which will ever be found inseparable from the perfection of the beautiful. Her right arm lay folded over her bosom. With her left she pointed downward to a curiously fashioned vase. One small, fairy foot, alone visible, barely touched the earth—and, scarcely discernible in the brilliant atmosphere which seemed to encircle and enshrine her loveliness, floated a pair of the most delicately imagined wings. My glance fell from the painting to the figure of my friend, and the vigorous words of Chapman's *Bussy D' Ambois* quivered instinctively upon my lips:

> "He is up
> There like a Roman statue! He will stand
> Till Death hath made him marble!"

"Come!" he said at length, turning toward a table of richly enameled and massive silver, upon which were a few goblets fantastically stained, together with two large Etruscan vases, fashioned in the same extraordinary model as that in the foreground of the portrait, and filled with what I supposed to be Johannisberger. "Come!" he said abruptly, "let us drink! It is early—but let us drink. It is indeed early," he continued, musingly, as a cherub with a heavy golden hammer made the apartment ring with the first hour after sunrise —"It is indeed early, but what matters it? let us drink! Let us pour out an offering to you solemn sun which these gaudy lamps and censers are so eager to subdue!" And, having made me pledge him in a bumper, he swallowed in rapid succession several goblets of the wine.

"To dream," he continued, resuming the tone of his desultory conversation, as he held up to the rich light of a censer one of the magnificent vases—"to dream has been the business of my life. I have therefore framed for myself, as you see, a bower of dreams. In the heart of Venice could I have erected a better? You behold around you, it is true, a medley of architectural embellishments. The chastity of Ionia is offended by antediluvian devices, and the sphinxes of Egypt are outstretched upon carpets of gold. Yet the effect is incongruous to the timid alone. Proprieties of place, and especially of time, are the bugbears which terrify mankind from the contemplation of the magnificent. Once I was myself a decorist: but that sublimation of folly has palled upon my soul. All this is now the fitter for my purpose. Like these arabesque censers, my spirit is writhing in fire, and the delirium of this scene is fashioning me for the wilder visions of that land of real dreams whither I am now rapidly departing." He here paused abruptly, bent his head to his bosom, and seemed to listen to a sound which I could not hear. At length, erecting his frame, he looked upward and ejaculated the lines of the Bishop of Chichester:

"Stay for me there! I will not fail
To meet thee in that hollow vale."

In the next instant, confessing the power of the wine, he threw himself at full length upon an ottoman.

A quick step was now heard upon the staircase, and a loud knock at the door rapidly succeeded. I was hastening to anticipate a second disturbance, when a page of Mentoni's household burst into the room, and faltered out, in a voice choking with emotion, the incoherent words, "My mistress!—my mistress!—poisoned!—poisoned! Oh beautiful—oh beautiful Aphrodite!"

Bewildered, I flew to the ottoman, and endeavored to arouse the sleeper to a sense of the startling intelligence. But his limbs were rigid—his lips were livid—his lately beaming eyes were riveted in *death*. I staggered back toward the table—my hand fell upon a cracked and blackened goblet—and a consciousness of the entire and terrible truth flashed suddenly over my soul.

BON-BON

Quand un bon vin meuble mon estomac
Je suis plus savant que Balzac—
Plus sage que Pibrac;
Mon bras seul faisant l'attaque
De la nation Cossaque,
La mettroit au sac;
De Charon je passerois le lac
En dormant dans son bac;
J'irois au fier Eac,
Sans que mon cœur fît tic ni tac,
Présenter du tabac.

French Vaudeville

THAT PIERRE BON-BON was a *restaurateur* of uncommon qualifications, no man who, during the reign of ———, frequented the little café in the cul-de-sac Le Febvre at Rouen, will, I imagine, feel himself at liberty to dispute. That Pierre Bon-Bon was, in an equal degree, skilled in the philosophy of that period is, I presume, still more especially undeniable. His *pâtés à la foie* were beyond doubt immaculate; but what pen can do justice to his essays *sur la Nature*—his thoughts sur *l'Ame*—his observations *sur l'Esprit*? If his omelettes—if his *fricandeaux* were inestimable, what *littérateur* of that day would not have given twice as much for an "*Idée de Bon-Bon*" as for all the trash of all the "*Idées*" of all the rest of the savants? Bon-Bon had ransacked libraries which no other man had ransacked—had read more than any other would have entertained a notion of reading—had understood more than any other would have conceived the possibility of understanding; and although, while he flourished, there were not wanting some authors at Rouen to assert "that his *dicta* evinced neither the purity of the Academy, nor the depth of the Lyceum"—although, mark me, his doctrines were by no means very generally comprehended, still it did not follow that they were difficult of comprehension. It was, I think, on account of their self-evidency that many persons were led to consider them abstruse. It is to Bon-Bon—but let this go no further—it is to Bon-Bon that Kant himself is mainly indebted for his metaphysics. The former was indeed not a Platonist, nor strictly speaking an Aristotelian—nor did he, like the modern Leibnitz, waste those precious hours which might be employed in the invention of a *fricassée* or, *facili gradu*, the analysis of a sensation, in frivolous attempts at reconciling the obstinate oils and waters of ethical discussion. Not at all. Bon-Bon was Ionic—Bon-Bon was equally Italic. He reasoned *a priori*—He reasoned *a posteriori*. His ideas were innate—or otherwise. He believed in George of Trebizond—He believed in Bossarion. Bon-Bon was emphatically a—*Bon-Bonist*.

I have spoken of the philosopher in his capacity of *restaurateur*. I would not, however, have any friend of mine imagine that, in fulfilling his hereditary duties in that line, our hero wanted a proper estimation of their dignity and importance. Far from it. It was impossible to say in which branch of his profession he took the greater pride. In his opinion the powers of the intellect held intimate connexion with the capabilities of the stomach. I am not sure, indeed, that he greatly disagreed with the Chinese, who hold that the soul lies in the abdomen. The Greeks at all events were right, he thought, who employed the same word for the mind and the diaphragm.[1] By this I do not mean to insinuate a charge of gluttony, or indeed any other serious charge to the prejudice of the metaphysician. If Pierre Bon-Bon had his failings—and what great man has not a thousand?—if Pierre Bon-Bon, I say, had his failings, they were failings of very little importance—faults indeed which, in other tempers, have often been looked upon rather in the light of virtues. As regards one of these foibles, I should not even have mentioned it in this history but for the remarkable prominency—the extreme *alto relievo*—in which it jutted out from the plane of his general disposition. He could never let slip an opportunity of making a bargain.

1 φρενες

Not that he was avaricious—no. It was by no means necessary to the satisfaction of the philosopher that the bargain should be to his own proper advantage. Provided a trade could be effected—a trade of any kind, upon any terms, or under any circumstances—a triumphant smile was seen for many days thereafter to enlighten his countenance, and a knowing wink of the eye to give evidence of his sagacity.

At any epoch it would not be very wonderful if a humor so peculiar as the one I have just mentioned, should elicit attention and remark. At the epoch of our narrative, had this peculiarity not attracted observation, there would have been room for wonder indeed. It was soon reported that, upon all occasions of the kind, the smile of Bon-Bon was found to differ widely from the downright grin with which he would laugh at his own jokes, or welcome an acquaintance. Hints were thrown out of an exciting nature; stories were told of perilous bargains made in a hurry and repented of at leisure; and instances were adduced of unaccountable capacities, vague longings, and unnatural inclinations implanted by the author of all evil for wise purposes of his own.

The philosopher had other weaknesses—but they are scarcely worthy our serious examination. For example, there are few men of extraordinary profundity who are found wanting in an inclination for the bottle. Whether this inclination be an exciting cause, or rather a valid proof, of such profundity, it is a nice thing to say. Bon-Bon, as far as I can learn, did not think the subject adapted to minute investigation;—nor do I. Yet in the indulgence of a propensity so truly classical, it is not to be supposed that the *restaurateur* would lose sight of that intuitive discrimination which was wont to characterize, at one and the same time, his *essais* and his *omelettes*. In his seclusions the *Vin de Bourgogne* had its allotted hour, and there were appropriate moments for the *Côtes du Rhone*. With him *Sauterne* was to *Médoc* what Catullus was to Homer. He would sport with a syllogism in sipping *St Péray*, but unravel an argument over *Clos de Vougéot*, and upset a theory in a torrent of *Chambertin*. Well had it been if the same quick sense of propriety had attended him in the peddling propensity to which I have formerly alluded—but this was by no means the case. Indeed, to say the truth, that trait of mind in the philosophic Bon-Bon *did* begin at length to assume a character of strange intensity and mysticism, and appeared deeply tinctured with the *diablerie* of his favorite German studies.

To enter the little *Café* in the *cul-de-sac* Le Febvre was, at the period of our tale, to enter the sanctum of a man of genius. Bon-Bon was a man of genius. There was not a *sous-cuisinier* in Rouen, who could not have told you that Bon-Bon was a man of genius. His very cat knew it, and forbore to whisk her tail in the presence of the man of genius. His large water-dog was acquainted with the fact, and upon the approach of his master, betrayed his sense of inferiority by a sanctity of deportment, a debasement of the ears, and a dropping of the lower jaw not altogether unworthy of a dog. It is, however, true that much of this habitual respect might have been attributed to the personal appearance of the metaphysician. A distinguished exterior will, I am constrained to say, have its way even with a beast; and I am willing to allow much in the outward man of the *restaurateur* calculated to impress the imagination of the quadruped. There is a peculiar majesty about the atmosphere of the little great—if I may be permitted so equivocal an expression—which mere physical bulk alone will be found at all times inefficient in creating. If, however, Bon-Bon was barely three feet in height, and if his head was diminutively small, still it was impossible to behold the rotundity of his stomach without a sense of magnificence nearly bordering upon the sublime. In its size both dogs and men must have seen a type of his acquirements—in its immensity a fitting habitation for his immortal soul.

I might here—if it so pleased me—dilate upon the matter of habiliment, and other mere circumstances of the external metaphysician. I might hint that the hair of our hero was worn short, combed smoothly over his forehead, and surmounted by a conical-shaped white flannel cap and tassels—that his pea-green jerkin was not after the fashion of those worn by the common class of *restaurateurs* at that day—that the sleeves were something fuller than the reigning costume permitted—that the cuffs were turned up, not as usual in that barbarous period, with cloth of the same quality and color as the garment, but faced in a more fanciful manner with the parti-colored velvet of Genoa—that his slippers were of a bright purple, curiously filigreed, and might have been manufactured in Japan, but for the exquisite pointing of the toes, and the brilliant tints of the binding and embroidery—that his breeches were of the yellow satin-like material called *aimable*—that his sky-blue cloak, resembling in form a dressing-wrapper, and richly bestudded all over with crimson devices, floated cavalierly upon his shoulders like a mist of the morning—and that his tout ensemble gave rise to the remarkable words of Benevenuta, the *Improvisatrice* of Florence, "that it was difficult to say whether Pierre Bon-Bon was indeed a bird of Paradise, or the rather a very Paradise of perfection." I might, I say, expatiate upon all these points if I pleased,—but I forbear; merely personal details may be left to historical novelists,—they are beneath the moral dignity of matter-of-fact.

I have said that "to enter the *Café* in the *cul-de-sac* Le Febvre was to enter the sanctum of a man of genius"—but then it was only the man of genius who could duly estimate the merits of the sanctum. A sign, consisting of a vast folio, swung before the entrance. On one side of the volume was painted a bottle; on the reverse a *pâté*. On the back were visible in large letters *Œuvres de Bon-Bon*. Thus was delicately shadowed forth the twofold occupation of the proprietor.

Upon stepping over the threshold, the whole interior of the building presented itself to view. A long, low-pitched room of antique construction, was indeed all the accommodation afforded by the *Café*. In a corner of the apartment stood the bed of the metaphysician. An array of curtains, together with a canopy *à la Grèque*, gave it an air at once classic and comfortable. In the corner diagonally opposite, appeared, in direct family communion, the properties of the kitchen and the *bibliothèque*. A dish of polemics stood peacefully upon the dresser. Here lay an ovenful of the latest ethics—there a kettle of duodecimo *mélanges*. Volumes of German morality were hand and glove with the gridiron—a toasting-fork might be discovered by the side of Eusebius—Plato reclined at his ease in the frying-pan—and contemporary manuscripts were filed away upon the spit.

In other respects the *Café de Bon-Bon* might be said to differ little from the usual restaurants of the period. A large fireplace yawned opposite the door. On the right of the fireplace an open cupboard displayed a formidable array of labelled bottles.

It was here, about twelve o'clock one night, during the severe winter of ——, that Pierre Bon-Bon, after having listened for some time to the comments of his neighbors upon his singular propensity—that Pierre Bon-Bon, I say, having turned them all out of his house, locked the door upon them with an oath, and betook himself in no very pacific mood to the comforts of a leather-bottomed arm-chair, and a fire of blazing faggots.

It was one of those terrific nights which are only met with once or twice during a century. It snowed fiercely, and the house tottered to its center with the floods of wind that, rushing through the crannies of the wall, and pouring impetuously down the chimney, shook awfully the curtains of the philosopher's bed, and disorganized the economy of his pâté-pans and paper. The huge folio sign that swung without, exposed to the fury of the tempest, creaked ominously, and gave out a moaning sound from its stanchions of solid oak.

It was in no placid temper, I say, that the metaphysician drew up his chair to its customary station by the hearth. Many circumstances of a perplexing nature had occurred during the day to disturb the serenity of his meditations. In attempting des *œufs à la Princesse*, he had unfortunately perpetrated an *omelette à la Reine*; the discovery of a principle in ethics had been frustrated by the overturning of a stew; and last, not least, he had been thwarted in one of those admirable bargains which he at all times took such especial delight in bringing to a successful termination. But in the chafing of his mind at these unaccountable vicissitudes, there did not fail to be mingled some degree of that nervous anxiety which the fury of a boisterous night is so well calculated to produce. Whistling to his more immediate vicinity the large black water-dog we have spoken of before, and settling himself uneasily in his chair, he could not help casting a wary and unquiet eye toward those distant recesses of the apartment whose inexorable shadows not even the red firelight itself could more than partially succeed in overcoming. Having completed a scrutiny whose exact purpose was perhaps unintelligible to himself, he drew close to his seat a small table covered with books and papers, and soon became absorbed in the task of retouching a voluminous manuscript, intended for publication on the morrow.

He had been thus occupied for some minutes, when "I am in no hurry, Monsieur Bon-Bon," suddenly whispered a whining voice in the apartment.

"The devil!" ejaculated our hero, starting to his feet, overturning the table at his side, and staring around him in astonishment.

"Very true," calmly replied the voice.

"Very true!—what is very true?—how came you here?" vociferated the metaphysician, as his eye fell upon something which lay stretched at full length upon the bed.

"I was saying," said the intruder, without attending to the interrogatories,—"I was saying that I am not at all pushed for time—that the business upon which I took the liberty of calling, is of no pressing importance—in short, that I can very well wait until you have finished your Exposition."

"My Exposition!—there now!—how do you know?—how came you to understand that I was writing an Exposition—good God!"

"Hush!" replied the figure, in a shrill undertone; and, arising quickly from the bed, he made a single step toward our hero, while an iron lamp that depended overhead swung convulsively back from his approach.

The philosopher's amazement did not prevent a narrow scrutiny of the stranger's dress and appearance. The outlines of his figure, exceedingly lean, but much above the common height, were rendered minutely distinct by means of a faded suit of black cloth which fitted tight to the skin, but was otherwise cut very much in the style of a century ago. These garments had evidently been intended for a much shorter person than their present owner. His ankles and wrists were left naked for several inches. In his shoes, however, a pair of very brilliant buckles gave the lie to the extreme poverty implied by the other portions of his dress. His head was bare, and entirely bald, with the exception of the hinder-part, from which depended a queue of considerable length. A pair of green spectacles, with side glasses, protected his eyes from the influence of the light, and at the same time prevented our hero from ascertaining either their color or their conformation. About the entire person there was no evidence of a shirt; but a white cravat, of filthy appearance, was tied with extreme precision around the throat, and the ends, hanging down formally side by side, gave (although I dare say unintentionally) the idea of an ecclesiastic. Indeed, many other points both in his appearance and demeanor might have very well sustained a conception of that nature. Over his left ear, he carried, after the fashion of a modern clerk, an instrument resembling the stylus of the ancients. In a breast-pocket of his coat appeared conspicuously a small black volume fastened with clasps of steel. This book, whether accidentally or not, was so turned outwardly from the person as to discover the words "*Rituel Catholique*" in white letters upon the back. His entire physiognomy was interestingly saturnine—even cadaverously pale. The forehead was lofty, and deeply furrowed with the ridges of contemplation. The corners of the mouth were drawn down into an expression of the most submissive humility. There was also a clasping of the hands, as he stepped toward our hero—a deep sigh—and altogether a look of such utter sanctity as could not have failed to be unequivocally prepossessing. Every shadow of anger faded from the countenance of the metaphysician, as, having completed a satisfactory survey of his visitor's person, he shook him cordially by the hand, and conducted him to a seat.

There would however be a radical error in attributing this instantaneous transition of feeling in the philosopher, to any one of those causes which might naturally be supposed to have had an influence. Indeed, Pierre Bon-Bon, from what I have been able to understand of his disposition, was of all men the least likely to be imposed upon by any speciousness of exterior deportment. It was impossible that so accurate an observer of men and things should have failed to discover, upon the moment, the real character of the personage who had thus intruded upon his hospitality. To say no more, the conformation of his visitor's feet was sufficiently remarkable—he maintained lightly upon his head an inordinately tall hat—there was a tremulous swelling about the hinder-part of his breeches—and the vibration of his coat tail was a palpable fact. Judge, then, with what feelings of satisfaction our hero found himself thrown thus at once into the society of a person for whom he had at all times entertained the most unqualified respect. He was, however, too much of the diplomatist to let escape him any intimation of his suspicions in regard to the true state of affairs. It was not his cue to appear at all conscious of the high honor he thus unexpectedly enjoyed; but, by leading his guest into conversation, to elicit some important ethical ideas, which might, in obtaining a place in his contemplated publication, enlighten the human race, and at the same time immortalize himself—ideas which I should have added, his visitor's great age, and well-known proficiency in the science of morals, might very well have enabled him to afford.

Actuated by these enlightened views, our hero bade the gentleman sit down, while he himself took occasion to throw some faggots upon the fire, and place upon the now re-established table some bottles of *Mousseux*. Having quickly completed these operations, he drew his chair *vis-à-vis* to his companion's, and waited until the latter should open the conversation. But plans, even the most skillfully matured, are often thwarted in the outset of their application—and the *restaurateur* found himself nonplussed by the very first words of his visitor's speech.

"I see you know me, Bon-Bon," said he; "ha! ha! ha!—he! he! he!—hi! hi! hi!—ho! ho! ho!—hu! hu! hu!"—and the Devil, dropping at once the sanctity of his demeanor, opened to its fullest extent a mouth from ear to ear, so as to display a set of jagged and fang-like teeth, and, throwing back his head laughed long, loudly, wickedly, and uproariously, while the black dog, crouching down upon his haunches, joined lustily in the chorus, and the tabby cat, flying off at a tangent, stood up on end, and shrieked in the farthest corner of the apartment.

Not so the philosopher: he was too much a man of the world either to laugh like the dog, or by shrieks to betray the indecorous trepidation of the cat. It must be confessed, he felt a little astonishment to see the white letters which formed the words "*Rituel Catholique*" on the book in his guest's pocket, momently changing both their color and their import, and in a few seconds, in place of the original title, the words "*Registre des Condamnés*" blaze forth in characters of red. This startling circumstance, when Bon-Bon replied to his visitor's remark, imparted to his manner an air of embarrassment which probably might not otherwise have been observed.

"Why, sir," said the philosopher, "why, sir, to speak sincerely—I believe you are—upon my word—the d——dest—that is to say, I think—I imagine—I have some faint—some very faint idea—of the remarkable honor——"

"Oh!—ah!—yes!—very well!" interrupted his Majesty; "say no more—I see how it is." And hereupon, taking off his green spectacles, he wiped the glasses carefully with the sleeve of his coat, and deposited them in his pocket.

If Bon-Bon had been astonished at the incident of the book, his amazement was now much increased by the spectacle which here presented itself to view. In raising his eyes, with a strong feeling of curiosity to ascertain the color of his guest's, he found them by no means black, as he had anticipated—nor gray, as might have been imagined—nor yet hazel nor blue—nor indeed yellow nor red—nor purple—nor white—nor green—nor any other color in the heavens above, or in the earth beneath, or in the waters under the earth. In short, Pierre Bon-Bon not only saw plainly that his Majesty had no eyes whatsoever, but could discover no indications of their having existed at any previous period—for the space where eyes should naturally have been was, I am constrained to say, simply a dead level of flesh.

It was not in the nature of the metaphysician to forbear making some inquiry into the sources of so strange a phenomenon; and the reply of his Majesty was at once prompt, dignified, and satisfactory.

"Eyes! my dear Bon-Bon—eyes did you say?—oh!—ah!—I perceive! The ridiculous prints, eh, which are in circulation, have given you a false idea of my personal appearance? Eyes!—true. Eyes, Pierre Bon-Bon, are very well in their proper place—that, you would say, is the head?—right—the head of a worm. To you, likewise, these optics are indispensable—yet I will convince you that my vision is more penetrating than your own. There is a cat I see in the corner—a pretty cat—look at her—observe her well. Now, Bon-Bon, do you behold the thoughts—the thoughts, I say—the ideas—the reflections—which are being engendered in her pericranium? There it is, now—you do not! She is thinking we admire the length of her tail and the profundity of her mind. She has just concluded that I am the most distinguished of ecclesiastics, and that you are the most superficial of metaphysicians. Thus you see I am not altogether blind; but to one of my profession, the eyes you speak of would be merely an incumbrance, liable at any time to be put out by a toasting-iron or a pitchfork. To you, I allow, these optical affairs are indispensable. Endeavor, Bon-Bon, to use them well;—*my* vision is the soul."

Hereupon the guest helped himself to the wine upon the table, and pouring out a bumper for Bon-Bon, requested him to drink it without scruple, and make himself perfectly at home.

"A clever book that of yours, Pierre," resumed his Majesty, tapping our friend knowingly upon the shoulder, as the latter put down his glass after a thorough compliance with his visitor's injunction. "A clever book that of yours, upon my honor. It's a work after my own heart. Your arrangement of the matter, I think, however, might be improved, and many of your notions remind me of Aristotle. That philosopher was one of my most intimate acquaintances. I liked him as much for his terrible ill temper, as for his happy knack at making a blunder. There is only one solid truth in all that he has written, and for that I gave him the hint out of pure compassion for his absurdity. I suppose, Pierre Bon-Bon, you very well know to what divine moral truth I am alluding?"

"Cannot say that I——"

"Indeed!—why it was I who told Aristotle that, by sneezing, men expelled superfluous ideas through the proboscis."

"Which is—hiccup!—undoubtedly the case," said the metaphysician, while he poured out for himself another bumper of *Mousseux*, and offered his snuff-box to the fingers of his visitor.

"There was Plato, too," continued his Majesty, modestly declining the snuff-box and the compliment it implied—"there was Plato, too, for whom I, at one time, felt all the affection of a friend. You knew Plato, Bon-Bon?—ah, no, I beg a thousand pardons. He met me at Athens, one day, in the Parthenon, and told me he was distressed for an idea. I bade him write down that 'ο νους εστιν αυλος.' He said that he would do so, and went home, while I stepped over to the pyramids. But my conscience smote me for having uttered a truth, even to aid a friend, and hastening back to Athens, I arrived behind the philosopher's chair as he was inditing the 'αυλος.' "Giving the lambdaa a fillip with my finger, I turned it upside down. So the sentence now reads and is, you perceive, the fundamental doctrine in his metaphysics."

"Were you ever at Rome?" asked the *restaurateur*, as he finished his second bottle of *Mousseux*, and drew from the closet a larger supply of *Chambertin*.

"But once, Monsieur Bon-Bon, but once. There was a time," said the Devil, as if reciting some passage from a book—"there was a time when occurred an anarchy of five years, during which the republic, bereft of all its officers, had no magistracy besides the tribunes of the people, and these were not legally vested with any degree of executive power—at that time, Monsieur Bon-Bon—at that time only I was in Rome, and I have no earthly acquaintance, consequently, with any of its philosophy."[1]

"What do you think of—what do you think of—hiccup!—Epicurus!"

1 *Ils écrivaient sur la philosophie* (Cicero, Lucretius, Seneca) *mais c'était la philosophie grècque.*—Condorcet. [They wrote on philosophy, but it was Greek philosophy.]]

"What do I think of *whom?*" said the Devil, in astonishment; "you surely do not mean to find any fault with Epicurus! What do I think of Epicurus! Do you mean me, sir?—I am Epicurus! I am the same philosopher who wrote each of the three hundred treatises commemorated by Diogenes Laertes."

"That's a lie!" said the metaphysician, for the wine had gotten a little into his head.

"Very well!—very well, sir!—very well, indeed, sir!" said his Majesty, apparently much flattered.

"That's a lie!" repeated the *restaurateur*, dogmatically; "that's a—hiccup!—a lie!"

"Well, well, have it your own way!" said the Devil, pacifically, and Bon-Bon, having beaten his Majesty at an argument, thought his duty to conclude a second bottle of Chambertin.

"As I was saying," resumed the visitor—"as I was observing a little while ago, there are some very *outré* notions in that book of yours, Monsieur Bon-Bon. What, for instance, do you mean by all that humbug about the soul? Pray, sir, what is the soul?"

"The—hiccup!—soul," replied the metaphysician, referring to his MS., "is undoubtedly——"

"No, sir!"

"Indubitably——"

"No, sir!"

"Indisputably——"

"No, sir!"

"Evidently——"

"No, sir!"

"Incontrovertibly——"

"No, sir!"

"Hiccup!"

"No, sir!"

"And beyond all question, a——"

"No, sir, the soul is no such thing!". (Here the philosopher, looking daggers, took occasion to make an end, upon the spot, of his third bottle of Chambertin.)

"Then—hiccup!—pray, sir—what—what is it?"

"That is neither here nor there, Monsieur Bon-Bon," replied his

Majesty, musingly. "I have tasted—that is to say, I have known some very bad souls, and some too—pretty good ones." Here he smacked his lips, and, having unconsciously let fall his hand upon the volume in his pocket, was seized with a violent fit of sneezing.

He continued:

"There was the soul of Cratinus—passable; Aristophanes—racy; Plato—exquisite—not your Plato, but Plato the comic poet; your Plato would have turned the stomach of Cerberus—faugh! Then let me see! there were Nævius, and Andronicus, and Plautus, and Terentius. Then there was Lucilius, and Catullus, and Naso, and Quintius Flaccus—dear Quinty! as I called him when he sung a *seculare* for my amusement, while I toasted him, in pure good-humor on a fork. But they want *flavor*, these Romans. One fat Greek is worth a dozen of them, and besides will keep, which cannot be said of a Quirite. Let us taste your *Sauterne*."

Bon-Bon had by this time made up his mind to the *nil admirari*, and endeavored to hand down the bottles in question. He was, however, conscious of a strange sound in the room like the wagging of a tail. Of this, although extremely indecent in his Majesty, the philosopher took no notice:—simply kicking the dog, and requesting him to be quiet. The visitor continued:

"I found that Horace tasted very much like Aristotle;—you know I am fond of variety. Terentius I could not have told from Menander. Naso, to my astonishment, was Nicander in disguise. Virgilius had a strong twang of Theocritus. Martial put me much in mind of Archilochus—and Titus Livius was positively Polybius and none other."

"Hiccup!" here replied Bon-Bon, and his Majesty proceeded:

"But if I have a penchant, Monsieur Bon-Bon—if I have a penchant, it is for a philosopher. Yet, let me tell you, sir, it is not every dev—I mean it is not every gentleman who knows how to *choose* a philosopher. Long ones are *not* good; and the best, if not carefully shelled, are apt to be a little rancid on account of the gall."

"Shelled!"

"I mean taken out of the carcass."

"What do you think of a—hiccup!—physician?"

"*Don't* mention them!—ugh! ugh!" (Here his Majesty retched violently.) "I never tasted but one—that rascal Hippocrates!—smelt of *asafœtida*—ugh! ugh! ugh!—caught a wretched cold washing him in the Styx—and after all he gave me the *cholera-morbus*."

"The—hiccup!—wretch!" ejaculated Bon-Bon, "the—hiccup!—abortion of a pill-box!"—and the philosopher dropped a tear.

"After all," continued the visitor, "after all, if a dev—if a gentleman wishes to *live*, he must have more talents than one or two; and with us a fat face is an evidence of diplomacy."

"How so?"

"Why, we are sometimes exceedingly pushed for provisions. You must know, in a climate so sultry as mine, it is frequently impossible to keep a spirit alive for more than two or three hours; and after death, unless pickled immediately (and a pickled spirit is *not* good), they will—smell—you understand, eh? Putrefaction is always to be apprehended when the souls are consigned to us in the usual way."

"Hiccup!—hiccup!—good God! how do you manage?"

Here the iron lamp commenced swinging with redoubled violence, and the Devil half started from his seat;—however, with a slight sigh, he recovered his composure, merely saying to our hero in a low tone: "I tell you what, Pierre Bon-Bon, we must have no more swearing."

The host swallowed another bumper, by way of denoting thorough comprehension and acquiescence, and the visitor continued:

"Why, there are several ways of managing. The most of us starve: some put up with the pickle: for my part I purchase my spirits *vivente corpore*, in which case I find they keep very well."

"But the body!—hiccup!—the body!"

"The body, the body—well, what of the body?—oh! ah! I perceive. Why, sir, the body is not at all affected by the transaction. I have made innumerable purchases of the kind in my day, and the parties never experienced any inconvenience. There were Cain and Nimrod, and Nero, and Caligula, and Dionysius, and Pisistratus, and—and a thousand others, who never knew what it was to have a soul during the latter part of their lives; yet, sir, these men adorned society. Why isn't there A——, now, whom you know as well as I? Is *he* not in possession of all his faculties, mental and corporeal? Who writes a keener epigram? Who reasons more wittily? Who—but, stay! I have his agreement in my pocket-book."

Thus saying, he produced a red leather wallet, and took from it a number of papers. Upon some of these Bon-Bon caught a glimpse of the letters Machi—Maza—Robesp—with the words Caligula, George, Elizabeth. His Majesty selected a narrow slip of parchment, and from it read aloud the following words:

"In consideration of certain mental endowments which it is unnecessary to specify, and in further consideration of one thousand *louis d'or*, I being aged one year and one month, do hereby make over to the bearer of this agreement all my right, title, and appurtenance in the shadow called my soul. (Signed) A. . . ."[1] (Here his Majesty repeated a name which I do not feel myself justified in indicating more unequivocally.)

"A clever fellow that," he resumed; "but, like you, Monsieur Bon-Bon, he was mistaken about the soul. The soul a shadow, truly! The soul a shadow! Ha! ha! ha!—he! he! he!—hu! hu! hu! Only think of a *fricasséed* shadow!"

"Only think—hiccup!—of a *fricasséed* shadow!" exclaimed our hero, whose faculties were becoming much illuminated by the profundity of his Majesty's discourse. "Only think of a—hiccup!—*fricasséed* shadow!! Now, *damme*!—hiccup!—humph! If I would have been such a—hiccup!—nincompoop! My soul, Mr.—humph!"

"*Your* soul, Monsieur Bon-Bon?"

"Yes, sir—hiccup!—*my* soul is——"

"What, sir?"

"No shadow, *damme*!"

"Did you mean to say——"

"Yes, sir, my soul is—hiccup!—humph!—yes, sir."

"Did you not intend to assert——"

"My soul is—hiccup!—peculiarly qualified for—hiccup!—a——"

"What, sir?"

"Stew."

"Ha!"

"*Soufflée.*"

"Eh!"

"*Fricassée.*"

"Indeed!"

"*Ragout* and *fricandeau*—and see here, my good fellow! I'll let you have it— hiccup!—a bargain." Here the philosopher slapped his Majesty upon the back.

"Couldn't think of such a thing," said the latter calmly, at the same time rising from his seat. The metaphysician stared.

"Am supplied at present," said his Majesty.

"Hic-cup!—e-h?" said the philosopher.

"Have no funds on hand."

"What?"

"Besides, very unhandsome in me——"

"Sir!"

"To take advantage of——"

"Hic-cup!"

"Your present disgusting and ungentlemanly situation."

Here the visitor bowed and withdrew—in what manner could not precisely be ascertained—but in a well-concerted effort to discharge a bottle at "the villain," the slenderchain was severed that depended from the ceiling, and the metaphysician prostrated by the downfall of the lamp.

KING PEST

A TALE CONTAINING AN ALLEGORY

The gods do bear and will allow in kings
The things which they abhor in rascal routes.
Buckhurst's *Tragedy of Ferrex and Porrex*

ABOUT TWELVE O'CLOCK, one night in the month of October, and during the chivalrous reign of the third Edward, two seamen belonging to the crew of the *Free and Easy*, a trading schooner plying between Sluys and the Thames, and then at anchor in that river, were much astonished to find themselves seated in the taproom of an alehouse in the parish of St Andrews, London—which alehouse bore for sign the portraiture of a "Jolly Tar."

The room, though ill-contrived, smoke-blackened, low-pitched, and in every other respect agreeing with the general character of such places at the period—was nevertheless, in the opinion of the grotesque groups scattered here and there within it, sufficiently well adapted to its purpose.

Of these groups our two seamen formed, I think, the most interesting, if not the most conspicuous.

The one who appeared to be the elder, and whom his companion addressed by the characteristic appellation of "Legs," was at the same time much the taller of the two. He might have measured six feet and a half, and an habitual stoop in the shoulders seemed to have been the necessary consequence of an altitude so enormous. Superfluities in height were, however, more than accounted for by deficiencies in other respects.

He was exceedingly thin; and might, as his associates asserted, have answered, when drunk, for a pennant at the mast-head, or, when sober, have served for a jib-boom. But these jests, and others of a similar nature, had evidently produced, at no time, any effect upon the cachinnatory muscles of the tar. With high cheek-bones, a large hawk-nose, retreating chin, fallen under-jaw, and huge protruding white eyes, the expression of his countenance, although tinged with a species of dogged indifference to matters and things in general, was not the less utterly solemn and serious beyond all attempts at imitation or description.

The younger seaman was, in all outward appearance, the converse of his companion. His stature could not have exceeded four feet. A pair of stumpy bow legs supported his squat, unwieldy figure, while his unusually short and thick arms, with no ordinary fists at their extremities, swung off dangling from his sides like the fins of a sea-turtle. Small eyes, of no particular color, twinkled far back in his head. His nose remained buried in the mass of flesh which enveloped his round, full, and purple face; and his thick upper-lip rested upon the still thicker one beneath with an air of complacent self-satisfaction, much heightened by the owner's habit of licking them at intervals. He evidently regarded his tall shipmate with a feeling half-wondrous, half-quizzical; and stared up occasionally in his face as the red setting sun stares up at the crags of Ben Nevis.

Various and eventful, however, had been the peregrinations of the worthy couple in and about the different tap-houses of the neighborhood during the earlier hours of the night. Funds, even the most ample, are not always everlasting; and it was with empty pockets our friends had ventured upon the present hostelry.

At the precise period, then, when this history properly commences, Legs, and his fellow, Hugh Tarpaulin, sat, each with both elbows resting upon the large oaken table in the middle of the floor, and with a hand upon either cheek. They were eyeing, from behind a huge flagon of unpaid-for "humming-stuff," the portentous words, "No Chalk," which to their indignation and astonishment were scored over the doorway by means of that very mineral whose presence they purported to deny. Not that the gift of deciphering written characters—a gift among the commonalty of that day considered little less cabalistical than the art of inditing—could, in strict justice, have been laid to the charge of either disciple of the sea; but there was, to say the truth, a certain twist in the formation of the letters—an indescribable lee-lurch about the whole—which foreboded, in the opinion of both seamen, a long run of dirty weather; and determined them at once, in the allegorical words of Leg himself, to "clew up all sail, and scud before the wind."

Having accordingly disposed of what remained of the ale, and looped up the points of their short doublets, they finally made a bolt for the street. Although Tarpaulin rolled twice into the fireplace, mistaking it for the door, yet their escape was at length happily effected—and half after twelve o'clock found our heroes ripe for mischief, and running for life down a dark alley in the direction of St Andrew's Stair, hotly pursued by the landlady of the "Jolly Tar."

At the epoch of this eventful tale, and periodically, for many years before and after, all England, but more especially the metropolis resounded with the fearful cry of "Plague!" The city was in a great measure depopulated—and in those horrible regions, in the vicinity of the Thames, where, amid the dark, narrow, and filthy lanes and alleys, the Demon of Disease was supposed to have had his nativity, Awe, Terror, and Superstition were alone to be found stalking abroad.

By authority of the king such districts were placed under ban, and all persons forbidden, under pain of death, to intrude upon their dismal solitude. Yet neither the mandate of the monarch, nor the huge barriers erected at the entrances of the streets, nor the prospect of that loathsome death which, with almost absolute certainty, overwhelmed the wretch whom no peril could deter from the adventure, prevented the unfurnished and untenanted dwellings from being stripped, by the hand of nightly rapine, of every article, such as iron, brass, or leadwork, which could in any manner be turned to a profitable account.

Above all, it was usually found, upon the annual winter opening of the barriers, that locks, bolts, and secret cellars had proved but slender protection to those rich stores of wines and liquors which, in consideration of the risk and trouble of removal, many of the numerous dealers having shops in the neighborhood had consented to trust, during the period of exile, to so insufficient a security.

But there were very few of the terror-stricken people who attributed these doings to the agency of human hands. Pest-spirits, plague-goblins, and fever-demons were the popular imps of mischief; and tales so blood-chilling were hourly told, that the whole mass of forbidden buildings was, at length, enveloped in terror as in a shroud, and the plunderer himself was often scared away by the horrors his own depredations had created; leaving the entire vast circuit of prohibited district to gloom, silence, pestilence, and death.

It was by one of the terrific barriers already mentioned, and which indicated the region beyond to be under the Pest-ban, that, in scrambling down an alley, Legs and the worthy Hugh Tarpaulin found their progress suddenly impeded. To return was out of the question, and no time was to be lost, as their pursuers were close upon their heels. With thorough-bred seamen to clamber up the roughly fashioned plank-work was a trifle; and maddened with the twofold excitement of exercise and liquor, they leaped unhesitatingly down within the enclosure, and holding on their drunken course with shouts and yellings, were soon bewildered in its noisome and intricate recesses.

Had they not, indeed, been intoxicated beyond moral sense, their reeling footsteps must have been palsied by the horrors of their situation. The air was cold and misty. The paving-stones, loosened from their beds, lay in wild disorder amid the tall, rank grass, which sprang up around the feet and ankles. Fallen houses choked up the streets. The most fetid and poisonous smells everywhere prevailed: and by the aid of that ghastly light which, even at midnight, never fails to emanate from a vapory and pestilential atmosphere, might be discerned lying in the bypaths and alleys, or rotting in the windowless habitations, the carcass of many a nocturnal plunderer arrested by the hand of the plague in the very perpetration of his robbery.

But it lay not in the power of images, or sensations, or impediments such as these, to stay the course of men who, naturally brave, and at that time especially, brimful of courage and of "humming-stuff," would have reeled, as straight as their condition might have permitted, undauntedly into the very jaws of Death. Onward—still onward stalked the grim Legs, making the desolate solemnity echo and re-echo with yells like the terrific war-whoop of the Indian; and onward, still onward rolled the dumpy Tarpaulin, hanging on to the doublet of his more active companion, and far surpassing the latter's most strenuous exertions in the way of vocal music, by bull-roarings in basso, from the profundity of his stentorian lungs.

They had now evidently reached the stronghold of the pestilence. Their way at every step or plunge grew more noisome and more horrible—the paths more narrow and more intricate. Huge stones and beams falling momently from the decaying roofs above them, gave evidence, by their sullen and heavy descent, of the vast height of the surrounding houses; and while actual exertion became necessary to force a passage through frequent heaps of rubbish, it was by no means seldom that the hand fell upon a skeleton or rested upon a more fleshy corpse.

Suddenly, as the seamen stumbled against the entrance of a tall and ghastly-looking building, a yell more than usually shrill from the throat of the excited Legs, was replied to from within, in a rapid succession of wild, laughter-like, and fiendish shrieks. Nothing daunted at sounds which, of such a nature, at such a time, and in such a place, might have curdled the very blood in hearts less irrevocably on fire, the drunken couple rushed headlong against the door, burst it open, and staggered into the midst of things with a volley of curses.

The room within which they found themselves proved to be the shop of an undertaker; but an open trap-door, in the corner of the floor near the entrance, looked down upon a long range of wine-cellars, whose depths the occasional sound of bursting bottles proclaimed to be well stored with their appropriate contents. In the middle of the room stood a table—in the center of which again arose a huge tub of what appeared to be punch. Bottles of various wines and cordials, together with jugs, pitchers, and flagons of every shape and quality, were scattered profusely upon the board. Around it, upon coffin-trestles, was seated a company of six. This company I will endeavor to delineate one by one.

Fronting the entrance, and elevated a little above his companions, sat a personage who appeared to be the president of the table. His stature was gaunt and tall, and Legs was confounded to behold in him a figure more emaciated than himself. His face was as yellow as saffron—but no feature, excepting one alone, was sufficiently marked to merit a particular description. This one consisted in a forehead so unusually and hideously lofty, as to have the appearance of a bonnet or crown of flesh superadded upon the natural head. His mouth was puckered and dimpled into an expression of ghastly affability, and his eyes, as indeed the eyes of all at table, were glazed over with the fumes of intoxication. This gentleman was clothed from head to foot in a richly embroidered black silk-velvet pall wrapped negligently around his form after the fashion of a Spanish cloak. His head was stuck full of sable hearse-plumes, which he nodded to and fro with a jaunty and knowing air; and, in his right hand, he held a huge human thigh-bone, with which he appeared to have been just knocking down some member of the company for a song.

Opposite him, and with her back to the door, was a lady of no whit less extraordinary character. Although quite as tall as the person just described, she had no right to complain of his unnatural emaciation. She was evidently in the last stage of a dropsy; and her figure resembled nearly that of the huge puncheon of October beer which stood, with the head driven in, close by her side, in a corner of the chamber. Her face was exceedingly round, red, and full; and the same peculiarity, or rather want of peculiarity, attached itself to her countenance, which I before mentioned in the case of the president—that is to say, only one feature of her face was sufficiently distinguished to need a separate characterization: indeed the acute Tarpaulin immediately observed that the same remark might have applied to each individual person of the party, every one of whom seemed to possess a monopoly of some particular portion of physiognomy. With the lady in question this portion proved to be the mouth. Commencing at the right ear, it swept with a terrific chasm to the left—the short pendants which she wore in either auricle continually bobbing into the aperture. She made, however, every exertion to keep her mouth closed and look dignified, in a dress consisting of a newly-starched and ironed shroud coming up close under her chin, with a crumpled ruffle of cambric muslin.

At her right hand sat a diminutive young lady whom she appeared to patronize. This delicate little creature, in the trembling of her wasted fingers, in the livid hue of her lips, and in the slight hectic spot which tinged her otherwise leaden complexion, gave evident indications of a galloping consumption. An air of extreme *haut ton*, however, pervaded her whole appearance; she wore, in a graceful and *dégagé* manner, a large and beautiful winding-sheet of the finest India lawn; her hair hung in ringlets over her neck; a soft smile played about her mouth; but her nose, extremely long, thin, sinuous, flexible, and pimpled, hung down far below her under-lip, and, in spite of the delicate manner in which she now and then moved it to one side or the other with her tongue, gave to her countenance a somewhat equivocal expression.

Over against her, and upon the left of the dropsical lady, was seated a little puffy, wheezing, and gouty old man, whose cheeks reposed upon the shoulders of their owner, like two huge bladders of Oporto wine. With his arms folded, and with one bandaged leg deposited upon the table, he seemed to think himself entitled to some consideration. He evidently prided himself much upon every inch of his personal appearance, but took more especial delight in calling attention to his gaudy-colored surtout. This, to say the truth, must have cost him no little money, and was made to fit him exceedingly well—being fashioned from one of the curiously embroidered silken covers appertaining to those glorious escutcheons which, in England and elsewhere, are customarily hung up, in some conspicuous place, upon the dwellings of departed aristocracy.

Next to him, and at the right hand of the president, was a gentleman in long white hose and cotton drawers. His frame shook, in a ridiculous manner, with a fit of what Tarpaulin called "the horrors." His jaws, which had been newly shaved, were tightly tied up by a bandage of muslin; and his arms being fastened in a similar way at the wrists, prevented him from helping himself too freely to the liquors upon the table; a precaution rendered necessary, in the opinion of Legs, by the peculiarly sottish and wine-bibbing cast of his visage. A pair of prodigious ears, nevertheless, which it was no doubt found impossible to confine, towered away into the atmosphere of the apartment, and were occasionally pricked up in a spasm at the sound of the drawing of a cork.

Fronting him, sixthly and lastly, was situated a singularly stiff-looking personage, who, being afflicted with paralysis, must, to speak seriously, have felt very ill at ease in his unaccommodating habiliments. He was habited, somewhat uniquely, in a new and handsome mahogany coffin. Its top or head-piece pressed upon the skull of the wearer, and extended over it in the fashion of a hood, giving to the entire face an air of indescribable interest. Arm-holes had been cut in the sides for the sake not more of elegance than of convenience; but the dress, nevertheless, prevented its proprietor from sitting as erect as his associates; and as he lay reclining against his trestle, at an angle of forty-five degrees, a pair of huge goggle eyes rolled up their awful whites toward the ceiling in absolute amazement at their own enormity.

Before each of the party lay a portion of a skull, which was used as a drinking-cup. Overhead was suspended a human skeleton, by means of a rope tied round one of the legs and fastened to a ring in the ceiling. The other limb, confined by no such fetter, stuck off from the body at right angles, causing the whole loose and rattling frame to dangle and twirl about at the caprice of every occasional puff of wind which found its way into the apartment. In the cranium of this hideous thing lay a quantity of ignited charcoal, which threw a fitful but vivid light over the entire scene; while coffins, and other wares appertaining to the shop of an undertaker, were piled high up around the room, and against the windows, preventing any ray from escaping into the street.

At sight of this extraordinary assembly, and of their still more extraordinary paraphernalia, our two seamen did not conduct themselves with that degree of decorum which might have been expected. Legs, leaning against the wall near which he happened to be standing, dropped his lower jaw still lower than usual, and spread open his eyes to their fullest extent; while Hugh Tarpaulin, stooping down so as to bring his nose upon a level with the table, and spreading out a palm upon either knee, burst into a long, loud, and obstreperous roar of very ill-timed and immoderate laughter.

Without, however, taking offense at behavior so excessively rude, the tall president smiled very graciously upon the intruders—nodded to them in a dignified manner with his head of sable plumes—and, arising, took each by an arm, and led him to a seat which some others of the company had placed in the meantime for his accommodation. Legs to all this offered not the slightest resistance, but sat down as he was directed; while the gallant Hugh, removing his coffin-trestle from its station near the head of the table, to the vicinity of the little consumptive lady in the winding-sheet, plumped down by her side in high glee, and pouring out a skull of red wine, quaffed it to their better acquaintance. But at this presumption the stiff gentleman in the coffin seemed exceedingly nettled; and serious consequences might have ensued, had not the president, rapping upon the table with his truncheon, diverted the attention of all present to the following speech:

"It becomes our duty upon the present happy occasion——"

"Avast there!" interrupted Legs, looking very serious, "avast there a bit, I say, and tell us who the devil ye all are, and what business ye have here, rigged off like the foul fiends, and swilling the snug blue ruin stowed away for the winter by my honest shipmate, Will Wimble, the undertaker!"

At this unpardonable piece of ill-breeding, all the original company half-started to their feet, and uttered the same rapid succession of wild fiendish shrieks which had before caught the attention of the seamen. The president, however, was the first to recover his composure, and at length, turning to Legs with great dignity, recommenced:

"Most willingly will we gratify any reasonable curiosity on the part of guests so illustrious, unbidden though they be. Know then that in these dominions I am monarch, and here rule with undivided empire under the title of 'King Pest the First.'

"This apartment, which you no doubt profanely suppose to be the shop of Will Wimble the undertaker—a man whom we know not, and whose plebeian appellation has never before this night thwarted our royal ears—this apartment, I say, is the Dais-Chamber of our Palace, devoted to the councils of our kingdom, and to other sacred and lofty purposes.

"The noble lady who sits opposite is Queen Pest, our Serene Consort. The other exalted personages whom you behold are all of our family, and wear the insignia of the blood royal under the respective titles of 'His Grace the Arch Duke Pest-Iferous,'—'His Grace the Duke Pest-Ilential'—'His Grace the Duke Tem-Pest'—'and Her Serene Highness the Arch Duchess Ana-Pest.'

"As regards," continued he, "your demand of the business upon which we sit here in council, we might be pardoned for replying that it concerns, and concerns alone, our own private and regal interest, and is in no manner important to any other than ourself. But in consideration of those rights to which as guests and strangers you may feel yourselves entitled, we will furthermore explain that we are here this night, prepared, by deep research and accurate investigation, to examine, analyze, and thoroughly determine the indefinable spirit—the incomprehensible qualities and nature—of those inestimable treasures of the palate, the wines, ales and liqueurs of this goodly metropolis: by so doing to advance not more our own designs than the true welfare of that unearthly sovereign whose reign is over us all, whose dominions are unlimited, and whose name is 'Death.'"

"Whose name is Davy Jones!" ejaculated Tarpaulin, helping the lady by his side to a skull of liqueur, and pouring out a second for himself.

"Profane varlet!" said the president, now turning his attention to the worthy Hugh, "profane and execrable wretch!—we have said, that, in consideration of those rights which, even in thy filthy person, we feel no inclination to violate, we have condescended to make reply to thy rude and unreasonable inquiries. We nevertheless, for your unhallowed intrusion upon our councils, believe it our duty to mulct thee and thy companion in each a gallon of Black Strap—having imbibed which to the prosperity of our kingdom—at a single draft—and upon your bended knees—ye shall be forthwith free either to proceed upon your way, or remain and be admitted to the privileges of our table, according to your respective and individual pleasures."

"It would be a matter of utter impossibility," replied Legs, whom the assumptions and dignity of King Pest the First had evidently inspired with some feelings of respect, and who arose and steadied himself by the table as he spoke—"it would, please your majesty, be a matter of utter impossibility to stow away in my hold even one-fourth part of that same liquor which your majesty has just mentioned. To say nothing of the stuffs placed on board in the forenoon by way of ballast, and not to mention the various ales and liqueurs shipped this evening at various seaports, I have, at present, a full cargo of 'humming-stuff' taken in and duly paid for at the sign of the 'Jolly Tar.' You will, therefore, please your majesty, be so good as to take the will for the deed—for by no manner of means either can I or will I swallow another drop—least of all a drop of that villainous bilge-water that answers to the name of 'Black Strap.'"

"Belay that," interrupted Tarpaulin, astonished not more at the length of his companion's speech than at the nature of his refusal—"Belay that, you lubber!—and I say, Legs, none of your palaver. My hull is still light, although I confess you yourself seem to be a little top-heavy; and as for the matter of your share of the cargo, why rather than raise a squall I would find stowage-room for it myself, but——"

"This proceeding," interposed the president, "is by no means in accordance with the terms of the mulct or sentence, which is in its nature Median, and not to be altered or recalled. The conditions we have imposed must be fulfilled to the letter, and that without a moment's hesitation—in failure of which fulfillment we decree that you do here be tied neck and heels together, and duly drowned as rebels in yon hogshead of October beer!"

"A sentence!—a sentence!—a righteous and just sentence!—a glorious decree!—a most worthy and upright and holy condemnation!" shouted the Pest family altogether. The king elevated his forehead into innumerable wrinkles; the gouty little old man puffed like a pair of bellows; the lady of the winding-sheet waved her nose to and fro; the gentleman in the cotton drawers pricked up his ears; she of the shroud gasped like a dying fish; and he of the coffin looked stiff and rolled up his eyes.

"Ugh! ugh! ugh!" chuckled Tarpaulin, without heeding the general excitation, "ugh! ugh! ugh!—ugh! ugh! ugh! ugh!—ugh! ugh! ugh!—I was saying," said he—"I was saying when Mr. King Pest poked in his marlinspike, that as for the matter of two or three gallons more or less of Black Strap, it was a trifle to a tight sea-boat like myself not overstowed—but when it comes to drinking the health of the Devil (whom God assoilizie) and going down upon my marrow-bones to his ill-favored majesty there, whom I know, as well as I know myself to be a sinner, to be nobody in the whole world but Tim Hurlygurly the stage-player!—why! it's quite another guess sort of a thing, and utterly and altogether past my comprehension."

He was not allowed to finish this speech in tranquillity. At the name of Tim Hurlygurly the whole assembly leaped from their seats.

"Treason!" shouted his Majesty King Pest the First.

"Treason!" said the little man with the gout.

"Treason!" screamed the Arch Duchess Ana-Pest.

"Treason!" muttered the gentleman with his jaws tied up.

"Treason!" growled he of the coffin.

"Treason! treason!" shrieked her majesty of the mouth; and, seizing by the hinder-part of his breeches the unfortunate Tarpaulin, who had just commenced pouring out for himself a skull of liqueur, she lifted him high into the air, and let him fall without ceremony into the huge open puncheon of his beloved ale. Bobbing up and down, for a few seconds, like an apple in a bowl of toddy, he, at length, finally disappeared amid the whirlpool of foam which, in the already effervescent liquor, his struggles easily succeeded in creating.

Not tamely, however, did the tall seaman behold the discomfiture of his companion. Jostling King Pest through the open trap, the valiant

Legs slammed the door down upon him with an oath, and strode toward the center of the room. Here tearing down the skeleton which swung over the table, he laid it about him with so much energy and good-will that, as the last glimpses of light died away within the apartment, he succeeded in knocking out the brains of the little gentleman with the gout. Rushing then with all his force against the fatal hogshead full of October ale and Hugh Tarpaulin, he rolled it over and over in an instant. Out poured a deluge of liquor so fierce—so impetuous—so overwhelming—that the room was flooded from wall to wall—the loaded table was overturned—the trestles were thrown upon their backs—the tub of punch into the fireplace—and the ladies into hysterics. Piles of death furniture floundered about. Jugs, pitchers, and carboys mingled promiscuously in the *mêlée*, and wicker flagons encountered desperately with bottles of junk. The man with the horrors was drowned upon the spot—the little stiff gentleman floated off in his coffin—and the victorious Legs, seizing by the waist the fat lady in the shroud, rushed out with her into the street, and made a bee-line for the *Free and Easy*, followed under easy sail by the redoubtable Hugh Tarpaulin, who, having sneezed three or four times, panted and puffed after him with the Arch Duchess Ana-Pest.

METZENGERSTEIN

Pestis eram vivus—moriens tua mors ero[1]—Martin Luther

HORROR AND FATALITY have been stalking abroad in all ages. Why then give a date to the story I have to tell? Let it suffice to say, that at the period of which I speak, there existed, in the interior of Hungary, a settled although hidden belief in the doctrines of the Metempsychosis. Of the doctrines themselves—that is, of their falsity, or of their probability—I say nothing. I assert, however, that much of our incredulity (as La Bruyère says of all our unhappiness) "*vient de ne pouvoir être seuls.*"[2]

But there were some points in the Hungarian superstition which were fast verging to absurdity. They—the Hungarians—differed very essentially from their Eastern authorities. For example. "The soul," said the former—I give the words of an acute and intelligent Parisian—"*ne demeure qu'une seule fois dans un corps sensible: au reste—un cheval, un chien, un homme même, n'est que la ressemblance peu tangible de ces animaux.*" [3]

The families at Berlifitzing and Metzengerstein had been at variance for centuries. Never before were two houses, so illustrious, mutually embittered by hostility so deadly. The origin of this enmity seems to be found in the words of an ancient prophecy—"A lofty name shall have a

1 "Living I was your plague, dying I shall be your death."

2 Mercier, in *L'An deux mille quatre cent quarante*, seriously maintains the doctrines of the Metempsychosis and J. D'Israeli says that "no system is so simple and so little repugnant to the understanding." Colonel Ethan Allen, the "Green Mountain Boy," is also said to have been a serious metempsychosist.

3 The soul resides only once in a sentient body: in fact—a horse, a dog, even a man, is only the scarcely tangible resemblances of these animals."

fearful fall when, as the rider over his horse, the mortality of Metzengerstein shall triumph over the immortality of Berlifitzing."

To be sure, the words themselves had little or no meaning. But more trivial causes have given rise—and that no long while ago—to consequences equally eventful. Besides, the estates, which were contiguous, had long exercised a rival influence in the affairs of a busy government. Moreover, near neighbors are seldom friends; and the inhabitants of the Castle Berlifitzing might look from their lofty buttresses into the very windows of the Palace Metzengerstein. Least of all had the more than feudal magnificence, thus discovered, a tendency to allay the irritable feelings of the less ancient and less wealthy Berlifitzings. What wonder, then, that the words, however silly, of that prediction, should have succeeded in setting and keeping at variance two families already predisposed to quarrel by every instigation of hereditary jealousy? The prophecy seemed to imply—if it implied anything—a final triumph on the part of the already more powerful house; and was of course remembered with the more bitter animosity by the weaker and less influential.

Wilhelm, Count Berlifitzing, although loftily descended, was, at the epoch of this narrative, an infirm and doting old man, remarkable for nothing but an inordinate and inveterate personal antipathy to the family of his rival, and so passionate a love of horses, and of hunting, that neither bodily infirmity, great age, nor mental incapacity, prevented his daily participation in the dangers of the chase.

Frederick, Baron Metzengerstein, was, on the other hand, not yet of age. His father, the Minister G——, died young. His mother, the Lady Mary, followed him quickly. Frederick was, at that time, in his eighteenth year. In a city, eighteen years are no long period; but in a wilderness—in so magnificent a wilderness as that old principality, the pendulum vibrates with a deeper meaning.

From some peculiar circumstances attending the administration of his father, the young Baron, at the decease of the former, entered immediately upon his vast possessions. Such estates were seldom held before by a nobleman of Hungary. His castles were without number. The chief in point of splendor and extent was the "Palace Metzengerstein." The boundary line of his dominions was never clearly defined; but his principal park embraced a circuit of fifty miles.

Upon the succession of a proprietor so young, with a character so well known, to a fortune so unparalleled, little speculation was afloat in regard to his probable course of conduct. And, indeed, for the space of three days the behavior of the heir out-Heroded Herod, and fairly surpassed the expectations of his most enthusiastic admirers. Shameful debaucheries—flagrant treacheries—unheard-of atrocities—gave his trembling vassals quickly to understand that no servile submission on their part—no punctilios of conscience on his own—were thenceforward to prove any security against the remorseless fangs of a petty Caligula. On the night of the fourth day, the stables of the Castle Berlifitzing were discovered to be on fire; and the unanimous opinion of the neighborhood added the crime of the incendiary to the already hideous list of the Baron's misdemeanors and enormities.

But during the tumult occasioned by this occurrence, the young nobleman himself sat apparently buried in meditation, in a vast and desolate upper apartment of the family palace of Metzengerstein. The rich although faded tapestry hangings which swung gloomily upon the walls represented the shadowy and majestic forms of a thousand illustrious ancestors. Here, rich-ermined priests and pontifical dignitaries, familiarly seated with the autocrat and the sovereign, put a veto on the wishes of a temporal king, or restrained with the fiat of papal supremacy the rebellious sceptre of the Arch-enemy. There, the dark, tall statures of the Princes Metzengerstein—their muscular war-courses plunging over the carcasses of fallen foes—startled the steadiest nerves with their vigorous expression; and here, again, the voluptuous and swan-like figures of the dames of days gone by floated away in the mazes of an unreal dance to the strains of imaginary melody.

But as the Baron listened, or affected to listen, to the gradually increasing uproar in the stables of Berlifitzing—or perhaps pondered upon some more novel, some more decided act of audacity—his eyes were turned unwittingly to the figure of an enormous, and unnaturally colored horse, represented in the tapestry as belonging to a Saracen ancestor of the family of his rival. The horse itself, in the foreground of the design, stood motionless and statue-like—while, farther back, its discomfited rider perished by the dagger of a Metzengerstein.

On Frederick's lip arose a fiendish expression, as he became aware of the direction which his glance had, without his consciousness, assumed. Yet he did not remove it. On the contrary, he could by no means account for the overwhelming anxiety which appeared falling like a pall upon his senses. It was with difficulty that he reconciled his dreamy and incoherent feelings with the certainty of being awake. The longer he gazed the more absorbing became the spell—the more impossible did it appear that he could ever withdraw his glance from the fascination of that tapestry. But the tumult without becoming suddenly more violent, with a compulsory exertion he diverted his attention to the glare of ruddy light thrown full by the flaming stables upon the windows of the apartment.

The action, however, was but momentary; his gaze returned mechanically to the wall. To his extreme horror and astonishment, the head of the gigantic steed had, in the meantime, altered its position. The neck of the animal, before arched, as if in compassion, over the prostrate body of its lord, was now extended at full length, in the direction of the Baron. The eyes, before invisible, now wore an energetic and human expression, while they gleamed with a fiery and unusual red; and the distended lips of the apparently enraged horse left in full view his sepulchral and disgusting teeth.

Stupefied with terror, the young nobleman tottered to the door. As he threw it open, a flash of red light, streaming far into the chamber, flung his shadow with a clear outline against the quivering tapestry; and he shuddered to perceive that shadow—as he staggered awhile upon the threshold—assuming the exact position, and precisely filling up the contour, of the relentless and triumphant murderer of the Saracen Berlifitzing.

To lighten the depression of his spirits, the Baron hurried into the open air. At the principal gate of the palace he encountered three equerries. With much difficulty, and at the imminent peril of their lives, they were restraining the convulsive plunges of a gigantic and fiery-colored horse.

"Whose horse? Where did you get him?" demanded the youth, in a querulous and husky tone, as he became instantly aware that the mysterious steed in the tapestried chamber was the very counterpart of the furious animal before his eyes.

"He is your own property, sire," replied one of the equerries, "at least he is claimed by no other owner. We caught him flying, all smoking and foaming with rage, from the burning stables of the Castle Berlifitzing. Supposing him to have belonged to the old Count's stud of foreign horses, we led him back as an estray. But the grooms there disclaim any title to the creature; which is strange, since he bears evident marks of having made a narrow escape from the flames."

"The letters W. V. B. are also branded very distinctly on his forehead," interrupted a second equerry; "I suppose them, of course, to be the initials of William Von Berlifitzing—but all at the castle are positive in denying any knowledge of the horse."

"Extremely singular!" said the young Baron, with a musing air, and apparently unconscious of the meaning of his words. "He is, as you say, a remarkable horse—a prodigious horse! although, as you very justly observe, of a suspicious and untractable character; let him be mine, however," he added, after a pause, "perhaps a rider like Frederick of Metzengerstein may tame even the devil from the stables of Berlifitzing."

"You are mistaken, my lord; the horse, as I think we mentioned, is not from the stables of the Count. If such had been the case, we know our duty better than to bring him into the presence of a noble of your family."

"True!" observed the Baron, dryly; and at that instant a page of the bedchamber came from the palace with a heightened color, and a precipitate step. He whispered into his master's ear an account of the sudden disappearance of a small portion of the tapestry in an apartment which he designated; entering, at the same time, into particulars of a minute and circumstantial character; but from the low tone of voice in which these latter were communicated, nothing escaped to gratify the excited curiosity of the equerries.

The young Frederick, during the conference, seemed agitated by a variety of emotions. He soon, however, recovered his composure, and an expression of determined malignancy settled upon his countenance, as he gave peremptory orders that the apartment in question should be immediately locked up, and the key placed in his own possession.

"Have you heard of the unhappy death of the old hunter, Berlifitzing?"

said one of his vassals to the Baron, as, after the departure of the page, the huge steed which that nobleman had adopted as his own, plunged and curveted, with redoubled fury, down the long avenue which extended from the palace to the stables of Metzengerstein.

"No!" said the Baron, turning abruptly toward the speaker, "dead! say you?"

"It is indeed true, my lord; and, to the noble of your name, will be, I imagine, no unwelcome intelligence."

A rapid smile shot over the countenance of the listener. "How died he?"

"In his rash exertions to rescue a favorite portion of the hunting stud, he has himself perished miserably in the flames."

"I—n—d—e—e—d—!" ejaculated the Baron, as if slowly and deliberately impressed with the truth of some exciting idea.

"Indeed," repeated the vassal.

"Shocking!" said the youth, calmly, and turned quietly into the palace.

From this date a marked alteration took place in the outward demeanor of the dissolute young Baron Frederick Von Metzengerstein. Indeed, his behavior disappointed every expectation, and proved little in accordance with the views of many a maneuvering mamma; while his habits and manner, still less than formerly, offered anything congenial with those of the neighboring aristocracy. He was never to be seen beyond the limits of his own domain, and, in this wide and social world, was utterly companionless—unless, indeed, that unnatural, impetuous, and fiery-colored horse, which he henceforward continually bestrode, had any mysterious right to the title of his friend.

Numerous invitations on the part of the neighborhood for a long time, however, periodically came in. "Will the Baron honor our festivals with his presence?" "Will the Baron join us in a hunting of the boar?"—"Metzengerstein does not hunt;" "Metzengerstein will not attend," were the haughty and laconic answers.

These repeated insults were not to be endured by an imperious nobility. Such invitations became less cordial—less frequent—in time they ceased altogether. The widow of the unfortunate Count Berlifitzing was even heard to express a hope "that the Baron might be at home when he did not wish to be at home, since he disdained the company of his equals; and ride when he did not wish to ride, since he preferred the society of a horse." This, to be sure, was a very silly explosion of hereditary pique; and merely proved how singularly unmeaning our sayings are apt to become, when we desire to be unusually energetic.

The charitable, nevertheless, attributed the alteration in the conduct of the young nobleman to the natural sorrow of a son for the untimely loss of his parents;—forgetting, however, his atrocious and reckless behavior during the short period immediately succeeding that bereavement. Some there were, indeed, who suggested a too haughty idea of self-consequence and dignity. Others again (among whom may be mentioned the family physician) did not hesitate in speaking of morbid melancholy, and hereditary ill-health; while dark hints, of a more equivocal nature, were current among the multitude.

Indeed, the Baron's perverse attachment to his lately acquired charger—an attachment which seemed to attain new strength from every fresh example of the animal's ferocious and demon-like propensities—at length became, in the eyes of all reasonable men, a hideous and unnatural fervor. In the glare of noon—at the dead hour of night—in sickness or in health—in calm or in tempest—the young Metzengerstein seemed riveted to the saddle of that colossal horse, whose intractable audacities so well accorded with his own spirit.

There were circumstances, moreover, which, coupled with late events, gave an unearthly and portentous character to the mania of the rider, and to the capabilities of the steed. The space passed over in a single leap had been accurately measured, and was found to exceed, by an astounding difference, the wildest expectations of the most imaginative. The Baron, besides, had no particular name for the animal, although all the rest in his collection were distinguished by characteristic appellations. His stable, too, was appointed at a distance from the rest; and, with regard to grooming and other necessary offices, none but the owner in person had ventured to officiate, or even to enter the enclosure of that horse's particular stall. It was also to be observed, that although the three grooms, who had caught the steed as he fled from the conflagration at Berlifitzing, had succeeded in arresting his course by means of a chain-bridle and noose—yet not one of the three could with any certainty affirm that he had, during that dangerous struggle, or at any period thereafter, actually placed his hand upon the body of the beast. Instances of peculiar intelligence in the demeanor of a noble and high-spirited horse are not to be supposed capable of exciting unreasonable attention, but there were certain circumstances which intruded themselves perforce upon the most skeptical and phlegmatic; and it is said there were times when the animal caused the gaping crowd who stood around to recoil in horror from the deep and impressive meaning of his terrible stamp—times when the young Metzengerstein turned pale and shrunk away from the rapid and searching expression of his human-looking eye.

Among all the retinue of the Baron, however, none were found to doubt the ardor of that extraordinary affection which existed on the part of the young nobleman for the fiery qualities of his horse; at least, none but an insignificant and misshapen little page, whose deformities were in everybody's way, and whose opinions were of the least possible importance. He (if his ideas are worth mentioning at all) had the effrontery to assert that his master never vaulted into the saddle without an unaccountable and almost imperceptible shudder; and that, upon his return from every long-continued and habitual ride, an expression of triumphant malignity distorted every muscle in his countenance.

One tempestuous night, Metzengerstein, awakening from a heavy slumber, descended like a maniac from his chamber, and, mounting in hot haste, bounded away into the mazes of the forest. An occurrence so common attracted no particular attention, but his return was looked for with intense anxiety on the part of his domestics, when, after some hours' absence, the stupendous and magnificent battlements of the Palace Metzengerstein were discovered crackling and rocking to their very foundation, under the influence of a dense and livid mass of ungovernable fire.

As the flames, when first seen, had already made so terrible a progress that all efforts to save any portion of the building were evidently futile, the astonished neighborhood stood idly around in silent if not apathetic wonder. But a new and fearful object soon riveted the attention of the multitude, and proved how much more intense is the excitement wrought in the feelings of a crowd by the contemplation of human agony, than that brought about by the most appalling spectacles of inanimate matter.

Up the long avenue of aged oaks which led from the forest to the main entrance of the Palace Metzengerstein, a steed, bearing an unbonneted and disordered rider, was seen leaping with an impetuosity which outstripped the very Demon of the Tempest.

The career of the horseman was indisputably, on his own part, uncontrollable. The agony of his countenance, the convulsive struggle of his frame, gave evidence of superhuman exertion; but no sound, save a solitary shriek, escaped from his lacerated lips, which were bitten through and through in the intensity of terror. One instant, and the clattering of hoofs resounded sharply and shrilly above the roaring of the flames and the shrieking of the winds—another, and, clearing at a single plunge the gateway and the moat, the steed bounded far up the tottering staircases of the palace, and, with its rider, disappeared amid the whirlwind of chaotic fire.

The fury of the tempest immediately died away, and a dead calm sullenly succeeded. A white flame still enveloped the building like a shroud, and, streaming far away into the quiet atmosphere, shot forth a glare of preternatural light; while a cloud of smoke settled heavily over the battlements in the distinct colossal figure of—*a horse*.

SILENCE—A FABLE

'Eudosin d'orheon korhuphai te kai pharhagges.
Prhones te kai charhadrhai.'
The mountain pinnacles slumber; valleys, crags, and caves are silent.
Alcman *[60 (10), 646]*

LISTEN TO ME," said the Demon, as he placed his hand upon my head. "The region of which I speak is a dreary region in Libya, by the borders of the river Zaïre. And there is no quiet there, nor silence.

"The waters of the river have a saffron and sickly hue; and they flow not onward to the sea, but palpitate for ever and for ever beneath the red eye of the sun with a tumultuous and convulsive motion. For many miles on either side of the river's oozy bed is a pale desert of gigantic water-lilies. They sigh one unto the other in that solitude, and stretch toward the heaven their long and ghastly necks, and nod to and fro their everlasting heads. And there is an indistinct murmur which cometh out from among them like the rushing of subterrene water. And they sigh one unto the other.

"But there is a boundary to their realm—the boundary of the dark, horrible, lofty forest. There, like the waves about the Hebrides, the low underwood is agitated continually. But there is no wind throughout the heaven. And the tall primeval trees rock eternally hither and thither with a crashing and mighty sound. And from their high summits, one by one, drop everlasting dews. And at the roots strange poisonous flowers lie writhing in perturbed slumber. And overhead, with a rustling and loud noise, the gray clouds rush westwardly for ever, until they roll, a cataract, over the fiery wall of the horizon. But there is no wind throughout the heaven. And by the shores of the river Zaïre there is neither quiet nor silence.

"It was night, and the rain fell; and, falling, it was rain, but, having fallen, it was blood. And I stood in the morass among the tall lilies, and the rain fell upon my head—and the lilies sighed one unto the other in the solemnity of their desolation.

"And, all at once, the moon arose through the thin ghastly mist, and was crimson in color. And mine eyes fell upon a huge gray rock which stood by the shore of the river, and was lighted by the light of the moon. And the rock was gray, and ghastly, and tall,—and the rock was gray. Upon its front were characters engraven in the stone; and I walked through the morass of water-lilies, until I came close unto the shore, that I might read the characters upon the stone. But I could not decipher them. And I was going back into the morass, when the moon shone with a fuller red, and I turned and looked again upon the rock, and upon the characters;—and the characters were desolation.

"And I looked upward, and there stood a man upon the summit of the rock; and I hid myself among the water-lilies that I might discover the actions of the man. And the man was tall and stately in form, and was wrapped up from his shoulders to his feet in the toga of old Rome. And the outlines of his figure were indistinct—but his features were the features of a deity; for the mantle of the night, and of the mist, and of the moon, and of the dew, had left uncovered the features of his face. And his brow was lofty with thought, and his eye wild with care; and in the few furrows upon his cheek I read the fables of sorrow, and weariness, and disgust with mankind, and a longing after solitude.

"And the man sat upon the rock, and leaned his head upon his hand, and looked out upon the desolation. He looked down into the low unquiet shrubbery, and up into the tall primeval trees, and up higher at the rustling heaven, and into the crimson moon. And I lay close within shelter of the lilies, and observed the actions of the man. And the man trembled in the solitude;—but the night waned, and he sat upon the rock.

"And the man turned his attention from the heaven, and looked out upon the dreary river Zaïre, and upon the yellow ghastly waters, and upon the pale legions of the water-lilies. And the man listened to the sighs of the water-lilies, and to the murmur that came up from among them. And I lay close within my covert and observed the actions of the man. And the man trembled in the solitude;—but the night waned, and he sat upon the rock.

"Then I went down into the recesses of the morass, and waded afar in among the wilderness of the lilies, and called unto the hippopotami which dwelt among the fens in the recesses of the morass. And the hippopotami heard my call, and came, with the behemoth, unto the foot of the rock, and roared loudly and fearfully beneath the moon. And I lay close within my covert and observed the actions of the man. And the man trembled in the solitude;—but the night waned, and he sat upon the rock.

"Then I cursed the elements with the curse of tumult; and a frightful tempest gathered in the heaven where, before, there had been no wind. And the heaven became livid with the violence of the tempest—and the rain beat upon the head of the man—and the floods of the river came down—and the river was tormented into foam—and the water-lilies shrieked within their beds—and the forest crumbled before the wind—and the thunder rolled—and the lightning fell—and the rock rocked to its foundation. And I lay close within my covert and observed the actions of the man. And the man trembled in the solitude;—but the night waned, and he sat upon the rock.

"Then I grew angry and cursed, with the curse of silence, the river, and the lilies, and the wind, and the forest, and the heaven, and the thunder, and the sighs of the water-lilies. And they became accursed, and were still. And the moon ceased to totter up its pathway to heaven—and the thunder died away—and the lightning did not flash—and the clouds hung motionless—and the waters sunk to their level and remained—and the trees ceased to rock—and the water-lilies sighed no more—and the murmur was heard no longer from among them, nor any shadow of sound throughout the vast illimitable desert. And I looked upon the characters of the rock, and they were changed;—and the characters were silence.

"And mine eyes fell upon the countenance of the man, and his countenance was wan with terror. And, hurriedly, he raised his head from his hand, and stood forth upon the rock and listened. But there was no voice throughout the vast, illimitable desert, and the characters upon the rock were silence. And the man shuddered, and turned his face away, and fled afar off, in haste, so that I beheld him no more."

*

Now there are fine tales in the volumes of the Magi—in the iron-bound, melancholy volumes of the Magi. Therein, I say, are glorious histories of the Heaven, and of the Earth, and of the mighty sea—and of the Genii that overruled the sea, and the earth, and the lofty heaven. There was much lore too in the sayings which were said by the Sibyls; and holy, holy things were heard of old by the dim leaves that trembled around Dodona—but, as Allah liveth, that fable which the Demon told me as he sat by my side in the shadow of the tomb, I hold to be the most wonderful of all! And as the Demon made an end of his story, he fell back within the cavity of the tomb and laughed. And I could not laugh with the Demon, and he cursed me because I could not laugh. And the lynx which dwelleth for ever in the tomb came out therefrom, and lay down at the feet of the Demon, and looked at him steadily in the face.

A DESCENT INTO THE MAELSTROM

The Ways of God in nature, as in Providence, are not as our *ways; nor are the models that we frame in any way commensurate to the vastness, profundity, and unsearchableness of His works, which have a depth in them greater than the well of Democritus.*

Joseph Glanvill

WE HAD NOW reached the summit of the loftiest crag. For some minutes the old man seemed too much exhausted to speak.

"Not long ago," said he at length, "and I could have guided you on this route as well as the youngest of my sons; but, about three years past, there happened to me an event such as never happened before to mortal man—or, at least, such as no man ever survived to tell of—and the six hours of deadly terror which I then endured have broken me up body and soul. You suppose me a *very* old man—but I am not. It took less than a single day to change these hairs from a jetty black to white, to weaken my limbs, and to unstring my nerves, so that I tremble at the least exertion, and am frightened at a shadow. Do you know I can scarcely look over this little cliff without getting giddy?"

The "little cliff," upon whose edge he had so carelessly thrown himself down to rest that the weightier portion of his body hung over it, while he was only kept from falling by the tenure of his elbow on its extreme and slippery edge—this "little cliff" arose, a sheer unobstructed precipice of black shining rock, some fifteen or sixteen hundred feet from the world of crags beneath us. Nothing would have tempted me to within half a dozen yards of its brink. In truth so deeply was I excited by the perilous position of my companion, that I fell at full length upon the ground, clung to the shrubs around me, and dared not even glance upward at the sky—while I struggled in vain to divest myself of the idea that the very foundations of the mountain were in danger from the fury of the wind. It was long before I could reason myself into sufficient courage to sit up and look out into the distance.

"You must get over these fancies," said the guide, "for I have brought you here that you might have the best possible view of the scene of that event I mentioned—and to tell you the whole story with the spot just under your eye."

"We are now," he continued, in that particularizing manner which distinguished him—"we are now close upon the Norwegian coast—in the sixty-eighth degree of latitude—in the great province of Nordland—and in the dreary district of Lofoden. The mountain upon whose top we sit is Helseggen, the Cloudy. Now raise yourself up a little higher—hold on to the grass if you feel giddy—so—and look out, beyond the belt of vapor beneath us, into the sea."

I looked dizzily, and beheld a wide expanse of ocean, whose waters wore so inky a hue as to bring at once to my mind the Nubian geographer's account of the *Mare Tenebrarum*. A panorama more deplorably desolate no human imagination can conceive. To the right and left, as far as the eye could reach, there lay outstretched, like ramparts of the world, lines of horridly black and beetling cliff, whose character of gloom was but the more forcibly illustrated by the surf which reared high up against it its white and ghastly crest, howling and shrieking for ever. Just opposite the promontory upon whose apex we were placed, and at a distance of some five or six miles out at sea, there was visible a small, bleak-looking island; or, more properly, its position was discernible through the wilderness of surge in which it was enveloped. About two miles nearer the land, arose another of smaller size, hideously craggy and barren, and encompassed at various intervals by a cluster of dark rocks.

The appearance of the ocean, in the space between the more distant island and the shore, had something very unusual about it. Although, at the time, so strong a gale was blowing landward that a brig in the remote offing lay to under a double-reefed trysail, and constantly plunged her whole hull out of sight, still there was here nothing like a regular swell, but only a short, quick, angry cross dashing of water in every direction—as well in the teeth of the wind as otherwise. Of foam there was little except in the immediate vicinity of the rocks.

"The island in the distance," resumed the old man, "is called by the Norwegians Vurrgh. The one midway is Moskoe. That a mile to the northward is Ambaaren. Yonder are Islesen. Hotholm, Keildhelm, Suarven, and Buckholm. Farther off—between Moskoe and Vurrgh—are Otterholm, Flimen, Sandflesen, and Stockholm. These are the true names of the places—but why it has been thought necessary to name them at all, is more than either you or I can understand. Do you hear anything? Do you see any change in the water?"

We had now been about ten minutes upon the top of Helseggen, to which we had ascended from the interior of Lofoden, so that we had caught no glimpse of the sea until it had burst upon us from the summit. As the old man spoke, I became aware of a loud and gradually increasing sound, like the moaning of a vast herd of buffaloes upon an American prairie; and at the same moment I perceived that what seamen term the *chopping* character of the ocean beneath us, was rapidly changing into a current which set to the eastward. Even while I gazed, this current acquired a monstrous velocity. Each moment added to its speed—to its headlong impetuosity. In five minutes the whole sea as far as Vurrgh, was lashed into ungovernable fury; but it was between Moskoe and the coast that the main uproar held its sway. Here the vast bed of the waters, seamed and scarred into a thousand conflicting channels, burst suddenly into frenzied convulsion—heaving, boiling, hissing—gyrating in gigantic and innumerable vortices, and all whirling and plunging on to the eastward with a rapidity which water never elsewhere assumes, except in precipitous descents.

In a few minutes more, there came over the scene another radical alteration. The general surface grew somewhat more smooth, and the whirlpools, one by one, disappeared, while prodigious streaks of foam became apparent where none had been seen before. These streaks, at length, spreading out to a great distance, and entering into combination, took unto themselves the gyratory motion of the subsided vortices, and seemed to form the germ of another more vast. Suddenly—very suddenly—this assumed a distinct and definite existence, in a circle of more than half a mile in diameter. The edge of the whirl was represented by a broad belt of gleaming spray; but no particle of this slipped into the mouth of the terrific funnel, whose interior, as far as the eye could fathom it, was a smooth, shining, and jet-black wall of water, inclined to the horizon at an angle of some forty-five degrees, speeding dizzily round and round with a swaying and sweltering motion, and sending forth to the winds an appalling voice, half shriek, half roar, such as not even the mighty cataract of Niagara ever lifts up in its agony to Heaven.

The mountain trembled to its very base, and the rock rocked. I threw myself upon my face, and clung to the scant herbage in an excess of nervous agitation.

"This," said I at length, to the old man—"this *can* be nothing else than the great whirlpool of the Maelstrom."

"So it is sometimes termed," said he. "We Norwegians call it the Moskoe-storm, from the island of Moskoe in the midway."

The ordinary accounts of this vortex had by no means prepared me for what I saw. That of Jonas Ramus, which is perhaps the most circumstantial of any, cannot impart the faintest conception either of the magnificence, or of the horror of the scene—or of the wild bewildering sense of *the novel* which confounds the beholder. I am not sure from what point of view the writer in question surveyed it, nor at what time; but it could neither have been from the summit of Helseggen, nor during a storm. There are some passages of his description, nevertheless, which may be quoted for their details, although their effect is exceedingly feeble in conveying an impression of the spectacle.

"Between Lofoden and Moskoe," he says, "the depth of the water is between thirty-six and forty fathoms; but on the other side, toward Ver (Vurrgh) this depth decreases so as not to afford a convenient passage for a vessel, without the risk of splitting on the rocks, which happens even in the calmest weather. When it is flood, the stream runs up the country between Lofoden and Moskoe with a boisterous rapidity; but the roar of its impetuous ebb to the sea is scarce equaled by the loudest and most dreadful cataracts; the noise being heard several leagues off, and the vortices or pits are of such an extent and depth, that if a ship comes within its attraction, it is inevitably absorbed and carried down to the bottom, and there beat to pieces against the rocks; and when the water relaxes, the fragments thereof are thrown up again. But these intervals of tranquillity are only at the turn of the ebb and flood, and in calm weather, and last but a quarter of an hour, its violence gradually returning. When the stream is most boisterous, and its fury heightened by a storm, it is dangerous to come within a Norway mile of it. Boats, yachts, and ships have been carried away by not guarding against it before they were carried within its reach. It likewise happens frequently, that whales come too near the stream, and are overpowered by its violence; and then it is impossible to describe their howlings and bellowings in their fruitless struggles to disengage themselves. A bear once, attempting to swim from Lofoden to Moskoe, was caught by the stream and borne down, while he roared terribly, so as to be heard on shore. Large stocks of firs and pine-trees, after being absorbed by the current, rise again broken and torn to such a degree as if bristles grew upon them. This plainly shows the bottom to consist of craggy rocks, among which they are whirled to and fro. This stream is regulated by the flux and reflux of the sea—it being constantly high and low water every six hours. In the year 1645, early in the morning of Sexagesima Sunday, it raged with such noise and impetuosity that the very stones of the houses on the coast fell to the ground."

In regard to the depth of the water, I could not see how this could have been ascertained at all in the immediate vicinity of the vortex. The "forty fathoms" must have reference only to portions of the channel close upon the shore either of Moskoe or Lofoden. The depth in the center of the Moskoe-ström must be unmeasurably greater; and no better proof of this fact is necessary than can be obtained from even the sidelong glance into the abyss of the whirl which may be had from the highest crag of Helseggen. Looking down from this pinnacle upon the howling Phlegethon below, I could not help smiling at the simplicity with which the honest Jonas Ramus records, as a matter difficult of belief, the anecdotes of the whales and the bears, for it appeared to me, in fact, a self-evident thing, that the largest ships of the line in existence, coming within the influence of that deadly attraction, could resist it as little as a feather the hurricane, and must disappear bodily and at once.

The attempts to account for the phenomenon—some of which, I remember, seemed to me sufficiently plausible in persual—now wore a very different and unsatisfactory aspect. The idea generally received is that this, as well as three smaller vortices among the Ferroe Islands, "have no other cause than the collision of waves rising and falling, at flux and reflux, against a ridge of rocks and shelves, which confines the water so that it precipitates itself like a cataract; and thus the higher the flood rises, the deeper must the fall be, and the natural result of all is a whirlpool or vortex, the prodigious suction of which is sufficiently known by lesser experiments."—These are the words of the *Encyclopaedia Britannica*. Kircher and others imagine that in the center of the channel of the Maelstrom is an abyss penetrating the globe, and issuing in some very remote part—the Gulf of Bothnia being somewhat decidedly named in one instance. This opinion, idle in itself, was the one to which, as I gazed, my imagination most readily assented; and, mentioning it to the guide, I was rather surprised to hear him say that, although it was the view almost universally entertained of the subject by the Norwegians, it nevertheless was not his own. As to the former notion he confessed his inability to comprehend it; and here I agreed with him—for, however conclusive on paper, it becomes altogether unintelligible, and even absurd, amid the thunder of the abyss.

"You have had a good look at the whirl now," said the old man, "and if you will creep round this crag, so as to get in its lee, and deaden the roar of the water, I will tell you a story that will convince you I ought to know something of the Moskoe-ström."

I placed myself as desired, and he proceeded.

"Myself and my two brothers once owned a schooner-rigged smack of about seventy tons burthen, with which we were in the habit of fishing among the islands beyond Moskoe, nearly to Vurrgh. In all violent eddies at sea there is good fishing, at proper opportunities, if one has only the courage to attempt it: but among the whole of the Lofoden coastmen, we three were the only ones who made a regular business of going out to the islands, as I tell you. The usual grounds are a great way lower down to the southward. There fish can be got at all hours, without much risk, and therefore these places are preferred. The choice spots over here among the rocks, however, not only yield the finest variety, but in far greater abundance; so that we often got in a single day, what the more timid of the craft could not scrape together in a week. In fact, we made it a matter of desperate speculation—the risk of life standing instead of labor, and courage answering for capital.

"We kept the smack in a cove about five miles higher up the coast than this; and it was our practice, in fine weather, to take advantage of the fifteen minutes' slack to push across the main channel of the Moskoe-ström, far above the pool, and then drop down upon anchorage somewhere near Otterholm, or Sandflesen where the eddies are not so violent as elsewhere. Here we used to remain until nearly time for slack-water again, when we weighed and made for home. We never set out upon this expedition without a steady side wind for going and coming—one that we felt sure would not fail us before our return—and we seldom made a miscalculation upon this point. Twice, during six years, we were forced to stay all night at anchor on account of a dead calm, which is a rare thing indeed just about here; and once we had to remain on the grounds nearly a week, starving to death, owing to a gale which blew up shortly after our arrival, and made the channel too boisterous to be thought of. Upon this occasion we should have been driven out to sea in spite of everything (for the whirlpools threw us round and round so violently, that, at length, we fouled our anchor and dragged it) if it had not been that we drifted into one of the innumerable cross currents—here to-day and gone to-morrow—which drove us under the lee of Flimen, where, by good luck, we brought up.

"I could not tell you the twentieth part of the difficulties we encountered 'on the ground'—it is a bad spot to be in, even in good weather—but we made shift always to run the gauntlet of the Moskoe-ström itself without accident: although at times my heart has been in my mouth when we happened to be a minute or so behind or before the slack. The wind sometimes was not as strong as we thought it at starting, and then we made rather less way than we could wish, while the current rendered the smack unmanageable. My eldest brother had a son eighteen years old, and I had two stout boys of my own. These would have been of great assistance at such times, in using the sweeps as well as afterward in fishing—but, somehow, although we ran the risk ourselves, we had not the heart to let the young ones get into the danger—for, after all said and done, it was a horrible danger, and that is the truth.

"It is now within a few days of three years since what I am going to tell you occurred. It was on July 10, 18—, a day which the people of this part of the world will never forget—for it was one in which blew the most terrible hurricane that ever came out of the heavens. And yet all the morning, and indeed until late in the afternoon, there was a gentle and steady breeze from the southwest, while the sun shone brightly, so that the oldest seaman among us could not have foreseen what was to follow.

"The three of us—my two brothers and myself—had crossed over to the islands about two o'clock p.m., and soon nearly loaded the smack with fine fish, which, we all remarked, were more plenty that day than we had ever known them. It was just seven, *by my watch*, when we weighed and started for home, so as to make the worst of the Strom at slack-water, which we knew would be at eight.

"We set out with a fresh wind on our starboard quarter, and for some time spanked along at a great rate, never dreaming of danger, for indeed we saw not the slightest reason to apprehend it. All at once we were taken aback by a breeze from over Helseggen. This was most unusual—something that had never happened to us before—and I began to feel a little uneasy, without exactly knowing why. We put the boat on the wind, but could make no headway at all for the eddies, and I was upon the point of proposing to return to the anchorage, when, looking astern, we saw the whole horizon covered with a singular copper-colored cloud that rose with the most amazing velocity.

"In the meantime the breeze that had headed us off fell away and we were dead becalmed, drifting about in every direction. This state of things, however, did not last long enough to give us time to think about it. In less than a minute the storm was upon us—in less than two the sky was entirely overcast—and what with this and the driving spray, it became suddenly so dark that we could not see each other in the smack.

"Such a hurricane as then blew it is folly to attempt describing. The oldest seaman in Norway never experienced anything like it. We had let our sails go by the run before it cleverly took us; but, at the first puff, both our masts went by the board as if they had been sawed off—the mainmast taking with it my youngest brother, who had lashed himself to it for safety.

"Our boat was the lightest feather of a thing that ever sat upon water. It had a complete flush deck, with only a small hatch near the bow, and this hatch it had always been our custom to batten down when about to cross the Strom, by way of precaution against the chopping seas. But for this circumstance we should have foundered at once—for we lay entirely buried for some moments. How my elder brother escaped destruction I cannot say, for I never had an opportunity of ascertaining. For my part, as soon as I had let the foresail run, I threw myself flat on deck, with my feet against the narrow gunwale of the bow, and with my hands grasping a ring-bolt near the foot of the foremast. It was mere instinct that prompted me to do this—which was undoubtedly the very best thing I could have done—for I was too much flurried to think.

"For some moments we were completely deluged, as I say, and all this time I held my breath, and clung to the bolt. When I could stand it no longer I raised myself upon my knees, still keeping hold with my hands, and thus got my head clear. Presently our little boat gave herself a shake, just as a dog does in coming out of the water, and thus rid herself, in some measure, of the seas. I was now trying to get the better of the stupor that had come over me, and to collect my senses so as to see what was to be done, when I felt somebody grasp my arm. It was my elder brother, and my heart leaped for joy, for I had made sure that he was overboard—but the next moment all this joy was turned into horror—for he put his mouth close to my ear, and screamed out the word '*Moskoe-ström!*'

"No one ever will know what my feelings were at that moment. I shook from head to foot as if I had had the most violent fit of the ague. I knew what he meant by that one word well enough—I knew what he wished to make me understand. With the wind that now drove us on, we were bound for the whirl of the Ström, and nothing could save us!

"You perceive that in crossing the Ström *channel*, we always went a long way up above the whirl, even in the calmest weather, and then had to wait and watch carefully for the slack—but now we were driving right upon the pool itself, and in such a hurricane as this! 'To be sure,' I thought, 'we shall get there just about the slack—there is some little hope in that'—but in the next moment I cursed myself for being so great a fool as to dream of hope at all. I knew very well that we were doomed, had we been ten times a ninety-ton ship.

"By this time the first fury of the tempest had spent itself, or perhaps we did not feel it so much, as we scudded before it, but at all events the sea which at first had been kept down by the wind, and lay flat and frothing, now got up into absolute mountains. A singular change, too, had come over the heavens. Around in every direction it was still as black as pitch, but nearly overhead there burst out, all at once, a circular rift of clear sky—as clear as I ever saw—and of a deep bright blue—and through it there blazed forth the full moon with a luster that I never before knew her to wear. She lit up everything about us with the greatest distinctness—but, oh God, what a scene it was to light up!

"I now made one or two attempts to speak to my brother—but in some manner which I could not understand, the din had so increased that I could not make him hear a single word, although I screamed at the top of my voice in his ear. Presently he shook his head, looking as pale as death, and held up one of his fingers, as if to say *'listen!'*

"At first I could not make out what he meant—but soon a hideous thought flashed upon me. I dragged my watch from its fob. It was not going. I glanced at its face by the moonlight, and then burst into tears as I flung it far away into the ocean. *It had run down at seven o'clock! We were behind the time of the slack, and the whirl of the Ström was in full fury!*

"When a boat is well built, properly trimmed, and not deep laden, the waves in a strong gale, when she is going large, seem always to slip from beneath her—which appears strange to a landsman—and this is what is called *riding*, in sea phrase.

"Well, so far we had ridden the swells very cleverly; but presently a gigantic sea happened to take us right under the counter, and bore us with it as it rose—up—up—as if into the sky. I would not have believed that any wave could rise so high. And then down we came with a sweep, a slide, and a plunge that made me feel sick and dizzy, as if I was falling from some lofty mountain-top in a dream. But while we were up I had thrown a quick glance around—and that one glance was all-sufficient. I saw our exact position in an instant. The Moskoe-ström whirlpool was about a quarter of a mile dead ahead—but no more like the everyday Moskoe-ström than the whirl, as you now see it, is like a mill-race. If I had not known where we were, and what we had to expect, I should not have recognized the place at all. As it was, I involuntarily closed my eyes in horror. The lids clenched themselves together as if in a spasm.

"It could not have been more than two minutes afterward until we suddenly felt the waves subside, and were enveloped in foam. The boat made a sharp half-turn to larboard, and then shot off in its new direction like a thunderbolt. At the same moment the roaring noise of the water was completely drowned in a kind of shrill shriek—such a sound as you might imagine given out by the water-pipes of many thousand steam-vessels letting off their steam all together. We were now in the belt of surf that always surrounds the whirl; and I thought, of course, that another moment would plunge us into the abyss, down which we could only see indistinctly on account of the amazing velocity with which we were borne along. The boat did not seem to sink into the water at all, but to skim like an air-bubble upon the surface of the surge. Her starboard side was next the whirl, and on the larboard arose the world of ocean we had left. It stood like a huge writhing wall between us and the horizon.

"It may appear strange, but now, when we were in the very jaws of the gulf, I felt more composed than when we were only approaching it. Having made up my mind to hope no more, I got rid of a great deal of that terror which unmanned me at first. I supposed it was despair that strung my nerves.

"It may look like boasting—but what I tell you is truth—I began to reflect how magnificent a thing it was to die in such a manner, and how foolish it was in me to think of so paltry a consideration as my own individual life, in view of so wonderful a manifestation of God's power. I do believe that I blushed with shame when this idea crossed my mind. After a little while I became possessed with the keenest curiosity about the whirl itself. I positively felt a *wish* to explore its depths, even at the sacrifice I was going to make; and my principal grief was that I should never be able to tell my old companions on shore about the mysteries I should see. These, no doubt, were singular fancies to occupy a man's mind in such extremity—and I have often thought since, that the revolutions of the boat around the pool might have rendered me a little light-headed.

"There was another circumstance which tended to restore my self-possession; and this was the cessation of the wind, which could not reach us in our present situation—for, as you saw for yourself, the belt of surf is considerably lower than the general bed of the ocean, and this latter now towered above us, a high, black, mountainous ridge. If you have never been at sea in a heavy gale, you can form no idea of the confusion of mind occasioned by the wind and spray together. They blind, deafen, and strangle you, and take away all power of action or reflection. But we were now, in a great measure, rid of these annoyances—just as death-condemned felons in prison are allowed petty indulgences, forbidden them while their doom is yet uncertain.

"How often we made the circuit of the belt it is impossible to say. We careered round and round for perhaps an hour, flying rather than floating, getting gradually more and more into the middle of the surge, and then nearer and nearer to its horrible inner edge. All this time I had never let go of the ring-bolt. My brother was at the stern, holding on to a large empty water-cask which had been securely lashed under the coop of the counter, and was the only thing on deck that had not been swept overboard when the gale first took us. As we approached the brink of the pit he let go his hold upon this, and made for the ring, from which, in the agony of his terror, he endeavored to force my hands, as it was not large enough to afford us both a secure grasp. I never felt deeper grief than when I saw him attempt this act—although I knew he was a madman when he did it—a raving maniac through sheer fright. I did not care, however, to contest the point with him. I knew it could make no difference whether either of us held on at all; so I let him have the bolt, and went astern to the cask. This there was no great difficulty in doing; for the smack flew round steadily enough, and upon an even keel—only swaying to and fro with the immense sweeps and swelters of the whirl. Scarcely had I secured myself in my new position, when we gave a wild lurch to starboard, and rushed headlong into the abyss. I muttered a hurried prayer to God, and thought all was over.

"As I felt the sickening sweep of the descent, I had instinctively tightened my hold upon the barrel, and closed my eyes. For some seconds I dared not open them—while I expected instant destruction, and wondered that I was not already in my death-struggles with the water. But moment after moment elapsed. I still lived. The sense of falling had ceased; and the motion of the vessel seemed much as it had been before, while in the belt of foam, with the exception that she now lay more along. I took courage and looked once again upon the scene.

"Never shall I forget the sensations of awe, horror, and admiration with which I gazed about me. The boat appeared to be hanging, as if by magic, midway down, upon the interior surface of a funnel vast in circumference, prodigious in depth, and whose perfectly smooth sides might have been mistaken for ebony, but for the bewildering rapidity with which they spun around, and for the gleaming and ghastly radiance they shot forth, as the rays of the full moon, from that circular rift amid the clouds which I have already described, streamed in a flood of golden glory along the black walls, and far away down into the inmost recesses of the abyss.

"At first I was too much confused to observe anything accurately. The general burst of terrific grandeur was all that I beheld. When I recovered myself a little, however, my gaze fell instinctively downward. In this direction I was able to obtain an unobstructed view, from the manner in which the smack hung on the inclined surface of the pool. She was quite upon an even keel—that is to say, her deck lay in a plane parallel with that of the water—but this latter sloped at an angle of more than forty-five degrees, so that we seemed to be lying upon our beam ends. I could not help observing, nevertheless, that I had scarcely more difficulty in maintaining my hold and footing in this situation, than if we had been upon a dead level; and this, I suppose, was owing to the speed at which we revolved.

"The rays of the moon seemed to search the very bottom of the profound gulf: but still I could make out nothing distinctly on account of a thick mist in which everything there was enveloped, and over which there hung a magnificent rainbow, like that narrow and tottering bridge which Mussulmans say is the only pathway between Time and Eternity. This mist, or spray, was no doubt occasioned by the clashing of the great walls of the funnel, as they all met together at the bottom—but the yell that went up to the heavens from out of that mist I dare not attempt to describe.

"Our first slide into the abyss itself, from the belt of foam above, had carried us to a great distance down the slope; but our further descent was by no means proportionate. Round and round we swept—not with any uniform movement—but in dizzying swings and jerks, that sent us sometimes only a few hundred yards—sometimes nearly the complete circuit of the whirl. Our progress downward, at each revolution, was slow, but very perceptible.

"Looking about me upon the wide waste of liquid ebony on which we were thus borne, I perceived that our boat was not the only object in the embrace of the whirl. Both above and below us were visible fragments of vessels, large masses of building-timber and trunks of trees, with many smaller articles, such as pieces of house furniture, broken boxes, barrels and staves. I have already described the unnatural curiosity which had taken the place of my original terrors. It appeared to grow upon me as I drew nearer and nearer to my dreadful doom. I now began to watch, with a strange interest, the numerous things that floated in our company. I *must* have been delirious, for I even sought *amusement* in speculating upon the relative velocities of their several descents toward the foam below. 'This fir-tree,' I found myself at one time saying, 'will certainly be the next thing that takes the awful plunge and disappears,'—and then I was disappointed to find that the wreck of a Dutch merchant ship overtook it and went down before. At length, after making several guesses of this nature, and being deceived in all—this fact—the fact of my invariable miscalculation, set me upon a train of reflection that made my limbs again tremble, and my heart beat heavily once more.

"It was not a new terror that thus affected me, but the dawn of a more exciting *hope*. This hope arose partly from memory, and partly from present observation. I called to mind the great variety of buoyant matter that strewed the coast of Lofoden, having been absorbed and then thrown forth by the Moskoe-ström. By far the greater number of the articles were shattered in the most extraordinary way—so chafed and roughened as to have the appearance of being stuck full of splinters—but then I distinctly recollected that there were *some* of them which were not disfigured at all. Now I could not account for this difference except by supposing that the roughened fragments were the only ones which had been *completely absorbed*—that the others had entered the whirl at so late a period of the tide, or, for some reason, had descended so slowly after entering, that they did not reach the bottom before the turn of the flood came, or of the ebb, as the case might be. I conceived it possible, in either instance, that they might thus be whirled up again to the level of the ocean, without undergoing the fate of those which had been drawn in more early or absorbed more rapidly. I made, also, three important observations. The first was, that as a general rule, the larger the bodies were, the more rapid their descent—the second, that, between two masses of equal extent, the one spherical, and the other of *any other shape*, the superiority in speed of descent was with the sphere—the third, that, between two masses of equal size, the one cylindrical, and the other of any other shape, the cylinder was absorbed the more slowly.

"Since my escape, I have had several conversations on this subject with an old schoolmaster of the district; and it was from him that I learned the use of the words 'cylinder' and 'sphere.' He explained to me—although I have forgotten the explanation—how what I observed was, in fact, the natural consequence of the forms of the floating fragments—and showed me how it happened that a cylinder, swimming in a vortex, offered more resistance to its suction, and was drawn in with greater difficulty than an equally bulky body, of any form whatever.[1]

"There was one startling circumstance which went a great way in enforcing these observations, and rendering me anxious to turn them to account, and this was that, at every revolution, we passed something like a barrel, or else the yard or the mast of a vessel, whilst many of these things, which had been on our level when I first opened my eyes upon the wonders of the whirlpool, were now high up above us, and seemed to have moved but little from their original station.

"I no longer hesitated what to do. I resolved to lash myself securely to the water-cask upon which I now held, to cut it loose from the counter, and to throw myself with it into the water. I attracted my brother's attention by signs, pointed to the floating barrels that came near us, and did everything in my power to make him understand what I was about to do. I thought at length that he comprehended my design—but, whether this was the case or not, he shook his head despairingly, and refused to move from his station by the ring bolt. It was impossible to reach him; the emergency admitted of no delay; and so, with a bitter struggle, I resigned him to his fate, fastened myself to the cask by means of the lashings which secured it to the counter, and precipitated myself with it into the sea, without another moment's hesitation.

"The result was precisely what I had hoped it might be. As it is myself who now tell you this tale—as you see that I *did* escape—and as you are already in possession of the mode in which this escape was effected, and must therefore anticipate all that I have further to say—I will bring my story quickly to conclusion. It might have been an hour, or thereabout, after my quitting the smack, when, having descended to a vast distance beneath me, it made three or four wild gyrations in rapid succession and, bearing my loved brother with it, plunged headlong, at

1 See Archimedes, *De Incidentibus in Fluido*, lib. 2.

once and for ever, into the chaos of foam below. The barrel to which I was attached sunk very little farther than half the distance between the bottom of the gulf and the spot at which I leaped overboard, before a great change took place in the character of the whirlpool. The slope of the sides of the vast funnel became momently less and less steep. The gyrations of the whirl grew, gradually, less and less violent. By degrees, the froth and the rainbow disappeared, and the bottom of the gulf seemed slowly to uprise. The sky was clear, the winds had gone down, and the full moon was setting radiantly in the west, when I found myself on the surface of the ocean, in full view of the shores of Lofoden, and above the spot where the pool of the Moskoe-ström *had been*. It was the hour of the slack—but the sea still heaved in mountainous waves from the effects of the hurricane. I was borne violently into the channel of the Ström, and in a few minutes, was hurried down the coast into the 'grounds' of the fishermen. A boat picked me up—exhausted from fatigue—and (now that the danger was removed) speechless from the memory of its horror. Those who drew me on board were my old mates and daily companions—but they knew me no more than they would have known a traveler from the spirit-land. My hair, which had been raven black the day before, was as white as you see it now. They say too that the whole expression of my countenance had changed. I told them my story—they did not believe it. I now tell it to *you*—and I can scarcely expect you to put more faith in it than did the merry fishermen of Lofoden."

LIGEIA

And the will therein lieth, which dieth not. Who knoweth the mysteries of the will, with its? For God is but a great will pervading all things by nature of its intentness. Man doth not yield himself to the angels, nor unto death utterly, save only through the weakness of his feeble will.

Joseph Glanvill

I CANNOT, FOR my soul, remember how, when, or even precisely where, I first became acquainted with the Lady Ligeia. Long years have since elapsed, and my memory is feeble through much suffering. Or, perhaps, I cannot now bring these points to mind, because, in truth, the character of my beloved, her rare learning, her singular yet placid cast of beauty, and the thrilling and enthralling eloquence of her low musical language, made their way into my heart by paces so steadily and stealthily progressive that they had been unnoticed and unknown. Yet I believe that I met her first and most frequently in some large, old, decaying city near the Rhine. Of her family—I have surely heard her speak. That it is of a remotely ancient date cannot be doubted. Ligeia! Ligeia! Buried in studies of a nature more than all else adapted to deaden impressions of the outward world, it is by that sweet word alone—by Ligeia—that I bring before mine eyes in fancy the image of her who is no more. And now, while I write, a recollection flashes upon me that I have never known the paternal name of her who was my friend and my betrothed, and who became the partner of my studies, and finally the wife of my bosom. Was it a playful charge on the part of my Ligeia? or was it a test of my strength of affection, that I should institute no inquiries upon this point? or was it rather a caprice of my own—a wildly romantic offering on the shrine of the most passionate devotion? I but distinctly recall the fact itself—what wonder that I have utterly forgotten the circumstances which originated or attended it? And, indeed, if ever that spirit which is entitled Romance—if ever she, the wan and the misty-winged Ashtophet of idolatrous Egypt, presided, as they tell, over marriages ill-omened, then most surely she presided over mine.

There is one dear topic, however, on which my memory fails me not. It is the person of Ligeia. In stature she was tall, somewhat slender, and, in her latter days, even emaciated. I would in vain attempt to portray the majesty, the quiet ease, of her demeanor, or the incomprehensible lightness and elasticity of her footfall. She came and departed as a shadow. I was never made aware of her entrance into my closed study save by the dear music of her low sweet voice, as she placed her marble hand upon my shoulder. In beauty of face no maiden ever equaled her. It was the radiance of an opium-dream—an airy and spirit-lifting vision more wildly divine than the fantasies which hovered about the slumbering souls of the daughters of Delos. Yet her features were not of that regular mold which we have been falsely taught to worship in the classical labors of the heathen. "There is no exquisite beauty," says Bacon, Lord Verulam, speaking truly of all the forms and genera of beauty, "without some strangeness in the proportion." Yet, although I saw that the features of Ligeia were not of a classic regularity—although I perceived that her loveliness was indeed "exquisite," and felt that there was much of "strangeness" pervading it, yet I have tried in vain to detect the irregularity and to trace home my own perception of "the strange." I examined the contour of the lofty and pale forehead—it was faultless—how cold indeed that word when applied to a majesty so divine!—the skin rivaling the purest ivory, the commanding extent and repose, the gentle prominence of the regions above the temples; and then the raven-black, the glossy, the luxuriant and naturally-curling tresses, setting forth the full force of the Homeric epithet, "hyacinthine"! I looked at the delicate outlines of the nose—and nowhere but in the graceful medallions of the Hebrews had I beheld a similar perfection. There were the same luxurious smoothness of surface, the same scarcely perceptible tendency to the aquiline, the same harmoniously curved nostrils speaking the free spirit. I regarded the sweet mouth. Here was indeed the triumph of all things heavenly—the magnificent turn of the short upper lip—the soft, voluptuous slumber of the under—the dimples which sported, and the color which spoke—the teeth glancing back, with a brilliancy almost startling, every ray of the holy light which fell upon them in her serene and placid, yet most exultingly radiant of all smiles. I scrutinized the formation of the chin—and here, too, I found the gentleness of breadth, the softness and the majesty, the fullness and the spirituality, of the Greek—the contour which the god Apollo revealed but in a dream, to Cleomenes, the son of the Athenian. And then I peered into the large eyes of Ligeia.

For eyes we have no models in the remotely antique. It might have been, too, that in these eyes of my beloved lay the secret to which Lord Verulam alludes. They were, I must believe, far larger than the ordinary eyes of our own race. They were even fuller than the fullest of the gazelle eyes of the tribe of the valley of Nourjahad. Yet it was only at intervals—in moments of intense excitement—that this peculiarity became more than slightly noticeable in Ligeia. And at such moments was her beauty—in my heated fancy thus it appeared perhaps—the beauty of beings either above or apart from the earth—the beauty of the fabulous Houri of the Turk. The hue of the orbs was the most brilliant of black, and, far over them, hung jetty lashes of great length. The brows, slightly irregular in outline, had the same tint. The "strangeness," however, which I found in the eyes, was of a nature distinct from the formation, or the color, or the brilliancy of the features, and must, after all, be referred to the expression. Ah, word of no meaning! behind whose vast latitude of mere sound we intrench our ignorance of so much of the spiritual. The expression of the eyes of Ligeia! How for long hours have I pondered upon it! How have I, through the whole of a midsummer night, struggled to fathom it! What was it—that something more profound than the well of Democritus—which lay far within the pupils of my beloved? What was it? I was possessed with a passion to discover. Those eyes! those large, those shining, those divine orbs! they became to me twin stars of Leda, and I to them devoutest of astrologers.

There is no point, among the many incomprehensible anomalies of the science of mind, more thrillingly exciting than the fact—never, I believe, noticed in the schools—that, in our endeavors to recall to memory something long forgotten, we often find ourselves upon the very verge of remembrance, without being able, in the end, to remember.

And thus how frequently, in my intense scrutiny of Ligeia's eyes, have I felt approaching the full knowledge of their expression—felt it approaching—yet not quite be mine—and so at length entirely depart! And (strange, oh strangest mystery of all!) I found, in the commonest objects of the universe, a circle of analogies to that expression. I mean to say that, subsequently to the period when Ligeia's beauty passed into my spirit, there dwelling as in a shrine, I derived from many existences in the material world, a sentiment such as I felt always aroused within me by her large and luminous orbs. Yet not the more could I define that sentiment, or analyze, or even steadily view it. I recognized it, let me repeat, sometimes in the survey of a rapidly-growing vine—in the contemplation of a moth, a butterfly, a chrysalis, a stream of running water. I have felt it in the ocean; in the falling of a meteor. I have felt it in the glances of unusually aged people. And there are one or two stars in heaven—(one especially, a star of the sixth magnitude, double and changeable, to be found near the large star in Lyra) in a telescopic scrutiny of which I have been made aware of the feeling. I have been filled with it by certain sounds from stringed instruments, and not unfrequently by passages from books. Among innumerable other instances, I well remember something in a volume of Joseph Glanvill, which (perhaps merely from its quaintness—who shall say?) never failed to inspire me with the sentiment;—"And the will therein lieth, which dieth not. Who knoweth the mysteries of the will, with its vigour? For God is but a great will pervading all things by nature of its intentness. Man doth not yield him to the angels, nor unto death utterly, save only through the weakness of his feeble will."

Length of years, and subsequent reflection, have enabled me to trace, indeed, some remote connexion between this passage in the English moralist and a portion of the character of Ligeia. An intensity in thought, action, or speech, was possibly, in her, a result, or at least an index, of that gigantic volition which, during our long intercourse, failed to give other and more immediate evidence of its existence. Of all the women whom I have ever known, she, the outwardly calm, the ever-placid Ligeia, was the most violently a prey to the tumultuous vultures of stern passion. And of such passion I could form no estimate, save by the miraculous expansion of those eyes which at once so delighted and appalled me—by the almost magical melody, modulation, distinctness, and placidity of her very low voice—and by the fierce energy (rendered doubly effective by contrast with her manner of utterance) of the wild words which she habitually uttered.

I have spoken of the learning of Ligeia: it was immense—such as I have never known in woman. In the classical tongues was she deeply proficient, and as far as my own acquaintance extended in regard to the modern dialects of Europe, I have never known her at fault. Indeed upon any theme of the most admired, because simply the most abstruse of the boasted erudition of the academy, have I ever found Ligeia at fault? How singularly—how thrillingly, this one point in the nature of my wife has forced itself, at this late period only, upon my attention! I said her knowledge was such as I have never known in woman—but where breathes the man who has traversed, and successfully, all the wide areas of moral, physical, and mathematical science? I saw not then what I now clearly perceive, that the acquisitions of Ligeia were gigantic, were astounding; yet I was sufficiently aware of her infinite supremacy to resign myself, with a childlike confidence, to her guidance through the chaotic world of metaphysical investigation at which I was most busily occupied during the earlier years of our marriage. With how vast a triumph—with how vivid a delight—with how much of all that is ethereal in hope—did I feel, as she bent over me in studies but little sought—but less known—that delicious vista by slow degrees expanding before me, down whose long, gorgeous, and all untrodden path, I might at length pass onward to the goal of a wisdom too divinely precious not to be forbidden!

How poignant, then, must have been the grief with which, after some years, I beheld my well-grounded expectations take wings to themselves and fly away! Without Ligeia I was but as a child groping benighted. Her presence, her readings alone, rendered vividly luminous the many mysteries of the transcendentalism in which we were immersed. Wanting the radiant luster of her eyes, letters, lambent and golden, grew duller than Saturnian lead. And now those eyes shone less and less frequently upon the pages over which I pored. Ligeia grew ill. The wild eyes blazed with a too—too glorious effulgence; the pale fingers became of the transparent waxen hue of the grave, and the blue veins upon the lofty forehead swelled and sank impetuously with the tides of the most gentle emotion. I saw that she must die—and I struggled desperately in spirit with the grim Azrael. And the struggles of the passionate wife were, to my astonishment, even more energetic than my own. There had been much in her stern nature to impress me with the belief that, to her, death would have come without its terrors;—but not so. Words are impotent to convey any just idea of the fierceness of resistance with which she wrestled with the Shadow. I groaned in anguish at the pitiable spectacle. I would have soothed—I would have reasoned; but, in the intensity of her wild desire for life,—for life—but for life—solace and reason were alike the uttermost of folly. Yet not until the last instance, amid the most convulsive writhings of her fierce spirit, was shaken the external placidity of her demeanor. Her voice grew more gentle—grew more low—yet I would not wish to dwell upon the wild meaning of the quietly uttered words. My brain reeled as I hearkened entranced, to a melody more than mortal—to assumptions and aspirations which mortality had never before known.

That she loved me I should not have doubted; and I might have been easily aware that, in a bosom such as hers, love would have reigned no ordinary passion. But in death only, was I fully impressed with the strength of her affection. For long hours, detaining my hand, would she pour out before me the overflowing of a heart whose more than passionate devotion amounted to idolatry. How had I deserved to be so blessed by such confessions?—how had I deserved to be so cursed with the removal of my beloved in the hour of her making them? But upon this subject I cannot bear to dilate. Let me say only, that in Ligeia's more than womanly abandonment to a love, alas! all unmerited, all unworthily bestowed, I at length recognized the principle of her longing with so wildly earnest a desire for the life which was now fleeing so rapidly away. It is this wild longing—it is this eager vehemence of desire for life—but for life—that I have no power to portray—no utterance capable of expressing.

At high noon of the night in which she departed, beckoning me, peremptorily, to her side, she bade me repeat certain verses composed by herself not many days before. I obeyed her.—They were these:

Lo! 'tis a gala night
Within the lonesome latter years!
An angel throng, bewinged, bedight

In veils, and drowned in tears,
Sit in a theater, to see
A play of hopes and fears,
While the orchestra breathes fitfully
The music of the spheres.

Mimes, in the form of God on high,
Mutter and mumble low,
And hither and thither fly—
Mere puppets they, who come and go
At bidding of vast formless things
That shift the scenery to and fro,
Flapping from out their Condor wings
Invisible Woe!

That motley drama!—oh, be sure
It shall not be forgot!
With its Phantom chased forever more,
By a crowd that seize it not,
Through a circle that ever returneth in
To the self-same spot,
And much of Madness and more of Sin
And Horror the soul of the plot.

But see, amid the mimic rout,
A crawling shape intrude!
A blood-red thing that writhes from out
The scenic solitude!
It writhes!—it writhes!—with mortal pangs
The mimes become its food,
And the seraphs sob at vermin fangs
In human gore imbued.

Out—out are the lights—out all!
And over each quivering form,
The curtain, a funeral pall,
Comes down with the rush of a storm,

And the angels, all pallid and wan,
Uprising, unveiling, affirm
That the play is the tragedy, "Man,"
And its hero the Conqueror Worm.

"Oh God!" half-shrieked Ligeia, leaping to her feet and extending her arms aloft with a spasmodic movement, as I made an end of these lines—"O God! O Divine Father!—shall these things be undeviatingly so?—shall this Conqueror be not once conquered? Are we not part and parcel in Thee? Who—who knoweth the mysteries of the will with its vigor? Man doth not yield him to the angels, nor unto death utterly, save only through the weakness of his feeble will."

And now, as if exhausted with emotion, she suffered her white arms to fall, and returned solemnly to her bed of death. And as she breathed her last sighs, there came mingled with them a low murmur from her lips. I bent to them my ear and distinguished, again, the concluding words of the passage in Glanvill—"Man doth not yield himself to the angels, nor unto death utterly, save only through the weakness of his feeble will."

She died;—and I, crushed into the very dust with sorrow, could no longer endure the lonely desolation of my dwelling in the dim and decaying city by the Rhine. I had no lack of what the world calls wealth. Ligeia had brought me far more, very far more than ordinarily falls to the lot of mortals. After a few months, therefore, of weary and aimless wandering, I purchased, and put in some repair, an abbey, which I shall not name, in one of the wildest and least frequented portions of fair England. The gloomy and dreary grandeur of the building, the almost savage aspect of the domain, the many melancholy and time-honored memories connected with both, had much in unison with the feelings of utter abandonment which had driven me into that remote and unsocial region of the country. Yet although the external abbey, with its verdant decay hanging about it, suffered but little alteration, I gave way, with a childlike perversity, and perchance with a faint hope of alleviating my sorrows, to a display of more than regal magnificence within.—For such follies, even in childhood, I had imbibed a taste, and now they came back to me as if in the dotage of grief. Alas, I feel how much even of incipient madness might have been discovered in the gorgeous and fantastic draperies, in the solemn carvings of Egypt, in the wild cornices and furniture, in the Bedlam patterns of the carpets of tufted gold! I had become a bounden slave in the trammels of opium, and my labors and my orders had taken a coloring from my dreams. But these absurdities I must not pause to detail. Let me speak only of that one chamber, ever accursed, whither in a moment of mental alienation, I led from the altar as my bride—as the successor of the unforgotten Ligeia—the fair-haired and blue-eyed Lady Rowena Trevanion, of Tremaine.

There is no individual portion of the architecture and decoration of that bridal chamber which is not now visibly before me. Where were the souls of the haughty family of the bride, when, through thirst of gold, they permitted to pass the threshold of an apartment so bedecked, a maiden and a daughter so beloved? I have said that I minutely remember the details of the chamber—yet I am sadly forgetful on topics of deep moment—and here there was no system, no keeping, in the fantastic display, to take hold upon the memory. The room lay in a high turret of the castellated abbey, was pentagonal in shape, and of capacious size. Occupying the whole southern face of the pentagon was the sole window—an immense sheet of unbroken glass from Venice—a single pane, and tinted of a leaden hue, so that the rays of either the sun or moon, passing through it, fell with a ghastly luster on the objects within. Over the upper portion of this huge window, extended the trellis-work of an aged vine, which clambered up the massy walls of the turret. The ceiling, of gloomy-looking oak, was excessively lofty, vaulted, and elaborately fretted with the wildest and most grotesque specimens of a semi-Gothic, semi-Druidical device. From out the most central recess of this melancholy vaulting, depended, by a single chain of gold with long links, a huge censer of the same metal, Saracenic in pattern, and with many perforations so contrived that there writhed in and out of them, as if endued with a serpent vitality, a continual succession of parti-colored fires.

Some few ottomans and golden candelabra, of Eastern figure, were in various stations about—and there was the couch, too—the bridal couch—of an Indian model, and low, and sculptured of solid ebony, with a pall-like canopy above. In each of the angles of the chamber stood on end a gigantic sarcophagus of black granite, from the tombs of the kings over against Luxor, with their aged lids full of immemorial sculpture. But in the draping of the apartment lay, alas! the chief fantasy of all. The lofty walls, gigantic in height—even unproportionably so—were hung from summit to foot, in vast folds, with a heavy and massive-looking tapestry—tapestry of a material which was found alike as a carpet on the floor, as a covering for the ottomans and the ebony bed, as a canopy for the bed, and as the gorgeous volutes of the curtains which partially shaded the window. The material was the richest cloth of gold. It was spotted all over, at irregular intervals, with arabesque figures, about a foot in diameter, and wrought upon the cloth in patterns of the most jetty black. But these figures partook of the true character of the arabesque only when regarded from a single point of view. By a contrivance now common, and indeed traceable to a very remote period of antiquity, they were made changeable in aspect. To one entering the room, they bore the appearance of simple monstrosities; but upon a farther advance, this appearance gradually departed; and step by step, as the visitor moved his station in the chamber, he saw himself surrounded by an endless succession of the ghastly forms which belong to the superstition of the Norman, or arise in the guilty slumbers of the monk. The phantasmagoric effect was vastly heightened by the artificial introduction of a strong continual current of wind behind the draperies—giving a hideous and uneasy animation to the whole.

In halls such as these—in a bridal chamber such as this—I passed, with the Lady of Tremaine, the unhallowed hours of the first month of our marriage—passed them with but little disquietude. That my wife dreaded the fierce moodiness of my temper—that she shunned me and loved me but little—I could not help perceiving; but it gave me rather pleasure than otherwise. I loathed her with a hatred belonging more to demon than to man. My memory flew back (oh, with what intensity of regret!) to Ligeia, the beloved, the august, the beautiful, the entombed. I reveled in recollections of her purity, of her wisdom, of her lofty, her ethereal nature, of her passionate, her idolatrous love. Now, then, did my spirit fully and freely burn with more than all the fires of her own. In the excitement of my opium dreams (for I was habitually fettered in the shackles of the drug) I would call aloud upon her name, during the silence of the night, or among the sheltered recesses of the glens by day, as if, through the wild eagerness, the solemn passion, the consuming ardor of my longing for the departed, I could restore her to the pathway she had abandoned—ah, could it be for ever?—upon the earth.

About the commencement of the second month of the marriage, the Lady Rowena was attacked with sudden illness, from which her recovery was slow. The fever which consumed her rendered her nights uneasy; and in her perturbed state of half-slumber, she spoke of sounds, and of motions, in and about the chamber of the turret, which I concluded had no origin save in the distemper of her fancy, or perhaps in the phantasmagoric influences of the chamber itself. She became at length convalescent—finally well. Yet but a brief period elapsed, ere a second more violent disorder again threw her upon a bed of suffering; and from this attack her frame, at all times feeble, never altogether recovered. Her illnesses were, after this epoch, of alarming character, and of more alarming recurrence, defying alike the knowledge and the great exertions of her physicians. With the increase of the chronic disease which had thus, apparently, taken too sure hold upon her constitution to be eradicated by human means, I could not fail to observe a similar increase in the nervous irritation of her temperament, and in her excitability by trivial causes of fear. She spoke again, and now more frequently and pertinaciously, of the sounds—of the slight sounds—and of the unusual motions among the tapestries, to which she had formerly alluded.

One night, near the closing in of September, she pressed this distressing subject with more than usual emphasis upon my attention. She had just awakened from an unquiet slumber, and I had been watching, with feelings half of anxiety, half of vague terror, the workings of her emaciated countenance. I sat by the side of her ebony bed, upon one of the ottomans of India. She partly arose, and spoke, in an earnest low whisper, of sounds which she then heard, but which I could not hear—of motions which she then saw, but which I could not perceive. The wind was rushing hurriedly behind the tapestries, and I wished to show her (what, let me confess it, I could not all believe) that those almost inarticulate breathings, and those very gentle variations of the figures upon the wall, were but the natural effects of that customary rushing of the wind. But a deadly pallor, overspreading her face, had proved to me that my exertions to reassure her would be fruitless. She appeared to be fainting, and no attendants were within call. I remembered where was deposited a decanter of light wine which had been ordered by her physicians, and hastened across the chamber to procure it. But, as I stepped beneath the light of the censer, two circumstances of a startling nature attracted my attention. I had felt that some palpable although invisible object had passed lightly by my person; and I saw that there lay upon the golden carpet, in the very middle of the rich luster thrown from the censer, a shadow—a faint, indefinite shadow of angelic aspect—such as might be fancied for the shadow of a shade. But I was wild with the excitement of an immoderate dose of opium, and heeded these things but little, nor spoke of them to Rowena. Having found the wine, I recrossed the chamber, and poured out a gobletful, which I held to the lips of the fainting lady. She had now partially recovered, however, and took the vessel herself, while I sank upon an ottoman near me, with my eyes fastened upon her person. It was then that I became distinctly aware of a gentle footfall upon the carpet, and near the couch; and in a second thereafter, as Rowena was in the act of raising the wine to her lips, I saw, or may have dreamed that I saw, fall within the goblet, as if from some invisible spring in the atmosphere of the room, three or four large drops of a brilliant and ruby-colored fluid. If this I saw—not so Rowena. She swallowed the wine unhesitatingly, and I forbore to speak to her of a circumstance which must after all, I considered, have been but the suggestion of a vivid imagination rendered morbidly active by the terror of the lady, by the opium, and by the hour.

Yet I cannot conceal it from my own perception that, immediately subsequent to the fall of the ruby-drops, a rapid change for the worse took place in the disorder of my wife; so that, on the third subsequent night, the hands of her menials prepared her for the tomb, and on the fourth, I sat alone, with her shrouded body, in that fantastic chamber which had received her as my bride. Wild visions, opium-engendered, flitted, shadow-like, before me. I gazed with unquiet eye upon the sarcophagi in the angles of the room, upon the varying figures of the drapery, and upon the writhing of the parti-colored fires in the censer overhead. My eyes then fell, as I called to mind the circumstances of a former night, to the spot beneath the glare of the censer where I had seen the faint traces of the shadow. It was there, however, no longer; and breathing with greater freedom, I turned my glances to the pallid and rigid figure upon the bed. Then rushed upon me a thousand memories of Ligeia—and then came back upon my heart, with the turbulent violence of a flood, the whole of that unutterable woe with which I had regarded her thus enshrouded. The night waned; and still, with a bosom full of bitter thoughts of the one only and supremely beloved, I remained gazing upon the body of Rowena.

It might have been midnight, or perhaps earlier, or later, for I had taken no note of time, when a sob, low, gentle, but very distinct, startled me from my reverie.—I felt that it came from the bed of ebony—the bed of death! I listened in an agony of superstitious terror—but there was no repetition of the sound. I strained my vision to detect any motion in the corpse—but there was not the slightest perceptible. Yet I could not have been deceived. I had heard the noise, however faint, and my soul was awakened within me. I resolutely and perseveringly kept my attention riveted upon the body. Many minutes elapsed before any circumstances occurred tending to throw light upon the mystery. At length it became evident that a slight, a very feeble, and barely noticeable tinge of color had flushed up within the cheeks, and along the sunken small veins of the eyelids. Through a species of unutterable horror and awe, for which the language of mortality has no sufficiently energetic expression, I felt my heart cease to beat, my limbs grow rigid where I sat. Yet a sense of duty finally operated to restore my self-possession. I could no longer doubt that we had been precipitate in our preparations—that Rowena still lived. It was necessary that some immediate exertion be made; yet the turret was altogether apart from the portion of the abbey tenanted by the servants—there were none within call—I had no means of summoning them to my aid without leaving the room for many minutes—and this I could not venture to do. I therefore struggled alone in my endeavors to call back the spirit still hovering. In a short period it was certain, however, that a relapse had taken place; the color disappeared from both eyelid and cheek, leaving a wanness even more than that of marble; the lips became doubly shriveled and pinched up in the ghastly expression of death; a repulsive clamminess and coldness overspread rapidly the surface of the body; and all the usual rigorous stiffness immediately supervened. I fell back with a shudder upon the couch from which I had been so startlingly aroused, and again gave myself up to passionate waking visions of Ligeia.

An hour thus elapsed when (could it be possible?) I was a second time aware of some vague sound issuing from the region of the bed. I listened—in extremity of horror. The sound came again—it was a sigh. Rushing to the corpse, I saw—distinctly saw—a tremor upon the lips. In a minute afterward they relaxed, disclosing a bright line of the pearly teeth. Amazement now struggled in my bosom with the profound awe which had hitherto reigned there alone. I felt that my vision grew dim, that my reason wandered; and it was only by a violent effort that I at length succeeded in nerving myself to the task which duty thus once more had pointed out. There was now a partial glow upon the forehead and upon the cheek and throat; a perceptible warmth pervaded the whole frame; there was even a slight pulsation at the heart. The lady lived; and with redoubled ardor I betook myself to the task of restoration. I chafed and bathed the temples and the hands, and used every exertion which experience, and no little medical reading, could suggest. But in vain. Suddenly, the color fled, the pulsation ceased, the lips resumed the expression of the dead, and, in an instant afterward, the whole body took upon itself the icy chilliness, the livid hue, the intense rigidity, the sunken outline, and all the loathsome peculiarities of that which has been, for many days, a tenant of the tomb.

And again I sunk into visions of Ligeia—and again (what marvel that I shudder while I write?) again there reached my ears a low sob from the region of the ebony bed. But why shall I minutely detail the unspeakable horrors of that night? Why shall I pause to relate how, time after time, until near the period of the gray dawn, this hideous drama of revivification was repeated; how each terrific relapse was only into a sterner and apparently more irredeemable death; how each agony wore the aspect of a struggle with some invisible foe; and how each struggle was succeeded by I know not what of wild change in the personal appearance of the corpse? Let me hurry to a conclusion.

The greater part of the fearful night had worn away, and she who had been dead, once again stirred—and now more vigorously than hitherto, although arousing from a dissolution more appalling in its utter hopelessness than any. I had long ceased to struggle or to move, and remained sitting rigidly upon the ottoman, a helpless prey to a whirl of violent emotions, of which extreme awe was perhaps the least terrible, the least consuming. The corpse, I repeat, stirred, and now more vigorously than before. The hues of life flushed up with unwonted energy into the countenance—the limbs relaxed—and, save that the eyelids were yet pressed heavily together, and that the bandages and draperies of the grave still imparted their charnel character to the figure, I might have dreamed that Rowena had indeed shaken off, utterly, the fetters of Death. But if this idea was not, even then, altogether adopted, I could at least doubt no longer, when arising from the bed, tottering, with feeble steps, with closed eyes, and with the manner of one bewildered in a dream, the thing that was enshrouded advanced boldly and palpably into the middle of the apartment.

I trembled not—I stirred not—for a crowd of unutterable fancies connected with the air, the stature, the demeanor of the figure, rushing hurriedly through my brain, had paralysed—had chilled me into stone. I stirred not—but gazed upon the apparition. There was a mad disorder in my thoughts—a tumult unappeasable. Could it, indeed, be the living Rowena who confronted me? Could it indeed be Rowena at all—the fair-haired, the blue-eyed Lady Rowena Trevanion of Tremaine? Why, why should I doubt it? The bandage lay heavily about the mouth—but then might it not be the mouth of the breathing Lady of Tremaine? And the cheeks—there were the roses as in her noon of life—yes, these might indeed be the fair cheeks of the living Lady of Tremaine. And the chin, with its dimples, as in health, might it not be hers?—but had she then grown taller since her malady? What inexpressible madness seized me with that thought? One bound, and I had reached her feet! Shrinking from my touch, she let fall from her head, unloosened, the ghastly cerements which had confined it, and there streamed forth, into the rushing atmosphere of the chamber, huge masses of long and dishevelled hair; *it was blacker than the raven wings of the midnight*! And now slowly opened the eyes of the figure which stood before me. “Here then, at least,” I shrieked aloud, “can I never—can I never be mistaken—these are the full, and the black, and the wild eyes—of my lost love—of the lady—of the LADY LIGEIA.”

THE FALL OF THE HOUSE OF USHER

Son cœur est un luth suspendu;
Sitôt qu'on le touche il résonne. [1]
De Béranger

DURING THE WHOLE of a dull, dark, and soundless day in the autumn of the year, when the clouds hung oppressively low in the heavens, I had been passing alone, on horseback, through a singularly dreary tract of country; and at length found myself, as the shades of the evening drew on, within view of the melancholy House of Usher. I know not how it was—but, with the first glimpse of the building, a sense of insufferable gloom pervaded my spirit. I say insufferable; for the feeling was unrelieved by any of that half-pleasureable, because poetic, sentiment, with which the mind usually receives even the sternest natural images of the desolate or terrible. I looked upon the scene before me—upon the mere house, and the simple landscape features of the domain—upon the bleak walls—upon the vacant eye-like windows—upon a few rank sedges—and upon a few white trunks of decayed trees—with an utter depression of soul which I can compare to no earthly sensation more properly than to the after-dream of the reveler upon opium—the bitter lapse into everyday life—the hideous dropping off of the veil. There was an iciness, a sinking, a sickening of the heart—an unredeemed dreariness of thought which no goading of the imagination

12 The heart is like a hanging lute; at the slightest touch, it resounds.

could torture into aught of the sublime. What was it—I paused to think—what was it that so unnerved me in the contemplation of the House of Usher? It was a mystery all insoluble; nor could I grapple with the shadowy fancies that crowded upon me as I pondered. I was forced to fall back upon the unsatisfactory conclusion, that while, beyond doubt, there are combinations of very simple natural objects which have the power of thus affecting us, still the analysis of this power lies among considerations beyond our depth. It was possible, I reflected, that a mere different arrangement of the particulars of the scene, of the details of the picture, would be sufficient to modify, or perhaps to annihilate its capacity for sorrowful impression; and, acting upon this idea, I reined my horse to the precipitous brink of a black and lurid tarn that lay in unruffled luster by the dwelling, and gazed down—but with a shudder even more thrilling than before—upon the remodeled and inverted images of the gray sedge, and the ghastly tree-stems, and the vacant and eye-like windows.

Nevertheless, in this mansion of gloom I now proposed to myself a sojourn of some weeks. Its proprietor, Roderick Usher, had been one of my boon companions in boyhood; but many years had elapsed since our last meeting. A letter, however, had lately reached me in a distant part of the country—a letter from him—which, in its wildly importunate nature, had admitted of no other than a personal reply. The MS. gave evidence of nervous agitation. The writer spoke of acute bodily illness—of a mental disorder which oppressed him—and of an earnest desire to see me, as his best, and indeed his only personal friend, with a view of attempting, by the cheerfulness of my society, some alleviation of his malady. It was the manner in which all this, and much more, was said—it was the apparent heart that went with his request—which allowed me no room for hesitation; and I accordingly obeyed forthwith what I still considered a very singular summons.

Although, as boys, we had been even intimate associates, yet I really knew little of my friend. His reserve had been always excessive and habitual. I was aware, however, that his very ancient family had been noted, time out of mind, for a peculiar sensibility of temperament, displaying itself, through long ages, in many works of exalted art, and manifested, of late, in repeated deeds of munificent yet unobtrusive charity, as well as in a passionate devotion to the intricacies, perhaps even more than to the orthodox and easily recognizable beauties, of musical science. I had learned, too, the very remarkable fact, that the stem of the Usher race, all time-honored as it was, had put forth, at no period, any enduring branch; in other words, that the entire family lay in the direct line of descent, and had always, with very trifling and very temporary variation, so lain. It was this deficiency, I considered, while running over in thought the perfect keeping of the character of the premises with the accredited character of the people, and while speculating upon the possible influence which the one, in the long lapse of centuries, might have exercised upon the other—it was this deficiency, perhaps, of collateral issue, and the consequent undeviating transmission, from sire to son, of the patrimony with the name, which had, at length, so identified the two as to merge the original title of the estate in the quaint and equivocal appellation of the "House of Usher"—an appellation which seemed to include, in the minds of the peasantry who used it, both the family and the family mansion.

I have said that the sole effect of my somewhat childish experiment—that of looking down within the tarn—had been to deepen the first singular impression. There can be no doubt that the consciousness of the rapid increase of my superstition—for why should I not so term it?—served mainly to accelerate the increase itself. Such, I have long known, is the paradoxical law of all sentiments having terror as a basis. And it might have been for this reason only, that, when I again uplifted my eyes to the house itself, from its image in the pool, there grew in my mind a strange fancy—a fancy so ridiculous, indeed, that I but mention it to show the vivid force of the sensations which oppressed me. I had so worked upon my imagination as really to believe that about the whole mansion and domain there hung an atmosphere peculiar to themselves and their immediate vicinity—an atmosphere which had no affinity with the air of heaven, but which had reeked up from the decayed trees, and the gray wall, and the silent tarn—a pestilent and mystic vapor, dull, sluggish, faintly discernible, and leaden-hued.

Shaking off from my spirit what must have been a dream, I scanned more narrowly the real aspect of the building. Its principal feature seemed to be that of an excessive antiquity. The discoloration of ages had been great. Minute fungi overspread the whole exterior, hanging in a fine tangled web-work from the eaves. Yet all this was apart from any extraordinary dilapidation. No portion of the masonry had fallen; and there appeared to be a wild inconsistency between its still perfect adaptation of parts, and the crumbling condition of the individual stones. In this there was much that reminded me of the specious totality of old woodwork which has rotted for long years in some neglected vault, with no disturbance from the breath of the external air. Beyond this indication of extensive decay, however, the fabric gave little token of instability. Perhaps the eye of a scrutinizing observer might have discovered a barely perceptible fissure, which, extending from the roof of the building in front, made its way down the wall in a zigzag direction, until it became lost in the sullen waters of the tarn.

Noticing these things, I rode over a short causeway to the house. A servant in waiting took my horse, and I entered the Gothic archway of the hall. A valet, of stealthy step, thence conducted me, in silence, through many dark and intricate passages in my progress to the studio of his master. Much that I encountered on the way contributed, I know not how, to heighten the vague sentiments of which I have already spoken. While the objects around me—while the carvings of the ceilings, the somber tapestries of the walls, the ebon blackness of the floors, and the phantasmagoric armorial trophies which rattled as I strode, were but matters to which, or to such as which, I had been accustomed from my infancy—while I hesitated not to acknowledge how familiar was all this—I still wondered to find how unfamiliar were the fancies which ordinary images were stirring up. On one of the staircases, I met the physician of the family. His countenance, I thought, wore a mingled expression of low cunning and perplexity. He accosted me with trepidation and passed on. The valet now threw open a door and ushered me into the presence of his master.

The room in which I found myself was very large and lofty. The windows were long, narrow, and pointed, and at so vast a distance from the black oaken floor as to be altogether inaccessible from within. Feeble gleams of encrimsoned light made their way through the trellised panes, and served to render sufficiently distinct the more prominent objects around; the eye, however, struggled in vain to reach the remoter angles of the chamber, or the recesses of the vaulted and fretted ceiling. Dark draperies hung upon the walls. The general furniture was profuse, comfortless, antique, and tattered. Many books and musical instruments lay scattered about, but failed to give any vitality to the scene. I felt that I breathed an atmosphere of sorrow. An air of stern, deep, and irredeemable gloom hung over and pervaded all.

Upon my entrance, Usher arose from a sofa on which he had been lying at full length, and greeted me with a vivacious warmth which had much in it, I at first thought, of an overdone cordiality—of the constrained effort of the ennuyé man of the world. A glance, however, at his countenance, convinced me of his perfect sincerity. We sat down; and for some moments, while he spoke not, I gazed upon him with a feeling half of pity, half of awe. Surely, man had never before so terribly altered, in so brief a period, as had Roderick Usher! It was with difficulty that I could bring myself to admit the identity of the wan being before me with the companion of my early boyhood. Yet the character of his face had been at all times remarkable. A cadaverousness of complexion; an eye large, liquid, and luminous beyond comparison; lips somewhat thin and very pallid, but of a surpassingly beautiful curve; a nose of a delicate Hebrew model, but with a breadth of nostril unusual in similar formations; a finely-molded chin, speaking, in its want of prominence, of a want of moral energy; hair of a more than web-like softness and tenuity; these features, with an inordinate expansion above the regions of the temple, made up altogether a countenance not easily to be forgotten. And now in the mere exaggeration of the prevailing character of these features, and of the expression they were wont to convey, lay so much of change that I doubted to whom I spoke. The now ghastly pallor of the skin, and the now miraculous luster of the eye, above all things startled and even awed me. The silken hair, too, had been suffered to grow all unheeded, and as, in its wild gossamer texture, it floated rather than fell about the face, I could not, even with effort, connect its arabesque expression with any idea of simple humanity.

In the manner of my friend I was at once struck with an incoherence—an inconsistency; and I soon found this to arise from a series of feeble and futile struggles to overcome an habitual trepidancy—an excessive nervous agitation. For something of this nature I had indeed been prepared, no less by his letter, than by reminiscences of certain boyish traits, and by conclusions deduced from his peculiar physical conformation and temperament. His action was alternately vivacious and sullen.

His voice varied rapidly from a tremulous indecision (when the animal spirits seemed utterly in abeyance) to that species of energetic concision—that abrupt, weighty, unhurried, and hollow-sounding enunciation—that leaden, self-balanced and perfectly modulated guttural utterance, which may be observed in the lost drunkard, or the irreclaimable eater of opium, during the periods of his most intense excitement.

It was thus that he spoke of the object of my visit, of his earnest desire to see me, and of the solace he expected me to afford him. He entered, at some length, into what he conceived to be the nature of his malady. It was, he said, a constitutional and a family evil, and one for which he despaired to find a remedy—a mere nervous affection, he immediately added, which would undoubtedly soon pass off. It displayed itself in a host of unnatural sensations. Some of these, as he detailed them, interested and bewildered me; although, perhaps, the terms, and the general manner of the narration had their weight. He suffered much from a morbid acuteness of the senses; the most insipid food was alone endurable; he could wear only garments of certain texture; the odors of all flowers were oppressive; his eyes were tortured by even a faint light; and there were but peculiar sounds, and these from stringed instruments, which did not inspire him with horror.

To an anomalous species of terror I found him a bounden slave. "I shall perish," said he, "I must perish in this deplorable folly. Thus, thus, and not otherwise, shall I be lost. I dread the events of the future, not in themselves, but in their results. I shudder at the thought of any, even the most trivial, incident, which may operate upon this intolerable agitation of soul. I have, indeed, no abhorrence of danger, except in its absolute effect—in terror. In this unnerved—in this pitiable condition—I feel that the period will sooner or later arrive when I must abandon life and reason together, in some struggle with the grim phantasm, Fear."

I learned, moreover, at intervals, and through broken and equivocal hints, another singular feature of his mental condition. He was enchained by certain superstitious impressions in regard to the dwelling which he tenanted, and whence, for many years, he had never ventured forth—in regard to an influence whose supposititious force was conveyed in terms too shadowy here to be restated—an influence which some peculiarities in the mere form and substance of his family mansion, had, by dint of long sufferance, he said, obtained over his spirit—an effect which the physique of the gray walls and turrets, and of the dim tarn into which they all looked down, had, at length, brought about upon the morale of his existence.

He admitted, however, although with hesitation, that much of the peculiar gloom which thus afflicted him could be traced to a more natural and far more palpable origin—to the severe and long-continued illness—indeed to the evidently approaching dissolution—of a tenderly beloved sister—his sole companion for long years—his last and only relative on earth. "Her decease," he said, with a bitterness which I can never forget, "would leave him (him the hopeless and the frail) the last of the ancient race of the Ushers." While he spoke, the Lady Madeline (for so was she called) passed slowly through a remote portion of the apartment, and, without having noticed my presence, disappeared. I regarded her with an utter astonishment not unmingled with dread—and yet I found it impossible to account for such feelings. A sensation of stupor oppressed me, as my eyes followed her retreating steps. When a door, at length, closed upon her, my glance sought instinctively and eagerly the countenance of the brother—but he had buried his face in his hands, and I could only perceive that a far more than ordinary wanness had overspread the emaciated fingers through which trickled many passionate tears.

The disease of the Lady Madeline had long baffled the skill of her physicians. A settled apathy, a gradual wasting away of the person, and frequent although transient affections of a partially cataleptical character, were the unusual diagnosis. Hitherto she had steadily borne up against the pressure of her malady, and had not betaken herself finally to bed; but, on the closing in of the evening of my arrival at the house, she succumbed (as her brother told me at night with inexpressible agitation) to the prostrating power of the destroyer; and I learned that the glimpse I had obtained of her person would thus probably be the last I should obtain—that the lady, at least while living, would be seen by me no more.

For several days ensuing, her name was unmentioned by either Usher or myself: and during this period I was busied in earnest endeavors to alleviate the melancholy of my friend. We painted and read together; or I listened, as if in a dream, to the wild improvisations of his speaking guitar. And thus, as a closer and still closer intimacy admitted me more unreservedly into the recesses of his spirit, the more bitterly did I perceive the futility of all attempt at cheering a mind from which darkness, as if an inherent positive quality, poured forth upon all objects of the moral and physical universe, in one unceasing radiation of gloom.

I shall ever bear about me a memory of the many solemn hours I thus spent alone with the master of the House of Usher. Yet I should fail in any attempt to convey an idea of the exact character of the studies, or of the occupations, in which he involved me, or led me the way. An excited and highly distempered ideality threw a sulfureous luster over all. His long improvised dirges will ring for ever in my ears. Among other things, I hold painfully in mind a certain singular perversion and amplification of the wild air of the last waltz of Von Weber. From the paintings over which his elaborate fancy brooded, and which grew, touch by touch, into vagueness at which I shuddered the more thrillingly, because I shuddered knowing not why;—from these paintings (vivid as their images now are before me) I would in vain endeavor to educe more than a small portion which should lie within the compass of merely written words. By the utter simplicity, by the nakedness of his designs, he arrested and overawed attention. If ever mortal painted an idea, that mortal was Roderick Usher. For me at least—in the circumstances then surrounding me—there arose out of the pure abstractions which the hypochondriac contrived to throw upon his canvas, an intensity of intolerable awe, no shadow of which felt I ever yet in the contemplation of the certainly glowing yet too concrete reveries of Fuseli.

One of the phantasmagoric conceptions of my friend, partaking not so rigidly of the spirit of abstraction, may be shadowed forth, although feebly, in words. A small picture presented the interior of an immensely long and rectangular vault or tunnel, with low walls, smooth, white, and without interruption or device. Certain accessory points of the design served well to convey the idea that this excavation lay at an exceeding depth below the surface of the earth. No outlet was observed in any portion of its vast extent, and no torch, or other artificial source of light was discernible; yet a flood of intense rays rolled throughout, and bathed the whole in a ghastly and inappropriate splendor.

I have just spoken of that morbid condition of the auditory nerve which rendered all music intolerable to the sufferer, with the exception of certain effects of stringed instruments. It was, perhaps, the narrow limits to which he thus confined himself upon the guitar, which gave birth in great measure, to the fantastic character of his performances. But the fervid facility of his impromptus could not be so accounted for. They must have been, and were, in the notes, as well as in the words of his wild fantasias (for he not unfrequently accompanied himself with rhymed verbal improvisations), the result of that intense mental collectedness and concentration to which I have previously alluded as observable only in particular moments of the highest artificial excitement. The words of one of these rhapsodies I have easily remembered. I was, perhaps, the more forcibly impressed with it, as he gave it, because, in the under or mystic current of its meaning, I fancied that I perceived, and for the first time, a full consciousness on the part of Usher, of the tottering of his lofty reason upon her throne. The verses, which were entitled "The Haunted Palace," ran very nearly, if not accurately, thus:

i

In the greenest of our valleys,
  By good angels tenanted,
Once a fair and stately palace—
  Radiant palace—reared its head.
In the monarch Thought's dominion—
  It stood there!
Never seraph spread a pinion
Over fabric half so fair.

ii

Banners yellow, glorious, golden,
On its roof did float and flow;
(This—all this—was in the olden
  Time long ago)
And every gentle air that dallied,
  In that sweet day,
Along the ramparts plumed and pallid,
  A wingèd odor went away.

iii

Wanderers in that happy valley
  Through two luminous windows saw

Spirits moving musically
  To a lute's well tunèd law,
Round about a throne, where sitting
  (Porphyrogene!)
In state his glory well befitting,
  The ruler of the realm was seen.

iv

And all with pearl and ruby glowing
  Was the fair palace door,
Through which came flowing, flowing, flowing
  And sparkling evermore,
A troop of echoes whose sweet duty
  Was but to sing,
In voices of surpassing beauty,
  The wit and wisdom of their king.

v

But evil things, in robes of sorrow,
  Assailed the monarch's high estate;
(Ah, let us mourn, for never morrow
  Shall dawn upon him, desolate!)
And, round about his home, the glory
  That blushed and bloomed
Is but a dim-remembered story
Of the old time entombed.

vi

And travelers now within that valley,
  Through the red-litten windows, see
Vast forms that move fantastically
  To a discordant melody;
While, like a rapid ghastly river,
  Through the pale door,
A hideous throng rush out forever,
And laugh—but smile no more.

I well remember that suggestions arising from this ballad, led us into a train of thought wherein there became manifest an opinion of Usher's which I mention not so much on account of its novelty (for other men[1] have thought thus), as on account of the pertinacity with which he maintained it. This opinion, in its general form, was that of the sentience of all vegetable things. But, in his disordered fancy, the idea had assumed a more daring character, and trespassed, under certain conditions, upon the kingdom of inorganization. I lack words to express the full extent, or the earnest abandon of his persuasion. The belief, however, was connected (as I have previously hinted) with the gray stones of the home of his forefathers. The conditions of the sentience had been here, he imagined, fulfilled in the method of collocation of these stones—in the order of their arrangement, as well as in that of the many fungi which overspread them, and of the decayed trees which stood around—above all, in the long undisturbed endurance of this arrangement, and in its reduplication in the still waters of the tarn. Its evidence—the evidence of the sentience—was to be seen, he said (and I here started as he spoke) in the gradual yet certain condensation of an atmosphere of their own about the waters and the walls. The result was discoverable, he added, in that silent, yet importunate and terrible influence which for centuries had molded the destinies of his family, and which made him what I now saw him—what he was. Such opinions need no comment, and I will make none.

Our books—the books which, for years, had formed no small portion of the mental existence of the invalid—were, as might be supposed, in strict keeping with this character of phantasm. We pored together over such works as the *Ververt et Chartreuse* of Gresset; the *Belphegor* of Machiavelli; the *Heaven and Hell* of Swedenborg; the *Subterranean Voyage of Nicholas Klimm* by Holberg; the *Chiromancy* of Robert Flud, of Jean D'Indaginé, and of De la Chambre; the *Journey into the Blue Distance* of Tieck; and the *City of the Sun* of Campanella. One favorite volume was a small octavo edition of the *Directorium Inquisitorum*, by the Dominican Eymeric de Gironne; and there were passages in *Pomponius Mela*, about the old African Satyrs and Ægipans, over which Usher would sit dreaming for hours. His chief delight, however, was found in the perusal of an

1 Watson, Dr. Percival, Spallanzani, and especially the Bishop of Landaff.

exceedingly rare and curious book in quarto Gothic—the manual of a forgotten church—the *Vigiliae Mortuorum secundum Chorum Ecclesiae Maguntinae*.

I could not help thinking of the wild ritual of this work, and of its probable influence upon the hypochondriac, when, one evening, having informed me abruptly that the Lady Madeline was no more, he stated his intention of preserving her corpse for a fortnight (previously to its final interment), in one of the numerous vaults within the main walls of the building. The worldly reason, however, assigned for this singular proceeding, was one which I did not feel at liberty to dispute. The brother had been led to his resolution (so he told me) by consideration of the unusual character of the malady of the deceased, of certain obtrusive and eager inquiries on the part of her medical men, and of the remote and exposed situation of the burial ground of the family. I will not deny that when I called to mind the sinister countenance of the person whom I met upon the staircase, on the day of my arrival at the house, I had no desire to oppose what I regarded as at best but a harmless, and by no means an unnatural, precaution.

At the request of Usher, I personally aided him in the arrangements for the temporary entombment. The body having been encoffined, we two alone bore it to its rest. The vault in which we placed it (and which had been so long unopened that our torches, half smothered in its oppressive atmosphere, gave us little opportunity for investigation) was small, damp, and entirely without means of admission for light; lying, at great depth, immediately beneath that portion of the building in which was my own sleeping apartment. It had been used, apparently, in remote feudal times, for the worst purpose of a donjon-keep, and, in later days, as a place of deposit for powder, or some other highly combustible substance, as a portion of its floor, and the whole interior of a long archway through which we reached it, were carefully sheathed with copper. The door, of massive iron, had been, also, similarly protected. Its immense weight caused an unusually sharp grating sound, as it moved upon its hinges.

Having deposited our mournful burden upon trestles within this region of horror, we partially turned aside the yet unscrewed lid of the coffin, and looked upon the face of the tenant. A striking similitude between the brother and sister now first arrested my attention; and

Usher, divining, perhaps, my thoughts, murmured out some few words from which I learned that the deceased and himself had been twins, and that sympathies of a scarcely intelligible nature had always existed between them. Our glances, however, rested not long upon the dead—for we could not regard her unawed. The disease which had thus entombed the lady in the maturity of youth, had left, as usual in all maladies of a strictly cataleptical character, the mockery of a faint blush upon the bosom and the face, and that suspiciously lingering smile upon the lip which is so terrible in death. We replaced and screwed down the lid, and, having secured the door of iron, made our way, with toil, into the scarcely less gloomy apartments of the upper portion of the house.

And now, some days of bitter grief having elapsed, an observable change came over the features of the mental disorder of my friend. His ordinary manner had vanished. His ordinary occupations were neglected or forgotten. He roamed from chamber to chamber with hurried, unequal, and objectless step. The pallor of his countenance had assumed, if possible, a more ghastly hue—but the luminousness of his eye had utterly gone out. The once occasional huskiness of his tone was heard no more; and a tremulous quaver, as if of extreme terror, habitually characterized his utterance. There were times, indeed, when I thought his unceasingly agitated mind was laboring with some oppressive secret, to divulge which he struggled for the necessary courage. At times, again, I was obliged to resolve all into the mere inexplicable vagaries of madness, for I beheld him gazing upon vacancy for long hours, in an attitude of the profoundest attention, as if listening to some imaginary sound. It was no wonder that his condition terrified—that it infected me. I felt creeping upon me, by slow yet certain degrees, the wild influences of his own fantastic yet impressive superstitions.

It was, especially, upon retiring to bed late in the night of the seventh or eighth day after the placing of the Lady Madeline within the donjon, that I experienced the full power of such feelings. Sleep came not near my couch—while the hours waned and waned away. I struggled to reason off the nervousness which had dominion over me. I endeavored to believe that much, if not all of what I felt, was due to the bewildering influence of the gloomy furniture of the room—of the dark and tattered draperies, which, tortured into motion by the breath of a rising tempest, swayed fitfully to and fro upon the walls, and rustled uneasily about the decorations of the bed. But my efforts were fruitless. An irrepressible tremor gradually pervaded my frame; and, at length, there sat upon my very heart an incubus of utterly causeless alarm. Shaking this off with a gasp and a struggle, I uplifted myself upon the pillows, and, peering earnestly within the intense darkness of the chamber, hearkened—I know not why, except that an instinctive spirit prompted me—to certain low and indefinite sounds which came, through the pauses of the storm, at long intervals, I knew not whence. Overpowered by an intense sentiment of horror, unaccountable yet unendurable, I threw on my clothes with haste (for I felt that I should sleep no more during the night), and endeavored to arouse myself from the pitiable condition into which I had fallen, by pacing rapidly to and fro through the apartment.

I had taken but few turns in this manner, when a light step on an adjoining staircase arrested my attention. I presently recognized it as that of Usher. In an instant afterward he rapped, with a gentle touch, at my door, and entered, bearing a lamp. His countenance was, as usual cadaverously wan—but, moreover, there was a species of mad hilarity in his eyes—an evident restrained hysteria in his whole demeanor. His air appalled me—but anything was preferable to the solitude which I had so long endured, and I even welcomed his presence as a relief.

"And you have not seen it?" he said abruptly, after having stared about him for some moments in silence—"you have not then seen it?—but, stay! you shall." Thus speaking, and having carefully shaded his lamp, he hurried to one of the casements, and threw it freely open to the storm.

The impetuous fury of the entering gust nearly lifted us from our feet. It was, indeed, a tempestuous yet sternly beautiful night, and one wildly singular in its terror and its beauty. A whirlwind had apparently collected its force in our vicinity; for there were frequent and violent alterations in the direction of the wind; and the exceeding density of the clouds (which hung so low as to press upon the turrets of the house) did not prevent our perceiving the lifelike velocity with which they flew careering from all points against each other, without passing away into the distance. I say that even their exceeding density did not prevent our perceiving this—yet we had no glimpse of the moon or stars—nor was there any flashing forth of the lighting. But the under surfaces of the huge masses of agitated vapor, as well as all terrestrial objects immediately around us, were glowing in the unnatural light of a faintly luminous and distinctly visible gaseous exhalation which hung about and enshrouded the mansion.

"You must not—you shall not behold this!" said I, shudderingly, to Usher, as I led him, with a gentle violence, from the window to a seat. "These appearances, which bewilder you, are merely electrical phenomena not uncommon—or it may be that they have their ghastly origin in the rank miasma of the tarn. Let us close this casement;—the air is chilling and dangerous to your frame. Here is one of your favorite romances. I will read, and you shall listen;—and so we will pass away this terrible night together."

The antique volume which I had taken up was the *Mad Trist* of Sir Launcelot Canning; but I had called it a favorite of Usher's more in sad jest than in earnest; for, in truth, there is little in its uncouth and unimaginative prolixity which could have had interest for the lofty and spiritual ideality of my friend. It was, however, the only book immediately at hand; and I indulged a vague hope that the excitement which now agitated the hypochondriac, might find relief (for the history of mental disorder is full of similar anomalies) even in the extremeness of the folly which I should read. Could I have judged, indeed, by the wild overstrained air of vivacity with which he hearkened, or apparently hearkened, to the words of the tale, I might well have congratulated myself upon the success of my design.

I had arrived at that well-known portion of the story where Ethelred, the hero of the *Trist*, having sought in vain for peaceable admission into the dwelling of the hermit, proceeds to make good an entrance by force. Here, it will be remembered, the words of the narrative run thus:

"And Ethelred, who was by nature of a doughty heart, and who was now mighty withal, on account of the powerfulness of the wine which he had drunken, waited no longer to hold parley with the hermit, who in sooth, was of an obstinate and maliceful turn, but, feeling the rain upon his shoulders, and fearing the rising of the tempest, uplifted his mace outright, and, with blows, made quickly room in the plankings of the door for his gauntleted hand; and now pulling therewith sturdily, he so cracked, and ripped, and tore all asunder, that the noise of the dry and hollow-sounding wood alarmed and reverberated throughout the forest."

At the termination of this sentence I started, and for a moment, paused; for it appeared to me (although I at once concluded that my excited fancy had deceived me)—it appeared to me that, from some very remote portion of the mansion, there came, indistinctly, to my ears, what might have been, in its exact similarity of character, the echo (but a stifled and dull one certainly) of the very cracking and ripping sound which Sir Launcelot had so particularly described. It was, beyond doubt, the coincidence alone which had arrested my attention; for, amid the rattling of the sashes of the casements, and the ordinary commingled noises of the still increasing storm, the sound, in itself, had nothing, surely, which should have interested or disturbed me. I continued the story:

"But the good champion Ethelred, now entering within the door, was sore enraged and amazed to perceive no signal of the maliceful hermit; but, in the stead thereof, a dragon of a scaly and prodigious demeanor, and of a fiery tongue, which sate in guard before a palace of gold, with a floor of silver; and upon the wall there hung a shield of shining brass with this legend enwritten—

> Who entereth herein, a conqueror hath bin;
> Who slayeth the dragon, the shield he shall win;

and Ethelred uplifted his mace, and struck upon the head of the dragon, which fell before him, and gave up his pesty breath, with a shriek so horrid and harsh, and withal so piercing, that Ethelred had fain to close his ears with his hands against the dreadful noise of it, the like whereof was never before heard."

Here again I paused abruptly, and now a feeling of wild amazement—for there could be no doubt whatever that, in this instance, I did actually hear (although from what direction it proceeded I found it impossible to say) a low and apparently distant, but harsh, protracted, and most unusual screaming or grating sound—the exact counterpart of what my fancy had already conjured up for the dragon's unnatural shriek as described by the romancer.

Oppressed, as I certainly was, upon the occurrence of the second and most extraordinary coincidence, by a thousand conflicting sensations, in which wonder and extreme terror were predominant, I still retained sufficient presence of mind to avoid exciting, by any observation, the sensitive nervousness of my companion. I was by no means certain that he had noticed the sounds in question; although, assuredly, a strange alteration had, during the last few minutes, taken place in his demeanor. From a position fronting my own, he had gradually brought round his chair, so as to sit with his face to the door of the chamber; and thus I could but partially perceive his features, although I saw that his lips trembled as if he were murmuring inaudibly. His head had dropped upon his breast—yet I knew that he was not asleep, from the wide and rigid opening of the eye as I caught a glance of it in profile. The motion of his body, too, was at variance with this idea—for he rocked from side to side with a gentle yet constant and uniform sway. Having rapidly taken notice of all this, I resumed the narrative of Sir Launcelot, which thus proceeded:

"And now, the champion, having escaped from the terrible fury of the dragon, bethinking himself of the brazen shield, and of the breaking up of the enchantment which was upon it, removed the carcass from out of the way before him, and approached valorously over the silver pavement of the castle to where the shield was upon the wall; which in sooth tarried not for his full coming, but fell down at his feet upon the silver floor, with a mighty great and terrible ringing sound."

No sooner had these syllables passed my lips, than—as if a shield of brass had indeed, at the moment, fallen heavily upon a floor of silver—I became aware of a distinct, hollow, metallic, and clangorous, yet apparently muffled reverberation. Completely unnerved, I leaped to my feet; but the measured rocking movement of Usher was undisturbed. I rushed to the chair in which he sat. His eyes were bent fixedly before him, and throughout his whole countenance there reigned a stony rigidity. But, as I placed my hand upon his shoulder, there came a strong shudder over his whole person; a sickly smile quivered about his lips; and I saw that he spoke in a low, hurried, and gibbering murmur, as if unconscious of my presence. Bending closely over him, I at length drank in the hideous import of his words.

"Not hear it?—yes, I hear it, and have heard it. Long—long—long—many minutes, many hours, many days, have I heard it—yet I dared not—oh, pity me, miserable wretch that I am!—I dared not—I dared not speak! We have put her living in the tomb! Said I not that my senses were acute? I now tell you that I heard her first feeble movements in the hollow coffin. I heard them—many, many days ago—yet I dared not—I dared not speak! And now—to-night—Ethelred—ha! ha!—the breaking of the hermit's door, and the death-cry of the dragon, and the clangour of the shield!—say, rather, the rending of her coffin, and the grating of the iron hinges of her prison, and her struggles within the coppered archway of the vault! Oh whither shall I fly? Will she not be here anon? Is she not hurrying to upbraid me for my haste? Have I not heard her footstep on the stair? Do I not distinguish that heavy and horrible beating of her heart? Madman!" here he sprang furiously to his feet, and shrieked out his syllables, as if in the effort he were giving up his soul—"Madman! I tell you that she now stands without the door!"

As if in the superhuman energy of his utterance there had been found the potency of a spell—the huge antique panels to which the speaker pointed, threw slowly back, upon the instant, their ponderous and ebony jaws. It was the work of the rushing gust—but then without those doors there did stand the lofty and enshrouded figure of the Lady Madeline of Usher. There was blood upon her white robes, and the evidence of some bitter struggle upon every portion of her emaciated frame. For a moment she remained trembling and reeling to and fro upon the threshold, then, with a low moaning cry, fell heavily inward upon the person of her brother, and in her violent and now final death-agonies, bore him to the floor a corpse, and a victim to the terrors he had anticipated.

From that chamber, and from that mansion, I fled aghast. The storm was still abroad in all its wrath as I found myself crossing the old causeway. Suddenly there shot along the path a wild light, and I turned to see whence a gleam so unusual could have issued; for the vast house and its shadows were alone behind me. The radiance was that of the full, setting, and blood-red moon which now shone vividly through that once barely discernible fissure of which I have before spoken as extending from the roof of the building, in a zigzag direction, to the base. While I gazed, this fissure rapidly widened—there came a fierce breath of the whirlwind—the entire orb of the satellite burst at once upon my sight—my brain reeled as I saw the mighty walls rushing asunder—there was a long tumultuous shouting sound like the voice of a thousand waters—and the deep and dank tarn at my feet closed sullenly and silently over the fragments of the "House of Usher."

WILLIAM WILSON

What say of it? what say of conscience grim,
That spectre in my path?
Chamberlayne's *Pharronida*

LET ME CALL myself, for the present, William Wilson. The fair page now lying before me need not be sullied with my real appellation. This has been already too much an object for the scorn—for the horror—for the detestation of my race. To the uttermost regions of the globe have not the indignant winds bruited its unparalleled infamy? Oh, outcast of all outcasts most abandoned!—to the earth art thou not for ever dead? to its honors, to its flowers, to its golden aspirations?—and a cloud, dense, dismal, and limitless, does it not hang eternally between thy hopes and heaven?

I would not, if I could, here or to-day, embody a record of my later years of unspeakable misery, and unpardonable crime. This epoch—these later years—took unto themselves a sudden elevation in turpitude, whose origin alone it is my present purpose to assign. Men usually grow base by degrees. From me, in an instant, all virtue dropped bodily as a mantle. From comparatively trivial wickedness I passed, with the stride of a giant, into more than the enormities of an Elah-Gabalus. What chance—what one event brought this evil thing to pass, bear with me while I relate. Death approaches; and the shadow which foreruns him has thrown a softening influence over my spirit. I long, in passing through the dim valley, for the sympathy—I had nearly said for the pity—of my fellow-men. I would fain have them believe that I have been, in some measure, the slave of circumstances beyond human control. I would wish them to seek out for me, in the details I am about to give, some little oasis of fatality amid a wilderness of error. I would have them allow—what they cannot refrain from allowing—that, although temptation may have erewhile existed as great, man was never thus, at least, tempted before—certainly, never thus fell. And is it therefore that he has never thus suffered? Have I not indeed been living in a dream? And am I not now dying a victim to the horror and the mystery of the wildest of all sublunary visions?

I am the descendant of a race whose imaginative and easily excitable temperament has at all times rendered them remarkable; and, in my earliest infancy, I gave evidence of having fully inherited the family character. As I advanced in years it was more strongly developed; becoming, for many reasons, a cause of serious disquietude to my friends, and of positive injury to myself. I grew self-willed, addicted to the wildest caprices, and a prey to the most ungovernable passions. Weak-minded, and beset with constitutional infirmities akin to my own, my parents could do but little to check the evil propensities which distinguished me. Some feeble and ill-directed efforts resulted in complete failure on their part, and, of course, in total triumphs on mine. Thenceforward my voice was a household law; and at an age when few children have abandoned their leading-strings, I was left to the guidance of my own will, and became, in all but name, the master of my own actions.

My earliest recollections of a school-life, are connected with a large, rambling, Elizabethan house, in a misty-looking village of England, where were a vast number of gigantic and gnarled trees, and where all the houses were excessively ancient. In truth, it was a dream-like and spirit-soothing place, that venerable old town. At this moment, in fancy, I feel the refreshing chilliness of its deeply-shadowed avenues, inhale the fragrance of its thousand shrubberies, and thrill anew with undefinable delight, at the deep hollow note of the church-bell, breaking, each hour, with sullen and sudden roar, upon the stillness of the dusky atmosphere in which the fretted Gothic steeple lay imbedded and asleep.

It gives me, perhaps, as much of pleasure as I can now in any manner experience, to dwell upon minute recollections of the school and its concerns. Steeped in misery as I am—misery, alas! only too real—I shall be pardoned for seeking relief, however slight and temporary, in the weakness of a few rambling details. These, moreover, utterly trivial, and even ridiculous in themselves, assume, to my fancy, adventitious importance, as connected with a period and a locality when and where I recognize the first ambiguous monitions of the destiny which afterward so fully overshadowed me. Let me then remember.

The house, I have said, was old and irregular. The grounds were extensive, and a high and solid brick wall, topped with a bed of mortar and broken glass, encompassed the whole. This prison-like rampart formed the limit of our domain; beyond it we saw but thrice a week—once every Saturday afternoon, when, attended by two ushers, we were permitted to take brief walks in a body through some of the neighboring fields—and twice during Sunday, when we were paraded in the same formal manner to the morning and evening service in the one church of the village. Of this church the principal of our school was pastor. With how deep a spirit of wonder and perplexity was I wont to regard him from our remote pew in the gallery, as, with step solemn and slow, he ascended the pulpit! This reverend man, with countenance so demurely benign, with robes so glossy and so clerically flowing, with wig so minutely powdered, so rigid and so vast,—could this be he who, of late, with sour visage, and in snuffy habiliments, administered, ferule in hand, the Draconian laws of the academy? Oh, gigantic paradox, too utterly monstrous for solution.

At an angle of the ponderous wall frowned a more ponderous gate. It was riveted and studded with iron bolts, and surmounted with jagged iron spikes. What impressions of deep awe did it inspire! It was never opened save for the three periodical egressions and ingressions already mentioned; then, in every creak of its mighty hinges, we found a plenitude of mystery—a world of matter for solemn remark, or for more solemn meditation.

The extensive enclosure was irregular in form, having many capacious recesses. Of these, three or four of the largest constituted the playground. It was level, and covered with fine hard gravel. I well remember it had no trees, nor benches, nor anything similar within it. Of course it was in the rear of the house. In front lay a small parterre, planted with box and other shrubs; but through this sacred division we passed only upon rare occasions indeed—such as a first advent to school or final departure thence, or perhaps, when a parent or friend having called for us, we joyfully took our way home for the Christmas or Midsummer holidays.

But the house!—how quaint an old building was this!—to me how veritably a palace of enchantment! There was really no end to its windings—to its incomprehensible subdivisions. It was difficult, at any given time, to say with certainty upon which of its two stories one happened to be. From each room to every other there were sure to be found three or four steps either in ascent or descent. Then the lateral branches were innumerable—inconceivable—and so returning in upon themselves, that our most exact ideas in regard to the whole mansion were not very far different from those with which we pondered upon infinity. During the five years of my residence here, I was never able to ascertain with precision in what remote locality lay the little sleeping apartment assigned to myself and some eighteen or twenty other scholars.

The school-room was the largest in the house—I could not help thinking, in the world. It was very long, narrow, and dismally low, with pointed Gothic windows and a ceiling of oak. In a remote and terror-inspiring angle was a square enclosure of eight or ten feet, comprising the sanctum, "during hours," of our principal, the Reverend Dr. Bransby. It was a solid structure, with massy door, sooner than open which in the absence of the "Dominie," we would all have willingly perished by the *peine forte et dure*. In other angles were two other similar boxes, far less reverenced, indeed, but still greatly matters of awe. One of these was the pulpit of the "classical" usher, one of the "English and mathematical." Interspersed about the room, crossing and recrossing in endless irregularity, were innumerable benches and desks, black, ancient, and time-worn, piled desperately with much-bethumbed books, and so beseamed with initial letters, names at full length, grotesque figures, and other multiplied efforts of the knife, as to have entirely lost what little of original form might have been their portion in days long departed. A huge bucket with water stood at one extremity of the room, and a clock of stupendous dimensions at the other.

Encompassed by the massy walls of this venerable academy, I passed, yet not in tedium or disgust, the years of the third lustrum of my life. The teeming brain of childhood requires no external world of incident to occupy or amuse it; and the apparently dismal monotony of a school was replete with more intense excitement than my riper youth has derived from luxury, or my full manhood from crime. Yet I must believe that my first mental development had in it much of the uncommon—even much of the outré. Upon mankind at large the events of very early existence rarely leave in mature age any definite impression. All is gray shadow—a weak and irregular remembrance—an indistinct regathering of feeble pleasures and phantasmagoric pains. With me this is not so. In childhood I must have felt with the energy of a man what I now find stamped upon memory in lines as vivid, as deep, and as durable as the exergues of the Carthaginian medals.

Yet in fact—in the fact of the world's view—how little was there to remember! The morning's awakening, the nightly summons to bed; the connings, the recitations; the periodical half-holidays, and perambulations; the playground, with its broils, its pastimes, its intrigues;—these, by a mental sorcery long forgotten, were made to involve a wilderness of sensation, a world of rich incident, a university of varied emotion, of excitement the most passionate and spirit-stirring. "*Oh, le bon temps, que ce siècle de fer!*"

In truth, the ardor, the enthusiasm, and the imperiousness of my disposition, soon rendered me a marked character among my schoolmates, and by slow, but natural gradations, gave me an ascendancy over all not greatly older than myself;—over all with a single exception. This exception was found in the person of a scholar, who, although no relation bore the same Christian and surname as myself;—a circumstance, in fact, little remarkable; for, notwithstanding a noble descent, mine was one of those every-day appellations which seem, by prescriptive right, to have been, time out of mind, the common property of the mob. In this narrative I have therefore designated myself as William Wilson,—a fictitious title not very dissimilar to the real. My namesake alone, of those who in school phraseology constituted "our set," presumed to compete with me in the studies of the class—in the sports and broils of the playground—to refuse implicit belief in my assertions, and submission to my will—indeed, to interfere with my arbitrary dictation in any respect whatsoever. If there is on earth a supreme and unqualified despotism, it is the despotism of a master mind in boyhood over the less energetic spirits of its companions.

Wilson's rebellion was to me a source of the greatest embarrassment;—the more so as, in spite of the bravado with which in public I made a point of treating him and his pretensions, I secretly felt that I feared him, and could not help thinking the equality which he maintained so easily with myself, a proof of his true superiority; since not to be overcome cost me a perpetual struggle. Yet this superiority—even this equality—was in truth acknowledged by no one but myself; our associates, by some unaccountable blindness, seemed not even to suspect it. Indeed, his competition, his resistance, and especially his impertinent and dogged interference with my purposes, were not more pointed than private. He appeared to be destitute alike of the ambition which urged, and of the passionate energy of mind which enabled me to excel. In his rivalry he might have been supposed actuated solely by a whimsical desire to thwart, astonish, or mortify myself; although there were times when I could not help observing, with a feeling made of wonder, abasement, and pique, that he mingled with his injuries, his insults, or his contradictions, a certain most inappropriate, and assuredly most unwelcome affectionateness of manner. I could only conceive this singular behavior to arise from a consummate self-conceit assuming the vulgar air of patronage and protection.

Perhaps it was this latter trait in Wilson's conduct, conjoined with our identity of name, and the mere accident of our having entered the school upon the same day, which set afloat the notion that we were brothers, among the senior classes in the academy. These do not usually inquire with much strictness into the affairs of their juniors. I have before said, or should have said, that Wilson was not, in the most remote degree connected with my family. But assuredly if we had been brothers we must have been twins; for, after leaving Dr. Bransby's, I casually learned that my namesake was born on the 19th of January, 1813—and this is a somewhat remarkable coincidence; for the day is precisely that of my own nativity.

It may seem strange that in spite of the continual anxiety occasioned me by the rivalry of Wilson, and his intolerable spirit of contradiction, I could not bring myself to hate him altogether. We had, to be sure, nearly every day a quarrel in which, yielding me publicly the palm of victory, he, in some manner, contrived to make me feel that it was he who had deserved it; yet a sense of pride on my part, and a veritable dignity on his own, kept us always upon what are called "speaking terms," while there were many points of strong congeniality in our tempers, operating to awake in me a sentiment which our position alone, perhaps, prevented from ripening into friendship. It is difficult, indeed, to define, or even to describe, my real feelings toward him. They formed a motley and heterogeneous admixture;—some petulant animosity, which was not yet hatred, some esteem, more respect, much fear, with a world of uneasy curiosity. To the moralist it will be unnecessary to say, in addition, that Wilson and myself were the most inseparable of companions.

It was no doubt the anomalous state of affairs existing between us, which turned all my attacks upon him (and they were many, either open or covert) into the channel of banter or practical joke (giving pain while assuming the aspect of mere fun) rather than into a more serious and determined hostility. But my endeavors on this head were by no means uniformly successful, even when my plans were the most wittily concocted; for my namesake had much about him, in character, of that unassuming and quiet austerity which, while enjoying the poignancy of its own jokes, has no heel of Achilles in itself, and absolutely refuses to be laughed at. I could find, indeed, but one vulnerable point, and that, lying in a personal peculiarity, arising, perhaps, from constitutional disease, would have been spared by any antagonist less at his wit's end than myself—my rival had a weakness in the faucial or gutteral organs, which precluded him from raising his voice at any time above a very low whisper. Of this defect I did not fail to take what poor advantage lay in my power.

Wilson's retaliations in kind were many; and there was one form of his practical wit that disturbed me beyond measure. How his sagacity first discovered at all that so petty a thing would vex me, is a question I never could solve; but, having discovered, he habitually practiced the annoyance. I had always felt aversion to my uncourtly patronymic, and its very common, if not plebeian prænomen. The words were venom in my ears; and when, upon the day of my arrival, a second William Wilson came also to the academy, I felt angry with him for bearing the name, and doubly disgusted with the name because a stranger bore it, who would be the cause of its two-fold repetition, who would be constantly in my presence, and whose concerns, in the ordinary routine of the school business, must inevitably, on account of the detestable coincidence, be often confounded with my own.

The feeling of vexation thus engendered grew stronger with every circumstance tending to show resemblance, moral or physical, between my rival and myself. I had not then discovered the remarkable fact that we were of the same age; but I saw that we were of the same height, and I perceived that we were even singularly alike in general contour of person and outline of feature. I was galled, too, by the rumor touching a relationship, which had grown current in the upper forms. In a word, nothing could more seriously disturb me (although I scrupulously concealed such disturbance), than any allusion to a similarity of mind, person, or condition existing between us. But, in truth, I had no reason to believe that (with the exception of the matter of relationship, and in the case of Wilson himself) this similarity had ever been made a subject of comment, or even observed at all by our schoolfellows. That he observed it in all its bearings, and as fixedly as I, was apparent; but that he could discover in such circumstances so fruitful a field of annoyance, can only be attributed, as I said before, to his more than ordinary penetration.

His cue, which was to perfect an imitation of myself, lay both in words and in actions; and most admirably did he play his part. My dress it was an easy matter to copy; my gait and general manner were, without difficulty, appropriated; in spite of his constitutional defect, even my voice did not escape him. My louder tones were, of course, unattempted, but then the key, it was identical; and his singular whisper, it grew the very echo of my own.

How greatly this most exquisite portraiture harassed me (for it could not justly be termed a caricature), I will not now venture to describe. I had but one consolation—in the fact that the imitation, apparently, was noticed by myself alone, and that I had to endure only the knowing and strangely sarcastic smiles of my namesake himself. Satisfied with having produced in my bosom the intended effect, he seemed to chuckle in secret over the sting he had inflicted, and was characteristically disregardful of the public applause which the success of his witty endeavors might have so easily elicited. That the school, indeed, did not feel his design, perceive its accomplishment, and participate in his sneer, was, for many anxious months, a riddle I could not resolve. Perhaps the gradation of his copy rendered it not so readily perceptible; or, more possibly, I owed my security to the masterly air of the copyist, who, disdaining the letter (which in a painting is all the obtuse can see), gave but the full spirit of his original for my individual contemplation and chagrin.

I have already more than once spoken of the disgusting air of patronage which he assumed toward me, and of his frequent officious interference with my will. This interference often took the ungracious character of advice; advice not openly given, but hinted or insinuated. I received it with a repugnance which gained strength as I grew in years. Yet, at this distant day, let me do him the simple justice to acknowledge that I can recall no occasion when the suggestions of my rival were on the side of those errors or follies so usual to his immature age and seeming inexperience; that his moral sense, at least, if not his general talents and worldly wisdom, was far keener than my own; and that I might, to-day, have been a better, and thus a happier man, had I less frequently rejected the counsels embodied in those meaning whispers which I then but too cordially hated and too bitterly despised.

As it was, I at length grew restive in the extreme under his distasteful supervision, and daily resented more and more openly what I considered his intolerable arrogance. I have said that, in the first years of our connexion as schoolmates, my feelings in regard to him might have been easily ripened into friendship: but, in the latter months of my residence at the academy, although the intrusion of his ordinary manner had, beyond doubt, in some measure, abated, my sentiments, in nearly similar proportion, partook very much of positive hatred. Upon one occasion he saw this, I think, and afterward avoided, or made a show of avoiding me.

It was about the same period, if I remember aright, that, in an altercation of violence with him, in which he was more than usually thrown off his guard, and spoke and acted with an openness of demeanor rather foreign to his nature, I discovered, or fancied I discovered, in his accent, his air, and general appearance, a something which first startled, and then deeply interested me, by bringing to mind dim visions of my earliest infancy—wild, confused, and thronging memories of a time when memory herself was yet unborn. I cannot better describe the sensation which oppressed me than by saying that I could with difficulty shake off the belief of my having been acquainted with the being who stood before me, at some epoch very long ago—some point of the past even infinitely remote. The delusion, however, faded rapidly as it came; and I mention it at all but to define the day of the last conversation I there held with my singular namesake.

The huge old house, with its countless subdivisions, had several large chambers communicating with each other, where slept the greater number of the students. There were, however (as must necessarily happen in a building so awkwardly planned), many little nooks or recesses, the odds and ends of the structure; and these the economic ingenuity of Dr. Bransby had also fitted up as dormitories; although, being the merest closets, they were capable of accommodating but a single individual. One of these small apartments was occupied by Wilson.

One night, about the close of my fifth year at the school, and immediately after the altercation just mentioned, finding everyone wrapped in sleep, I arose from bed, and, lamp in hand, stole through a wilderness of narrow passages from my own bedroom to that of my rival. I had long been plotting one of those ill-natured pieces of practical wit at his expense in which I had hitherto been so uniformly unsuccessful. It was my intention, now, to put my scheme in operation, and I resolved to make him feel the whole extent of the malice with which I was imbued. Having reached his closet, I noiselessly entered, leaving the lamp, with a shade over it, on the outside. I advanced a step, and listened to the sound of his tranquil breathing. Assured of his being asleep, I returned, took the light, and with it again approached the bed. Close curtains were around it, which, in the prosecution of my plan, I slowly and quietly withdrew, when the bright rays fell vividly upon the sleeper, and my eyes, at the same moment, upon his countenance. I looked;—and a numbness, an iciness of feeling instantly pervaded my frame. My breast heaved, my knees tottered, my whole spirit became possessed with an objectless yet intolerable horror. Gasping for breath, I lowered the lamp in still nearer proximity to the face. Were these—these the lineaments of William Wilson? I saw, indeed, that they were his, but I shook as if with a fit of the ague in fancying they were not. What was there about them to confound me in this manner? I gazed;—while my brain reeled with a multitude of incoherent thoughts. Not thus he appeared—assuredly not thus—in the vivacity of his waking hours. The same name! the same contour of person! the same day of arrival at the academy! And then his dogged and meaningless imitation of my gait, my voice, my habits, and my manner! Was it, in truth, within the bounds of human possibility, that what I now saw was the result, merely, of the habitual practice of this sarcastic imitation? Awestricken, and with a creeping shudder, I extinguished the lamp, passed silently from the chamber, and left, at once, the halls of that old academy, never to enter them again.

After a lapse of some months, spent at home in mere idleness, I found myself a student at Eton. The brief interval had been sufficient to enfeeble my remembrance of the events at Dr. Bransby's, or at least to effect a material change in the nature of the feelings with which I remembered them. The truth—the tragedy—of the drama was no more. I could now find room to doubt the evidence of my senses; and seldom called up the subject at all but with wonder at the extent of human credulity, and a smile at the vivid force of the imagination which I hereditarily possessed. Neither was this species of skepticism likely to be diminished by the character of the life I led at Eton. The vortex of thoughtless folly into which I there so immediately and so recklessly plunged, washed away all but the froth of my past hours, engulfed at once every solid or serious impression, and left to memory only the veriest levities of a former existence.

I do not wish, however, to trace the course of my miserable profligacy here—a profligacy which set at defiance the laws, while it eluded the vigilance of the institution. Three years of folly, passed without profit, had but given me rooted habits of vice, and added, in a somewhat unusual degree, to my bodily stature, when, after a week of soulless dissipation, I invited a small party of the most dissolute students to a secret carousal in my chambers. We met at a late hour of the night; for our debaucheries were to be faithfully protracted until morning. The wine flowed freely, and there were not wanting other and perhaps more dangerous seductions; so that the gray dawn had already faintly appeared in the east, while our delirious extravagance was at its height. Madly flushed with cards and intoxication, I was in the act of insisting upon a toast of more than wonted profanity, when my attention was suddenly diverted by the violent, although partial unclosing of the door of the apartment, and by the eager voice of a servant from without. He said that some person, apparently in great haste, demanded to speak with me in the hall.

Wildly excited with wine, the unexpected interruption rather delighted than surprised me. I staggered forward at once, and a few steps brought me to the vestibule of the building. In this low and small room there hung no lamp; and now no light at all was admitted, save that of the exceedingly feeble dawn which made its way through the semi-circular window. As I put my foot over the threshold, I became aware of the figure of a youth about my own height, and habited in a white kerseymere morning frock, cut in the novel fashion of the one I myself wore at the moment. This the faint light enabled me to perceive; but the features of his face I could not distinguish. Upon my entering he strode hurriedly up to me, and, seizing me by the arm with a gesture of petulant impatience, whispered the words "William Wilson!" in my ear.

I grew perfectly sober in an instant.

There was that in the manner of the stranger, and in the tremulous shake of his uplifted finger, as he held it between my eyes and the light, which filled me with unqualified amazement; but it was not this which had so violently moved me. It was the pregnancy of solemn admonition in the singular, low, hissing utterance; and, above all, it was the character, the tone, the key, of those few, simple, and familiar, yet whispered syllables, which came with a thousand thronging memories of bygone days, and struck upon my soul with the shock of a galvanic battery. Ere I could recover the use of my senses he was gone.

Although this event failed not of a vivid effect upon my disordered imagination, yet was it evanescent as vivid. For some weeks, indeed, I busied myself in earnest inquiry, or was wrapped in a cloud of morbid speculation. I did not pretend to disguise from my perception the identity of the singular individual who thus perseveringly interfered with my affairs, and harassed me with his insinuated counsel. But who and what was this Wilson?—and whence came he?—and what were his purposes? Upon neither of these points could I be satisfied; merely ascertaining, in regard to him, that a sudden accident in his family had caused his removal from Dr. Bransby's academy on the afternoon of the day in which I myself had eloped. But in a brief period I ceased to think upon the subject; my attention being all absorbed in a contemplated departure for Oxford. Thither I soon went; the uncalculating vanity of my parents furnishing me with an outfit and annual establishment, which would enable me to indulge at will in the luxury already so dear to my heart,—to vie in profuseness of expenditure with the haughtiest heirs of the wealthiest earldoms in Great Britain.

Excited by such appliances to vice, my constitutional temperament broke forth with redoubled ardor, and I spurned even the common restraints of decency in the mad infatuation of my revels. But it were absurd to pause in the detail of my extravagance. Let it suffice, that among spendthrifts I out-Heroded Herod, and that, giving name to a multitude of novel follies, I added no brief appendix to the long catalog of vices then usual in the most dissolute university of Europe.

It could hardly be credited, however, that I had, even here, so utterly fallen from the gentlemanly estate, as to seek acquaintance with the vilest arts of the gambler by profession, and, having become an adept in his despicable science, to practice it habitually as a means of increasing my already enormous income at the expense of the weak-minded among my fellow-collegians. Such, nevertheless, was the fact. And the very enormity of this offense against all manly and honorable sentiment proved, beyond doubt, the main if not the sole reason of the impunity with which it was committed. Who, indeed, among my most abandoned associates, would not rather have disputed the clearest evidence of his senses, than have suspected of such courses, the gay, the frank, the generous William Wilson—the noblest and most liberal commoner at Oxford—him whose follies (said his parasites) were but the follies of youth and unbridled fancy—whose errors but inimitable whim—whose darkest vice but a careless and dashing extravagance?

I had been now two years successfully busied in this way, when there came to the university a young parvenu nobleman, Glendinning—rich, said report, as Herodes Atticus—his riches, too, as easily acquired. I soon found him of weak intellect, and, of course, marked him as a fitting subject for my skill. I frequently engaged him in play, and contrived, with the gambler's usual art, to let him win considerable sums, the more effectually to entangle him in my snares. At length, my schemes being ripe, I met him (with the full intention that this meeting should be final and decisive) at the chambers of a fellow-commoner (Mr. Preston), equally intimate with both, but who, to do him justice, entertained not even a remote suspicion of my design. To give to this a better coloring, I had contrived to have assembled a party of some eight or ten, and was solicitously careful that the introduction of cards should appear accidental, and originate in the proposal of my contemplated dupe himself. To be brief upon a vile topic, none of the low finesse was omitted, so customary upon similar occasions that it is a just matter for wonder how any are still found so besotted as to fall its victim.

We had protracted our sitting far into the night, and I had at length effected the manœuvre of getting Glendinning as my sole antagonist. The game, too, was my favorite écarté. The rest of the company, interested in the extent of our play, had abandoned their own cards, and were standing around us as spectators. The parvenu, who had been induced by my artifices in the early part of the evening, to drink deeply, now shuffled, dealt, or played, with a wild nervousness of manner for which his intoxication, I thought, might partially, but could not altogether account. In a very short period he had become my debtor to a large amount, when, having taken a long draft of port, he did precisely what I had been coolly anticipating—he proposed to double our already extravagant stakes. With a well-feigned show of reluctance, and not until after my repeated refusal had seduced him into some angry words which gave a color of pique to my compliance, did I finally comply. The result, of course, did but prove how entirely the prey was in my toils; in less than an hour he had quadrupled his debt. For some time his countenance had been losing the florid tinge lent it by the wine; but now, to my astonishment, I perceived that it had grown to a pallor truly fearful. I say to my astonishment. Glendinning had been represented to my eager inquiries as immeasurably wealthy; and the sums which he had as yet lost, although in themselves vast, could not, I supposed, very seriously annoy, much less so violently affect him. That he was overcome by the wine just swallowed, was the idea which most readily presented itself; and, rather with a view to the preservation of my own character in the eyes of my associates, than from any less interested motive, I was about to insist, peremptorily, upon a discontinuance of the play, when some expressions at my elbow from among the company, and an ejaculation evincing utter despair on the part of Glendinning, gave me to understand that I had effected his total ruin under circumstances which, rendering him an object for the pity of all, should have protected him from the ill offices even of a fiend.

What now might have been my conduct it is difficult to say. The pitiable condition of my dupe had thrown an air of embarrassed gloom over all; and, for some moments, a profound silence was maintained, during which I could not help feeling my cheeks tingle with the many burning glances of scorn or reproach cast upon me by the less abandoned of the party. I will even own that an intolerable weight of anxiety was for a brief instant lifted from my bosom by the sudden and extraordinary interruption which ensued. The wide, heavy folding-doors of the apartment were all at once thrown open, to their full extent, with a vigorous and rushing impetuosity that extinguished, as if by magic, every candle in the room. Their light, in dying, enabled us just to perceive that a stranger had entered, about my own height, and closely muffled in a cloak. The darkness, however, was now total; and we could only feel that he was standing in our midst. Before any one of us could recover from the extreme astonishment into which this rudeness had thrown all, we heard the voice of the intruder.

"Gentlemen," he said, in a low, distinct, and never-to-be-forgotten whisper which thrilled to the very marrow of my bones, "Gentlemen, I make no apology for this behavior, because in thus behaving, I am but fulfilling a duty. You are, beyond doubt, uninformed of the true character of the person who has to-night won at écarté a large sum of money from Lord Glendinning. I will therefore put you upon an expeditious and decisive plan of obtaining this very necessary information. Please to examine, at your leisure, the inner linings of the cuff of his left sleeve, and the several little packages which may be found in the somewhat capacious pockets of his embroidered morning wrapper."

While he spoke, so profound was the stillness that one might have heard a pin drop upon the floor. In ceasing, he departed at once, and as abruptly as he had entered. Can I—shall I describe my sensations? —must I say that I felt all the horrors of the damned? Most assuredly I had little time given for reflection. Many hands roughly seized me upon the spot, and lights were immediately re-procured. A search ensued. In the lining of my sleeve were found all the court cards essential in écarté, and, in the pockets of my wrapper, a number of packs, facsimiles of those used at our sittings, with the single exception that mine were of the species called, technically, arrondées; the honors being slightly convex at the ends, the lower cards slightly convex at the sides. In this disposition, the dupe who cuts, as customary, at the length of the pack, will, invariably find that he cuts his antagonist an honor; while the gambler, cutting at the breadth, will, as certainly, cut nothing for his victim which may count in the records of the game.

Any burst of indignation upon this discovery would have affected me less than the silent contempt, or the sarcastic composure, with which it was received.

"Mr. Wilson," said our host, stooping to remove from beneath his feet an exceedingly luxurious cloak of rare furs, "Mr. Wilson, this is your property." (The weather was cold; and, upon quitting my own room, I had thrown a cloak over my dressing-wrapper, putting it off upon reaching the scene of play.) "I presume it is supererogatory to seek here" (eyeing the folds of the garment with a bitter smile) "for any farther evidence of your skill. Indeed, we have had enough. You will see the necessity, I hope, of quitting Oxford—at all events, of quitting instantly my chambers."

Abased, humbled to the dust as I then was, it is probable that I should have resented this galling language by immediate personal violence, had not my whole attention been at the moment arrested by a fact of the most startling character. The cloak which I had worn was of a rare description of fur; how rare, how extravagantly costly, I shall not venture to say. Its fashion, too, was of my own fantastic invention; for I was fastidious to an absurd degree of coxcombry, in matters of this frivolous nature. When, therefore, Mr. Preston reached me that which he had picked up upon the floor, and near the folding-doors of the apartment, it was with an astonishment nearly bordering upon terror, that I perceived my own already hanging on my arm (where I had no doubt unwittingly placed it), and that the one presented me was but its exact counterpart in every, in even the minutest possible particular. The singular being who had so disastrously exposed me, had been muffled, I remembered, in a cloak; and none had been worn at all by any of the members of our party with the exception of myself. Retaining some presence of mind, I took the one offered me by Preston;

placed it, unnoticed, over my own; left the apartment with a resolute scowl of defiance; and, next morning ere dawn of day, commenced a hurried journey from Oxford to the continent, in a perfect agony of horror and of shame.

I fled in vain. My evil destiny pursued me as if in exultation, and proved, indeed, that the exercise of its mysterious dominion had as yet only begun. Scarcely had I set foot in Paris ere I had fresh evidence of the detestable interest taken by this Wilson in my concerns. Years flew, while I experienced no relief. Villain!—at Rome, with how untimely, yet with how spectral an officiousness, stepped he in between me and my ambition! At Vienna, too—at Berlin—and at Moscow! Where, in truth, had I not bitter cause to curse him within my heart? From his inscrutable tyranny did I at length flee, panic-stricken, as from a pestilence; and to the very ends of the earth I fled in vain.

And again, and again, in secret communion with my own spirit, would I demand the questions "Who is he?—whence came he?—and what are his objects?" But no answer was there found. And then I scrutinized, with a minute scrutiny, the forms, and the methods, and the leading traits of his impertinent supervision. But even here there was very little upon which to base a conjecture. It was noticeable, indeed, that, in no one of the multiplied instances in which he had of late crossed my path, had he so crossed it except to frustrate those schemes, or to disturb those actions, which, if fully carried out, might have resulted in bitter mischief. Poor justification this, in truth, for an authority so imperiously assumed! Poor indemnity for natural rights of self-agency so pertinaciously, so insultingly denied!

I had also been forced to notice that my tormentor, for a very long period of time (while scrupulously and with miraculous dexterity maintaining his whim of an identity of apparel with myself) had so contrived it, in the execution of his varied interference with my will, that I saw not, at any moment, the features of his face. Be Wilson what he might, this, at least, was but the veriest of affectation, or of folly. Could he, for an instant, have supposed that, in my admonisher at Eton—in the destroyer of my honor at Oxford—in him who thwarted my ambition at Rome, my revenge at Paris, my passionate love at Naples, or what he falsely termed my avarice in Egypt,—that in this, my arch-enemy and evil genius, I could fail to recognize the William Wilson of my school-boy days,—the namesake, the companion, the rival,—the hated and dreaded rival at Dr. Bransby's? Impossible!—But let me hasten to the last eventful scene of the drama.

Thus far I had succumbed supinely to this imperious domination. The sentiments of deep awe with which I habitually regarded the elevated character, the majestic wisdom, the apparent omnipresence and omnipotence of Wilson, added to a feeling of even terror, with which certain other traits in his nature and assumptions inspired me, had operated, hitherto, to impress me with an idea of my own utter weakness and helplessness, and to suggest an implicit, although bitterly reluctant submission to his arbitrary will. But, of late days, I had given myself up entirely to wine; and its maddening influence upon my hereditary temper rendered me more and more impatient of control. I began to murmur,—to hesitate,—to resist. And was it only fancy which induced me to believe that, with the increase of my own firmness, that of my tormentor underwent a proportional diminution? Be this as it may, I now began to feel the inspiration of a burning hope, and at length nurtured in my secret thoughts a stern and desperate resolution that I would submit no longer to be enslaved.

It was at Rome, during the Carnival of 18—, that I attended a masquerade in the palazzo of the Neapolitan Duke Di Broglio. I had indulged more freely than usual in the excesses of the wine-table; and now the suffocating atmosphere of the crowded rooms irritated me beyond endurance. The difficulty, too, of forcing my way through the mazes of the company contributed not a little to the ruffling of my temper; for I was anxiously seeking (let me not say with what unworthy motive) the young, the gay, the beautiful wife of the aged and doting Di Broglio. With a too unscrupulous confidence she had previously communicated to me the secret of the costume in which she would be habited, and now, having caught a glimpse of her person, I was hurrying to make my way into her presence.—At this moment I felt a light hand placed upon my shoulder, and that ever-remembered, low, damnable whisper within my ear.

In an absolute frenzy of wrath, I turned at once upon him who had thus interrupted me, and seized him violently by the collar. He was attired, as I had expected, in a costume altogether similar to my own; wearing a Spanish cloak of blue velvet, begirt about the waist with a crimson belt sustaining a rapier. A mask of black silk entirely covered his face.

"Scoundrel!" I said, in a voice husky with rage, while every syllable I uttered seemed as new fuel to my fury, "scoundrel! impostor! accursed villain! you shall not—you shall not dog me unto death! Follow me, or I stab you where you stand!"—and I broke my way from the ballroom into a small antechamber adjoining—dragging him unresistingly with me as I went.

Upon entering, I thrust him furiously from me. He staggered against the wall, while I closed the door with an oath, and commanded him to draw. He hesitated but for an instant; then, with a slight sigh, drew in silence, and put himself upon his defense.

The contest was brief indeed. I was frantic with every species of wild excitement, and felt within my single arm the energy and power of a multitude. In a few seconds I forced him by sheer strength against the wainscoting, and thus, getting him at mercy, plunged my sword, with brute ferocity, repeatedly through and through his bosom.

At that instant some person tried the latch of the door. I hastened to prevent an intrusion, and then immediately returned to my dying antagonist. But what human language can adequately portray that astonishment, that horror which possessed me at the spectacle then presented to view? The brief moment in which I averted my eyes had been sufficient to produce, apparently, a material change in the arrangements at the upper or farther end of the room. A larger mirror,—so at first it seemed to me in my confusion—now stood where none had been perceptible before; and, as I stepped up to it in extremity of terror, mine own image, but with features all pale and dabbled in blood, advanced to meet me with a feeble and tottering gait.

Thus it appeared, I say, but was not. It was my antagonist—it was Wilson, who then stood before me in the agonies of his dissolution. His mask and cloak lay, where he had thrown them, upon the floor. Not a thread in all his raiment—not a line in all the marked and singular lineaments of his face which was not, even in the most absolute identity, mine own!

It was Wilson; but he spoke no longer in a whisper, and I could have fancied that I myself was speaking while he said:

"*You have conquered, and I yield. Yet, henceforward art thou also dead—dead to the World, to Heaven, and to hope! In me didst thou exist—and, in my death, see by this image, which is thine own, how utterly thou hast murdered thyself.*"

THE CONVERSATION OF EIROS AND CHARMION

Πυρ σοι προσοισω
I will bring fire to thee.
Euripides, *Andromache*

EIROS. WHY DO you call me Eiros?

CHARMION. So henceforward will you always be called. You must forget, too, my earthly name, and speak to me as Charmion.

EIROS. This is indeed no dream!

CHARMION. Dreams are with us no more; but of these mysteries anon. I rejoice to see you looking life-like and rational. The film of the shadow has already passed off from your eyes. Be of heart, and fear nothing. Your allotted days of stupor have expired; and, to-morrow, I will myself induct you into the full joys and wonders of your novel existence.

EIROS. True, I feel no stupor, none at all. The wild sickness and the terrible darkness have left me, and I hear no longer that mad, rushing, horrible sound, "like the voice of many waters." Yet my senses are bewildered, Charmion, with the keenness of their perception of the new.

CHARMION. A few days will remove all this;—but I fully understand you, and feel for you. It is now ten earthly years since I underwent what you undergo, yet the remembrance of it hangs by me still. You have now suffered all of pain, however, which you will suffer in Aidenn.

EIROS. In Aidenn?

CHARMION. In Aidenn.

EIROS. Oh, God!—pity me, Charmion!—I am overburdened with the majesty of all things—of the unknown now known—of the speculative Future merged in the august and certain Present.

CHARMION. Grapple not now with such thoughts. To-morrow we will speak of this. Your mind wavers, and its agitation will find relief in the exercise of simple memories. Look not around, nor forward—but back. I am burning with anxiety to hear the details of that stupendous event which threw you among us. Tell me of it. Let us converse of familiar things, in the old familiar language of the world which has so fearfully perished.

EIROS. Most fearfully, fearfully!—this is indeed no dream.

CHARMION. Dreams are no more. Was I much mourned, my Eiros?

EIROS. Mourned, Charmion?—oh, deeply. To that last hour of all, there hung a cloud of intense gloom and devout sorrow over your household.

CHARMION. And that last hour—speak of it. Remember that, beyond the naked fact of the catastrophe itself, I know nothing. When, coming out from among mankind, I passed into Night through the Grave—at that period, if I remember aright, the calamity which overwhelmed you was utterly unanticipated. But, indeed, I knew little of the speculative philosophy of the day.

EIROS. The individual calamity was, as you say, entirely unanticipated; but analogous misfortunes had been long a subject of discussion with astronomers. I need scarce tell you, my friend, that, even when you left us, men had agreed to understand those passages in the most holy writings which speak of the final destruction of all things by fire, as having reference to the orb of the earth alone. But in regard to the immediate agency of the ruin, speculation had been at fault from that epoch in astronomical knowledge in which the comets were divested of the terrors of flame. The very moderate density of these bodies had been well established. They had been observed to pass among the satellites of Jupiter, without bringing about any sensible alterations either in the masses or in the orbits of these secondary planets. We had long regarded the wanderers as vapory creations of inconceivable tenuity, and as altogether incapable of doing injury to our substantial globe, even in the event of contact. But contact was not in any degree dreaded; for the elements of all the comets were accurately known. That among them we should look for the agency of the threatened fiery destruction had been for many years considered an inadmissible idea. But wonders and wild fancies had been, of late days, strangely rife among mankind; and although it was only with a few of the ignorant that actual apprehension prevailed, upon the announcement by astronomers of a new comet, yet this announcement was generally received with I know not what of agitation and mistrust.

The elements of the strange orb were immediately calculated, and it was at once conceded by all observers, that its path, at perihelion, would bring it into very close proximity with the earth. There were two or three astronomers, of secondary note, who resolutely maintained that a contact was inevitable. I cannot very well express to you the effect of this intelligence upon the people. For a few short days they would not believe an assertion which their intellect, so long employed among worldly considerations, could not in any manner grasp. But the truth of a vitally important fact soon makes its way into the understanding of even the most stolid. Finally, all men saw that astronomical knowledge lied not, and they awaited the comet. Its approach was not, at first, seemingly rapid; nor was its appearance of very unusual character. It was of a dull red, and had little perceptible train. For seven or eight days we saw no material increase in its apparent diameter, and but a partial alteration in its color. Meanwhile the ordinary affairs of men were discarded, and all interests absorbed in a growing discussion, instituted by the philosophic, in respect to the cometary nature. Even the grossly ignorant aroused their sluggish capacities to such considerations. The learned now gave their intellect—their soul—to no such points as the allaying of fear, or to the sustenance of loved theory. They sought—they panted for right views. They groaned for perfected knowledge. Truth arose in the purity of her strength and exceeding majesty, and the wise bowed down and adored.

That material injury to our globe or to its inhabitants would result from the apprehended contact, was an opinion which hourly lost ground among the wise; and the wise were now freely permitted to rule the reason and the fancy of the crowd. It was demonstrated, that the density of the comet's nucleus was far less than that of our rarest gas; and the harmless passage of a similar visitor among the satellites of Jupiter was a point strongly insisted upon, and which served greatly to allay terror. Theologists, with an earnestness fear-enkindled, dwelt upon the biblical prophecies, and expounded them to the people with a directness and simplicity of which no previous instance had been known. That the final destruction of the earth must be brought about by the agency of fire, was urged with a spirit that enforced everywhere conviction; and that the comets were of no fiery nature (as all men now knew) was a truth which relieved all, in a great measure, from the apprehension of the great calamity foretold. It is noticeable that the popular prejudices and vulgar errors in regard to pestilences and wars—errors which were wont to prevail upon every appearance of a comet—were now altogether unknown. As if by some sudden convulsive exertion, reason had at once hurled superstition from her throne. The feeblest intellect had derived vigor from excessive interest.

What minor evils might arise from the contact were points of elaborate question. The learned spoke of slight geological disturbances, of probable alterations in climate, and consequently in vegetation; of possible magnetic and electric influences. Many held that no visible or perceptible effect would in any manner be produced. While such discussions were going on, their subject gradually approached, growing larger in apparent diameter, and of a more brilliant luster. Mankind grew paler as it came. All human operations were suspended.

There was an epoch in the course of the general sentiment when the comet had attained, at length, a size surpassing that of any previously recorded visitation. The people now, dismissing any lingering hope that the astronomers were wrong, experienced all the certainty of evil. The chimerical aspect of their terror was gone. The hearts of the stoutest of our race beat violently within their bosoms. A very few days sufficed, however, to merge even such feelings in sentiments more unendurable. We could no longer apply to the strange orb any accustomed thoughts. Its historical attributes had disappeared. It oppressed us with a hideous novelty of emotion. We saw it not as an astronomical phenomenon in the heavens, but as an incubus upon our hearts, and a shadow upon our brains. It had taken, with inconceivable rapidity, the character of a gigantic mantle of rare flame, extending from horizon to horizon.

Yet a day, and men breathed with greater freedom. It was clear that we were already within the influence of the comet; yet we lived. We even felt an unusual elasticity of frame and vivacity of mind. The exceeding tenuity of the object of our dread was apparent; for all heavenly objects were plainly visible through it. Meantime, our vegetation had perceptibly altered; and we gained faith, from this predicted circumstance, in the foresight of the wise. A wild luxuriance of foliage, utterly unknown before, burst out upon every vegetable thing.

Yet another day—and the evil was not altogether upon us. It was now evident that its nucleus would first reach us. A wild change had come over all men; and the first sense of pain was the wild signal for general lamentation and horror. This first sense of pain lay in a rigorous constriction of the breast and lungs, and an insufferable dryness of the skin. It could not be denied that our atmosphere was radically affected; the conformation of this atmosphere and the possible modifications to which it might be subjected, were now the topics of discussion. The result of investigation sent an electric thrill of the intensest horror through the universal heart of man.

It had been long known that the air which encircled us was a compound of oxygen and nitrogen gases, in the proportion of twenty-one measures of oxygen and seventy-nine of nitrogen, in every one hundred of the atmosphere. Oxygen, which was the principle of combustion, and the vehicle of heat, was absolutely necessary to the support of animal life, and was the most powerful and energetic agent in nature. Nitrogen, on the contrary, was incapable of supporting either animal life or flame. An unnatural excess of oxygen would result, it had been ascertained, in just such an elevation of the animal spirits as we had latterly experienced. It was the pursuit, the extension of the idea, which had engendered awe. What would be the result of a total extraction of the nitrogen? A combustion irresistible, all-devouring, omni-prevalent, immediate;—the entire fulfillment, in all their minute and terrible details, of the fiery and horror-inspiring denunciations of the prophecies of the Holy Book.

Why need I paint, Charmion, the now disenchained frenzy of mankind? That tenuity in the comet which had previously inspired us with hope, was now the source of the bitterness of despair. In its impalpable gaseous character we clearly perceived the consummation of Fate. Meantime a day again passed, bearing away with it the last shadow of Hope. We gasped in the rapid modification of the air. The red blood bounded tumultuously through its strict channels. A furious delirium possessed all men; and, with arms rigidly outstretched toward the threatening heavens, they trembled and shrieked aloud. But the nucleus of the destroyer was now upon us: even here in Aidenn, I shudder while I speak. Let me be brief—brief as the ruin that overwhelmed. For a moment there was a wild lurid light alone, visiting and penetrating all things. Then—let us bow down, Charmion, before the excessive majesty of the great God!—then, there came a shouting and pervading sound, as if from the mouth itself of HIMS; while the whole incumbent mass of ether in which we existed, burst at once into a species of intense flame, for whose surpassing brilliancy and all-fervid heat even the angels in the high Heaven of pure knowledge have no name. Thus ended all.

THE MAN OF THE CROWD

Ce grand malheur, de ne pouvoir être seul.[1]—La Bruyère

IT WAS WELL said of a certain German book that "*es lässt sich nicht lesen*"—it does not permit itself to be read. There are some secrets which do not permit themselves to be told. Men die nightly in their beds, wringing the hands of ghostly confessors, and looking them piteously in the eyes—die with despair of heart and convulsion of throat, on account of the hideousness of mysteries which will not suffer themselves to be revealed. Now and then, alas, the conscience of man takes up a burthen so heavy in horror that it can be thrown down only into the grave. And thus the essence of all crime is undivulged.

Not long ago, about the closing in of an evening in autumn, I sat at the large bow window of the D—— Coffee-House in London. For some months I had been ill in health, but was now convalescent, and, with returning strength, found myself in one of those happy moods which are so precisely the converse of ennui—moods of the keenest appetency, when the film from the mental vision departs—the αχλυς ος πριν επηεν—and the intellect, electrified, surpasses as greatly its everyday condition, as does the vivid yet candid reason of Leibnitz, the mad and flimsy rhetoric of Gorgias. Merely to breathe was enjoyment; and I derived positive pleasure even from many of the legitimate sources of pain. I felt a calm but inquisitive interest in everything. With a cigar in my mouth and a newspaper in my lap, I had been amusing myself for the greater part of the afternoon, now in poring

1 Such a great misfortune, not to be able to be alone.

over advertisements, now in observing the promiscuous company in the room, and now in peering through the smoky panes into the street.

This latter is one of the principal thoroughfares of the city, and had been very much crowded during the whole day. But, as the darkness came on, the throng momently increased; and, by the time the lamps were well lighted, two dense and continuous tides of population were rushing past the door. At this particular period of the evening I had never before been in a similar situation, and the tumultuous sea of human heads filled me, therefore, with a delicious novelty of emotion. I gave up, at length, all care of things within the hotel, and became absorbed in contemplation of the scene without.

At first my observations took an abstract and generalizing turn. I looked at the passengers in masses, and thought of them in their aggregate relations. Soon, however, I descended to details, and regarded with minute interest the innumerable varieties of figure, dress, air, gait, visage, and expression of countenance.

By far the greater number of those who went by had a satisfied business-like demeanor, and seemed to be thinking only of making their way through the press. Their brows were knit, and their eyes rolled quickly; when pushed against by fellow-wayfarers they evinced no symptom of impatience, but adjusted their clothes and hurried on. Others, still a numerous class, were restless in their movements, had flushed faces, and talked and gesticulated to themselves, as if feeling in solitude on account of the very denseness of the company around. When impeded in their progress, these people suddenly ceased muttering, but redoubled their gesticulations, and waited, with an absent and overdone smile upon the lips, the course of the persons impeding them. If jostled, they bowed profusely to the jostlers, and appeared overwhelmed with confusion.—There was nothing very distinctive about these two large classes beyond what I have noted. Their habiliments belonged to that order which is pointedly termed the decent. They were undoubtedly noblemen, merchants, attorneys, tradesmen, stock-jobbers—the Eupatrids and the commonplaces of society—men of leisure and men actively engaged in affairs of their own—conducting business upon their own responsibility. They did not greatly excite my attention.

The tribe of clerks was an obvious one; and here I discerned two remarkable divisions. There were the junior clerks of flash houses—young gentlemen with tight coats, bright boots, well-oiled hair, and supercilious lips. Setting aside a certain dapperness of carriage, which may be termed deskism for want of a better word, the manner of these persons seemed to me an exact facsimile of what had been the perfection of *bon ton* about twelve or eighteen months before. They wore the cast-off graces of the gentry;—and this, I believe, involves the best definition of the class.

The division of the upper clerks of staunch firms, or of the "steady old fellows," it was not possible to mistake. These were known by their coats and pantaloons of black or brown, made to sit comfortably, with white cravats and waistcoats, broad solid-looking shoes, and thick hose or gaiters.—They had all slightly bald heads, from which the right ears, long used to pen-holding, had an odd habit of standing off on end. I observed that they always removed or settled their hats with both hands, and wore watches, with short gold chains of a substantial and ancient pattern. Theirs was the affectation of respectability;—if indeed there be an affectation so honorable.

There were many individuals of dashing appearance, whom I easily understood as belonging to the race of swell pickpockets, with which all great cities are infested. I watched these gentry with much inquisitiveness, and found it difficult to imagine how they should ever be mistaken for gentlemen by gentlemen themselves. Their voluminousness of wristband, with an air of excessive frankness, should betray them at once.

The gamblers, of whom I descried not a few, were still more easily recognizable. They wore every variety of dress, from that of the desperate thimble-rig bully, with velvet waistcoat, fancy neckerchief, gilt chains, and filagreed buttons, to that of the scrupulously inornate clergyman than which nothing could be less liable to suspicion. Still all were distinguished by a certain sodden swarthiness of complexion, a filmy dimness of eye, and pallor and compression of lip. There were two other traits, moreover, by which I could always detect them;—a guarded lowness of tone in conversation, and a more than ordinary extension of the thumb in a direction at right angles with the fingers.—Very often, in company with these sharpers, I observed an order of men somewhat different in habits, but still birds of a kindred feather. They may be defined as the gentlemen who live by their wits. They seem to prey upon the public in two battalions—that of the dandies and that of the military men. Of the first grade the leading features are long locks and smiles; of the second frogged coats and frowns.

Descending in the scale of what is termed gentility, I found darker and deeper themes for speculation. I saw Jew pedlars, with hawk eyes flashing from countenances whose every other feature wore only an expression of abject humility; sturdy professional street beggars scowling upon mendicants of a better stamp, whom despair alone had driven forth into the night for charity; feeble and ghastly invalids, upon whom death had placed a sure hand, and who sidled and tottered through the mob, looking every one beseechingly in the face, as if in search of some chance consolation, some lost hope; modest young girls returning from long and late labour to a cheerless home, and shrinking more tearfully than indignantly from the glances of ruffians, whose direct contact, even, could not be avoided; women of the town of all kinds and of all ages—the unequivocal beauty in the prime of her womanhood, putting one in mind of the statue in Lucian, with the surface of Parian marble, and the interior filled with filth—the loathsome and utterly lost leper in rags—the wrinkled, bejewelled and paint-begrimed beldame, making a last effort at youth—the mere child of immature form, yet from long association, an adept in the dreadful coquetries of her trade, and burning with a rabid ambition to be ranked the equal of her elders in vice; drunkards innumerable and indescribable—some in shreds and patches, reeling, inarticulate, with bruised visage and lack-luster eyes—some in whole although filthy garments, with a slightly unsteady swagger, thick, sensual lips, and hearty-looking rubicund faces—others clothed in materials which had once been good, and which even now were scrupulously well brushed—men who walked with a more than naturally firm and springy step, but whose countenances were fearfully pale, whose eyes hideously wild and red, and who clutched with quivering fingers, as they strode through the crowd, at every object which came within their reach; beside these, pie-men, porters, coal-heavers, sweeps; organ-grinders, monkey-exhibitors, and ballad-mongers, those who vended with those who sang; ragged artisans and exhausted laborers of every description, and all full of a noisy and inordinate vivacity which jarred discordantly upon the ear, and gave an aching sensation to the eye.

As the night deepened, so deepened to me the interest of the scene; for not only did the general character of the crowd materially alter (its gentler features retiring in the gradual withdrawal of the more orderly portion of the people, and its harsher ones coming out into bolder relief, as the late hour brought forth every species of infamy from its den), but the rays of the gas-lamps, feeble at first in their struggle with the dying day, had now at length gained ascendancy, and threw over everything a fitful and garish luster. All was dark yet splendid—as that ebony to which has been likened the style of Tertullian.

The wild effects of the light enchained me to an examination of individual faces; and although the rapidity with which the world of light flitted before the window, prevented me from casting more than a glance upon each visage, still it seemed that, in my then peculiar mental state, I could frequently read, even in that brief interval of a glance, the history of long years.

With my brow to the glass, I was thus occupied in scrutinizing the mob, when suddenly there came into view a countenance (that of a decrepit old man, some sixty-five or seventy years of age)—a countenance which at once arrested and absorbed my whole attention, on account of the absolute idiosyncrasy of its expression. Anything even remotely resembling that expression I had never seen before. I well remember that my first thought, upon beholding it, was that Retszch, had he viewed it, would have greatly preferred it to his own pictural incarnations of the fiend. As I endeavored, during the brief minute of my original survey, to form some analysis of the meaning conveyed, there arose confusedly and paradoxically within my mind, the ideas of vast mental power, of caution, of penuriousness, of avarice, of coolness, of malice, of bloodthirstiness, of triumph, of merriment, of excessive terror, of intense—of extreme despair. I felt singularly aroused, startled, fascinated. "How wild a history," I said to myself, "is written within that bosom!" Then came a craving desire to keep the man in view—to know more of him. Hurriedly putting on an overcoat, and seizing my hat and cane, I made my way into the street, and pushed through the crowd in the direction which I had seen him take; for he had already disappeared. With some little difficulty I at length came within sight of him, approached, and followed him closely, yet cautiously, so as not to attract his attention.

I had now a good opportunity of examining his person. He was short in stature, very thin, and apparently very feeble. His clothes, generally, were filthy and ragged; but as he came, now and then, within the strong glare of a lamp, I perceived that his linen, although dirty, was of beautiful texture; and my vision deceived me, or, through a rent in a closely-buttoned and evidently second-handed roquelaure which enveloped him, I caught a glimpse both of a diamond and of a dagger. These observations heightened my curiosity, and I resolved to follow the stranger whithersoever he should go.

It was now fully nightfall, and a thick humid fog hung over the city, soon ending in a settled and heavy rain. This change of weather had an odd effect upon the crowd, the whole of which was at once put into new commotion, and overshadowed by a world of umbrellas. The waver, the jostle, and the hum increased in a tenfold degree. For my own part I did not much regard the rain—the lurking of an old fever in my system rendering the moisture somewhat too dangerously pleasant. Tying a handkerchief about my mouth, I kept on. For half an hour the old man held his way with difficulty along the great thoroughfare; and I here walked close at his elbow through fear of losing sight of him. Never once turning his head to look back, he did not observe me. By and by he passed into a cross street, which, although densely filled with people, was not quite so much thronged as the main one he had quitted. Here a change in his demeanor became evident. He walked more slowly and with less object than before—more hesitatingly. He crossed and recrossed the way repeatedly without apparent aim; and the press was still so thick, that, at every such movement, I was obliged to follow him closely. The street was a narrow and long one, and his course lay within it for nearly an hour, during which the passengers had gradually diminished to about that number which is ordinarily seen at noon in Broadway near the Park—so vast a difference is there between a London populace and that of the most frequented American city. A second turn brought us into a square, brilliantly lighted, and overflowing with life. The old manner of the stranger reappeared. His chin fell upon his breast, while his eyes rolled wildly from under his knit brows, in every direction, upon those who hemmed him in. He urged his way steadily and perseveringly. I was surprised, however, to find, upon his having made the circuit of the square, that he turned and retraced his steps. Still more was I astonished to see him repeat the same walk several times—once nearly detecting me as he came round with a sudden movement.

In this exercise he spent another hour, at the end of which we met with far less interruption from passengers than at first. The rain fell fast; the air grew cool; and the people were retiring to their homes. With a gesture of impatience, the wanderer passed into a by-street comparatively deserted. Down this, some quarter of a mile long, he rushed with an activity I could not have dreamed of seeing in one so aged, and which put me to much trouble in pursuit. A few minutes brought us to a large and busy bazaar, with the localities of which the stranger appeared well acquainted, and where his original demeanor again became apparent, as he forced his way to and fro, without aim, among the host of buyers and sellers.

During the hour and a half, or thereabouts, which we passed in this place, it required much caution on my part to keep him within reach without attracting his observation. Luckily I wore a pair of caoutchouc overshoes, and could move about in perfect silence. At no moment did he see that I watched him. He entered shop after shop, priced nothing, spoke no word, and looked at all objects with a wild and vacant stare. I was now utterly amazed at his behavior, and firmly resolved that we should not part until I had satisfied myself in some measure respecting him.

A loud-toned clock struck eleven, and the company were fast deserting the bazaar. A shopkeeper, in putting up a shutter, jostled the old man, and at the instant I saw a strong shudder come over his frame. He hurried into the street, looked anxiously around him for an instant, and then ran with incredible swiftness through many crooked and people-less lanes, until we emerged once more upon the great thoroughfare whence we had started—the street of the D—— Hotel. It no longer wore, however, the same aspect. It was still brilliant with gas; but the rain fell fiercely, and there were few persons to be seen.

The stranger grew pale. He walked moodily some paces up the once populous avenue, then, with a heavy sigh, turned in the direction of the river, and, plunging through a great variety of devious ways, came out, at length, in view of one of the principal theaters. It was about being closed, and the audience were thronging from the doors. I saw the old man gasp as if for breath while he threw himself amid the crowd; but I thought that the intense agony of his countenance had, in some measure, abated. His head again fell upon his breast; he appeared as I had seen him at first. I observed that he now took the course in which had gone the greater number of the audience—but, upon the whole, I was at a loss to comprehend the waywardness of his actions.

As he proceeded, the company grew more scattered, and his old uneasiness and vacillation were resumed. For some time he followed closely a party of some ten or twelve roysterers; but from this number one by one dropped off, until three only remained together, in a narrow and gloomy lane little frequented. The stranger paused, and, for a moment, seemed lost in thought; then, with every mark of agitation, pursued rapidly a route which brought us to the verge of the city, amid regions very different from those we had hitherto traversed. It was the most noisome quarter of London, where everything wore the worst impress of the most deplorable poverty, and of the most desperate crime. By the dim light of an accidental lamp, tall, antique, worm-eaten, wooden tenements were seen tottering to their fall, in directions so many and capricious that scarce the semblance of a passage was discernible between them. The paving stones lay at random, displaced from their beds by the rankly-growing grass. Horrible filth festered in the dammed-up gutters. The whole atmosphere teemed with desolation. Yet, as we proceeded, the sounds of human life revived by sure degrees, and at length large bands of the most abandoned of a London populace were seen reeling to and fro. The spirits of the old man again flickered up, as a lamp which is near its death-hour. Once more he strode onward with elastic tread. Suddenly a corner was turned, a blaze of light burst upon our sight, and we stood before one of the huge suburban temples of Intemperance—one of the palaces of the fiend, Gin.

It was now nearly daybreak; but a number of wretched inebriates still pressed in and out of the flaunting entrance. With a half shriek of joy the old man forced a passage within, resumed at once his original bearing, and stalked backward and forward, without apparent object, among the throng. He had not been thus long occupied, however, before a rush to the doors gave token that the host was closing them for the night. It was something even more intense than despair that I then observed upon the countenance of the singular being whom I had watched so pertinaciously. Yet he did not hesitate in his career, but, with a mad energy, retraced his steps at once, to the heart of the mighty London. Long and swiftly he fled, while I followed him in the wildest amazement, resolute not to abandon a scrutiny in which I now felt an interest all-absorbing. The sun arose while we proceeded, and, when we had once again reached that most thronged mart of the populous town, the street of the D—— Hotel, it presented an appearance of human bustle and activity scarcely inferior to what I had seen on the evening before. And here, long, amid the momently increasing confusion, did I persist in my pursuit of the stranger. But, as usual, he walked to and fro, and during the day did not pass from out the turmoil of that street. And, as the shades of the second evening came on, I grew wearied unto death, and, stopping fully in front of the wanderer, gazed at him steadfastly in the face. He noticed me not, but resumed his solemn walk, while I, ceasing to follow, remained absorbed in contemplation. "This old man," I said at length, "is the type and the genius of deep crime. He refuses to be alone. *He is the man of the crowd.* It will be in vain to follow; for I shall learn no more of him, nor of his deeds. The worst heart of the world is a grosser book than the *Hortulus Animae*, and perhaps it is but one of the great mercies of God that *es lässt sich nicht lesen*."

THE MURDERS IN THE RUE MORGUE

What song the Syrens sang, or what name Achilles assumed when he hid himself among women, although puzzling questions are not beyond all *conjecture.*

—Sir Thomas Browne, *Urn Burial*

THE MENTAL FEATURES discoursed of as the analytical, are, in themselves, but little susceptible of analysis. We appreciate them only in their effects. We know of them, among other things, that they are always to their possessor, when inordinately possessed, a source of the liveliest enjoyment. As the strong man exults in his physical ability, delighting in such exercises as call his muscles into action, so glories the analyst in that moral activity which disentangles. He derives pleasure from even the most trivial occupations bringing his talents into play. He is fond of enigmas, of conundrums, of hieroglyphics; exhibiting in his solutions of each a degree of acumen which appears to the ordinary apprehension preternatural. His results, brought about by the very soul and essence of method, have, in truth, the whole air of intuition. The faculty of re-solution is possibly much invigorated by mathematical study, and especially by that highest branch of it which, unjustly, and merely on account of its retrograde operations, has been called, as if *par excellence*, analysis. Yet to calculate is not in itself to analyze. A chess-player, for example, does the one without effort at the other. It follows that the game of chess, in its effects upon mental character, is greatly misunderstood. I am not now writing a treatise, but simply prefacing a somewhat peculiar narrative by observations very much at random; I will, therefore, take occasion to assert that the higher powers of the reflective intellect are more decidedly and more usefully tasked by the unostentatious game of drafts than by all the elaborate frivolity of chess. In this latter, where the pieces have different and *bizarre* motions, with various and variable values, what is only complex is mistaken (a not unusual error) for what is profound. The *attention* is here called powerfully into play. If it flag for an instant, an oversight is committed, resulting in injury or defeat. The possible moves being not only manifold but involute, the chances of such oversights are multiplied; and in nine cases out of ten it is the more concentrative rather than the more acute player who conquers. In drafts, on the contrary, where the moves are *unique* and have but little variation, the probabilities of inadvertence are diminished, and the mere attention being left comparatively unemployed, what advantages are obtained by either party are obtained by superior *acumen*. To be less abstract—Let us suppose a game of drafts where the pieces are reduced to four kings, and where, of course, no oversight is to be expected. It is obvious that here the victory can be decided (the players being at all equal) only by some *recherché* movement, the result of some exertion of the intellect. Deprived of ordinary resources, the analyst throws himself into the spirit of his opponent, identifies himself therewith, and not unfrequently sees thus, at a glance, the sole methods (sometimes indeed absurdly simple ones) by which he may seduce into error or hurry into miscalculation.

Whist had long been noted for its influence upon what is termed the calculating power; and men of the highest order of intellect have been known to take an apparently unaccountable delight in it, while eschewing chess as frivolous. Beyond doubt there is nothing of a similar nature so greatly tasking the faculty of analysis. The best chess-player in Christendom *may* be little more than the best player of chess; but proficiency in whist implies capacity for success in all these more important undertakings where mind struggles with mind. When I say proficiency, I mean that perfection in the game which includes a comprehension of *all* the sources whence legitimate advantage may be derived. These are not only manifold but multiform, and lie frequently among the recesses of thought altogether inaccessible to the ordinary understanding. To observe attentively is to remember distinctly; and, so far, the concentrative chess-player will do very well at whist; while the rules of Hoyle (themselves based upon the mere mechanism of the game) are sufficiently and generally comprehensible. Thus to have a retentive memory, and to proceed by "the book," are points commonly regarded as the sum total of good playing. But it is in matters beyond the limits of mere rule that the skill of the analyst is evinced. He makes, in silence, a host of observations and inferences. So, perhaps, do his companions; and the difference in the extent of the information obtained, lies not so much in the validity of the inference as in the quality of the observation. The necessary knowledge is that of *what* to observe. Our player confines himself not at all; nor, because the game is the object, does he reject deductions from things external to the game. He examines the countenance of his partner, comparing it carefully with that of each of his opponents. He considers the mode of assorting the cards in each hand; often counting trump by trump, and honor by honor, through the glances bestowed by their holders upon each. He notes every variation of face as the play progresses, gathering a fund of thought from the differences in the expression of certainty, of surprise, of triumph, or chagrin. From the manner of gathering up a trick he judges whether the person taking it can make another in the suit. He recognizes what is played through feint, by the air with which it is thrown upon the table. A casual or inadvertent word; the accidental dropping or turning of a card, with the accompanying anxiety or carelessness in regard to its concealment; the counting of the tricks, with the order of their arrangement; embarrassment, hesitation, eagerness or trepidation—all afford, to his apparently intuitive perception, indications of the true state of affairs. The first two or three rounds having been played, he is in full possession of the contents of each hand, and thenceforward puts down his cards with as absolute a precision of purpose as if the rest of the party had turned outward the faces of their own.

The analytical power should not be confounded with simple ingenuity; for while the analyst is necessarily ingenious, the ingenious man is often remarkably incapable of analysis. The consecutive or combining power, by which ingenuity is usually manifested, and to which the phrenologists (I believe erroneously) have assigned a separate organ, supposing it a primitive faculty, has been so frequently seen in those whose intellect bordered otherwise upon idiocy, as to have attracted general observation among writers on morals. Between ingenuity and the analytic ability there exists a difference far greater, indeed, than that between the fancy and the imagination, but of a character very strictly analogous. It will be found, in fact, that the ingenious are always fanciful, and the *truly* imaginative never otherwise than analytic.

The narrative which follows will appear to the reader somewhat in the light of a commentary upon the propositions just advanced.

Residing in Paris during the spring and part of the summer of 18—, I there became acquainted with a Monsieur C. Auguste Dupin. This young gentleman was of an excellent—indeed of an illustrious family, but, by a variety of untoward events, had been reduced to such poverty that the energy of his character succumbed beneath it, and he ceased to bestir himself in the world, or to care for the retrieval of his fortunes. By courtesy of his creditors, there still remained in his possession a small remnant of his patrimony; and upon the income arising from this, he managed, by means of a rigorous economy, to procure the necessaries of life, without troubling himself about its superfluities. Books, indeed, were his sole luxuries, and in Paris these are easily obtained.

Our first meeting was at an obscure library in the Rue Montmartre, where the accident of our both being in search of the same very rare and very remarkable volume, brought us into closer communion. We saw each other again and again. I was deeply interested in the little family history which he detailed to me with all that candour which a Frenchman indulges whenever mere self is the theme. I was astonished, too, at the vast extent of his reading; and, above all, I felt my soul enkindled within me by the wild fervor, and the vivid freshness of his imagination. Seeking in Paris the objects I then sought, I felt that the society of such a man would be to me a treasure beyond price; and this feeling I frankly confided to him. It was at length arranged that we should live together during my stay in the city; and as my worldly circumstances were somewhat less embarrassed than his own, I was permitted to be at the expense of renting, and furnishing in a style which suited the rather fantastic gloom of our common temper, a time-eaten and grotesque mansion, long deserted through superstitions into which we did not inquire, and tottering to its fall in a retired and desolate portion of the Faubourg Saint-Germain.

Had the routine of our life at this place been known to the world, we should have been regarded as madmen—although, perhaps, as madmen of a harmless nature. Our seclusion was perfect. We admitted no visitors.

Indeed the locality of our retirement had been carefully kept a secret from my own former associates; and it had been many years since Dupin had ceased to know or be known in Paris. We existed within ourselves alone.

It was a freak of fancy in my friend (for what else shall I call it?) to be enamored of the Night for her own sake; and into this bizarrerie, as into all his others, I quietly fell; giving myself up to his wild whims with a perfect *abandon*. The sable divinity would not herself dwell with us always; but we could counterfeit her presence. At the first dawn of the morning we closed all the massy shutters of our old building; lighted a couple of tapers which, strongly perfumed, threw out only the ghastliest and feeblest of rays. By the aid of these we then busied our souls in dreams—reading, writing, or conversing, until warned by the clock of the advent of the true Darkness. Then we sallied forth into the streets, arm in arm, continuing the topics of the day, or roaming far and wide until a late hour, seeking, amid the wild lights and shadows of the populous city, that infinity of mental excitement which quiet observation can afford.

At such times I could not help remarking and admiring (although from his rich ideality I had been prepared to expect it) a peculiar analytic ability in Dupin. He seemed, too, to take an eager delight in its exercise—if not exactly in its display—and did not hesitate to confess the pleasure thus derived. He boasted to me, with a low chuckling laugh, that most men, in respect to himself, wore windows in their bosoms, and was wont to follow up such assertions by direct and very startling proofs of his intimate knowledge of my own. His manner at these moments was frigid and abstract; his eyes were vacant in expression; while his voice, usually a rich tenor, rose into a treble which would have sounded petulantly but for the deliberateness and entire distinctness of the enunciation. Observing him in these moods, I often dwelt meditatively upon the old philosophy of the Bi-Part Soul, and amused myself with the fancy of a double Dupin—the creative and the resolvent.

Let it not be supposed, from what I have just said, that I am detailing any mystery, or penning any romance. What I have described in the Frenchman, was merely the result of an excited, or perhaps of a diseased intelligence. But of the character of his remarks at the periods in question an example will best convey the idea.

We were strolling one night down a long dirty street, in the vicinity of the Palais Royal. Being both, apparently, occupied with thought, neither of us had spoken a syllable for fifteen minutes at least. All at once Dupin broke forth with these words:

"He is a very little fellow, that's true, and would do better for the *Théâtre des Variétés*."

"There can be no doubt of that," I replied unwittingly, and not at first observing (so much had I been absorbed in reflection) the extraordinary manner in which the speaker had chimed in with my meditations. In an instant afterward I recollected myself, and my astonishment was profound.

"Dupin," said I, gravely, "this is beyond my comprehension. I do not hesitate to say that I am amazed, and can scarcely credit my senses. How was it possible you should know I was thinking of——?" Here I paused, to ascertain beyond a doubt whether he really knew of whom I thought.

——"of Chantilly," said he, "why do you pause? You were remarking to yourself that his diminutive figure unfitted him for tragedy."

This was precisely what had formed the subject of my reflections. Chantilly was a *quondam* cobbler of the Rue Saint-Denis, who, becoming stage-mad, had attempted the *rôle* of Xerxes, in Crébillion's tragedy so called, and been notoriously Pasquinaded for his pains.

"Tell me, for Heaven's sake," I exclaimed, "the method—if method there is—by which you have been enabled to fathom my soul in this matter." In fact I was even more startled than I would have been willing to express.

"It was the fruiterer," replied my friend, "who brought you to the conclusion that the mender of soles was not of sufficient height for Xerxes *et id genus omne*."

"The fruiterer—you astonish me—I know no fruiterer whomsoever."

"The man who ran up against you as we entered the street—it may have been fifteen minutes ago."

I now remembered that, in fact, a fruiterer, carrying upon his head a large basket of apples, had nearly thrown me down, by accident, as we passed from the Rue C—— into the thoroughfare where we stood; but what this had to do with Chantilly I could not possibly understand.

There was not a particle of *charlatanerie* about Dupin. "I will explain," he said, "and that you may comprehend all clearly, we will first retrace the course of your meditations, from the moment in which I spoke to you until that of the *rencontre* with the fruiterer in question. The larger links of the chain run thus—Chantilly, Orion, Dr. Nichols, Epicurus, Stereotomy, the street stones, the fruiterer."

There are few persons who have not, at some period of their lives, amused themselves in retracing the steps by which particular conclusions of their own minds have been attained. The occupation is often full of interest; and he who attempts it for the first time is astonished by the apparently illimitable distance and incoherence between the starting-point and the goal. What, then, must have been my amazement when I heard the Frenchman speak what he had just spoken, and when I could not help acknowledging that he had spoken the truth. He continued:

"We had been talking of horses, if I remember aright, just before leaving the Rue C——. This was the last subject we discussed. As we crossed into this street, a fruiterer, with a large basket upon his head, brushing quickly past us, thrust you upon a pile of paving-stones collected at a spot where the causeway is undergoing repair. You stepped upon one of the loose fragments, slipped, slightly strained your ankle, appeared vexed or sulky, muttered a few words, turned to look at the pile, and then proceeded in silence. I was not particularly attentive to what you did; but observation has become with me, of late, a species of necessity.

"You kept your eyes upon the ground—glancing, with a petulant expression, at the holes and ruts in the pavement (so that I saw you were still thinking of the stones), until we reached the little alley called Lamartine, which has been paved, by way of experiment, with the overlapping and riveted blocks. Here your countenance brightened up, and, perceiving your lips move, I could not doubt that you murmured the word 'stereotomy,' a term very affectedly applied to this species of pavement. I knew that you could not say to yourself 'stereotomy' without being brought to think of atomies, and thus of the theories of Epicurus; and since, when we discussed this subject not very long ago, I mentioned to you how singularly, yet with how little notice, the vague guesses of that noble Greek had met with confirmation in the late nebular cosmogony, I felt that you could not avoid casting your eyes upward to the great nebula in Orion, and I certainly expected that you would do so. You did look up; and I was now assured that I had correctly followed your steps. But in that bitter *tirade* upon Chantilly, which appeared in yesterday's '*Musée*,' the satirist, making some disgraceful allusions to the cobbler's change of name upon assuming the buskin, quoted a Latin line about which we have often conversed. I mean the line

Perdidit antiquum litera prima sonum.

I had told you that this was in reference to Orion, formerly written Urion; and, from certain pungencies connected with this explanation, I was aware that you could not have forgotten it. It was clear, therefore, that you would not fail to combine the two ideas of Orion and Chantilly. That you did combine them I saw by the character of the smile which passed over your lips. You thought of the poor cobbler's immolation. So far, you had been stooping in your gait; but now I saw you draw yourself up to your full height. I was then sure that you reflected upon the diminutive figure of Chantilly. At this point I interrupted your meditations to remark that as, in fact, he was a very little fellow—that Chantilly—he would do better at the *Théâtre des Variétés*."

Not long after this, we were looking over an evening edition of the *Gazette des Tribunaux*, when the following paragraphs arrested our attention.

"Extraordinary Murders.—This morning, about three o'clock, the inhabitants of the Quartier Saint-Roch were aroused from sleep by a succession of terrific shrieks, issuing, apparently, from the fourth story of a house in the Rue Morgue, known to be in the sole occupancy of one Madame L'Espanaye, and her daughter, Mademoiselle Camille L'Espanaye. After some delay, occasioned by a fruitless attempt to procure admission in the usual manner, the gateway was broken in with a crowbar, and, eight or ten of the neighbors entered, accompanied by two gendarmes. By this time the cries had ceased; but, as the party rushed up the first flight of stairs, two or more rough voices, in angry contention, were distinguished, and seemed to proceed from the upper part of the house. As the second landing was reached, these sounds, also, had ceased, and everything remained perfectly quiet. The party spread themselves, and hurried from room to room. Upon arriving at a large back chamber in the fourth story (the door of which, being found locked, with the key inside, was forced open), a spectacle presented itself which struck every one present not less with horror than with astonishment.

"The apartment was in the wildest disorder—the furniture broken and thrown about in all directions. There was only one bedstead; and from this the bed had been removed, and thrown into the middle of the floor. On a chair lay a razor, besmeared with blood. On the hearth were two or three long and thick tresses of gray human hair, also dabbled in blood, and seeming to have been pulled out by the roots. Upon the floor were found four Napoleons, an ear-ring of topaz, three large silver spoons, three smaller of métal d'Alger, and two bags containing nearly four thousand francs in gold. The drawers of a *bureau*, which stood in one corner, were open, and had been, apparently, rifled, although many articles still remained in them. A small iron safe was discovered under the *bed* (not under the bedstead). It was open, with the key still in the door. It had no contents beyond a few old letters, and other papers of little consequence.

"Of Madame L'Espanaye no traces were here seen; but an unusual quantity of soot being observed in the fireplace, a search was made in the chimney, and (horrible to relate!) the corpse of the daughter, head downward, was dragged therefrom; it having been thus forced up the narrow aperture for a considerable distance. The body was quite warm. Upon examining it, many excoriations were perceived, no doubt occasioned by the violence with which it had been thrust up and disengaged. Upon the face were many severe scratches, and, upon the throat, dark bruises, and deep indentations of finger-nails, as if the deceased had been throttled to death.

"After a thorough investigation of every portion of the house, without further discovery, the party made its way into a small paved yard in the rear of the building, where lay the corpse of the old lady, with her throat so entirely cut that, upon an attempt to raise her, the head fell off. The body, as well as the head, was fearfully mutilated—the former so much so as scarcely to retain any semblance of humanity.

"To this horrible mystery there is not as yet, we believe, the slightest clue."

The next day's paper had these additional particulars.

"*The Tragedy in the Rue Morgue*. Many individuals have been examined in relation to this most extraordinary and frightful affair" (the word '*affaire*' has not yet, in France, that levity of import which it conveys with us), "but nothing whatever has transpired to throw light upon it. We give below all the material testimony elicited.

"*Pauline Dubourg*, laundress, deposes that she has known both the deceased for three years, having washed for them during that period. The old lady and her daughter seemed on good terms—very affectionate toward each other. They were excellent pay. Could not speak in regard to their mode or means of living. Believed that Madame L. told fortunes for a living. Was reputed to have money put by. Never met any persons in the house when she called for the clothes or took them home. Was sure that they had no servant in employ. There appeared to be no furniture in any part of the building except in the fourth story.

"*Pierre Moreau*, tobacconist, deposes that he has been in the habit of selling small quantities of tobacco and snuff to Madame L'Espanaye for nearly four years. Was born in the neighborhood, and has always resided there. The deceased and her daughter had occupied the house in which the corpses were found, for more than six years. It was formerly occupied by a jeweler, who under-let the upper rooms to various persons. The house was the property of Madame L. She became dissatisfied with the abuse of the premises by her tenant, and moved into them herself, refusing to let any portion. The old lady was childish. Witness had seen the daughter some five or six times during the six years. The two lived an exceedingly retired life—were reputed to have money. Had heard it said among the neighbors that Madame L. told fortunes—did not believe it. Had never seen any person enter the door except the old lady and her daughter, a porter once or twice, and a physician some eight or ten times.

"Many other persons, neighbors, gave evidence to the same effect. No one was spoken of as frequenting the house. It was not known whether there were any living connexions of Madame L. and her daughter. The shutters of the front windows were seldom opened. Those in the rear were always closed, with the exception of the large back room, fourth story. The house was a good house—not very old.

"*Isidore Musèt, gendarme*, deposes that he was called to the house about three o'clock in the morning, and found some twenty or thirty persons at the gateway, endeavoring to gain admittance. Forced it open, at length, with a bayonet—not with a crowbar. Had but little difficulty in getting it open, on account of its being a double or folding gate, and bolted neither at bottom nor top. The shrieks were continued until the gate was forced—and then suddenly ceased. They seemed to be screams of some person (or persons) in great agony—were loud and drawn out, not short and quick. Witness led the way upstairs. Upon reaching the first landing, heard two voices in loud and angry contention—the one a gruff voice, the other much shriller—a very strange voice. Could distinguish some words of the former, which was that of a Frenchman. Was positive that it was not a woman's voice. Could distinguish the words '*sacré*' and '*diable*.' The shrill voice was that of a foreigner. Could not be sure whether it was the voice of a man or of a woman. Could not make out what was said, but believed the language to be Spanish. The state of the room and of the bodies was described by this witness as we described them yesterday.

"*Henri Duval*, a neighbor, and by trade a silversmith, deposes that he was one of the party who first entered the house. Corroborates the testimony of Musèt in general. As soon as they forced an entrance, they reclosed the door, to keep out the crowd, which collected very fast, notwithstanding the lateness of the hour. The shrill voice, the witness thinks, was that of an Italian. Was certain it was not French. Could not be sure that it was a man's voice. It might have been a woman's. Was not acquainted with the Italian language. Could not distinguish the words, but was convinced by the intonation that the speaker was an Italian. Knew Madame L. and her daughter. Had conversed with both frequently. Was sure that the shrill voice was not that of either of the deceased.

"—*Odenheimer, restaurateur*. This witness volunteered his testimony. Not speaking French, was examined through an interpreter. Is a native of Amsterdam. Was passing the house at the time of the shrieks. They lasted for several minutes—probably ten. They were long and loud—very awful and distressing. Was one of those who entered the building. Corroborated the previous evidence in every respect but one. Was sure that the shrill voice was that of a man—of a Frenchman. Could not distinguish the words uttered. They were loud and quick—unequal—spoken apparently in fear as well as in anger. The voice was harsh—not so much shrill as harsh. Could not call it a shrill voice. The gruff voice said repeatedly '*sacré*,' '*diable*,' and once '*mon Dieu*.'

"*Jules Mignaud*, banker, of the firm of Mignaud et Fils, Rue Deloraine. Is the elder Mignaud. Madame L'Espanaye had some property. Had opened an account with his banking house in the spring of the year—(eight years previously). Made frequent deposits in small sums. Had checked for nothing until the third day before her death, when she took out in person the sum of four thousand francs. This sum was paid in gold, and a clerk sent home with the money.

"*Adolphe Le Bon*, clerk to Mignaud et Fils, deposes that on the day in question, about noon, he accompanied Madame L'Espanaye to her residence with the four thousand francs, put up in two bags. Upon the door being opened, Mademoiselle L. appeared and took from his hands one of the bags, while the old lady relieved him of the other. He then bowed and departed. Did not see any person in the street at the time. It is a bye-street—very lonely.

"*William Bird*, tailor, deposes that he was one of the party who entered the house. Is an Englishman. Has lived in Paris two years. Was one of the first to ascend the stairs. Heard the voices in contention. The gruff voice was that of a Frenchman. Could make out several words, but cannot now remember all. Heard distinctly '*sacré*' and '*mon Dieu*.' There was a sound at the moment as if of several persons struggling—a scraping and scuffling sound. The shrill voice was very loud—louder than the gruff one. Is sure that it was not the voice of an Englishman. Appeared to be that of a German. Might have been a woman's voice. Does not understand German.

"Four of the above-named witnesses, being recalled, deposed that the door of the chamber in which was found the body of Mademoiselle L. was locked on the inside when the party reached it. Everything was perfectly silent—no groans or noises of any kind. Upon forcing the door no person was seen. The windows, both of the back and front room, were down and firmly fastened from within. A door between the two rooms was closed, but not locked. The door leading from the front room into the passage was locked, with the key on the inside. A small room in the front of the house, on the fourth story, at the head of the passage, was open, the door being ajar. This room was crowded with old beds, boxes, and so forth. These were carefully removed and searched. There was not an inch of any portion of the house which was not carefully searched. Sweeps were sent up and down the chimneys. The house was a four-story one, with garrets (*mansardes*). A trap-door on the roof was nailed down very securely—did not appear to have been opened for years. The time elapsing between the hearing of the voices in contention and the breaking open of the room door, was variously stated by the witnesses. Some made it as short as three minutes—some as long as five. The door was opened with difficulty.

"*Alfonzo Garcio*, undertaker, deposes that he resides in the Rue Morgue. Is a native of Spain. Was one of the party who entered the house. Did not proceed upstairs. Is nervous, and was apprehensive of the consequences of agitation. Heard the voices in contention. The gruff voice was that of a Frenchman. Could not distinguish what was said. The shrill voice was that of an Englishman—is sure of this. Does not understand the English language, but judges by the intonation.

"*Alberto Montani*, confectioner, deposes that he was among the first to ascend the stairs. Heard the voices in question. The gruff voice was that of a Frenchman. Distinguished several words. The speaker appeared to be expostulating. Could not make out the words of the shrill voice. Spoke quickly and unevenly. Thinks it the voice of a Russian. Corroborates the general testimony. Is an Italian. Never conversed with a native of Russia.

"Several witnesses, recalled, here testified that the chimneys of all the rooms on the fourth story were too narrow to admit the passage of a human being. By 'sweeps' were meant cylindrical sweeping-brushes, such as are employed by those who clean chimneys. These brushes were passed up and down every flue in the house. There is no back passage by which any one could have descended while the party proceeded upstairs. The body of Mademoiselle L'Espanaye was so firmly wedged in the chimney that it could not be got down until four or five of the party united their strength.

"*Paul Dumas*, physician, deposes that he was called to view the bodies about daybreak. They were both then lying on the sacking of the bed-stead in the chamber where Mademoiselle L. was found.

The corpse of the young lady was much bruised and excoriated. The fact that it had been thrust up the chimney would sufficiently account for these appearances. The throat was greatly chafed. There were several deep scratches just below the chin, together with a series of livid spots which were evidently the impression of fingers. The face was fearfully discolored, and the eyeballs protruded. The tongue had been partially bitten through. A large bruise was discovered upon the pit of the stomach, produced, apparently, by the pressure of a knee. In the opinion of M. Dumas, Mademoiselle L'Espanaye had been throttled to death by some person or persons unknown. The corpse of the mother was horribly mutilated. All the bones of the right leg and arm were more or less shattered. The left *tibia* much splintered, as well as all of the ribs of the left side. Whole body dreadfully bruised and discolored. It was not possible to say how the injuries had been inflicted. A heavy club of wood, or a broad bar of iron—a chair—any large, heavy, and obtuse weapon would have produced such results, if wielded by the hands of a very powerful man. No woman could have inflicted the blows with any weapon. The head of the deceased, when seen by witness, was entirely separated from the body, and was also greatly shattered. The throat had evidently been cut with some very sharp instrument—probably with a razor.

"*Alexandre Etienne*, surgeon, was called with M. Dumas to view the bodies. Corroborated the testimony, and the opinions of M. Dumas.

"Nothing further of importance was elicited, although several other persons were examined. A murder so mysterious, and so perplexing in all its particulars, was never before committed in Paris—if indeed a murder has been committed at all. The police are entirely at fault—an unusual occurrence in affairs of this nature. There is not, however, the shadow of a clue apparent."

The evening edition of the paper stated that the greatest excitement still continued in the Quartier Saint-Roch—that the premises in question had been carefully re-searched, and fresh examinations of witnesses instituted, but all to no purpose. A postscript, however, mentioned that Adolphe Le Bon had been arrested and imprisoned—although nothing appeared to criminate him, beyond the facts already detailed.

Dupin seemed singularly interested in the progress of this affair—at least so I judged from his manner, for he made no comments. It was only after the announcement that Le Bon had been imprisoned, that he asked me my opinion respecting the murders.

I could merely agree with all Paris in considering them an insoluble mystery. I saw no means by which it would be possible to trace the murderer.

"We must not judge of the means," said Dupin, "by this shell of an examination. The Parisian police, so much extolled for acumen, are cunning, but no more. There is no method in their proceedings, beyond the method of the moment. They make a vast parade of measures; but, not unfrequently, these are so ill adapted to the objects proposed, as to put us in mind of Monsieur Jourdain's calling for his *robe-de-chambre—pour mieux entendre la musique*. The results attained by them are not unfrequently surprising, but, for the most part, are brought about by simple diligence and activity. When these qualities are unavailing, their schemes fail. Vidocq, for example, was a good guesser, and a persevering man. But, without educated thought, he erred continually by the very intensity of his investigations. He impaired his vision by holding the object too close. He might see, perhaps, one or two points with unusual clearness, but in so doing he, necessarily, lost sight of the matter as a whole. Thus there is such a thing as being too profound. Truth is not always in a well. In fact, as regards the more important knowledge, I do believe that she is invariably superficial. The depth lies in the valleys where we seek her, and not upon the mountain-tops where she is found. The modes and sources of this kind of error are well typified in the contemplation of the heavenly bodies. To look at a star by glances—to view it in a side-long way, by turning toward it the exterior portions of the *retina* (more susceptible of feeble impressions of light than the interior), is to behold the star distinctly—is to have the best appreciation of its luster—a luster which grows dim just in proportion as we turn our vision *fully* upon it. A greater number of rays actually fall upon the eye in the latter case, but, in the former, there is the more refined capacity for comprehension. By undue profundity we perplex and enfeeble thought; and it is possible to make even Venus herself vanish from the firmament by a scrutiny too sustained, too concentrated, or too direct.

"As for these murders, let us enter into some examinations for ourselves, before we make up an opinion respecting them. An inquiry will afford us amusement" (I thought this an odd term, so applied, but said nothing), "and, besides, Le Bon once rendered me a service for which I am not ungrateful. We will go and see the premises with our own eyes. I know G——, the Prefect of Police, and shall have no difficulty in obtaining the necessary permission."

The permission was obtained, and we proceeded at once to the Rue Morgue. This is one of those miserable thoroughfares which intervene between the Rue Richelieu and the Rue Saint-Roch. It was late in the afternoon when we reached it; as this quarter is at a great distance from that in which we resided. The house was readily found; for there were still many persons gazing up at the closed shutters, with an objectless curiosity, from the opposite side of the way. It was an ordinary Parisian house, with a gateway, on one side of which was a glazed watch-box, with a sliding panel in the window, indicating a *loge de concierge*. Before going in we walked up the street, turned down an alley, and then, again turning, passed in the rear of the building—Dupin, meanwhile, examining the whole neighborhood, as well as the house, with a minuteness of attention for which I could see no possible object.

Retracing our steps, we came again to the front of the dwelling, rang, and, having shown our credentials, were admitted by the agents in charge. We went upstairs—into the chamber where the body of Mademoiselle L'Espanaye had been found, and where both the deceased still lay. The disorders of the room had, as usual, been suffered to exist. I saw nothing beyond what had been stated in the *Gazette des Tribunaux*. Dupin scrutinized everything—not excepting the bodies of the victims. We then went into the other rooms, and into the yard; a *gendarme* accompanying us throughout. The examination occupied us until dark, when we took our departure. On our way home my companion stepped in for a moment at the office of one of the daily papers.

I have said that the whims of my friend were manifold, and that *Je les ménageais:*—for this phrase there is no English equivalent. It was his humor, now, to decline all conversation on the subject of the murder, until about noon the next day. He then asked me, suddenly, if I had observed anything *peculiar* at the scene of the atrocity.

There was something in his manner of emphasizing the word "peculiar," which caused me to shudder, without knowing why.

"No, nothing *peculiar*," I said; "nothing more, at least, than we both saw stated in the paper."

"The *Gazette*," he replied, "has not entered, I fear, into the unusual horror of the thing. But dismiss the idle opinions of this print. It appears to me that this mystery is considered insoluble, for the very reason which should cause it to be regarded as easy of solution—I mean for the *outré* character of its features. The police are confounded by the seeming absence of motive—not for the murder itself—but for the atrocity of the murder. They are puzzled, too, by the seeming impossibility of reconciling the voices heard in contention, with the facts that no one was discovered upstairs but the assassinated Mademoiselle L'Espanaye, and that there were no means of egress without the notice of the party ascending. The wild disorder of the room; the corpse thrust, with the head downward, up the chimney; the frightful mutilation of the body of the old lady; these considerations, with those just mentioned, and others which I need not mention, have sufficed to paralyse the powers, by putting completely at fault the boasted acumen, of the government agents. They have fallen into the gross but common error of confounding the unusual with the abstruse. But it is by these deviations from the plane of the ordinary, that reason feels its way, if at all, in its search for the true. In investigations such as we are now pursuing, it should not be so much asked 'what has occurred,' as 'what has occurred that has never occurred before.' In fact, the facility with which I shall arrive, or have arrived, at the solution of this mystery, is in the direct ratio of its apparent insolubility in the eyes of the police."

I stared at the speaker in mute astonishment.

"I am now awaiting," continued he, looking toward the door of our apartment—"I am now awaiting a person who, although perhaps not the perpetrator of these butcheries, must have been in some measure implicated in their perpetration. Of the worst portion of the crimes committed, it is probable that he is innocent. I hope that I am right in this supposition; for upon it I build my expectation of reading the entire riddle. I look for the man here—in this room—every moment. It is true that he may not arrive; but the probability is that he will. Should he come, it will be necessary to detain him. Here are pistols; and we both know how to use them when occasion demands their use."

I took the pistols, scarcely knowing what I did, or believing what I heard, while Dupin went on, very much as if in a soliloquy. I have already spoken of his abstract manner at such times. His discourse was addressed to myself; but his voice, although by no means loud, had that intonation which is commonly employed in speaking to some one at a great distance. His eyes, vacant in expression, regarded only the wall.

"That the voices heard in contention," he said, "by the party upon the stairs, were not the voices of the women themselves, was fully proved by the evidence. This relieves us of all doubt upon the question whether the old lady could have first destroyed the daughter, and afterward have committed suicide. I speak of this point chiefly for the sake of method; for the strength of Madame L'Espanaye would have been utterly unequal to the task of thrusting her daughter's corpse up the chimney as it was found; and the nature of the wounds upon her own person entirely preclude the idea of self-destruction. Murder, then, has been committed by some third party; and the voices of this third party were those heard in contention. Let me now advert—not to the whole testimony respecting these voices—but to what was *peculiar* in that testimony. Did you observe anything peculiar about it?"

I remarked that, while all the witnesses agreed in supposing the gruff voice to be that of a Frenchman, there was much disagreement in regard to the shrill, or, as one individual termed it, the harsh voice.

"That was the evidence itself," said Dupin, "but it was not the peculiarity of the evidence. You have observed nothing distinctive. Yet there was something to be observed. The witnesses, as you remark, agreed about the gruff voice; they were here unanimous. But in regard to the shrill voice, the peculiarity is—not that they disagreed—but that, while an Italian, an Englishman, a Spaniard, a Hollander, and a Frenchman attempted to describe it, each one spoke of it as that *of a foreigner*. Each is sure that it was not the voice of one of his own countrymen. Each likens it—not to the voice of an individual of any nation with whose language he is conversant—but the converse. The Frenchman supposes it the voice of a Spaniard, and 'might have distinguished some words *had he been acquainted with the Spanish*.' The Dutchman maintains it to have been that of a Frenchman; but we find it stated that '*not understanding French this witness was examined through an interpreter.*' The Englishman thinks it the voice of a German, and '*does not understand German.*' The Spaniard 'is sure' that it was that of an Englishman, but 'judges by the intonation' altogether, '*as he has no knowledge of the English.*' The Italian believes it the voice of a Russian, but '*has never conversed with a native of Russia.*' A second Frenchman differs, moreover, with the first, and is positive that the voice was that of an Italian, but, *not being cognizant of that tongue*, is, like the Spaniard, 'convinced by the intonation.' Now, how strangely unusual must that voice have really been, about which such testimony as this *could* have been elicited!—in whose *tones*, even, denizens of the five great divisions of Europe could recognize nothing familiar! You will say that it might have been the voice of an Asiatic—of an African. Neither Asiatics nor Africans abound in Paris; but, without denying the inference, I will now merely call your attention to three points. The voice is termed by one witness 'harsh rather than shrill.' It is represented by two others to have been 'quick and *unequal.*' No words—no sounds resembling words—were by any witness mentioned as distinguishable.

"I know not," continued Dupin, "what impression I may have made, so far, upon your own understanding; but I do not hesitate to say that legitimate deductions even from this portion of the testimony—the portion respecting the gruff and shrill voices—are in themselves sufficient to engender a suspicion which should give direction to all further progress in the investigation of the mystery. I said 'legitimate deductions'; but my meaning is not thus fully expressed. I designed to imply that the deductions are the *sole* proper ones, and that the suspicion arises *inevitably* from them as the single result. What the suspicion is, however, I will not say just yet. I merely wish you to bear in mind that, with myself, it was sufficiently forcible to give a definite form—a certain tendency—to my inquiries in the chamber.

"Let us now transport ourselves, in fancy, to this chamber. What shall we first seek here? The means of egress employed by the murderers. It is not too much to say that neither of us believe in preternatural events. Madame and Mademoiselle L'Espanaye were not destroyed by spirits. The doers of the deed were material, and escaped materially. Then how? Fortunately, there is but one mode of reasoning upon the point, and that mode must lead us to a definite decision.—Let us examine, each by each, the possible means of egress. It is clear that the assassins were in the room where Mademoiselle L'Espanaye was found, or at least in the room adjoining, when the party ascended the stairs. It is then only from these two apartments that we have to seek issues. The police have laid bare the floors, the ceilings, and the masonry of the walls, in every direction. No *secret* issues could have escaped their vigilance. But not trusting to *their* eyes, I examined with my own. There were, then, no secret issues. Both doors leading from the rooms into the passage were securely locked, with the keys inside. Let us turn to the chimneys. These, although of ordinary width for some eight or ten feet above the hearths, will not admit throughout their extent, the body of a large cat. The impossibility of egress, by means already stated, being thus absolute, we are reduced to the windows. Through those of the front room no one could have escaped without notice from the crowd in the street. The murderers *must* have passed, then, through those of the back room. Now, brought, to this conclusion in so unequivocal a manner as we are, it is not our part, as reasoners, to reject it on account of apparent impossibilities. It is only for us to prove that these apparent 'impossibilities' are, in reality, not such.

"There are two windows in the chamber. One of them is unobstructed by furniture, and is wholly visible. The lower portion of the other is hidden from view by the head of the unwieldy bedstead which is thrust close up against it. The former was found securely fastened from within. It resisted the utmost force of those who endeavored to raise it. A large gimlet-hole had been pierced in its frame to the left, and a very stout nail was found fitted therein, nearly to the head. Upon examining the other window, a similar nail was seen similarly fitted in it; and a vigorous attempt to raise this sash, failed also. The police were now entirely satisfied that egress had not been in these directions. And, *therefore*, it was thought a matter of supererogation to withdraw the nails and open the windows.

"My own examination was somewhat more particular, and was so for the reason I have just given—because here it was, I knew, that all apparent impossibilities *must* be proved to be not such in reality.

"I proceeded to think thus—*a posteriori*. The murderers did escape from one of these windows. This being so, they could not have refastened the sashes from the inside, as they were found fastened;—the consideration which put a stop, through its obviousness, to the scrutiny of the police in this quarter. Yet the sashes *were* fastened. They *must*, then, have the power of fastening themselves. There was no escape from this conclusion. I stepped to the unobstructed casement, withdrew the nail with some difficulty, and attempted to raise the sash. It resisted all my efforts, as I had anticipated. A concealed spring must, I now knew, exist; and this corroboration of my idea convinced me that my premises, at least, were correct, however mysterious still appeared the circumstances attending the nails. A careful search soon brought to light the hidden spring. I pressed it, and, satisfied with the discovery, forbore to upraise the sash.

"I now replaced the nail and regarded it attentively. A person passing out through this window might have reclosed it, and the spring would have caught—buts the nail could not have been replaced. The conclusion was plain, and again narrowed in the field of my investigations. The assassins *must* have escaped through the other window. Supposing, then, the springs upon each sash to be the same, as was probable, there must be found a difference between the nails, or at least between the modes of their fixture. Getting upon the sacking of the bedstead, I looked over the head-board minutely at the second casement. Passing my hand down behind the board, I readily discovered and pressed the spring, which was, as I had supposed, identical in character with its neighbor. I now looked at the nail. It was as stout as the other, and apparently fitted in the same manner—driven in nearly up to the head.

"You will say that I was puzzled; but, if you think so, you must have misunderstood the nature of the inductions. To use a sporting phrase, I had not been once 'at fault.' The scent had never for an instant been lost. There was no flaw in any link of the chain. I had traced the secret to its ultimate result,—and that result was *the nail*. It had, I say, in every respect, the appearance of its fellow in the other window; but this fact was an absolute nullity (conclusive as it might seem to be) when compared with the consideration that here, at this point, terminated the clue. 'There *must* be something wrong,' I said, 'about the nail.' I touched it; and the head, with about a quarter of an inch of the shank, came off in my fingers. The rest of the shank was in the gimlet-hole, where it had been broken off. The fracture was an old one (for its edges were incrusted with rust), and had apparently been accomplished by the blow of a hammer, which had partially imbedded, in the top of the bottom sash, the head portion of the nail. I now carefully replaced this head portion in the indentation whence I had taken it, and the resemblance to a perfect nail was complete—the fissure was invisible. Pressing the spring, I gently raised the sash for a few inches; the head went up with it, remaining firm in its bed. I closed the window, and the semblance of the whole nail was again perfect.

"The riddle, so far, was now unriddled. The assassin had escaped through the window which looked upon the bed. Dropping of its own accord upon his exit (or perhaps purposely closed), it had become fastened by the spring; and it was the retention of this spring which had been mistaken by the police for that of the nail,—further inquiry being thus considered unnecessary.

"The next question is that of the mode of descent. Upon this point I had been satisfied in my walk with you around the building. About five feet and a half from the casement in question there runs a lightning-rod. From this rod it would have been impossible for any one to reach the window itself, to say nothing of entering it. I observed, however, that the shutters of the fourth story were of a peculiar kind called by Parisian carpenters *ferrades*—a kind rarely employed at the present day, but frequently seen upon very old mansions at Lyons and Bordeaux. They are in the form of an ordinary door (a single, not a folding door), except that the upper half is latticed or worked in open trellis—thus affording an excellent hold for the hands. In the present instance these shutters are fully three feet and a half broad. When we saw them from the rear of the house, they were both about half open—that is to say, they stood off at right angles from the wall. It is probable that the police, as well as myself, examined the back of the tenement; but, if so, in looking at these *ferrades* in the line of their breadth (as they must have done), they did not perceive this great breadth itself, or, at all events, failed to take it into due consideration. In fact, having once satisfied themselves that no egress could have been made in this quarter, they would naturally bestow here a very cursory examination. It was clear to me, however, that the shutter belonging to the window at the head of the bed, would, if swung fully back to the wall, reach to within two feet of the lightning-rod. It was also evident that, by exertion of a very unusual degree of activity and courage, an entrance into the window, from the rod, might have been thus effected.—By reaching to the distance of two feet and a half (we now suppose the shutter open to its whole extent) a robber might have taken a firm grasp upon the trellis-work. Letting go, then, his hold upon the rod, placing his feet securely against the wall, and springing boldly from it, he might have swung the shutter so as to close it, and, if we imagine the window open at the time, might even have swung himself into the room.

"I wish you to bear especially in mind that I have spoken of a *very* unusual degree of activity as requisite to success in so hazardous and so difficult a feat. It is my design to show you, first, that the thing might possibly have been accomplished:—but, secondly and *chiefly*, I wish to impress upon your understanding the *very extraordinary*—the almost preternatural character of that agility which could have accomplished it.

"You will say, no doubt, using the language of the law, that 'to make out my case' I should rather undervalue, than insist upon a full estimation of the activity required in this matter. This may be the practice in law, but it is not the usage of reason. My ultimate object is only the truth. My immediate purpose is to lead you to place in juxtaposition that very unusual activity of which I have just spoken, with that *very peculiar* shrill (or harsh) and *unequal* voice, about whose nationality no two persons could be found to agree, and in whose utterance no syllabification could be detected."

At these words a vague and half-formed conception of the meaning of Dupin flitted over my mind. I seemed to be upon the verge of comprehension, without power to comprehend—as men, at times, find themselves upon the brink of remembrance, without being able, in the end, to remember. My friend went on with his discourse.

"You will see," he said, "that I have shifted the question from the mode of egress to that of ingress. It was my design to suggest that both were effected in the same manner, at the same point. Let us now revert to the interior of the room. Let us survey the appearances here. The drawers of the bureau, it is said, had been rifled, although many articles of apparel still remained within them. The conclusion here is absurd. It is a mere guess—a very silly one—and no more. How are we to know that the articles found in the drawers were not all these drawers had originally contained? Madame L'Espanaye and her daughter lived an exceedingly retired life—saw no company—seldom went out—had little use for numerous changes of habiliment. Those found were at least of as good quality as any likely to be possessed by these ladies. If a thief had taken any, why did he not take the best—why did he not take all? In a word, why did he abandon four thousand francs in gold to encumber himself with a bundle of linen? The gold *was* abandoned. Nearly the whole sum mentioned by Monsieur Mignaud, the banker, was discovered, in bags, upon the floor. I wish you, therefore, to discard from your thoughts the blundering idea of *motive*, engendered in the brains of the police by that portion of the evidence which speaks of money delivered at the door of the house. Coincidences ten times as remarkable as this (the delivery of the money, and murder committed within three days upon the party receiving it), happen to all of us every hour of our lives, without attracting even momentary notice. Coincidences, in general, are great stumbling-blocks in the way of that class of thinkers who have been educated to know nothing of the theory of probabilities—that theory to which the most glorious objects of human research are indebted for the most glorious of illustration. In the present instance, had the gold been gone, the fact of its delivery three days before would have formed something more than a coincidence. It would have been corroborative of this idea of motive. But, under the real circumstances of the case, if we are to suppose gold the motive of this outrage, we must also imagine the perpetrator so vacillating an idiot as to have abandoned his gold and his motive together.

"Keeping now steadily in mind the points to which I have drawn your attention— that peculiar voice, that unusual agility, and that startling absence of motive in a murder so singularly atrocious as this—let us glance at the butchery itself. Here is a woman strangled to death by manual strength, and thrust up a chimney, head downward. Ordinary assassins employ no such modes of murder as this. Least of all, do they thus dispose of the murdered. In the manner of thrusting the corpse up the chimney, you will admit that there was something *excessively outré*—something altogether irreconcilable with our common notions of human action, even when we suppose the actors the most depraved of men. Think, too, how great must have been that strength which could have thrust the body *up* such an aperture so forcibly that the united vigor of several persons was found barely sufficient to drag it *down*!

"Turn, now, to other indications of the employment of a vigor most marvelous. On the hearth were thick tresses—very thick tresses—of gray human hair. These had been torn out by the roots. You are aware of the great force in tearing thus from the head even twenty or thirty hairs together. You saw the locks in question as well as myself. Their roots (a hideous sight!) were clotted with fragments of the flesh of the scalp—sure token of the prodigious power which had been exerted in uprooting perhaps half a million of hairs at a time. The throat of the old lady was not merely cut, but the head absolutely severed from the body: the instrument was a mere razor. I wish you also to look at the brutal ferocity of these deeds. Of the bruises upon the body of Madame L'Espanaye I do not speak. Monsieur Dumas, and his worthy coadjutor Monsieur Etienne, have pronounced that they were inflicted by some obtuse instrument; and so far these gentlemen are very correct. The instrument was clearly the stone pavement in the yard, upon which the victim had fallen from the window which looked in upon the bed. This idea, however simple it may now seem, escaped the police for the same reason that the breadth of the shutters escaped them—because, by the affair of the nails, their perceptions had been hermetically sealed against the possibility of the windows having ever been opened at all.

"If now, in addition to all these things, you have properly reflected upon the odd disorder of the chamber, we have gone so far as to combine the ideas of an agility astounding, a strength superhuman, a ferocity brutal, a butchery without motive, a *grotesquerie* in horror absolutely alien from humanity, and a voice foreign in tone to the ears of men of many nations, and devoid of all distinct or intelligible syllabification. What result, then, has ensued? What impression have I made upon your fancy?"

I felt a creeping of the flesh as Dupin asked me the question. "A madman," I said, "has done this deed—some raving maniac, escaped from a neighboring *Maison de Santé*."

"In some respects," he replied, "your idea is not irrelevant. But the voices of madmen, even in their wildest paroxysms, are never found to tally with that peculiar voice heard upon the stairs. Madmen are of some nation, and their language, however incoherent in its words, has always the coherence of syllabification. Besides, the hair of a madman is not such as I now hold in my hand. I disentangled this little tuft from the rigidly clutched fingers of Madame L'Espanaye. Tell me what you can make of it."

"Dupin!" I said, completely unnerved; "this hair is most unusual—this is no *human* hair."

"I have not asserted that it is," said he; "but, before we decide this point, I wish you to glance at the little sketch I have here traced upon this paper. It is a *facsimile* drawing of what has been described in one portion of the testimony as 'dark bruises, and deep indentations of finger-nails,' upon the throat of Mademoiselle L'Espanaye, and in another (by Messrs Dumas and Etienne), as a 'series of livid spots, evidently the impression of fingers.'

"You will perceive," continued my friend, spreading out the paper upon the table before us, "that this drawing gives the idea of a firm and fixed hold. There is no *slipping* apparent. Each finger has retained—

possibly until the death of the victim—the fearful grasp by which it originally imbedded itself. Attempt, now, to place all your fingers, at the same time, in the respective impressions as you see them."

I made the attempt in vain.

"We are possibly not giving this matter a fair trial," he said. "The paper is spread out upon a plane surface; but the human throat is cylindrical. Here is a billet of wood, the circumference of which is about that of the throat. Wrap the drawing around it, and try the experiment again."

I did so; but the difficulty was even more obvious than before.

"This," I said, "is the mark of no human hand."

"Read now," replied Dupin, "this passage from Cuvier."

It was a minute anatomical and generally descriptive account of the large fulvous Ourang-Outang of the East Indian Islands. The gigantic stature, the prodigious strength and activity, the wild ferocity, and the imitative propensities of these mammalia are sufficiently well known to all. I understood the full horrors of the murder at once.

"The description of the digits," said I, as I made an end of reading, "is in exact accordance with this drawing. I see that no animal but an Ourang-Outang, of the species here mentioned, could have impressed the indentations as you have traced them. This tuft of tawny hair, too, is identical with that of the beast of Cuvier. But I cannot possibly comprehend the particulars of this frightful mystery. Besides, there were two voices heard in contention, and one of them was unquestionably the voice of a Frenchman."

"True; and you will remember an expression attributed almost unanimously, by the evidence, to this voice,—the expression, '*mon Dieu!*' This, under the circumstances, has been justly characterized by one of the witnesses (Montani, the confectioner), as an expression of remonstrance or expostulation. Upon these two words, therefore, I have mainly built my hopes of a full solution of the riddle. A Frenchman was cognizant of the murder. It is possible—indeed it is far more than probable—that he was innocent of all participation in the bloody transactions which took place. The Ourang-Outang may have escaped from him. He may have traced it to the chamber; but, under the agitating circumstances which ensued, he could never have recaptured it. It is still at large. I will not pursue these guesses—for I have no right to call them more—since the shades of reflection upon which they are based are scarcely of sufficient depth to be appreciable by my own intellect, and since I could not pretend to make them intelligible to the understanding of another. We will call them guesses then, and speak of them as such. If the Frenchman in question is indeed, as I suppose, innocent of this atrocity, this advertisement, which I left last night, upon our return home, at the office of *Le Monde* (a paper devoted to the shipping interest, and much sought by sailors), will bring him to our residence."

He handed me a paper, and I read thus:

> CAUGHT.—In the Bois de Boulogne, early in the morning of the — inst. [the morning of the murder], a very large, tawny Ourang-Outang of the Bornese species. The owner (who is ascertained to be a sailor, belonging to a Maltese vessel) may have the animal again, upon identifying it satisfactorily and paying a few charges arising from its capture and keeping. Call at No. —, Rue ——, Faubourg Saint-Germain —— au troisième.

"How was it possible," I asked, "that you should know the man to be a sailor, and belonging to a Maltese vessel?"

"I do *not* know it," said Dupin. "I am not *sure* of it. Here, however, is a small piece of ribbon, which from its form, and from its greasy appearance, has evidently been used in tying the hair in one of those long queues of which sailors are so fond. Moreover, this knot is one which few besides sailors can tie, and is peculiar to the Maltese. I picked the ribbon up at the foot of the lightning-rod. It could not have belonged to either of the deceased. Now if, after all, I am wrong in my deduction from this ribbon. that the Frenchman was a sailor belonging to a Maltese vessel, still I can have done no harm in saying what I did in the advertisement. If I am in error, he will merely suppose that I have been misled by some circumstance into which he will not take the trouble to inquire. But if I am right, a great point is gained. Cognizant although innocent of the murder, the Frenchman will naturally hesitate about replying to the advertisement—about demanding the Ourang-Outang. He will reason thus:—'I am innocent; I am poor; my Ourang-Outang is of great value—to one in my circumstances a fortune of itself—why should I lose it through idle apprehensions of danger? Here it is, within my grasp. It was found in the Bois de Boulogne—at a vast distance from the scene of that butchery. How can it ever be suspected that a brute beast should have done the deed? The police are at fault—they have failed to procure the slightest clue. Should they even trace the animal, it would be impossible to prove me cognizant of the murder, or to implicate me in guilt on account of that cognizance. Above all, *I am known*. The advertiser designates me as the possessor of the beast. I am not sure to what limit his knowledge may extend. Should I avoid claiming a property of so great value, which it is known that I possess, I will render the animal, at least, liable to suspicion. It is not my policy to attract attention either to myself or to the beast. I will answer the advertisement, get the Ourang-Outang, and keep it close until this matter has blown over.'"

At this moment we heard a step upon the stairs.

"Be ready," said Dupin, "with your pistols, but neither use them nor show them until at a signal from myself."

The front door of the house had been left open, and the visitor had entered, without ringing, and advanced several steps upon the staircase. Now, however, he seemed to hesitate. Presently we heard him descending. Dupin was moving quickly to the door, when we again heard him coming up. He did not turn back a second time, but stepped up with decision and rapped at the door of our chamber.

"Come in," said Dupin, in a cheerful and hearty tone.

A man entered. He was a sailor, evidently,—a tall, stout, and muscular-looking person, with a certain daredevil expression of countenance, not altogether unprepossessing. His face, greatly sunburnt, was more than half hidden by whisker and *mustachio*. He had with him a huge oaken cudgel, but appeared to be otherwise unarmed. He bowed awkwardly, and bade us "good evening," in French accents, which, although somewhat Neufchatelish, were still sufficiently indicative of a Parisian origin.

"Sit down, my friend," said Dupin. "I suppose you have called about the Ourang-Outang. Upon my word, I almost envy you the possession of him; a remarkably fine, and no doubt a very valuable animal. How old do you suppose him to be?"

The sailor drew a long breath, with the air of a man relieved of some intolerable burthen, and then replied, in an assured tone:

"I have no way of telling—but he can't be more than four or five years old. Have you got him here?"

"Oh no; we had no conveniences for keeping him here. He is at a livery stable in the Rue Dubourg, just by. You can get him in the morning. Of course you are prepared to identify the property?"

"To be sure I am, sir."

"I shall be sorry to part with him," said Dupin.

"I don't mean that you should be at all this trouble for nothing, sir," said the man. "Couldn't expect it. Am very willing to pay a reward for the finding of the animal—that is to say, anything in reason."

"Well," replied my friend, "that is all very fair, to be sure. Let me think!—what should I have? Oh! I will tell you. My reward shall be this. You shall give me all the information in your power about these murders in the Rue Morgue."

Dupin said the last words in a very low tone, and very quietly. Just as quietly, too, he walked toward the door, locked it, and put the key in his pocket. He then drew a pistol from his bosom and placed it, without the least flurry, upon the table.

The sailor's face flushed up as if he were struggling with suffocation. He started to his feet and grasped his cudgel; but the next moment he fell back into his seat, trembling violently, and with the countenance of death itself. He spoke not a word. I pitied him from the bottom of my heart.

"My friend," said Dupin, in a kind tone, "you are alarming yourself unnecessarily—you are indeed. We mean you no harm whatever. I pledge you the honor of a gentleman, and of a Frenchman, that we intend you no injury. I perfectly well know that you are innocent of the atrocities in the Rue Morgue. It will not do, however, to deny that you are in some measure implicated in them. From what I have already said, you must know that I have had means of information about this matter—means of which you could never have dreamed. Now the thing stands thus. You have done nothing which you could have avoided—nothing, certainly, which renders you culpable. You were not even guilty of robbery, when you might have robbed with impunity. You have nothing to conceal. You have no reason for concealment. On the other hand, you are bound by every principle of honor to confess all you know. An innocent man is now imprisoned, charged with that crime of which you can point out the perpetrator."

The sailor had recovered his presence of mind, in a great measure, while Dupin uttered these words; but his original boldness of bearing was all gone.

"So help me God," said he, after a brief pause, "I will tell you all I know about this affair;—but I do not expect you to believe one half I say—I would be a fool indeed if I did. Still, I am innocent, and I will make a clean breast if I die for it."

What he stated was, in substance, this. He had lately made a voyage to the Indian Archipelago. A party, of which he formed one, landed at Borneo, and passed into the interior on an excursion of pleasure. Himself and a companion had captured the Ourang-Outang. This companion dying, the animal fell into his own exclusive possession. After great trouble, occasioned by the intractable ferocity of his captive during the home voyage, he at length succeeded in lodging it safely at his own residence in Paris, where, not to attract toward himself the unpleasant curiosity of his neighbors, he kept it carefully secluded, until such time as it should recover from a wound in the foot, received from a splinter on board ship. His ultimate design was to sell it.

Returning home from some sailors' frolic on the night, or rather in the morning of the murder, he found the beast occupying his own bedroom, into which it had broken from a closet adjoining, where it had been, as was thought, securely confined. Razor in hand, and fully lathered, it was sitting before a looking-glass, attempting the operation of shaving, in which it had no doubt previously watched its master through the keyhole of the closet. Terrified at the sight of so dangerous a weapon in the possession of an animal so ferocious, and so well able to use it, the man, for some moments, was at a loss what to do. He had been accustomed, however, to quiet the creature, even in its fiercest moods, by the use of a whip, and to this he now resorted. Upon sight of it, the Ourang-Outang sprang at once through the door of the chamber, down the stairs, and thence, through a window, unfortunately open, into the street.

The Frenchman followed in despair; the ape, razor still in hand, occasionally stopping to look back and gesticulate at its pursuer, until the latter had nearly come up with it. It then again made off. In this manner the chase continued for a long time. The streets were profoundly quiet, as it was nearly three o'clock in the morning. In passing down an alley in the rear of the Rue Morgue, the fugitive's attention was arrested by a light gleaming from the open window of Madame L'Espanaye's chamber, in the fourth story of her house. Rushing to the building, it perceived the lightning-rod, clambered up with inconceivable agility, grasped the shutter, which was thrown fully back against the wall, and, by its means, swung itself directly upon the head-board of the bed. The whole feat did not occupy a minute. The shutter was kicked open again by the Ourang-Outang as it entered the room.

The sailor, in the meantime, was both rejoiced and perplexed. He had strong hopes of now capturing the brute, as it could scarcely escape from the trap into which it had ventured, except by the rod, where it might be intercepted as it came down. On the other hand, there was much cause for anxiety as to what it might do in the house. This latter reflection urged the man still to follow the fugitive. A lightning-rod is ascended without difficulty, especially by a sailor; but, when he had arrived as high as the window, which lay far to his left, his career was stopped; the most that he could accomplish was to reach over so as to obtain a glimpse of the interior of the room. At this glimpse he nearly fell from his hold through excess of horror. Now it was that those hideous shrieks arose upon the night, which had startled from slumber the inmates of the Rue Morgue. Madame L'Espanaye and her daughter, habited in their night clothes, had apparently been arranging some papers in the iron chest already mentioned, which had been wheeled into the middle of the room. It was open, and its contents lay beside it on the floor. The victims must have been sitting with their backs toward the window; and, from the time elapsing between the ingress of the beast and the screams, it seems probable that it was not immediately perceived. The flapping-to of the shutter would naturally have been attributed to the wind.

As the sailor looked in, the gigantic animal had seized Madame L'Espanaye by the hair (which was loose, as she had been combing it), and was flourishing the razor about her face, in imitation of the motions of a barber. The daughter lay prostrate and motionless; she had swooned. The screams and struggles of the old lady (during which the hair was torn from her head) had the effect of changing the probably pacific purposes of the Ourang-Outang into those of wrath. With one determined sweep of its muscular arm it nearly severed her head from her body. The sight of blood inflamed its anger into frenzy. Gnashing its teeth, and flashing fire from its eyes, it flew upon the body of the girl, and imbedded its fearful talons in her throat, retaining its grasp until she expired. Its wandering and wild glances fell at this moment upon the head of the bed, over which the face of its master, rigid with horror, was just discernible. The fury of the beast, who no doubt bore still in mind the dreaded whip, was instantly converted into fear. Conscious of having deserved punishment, it seemed desirous of concealing its bloody deeds, and skipped about the chamber in an agony of nervous agitation; throwing down and breaking the furniture as it moved, and dragging the bed from the bedstead. In conclusion, it seized first the corpse of the daughter, and thrust it up the chimney, as it was found; then that of the old lady, which it immediately hurled through the window headlong.

As the ape approached the casement with its mutilated burthen, the sailor shrank aghast to the rod, and, rather gliding than clambering down it, hurried at once home—dreading the consequences of the butchery and gladly abandoning, in his terror, all solicitude about the fate of the Ourang-Outang. The words heard by the party upon the staircase were the Frenchman's exclamations of horror and affright, commingled with the fiendish jabberings of the brute.

I have scarcely anything to add. The Ourang-Outang must have escaped from the chamber by the rod, just before the breaking of the door. It must have closed the window as it passed through it. It was subsequently caught by the owner himself, who obtained for it a very large sum at the *Jardin des Plantes*. Le Bon was instantly released, upon our narration of the circumstances (with some comments from Dupin) at the bureau of the Prefect of Police. This functionary, however well disposed to my friend, could not altogether conceal his chagrin at the turn which affairs had taken, and was fain to indulge in a sarcasm or two, about the propriety of every person minding his own business.

"Let him talk," said Dupin, who had not thought it necessary to reply. "Let him discourse; it will ease his conscience. I am satisfied with having defeated him in his own castle. Nevertheless, that he failed in the solution of this mystery is by no means that matter for wonder which he supposes it; for in truth, our friend the Prefect is somewhat too cunning to be profound. In his wisdom is no stamen. It is all head and no body, like the pictures of the Goddess Laverna,—or, at best, all head and shoulders, like a codfish. But he is a good creature after all. I like him especially for one master-stroke of cant, by which he has attained his reputation for ingenuity. I mean the way he was '*de nier ce qui est, et d' expliquer ce qui n'est pas.*'"[1]

1 Rousseau, *Nouvelle Héloïse*.

THE MYSTERY OF MARIE RÔGET

A Sequel To "The Murders In The Rue Morgue"[1]

Es giebt eine Reihe idealischer Begebenheiten, die der Wirklichkeit parallel läuft. Selten fallen sie zusammen. Menschen und Zufälle modificiren gewöhnlich die idealische Begebenheit, so dass sie unvollkommen erscheint, und ihre Folgen gleichfalls unvollkommen sind. So bei der Reformation; statt des Protestantismus kam das Lutherthum hervor.

There are ideal series of events which run parallel with the real ones. They rarely coincide. Men and circumstances generally modify the ideal train of events, so that it seems imperfect,

1 Upon the original publication of *Marie Rogêt*, the footnotes now appended were considered unnecessary; but the lapse of several years since the tragedy upon which the tale is based, renders it expedient to give them, and also to say a few words in explanation of the general design. A young girl, Mary Cecilia Rogers, was murdered in the vicinity of New York; and although her death occasioned an intense and long-enduring excitement, the mystery attending it had remained unsolved at the period when the present paper was written and published (November, 1842). Herein, under pretence of relating the fate of a Parisian *grisette*, the author has followed, in minute detail, the essential, while merely paralleling the inessential, facts of the real murder of Mary Rogers. Thus all argument upon the fiction is applicable to the truth: and the investigation of the truth was the object.

The Mystery of Marie Rogêt was composed at a distance from the scene of the atrocity, and with no other means of investigation than the newspapers afforded. Thus much escaped the writer of which he could have availed himself had he been upon the spot and visited the localities. It may not be improper to record, nevertheless, that the confessions of two persons (one of them the Madame Deluc of the narrative), made, at different periods, long subsequent to the publication, confirmed, in full, not only the general conclusion, but absolutely *all* the chief hypothetical details by which that conclusion was attained.

> *and its consequences are equally imperfect. Thus with the Reformation; instead of Protestantism came Lutheranism.*
>
> Novalis, *Moral Ansichten*

THERE ARE FEW persons, even among the calmest thinkers, who have not occasionally been startled into a vague yet thrilling half-credence in the supernatural, by coincidences of so seemingly marvelous a character that, as mere coincidences, the intellect has been unable to receive them. Such sentiments—for the half-credences of which I speak have never the full force of thought—such sentiments are seldom thoroughly stifled unless by reference to the doctrine of chance, or, as it is technically termed, the Calculus of Probabilities. Now this Calculus is, in its essence, purely mathematical; and thus we have the anomaly of the most rigidly exact in science applied to the shadow and spirituality of the most intangible in speculation.

The extraordinary details which I am now called upon to make public, will be found to form, as regards sequence of time, the primary branch of a series of scarcely intelligible coincidences, whose secondary or concluding branch will be recognized by all readers in the late murder of Mary Cecilia Rogers, at New York.

When, in an article entitled, *The Murders in the Rue Morgue*, I endeavored, about a year ago, to depict some very remarkable features in the mental character of my friend, the Chevalier C. Auguste Dupin, it did not occur to me that I should ever resume the subject. This depicting of character constituted my design; and this design was thoroughly fulfilled in the wild train of circumstances brought to instance Dupin's idiosyncrasy. I might have adduced other examples, but I should have proven no more. Late events, however, in their surprising development, have startled me into some further details, which will carry with them the air of extorted confession. Hearing what I have lately heard, it would be indeed strange should I remain silent in regard to what I both heard and saw long ago.

Upon the winding up of the tragedy involved in the deaths of Madame L'Espanaye and her daughter, the Chevalier dismissed the affair at once from his attention, and relapsed into his old habits of moody reverie. Prone, at all times, to abstraction, I readily fell in with his humor; and, continuing to occupy our chambers in the Faubourg Saint-Germain, we gave the Future to the winds, and slumbered tranquilly in the Present, weaving the dull world around us into dreams.

But these dreams were not altogether uninterrupted. It may readily be supposed that the part played by my friend, in the drama at the Rue Morgue, had not failed of its impression upon the fancies of the Parisian police. With its emissaries, the name of Dupin had grown into a household word. The simple character of those inductions by which he had disentangled the mystery never having been explained even to the Prefect, or to any other individual than myself, of course it is not surprising that the affair was regarded as little less than miraculous, or that the Chevalier's analytical abilities acquired for him the credit of intuition. His frankness would have led him to disabuse every inquirer of such prejudice; but his indolent humor forbade all further agitation of a topic whose interest to himself had long ceased. It thus happened that he found himself the cynosure of the political eyes; and the cases were not few in which attempt was made to engage his services at the Prefecture. One of the most remarkable instances was that of the murder of a young girl named Marie Rogêt.

This event occurred about two years after the atrocity in the Rue Morgue. Marie, whose Christian and family name will at once arrest attention from their resemblance to those of the unfortunate "cigar-girl," was the only daughter of the widow Estelle Rogêt. The father had died during the child's infancy, and from the period of his death, until within eighteen months before the assassination which forms the subject of our narrative, the mother and daughter had dwelt together in the Rue Pavée Sainte-Andrée;[1] Madame there keeping a pension, assisted by Marie. Affairs went on thus until the latter had attained her twenty-second year, when her great beauty attracted the notice of a perfumer, who occupied one of the shops in the basement of the Palais-Royal, and whose custom lay chiefly among the desperate adventurers infesting that neighborhood. Monsieur Le Blanc[2] was not unaware of the advantages to be derived from the attendance of the fair Marie in his perfumery; and his liberal proposals were accepted eagerly by the girl, although with somewhat more of hesitation by Madame.

1 Nassau Street.
2 Anderson.

The anticipations of the shopkeeper were realized, and his rooms soon became notorious through the charms of the sprightly *grisette*. She had been in his employ about a year, when her admirers were thrown into confusion by her sudden disappearance from the shop. Monsieur Le Blanc was unable to account for her absence, and Madame Rogêt was distracted with anxiety and terror. The public papers immediately took up the theme, and the police were upon the point of making serious investigations, when, one morning, after a lapse of a week, Marie, in good health, but with a somewhat saddened air, made her reappearance at her usual counter in the perfumery. All inquiry, except that of a private character, was, of course, immediately hushed. Monsieur Le Blanc professed total ignorance, as before. Marie, with Madame, replied to all questions, that the last week had been spent at the house of a relation in the country. Thus the affair died away, and was generally forgotten; for the girl, ostensibly to relieve herself from the impertinence of curiosity, soon bade a final adieu to the perfumer, and sought the shelter of her mother's residence in the Rue Pavée Sainte-Andrée.

It was about five months after this return home, that her friends were alarmed by her sudden disappearance for the second time. Three days elapsed, and nothing was heard of her. On the fourth her corpse was found floating in the Seine,[1] near the shore which is opposite the Quartier of the Rue Sainte-Andrée, and at a point not very far distant from the secluded neighborhood of the Barrière du Roule.[2]

The atrocity of this murder (for it was at once evident that murder had been committed), the youth and beauty of the victim, and, above all, her previous notoriety, conspired to produce intense excitement in the minds of the sensitive Parisians. I can call to mind no similar occurrence producing so general and so intense an effect. For several weeks, in the discussion of this one absorbing theme, even the momentous political topics of the day were forgotten. The Prefect made unusual exertions; and the powers of the whole Parisian police were, of course, tasked to the utmost extent.

Upon the first discovery of the corpse, it was not supposed that the murderer would be able to elude, for more than a very brief period, the inquisition which was immediately set on foot. It was not until the expi-

1 The Hudson.
2 Weehawken.

ration of a week that it was deemed necessary to offer a reward; and even then this reward was limited to a thousand francs. In the meantime the investigation proceeded with vigor, if not always with judgment, and numerous individuals were examined to no purpose; while, owing to the continual absence of all clue to the mystery, the popular excitement greatly increased. At the end of the tenth day it was thought advisable to double the sum originally proposed; and, at length, the second week having elapsed without leading to any discoveries, and the prejudice which always exists in Paris against the police having given vent to itself in several serious *émeutes*, the Prefect took it upon himself to offer the sum of twenty thousand francs "for the conviction of the assassin," or, if more than one should prove to have been implicated, "for the conviction of any one of the assassins." In the proclamation setting forth this reward, a full pardon was promised to any accomplice who should come forward in evidence against his fellow; and to the whole was appended, wherever it appeared, the private placard of a committee of citizens, offering ten thousand francs, in addition to the amount proposed by the Prefecture. The entire reward thus stood at no less than thirty thousand francs, which will be regarded as an extraordinary sum when we consider the humble condition of the girl, and the great frequency, in large cities, of such atrocities as the one described.

No one doubted now that the mystery of this murder would be immediately brought to light. But although, in one or two instances, arrests were made which promised elucidation, yet nothing was elicited which could implicate the parties suspected; and they were discharged forthwith. Strange as it may appear, the third week from the discovery of the body had passed, and passed without any light being thrown upon the subject, before even a rumor of the events which had so agitated the public mind reached the ears of Dupin and myself. Engaged in researches which had absorbed our whole attention, it had been nearly a month since either of us had gone abroad, or received a visitor, or more than glanced at the leading political articles in one of the daily papers. The first intelligence of the murder was brought us by G——, in person. He called upon us early in the afternoon of the 13th of July, 18—, and remained with us until late in the night. He had been piqued by the failure of all his endeavors to ferret out the assassins. His reputation—so he said with a peculiarly Parisian air—was at stake. Even his honor was concerned. The eyes of the public were upon him; and there was really no sacrifice which he would not be willing to make for the development of the mystery. He concluded a somewhat droll speech with a compliment upon what he was pleased to term the *tact* of Dupin, and made him a direct and certainly a liberal proposition, the precise nature of which I do not feel myself at liberty to disclose, but which has no bearing upon the proper subject of my narrative.

The compliment my friend rebutted as best he could, but the proposition he accepted at once, although its advantages were altogether provisional. This point being settled, the Prefect broke forth at once into explanations of his own views, interspersing them with long comments upon the evidence; of which latter we were not yet in possession. He discoursed much and, beyond doubt, learnedly; while I hazarded an occasional suggestion as the night wore drowsily away. Dupin, sitting steadily in his accustomed arm-chair, was the embodiment of respectful attention. He wore spectacles, during the whole interview; and an occasional glance beneath their green glasses sufficed to convince me that he slept not the less soundly, because silently, throughout the seven or eight leaden-footed hours which immediately preceded the departure of the Prefect.

In the morning, I procured, at the Prefecture, a full report of all the evidence elicited, and, at the various newspaper offices, a copy of every paper in which, from first to last, had been published any decisive information in regard to this sad affair. Freed from all that was positively disproved, the mass of information stood thus:

Marie Rogêt left the residence of her mother, in the Rue Pavée Sainte-Andrée, about nine o'clock in the morning of Sunday, the 22nd June, 18—. In going out, she gave notice to a Monsieur Jacques Saint-Eustache,[1] and to him only, of her intention to spend the day with an aunt, who resided in the Rue des Drômes. The Rue des Drômes is a short and narrow but populous thoroughfare, not far from the banks of the river, and at a distance of some two miles, in the most direct course possible, from the pension of Madame Rogêt. Saint-Eustache was the accepted suitor of Marie, and lodged, as well as took his meals, at the pension. He was to have gone for his betrothed at dusk, and to have escorted her home. In the afternoon, however, it came on to rain heavily; and, supposing that she would remain at her aunt's (as she had done under similar circum-

1 Payne.

stances before), he did not think it necessary to keep his promise. As night drew on, Madame Rogêt (who was an infirm old lady, seventy years of age) was heard to express a fear "that she should never see Marie again"; but this observation attracted little attention at the time.

On Monday it was ascertained that the girl had not been to the Rue des Drômes; and when the day elapsed without tidings of her, a tardy search was instituted at several points in the city and its environs. It was not, however, until the fourth day from the period of her disappearance that anything satisfactory was ascertained respecting her. On this day (Wednesday, June the 25th) a Monsieur Beauvais,[1] who, with a friend, had been making inquiries for Marie near the Barrière du Roule, on the shore of the Seine which is opposite the Rue Pavée Sainte-André, was informed that a corpse had just been towed ashore by some fishermen, who had found it floating in the river. Upon seeing the body, Beauvais, after some hesitation, identified it as that of the perfumery-girl. His friend recognized it more promptly.

The face was suffused with dark blood, some of which issued from the mouth. No foam was seen, as in the case of the merely drowned. There was no discoloration in the cellular tissue. About the throat were bruises and impressions of fingers. The arms were bent over on the chest, and were rigid. The right hand was clenched; the left partially open. On the left wrist were two circular excoriations, apparently the effect of ropes, or of a rope in more than one volution. A part of the right wrist, also, was much chafed, as well as the back throughout its extent, but more especially at the shoulder-blades. In bringing the body to the shore the fishermen had attached to it a rope, but none of the excoriations had been effected by this. The flesh of the neck was much swollen. There were no cuts apparent, or bruises which appeared the effect of blows. A piece of lace was found tied so tightly around the neck as to be hidden from sight; it was completely buried in the flesh, and was fastened by a knot which lay just under the left ear. This alone would have sufficed to produce death. The medical testimony spoke confidently of the virtuous character of the deceased. She had been subjected, it said, to brutal violence. The corpse was in such condition when found that there could have been no difficulty in its recognition by friends.

1 Crommelin.

The dress was much torn and otherwise disordered. In the outer garment, a slip, about a foot wide, had been torn upward from the bottom hem to the waist, but not torn off. It was wound three times around the waist, and secured by a sort of hitch in the back. The dress immediately beneath the frock was of fine muslin; and from this a slip eighteen inches wide had been torn entirely out—torn very evenly and with great care. It was found around her neck, fitting loosely, and secured with a hard knot. Over this muslin slip and the slip of lace, the strings of a bonnet were attached, the bonnet being appended. The knot by which the strings of the bonnet were fastened was not a lady's but a slip or sailor's knot.

After the recognition of the corpse, it was not, as usual, taken to the Morgue (this formality being superfluous), but hastily interred not far from the spot at which it was brought ashore. Through the exertions of Beauvais, the matter was industriously hushed up, as far as possible; and several days had elapsed before any public emotion resulted. A weekly paper,[1] however, at length took up the theme; the corpse was disinterred, and a re-examination instituted; but nothing was elicited beyond what has been already noted. The clothes, however, were now submitted to the mother and friends of the deceased, and fully identified as those worn by the girl upon leaving home.

Meantime, the excitement increased hourly. Several individuals were arrested and discharged. Saint-Eustache fell especially under suspicion; and he failed, at first, to give an intelligible account of his whereabouts during the Sunday on which Marie left home. Subsequently, however, he submitted to Monsieur G——, affidavits, accounting satisfactorily for every hour of the day in question. As time passed and no discovery ensued, a thousand contradictory rumors were circulated, and journalists busied themselves in suggestions. Among these, the one which attracted the most notice, was the idea that Marie Rogêt still lived—that the corpse found in the Seine was that of some other unfortunate. It will be proper that I submit to the reader some passages which embody the suggestion alluded to. These passages are literal translations from *L'Etoile*,[2] a paper conducted, in general, with much ability.

1 The New York *Mercury*.
2 The New York *Brother Jonathan*, edited by H. Hastings Weld, Esq.

"Mademoiselle Rogêt left her mother's house on Sunday morning, June the 22nd, 18—, with the ostensible purpose of going to see her aunt, or some other connexion, in the Rue des Drômes. From that hour, nobody is proved to have seen her. There is no trace or tidings of her at all. . . . There has no person, whatever, come forward, so far, who saw her at all, on that day, after she left her mother's door. . . . Now, though we have no evidence that Marie Rogêt was in the land of the living after nine o'clock on Sunday, June the 22nd, we have proof that, up to that hour, she was alive. On Wednesday noon, at twelve, a female body was discovered afloat on the shore of the Barrière du Roule. This was, even if we presume that Marie Rogêt was thrown into the river within three hours after she left her mother's house, only three days from the time she left her home—three days to an hour. But it is folly to suppose that the murder, if murder was committed on her body, could have been consummated soon enough to have enabled her murderers to throw the body into the river before midnight. Those who are guilty of such horrid crimes choose darkness rather than light. . . . Thus we see that if the body found in the river was that of Marie Rogêt, it could only have been in the water two and a half days, or three at the outside. All experience has shown that drowned bodies, or bodies thrown into the water immediately after death by violence, require from six to ten days for sufficient decomposition to take place to bring them to the top of the water. Even where a cannon is fired over a corpse, and it rises before, at least, five or six days' immersion, it sinks again, if let alone. Now, we ask what was there in this case to cause a departure from the ordinary course of nature? . . . If the body had been kept in its mangled state on shore until Tuesday night, some trace would be found on shore of the murderers. It is a doubtful point, also, whether the body would be so soon afloat, even were it thrown in after having been dead two days. And, furthermore, it is exceedingly improbable that any villains who had committed such a murder as is here supposed, would have thrown the body in without weight to sink it, when such a precaution could have so easily been taken."

The editor here proceeds to argue that the body must have been in water "not three days merely, but, at least, five times three days," because it was so far decomposed that Beauvais had great difficulty in recognizing it. This latter point, however, was fully disproved. I continue the translation:

> "What, then, are the facts on which M. Beauvais says that he has no doubt the body was that of Marie Rogêt? He ripped up the gown sleeve, and says he found marks which satisfied him of the identity. The public generally supposed those marks to have consisted of some description of scars. He rubbed the arm and found hair upon it—something as indefinite, we think, as can readily be imagined—as little conclusive as finding an arm in the sleeve. M. Beauvais did not return that night, but sent word to Madame Rogêt, at seven o'clock, on Wednesday evening, that an investigation was still in progress respecting her daughter. If we allow that Madame Rogêt, from her age and grief, could not go over (which is allowing a great deal), there certainly must have been some one who would have thought it worth while to go over and attend the investigation, if they thought the body was that of Marie. Nobody went over. There was nothing said or heard about the matter in the Rue Pavée Sainte-Andrée, that reached even the occupants of the same building. M. Saint-Eustache, the lover and intended husband of Marie, who boarded in her mother's house, deposes that he did not hear of the discovery of the body of his intended until the next morning, when M. Beauvais came into his chamber and told him of it. For an item of news like this, it strikes us it was very coolly received."

In this way the journal endeavored to create the impression of an apathy on the part of the relatives of Marie, inconsistent with the supposition that these relatives believed the corpse to be hers. Its insinuations amount to this: that Marie, with the connivance of her friends, had absented herself from the city for reasons involving a charge against her chastity; and that these friends upon the discovery of a corpse in the Seine, somewhat resembling that of the girl, had availed themselves of the opportunity to impress the public with the belief of her death. But *L'Etoile* was again overhasty. It was distinctly proved that no apathy, such as was imagined, existed; that the old lady was exceedingly feeble, and so agitated as to be unable to attend to any duty; that Saint-Eustache, so far from receiving the news coolly, was distracted with grief, and bore himself so frantically, that M. Beauvais prevailed upon a friend and relative to take charge of him, and prevent his attending the examination at the disinterment. Moreover, although it was stated by *L'Etoile*, that the corpse was reinterred at the public expense, that an advantageous offer of private sepulture was absolutely declined by the family, and that no member of the family attended the ceremonial;—although, I say, all this was asserted by *L'Etoile* in furtherance of the impression it designed to convey—yet all this was satisfactorily disproved. In a subsequent number of the paper, an attempt was made to throw suspicion upon Beauvais himself. The editor says:

> "Now, then, a change comes over the matter. We are told that, on one occasion, while a Madame B— was at Madame Rogêt's house, M. Beauvais, who was going out, told her that a gendarme was expected there, and that she, Madame B—, must not say anything to the gendarme until he returned, but let the matter be for him. . . . In the present posture of affairs M. Beauvais appears to have the whole matter locked up in his head. A single step cannot be taken without M. Beauvais, for go which way you will, you run against him. . . . For some reason he determined that nobody shall have anything to do with the proceedings but himself, and he has elbowed the male relatives out of the way, according to their representations, in a very singular manner. He seems to have been very much averse to permitting the relatives to see the body."

By the following fact, some color was given to the suspicion thus thrown upon Beauvais. A visitor at his office, a few days prior to the girl's disappearance, and during the absence of its occupant, had observed a rose in the keyhole of the door, and the name '*Marie*' inscribed upon a slate which hung near at hand.

The general impression, so far as we were enabled to glean it from the newspapers, seemed to be, that Marie had been the victim of a gang of desperadoes—that by these she had been borne across the river, maltreated, and murdered. *Le Commerciel*,[1] however, a print of extensive

1 New York *Journal of Commerce*.

influence, was earnest in combating this popular idea. I quote a passage or two from its columns:

> "We are persuaded that pursuit has hitherto been on a false scent so far as it has been directed to the Barrière du Roule. It is impossible that a person so well known to thousands as this young woman was, should have passed three blocks without some one having seen her; and any one who saw her would have remembered it, for she interested all who knew her. It was when the streets were full of people, when she went out. . . . It is impossible that she could have gone to the Barrière du Roule, or to the Rue des Drômes, without being recognized by a dozen persons; yet no one has come forward who saw her outside her mother's door, and there is no evidence except the testimony concerning her *expressed intentions*, that she did go out at all. Her gown was torn, bound round her, and tied; and by that the body was carried as a bundle. If the murder had been committed at the Barrière du Roule, there would have been no necessity for any such arrangement. The fact that the body was found floating near the Barrière is no proof as to where it was thrown into the water. . . . A piece of one of the unfortunate girl's petticoats, two feet long and one foot wide, was torn out and tied under her chin around the back of her head, probably to prevent screams. This was done by fellows who had no pocket-handkerchiefs."

A day or two before the Prefect called upon us, however, some important information reached the police, which seemed to overthrow, at least, the chief portion of *Le Commerciel's* argument. Two small boys, sons of a Madame Deluc, while roaming among the woods near the Barrière du Roule, chanced to penetrate a close thicket, within which were three or four large stones, forming a kind of seat with a back and footstool. On the upper stone lay a white petticoat; on the second, a silk scarf. A parasol, gloves, and a pocket-handkerchief were also here found. The handkerchief bore the name 'Marie Rogêt.' Fragments of dress were discovered on the brambles around. The earth was trampled, the bushes were broken, and there was every evidence of a struggle. Between the thicket and the river, the fences were found taken down, and the ground bore evidence of some heavy burthen having been dragged along it.

A weekly paper, *Le Soleil*,[1] had the following comments upon this discovery—comments which merely echoed the sentiment of the whole Parisian press:

> "The things had all evidently been there at least three or four weeks; they were all mildewed down hard with the action of the rain, and stuck together from mildew. The grass had grown around and over some of them. The silk on the parasol was strong, but the threads of it were run together within. The upper part, where it had been doubled and folded, was all mildewed and rotten, and tore on its being opened. . . . The pieces of her frock torn out by the bushes were about three inches wide and six inches long. One part was the hem of the frock, and it had been mended; the other piece was part of the skirt, not the hem. They looked like strips torn off, and were on the thorn bush, about a foot from the ground. . . . There can be no doubt, therefore, that the spot of this appalling outrage has been discovered."

Consequent upon this discovery, new evidence appeared. Madame Deluc testified that she keeps a roadside inn not far from the bank of the river, opposite the Barrière du Roule. The neighborhood is secluded—particularly so. It is the usual Sunday resort of blackguards from the city, who cross the river in boats. About three o'clock, in the afternoon of the Sunday in question, a young girl arrived at the inn accompanied by a young man of dark complexion. The two remained here for some time. On their departure, they took the road to some thick woods in the vicinity. Madame Deluc's attention was called to the dress worn by the girl, on account of its resemblance to one worn by a deceased relative. A scarf was particularly noticed. Soon after the departure of the couple, a gang of miscreants made their appearance, behaved boisterously, ate and drank without making payment, followed in the route of the young man and girl, returned to the inn about dusk, and recrossed the river as if in great haste.

It was soon after dark, upon this same evening, that Madame Deluc,

1 Philadelphia *Saturday Evening Post*, edited by C. I. Peterson, Esq.

as well as her eldest son, heard the screams of a female in the vicinity of the inn. The screams were violent but brief. Madame D. recognized not only the scarf which was found in the thicket, but the dress which was discovered upon the corpse. An omnibus driver, Valence,[1] now also testified that he saw Marie Rogêt cross a ferry on the Seine, on the Sunday in question, in company with a young man of dark complexion. He, Valence, knew Marie, and could not be mistaken in her identity. The articles found in the thicket were fully identified by the relatives of Marie.

The items of evidence and information thus collected by myself, from the newspapers, at the suggestion of Dupin, embraced only one more point—but this was a point of seemingly vast consequence. It appears that, immediately after the discovery of the clothes as above described, the lifeless or nearly lifeless body of Saint-Eustache, Marie's betrothed, was found in the vicinity of what all now supposed the scene of the outrage. A phial labelled 'laudanum,' and emptied, was found near him. His breath gave evidence of the poison. He died without speaking. Upon his person was found a letter, briefly stating his love for Marie, with his design of self-destruction.

"I need scarcely tell you," said Dupin, as he finished the perusal of my notes, "that this is a far more intricate case than that of the Rue Morgue; from which it differs in one important respect. This is an ordinary, although an atrocious, instance of crime. There is nothing peculiarly outré about it. You will observe that, for this reason, the mystery has been considered easy, when, for this reason, it should have been considered difficult of solution. Thus, at first, it was thought unnecessary to offer a reward. The myrmidons of G—— were able at once to comprehend how and why such an atrocity might have been committed. They could picture to their imaginations a mode—many modes,—and a motive—many motives; and because it was not impossible that either of these numerous modes and motives could have been the actual one, they have taken it for granted that one of them must. But the ease with which these variable fancies were entertained, and the very plausibility which each assumed, should have been understood as indicative rather of the difficulties than of the facilities which must attend elucidation. I have therefore observed that it is by prominences above the plane of the ordinary, that reason feels her

1 Adam.

way, if at all, in her search for the true, and that the proper question in cases such as this is not so much 'what has occurred?' as 'what has occurred that has never occurred before?' In the investigations at the house of Madame L'Espanaye,[1] the agents of G—— were discouraged and confounded by that very unusualness which, to a properly regulated intellect, would have afforded the surest omen of success; while this same intellect might have been plunged in despair at the ordinary character of all that met the eye in the case of the perfumery-girl, and yet told of nothing but easy triumph to the functionaries of the Prefecture.

"In the case of Madame L'Espanaye and her daughter, there was, even at the beginning of our investigation, no doubt that murder had been committed. The idea of suicide was excluded at once. Here, too, we are freed, at the commencement, from all supposition of self-murder. The body found at the Barrière du Roule was found under such circumstances as to leave us no room for embarrassment upon this important point. But it has been suggested that the corpse discovered is not that of the Marie Rogêt for the conviction of whose assassin, or assassins, the reward is offered, and respecting whom, solely, our agreement has been arranged with the Prefect. We both know this gentleman well. It will not do to trust him too far. If, dating our inquiries from the body found, and then tracing a murderer, we yet discover this body to be that of some other individual than Marie; or if, starting from the living Marie, we find her, yet find her unassassinated—in either case we lose our labor; since it is Monsieur G—— with whom we have to deal. For our own purpose, therefore, if not for the purpose of justice, it is indispensable that our first step should be the determination of the identity of the corpse with the Marie Rogêt who is missing.

"With the public the arguments of *L'Etoile* have had weight; and that the journal itself is convinced of their importance would appear from the manner in which it commences one of its essays upon the subject.—'Several of the morning papers of the day,' it says, 'speak of the *conclusive* article in Monday's *Etoile*.' To me, this article appears conclusive of little beyond the zeal of its inditer. We should bear in mind that, in general, it is the object of our newspapers rather to create a sensation—to make a point—than to further the cause of truth. The latter end is only pursued

1 See *The Murders in the Rue Morgue.*

when it seems coincident with the former. The print which merely falls in with ordinary opinion (however well founded this opinion may be) earns for itself no credit with the mob. The mass of the people regard as profound only him who suggests *pungent contradictions* of the general idea. In ratiocination, not less than in literature, it is the epigram which is the most immediately and the most universally appreciated. In both, it is of the lowest order of merit.

"What I mean to say is, that it is the mingled epigram and melodrame of the idea, that Marie Rogêt still lives, rather than any true plausibility in this idea, which have suggested it to *L'Etoile*, and secured it a favorable reception with the public. Let us examine the heads of this journal's argument; endeavoring to avoid the incoherence with which it is originally set forth.

"The first aim of the writer is to show, from the brevity of the interval between Marie's disappearance and the finding of the floating corpse, that this corpse cannot be that of Marie. The reduction of this interval to its smallest possible dimension, becomes thus, at once, an object with the reasoner. In the rash pursuit of this object, he rushes into mere assumption at the outset. 'It is folly to suppose,' he says, 'that the murder, if murder was committed on her body, could have been consummated soon enough to have enabled her murderers to throw the body into the river before midnight.' We demand at once, and very naturally, why? Why is it folly to suppose that the murder was committed *within five minutes* after the girl's quitting her mother's house? Why is it folly to suppose that the murder was committed at any given period of the day? There have been assassinations at all hours. But, had the murder taken place at any moment between nine o'clock in the morning of Sunday and a quarter before midnight, there would still have been time enough 'to throw the body into the river before midnight.' This assumption, then, amounts precisely to this—that the murder was not committed on Sunday at all—and, if we allow *L'Etoile* to assume this, we may permit it any liberties whatever. The paragraph beginning 'It is folly to suppose that the murder, etc.,' however it appears as printed in *L'Etoile*, may be imagined to have existed actually thus in the brain of the inditer: 'It is folly to suppose that the murder, if murder was committed on the body, could have been committed soon enough to have enabled her murderers to throw the body into the river before midnight; it is folly, we say, to suppose all this, and to suppose at the same time (as we are resolved to suppose), that the body was not thrown in until after midnight'—a sentence sufficiently inconsequential in itself, but not so utterly preposterous as the one printed.

"Were it my purpose," continued Dupin, "merely to *make out a case* against this passage of *L'Etoile*'s argument, I might safely leave it where it is. It is not, however, with *L'Etoile* that we have to do, but with the truth. The sentence in question has but one meaning, as it stands; and this meaning I have fairly stated; but it is material that we go behind the mere words for an idea which these words have obviously intended, and failed to convey. It was the design of the journalists to say that at whatever period of the day or night of Sunday this murder was committed, it was improbable that the assassins would have ventured to bear the corpse to the river before midnight. And herein lies, really, the assumption of which I complain. It is assumed that the murder was committed at such a position, and under such circumstances, that the bearing it to the river became necessary. Now, the assassination might have taken place upon the river's brink, or on the river itself; and, thus, the throwing the corpse in the water might have been resorted to at any period of the day or night, as the most obvious and most immediate mode of disposal. You will understand that I suggest nothing here as probable, or as coincident with my own opinion. My design, so far, has no reference to the facts of the case. I wish merely to caution you against the whole tone of *L'Etoile*'s suggestion, by calling your attention to its ex-parte character at the outset.

"Having prescribed thus a limit to suit its own preconceived notions; having assumed that, if this were the body of Marie, it could have been in the water but a very brief time, the journal goes on to say:

> " 'All experience has shown that drowned bodies, or bodies thrown into the water immediately after death by violence, require from six to ten days for sufficient decomposition to take place to bring them to the top of the water. Even when a cannon is fired over a corpse, and it rises before at least five or six days' immersion, it sinks again if let alone.'

"These assertions have been tacitly received by every paper in Paris, with the exception of *Le Moniteur*.[1] This latter print endeavors to combat that portion of the paragraph which has reference to 'drowned bodies' only, by citing some five or six instances in which the bodies of individuals known to be drowned were found floating after the lapse of less time than is insisted upon by *L'Etoile*. But there is something excessively unphilosophical in the attempt, on the part of *Le Moniteur*, to rebut the general assertion of *L'Etoile*, by a citation of particular instances militating against that assertion. Had it been possible to adduce fifty instead of five examples of bodies found floating at the end of two or three days, these fifty examples could still have been properly regarded only as exceptions to *L'Etoile*'s rule, until such time as the rule itself should be confuted. Admitting the rule (and this *Le Moniteur* does not deny, insisting merely upon its exceptions), the argument of *L'Etoile* is suffered to remain in full force; for this argument does not pretend to involve more than a question of the probability of the body having risen to the surface in less than three days; and this probability will be in favor of *L'Etoile*'s position until the instances so childishly adduced shall be sufficient in number to establish an antagonistical rule.

"You will see at once that all argument upon this head should be urged, if at all, against the rule itself; and for this end we must examine the rationale of the rule. Now the human body, in general, is neither much lighter nor much heavier than the water of the Seine; that is to say, the specific gravity of the human body, in its natural condition, is about equal to the bulk of fresh water which it displaces. The bodies of fat and fleshy persons, with small bones, and of women generally, are lighter than those of the lean and large-boned, and of men; and the specific gravity of the water of a river is somewhat influenced by the presence of the tide from the sea. But, leaving this tide out of the question, it may be said that very few human bodies will sink at all, even in fresh water, of their own accord. Almost anyone, falling into a river, will be enabled to float, if he suffer the specific gravity of the water fairly to be adduced in comparison with his own—that is to say, if he suffer his whole person to be immersed, with as little exception as possible. The proper position for one who cannot swim, is the upright position of the walker on land, with the head thrown fully back, and immersed;

1 The New York *Commercial Advertiser*, edited by Col. Stone.

the mouth and nostrils alone remaining above the surface. Thus circumstanced, we shall find that we float without difficulty and without exertion. It is evident, however, that the gravities of the body, and of the bulk of water displaced, are very nicely balanced, and that a trifle will cause either to preponderate. An arm, for instance, uplifted from the water, and thus deprived of its support, is an additional weight sufficient to immerse the whole head, while the accidental aid of the smallest piece of timber will enable us to elevate the head so as to look about. Now, in the struggles of one unused to swimming, the arms are invariably thrown upward, while an attempt is made to keep the head in its usual perpendicular position. The result is the immersion of the mouth and nostrils, and the inception, during efforts to breathe while beneath the surface, of water into the lungs. Much is also received into the stomach, and the whole body becomes heavier by the difference between the weight of the air originally distending these cavities, and that of the fluid which now fills them. This difference is sufficient to cause the body to sink, as a general rule; but is insufficient in the cases of individuals with small bones and an abnormal quantity of flaccid or fatty matter. Such individuals float even after drowning.

"The corpse, being supposed at the bottom of the river, will there remain until, by some means, its specific gravity again becomes less than that of the bulk of water which it displaces. This effect is brought about by decomposition, or otherwise. The result of decomposition is the generation of gas, distending the cellular tissues and all the cavities, and giving the puffed appearance which is so horrible. When this distention has so far progressed that the bulk of the corpse is materially increased without a corresponding increase of mass or weight, its specific gravity becomes less than that of the water displaced, and it forthwith makes its appearance at the surface. But decomposition is modified by innumerable circumstances—is hastened or retarded by innumerable agencies; for example, by the heat or cold of the season, by the mineral impregnation or purity of the water, by its depth or shallowness, by its currency or stagnation, by the temperament of the body, by its infection or freedom from disease before death. Thus it is evident that we can assign no period, with anything like accuracy, at which the corpse shall rise through decomposition. Under certain conditions this result would be brought about within an hour; under others it might not take place at all. There are chemical infusions by which the animal frame can be preserved for ever from corruption; the bichloride of mercury is one. But, apart from decomposition, there may be, and very usually is, a generation of gas within the stomach, from the acetous fermentation of vegetable matter (or within other cavities from other causes), sufficient to induce a distension which will bring the body to the surface. The effect produced by the firing of a cannon is that of simple vibration. This may either loosen the corpse from the soft mud or ooze in which it is embedded, thus permitting it to rise when other agencies have already prepared it for so doing; or it may overcome the tenacity of some putrescent portions of the cellular tissues, allowing the cavities to distend under the influence of the gas.

"Having thus before us the whole philosophy of this subject, we can easily test by it the assertions of *L'Etoile*. 'All experience shows,' says this paper, 'that drowned bodies, or bodies thrown into the water immediately after death by violence, require from six to ten days for sufficient decomposition to take place to bring them to the top of the water. Even when a cannon is fired over a corpse, and it rises before at least five or six days' immersion, it sinks again if let alone.'

"The whole of this paragraph must now appear a tissue of inconsequence and incoherence. All experience does not show that 'drowned bodies' require from six to ten days for sufficient decomposition to take place to bring them to the surface. Both science and experience show that the period of their rising is, and necessarily must be, indeterminate. If, moreover, a body has risen to the surface through firing of cannon, it will not 'sink again if let alone,' until decomposition has so far progressed as to permit the escape of the generated gas. But I wish to call your attention to the distinction which is made between 'drowned bodies,' and 'bodies thrown into water immediately after death by violence.' Although the writer admits the distinction, he yet includes them all in the same category. I have shown how it is that the body of a drowning man becomes specifically heavier than its bulk of water, and that he would not sink at all, except for the struggle by which he elevates his arms above the surface, and his gasps for breath while beneath the surface—gasps which supply by water the place of the original air in the lungs. But these struggles and these gasps would not occur in the body 'thrown into the water immediately after death by violence.' Thus, in the latter instance, the body, as a general rule, would not sink at all—a fact of which *L'Etoile* is evidently ignorant. When decomposition had proceeded to a very great extent—when the flesh had in a great measure left the bones—then, indeed, but not till then, should we lose sight of the corpse.

"And now what are we to make of the argument, that the body found could not be that of Marie Rogêt, because, three days only having elapsed, this body was found floating? If drowned, being a woman, she might never have sunk; or, having sunk, might have reappeared in twenty-four hours or less. But no one supposes her to have been drowned, and, dying before being thrown into the river, she might have been found floating at any period afterward whatever.

" 'But,' says *L'Etoile*, 'if the body had been kept in its mangled state on shore until Tuesday night, some trace would be found on shore of the murderers.' Here it is at first difficult to perceive the intention of the reasoner. He means to anticipate what he imagines would be an objection to his theory—viz., that the body was kept on shore two days, suffering rapid decomposition—more rapid than if immersed in water. He supposes that, had this been the case, it might have appeared at the surface on the Wednesday, and thinks that only under such circumstances it could have so appeared. He is accordingly in haste to show that it was not kept on shore; for, if so, 'some trace would be found on shore of the murderers.' I presume you smile at the sequitur. You cannot be made to see how the mere duration of the corpse on the shore could operate to multiply traces of the assassins. Nor can I.

" 'And furthermore it is exceedingly improbable,' continues our journal, 'that any villains who had committed such a murder as is here supposed, would have thrown the body in without weight to sink it, when such a precaution could have so easily been taken.' Observe, here, the laughable confusion of thought! No one—not even *L'Etoile*—disputes the murder committed *on the body found*. The marks of violence are too obvious. It is our reasoner's object merely to show that this body is not Marie's. He wishes to prove that Marie is not assassinated—not that the corpse was not. Yet his observation proves only the latter point. Here is a corpse without weight attached. Murderers, casting it in, would not have failed to attach a weight. Therefore it was not thrown in by murderers. This is all which is proved, if anything is. The question of identity is not even approached, and L'Etoile has been at great pains merely to gainsay now what it has admitted only a moment before. 'We are perfectly convinced,' it says, 'that the body found was that of a murdered female.'

"Nor is this the sole instance, even in this division of his subject, where our reasoner unwittingly reasons against himself. His evident object, I have already said, is to reduce, as much as possible, the interval between Marie's disappearance and the finding of the corpse. Yet we find him urging the point that no person saw the girl from the moment of her leaving her mother's house. 'We have no evidence,' he says, 'that Marie Rogêt was in the land of the living after nine o'clock on Sunday, June the 22nd.' As his argument is obviously an *ex parte* one, he should, at least, have left this matter out of sight; for had anyone been known to see Marie, say on Monday, or on Tuesday, the interval in question would have been much reduced, and, by his own ratiocination, the probability much diminished of the corpse being that of the grisette. It is, nevertheless, amusing to observe that *L'Etoile* insists upon its point in the full belief of its furthering its general argument.

"Re-peruse now that portion of this argument which has reference to the identification of the corpse by Beauvais. In regard to the hair upon the arm, *L'Etoile* has been obviously disingenuous. M. Beauvais, not being an idiot, could never have urged in identification of the corpse, simply hair upon its arm. No arm is without hair. The generality of the expression of *L'Etoile* is a mere perversion of the witness's phraseology. He must have spoken of some peculiarity in this hair. It must have been a peculiarity of color, of quantity, of length, or of situation.

" 'Her foot,' says the journal, 'was small—so are thousands of feet. Her garter is no proof whatever—nor is her shoe—for shoes and garters are sold in packages. The same may be said of the flowers in her hat. One thing upon which M. Beauvais strongly insists is, that the clasp on the garter found had been set back to take it in. This amounts to nothing; for most women find it proper to take a pair of garters home and fit them to the size of the limbs they are to encircle, rather than to try them in the store where they purchase.' Here it is difficult to suppose the reasoner in earnest. Had M. Beauvais, in his search for the body of Marie, discovered a corpse corresponding in general size and appearance to the missing girl, he would have been warranted (without reference to the question of habiliment at all) in forming an opinion that his search had been successful. If, in addition to the point of general size and contour, he had found upon the arm a peculiar hairy appearance which he had observed upon the living Marie, his opinion might have been justly strengthened; and the increase of positiveness might well have been in the ratio of the peculiarity, or unusualness of the hairy mark. If, the feet of Marie being small, those of the corpse were also small, the increase of probability that the body was that of Marie would not be an increase in a ratio merely arithmetical, but in one highly geometrical, or accumulative. Add to all this shoes such as she had been known to wear upon the day of her disappearance, and, although these shoes may be 'sold in packages,' you so far augment the probability as to verge upon the certain. What, of itself, would be no evidence of identity, becomes, through its corroborative position, proof most sure. Give us, then, flowers in the hat corresponding to those worn by the missing girl, and we seek for nothing further. If only one flower, we seek for nothing further—what then if two or three, or more? Each successive one is multiple evidence—proof not *added* to proof, but multiplied by hundreds or thousands. Let us now discover, upon the deceased, garters such as the living used, and it is almost folly to proceed. But these garters are found to be tightened, by the setting back of a clasp, in just such a manner as her own had been tightened by Marie shortly previous to her leaving home. It is now madness or hypocrisy to doubt. What *L'Etoile* says in respect to this abbreviation of the garters being an unusual occurrence, shows nothing beyond its own pertinacity in error. The elastic nature of the claspgarter is self-demonstration of the unusualness of the abbreviation. What is made to adjust itself, must of necessity require foreign adjustment but rarely. It must have been by an accident, in its strictest sense, that these garters of Marie needed the tightening described. They alone would have amply established her identity. But it is not that the corpse was found to have the garters of the missing girl, or found to have her shoes, or her bonnet, or the flowers of her bonnet, or her feet, or a peculiar mark upon the arm, or her general size and appearance—it is that the corpse had each, and *all collectively*. Could it be proved that the editor of *L'Etoile* really entertained a doubt, under the circumstances, there would be no need, in his case, of a commission *de lunatico inquirendo*. He has thought it sagacious to echo the small talk of the lawyers, who, for the most part, content themselves with echoing the rectangular precepts of the courts. I would here observe that very much of what is rejected as evidence by a court is the best of evidence to the intellect. For the court, guided itself by the general principles of evidence—the recognized and *booked* principles—is averse from swerving at particular instances. And this steadfast adherence to principle, with rigorous disregard of the conflicting exception, is a sure mode of attaining the maximum of attainable truth, in any long sequence of time. The practice, en masse, is therefore philosophical; but it is not the less certain that it engenders vast individual error.[1]

"In respect to the insinuations leveled at Beauvais, you will be willing to dismiss them in a breath. You have already fathomed the true character of this good gentleman. He is a busy-body, with much of romance and little of wit. Anyone so constituted will readily so conduct himself, upon occasion of real excitement, as to render himself liable to suspicion on the part of the overacute, or the ill-disposed. M. Beauvais (as it appears from your notes) had some personal interviews with the editor of *L'Etoile*, and offended him by venturing an opinion that the corpse, notwithstanding the theory of the editor, was, in sober fact, that of Marie. 'He persists,' says the paper, 'in asserting the corpse to be that of Marie, but cannot give a circumstance, in addition to those which we have commented upon, to make others believe.' Now, without re-adverting to the fact that stronger evidence 'to make others believe,' could never have been adduced, it may be remarked that a man may very well be understood to believe, in a case of this kind, without the ability to advance a single reason for the belief of a second party. Nothing is more vague than impressions of individual identity. Each man recognizes his neighbor, yet there are few instances in which anyone is prepared to give a reason for his recognition. The editor of *L'Etoile* had no right to be offended at M. Beauvais' unreasoning belief.

"The suspicious circumstances which invest him, will be found to tally much better with my hypothesis of romantic busy-bodyism, than with the reasoner's suggestion of guilt. Once adopting the more charitable interpretation, we shall find no difficulty in comprehending the rose in the

1 "A theory based on the qualities of an object, will prevent its being unfolded according to its objects; and he who arranges topics in reference to their causes, will cease to value them according to their results. Thus the jurisprudence of every nation will show that, when law becomes a science and a system, it ceases to be justice. The errors into which a blind devotion to principles of classification has led the common law, will be seen by observing how often the legislature has been obliged to come forward to restore the equity its scheme had lost."—Landor.

keyhole; the 'Marie' upon the slate; the 'elbowing the male relatives out of the way'; the 'aversion to permitting them to see the body'; the caution given to Madame B——, that she must hold no conversation with the gendarme until his (Beauvais') return; and, lastly, his apparent determination 'that nobody should have anything to do with the proceedings except himself.' It seems to me unquestionable that Beauvais was a suitor of Marie's; that she coquetted with him; and that he was ambitious of being thought to enjoy her fullest intimacy and confidence. I shall say nothing more upon this point; and, as the evidence fully rebuts the assertion of *L'Etoile*, touching the matter of apathy on the part of the mother and other relatives—an apathy inconsistent with the supposition of their believing the corpse to be that of the perfumery-girl—we shall now proceed as if the question of identity were settled to our perfect satisfaction."

"And what," I here demanded, "do you think of the opinions of *Le Commerciel*?"

"That, in spirit, they are far more worthy of attention than any which have been promulgated upon the subject. The deductions from the premises are philosophical and acute; but the premises, in two instances, at least, are founded in imperfect observation. *Le Commerciel* wishes to intimate that Marie was seized by some gang of low ruffians not far from her mother's door. 'It is impossible,' it urges, 'that a person so well known to thousands as this young woman was, should have passed three blocks without someone having seen her.' This is the idea of a man long resident in Paris—a public man—and one whose walks to and fro in the city have been mostly limited to the vicinity of the public offices. He is aware that he seldom passes so far as a dozen blocks from his own bureau, without being recognized and accosted. And, knowing the extent of his personal acquaintance with others, and of others with him, he compares his notoriety with that of the perfumery-girl, finds no great difference between them, and reaches at once the conclusion that she, in her walks, would be equally liable to recognition with himself in his. This could only be the case were her walks of the same unvarying methodical character, and within the same species of limited region as are his own. He passes to and fro, at regular intervals, within a confined periphery, abounding in individuals who are led to observation of his person through interest in the kindred nature of his occupation with their own. But the walks of Marie may, in general, be supposed discursive. In this particular instance, it will be understood as most probable that she proceeded upon a route of more than average diversity, from her accustomed ones. The parallel which we imagine to have existed in the mind of *Le Commerciel* would only be sustained in the event of the two individuals traversing the whole city. In this case, granting the personal acquaintances to be equal, the chances would be also equal that an equal number of personal rencontres would be made. For my own part, I should hold it not only as possible, but as far more than probable, that Marie might have proceeded, at any given period, by any one of the many routes between her own residence and that of her aunt, without meeting a single individual whom she knew, or by whom she was known. In viewing this question in its full and proper light, we must hold steadily in mind the great disproportion between the personal acquaintances of even the most noted individual in Paris, and the entire population of Paris itself.

"But whatever force there may still appear to be in the suggestion of *Le Commerciel*, will be much diminished when we take into consideration the hour at which the girl went abroad. 'It was when the streets were full of people,' says *Le Commerciel*, 'that she went out.' But not so. It was at nine o'clock in the morning. Now at nine o'clock of every morning in the week, *with the exception of Sunday*, the streets in the city are, it is true, thronged with people. At nine on Sunday, the populace are chiefly within doors *preparing for church*. No observing person can have failed to notice the peculiarly deserted air of the town, from about eight until ten on the morning of every Sabbath. Between ten and eleven the streets are thronged, but not at so early a period as that designated.

"There is another point at which there seems a deficiency of observation on the part of *Le Commerciel*. 'A piece,' it says, 'of one of the unfortunate girl's petticoats, two feet long and one foot wide, was torn out and tied under her chin, and around the back of her head, probably to prevent screams. This was done by fellows who had no pocket-handkerchiefs.' Whether this idea is or is not well founded, we will endeavor to see hereafter; but by 'fellows who have no pocket-handkerchiefs,' the editor intends the lowest class of ruffians. These, however, are the very description of people who will always be found to have handkerchiefs even when destitute of shirts. You must have had occasion to observe how absolutely indispensable, of late years, to the thorough blackguard, has become the pocket-handkerchief."

"And what are we to think," I asked, "of the article in *Le Soleil*?"

"That it is a vast pity its inditer was not born a parrot—in which case he would have been the most illustrious parrot of his race. He has merely repeated the individual items of the already published opinion; collecting them, with a laudable industry, from this paper and from that. 'The things had all evidently been there,' he says, 'at least three or four weeks, and there can be *no doubt* that the spot of this appalling outrage has been discovered.' The facts here restated by *Le Soleil* are very far indeed from removing my own doubts upon this subject, and we will examine them more particularly hereafter in connexion with another division of the theme.

"At present we must occupy ourselves with other investigations. You cannot fail to have remarked the extreme laxity of the examination of the corpse. To be sure, the question of identity was readily determined, or should have been; but there were other points to be ascertained. Had the body been in any respect despoiled? Had the deceased any articles of jewelry about her person upon leaving home? if so, had she any when found? These are important questions utterly untouched by the evidence; and there are others of equal moment, which have met with no attention. We must endeavor to satisfy ourselves by personal inquiry. The case of Saint Eustache must be re examined. I have no suspicion of this person; but let us proceed methodically. We will ascertain beyond a doubt the validity of the affidavits in regard to his whereabouts on the Sunday. Affidavits of this character are readily made matter of mystification. Should there be nothing wrong here, however, we will dismiss Saint-Eustache from our investigations. His suicide, however, corroborative of suspicion, were there found to be deceit in the affidavits, is, without such deceit, in no respect an unaccountable circumstance, or one which need cause us to deflect from the line of ordinary analysis.

"In that which I now propose, we will discard the interior points of this tragedy, and concentrate our attention upon its outskirts. Not the least usual error in investigations such as this is the limiting of inquiry to the immediate, with total disregard of the collateral or circumstantial events. It is the malpractice of the courts to confine evidence and discussion to the bounds of apparent relevancy. Yet experience has shown, and a true philosophy will always show, that a vast, perhaps the larger, portion of truth arises from the seemingly irrelevant. It is through the spirit of this principle, if not precisely through its letter, that modern science has resolved to calculate upon the unforeseen. But perhaps you do not comprehend me. The history of human knowledge has so uninterruptedly shown that to collateral, or incidental, or accidental events we are indebted for the most numerous and most valuable discoveries, that it has at length become necessary, in prospective view of improvement, to make not only large, but the largest, allowances for inventions that shall arise by chance, and quite out of the range of ordinary expectation. It is no longer philosophical to base upon what has been a vision of what is to be. Accident is admitted as a portion of the substructure. We make chance a matter of absolute calculation. We subject the unlooked-for and unimagined to the mathematical *formulae* of the schools.

"I repeat that it is no more than fact that the larger portion of all truth has sprung from the collateral; and it is but in accordance with the spirit of the principle involved in this fact that I would divert inquiry, in the present case, from the trodden and hitherto unfruitful ground of the event itself to the contemporary circumstances which surround it. While you ascertain the validity of the affidavits, I will examine the newspapers more generally than you have as yet done. So far, we have only reconnoitred the field of investigation; but it will be strange, indeed, if a comprehensive survey, such as I propose, of the public prints will not afford us some minute points which shall establish a direction for inquiry."

In pursuance of Dupin's suggestion, I made scrupulous examination of the affair of the affidavits. The result was a firm conviction of their validity, and of the consequent innocence of Saint-Eustache. In the meantime my friend occupied himself, with what seemed to me a minuteness altogether objectless, in a scrutiny of the various newspaper files. At the end of a week he placed before me the following extracts:

> "About three years and a half ago, a disturbance very similar to the present was caused by the disappearance of this same Marie Rogêt from the parfumerie of Monsieur Le Blanc, in the Palais-Royal. At the end of a week, however, she reappeared at her customary comptoir, as well as ever, with the exception of a slight paleness not altogether usual. It was given out by Monsieur Le Blanc and her mother that she had merely been on a visit to some friend in the country; and the affair was speedily hushed up. We presume

that the present absence is a freak of the same nature, and that, at the expiration of a week, or perhaps of a month, we shall have her among us again."—*Evening Paper*, Monday, June the 23rd.[1]

"An evening journal of yesterday refers to a former mysterious disappearance of Mademoiselle Rogêt. It is well known that, during the week of her absence from Le Blanc's parfumerie, she was in the company of a young naval officer much noted for his debaucheries. A quarrel, it is supposed, providentially led to her return home. We have the name of the Lothario in question, who is at present stationed in Paris, but for obvious reasons forbear to make it public."—*La Mercure*, Tuesday morning, June the 24th.[2]

"An outrage of the most atrocious character was perpetrated near this city the day before yesterday. A gentleman, with his wife and daughter, engaged, about dusk, the services of six young men, who were idly rowing a boat to and fro near the banks of the Seine, to convey him across the river. Upon reaching the opposite shore the three passengers stepped out, and had proceeded so far as to be beyond the view of the boat, when the daughter discovered that she had left in it her parasol. She returned for it, was seized by the gang, carried out into the stream, gagged, brutally treated, and finally taken to the shore at a point not far from that at which she had originally entered the boat with her parents. The villains have escaped for the time, but the police are upon their trail, and some of them will soon be taken."—*Morning Paper*, June the 25th.[3]

"We have received one or two communications, the object of which is to fasten the crime of the late atrocity upon Mennais;[4] but as this gentleman has been fully exonerated by a legal inquiry, and as the arguments of our several correspondents appear to be more zealous than profound, we do not think it advisable to make them public."—*Morning Paper*, June the 28th.[5]

"We have received several forcibly written communications, apparently from various sources, and which go far to render it a

1 New York *Express*.
2 New York *Herald*.
3 New York *Courier and Inquirer*.
4 Mennais was one of the parties originally suspected and arrested, but discharged through total lack of evidence.
5 New York *Courier and Inquirer*.

matter of certainty that the unfortunate Marie Rogêt has become a victim of one of the numerous bands of blackguards which infest the vicinity of the city upon Sunday. Our own opinion is decidedly in favor of this supposition. We shall endeavor to make room for some of these arguments hereafter."—*Evening Paper*, Tuesday, June the 31st.[1]

"On Monday, one of the bargemen connected with the revenue service saw an empty boat floating down the Seine. Sails were lying in the bottom of the boat. The bargeman towed it under the barge office. The next morning it was taken from thence without the knowledge of any of the officers. The rudder is now at the barge office."—*La Diligence*, Thursday, June the 26th.[2]

Upon reading these various extracts, they not only seemed to me irrelevant, but I could perceive no mode in which any one of them could be brought to bear upon the matter in hand. I waited for some explanation from Dupin.

"It is not my present design," he said, "to dwell upon the first and second of these extracts. I have copied them chiefly to show you the extreme remissness of the police, who, as far as I can understand from the Prefect, have not troubled themselves, in any respect, with an examination of the naval officer alluded to. Yet it is mere folly to say that between the first and second disappearance of Marie there is no *supposable* connexion. Let us admit the first elopement to have resulted in a quarrel between the lovers, and the return home of the betrayed. We are now prepared to view a second elopement (if we know that an elopement has again taken place) as indicating a renewal of the betrayer's advances, rather than as the result of new proposals by a second individual—we are prepared to regard it as a 'making up' of the old amour, rather than as the commencement of a new one. The chances are ten to one, that he who had once eloped with Marie would again propose an elopement, rather than that she to whom proposals of elopement had been made by one individual, should have them made to her by another. And here let me call your attention to the fact, that the time elapsing between the

1 New York *Evening Post*.
2 New York *Standard*.

first ascertained and the second supposed elopement is a few months more than the general period of the cruises of our men-of-war. Had the lover been interrupted in his first villainy by the necessity of departure to sea, and had he seized the first moment of his return to renew the base designs not yet altogether accomplished—or not yet altogether accomplished by *him*? Of all these things we know nothing.

"You will say, however, that, in the second instance, there was no elopement as imagined. Certainly not—but are we prepared to say that there was not the frustrated design? Beyond Saint-Eustache, and perhaps Beauvais, we find no recognized, no open, no honorable suitors of Marie. Of none other is there anything said. Who, then, is the secret lover, of whom the relatives (at least most of them) know nothing, but whom Marie meets upon the morning of Sunday, and who is so deeply in her confidence, that she hesitates not to remain with him until the shades of the evening descend, amid the solitary groves of the Barrière du Roule? Who is that secret lover, I ask, of whom, at least, most of the relatives know nothing? And what means the singular prophecy of Madame Rogêt on the morning of Marie's departure—'I fear that I shall never see Marie again.'

"But if we cannot imagine Madame Rogêt privy to the design of elopement, may we not at least suppose this design entertained by the girl? Upon quitting home, she gave it to be understood that she was about to visit her aunt in the Rue des Drômes, and Saint-Eustache was requested to call for her at dark. Now, at first glance, this fact strongly militates against my suggestion;—but let us reflect. That she did meet some companion, and proceed with him across the river, reaching the Barrière du Roule at so late an hour as three o'clock in the afternoon, is known. But in consenting so to accompany this individual (*for whatever purpose—to her mother known or unknown*), she must have thought of her expressed intention when leaving home, and of the surprise and suspicion aroused in the bosom of her affianced suitor, Saint-Eustache, when, calling for her, at the hour appointed, in the Rue des Drômes, he should find that she had not been there, and when, moreover, upon returning to the pension with this alarming intelligence, he should become aware of her continued absence from home. She must have thought of these things, I say. She must have foreseen the chagrin of Saint-Eustache, the suspicion of all. She could not have thought of returning to brave this suspicion; but the suspicion becomes a point of trivial importance to her, if we suppose her not intending to return.

"We may imagine her thinking thus—'I am to meet a certain person for the purpose of elopement, or for certain other purposes known only to myself. It is necessary that there be no chance of interruption—there must be a sufficient time given us to elude pursuit—I will give it to be understood that I shall visit and spend the day with my aunt at the Rue des Drômes—I will tell Saint-Eustache not to call for me until dark—in this way, my absence from home for the longest possible period, without causing suspicion or anxiety, will be accounted for, and I shall gain more time than in any other manner. If I bid Saint-Eustache call for me at dark, he will be sure not to call before; but if I wholly neglect to bid him call, my time for escape will be diminished, since it will be expected that I return the earlier, and my absence will the sooner excite anxiety. Now, if it were my design to return at all—if I had in contemplation merely a stroll with the individual in question—it would not be my policy to bid Saint-Eustache call; for, calling, he will be sure to ascertain that I have played him false—a fact of which I might keep him for ever in ignorance, by leaving home without notifying him of my intention, by returning before dark, and by then stating that I had been to visit my aunt in the Rue des Drômes. But, as it is my design never to return—or not for some weeks—or not until certain concealments are effected—the gaining of time is the only point about which I need give myself any concern.'

"You have observed, in your notes, that the most general opinion in relation to this sad affair is, and was from the first, that the girl had been the victim of a gang of blackguards. Now, the popular opinion, under certain conditions, is not to be disregarded. When arising of itself—when manifesting itself in a strictly spontaneous manner—we should look upon it as analogous with that *intuition* which is the idiosyncrasy of the individual man of genius. In ninety-nine cases from the hundred I would abide by its decision. But it is important that we find no palpable traces of *suggestion*. The opinion must be rigorously *the public's own*; and the distinction is often exceedingly difficult to perceive and to maintain. In the present instance, it appears to me that this 'public opinion,' in respect to a gang, has been superinduced by the collateral event which is detailed in the third of my extracts. All Paris is excited by the discovered corpse of Marie, a girl young, beautiful, and notorious. This corpse is found, bearing marks of violence, and floating in the river. But it is now made known that, at the very period, or about the very period, in which it is supposed that the girl was assassinated, an outrage similar in nature to that endured by the deceased, although less in extent, was perpetrated, by a gang of young ruffians, upon the person of a second young female. Is it wonderful that the one known atrocity should influence the popular judgment in regard to the other unknown? This judgment awaited direction, and the known outrage seemed so opportunely to afford it! Marie, too, was found in the river; and upon this very river was this known outrage committed. The connexion of the two events had about it so much of the palpable, that the true wonder would have been a failure of the populace to appreciate and to seize it. But, in fact, the one atrocity, known to be so committed, is, if anything, evidence that the other, committed at a time nearly coincident, was not so committed. It would have been a miracle indeed, if, while a gang of ruffians were perpetrating, at a given locality, a most unheard-of wrong, there should have been another similar gang, in a similar locality, in the same city, under the same circumstances, with the same means and appliances, engaged in a wrong of precisely the same aspect, at precisely the same period of time! Yet in what, if not in this marvelous train of coincidence, does the accidentally suggested opinion of the populace call upon us to believe?

"Before proceeding further, let us consider the supposed scene of the assassination, in the thicket at the Barrière du Roule. This thicket, although dense, was in the close vicinity of a public road. Within were three or four large stones, forming a kind of seat with a back and a footstool. On the upper stone was discovered a white petticoat; on the second, a silk scarf. A parasol, gloves, and a pocket-handkerchief were also here found. The handkerchief bore the name 'Marie Rogêt.' Fragments of dress were seen on the branches around. The earth was trampled, the bushes were broken, and there was every evidence of a violent struggle.

"Notwithstanding the acclamation with which the discovery of this thicket was received by the press, and the unanimity with which it was supposed to indicate the precise scene of the outrage, it must be admitted that there was some very good reason for doubt. That it was the scene, I may or may not believe—but there was excellent reason for doubt. Had the true scene been, as *Le Commerciel* suggested, in the neighborhood of the Rue Pavée Sainte-André, the perpetrators of the crime, supposing them still resident in Paris, would naturally have been stricken with terror at the public attention thus acutely directed into the proper channel; and, in certain classes of minds, there would have arisen, at once, a sense of the necessity of some exertion to redivert the attention. And thus, the thicket of the Barrière du Roule having been already suspected, the idea of placing the articles where they were found, might have been naturally entertained. There is no real evidence, although *Le Soleil* so supposes, that the articles discovered had been more than a few days in the thicket; while there is much circumstantial proof that they could not have remained there, without attracting attention, during the twenty days elapsing between the fatal Sunday and the afternoon upon which they were found by the boys. 'They were all *mildewed* down hard,' says *Le Soleil*, adopting the opinions of its predecessors, 'with the action of the rain and stuck together from *mildew*. The grass had grown around and over some of them. The silk of the parasol was strong, but the threads of it were run together within. The upper part, where it had been doubled and folded, was all *mildewed* and rotten, and tore on being opened.' In respect to the grass having 'grown around and over some of them,' it is obvious that the fact could only have been ascertained from the words, and thus from the recollections, of two small boys; for these boys removed the articles and took them home before they had been seen by a third party. But the grass will grow, especially in warm and damp weather (such as was that of the period of the murder) as much as two or three inches in a single day. A parasol lying upon a newly turfed ground, might, in a single week, be entirely concealed from sight by the upspringing grass. And touching that mildew, upon which the editor of *Le Soleil* so pertinaciously insists, that he employs the word no less than three times in the brief paragraph just quoted, is he really unaware of the nature of this mildew? Is he to be told that it is one of many classes of fungus, of which the most ordinary feature is its upspringing and decadence within twenty-four hours?

"Thus we see, at a glance, that what has been most triumphantly adduced in support of the idea that the articles had been 'for at least three or four weeks' in the thicket, is most absurdly null as regards any evidence of that fact. On the other hand, it is exceedingly difficult to believe that these articles could have remained in the thicket specified for a longer period than a single week—for a longer period than from one Sunday to the next. Those who know anything of the vicinity of Paris, know the extreme difficulty of finding seclusion, unless at a great distance from its suburbs. Such a thing as an unexplored or even an unfrequently visited recess, amid its woods or groves, is not for a moment to be imagined. Let anyone who, being at heart a lover of nature, is yet chained by duty to the dust and heat of this great metropolis—let any such one attempt, even during the week-days, to slake his thirst for solitude amid the scenes of natural loveliness which immediately surround us. At every second step, he will find the growing charm dispelled by the voice and personal intrusion of some ruffian or party of carousing blackguards. He will seek privacy amid the densest foliage all in vain. Here are the very nooks where the unwashed most abound—here are the temples most desecrate. With sickness of the heart the wanderer will flee back to the polluted Paris as to a less odious because less incongruous sink of pollution. But if the vicinity of the city is so beset during the working days of the week, how much more so on the Sabbath! It is now especially that, released from the claims of labor, or deprived of the customary opportunities of crime, the town blackguard seeks the precincts of the town, not through love of the rural, which in his heart he despises, but by way of escape from the restraints and conventionalities of society. He desires less the fresh air and the green trees, than the utter license of the country. Here, at the roadside inn, or beneath the foliage of the woods, he indulges, unchecked by any eye except those of his boon companions, in all the mad excess of a counterfeit hilarity—the joint offspring of liberty and of rum. I say nothing more than what must be obvious to every dispassionate observer, when I repeat that the circumstance of the articles in question having remained undiscovered, for a longer period than from one Sunday to another, in any thicket in the immediate neighborhood of Paris, is to be looked upon as little less than miraculous.

"But there are not wanting other grounds for the suspicion that the articles were placed in the thicket with the view of diverting attention from the real scene of the outrage. And, first, let me direct your notice to the date of the discovery of the articles. Collate this with the date of the fifth extract made by myself from the newspapers. You will find that the discovery followed, almost immediately, the urgent communications sent to the evening paper. These communications, although various, and apparently from various sources, tended all to the same point—viz., the directing of attention to a gang as the perpetrators of the outrage, and to the neighborhood of the Barrière du Roule as its scene. Now, here, of course, the situation is not that, in consequence of these communications, or of the public attention by them directed, the articles were found by the boys; but the suspicion might and may well have been that the articles were not before found by the boys, for the reason that the articles had not before been in the thicket; having been deposited there only at so late a period as at the date, or shortly prior to the date of the communications, by the guilty authors of these communications themselves.

"This thicket was a singular—an exceedingly singular one. It was unusually dense. Within its naturally walled enclosure were three extraordinary stones, forming a seat with a back and a footstool. And this thicket, so full of art, was in the immediate vicinity, within a few rods, of the dwelling of Madame Deluc, whose boys were in the habit of closely examining the shrubberies about them in search of the bark of the sassafras. Would it be a rash wager—a wager of one thousand to one—that a day never passed over the heads of these boys without finding at least one of them ensconced in the umbrageous hall, and enthroned upon its natural throne? Those who would hesitate at such a wager, have either never been boys themselves, or have forgotten the boyish nature. I repeat—it is exceedingly hard to comprehend how the articles could have remained in this thicket, undiscovered, for a longer period than one or two days; and that thus there is good ground for suspicion, in spite of the dogmatic ignorance of *Le Soleil*, that they were, at a comparatively late date, deposited where found.

"But there are still other and stronger reasons for believing them so deposited, than any which I have as yet urged. And, now, let me beg your notice to the highly artificial arrangement of the articles. On the upper stone lay a white petticoat; on the second, a silk scarf; scattered around, were a parasol, gloves, and a pocket-handkerchief bearing the name 'Marie Rogêt.' Here is just such an arrangement as would naturally be made by a not-overacute person wishing to dispose the articles naturally. But it is by no means a really natural arrangement. I should rather have looked to see the things all lying on the ground and trampled under foot. In the narrow limits of that bower, it would have been scarcely possible that the petticoat and scarf should have retained a position upon the stones, when subjected to the brushing to and fro of many struggling persons. 'There was evidence,' it is said, 'of a struggle; and the earth was trampled, the bushes were broken,'—but the petticoat and the scarf are found deposited as if upon shelves. 'The pieces of the frock torn out by the bushes were about three inches wide and six inches long. One part was the hem of the frock, and it had been mended. They looked like strips torn off.' Here, inadvertently, *Le Soleil* has employed an exceedingly suspicious phrase. The pieces, as described, do indeed 'look like strips torn off'; but purposely and by hand. It is one of the rarest of accidents that a piece is 'torn off,' from any garment such as is now in question, by the agency of a thorn. From the very nature of such fabrics, a thorn or nail becoming entangled in them, tears them rectangularly—divides them into two longitudinal rents, at right angles with each other, and meeting at an apex where the thorn enters—but it is scarcely possible to conceive the piece 'torn off.' I never so knew it, nor did you. To tear a piece off from such fabric, two distinct forces, in different directions, will be, in almost every case, required. If there be two edges to the fabric—if, for example, it be a pocket-handkerchief, and it is desired to tear from it a slip, then, and then only, will the one force serve the purpose. But in the present case the question is of a dress, presenting but one edge. To tear a piece from the interior, where no edge is presented could only be effected by a miracle through the agency of thorns, and no one thorn could accomplish it. But, even where an edge is presented, two thorns will be necessary, operating, the one in two distinct directions, and the other in one. And this in the supposition that the edge is unhemmed. If hemmed, the matter is nearly out of the question. We thus see the numerous and great obstacles in the way of pieces being 'torn off' through the simple agency of 'thorns'; yet we are required to believe not only that one piece but that many have been so torn. 'And one part,' too, 'was the hem of the frock!' Another piece was 'part of the skirt, not the hem,'—that is to say, was torn completely out, through the agency of thorns, from the unedged interior of the dress! These, I say, are things which one may well be pardoned for disbelieving; yet, taken collectively, they form, perhaps, less of reasonable ground for suspicion than the one startling circumstance of the articles having been left in this thicket at all, by any murderers who had enough precaution to think of removing the corpse. You will not have apprehended me rightly, however, if you suppose it my design to deny this thicket as the scene of the outrage. There might have been a wrong here, or, more possibly, an accident at Madame Deluc's. But, in fact, this is a point of minor importance. We are not engaged in an attempt to discover the scene, but to produce the perpetrators of the murder. What I have adduced, notwithstanding the minuteness with which I have adduced it, has been with the view, first, to show the folly of the positive and headlong assertions of *Le Soleil*, but secondly and chiefly, to bring you, by the most natural route, to a further contemplation of the doubt whether this assassination has, or has not, been the work of a gang.

"We will resume this question by mere allusion to the revolting details of the surgeon examined at the inquest. It is only necessary to say that his published inferences, in regard to the number of the ruffians, have been properly ridiculed as unjust and totally baseless, by all the reputable anatomists of Paris. Not that the matter might not have been as inferred, but that there was no ground for the inference:—was there not much for another?

"Let us reflect now upon 'the traces of a struggle'; and let me ask what these traces have been supposed to demonstrate. A gang. But do they not rather demonstrate the absence of a gang? What struggle could have taken place—what struggle so violent and so enduring as to have left its 'traces' in all directions—between a weak and defenseless girl and the gang of ruffians imagined? The silent grasp of a few rough arms and all would have been over. The victim must have been absolutely passive at their will. You will here bear in mind that the arguments used against the thicket as the scene, are applicable, in chief part, only against it as the scene of an outrage committed by more than a single individual. If we imagine but one violator, we can conceive, and thus only conceive, the struggle of so violent and so obstinate a nature as to have left the 'traces' apparent.

"And again. I have already mentioned the suspicion to be excited by the fact that the articles in question were suffered to remain at all in the thicket where discovered. It seems almost impossible that these evidences of guilt should have been accidentally left where found. There was sufficient presence of mind (it is supposed) to remove the corpse; and yet a more positive evidence than the corpse itself (whose features might have been quickly obliterated by decay), is allowed to lie conspicuously in the scene of the outrage—I allude to the handkerchief with the name of the deceased. If this was accident, it was not the accident of a gang. We can imagine it only the accident of an individual. Let us see. An individual has committed the murder. He is alone with the ghost of the departed. He is appalled by what lies motionless before him. The fury of his passion is over, and there is abundant room in his heart for the natural awe of the deed. His is none of that confidence which the presence of numbers inevitably inspires. He is alone with the dead. He trembles and is bewildered. Yet there is a necessity for disposing of the corpse. He bears it to the river, and leaves behind him the other evidences of his guilt; for it is difficult, if not impossible, to carry all the burden at once, and it will be easy to return for what is left. But in his toilsome journey to the water his fears redouble within him. The sounds of life encompass his path. A dozen times he hears or fancies he hears the step of an observer. Even the very lights from the city bewilder him. Yet, in time, and by long and frequent pauses of deep agony, he reaches the river's brink, and disposes of his ghastly charge—perhaps through the medium of a boat. But now what treasure does the world hold—what threat of vengeance could it hold out—which would have power to urge the return of that lonely murderer over that toilsome and perilous path, to the thicket and its blood-chilling recollections? He returns not, let the consequences be what they may. He could not return if he would. His sole thought is immediate escape. He turns his back for ever upon those dreadful shrubberies, and flees as from the wrath to come.

"But how with a gang? Their number would have inspired them with confidence; if, indeed, confidence is ever wanting in the breast of the arrant blackguard; and of arrant blackguards alone are the supposed gangs ever constituted. Their number, I say, would have prevented the bewildering and unreasoning terror which I have imagined to paralyse the single man. Could we suppose an oversight in one, or two, or three, this oversight would have been remedied by a fourth. They would have left nothing behind them; for their number would have enabled them to carry all at once. There would have been no need of return.

"Consider now the circumstance that, in the outer garment of the corpse when found, 'a slip, about a foot wide, had been torn upward from the bottom hem to the waist, wound three times round the waist, and secured by a sort of hitch in the back.' This was done with the obvious design of affording a handle by which to carry the body. But would any number of men have dreamed of resorting to such an expedient? To three or four, the limbs of the corpse would have afforded not only a sufficient, but the best possible, hold. The device is that of a single individual; and this brings us to the fact that 'between the thicket and the river the rails of the fences were found taken down, and the ground bore evident traces of some heavy burden having been dragged along it!' But would a number of men have put themselves to the superfluous trouble of taking down a fence, for the purpose of dragging through it a corpse which they might have lifted over any fence in an instant? Would a number of men have so dragged a corpse at all as to have left evident traces of the dragging?

"And here we must refer to an observation of *Le Commerciel*; an observation upon which I have already, in some measure, commented. 'A piece,' says this journal, 'of one of the unfortunate girl's petticoats was torn out and tied under her chin, and around the back of her head, probably to prevent screams. This was done by fellows who had no pocket-handkerchiefs.'

"I have before suggested that a genuine blackguard is never without a pocket-handkerchief. But it is not to this fact that I now specially advert. That it was not through want of a handkerchief for the purpose imagined by *Le Commerciel*, that this bandage was employed, is rendered apparent by the handkerchief left in the thicket; and that the object was not 'to prevent screams' appears, also, from the bandage having been employed in preference to what would so much better have answered the purpose. But the language of the evidence speaks of the strip in question as 'found around the neck, fitting loosely, and secured with a hard knot.' These words are sufficiently vague, but differ materially from those of *Le Commerciel*. The slip was eighteen inches wide, and therefore, although of muslin, would form a strong band when folded or rumpled longitudinally. And thus rumpled it was discovered. My inference is this. The solitary murderer, having borne the corpse for some distance (whether from the thicket or elsewhere) by means of the bandage hitched around its middle, found the weight, in this mode of procedure, too much for his strength. He resolved to drag the burden—the evidence goes to show that it was dragged. With this object in view, it became necessary to attach something like a rope to one of the extremities. It could be best attached about the neck, where the head would prevent its slipping off. And now the murderer bethought him, unquestionably, of the bandage about the loins. He would have used this, but for its volution about the corpse, the hitch which embarrassed it, and the reflection that it had not been 'torn off' from the garment. It was easier to tear a new slip from the petticoat. He tore it, made it fast about the neck, and so dragged his victim to the brink of the river. That this 'bandage,' only attainable with trouble and delay, and but imperfectly answering its purpose—that this bandage was employed at all, demonstrates that the necessity for its employment sprang from circumstances arising at a period when the handkerchief was no longer attainable—that is to say, arising, as we have imagined, after quitting the thicket (if the thicket it was), and on the road between the thicket and the river.

"But the evidence, you will say, of Madame Deluc(!) points especially to the presence of a gang in the vicinity of the thicket, at or about the epoch of the murder. This I grant. I doubt if there were not a dozen gangs, such as described by Madame Deluc, in and about the vicinity of the Barrière du Roule at or about the period of this tragedy. But the gang which has drawn upon itself the pointed animadversion, through the somewhat tardy and very suspicious evidence of Madame Deluc, is the only gang which is represented by that honest and scrupulous old lady as having eaten her cakes, and swallowed her brandy, without putting themselves to the trouble of making her payment. *Et hinc illae irae?*

"But what is the precise evidence of Madame Deluc. A gang of miscreants made their appearance, behaved boisterously, ate and drank without making payment, followed in the route of the young man and the girl, returned to the inn about dusk, and recrossed the river as if in great haste.'

"Now, this 'great haste' very possibly seemed greater haste in the eyes of Madame Deluc, since she dwelt lingeringly and lamentingly upon her violated cakes and ale,—cakes and ale for which she might still have entertained a faint hope of compensation. Why, otherwise, since it was about dusk, should she make a point of the haste? It is no cause for wonder surely, that a gang of blackguards should make haste to get home when a wide river is to be crossed in small boats, when storm impends, and when night approaches.

"I say approaches; for the night had not yet arrived. It was only about dusk that the indecent haste of these 'miscreants' offended the sober eyes of Madame Deluc. But we are told that it was upon this very evening that Madame Deluc, as well as her eldest son, 'heard the screams of a female in the vicinity of the inn.' And in what words does Madame Deluc designate the period of the evening at which these screams were heard? 'It was soon after dark,' she says. But 'soon after dark' is at least dark;

and 'about dusk' is as certainly daylight. Thus it is abundantly clear that the gang quitted the Barrière du Roule prior to the screams overheard (?) by Madame Deluc. And although, in all the many reports of the evidence, the relative expressions in question are distinctly and invariably employed just as I have employed them in this conversation with yourself, no notice whatever of the gross discrepancy has, as yet, been taken by any of the public journals, or by any of the myrmidons of police.

"I shall add but one to the arguments against a gang; but this one has, to my own understanding at least, a weight altogether irresistible. Under the circumstances of large reward offered, and full pardon to any king's evidence, it is not to be imagined, for a moment, that some member of a gang of low ruffians, or of any body of men, would not long ago have betrayed his accomplices. Each one of a gang, so placed, is not so much greedy of reward, or anxious for escape, as fearful of betrayal. He betrays eagerly and early that he may not himself be betrayed. That the secret has not been divulged is the very best of proof that it is, in fact, a secret. The horrors of this dark deed are known only to one, or two, living human beings, and to God.

"Let us sum up now the meagre yet certain fruits of our long analysis. We have attained the idea either of a fatal accident under the roof of Madame Deluc, or of a murder perpetrated in the thicket at the Barrière du Roule, by a lover, or at least by an intimate and secret associate of the deceased. The associate is of swarthy complexion. This complexion, the 'hitch' in the bandage, and the 'sailor's knot' with which the bonnet-ribbon is tied, point to a seaman. His companionship with the deceased—a gay but not abject young girl—designates him as above the grade of the common sailor. Here the well-written and urgent communications to the journals are much in the way of corroboration. The circumstance of the first elopement, as mentioned by *La Mercure*, tends to blend the idea of this seaman with that of the 'naval officer' who is first known to have led the unfortunate into crime.

"And here, most fitly, comes the consideration of the continued absence of him of the dark complexion. Let me pause to observe that the complexion of this man is dark and swarthy; it was no common swarthiness which constituted the sole point of resemblance, both as regards Valence and Madame Deluc. But why is this man absent? Was he murdered by the gang? If so, why are there only traces of the assassinated girl? The scene of the two outrages will naturally be supposed identical. And where is his corpse? The assassins would most probably have disposed of both in the same way. But it may be said that this man lives, and is deterred from making himself known through dread of being charged with the murder. This consideration might be supposed to operate upon him now—at this late period—since it has been given in evidence that he was seen with Marie, but it would have had no force at the period of the deed. The first impulse of an innocent man would have been to announce the outrage, and to aid in identifying the ruffians. This, policy would have suggested. He had been seen with the girl. He had crossed the river with her in an open ferry-boat. The denouncing of the assassins would have appeared, even to an idiot, the surest and sole means of relieving himself from suspicion. We cannot suppose him, on the night of the fatal Sunday, both innocent himself and incognizant of an outrage committed. Yet only under such circumstances is it possible to imagine that he would have failed, if alive, in the denouncement of the assassins.

"And what means are ours of attaining the truth? We shall find these means of multiplying and gathering distinctness as we proceed. Let us sift to the bottom this affair of the first elopement. Let us know the full history of 'the officer,' with his present circumstances, and his whereabouts at the precise period of the murder. Let us carefully compare with each other the various communications sent to the evening paper, in which the object was to inculcate a gang. This done, let us compare these communications, both as regards style and MS., with those sent to the morning paper, at a previous period, and insisting so vehemently upon the guilt of Mennais. And, all this done, let us again compare these various communications with the known MSS. of the officer. Let us endeavor to ascertain, by repeated questionings of Madame Deluc and her boys, as well as of the omnibus-driver, Valence, something more of the personal appearance and bearing of the 'man of dark complexion.' Queries, skillfully directed, will not fail to elicit, from some of these parties, information on this particular point (or upon others)—information which the parties themselves may not even be aware of possessing. And let us now trace the boat picked up by the bargeman on the morning of Monday, the 23rd of June, and which was removed from the barge office, without the cognizance of the officer in attendance, and without the rudder, at some period prior to the discovery of the corpse. With a proper caution and perseverance we shall infallibly trace this boat; for not only can the bargeman who picked it up identify it, but the rudder is at hand. The rudder of a sail boat would not have been abandoned without inquiry, by one altogether at ease in heart. And here let me pause to insinuate a question. There was no advertisement of the picking up of this boat. It was silently taken to the barge office, and as silently removed. But its owner or employer—how happened he, at so early a period on Tuesday morning, to be informed, without the agency of advertisement, of the locality of the boat taken up on Monday, unless we imagine some connexion with the navy—some personal permanent connexion leading to cognizance of its minute interests—its petty local news?

"In speaking of the lonely assassin dragging his burden to the shore, I have already suggested the probability of his availing himself of a boat. Now we are to understand that Marie Rogêt was precipitated from a boat. This would naturally have been the case. The corpse could not have been trusted to the shallow waters of the shore. The peculiar marks on the back and shoulders of the victim tell of the bottom ribs of a boat. That the body was found without weight is also corroborative of the idea. If thrown from the shore a weight would have been attached. We can only account for its absence by supposing the murderer to have neglected the precaution of supplying himself with it before pushing off. In the act of consigning the corpse to the water he would unquestionably have noticed his oversight; but then no remedy would have been at hand. Any risk would have been preferred to a return to that accursed shore. Having rid himself of his ghastly charge, the murderer would have hastened to the city. There, at some obscure wharf, he would have leaped on land. But the boat, would he have secured it? He would have been in too great haste for such things as securing a boat. Moreover, in fastening it to the wharf, he would have felt as if securing evidence against himself. His natural thought would have been to cast from him, as far as possible, all that held connexion with his crime. He would not only have fled from the wharf, but he would not have permitted the boat to remain. Assuredly he would have cast it adrift. Let us pursue our fancies.—In the morning, the wretch is stricken with unutterable horror at finding that the boat has been picked up and detained at a locality which he is in the daily habit of frequenting—at a locality, perhaps, which his duty compels him to frequent. The next night, without daring to ask for the rudder, he removes it. Now where is that rudderless boat? Let it be one of our first purposes to discover. With the first glimpse we obtain of it, the dawn of our success shall begin. This boat shall guide us, with a rapidity which will surprise even ourselves, to him who employed it in the midnight of the fatal Sabbath. Corroboration will rise upon corroboration, and the murderer will be traced."

[For reasons which we shall not specify, but which to many readers will appear obvious, we have taken the liberty of here omitting, from the MSS. placed in our hands, such portion as details the following up of the apparently slight clue obtained by Dupin. We feel it advisable only to state, in brief, that the result desired was brought to pass; and that the Prefect fulfilled punctually, although with reluctance, the terms of his compact with the Chevalier. Mr. Poe's article concludes with the following words.—Eds.[1]]

It will be understood that I speak of coincidences and no more. What I have said above upon this topic must suffice. In my own heart there dwells no faith in præter-nature. That Nature and its God are two, no man who thinks will deny. That the latter, creating the former, can, at will, control or modify it, is also unquestionable. I say 'at will'; for the question is of will, and not, as the insanity of logic has assumed, of power. It is not that the Deity cannot modify His laws, but that we insult Him in imagining a possible necessity for modification. In their origin these laws were fashioned to embrace all contingencies which could lie in the future. With God all is Now.

I repeat, then, that I speak of these things only as of coincidences. And further: in what I relate it will be seen that between the fate of the unhappy Mary Cecilia Rogers, so far as that fate is known, and the fate of one Marie Rogêt up to a certain epoch in her history, there has existed a parallel in the contemplation of whose wonderful exactitude the reason becomes embarrassed. I say all this will be seen. But let it not for a moment be supposed that, in proceeding with the sad narrative of Marie from the epoch just mentioned, and in tracing to its dénouement the mystery which enshrouded her, it is my covert design to hint at an extension of the parallel, or even to suggest that the measures adopted in Paris for the discovery of the assassin of a grisette, or measures

1 Of Snowden's *Lady's Companion*, the magazine in which the article was originally published.

founded in any similar ratiocination, would produce any similar result.

For, in respect to the latter branch of the supposition, it should be considered that the most trifling variation in the facts of the two cases might give rise to the most important miscalculations, by diverting thoroughly the two courses of events; very much as, in arithmetic, an error which, in its own individuality, may be inappreciable, produces at length, by dint of multiplication at all points of the process, a result enormously at variance with truth. And, in regard to the former branch, we must not fail to hold in view that the very Calculus of Probabilities to which I have referred, forbids all idea of the extension of the parallel,—forbids it with a positiveness strong and decided just in proportion as this parallel has been already long-drawn and exact. This is one of those anomalous propositions which, seemingly, appealing to thought altogether apart from the mathematical, is yet one which only the mathematician can fully entertain. Nothing, for example, is more difficult than to convince the merely general reader that the fact of sixes having been thrown twice in succession by a player at dice, is sufficient cause for betting the largest odds that sixes will not be thrown in the third attempt. A suggestion to this effect is usually rejected by the intellect at once. It does not appear that the two throws which have been completed, and which lie now absolutely in the Past, can have influence upon the throw which exists only in the Future. The chance for throwing sixes seems to be precisely as it was at any ordinary time—that is to say, subject only to the influence of the various other throws which may be made by the dice. And this is a reflection which appears so exceedingly obvious that attempts to controvert it are received more frequently with a derisive smile than with anything like respectful attention. The error here involved—a gross error redolent of mischief—I cannot pretend to expose within the limits assigned me at present; and with the philosophical it needs no exposure. It may be sufficient here to say that it forms one of an infinite series of mistakes which arise in the path of Reason through her propensity for seeking truth *in detail.*

THE COLLOQUY OF MONOS AND UNA

Μελλοντα ταυτα
"These things are in the future."
Sophocles, *Antigone.*

UNA. "BORN AGAIN"?

Monos. Yes, fairest and best beloved Una, "born again." These were the words upon whose mystical meaning I had so long pondered, rejecting the explanation of the priesthood, until Death himself resolved for me the secret.

Una. Death!

Monos. How strangely, sweet Una, you echo my words! I observe, too, a vacillation in your step—a joyous inquietude in your eyes. You are confused and oppressed by the majestic novelty of the Life Eternal. Yes, it was of Death I spoke. And here how singularly sounds that word which of old was wont to bring terror to all hearts—throwing a mildew upon all pleasures!

Una. Ah, Death, the spectre which sat at all feasts. How often, Monos, did we lose ourselves in speculations upon its nature! How mysteriously did it act as a check to human bliss—saying unto it "thus far, and no farther!" That earnest mutual love, my own Monos, which burned within our bosoms—how vainly did we flatter ourselves, feeling happy in its first upspringing, that our happiness would strengthen with its strength! Alas! as it grew, so grew in our hearts the dread of that evil hour which was hurrying to separate us for ever! Thus, in time, it became painful to love. Hate would have been mercy then.

Monos. Speak not here of these griefs, dear Una—mine, mine for ever now!

Una. But the memory of past sorrow—is it not present joy? I have much to say yet of the things which have been. Above all, I burn to know the incidents of your own passage through the dark Valley and Shadow.

Monos. And when did the radiant Una ask anything of her Monos in vain? I will be minute in relating all—but at what point shall the weird narrative begin?

Una. At what point?

Monos. You have said.

Una. Monos, I comprehend you. In Death we have both learned the propensity of man to define the indefinable. I will not say, then, commence with the moment of life's cessation—but commence with that sad, sad instant when, the fever having abandoned you, you sank into a breathless and motionless torpor, and I pressed down your pallid eyelids with the passionate fingers of love.

Monos. One word first, my Una, in regard to man's general condition at this epoch. You will remember that one or two of the wise among our forefathers—wise in fact, although not in the world's esteem—had ventured to doubt the propriety of the term "improvement," as applied to the progress of our civilization. There were periods in each of the five or six centuries immediately preceding our dissolution, when arose some vigorous intellect, boldly contending for those principles whose truth appears now, to our disenfranchised reason, so utterly obvious—principles which should have taught our race to submit to the guidance of the natural laws, rather than attempt their control. At long intervals some master-minds appeared, looking upon each advance in practical science as a retrogradation in the true utility. Occasionally the poetic intellect—that intellect which we now feel to have been the most exalted of all—since those truths which to us were of the most enduring importance could only be reached by that *analogy* which speaks in proof-tones to the imagination alone, and to the unaided reason bears no weight—occasionally did this poetic intellect proceed a step farther in the evolving of the vague idea of the philosophic, and find in the mystic parable that tells of the tree of knowledge, and of its forbidden fruit, death-producing, a distinct intimation that knowledge was not meet for man in the infant condition of his soul. And these men, the poets, living and perishing amid the scorn of the "utilitarians"—of rough pedants, who arrogated to themselves a title which could have been properly applied only to the scorned—these men, the poets, pondered piningly, yet not unwisely, upon the ancient days when our wants were not more simple than our enjoyments were keen—days when *mirth* was a word unknown, so solemnly deep-toned was happiness—holy, august, and blissful days, when blue rivers ran undammed, between hills unhewn, into far forest solitudes, primeval, odorous, and unexplored.

Yet these noble exceptions from the general misrule served but to strengthen it by opposition. Alas! we have fallen upon the most evil of all our evil days. The great "movement"—that was the cant term—went on: a diseased commotion, moral and physical. Art—the Arts—arose supreme, and, once enthroned, cast chains upon the intellect which had elevated them to power. Man, because he could not but acknowledge the majesty of Nature, fell into childish exultation at his acquired and still-increasing dominion over her elements. Even while he stalked a God in his own fancy, an infantine imbecility came over him. As might be supposed from the origin of his disorder, he grew infected with system, and with abstraction. He enwrapped himself in generalities. Among other odd ideas, that of universal equality gained ground; and in the face of analogy and of God—in despite of the loud warning voice of the laws of *gradation* so visibly pervading all things in Earth and Heaven—wild attempts at an omni-prevalent Democracy were made. Yet this evil sprang necessarily from the leading evil—Knowledge. Man could not both know and succumb. Meantime huge smoking cities arose, innumerable. Green leaves shrank before the hot breath of furnaces. The fair face of Nature was deformed as with the ravages of some loathsome disease. And methinks, sweet Una, even our slumbering sense of the forced and of the far-fetched might have arrested us here. But now it appears that we had worked out our own destruction in the perversion of our taste, or rather in the blind neglect of its culture in the schools. For, in truth, it was at this crisis that taste alone—that faculty which, holding a middle position between the pure intellect and the moral sense, could never safely have been disregarded—it was now that taste alone could have led us gently back to Beauty, to Nature, and to Life. But alas for the pure contemplative spirit and majestic intuition of Plato! Alas for the *μουσιχη* which he justly regarded as an all-sufficient education for the soul! Alas for him and for it!—since both were most desperately needed when both were most entirely forgotten or despised.[1]

Pascal, a philosopher whom we both love, has said, how truly!—"*que tout notre raisonnement se réduit à céder au sentiment*"; and it is not impossible that the sentiment of the natural, had time permitted it, would have regained its old ascendancy over the harsh mathematical reason of the schools. But this thing was not to be. Prematurely induced by intemperance of knowledge, the old age of the world drew on. This the mass of mankind saw not, or, living lustily although unhappily, affected not to see. But, for myself, the Earth's records had taught me to look for widest ruin as the price of highest civilization. I had imbibed a prescience of our Fate from comparison of China the simple and enduring, with Assyria the architect, with Egypt the astrologer, with Nubia, more crafty than either, the turbulent mother of all Arts. In the history of these regions I met with a ray from the Future. The individual artificialities of the three latter were local diseases of the Earth, and in their individual overthrows we had seen local remedies applied; but for the infected world at large I could anticipate no regeneration save in death. That man, as a race, should not become extinct, I saw that he must be "*born again.*"

1 "It will be hard to discover a better [method of education] than that which the experience of so many ages has already discovered; and this may be summed up as consisting in gymnastics for the body, and music for the soul."—*Repub.*, lib. 2. "For this reason is a musical education most essential; since it causes Rhythm and Harmony to penetrate most intimately into the soul, taking the strongest hold upon it, filling it with beauty and making the man *beautiful-minded*. . . . He will praise and admire *the beautiful*; will receive it with joy into his soul, will feed upon it, and *assimilate his own condition with it.*"—Ibid., lib. 3. Music (*mousikh*) had, however, among the Athenians, a far more comprehensive signification than with us. It included not only the harmonies of time and of tune, but the poetic diction, sentiment, and creation, each in its widest sense. The study of music was with them, in fact, the general cultivation of the taste—of that which recognizes the beautiful—in contra-distinction from reason, which deals only with the true.

And now it was, fairest and dearest, that we wrapped our spirits, daily, in dreams. Now it was that, in twilight, we discoursed of the days to come, when the Art-scarred surface of the Earth, having undergone that purification[1] which alone could efface its rectangular obscenities, should clothe itself anew in the verdure and the mountain-slopes and the smiling waters of Paradise, and be rendered at length a fit dwelling-place for man:—for man the Death-purged—for man to whose now exalted intellect there should be poison in knowledge no more—for the redeemed, regenerated, blissful, and now immortal, but still for the *material*, man.

UNA. Well do I remember these conversations, dear Monos; but the epoch of the fiery overthrow was not so near at hand as we believed, and as the corruption you indicate did surely warrant us in believing. Men lived; and died individually. You yourself sickened, and passed into the grave; and thither your constant Una speedily followed you. And though the century which has since elapsed, and whose conclusion brings us thus together once more, tortured our slumbering senses with no impatience of duration, yet, my Monos, it was a century still.

MONOS. Say, rather, a point in the vague infinity. Unquestionably it was in the Earth's dotage that I died. Wearied at heart with anxieties which had their origin in the general turmoil and decay, I succumbed to the fierce fever. After some few days of pain, and many of dreamy delirium replete with ecstasy, the manifestations of which you mistook for pain, while I longed but was impotent to undeceive you—after some days there came upon me, as you have said, a breathless and motionless torpor, and this was termed Death, by those who stood around me.

Words are vague things. My condition did not deprive me of sentience. It appeared to me not greatly dissimilar to the extreme quiescence of him, who, having slumbered long and profoundly, lying motionless and fully prostrate in a midsummer noon, begins to steal slowly back into consciousness, through the mere sufficiency of his sleep, and without being awakened by external disturbances.

1 The word "purification" seems here to be used with reference to its root in the Greek *pyr* [πυρ], fire.

I breathed no longer. The pulses were still. The heart had ceased to beat. Volition had not departed, but was powerless. The senses were unusually active, although eccentrically so—assuming often each other's functions at random. The taste and the smell were inextricably confounded, and became one sentiment, abnormal and intense. The rose-water with which your tenderness had moistened my lips to the last, affected me with sweet fancies of flowers—fantastic flowers, far more lovely than any of the old Earth, but whose prototypes we have here blooming around us. The eyelids, transparent and bloodless, offered no complete impediment to vision. As volition was in abeyance the balls could not roll in their sockets—but all objects within the range of the visual hemisphere were seen with more or less distinctness; the rays which fell upon the external retina, or into the cornea of the eye, producing a more vivid effect than those which struck the front or anterior surface. Yet, in the former instance, this effect was so far anomalous that I appreciated it only as *sound*—sound sweet or discordant as the matters presenting themselves at my side were light or dark in shade—curved or angular in outline. The hearing at the same time, although excited in degree, was not irregular in action—estimating real sounds with an extravagance of precision, not less than of sensibility. Touch had undergone a modification more peculiar. Its impressions were tardily received, but pertinaciously retained, and resulted always in the highest physical pleasure. Thus the pressure of your sweet fingers upon my eyelids, at first only recognized through vision, at length, long after their removal, filled my whole being with a sensual delight immeasurable. I say with a sensual delight. *All* my perceptions were purely sensual. The materials furnished the passive brain by the senses were not in the least degree wrought into shape by the deceased understanding. Of pain there was some little; of pleasure there was much; but of moral pain or pleasure none at all. Thus your wild sobs floated into my ear with all their mournful cadences, and were appreciated in their every variation of sad tone; but they were soft musical sounds and no more; they conveyed to the extinct reason no intimation of the sorrows which gave them birth; while the large and constant tears which fell upon my face, telling the bystanders of a heart which broke, thrilled every fibre of my frame with ecstasy alone. And this was in truth the *Death* of which these bystanders spoke reverently, in low whispers—you, sweet Una, gaspingly, with loud cries.

They attired me for the coffin—three or four dark figures which flitted busily to and fro. As these crossed the direct line of my vision they affected me as *forms*; but upon passing to my side their images impressed me with the idea of shrieks, groans, and other dismal expressions of terror, of horror, or of woe. You alone, habited in a white robe, passed in all directions musically about me.

The day waned; and, as its light faded away, I became possessed by a vague uneasiness—an anxiety such as the sleeper feels when sad real sounds fall continuously within his ear—low distant bell tones, solemn, at long but equal intervals, and commingling with melancholy dreams. Night arrived; and with its shadows a heavy discomfort. It oppressed my limbs with the oppression of some dull weight, and was palpable. There was also a moaning sound, not unlike the distant reverberation of surf, but more continuous, which, beginning with the first twilight, had grown in strength with the darkness. Suddenly lights were brought into the room, and this reverberation became forthwith interrupted into frequent unequal bursts of the same sound, but less dreary and less distinct. The ponderous oppression was in a great measure relieved; and, issuing from the flame of each lamp (for there were many), there flowed unbrokenly into my ears a strain of melodious monotone. And when now, dear Una, approaching the bed upon which I lay outstretched, you sat gently by my side, breathing odor from your sweet lips, and pressing them upon my brow, there arose tremulously within my bosom, and mingling with the merely physical sensations which circumstances had called forth, a something akin to sentiment itself—a feeling that, half appreciating, half responded to your earnest love and sorrow; but this feeling took no root in the pulseless heart, and seemed indeed rather a shadow than a reality, and faded quickly away, first into extreme quiescence, and then into a purely sensual pleasure as before.

And now, from the wreck and the chaos of the usual senses, there appeared to have arisen within me a sixth, all perfect. In its exercise I found a wild delight—yet a delight still physical, inasmuch as the understanding in it had no part. Motion in the animal frame had fully ceased. No muscle quivered; no nerve thrilled; no artery throbbed. But there seemed to have sprung up in the brain, *that* of which no words could convey to the merely human intelligence even an indistinct conception. Let me term it a mental pendulous pulsation. It was the moral embodiment of man's abstract idea of *Time*. By the absolute equalization of this movement—or of such as this—had the cycles of the firmamental orbs themselves, been adjusted. By its aid I measured the irregularities of the clock upon the mantel, and of the watches of the attendants. Their tickings came sonorously to my ears. The slightest deviation from the true proportion—and these deviations were omni-prevalent—affected me just as violations of abstract truth are wont, on Earth, to affect the moral sense. Although no two of the time-pieces in the chamber struck individual seconds accurately together, yet I had no difficulty in holding steadily in mind the tones, and the respective momentary errors of each. And this—this keen, perfect, self-existing sentiment of *duration*—this sentiment existing (as man could not possibly have conceived it to exist) independently of any succession of events—this idea—this sixth sense upspringing from the ashes of the rest, was the first obvious and certain step of the intemporal soul upon the threshold of the temporal Eternity.

It was midnight; and you still sat by my side. All others had departed from the chamber of Death. They had deposited me in the coffin. The lamps burned flickeringly; for this I knew by the tremulousness of the monotonous strains. But, suddenly these strains diminished in distinctness and in volume. Finally they ceased. The perfume in my nostrils died away. Forms affected my vision no longer. The oppression of the Darkness uplifted itself from my bosom. A dull shock like that of electricity pervaded my frame, and was followed by total loss of the idea of contact. All of what man has termed sense was merged in the sole consciousness of entity, and in the one abiding sentiment of duration. The mortal body had been at length stricken with the hand of the deadly *Decay*.

Yet had not all sentience departed; for the consciousness and the sentiment remaining supplied some of its functions by a lethargic intuition. I appreciated the direful change now in operation upon the flesh, and, as the dreamer is sometimes aware of the bodily presence of one who leans over him, so, sweet Una, I still dully felt that you sat by my side. So, too, when the noon of the second day came, I was not unconscious of those movements which displaced you from my side, which confined me within the coffin, which deposited me within the hearse, which bore me to the grave, which lowered me within it, which heaped heavily the mold upon me, and which thus left me, in blackness and corruption, to my sad and solemn slumbers with the worm.

And here, in the prison-house which has few secrets to disclose, there rolled away days and weeks and months; and the soul watched narrowly each second as it flew, and, without effort, took record of its flight—without effort and without object.

A year passed. The consciousness of *being* had grown hourly more indistinct, and that of mere *locality* had, in great measure, usurped its position. The idea of entity was becoming merged in that of *place*. The narrow space immediately surrounding what had been the body, was now going to be the body itself. At length, as often happens to the sleepers (by sleep and its world alone is *Death* imaged)—at length, as sometimes happened on Earth to the deep slumberer, when some flitting light half startled him into awakening, yet left him half enveloped in dreams—so to me, in the strict embrace of the *Shadow* came *that* light which alone might have had power to startle—the light of enduring Love. Men toiled at the grave in which I lay darkling. They upthrew the damp earth. Upon my moldering bones there descended the coffin of Una.

And now again all was void. That nebulous light had been extinguished. That feeble thrill had vibrated itself into quiescence. Many *lustra* had supervened. Dust had returned to dust. The worm had food no more. The sense of being had at length utterly departed, and there reigned in its stead—instead of all things—dominant and perpetual—the autocrats *Place* and *Time*. For *that* which was *not*—for that which had no form—for that which had no thought—for that which had no sentience—for that which was soulless, yet of which matter formed no portion—for all this nothingness, yet for all this immortality, the grave was still a home, and the corrosive hours, co-mates.

THE MASQUE OF THE RED DEATH

THE "RED DEATH" had long devastated the country. No pestilence had ever been so fatal, or so hideous. Blood was its Avatar and its seal—the redness and horror of blood. There were sharp pains, and sudden dizziness, and then profuse bleeding at the pores, with dissolution. The scarlet stains upon the body and especially upon the face of the victim, were the pest ban which shut him out from the aid and from the sympathy of his fellow-men. And the whole seizure, progress, and termination of the disease, were the incidents of half an hour.

But the Prince Prospero was happy and dauntless and sagacious. When his dominions were half-depopulated, he summoned to his presence a thousand hale and light-hearted friends from among the knights and dames of his court, and with these retired to the deep seclusion of one of his castellated abbeys. This was an extensive and magnificent structure, the creation of the prince's own eccentric yet august taste. A strong and lofty wall girdled it in. This wall had gates of iron. The courtiers, having entered, brought furnaces and massy hammers and welded the bolts. They resolved to leave means neither of ingress nor egress to the sudden impulses of despair or of frenzy from within. The abbey was amply provisioned. With such precautions the courtiers might bid defiance to contagion. The external world could take care of itself. In the meantime it was folly to grieve, or to think. The prince had provided all the appliances of pleasure. There were buffoons, there were improvisatori, there were ballet-dancers, there were musicians, there was Beauty, there was wine. All these and security were within. Without was the "Red Death."

It was toward the close of the fifth or sixth month of his seclusion, and while the pestilence raged most furiously abroad, that the Prince Prospero entertained his thousand friends at a masked ball of the most unusual magnificence.

It was a voluptuous scene, that masquerade. But first let me tell of the rooms in which it was held. There were seven—an imperial suite. In many palaces, however, such suites form a long and straight vista, while the folding doors slide back nearly to the walls on either hand, so that the view of the whole extent is scarcely impeded. Here the case was very different, as might have been expected from the duke's love of the bizarre. The apartments were so irregularly disposed that the vision embraced but little more than one at a time. There was a sharp turn at every twenty or thirty yards, and at each turn a novel effect. To the right and left, in the middle of each wall, a tall and narrow Gothic window looked out upon a closed corridor which pursued the windings of the suite. These windows were of stained glass whose color varied in accordance with the prevailing hue of the decorations of the chamber into which it opened. That at the eastern extremity was hung, for example, in blue—and vividly blue were its windows. The second chamber was purple in its ornaments and tapestries, and here the panes were purple. The third was green throughout, and so were the casements. The fourth was furnished and lighted with orange—the fifth with white—the sixth with violet. The seventh apartment was closely shrouded in black velvet tapestries that hung all over the ceiling and down the walls, falling in heavy folds upon a carpet of the same material and hue. But in this chamber only, the color of the windows failed to correspond with the decorations. The panes here were scarlet—a deep blood color. Now in no one of the seven apartments was there any lamp or candelabrum, amid the profusion of golden ornaments that lay scattered to and fro or depended from the roof. There was no light of any kind emanating from lamp or candle within the suite of chambers. But in the corridors that followed the suite there stood, opposite to each window, a heavy tripod, bearing a brazier of fire, that projected its rays through the tinted glass and so glaringly illumined the room. And thus were produced a multitude of gaudy and fantastic appearances. But in the western or black chamber the effect of the firelight that streamed upon the dark hangings through the blood-tinted panes was ghastly in the extreme, and produced so wild a look upon the countenances of those who entered, that there were few of the company bold enough to set foot within its precincts at all.

It was in this apartment, also, that there stood against the western wall, a gigantic clock of ebony. Its pendulum swung to and fro with a dull, heavy, monotonous clang; and when the minute-hand made the circuit of the face, and the hour was to be stricken, there came from the brazen lungs of the clock a sound which was clear and loud and deep and exceedingly musical, but of so peculiar a note and emphasis that, at each lapse of an hour, the musicians of the orchestra were constrained to pause, momentarily, in their performance, to harken to the sound; and thus the waltzers perforce ceased their evolutions; and there was a brief disconcert of the whole gay company; and, while the chimes of the clock yet rang, it was observed that the giddiest grew pale, and the more aged and sedate passed their hands over their brows as if in confused reverie or meditation. But when the echoes had fully ceased, a light laughter at once pervaded the assembly; the musicians looked at each other and smiled as if at their own nervousness and folly, and made whispering vows, each to the other, that the next chiming of the clock should produce in them no similar emotion; and then, after the lapse of sixty minutes (which embrace three thousand and six hundred seconds of the Time that flies), there came yet another chiming of the clock, and then were the same disconcert and tremulousness and meditation as before.

But, in spite of these things, it was a gay and magnificent revel. The tastes of the duke were peculiar. He had a fine eye for colors and effects. He disregarded the decora of mere fashion. His plans were bold and fiery, and his conceptions glowed with barbaric luster. There are some who would have thought him mad. His followers felt that he was not. It was necessary to hear and see and touch him to be sure that he was not.

He had directed, in great part, the movable embellishments of the seven chambers, upon occasion of this great fête; and it was his own guiding taste which had given character to the masqueraders. Be sure they were grotesque. There were much glare and glitter and piquancy and phantasm—much of what has been since seen in Hernani. There were arabesque figures with unsuited limbs and appointments. There were delirious fancies such as the madman fashions. There were much of the beautiful, much of the wanton, much of the bizarre, something of the terrible, and not a little of that which might have excited disgust. To and fro in the seven chambers there stalked, in fact, a multitude of dreams. And these—the dreams—writhed in and about, taking hue from the rooms, and causing the wild music of the orchestra to seem as the echo of their steps. And, anon, there strikes the ebony clock which stands in the hall of the velvet. And then, for a moment, all is still, and all is silent save the voice of the clock. The dreams are stiff-frozen as they stand. But the echoes of the chime die away—they have endured but an instant—and a light, half-subdued laughter floats after them as they depart. And now again the music swells, and the dreams live, and writhe to and fro more merrily than ever, taking hue from the many-tinted windows through which stream the rays from the tripods. But to the chamber which lies most westwardly of the seven there are now none of the maskers who venture; for the night is waning away; and there flows a ruddier light through the blood-colored panes; and the blackness of the sable drapery appals; and to him whose foot falls upon the sable carpet, there comes from the near clock of ebony a muffled peal more solemnly emphatic than any which reaches their ears who indulged in the more remote gaieties of the other apartments.

But these other apartments were densely crowded, and in them beat feverishly the heart of life. And the revel went whirlingly on, until at length there commenced the sounding of midnight upon the clock. And then the music ceased, as I have told; and the evolutions of the waltzers were quieted; and there was an uneasy cessation of all things as before. But now there were twelve strokes to be sounded by the bell of the clock; and thus it happened, perhaps, that more of thought crept, with more of time, into the meditations of the thoughtful among those who reveled. And thus too, it happened, perhaps, that before the last echoes of the last chime had utterly sunk into silence, there were many individuals in the crowd who had found leisure to become aware of the presence of a masked figure which had arrested the attention of no single individual before. And the rumor of this new presence having spread itself whisperingly around, there arose at length from the whole company a buzz, or murmur, expressive of disapprobation and surprise—then finally, of terror, of horror, and of disgust.

In an assembly of phantasms such as I have painted, it may well be supposed that no ordinary appearance could have excited such sensation.

In truth the masquerade license of the night was nearly unlimited; but the figure in question had out-Heroded Herod, and gone beyond the bounds of even the prince's indefinite decorum. There are chords in the hearts of the most reckless which cannot be touched without emotion. Even with the utterly lost, to whom life and death are equally jests, there are matters of which no jest can be made. The whole company, indeed, seemed now deeply to feel that in the costume and bearing of the stranger neither wit nor propriety existed. The figure was tall and gaunt, and shrouded from head to foot in the habiliments of the grave. The mask which concealed the visage was made so nearly to resemble the countenance of a stiffened corpse that the closest scrutiny must have had difficulty in detecting the cheat. And yet all this might have been endured, if not approved, by the mad revelers around. But the mummer had gone so far as to assume the type of the Red Death. His vesture was dabbled in blood—and his broad brow, with all the features of the face, was be-sprinkled with the scarlet horror.

When the eyes of Prince Prospero fell upon this spectral image (which, with a slow and solemn movement, as if more fully to sustain its rôle, stalked to and fro among the waltzers) he was seen to be convulsed in the first moment with a strong shudder either of terror or distaste; but, in the next, his brow reddened with rage.

"Who dares,"—he demanded hoarsely of the courtiers who stood near him—"who dares insult us with this blasphemous mockery? Seize him and unmask him—that we may know whom we have to hang, at sunrise, from the battlements!"

It was in the eastern or blue chamber in which stood the Prince Prospero as he uttered these words. They rang throughout the seven rooms loudly and clearly—for the prince was a bold and robust man, and the music had become hushed at the waving of his hand.

It was in the blue room where stood the prince, with a group of pale courtiers by his side. At first, as he spoke, there was a slight rushing movement of this group in the direction of the intruder, who at the moment was also near at hand, and now, with deliberate and stately step, made closer approach to the speaker. But from a certain nameless awe with which the mad assumptions of the mummer had inspired the whole party, there were found none who put forth hand to seize him; so that, unimpeded, he passed within a yard of the prince's person; and, while the vast assembly, as if with one impulse, shrank from the centers of the rooms to the walls, he made his way uninterruptedly, but with the same solemn and measured step which had distinguished him from the first, through the blue chamber to the purple—through the purple to the green—through the green to the orange—through this again to the white—and even thence to the violet, ere a decided movement had been made to arrest him. It was then, however, that the Prince Prospero, maddening with rage and the shame of his own momentary cowardice, rushed hurriedly through the six chambers, while none followed him on account of a deadly terror that had seized upon all. He bore aloft a drawn dagger, and had approached, in rapid impetuosity, to within three or four feet of the retreating figure, when the latter, having attained the extremity of the velvet apartment, turned suddenly and confronted his pursuer. There was a sharp cry—and the dagger dropped gleaming upon the sable carpet, upon which, instantly afterward, fell prostrate in death the Prince Prospero. Then, summoning the wild courage of despair, a throng of the revelers at once threw themselves into the black apartment, and, seizing the mummer, whose tall figure stood erect and motionless within the shadow of the ebony clock, gasped in unutterable horror at finding the grave cerements and corpse-like mask, which they handled with so violent a rudeness, untenanted by any tangible form.

And now was acknowledged the presence of the Red Death. He had come like a thief in the night. And one by one dropped the revelers in the blood-bedewed halls of their revel, and died each in the despairing posture of his fall. And the life of the ebony clock went out with that of the last of the gay. And the flames of the tripods expired. And Darkness and Decay and the Red Death held illimitable dominion over all.

THE PIT AND THE PENDULUM

Impia tortorum longas hic turba furores
Sanguinis innocui, non satiata, aluit.
Sospite nunc patria, fracto nunc funeris antro,
Mors ubi dira fuit vita salusque patent.
Quatrain composed for the gates of a market to be erected
upon the site of the Jacobin Club House at Paris

I WAS SICK—SICK unto death with that long agony; and when they at length unbound me, and I was permitted to sit, I felt that my senses were leaving me. The sentence—the dread sentence of death—was the last of distinct accentuation which reached my ears. After that the sound of the inquisitorial voices seemed merged in one dreamy indeterminate hum. It conveyed to my soul the idea of revolution—perhaps from its association in fancy with the burr of a mill-wheel. This only for a brief period, for presently I heard no more. Yet, for a while, I saw—but with how terrible an exaggeration! I saw the lips of the black-robed judges. They appeared to me white—whiter than the sheet upon which I trace these words—and thin even to grotesqueness; thin with the intensity of their expression of firmness—of immovable resolution—of stern contempt of human torture. I saw that the decrees of what to me was Fate were still issuing from those lips. I saw them writhe with a deadly locution. I saw them fashion the syllables of my name; and I shuddered because no sound succeeded. I saw, too, for a few moments of delirious horror, the soft and nearly imperceptible waving of the sable draperies which enwrapped the walls of the apartment. And then my vision fell upon the seven tall candles upon the table. At first they wore the aspect of charity, and seemed white slender angels who would save me; but then, all at once, there came a most deadly nausea over my spirit, and I felt every fibre in my frame thrill as if I had touched the wire of a galvanic battery, while the angel forms became meaningless spectres, with heads of flame, and I saw that from them there would be no help. And then there stole into my fancy, like a rich musical note, the thought of what sweet rest there must be in the grave. The thought came gently and stealthily, and it seemed long before it attained full appreciation; but just as my spirit came at length properly to feel and entertain it, the figures of the judges vanished, as if magically, from before me; the tall candles sank into nothingness; their flames went out utterly; the blackness of darkness supervened; all sensations appeared swallowed up in a mad rushing descent as of the soul into Hades. Then silence and stillness and night were the universe.

I had swooned; but still will not say that all of consciousness was lost. What of it remained I will not attempt to define, or even to describe; yet all was not lost. In the deepest slumber—no! In delirium—no! In a swoon—no! In death—no! even in the grave all is not lost. Else there is no immortality for man. Arousing from the most profound of slumbers, we break the gossamer web of some dream. Yet in a second afterward (so frail may that web have been) we remember not that we have dreamed. In the return to life from the swoon there are two stages: first, that of the sense of mental or spiritual; secondly, that of the sense of physical, existence. It seems probable that if, upon reaching the second stage, we could recall the impressions of the first, we should find these impressions eloquent in memories of the gulf beyond. And that gulf is—what? How at least shall we distinguish its shadows from those of the tomb? But if the impressions of what I have termed the first stage are not at will recalled, yet, after long interval, do they not come unbidden, while we marvel whence they come? He who has never swooned, is not he who finds strange palaces and wildly familiar faces in coals that glow; is not he who beholds floating in mid-air the sad visions that the many may not view; is not he who ponders over the perfume of some novel flower; is not he whose brain grows bewildered with the meaning of some musical cadence which has never before arrested his attention.

Amid frequent and thoughtful endeavors to remember; amid earnest struggles to regather some token of the state of seeming nothingness into which my soul had lapsed, there have been moments when I have dreamed of success; there have been brief, very brief periods when I have conjured up remembrances which the lucid reason of a later epoch assures me could have had reference only to that condition of seeming unconsciousness. These shadows of memory tell, indistinctly, of tall figures that lifted and bore me in silence down—down—still down—till a hideous dizziness oppressed me at the mere idea of the interminableness of the descent. They tell also of a vague horror at my heart, on account of that heart's unnatural stillness. Then comes a sense of sudden motionlessness throughout all things; as if those who bore me (a ghastly train!) had outrun, in their descent, the limits of the limitless, and paused from the wearisomeness of their toil. After this I call to mind flatness and dampness; and then all is madness—the madness of a memory which busies itself among forbidden things.

Very suddenly there came back to my soul motion and sound—the tumultuous motion of my heart, and, in my ears, the sound of its beating. Then a pause in which all is blank. Then again sound, and motion, and touch—a tingling sensation pervading my frame. Then the mere consciousness of existence, without thought—a condition which lasted long. Then very suddenly, thought, and shuddering terror, and earnest endeavor to comprehend my true state. Then a strong desire to lapse into insensibility. Then a rushing revival of soul, and a successful effort to move. And now a full memory of the trial, of the judges, of the sable draperies, of the sentence, of the sickness, of the swoon. Then entire forgetfulness of all that followed; of all that a later day and much earnestness of endeavor have enabled me vaguely to recall.

So far, I had not opened my eyes. I felt that I lay upon my back, unbound. I had reached out my hand, and it fell heavily upon something damp and hard. There I suffered it to remain for many minutes, while I strove to imagine where and what I could be. I longed, yet dared not, to employ my vision. I dreaded the first glance at objects around me. It was not that I feared to look upon things horrible, but that I grew aghast lest there should be nothing to see. At length, with a wild desperation at heart, I quickly unclosed my eyes. My worst thoughts, then, were confirmed. The blackness of eternal night encompassed me. I struggled for breath. The intensity of the darkness seemed to oppress and stifle me. The atmosphere was intolerably close. I still lay quietly, and made effort to exercise my reason. I brought to mind the inquisitorial proceedings, and attempted from that point to deduce my real condition. The sentence had passed; and it appeared to me that a very long interval of time had since elapsed. Yet not for a moment did I suppose myself actually dead. Such a supposition, notwithstanding what we read in fiction, is altogether inconsistent with real existence;—but where and in what state was I? The condemned to death, I knew, perished usually at the auto-da-fés, and one of these had been held on the very night of the day of my trial. Had I been remanded to my dungeon, to await the next sacrifice, which would not take place for many months? This I at once saw could not be. Victims had been in immediate demand. Moreover, my dungeon, as well as all the condemned cells at Toledo, had stone floors, and light was not altogether excluded.

A fearful idea now suddenly drove the blood in torrents upon my heart, and for a brief period I once more relapsed into insensibility. Upon recovering, I at once started to my feet, trembling convulsively in every fibre. I thrust my arms wildly above and around me in all directions. I felt nothing; yet dreaded to move a step, lest I should be impeded by the walls of a tomb. Perspiration burst from every pore, and stood in cold big beads upon my forehead. The agony of suspense grew at length intolerable, and I cautiously moved forward, with my arms extended, and my eyes straining from their sockets in the hope of catching some faint ray of light. I proceeded for many paces; but still all was blackness and vacancy. I breathed more freely. It seemed evident that mine was not, at least, the most hideous of fates.

And now, as I still continued to step cautiously onward, there came thronging upon my recollection a thousand vague rumors of the horrors of Toledo. Of the dungeons there had been strange things narrated—fables I had always deemed them—but yet strange, and too ghastly to repeat, save in a whisper. Was I left to perish of starvation in this subterranean world of darkness; or what fate, perhaps even more fearful, awaited me? That the result would be death, and a death of more than customary bitterness, I knew too well the character of my judges to doubt. The mode and the hour were all that occupied or distracted me.

My outstretched hands at length encountered some solid obstruction. It was a wall, seemingly of stone masonry—very smooth, slimy, and cold. I followed it up; stepping with all the careful distrust with which certain antique narratives had inspired me. This process, however, afforded me no means of ascertaining the dimensions of my dungeon, as I might make its circuit and return to the point whence I set out without being aware of the fact, so perfectly uniform seemed the wall. I therefore sought the knife which had been in my pocket when led into the inquisitorial chamber; but it was gone; my clothes had been exchanged for a wrapper of coarse serge. I had thought of forcing the blade in some minute crevice of the masonry, so as to identify my point of departure. The difficulty, nevertheless, was but trivial; although, in the disorder of my fancy, it seemed at first insuperable. I tore a part of the hem from the robe and placed the fragment at full length, and at right angles to the wall. In groping my way around the prison, I could not fail to encounter this rag upon completing the circuit. So, at least, I thought; but I had not counted upon the extent of the dungeon, or upon my own weakness. The ground was moist and slippery. I staggered onward for some time, when I stumbled and fell. My excessive fatigue induced me to remain prostrate; and sleep soon overtook me as I lay.

Upon awaking, and stretching forth an arm, I found beside me a loaf and a pitcher with water. I was too much exhausted to reflect upon this circumstance, but ate and drank with avidity. Shortly afterward, I resumed my tour around the prison, and with much toil, came at last upon the fragment of the serge. Up to the period when I fell, I had counted fifty-two paces, and, upon resuming my walk, I had counted forty-eight more—when I arrived at the rag. There were in all, then, a hundred paces; and, admitting two paces to the yard, I presumed the dungeon to be fifty yards in circuit. I had met, however, with many angles in the wall, and thus I could form no guess at the shape of the vault, for vault I could not help supposing it to be.

I had little object—certainly no hope—in these researches; but a vague curiosity prompted me to continue them. Quitting the wall, I resolved to cross the area of the enclosure. At first, I proceeded with extreme caution, for the floor, although seemingly of solid material, was treacherous with slime. At length, however, I took courage, and did not hesitate to step firmly—endeavoring to cross in as direct a line as possible. I had advanced some ten or twelve paces in this manner, when the remnant of the torn hem of my robe became entangled between my legs. I stepped on it, and fell violently on my face.

In the confusion attending my fall, I did not immediately apprehend a somewhat startling circumstance, which yet, in a few seconds afterward, and while I still lay prostrate, arrested my attention. It was this: my chin rested upon the floor of the prison, but my lips, and the upper portion of my head, although seemingly at a less elevation than the chin, touched nothing. At the same time, my forehead seemed bathed in a clammy vapor, and the peculiar smell of decayed fungus arose to my nostrils. I put forward my arm, and shuddered to find that I had fallen at the very brink of a circular pit, whose extent, of course, I had no means of ascertaining at the moment. Groping about the masonry just below the margin, I succeeded in dislodging a small fragment, and let it fall into the abyss. For many seconds I hearkened to its reverberations as it dashed against the sides of the chasm in its descent; at length, there was a sullen plunge into water, succeeded by loud echoes. At the same moment, there came a sound resembling the quick opening and as rapid closing of a door overhead, while a faint gleam of light flashed suddenly through the gloom, and as suddenly faded away.

I saw clearly the doom which had been prepared for me, and congratulated myself upon the timely accident by which I had escaped. Another step before my fall, and the world had seen me no more. And the death just avoided was of that very character which I had regarded as fabulous and frivolous in the tales respecting the Inquisition. To the victims of its tyranny, there was the choice of death with its direst physical agonies, or death with its most hideous moral horrors. I had been reserved for the latter. By long suffering my nerves had been unstrung, until I trembled at the sound of my own voice, and had become in every respect a fitting subject for the species of torture which awaited me.

Shaking in every limb, I groped my way back to the wall—resolving there to perish rather than risk the terrors of the wells, of which my imagination now pictured many in various positions about the dungeon. In other conditions of mind, I might have had courage to end my misery at once, by a plunge into one of these abysses; but now I was the veriest of cowards. Neither could I forget what I had read of these pits—that the sudden extinction of life formed no part of their most horrible plan.

Agitation of spirit kept me awake for many long hours, but at length I again slumbered. Upon arousing, I found by my side, as before, a loaf and a pitcher of water. A burning thirst consumed me, and I emptied the vessel at a draft. It must have been drugged—for scarcely had I drunk, before I became irresistibly drowsy. A deep sleep fell upon me, a sleep like that of death. How long it lasted, of course I know not; but when, once again, I unclosed my eyes, the objects around me were visible. By a wild, sulfurous luster, the origin of which I could not at first determine, I was enabled to see the extent and aspect of the prison.

In its size I had been greatly mistaken. The whole circuit of its walls did not exceed twenty-five yards. For some minutes this fact occasioned me a world of vain trouble; vain indeed—for what could be of less importance, under the terrible circumstances which environed me, than the mere dimensions of my dungeon? But my soul took a wild interest in trifles, and I busied myself in endeavors to account for the error I had committed in my measurement. The truth at length flashed upon me. In my first attempt at exploration I had counted fifty-two paces, up to the period when I fell: I must then have been within a pace or two of the fragment of serge; in fact, I had nearly performed the circuit of the vault. I then slept—and upon awaking, I must have turned upon my steps—thus supposing the circuit nearly double what it actually was. My confusion of mind prevented me from observing that I began my tour with the wall to the left, and ended with the wall to the right.

I had been deceived, too, in respect to the shape of the enclosure. In feeling my way I had found many angles, and thus deduced an idea of great irregularity; so potent is the effect of total darkness upon one arousing from lethargy or sleep! The angles were simply those of a few slight depressions, or niches at odd intervals. The general shape of the prison was square. What I had taken for masonry seemed now to be iron, or some other metal, in huge plates, whose sutures or joints occasioned the depression. The entire surface of this metallic enclosure was rudely daubed in all the hideous and repulsive devices to which the charnel superstition of the monks has given rise. The figures of fiends in aspects of menace, with skeleton forms, and other more really fearful images, overspread and disfigured the walls. I observed that the outlines of these monstrosities were sufficiently distinct, but that the colors seemed faded and blurred, as if from the effects of a damp atmosphere. I now noticed the floor, too, which was of stone. In the center yawned the circular pit from whose jaws I had escaped; but it was the only one in the dungeon.

All this I saw indistinctly and by much effort—for my personal condition had been greatly changed during slumber. I now lay upon my back, and at full length, on a species of low framework of wood. To this I was securely bound by a long strap resembling a surcingle. It passed in many convolutions about my limbs and body, leaving at liberty only my head, and my left arm to such extent, that I could, by dint of much exertion, supply myself with food from an earthen dish which lay by my side on the floor. I saw, to my horror, that the pitcher had been removed. I say to my horror—for I was consumed with intolerable thirst. This thirst it appeared to be the design of my persecutors to stimulate—for the food in the dish was meat pungently seasoned.

Looking upward, I surveyed the ceiling of my prison. It was some thirty or forty feet overhead, and constructed much as the side walls. In one of its panels a very singular figure riveted my whole attention. It was the painted figure of Time as he is commonly represented, save that, in lieu of a scythe, he held what, at a casual glance, I supposed to be the pictured image of a huge pendulum, such as we see on antique clocks. There was something, however, in the appearance of this machine which caused me to regard it more attentively. While I gazed directly upward at it (for its position was immediately over my own) I fancied that I saw it in motion. In an instant afterward the fancy was confirmed. Its sweep was brief, and of course slow. I watched it for some minutes somewhat in fear, but more in wonder. Wearied at length with observing its dull movement, I turned my eyes upon the other objects in the cell.

A slight noise attracted my notice, and, looking to the floor, I saw several enormous rats traversing it. They had issued from the well which lay just within view to my right. Even then, while I gazed, they came up in troops, hurriedly, with ravenous eyes, allured by the scent of the meat. From this it required much effort and attention to scare them away.

It might have been half an hour, perhaps even an hour (for I could take but imperfect note of time), before I again cast my eyes upward. What I then saw confounded and amazed me. The sweep of the pendulum had increased in extent by nearly a yard. As a natural consequence its velocity was also much greater. But what mainly disturbed me was the idea that it had perceptibly *descended.* I now observed—with what horror it is needless to say—that its nether extremity was formed of a crescent of glittering steel, about a foot in length from horn to horn; the horns upward, and the under edge evidently as keen as that of a razor. Like a razor also, it seemed massive and heavy, tapering from the edge into a solid and broad structure above. It was appended to a weighty rod of brass, and the whole hissed as it swung through the air.

I could no longer doubt the doom prepared for me by monkish ingenuity in torture. My cognizance of the pit had become known to the inquisitorial agents—the pit, whose horrors had been destined for so bold a recusant as myself—the pit, typical of hell and regarded by rumor as the Ultima Thule of all their punishments. The plunge into this pit I had avoided by the merest of accidents, and I knew that surprise, or entrapment into torment, formed an important portion of all the grotesquerie of these dungeon deaths. Having failed to fall, it was no part of the demon plan to hurl me into the abyss; and thus (there being no alternative) a different and milder destruction awaited me. Milder! I half smiled in my agony as I thought of such application of such a term.

What boots it to tell of the long, long hours of horror more than mortal, during which I counted the rushing oscillations of the steel! Inch by inch—line by line—with a descent only appreciable at intervals that seemed ages—down and still down it came! Days passed—it might have been that many days passed—ere it swept so closely over me as to fan me with its acrid breath. The odor of the sharp steel forced itself into my nostrils. I prayed—I wearied heaven with my prayer for its more speedy descent. I grew frantically mad, and struggled to force myself upward against the sweep of the fearful scimitar. And then I fell suddenly calm, and lay smiling at the glittering death, as a child at some rare bauble.

There was another interval of utter insensibility; it was brief; for, upon again lapsing into life, there had been no perceptible descent in the pendulum. But it might have been long—for I knew there were demons who took note of my swoon, and who could have arrested the vibration at pleasure. Upon my recovery, too, I felt very—oh! inexpressibly—sick and weak, as if through long inanition. Even amid the agonies of that period the human nature craved food. With painful effort I outstretched my left arm as far as my bonds permitted, and took possession of the small remnant which had been spared me by the rats. As I put a portion of it within my lips, there rushed to my mind a half-formed thought of joy—of hope. Yet what business had I with hope? It was, as I say, a half-formed thought—man has many such, which are never completed. I felt that it was of joy—of hope; but I felt also that it had perished in its formation. In vain I struggled to perfect—to regain it. Long suffering had nearly annihilated all my ordinary powers of mind. I was an imbecile—an idiot.

The vibration of the pendulum was at right angles to my length. I saw that the crescent was designed to cross the region of the heart. It would fray the serge of my robe—it would return and repeat its operations—again—and again. Notwithstanding its terrifically wide sweep (some thirty feet or more), and the hissing vigor of its descent, sufficient to sunder these very walls of iron, still the fraying of my robe would be all that, for several minutes, it would accomplish. And at this thought I paused. I dared not go further than this reflection. I dwelt upon it with a pertinacity of attention—as if, in so dwelling, I could arrest here the descent of the steel. I forced myself to ponder upon the sound of the crescent as it should pass across the garment—upon the peculiar thrilling sensation which the friction of cloth produces on the nerves. I pondered over all this frivolity until my teeth were on edge.

Down—steadily down it crept. I took a frenzied pleasure in

contrasting its downward with its lateral velocity. To the right—to the left—far and wide—with the shriek of a damned spirit! to my heart, with the stealthy pace of the tiger! I alternately laughed and howled, as the one or the other idea grew predominant.

Down—certainly, relentlessly down! It vibrated within three inches of my bosom! I struggled violently—furiously—to free my left arm. This was free only from the elbow to the hand. I could reach the latter, from the platter beside me, to my mouth, with great effort, but no farther. Could I have broken the fastenings above the elbow, I would have seized and attempted to arrest the pendulum. I might as well have attempted to arrest an avalanche!

Down—still unceasingly—still inevitably down! I gasped and struggled at each vibration. I shrunk convulsively at its every sweep. My eyes followed its outward or upward whirls with the eagerness of the most unmeaning despair; they closed themselves spasmodically at the descent, although death would have been a relief, oh, how unspeakable! Still I quivered in every nerve to think how slight a sinking of the machinery would precipitate that keen, glistening ax upon my bosom. It was hope that prompted the nerve to quiver—the frame to shrink. It was hope—the hope that triumphs on the rack—that whispers to the death-condemned even in the dungeons of the Inquisition.

I saw that some ten or twelve vibrations would bring the steel in actual contact with my robe—and with this observation there suddenly came over my spirit all the keen, collected calmness of despair. For the first time during many hours—or perhaps days—I thought. It now occurred to me, that the bandage, or surcingle, which enveloped me, was unique. I was tied by no separate cord. The first stroke of the razor-like crescent athwart any portion of the band would so detach it that it might be unwound from my person by means of my left hand. But how fearful, in that case, the proximity of the steel! The result of the slightest struggle, how deadly! Was it likely, moreover, that the minions of the torturer had not foreseen and provided for this possibility? Was it probable that the bandage crossed my bosom in the track of the pendulum? Dreading to find my faint and, as it seemed, my last hope frustrated, I so far elevated my head as to obtain a distinct view of my breast. The surcingle enveloped my limbs and body close in all directions—*save in the path of the destroying crescent.*

Scarcely had I dropped my head back into its original position, when there flashed upon my mind what I cannot better describe than as the unformed half of that idea of deliverance to which I have previously alluded, and of which a moiety only floated indeterminately through my brain when I raised food to my burning lips. The whole thought was now present—feeble, scarcely sane, scarcely definite—but still entire. I proceeded at once, with the nervous energy of despair, to attempt its execution.

For many hours the immediate vicinity of the low framework upon which I lay had been literally swarming with rats. They were wild, bold, ravenous—their red eyes glaring upon me as if they waited but for motionlessness on my part to make me their prey. "To what food," I thought, "have they been accustomed in the well?"

They had devoured, in spite of all my efforts to prevent them, all but a small remnant of the contents of the dish. I had fallen into an habitual see-saw or wave of the hand about the platter; and, at length, the unconscious uniformity of the movement deprived it of effect. In their voracity, the vermin frequently fastened their sharp fangs in my fingers. With the particles of the oily and spicy viand which now remained, I thoroughly rubbed the bandage wherever I could reach it; then, raising my hand from the floor, I lay breathlessly still.

At first, the ravenous animals were startled and terrified at the change—at the cessation of movement. They shrank alarmedly back; many sought the well. But this was only for a moment. I had not counted in vain upon their voracity. Observing that I remained without motion, one or two of the boldest leaped upon the framework, and smelt at the surcingle. This seemed the signal for a general rush. Forth from the well they hurried in fresh troops. They clung to the wood—they overran it, and leaped in hundreds upon my person. The measured movement of the pendulum disturbed them not at all. Avoiding its strokes, they busied themselves with the anointed bandage. They pressed—they swarmed upon me in ever accumulating heaps. They writhed upon my throat; their cold lips sought my own; I was half stifled by their thronging pressure; disgust, for which the world has no name, swelled my bosom, and chilled, with a heavy clamminess, my heart. Yet one minute, and I felt that the struggle would be over. Plainly I perceived the loosening of the bandage. I knew that in more than one place it must be already severed. With a more than human resolution I lay still.

Nor had I erred in my calculations—nor had I endured in vain. I at length felt that I was free. The surcingle hung in ribands from my body. But the stroke of the pendulum already pressed upon my bosom. It had divided the serge of the robe. It had cut through the linen beneath. Twice again it swung, and a sharp sense of pain shot through every nerve. But the moment of escape had arrived. At a wave of my hand my deliverers hurried tumultuously away. With a steady movement—cautious sidelong, shrinking, and slow—I slid from the embrace of the bandage and beyond the reach of the scimitar. For the moment, at least, I was free.

Free!—and in the grasp of the Inquisition! I had scarcely stepped from my wooden bed of horror upon the stone floor of the prison, when the motion of the hellish machine ceased, and I beheld it drawn up, by some invisible force, through the ceiling. This was a lesson which I took desperately to heart. My every motion was undoubtedly watched. Free!—I had but escaped death in one form of agony, to be delivered unto worse than death in some other. With that thought I rolled my eyes nervously around on the barriers of iron that hemmed me in. Something unusual—some change, which, at first, I could not appreciate distinctly—it was obvious, had taken place in the apartment. For many minutes of a dreamy and trembling abstraction, I busied myself in vain, unconnected conjecture. During this period, I became aware, for the first time, of the origin of the sulfurous light which illumined the cell. It proceeded from a fissure, about half an inch in width, extending entirely around the prison at the base of the walls, which thus appeared, and were completely separated from the floor. I endeavored, but of course in vain, to look through the aperture.

As I arose from the attempt, the mystery of the alteration in the chamber broke at once upon my understanding. I have observed that, although the outlines of the figures upon the walls were sufficiently distinct, yet the colors seemed blurred and indefinite. These colors had now assumed, and were momentarily assuming a startling and most intense brilliancy, that gave to the spectral and fiendish portraitures an aspect that might have thrilled even firmer nerves than my own. Demon eyes, of a wild and ghastly vivacity, glared upon me in a thousand directions, where none had been visible before, and gleamed with the lurid luster of a fire that I could not force my imagination to regard as unreal.

Unreal!—Even while I breathed there came to my nostrils the breath of the vapor of heated iron! A suffocating odor pervaded the prison! A deeper glow settled each moment in the eyes that glared at my agonies! A richer tint of crimson diffused itself over the pictured horrors of blood. I panted! I gasped for breath! There could be no doubt of the design of my tormentors—oh! most unrelenting! oh! most demoniac of men! I shrank from the glowing metal to the center of the cell. Amid the thought of the fiery destruction that impended, the idea of the coolness of the well came over my soul like balm. I rushed to its deadly brink. I threw my straining vision below. The glare from the enkindled roof illumined its inmost recesses. Yet, for a wild moment, did my spirit refuse to comprehend the meaning of what I saw. At length it forced—it wrestled its way into my soul—it burned itself in upon my shuddering reason. Oh! for a voice to speak!—oh! horror!—oh! any horror but this! With a shriek, I rushed from the margin, and buried my face in my hands—weeping bitterly.

The heat rapidly increased, and once again I looked up, shuddering as with a fit of the ague. There had been a second change in the cell—and now the change was obviously in the form. As before, it was in vain that I at first endeavored to appreciate or understand what was taking place. But not long was I left in doubt. The Inquisitorial vengeance had been hurried by my twofold escape, and there was to be no more dallying with the King of Terrors. The room had been square. I saw that two of its iron angles were now acute—two, consequently, obtuse. The fearful difference quickly increased with a low rumbling or moaning sound. In an instant the apartment had shifted its form into that of a lozenge. But the alteration stopped not here—I neither hoped nor desired it to stop. I could have clasped the red walls to my bosom as a garment of eternal peace. "Death," I said, "any death but that of the pit!" Fool! might I not have known that into the pit it was the object of the burning iron to urge me? Could I resist its glow? or if even that, could I withstand its pressure? And now, flatter and flatter grew the lozenge, with a rapidity that left me no time for contemplation. Its center, and of course its greatest width, came just over the yawning gulf. I shrank back—but the closing walls pressed me resistlessly onward. At length for my seared and writhing body there was no longer an inch of foothold on the firm floor of the prison. I struggled no more, but the agony of my soul found vent in one loud, long, and final scream of despair. I felt that I tottered upon the brink—I averted my eyes—

There was a discordant hum of human voices! There was a loud blast as of many trumpets! There was a harsh grating as of a thousand thunders! The fiery walls rushed back! An outstretched arm caught my own as I fell, fainting, into the abyss. It was that of General Lasalle. The French army had entered Toledo. The Inquisition was in the hands of its enemies.

THE TELL-TALE HEART

TRUE!—NERVOUS—VERY, very dreadfully nervous I had been and am; but why will you say that I am mad? The disease had sharpened my senses—not destroyed—not dulled them. Above all was the sense of hearing acute. I heard all things in the heaven and in the earth. I heard many things in hell. How, then, am I mad? Hearken! and observe how healthily—how calmly I can tell you the whole story.

It is impossible to say how first the idea entered my brain; but once conceived, it haunted me day and night. Object there was none. Passion there was none. I loved the old man. He had never wronged me. He had never given me insult. For his gold I had no desire. I think it was his eye! yes, it was this! He had the eye of a vulture—a pale blue eye, with a film over it. Whenever it fell upon me, my blood ran cold; and so by degrees—very gradually—I made up my mind to take the life of the old man, and thus rid myself of the eye for ever.

Now this is the point. You fancy me mad. Madmen know nothing. But you should have seen me. You should have seen how wisely I proceeded—with what caution—with what foresight—with what dissimulation I went to work! I was never kinder to the old man than during the whole week before I killed him. And every night, about midnight, I turned the latch of his door and opened it—oh, so gently! And then, when I had made an opening sufficient for my head, I put in a dark lantern, all closed, closed, so that no light shone out, and then I thrust in my head. Oh, you would have laughed to see how cunningly I thrust it in! I moved it slowly—very, very slowly, so that I might not disturb the old man's sleep. It took me an hour to place my whole head within the opening so far that

I could see him as he lay upon his bed. Ha!—would a madman have been so wise as this? And then, when my head was well in the room, I undid the lantern cautiously—oh, so cautiously—cautiously (for the hinges creaked)—I undid it just so much that a single thin ray fell upon the vulture eye. And this I did for seven long nights—every night just at midnight—but I found the eye always closed; and so it was impossible to do the work; for it was not the old man who vexed me, but his Evil Eye. And every morning, when the day broke, I went boldly into the chamber, and spoke courageously to him, calling him by name in a hearty tone, and inquiring how he had passed the night. So you see he would have been a very profound old man, indeed, to suspect that every night, just at twelve, I looked in upon him while he slept.

Upon the eighth night I was more than usually cautious in opening the door. A watch's minute-hand moves more quickly than did mine. Never before that night, had I felt the extent of my own powers—of my sagacity. I could scarcely contain my feelings of triumph. To think that there I was, opening the door, little by little, and he not even to dream of my secret deeds or thoughts. I fairly chuckled at the idea; and perhaps he heard me; for he moved on the bed suddenly, as if startled. Now you may think that I drew back—but no. His room was as black as pitch with the thick darkness (for the shutters were close fastened, through fear of robbers), and so I knew that he could not see the opening of the door, and I kept pushing it on steadily, steadily.

I had my head in, and was about to open the lantern, when my thumb slipped upon the tin fastening, and the old man sprang up in bed, crying out—"Who's there?"

I kept quite still and said nothing. For a whole hour I did not move a muscle, and in the meantime I did not hear him lie down. He was still sitting up in the bed listening;—just as I have done, night after night, hearkening to the death-watches in the wall.

Presently I heard a slight groan, and I knew it was the groan of mortal terror. It was not a groan of pain or of grief—oh, no!—it was the low stifled sound that arises from the bottom of the soul when overcharged with awe. I knew the sound well. Many a night, just at midnight, when all the world slept, it has welled up from my own bosom, deepening, with its dreadful echo, the terrors that distracted me. I say I knew it well. I knew what the old man felt, and pitied him, although I chuckled at heart. I knew that he had been lying awake ever since the first slight noise, when he had turned in the bed. His fears had been ever since growing upon him. He had been trying to fancy them causeless, but could not. He had been saying to himself—"It is nothing but the wind in the chimney—it is only a mouse crossing the floor," or "it is merely a cricket which has made a single chirp." Yes, he had been trying to comfort himself with these suppositions: but he had found all in vain. All in vain; because Death, in approaching him had stalked with his black shadow before him, and enveloped the victim. And it was the mournful influence of the unperceived shadow that caused him to feel—although he neither saw nor heard—to feel the presence of my head within the room.

When I had waited a long time, very patiently, without hearing him lie down, I resolved to open a little—a very, very little crevice in the lantern. So I opened it—you cannot imagine how stealthily, stealthily—until, at length a single dim ray, like the thread of the spider, shot from out the crevice and fell full upon the vulture eye.

It was open—wide, wide open—and I grew furious as I gazed upon it. I saw it with perfect distinctness—all a dull blue, with a hideous veil over it that chilled the very marrow in my bones; but I could see nothing else of the old man's face or person: for I had directed the ray, as if by instinct, precisely upon the damned spot.

And have I not told you that what you mistake for madness is but overacuteness of the senses?—now, I say, there came to my ears a low, dull, quick sound, such as a watch makes when enveloped in cotton. I knew that sound well, too. It was the beating of the old man's heart. It increased my fury, as the beating of a drum stimulates the soldier into courage.

But even yet I refrained and kept still. I scarcely breathed. I held the lantern motionless. I tried how steadily I could maintain the ray upon the eye. Meantime the hellish tattoo of the heart increased. It grew quicker and quicker, and louder and louder every instant. The old man's terror must have been extreme! It grew louder, I say, louder every moment!—do you mark me well? I have told you that

I am nervous: so I am. And now at the dead hour of the night, amid the dreadful silence of that old house, so strange a noise as this excited me to uncontrollable terror. Yet, for some minutes longer I refrained and stood still. But the beating grew louder, louder! I thought the heart must burst. And now a new anxiety seized me—the sound would be heard by a neighbor! The old man's hour had come! With a loud yell, I threw open the lantern and leaped into the room. He shrieked once—once only. In an instant I dragged him to the floor, and pulled the heavy bed over him. I then smiled gaily, to find the deed so far done. But, for many minutes, the heart beat on with a muffled sound. This, however, did not vex me; it would not be heard through the wall. At length it ceased. The old man was dead. I removed the bed and examined the corpse. Yes, he was stone, stone dead. I placed my hand upon the heart and held it there many minutes. There was no pulsation. He was stone dead. His eye would trouble me no more.

If still you think me mad, you will think so no longer when I describe the wise precautions I took for the concealment of the body. The night waned, and I worked hastily, but in silence. First of all I dismembered the corpse. I cut off the head and the arms and the legs.

I then took up three planks from the flooring of the chamber, and deposited all between the scantlings. I then replaced the boards so cleverly, so cunningly, that no human eye—not even his—could have detected anything wrong. There was nothing to wash out—no stain of any kind—no blood-spot whatever. I had been too wary for that. A tub had caught all—ha! ha!

When I had made an end of these labors, it was four o'clock—still dark as midnight. As the bell sounded the hour, there came a knocking at the street door. I went down to open it with a light heart,—for what had I now to fear? There entered three men, who introduced themselves, with perfect suavity, as officers of the police. A shriek had been heard by a neighbor during the night; suspicion of foul play had been aroused; information had been lodged at the police office, and they (the officers) had been deputed to search the premises.

I smiled,—for what had I to fear? I bade the gentlemen welcome.

The shriek, I said, was my own in a dream. The old man, I mentioned, was absent in the country. I took my visitors all over the house. I bade them search—search well. I led them, at length, to his chamber. I showed them his treasures, secure, undisturbed. In the enthusiasm of my confidence, I brought chairs into the room, and desired them here to rest from their fatigues, while I myself, in the wild audacity of my perfect triumph, placed my own seat upon the very spot beneath which reposed the corpse of the victim.

The officers were satisfied. My manner had convinced them. I was singularly at ease. They sat, and while I answered cheerily, they chatted of familiar things. But, ere long, I felt myself getting pale and wished them gone. My head ached, and I fancied a ringing in my ears: but still they sat and still chatted. The ringing became more distinct:—it continued and became more distinct: I talked more freely to get rid of the feeling: but it continued and gained definiteness—until, at length, I found that the noise was not within my ears.

No doubt I now grew very pale;—but I talked more fluently, and with a heightened voice. Yet the sound increased—and what could I do? It was a low, dull, quick sound—much such a sound as a watch makes when enveloped in cotton. I gasped for breath—and yet the officers heard it not. I talked more quickly—more vehemently; but the noise steadily increased. I arose and argued about trifles, in a high key and with violent gesticulations; but the noise steadily increased. Why would they not be gone? I paced the floor to and fro with heavy strides, as if excited to fury by the observations of the men—but the noise steadily increased. Oh God! what could I do? I foamed—I raved—I swore! I swung the chair upon which I had been sitting, and grated it upon the boards, but the noise arose over all and continually increased. It grew louder—louder—louder! And still the men chatted pleasantly, and smiled. Was it possible they heard not? Almighty God!—no, no! They heard!—they suspected!—they knew!—they were making a mockery of my horror!—this I thought, and this I think. But anything was better than this agony! Anything was more tolerable than this derision! I could bear those hypocritical smiles no longer! I felt that I must scream or die! and now—again!—hark! louder! louder! louder! louder!

"Villains!" I shrieked, "dissemble no more! I admit the deed!—tear up the planks! here, here!—it is the beating of his hideous heart!"

THE GOLD BUG

What ho! what ho! this fellow is dancing mad!
He hath been bitten by the Tarantula.
All in the Wrong

MANY YEARS AGO, I contracted an intimacy with a Mr. William Legrand. He was of an ancient Huguenot family, and had once been wealthy; but a series of misfortunes had reduced him to want. To avoid the mortification consequent upon his disasters, he left New Orleans, the city of his forefathers, and took up his residence at Sullivan's Island, near Charleston, South Carolina.

This island is a very singular one. It consists of little else than the sea sand, and is about three miles long. Its breadth at no point exceeds a quarter of a mile. It is separated from the mainland by a scarcely perceptible creek, oozing its way through a wilderness of reeds and slime, a favorite resort of the marsh-hen. The vegetation, as might be supposed, is scant, or at least dwarfish. No trees of any magnitude are to be seen. Near the western extremity, where Fort Moultrie stands, and where are some miserable frame buildings, tenanted, during summer, by the fugitives from Charleston dust and fever, may be found, indeed, the bristly palmetto; but the whole island, with the exception of this western point, and a line of hard, white beach on the sea-coast, is covered with a dense under-growth of the sweet myrtle so much prized by the horticulturist of England. The shrub here often attains the height of fifteen or twenty feet, and forms an almost impenetrable coppice, burthening the air with its fragrance.

In the inmost recesses of this coppice, not far from the eastern or more remote end of the island, Legrand had built himself a small hut, which he occupied when I first, by mere accident, made his acquaintance. This soon ripened into friendship—for there was much in the recluse to excite interest and esteem. I found him well educated, with unusual powers of mind, but infected with misanthropy, and subject to perverse moods of alternate enthusiasm and melancholy. He had with him many books, but rarely employed them. His chief amusements were gunning and fishing, or sauntering along the beach and through the myrtles, in quest of shells or entomological specimens—his collection of the latter might have been envied by a Swammerdamm. In these excursions he was usually accompanied by an old negro, called Jupiter, who had been manumitted before the reverses of the family, but who could be induced, neither by threats nor by promises, to abandon what he considered his right of attendance upon the footsteps of his young "Massa Will." It is not improbable that the relatives of Legrand, conceiving him to be somewhat unsettled in intellect, had contrived to instil this obstinacy into Jupiter, with a view to the supervision and guardianship of the wanderer.

The winters in the latitude of Sullivan's Island are seldom very severe, and in the fall of the year it is a rare event indeed when a fire is considered necessary. About the middle of October, 18—, there occurred, however, a day of remarkable chilliness. Just before sunset I scrambled my way through the evergreens to the hut of my friend, whom I had not visited for several weeks—my residence being, at that time, in Charleston, a distance of nine miles from the island, while the facilities of passage and re-passage were very far behind those of the present day. Upon reaching the hut I rapped, as was my custom, and getting no reply, sought for the key where I knew it was secreted, unlocked the door, and went in. A fine fire was blazing upon the hearth. It was a novelty, and by no means an ungrateful one. I threw off an overcoat, took an arm-chair by the crackling logs, and awaited patiently the arrival of my hosts.

Soon after dark they arrived, and gave me a most cordial welcome. Jupiter, grinning from ear to ear, bustled about to prepare some marsh-hen for supper. Legrand was in one of his fits—how else shall I term them?—of enthusiasm. He had found an unknown bivalve, forming a new genus, and, more than this, he had hunted down and secured, with Jupiter's assistance, a scarabaeus which he believed to be totally new, but in respect to which he wished to have my opinion on the morrow.

"And why not to-night?" I asked, rubbing my hands over the blaze, and wishing the whole tribe of scarabaei at the devil.

"Ah, if I had only known you were here!" said Legrand, "but it's so long since I saw you; and how could I foresee that you would pay me a visit this very night of all others? As I was coming home I met Lieutenant G——, from the fort, and, very foolishly, I lent him the bug; so it will be impossible for you to see it until the morning. Stay here to-night, and I will send Jup down for it at sunrise. It is the loveliest thing in creation!"

"What?—sunrise?"

"Nonsense! no!—the bug. It is of a brilliant gold color—about the size of a large hickory-nut—with two jet black spots near one extremity of the back, and another, somewhat longer, at the other. The antennae are——"

"Dey ain't no tin in him, Massa Will, I keep a tellin' on you," here interrupted Jupiter; "de bug is a goole-bug, solid, ebery bit of him, inside and all, sep him wing—neber feel half so hebby a bug in my life."

"Well, suppose it is, Jup," replied Legrand, somewhat more earnestly, it seemed to me, than the case demanded; "is that any reason for your letting the birds burn? The color"—here he turned to me—"is really almost enough to warrant Jupiter's idea. You never saw a more brilliant metallic luster than the scales emit—but of this you cannot judge till to-morrow. In the meantime I can give you some idea of the shape." Saying this, he seated himself at a small table, on which were a pen and ink, but no paper. He looked for some in a drawer, but found none.

"Never mind," he said at length, "this will answer"; and he drew from his waistcoat pocket a scrap of what I took to be very dirty foolscap, and made upon it a rough drawing with the pen. While he did this, I retained my seat by the fire, for I was still chilly. When the design was complete, he handed it to me without rising. As I received it, a loud growl was heard, succeeded by scratching at the door. Jupiter opened it, and a large Newfoundland, belonging to Legrand, rushed in, leaped upon my shoulders, and loaded me with caresses; for I had shown him much attention during previous visits. When his gambols were over, I looked at the paper, and, to speak the truth, found myself not a little puzzled at what my friend had depicted.

"Well!" I said, after contemplating it for some minutes, "this is a strange scarabaeus, I must confess; new to me; never saw anything like it before—unless it was a skull, or a death's-head, which it more nearly resembles than anything else that has come under my observation."

"A death's-head!" echoed Legrand. "Oh—yes—well, it has something of that appearance upon paper, no doubt. The two upper black spots look like eyes, eh? and the longer one at the bottom like a mouth—and then the shape of the whole is oval."

"Perhaps so," said I; "but, Legrand, I fear you are no artist. I must wait until I see the beetle itself, if I am to form any idea of its personal appearance."

"Well, I don't know," said he, a little nettled, "I draw tolerably—should do it at least—have had good masters, and flatter myself that I am not quite a blockhead."

"But, my dear fellow, you are joking then," said I, "this is a very passable skull—indeed, I may say that it is a very excellent skull, according to the vulgar notions about such specimens of physiology—and your scarabaeus must be the queerest scarabaeus in the world if it resembles it. Why, we may get up a very thrilling bit of superstition upon this hint. I presume you will call the bug *scarabaeus caput hominis*, or something of that kind—there are many similar titles in the Natural Histories. But where are the antennae you spoke of?"

"The antennae!" said Legrand, who seemed to be getting unaccountably warm upon the subject; "I am sure you must see the antennae. I made them as distinct as they are in the original insect, and I presume that is sufficient."

"Well, well," I said, "perhaps you have—still I don't see them"; and I handed him the paper without additional remark, not wishing to ruffle his temper; but I was much surprised at the turn affairs had taken; his ill-humor puzzled me—and, as for the drawing of the beetle, there were positively no antennae visible, and the whole did bear a very close resemblance to the ordinary cuts of a death's-head.

He received the paper very peevishly, and was about to crumple it, apparently to throw it in the fire, when a casual glance at the design seemed suddenly to rivet his attention. In an instant his face grew violently red—in another as excessively pale. For some minutes he continued to scrutinize the drawing minutely where he sat. At length he arose, took a candle from the table, and proceeded to seat himself upon a sea-chest in the furthest corner of the room. Here again he made an anxious examination of the paper; turning it in all directions. He said nothing, however, and his conduct greatly astonished me; yet I thought it prudent not to exacerbate the growing moodiness of his temper by any comment. Presently he took from his coat-pocket a wallet, placed the paper carefully in it, and deposited both in a writing desk, which he locked. He now grew more composed in his demeanor; but his original air of enthusiasm had quite disappeared. Yet he seemed not so much sulky as abstracted. As the evening wore away he became more and more absorbed in reverie, from which no sallies of mine could arouse him. It had been my intention to pass the night at the hut, as I had frequently done before, but, seeing my host in this mood, I deemed it proper to take leave. He did not press me to remain, but, as I departed, he shook my hand with even more than his usual cordiality.

It was about a month after this (and during the interval I had seen nothing of Legrand) when I received a visit at Charleston, from his man, Jupiter. I had never seen the good old negro look so dispirited, and I feared that some serious disaster had befallen my friend.

"Well, Jup," said I, "what is the matter now?—how is your master?"

"Why, to speak de troof, massa, him not so berry well as mought be."

"Not well! I am truly sorry to hear it. What does he complain of?"

"Dar! dat's it!—he neber 'plain of notin'—but him berry sick for all dat."

"Very sick, Jupiter!—why didn't you say so at once? Is he confined to bed?"

"No, dat he ain't!—he ain't 'fin'd nowhar—dat's just whar de shoe pinch—my mind is got to be berry hebby 'bout poor Massa Will."

"Jupiter, I should like to understand what it is you are talking about. You say your master is sick. Hasn't he told you what ails him?"

"Why, massa, 'tain't worf while for to git mad about de matter—Massa Will say noffin at all ain't de matter wid him—but den what makes him go about looking dis here way, wid he head down and he soldiers up, and as white as a gose? And den he keep a syphon all de time——"

"Keep's a what, Jupiter?"

"Keeps a syphon wid de figgurs on de slate—de queerest figgurs I ebber did see. Ise gettin' to be skeered, I tell you. Hab for to keep mighty tight eye 'pon him 'noovers. Todder day he gib me slip fore de sun up and was gone the whole ob de blessed day. I had a big stick ready cut for to gib him deuced good beating when he did come—but Ise sich a fool dat I hadn't de heart arter all—he looked so berry poorly."

"Eh?—what?—ah yes!—upon the whole I think you had better not be too severe with the poor fellow—don't flog him, Jupiter—he can't very well stand it—but can you form no idea of what has occasioned this illness, or rather this change of conduct? Has anything unpleasant happened since I saw you?"

"No, massa, dey ain't bin noffin onpleasant since den—'twas 'fore den I'm feared—'twas de berry day you was dare."

"How? what do you mean?"

"Why, massa, I mean de bug—dare now."

"The what?"

"De bug—I'm berry sartain dat Massa Will bin bit somewhere 'bout de head by dat goole-bug."

"And what cause have you, Jupiter, for such a supposition?"

"Claws enuff, massa, and mouff too. I nebber did see sich a deuced bug—he kick and he bite ebery ting what cum near him. Massa Will cotch him fuss, but had for to let him go 'gin mighty quick, I tell you—den was de time he must ha' got de bite. I didn't like de look ob de bug mouff, myself, nohow, so I wouldn't take hold ob him wid my finger, but I cotch him wid a piece ob paper dat I found. I rap him up in de paper and stuff a piece of it in he mouff—dat was de way."

"And you think, then, that your master was really bitten by the beetle, and that the bite made him sick?"

"I don't think noffin' about it—I nose it. What make him dream 'bout de goole so much, if 'tain't 'cause he bit by the goole-bug? Ise heerd 'bout dem goole-bugs 'fore dis."

"But how do you know he dreams about gold?"

"How I know? why, 'cause he talk about it in he sleep—dat's how I nose."

"Well, Jup, perhaps you are right; but to what fortunate circumstances am I to attribute the honor of a visit from you to-day?"

"What de matter, massa?"

"Did you bring any message from Mr. Legrand?"

"No, massa, I bring dis here pissel"; and here Jupiter handed me a note which ran thus:

My Dear—,

Why have I not seen you for so long a time? I hope you have not been so foolish as to take offense at any little brusquerie of mine; but no, that is improbable.

Since I saw you I have had great cause for anxiety. I have something to tell you, yet scarcely know how to tell it, or whether I should tell it at all.

I have not been quite well for some days past, and poor old Jup annoys me, almost beyond endurance, by his well-meant attentions. Would you believe it?—he had prepared a huge stick, the other day, with which to chastise me for giving him the slip, and spending the day, solus, among the hills on the mainland. I verily believe that my ill looks alone saved me a flogging.

I have made no addition to my cabinet since we met.

If you can, in any way, make it convenient, come over with Jupiter. Do come. I wish to see you to-night, upon business of importance. I assure you that it is of the highest importance.

Ever yours,
William Legrand

There was something in the tone of this note which gave me great uneasiness. Its whole style differed materially from that of Legrand. What could he be dreaming of? What new crotchet possessed his excitable brain? What "business of the highest importance" could he possibly have to transact? Jupiter's account of him boded no good. I dreaded lest the continued pressure of misfortune had, at length, fairly unsettled the reason of my friend. Without a moment's hesitation, therefore, I prepared to accompany the negro.

Upon reaching the wharf, I noticed a scythe and three spades, all apparently new, lying in the bottom of the boat in which we were to embark.

"What is the meaning of all this, Jup?" I inquired.

"Him syfe, massa, and spade."

"Very true; but what are they doing here?"

"Him de syfe and de spade what Massa Will sis 'pon my buying for him in de town, and de debbil's own lot of money I had to gib for 'em."

"But what, in the name of all that is mysterious, is your 'Massa Will' going to do with scythes and spades?"

"Dat's more dan I know, and debbil take me if I don't b'lieve 'tis more dan he know too. But it's all cum ob de bug."

Finding that no satisfaction was to be obtained of Jupiter, whose whole intellect seemed to be absorbed by "de bug," I now stepped into the boat, and made sail. With a fair and strong breeze we soon ran into the little cove to the northward of Fort Moultrie, and a walk of some two miles brought us to the hut. It was about three in the afternoon when we arrived. Legrand had been awaiting us in eager expectation. He grasped my hand with a nervous empressement which alarmed me and strengthened the suspicions already entertained. His countenance was pale even to ghastliness, and his deep-set eyes glared with unnatural luster. After some inquiries respecting his health, I asked him, not knowing what better to say, if he had yet obtained the scarabaeus from Lieutenant G——.

"Oh, yes," he replied, coloring violently, "I got it from him the next morning. Nothing should tempt me to part with that scarabaeus. Do you know that Jupiter is quite right about it?"

"In what way?" I asked, with a sad foreboding at heart.

"In supposing it to be a bug of real gold." He said this with an air of profound seriousness, and I felt inexpressibly shocked.

"This bug is to make my fortune," he continued, with a triumphant smile; "to reinstate me in my family possessions. Is it any wonder, then, that I prize it? Since Fortune has thought fit to bestow it upon me, I have only to use it properly, and I shall arrive at the gold of which it is the index. Jupiter, bring me that scarabaeus!"

"What! de bug, massa? I'd rudder not go fer trubble dat bug; you mus' git him for your own self." Hereupon Legrand arose, with a grave and stately air, and brought me the beetle from a glass case in which it was enclosed. It was a beautiful scarabaeus, and, at that time, unknown to naturalists—of course a great prize in a scientific point of view. There were two round black spots near one extremity of the back, and a long one near the other. The scales were exceedingly hard and glossy, with all the appearance of burnished gold. The weight of the insect was very remarkable, and, taking all things into consideration, I could hardly blame Jupiter for his opinion respecting it; but what to make of Legrand's concordance with that opinion, I could not, for the life of me, tell.

"I sent for you," said he, in a grandiloquent tone, when I had completed my examination of the beetle, "I sent for you that I might have your counsel and assistance in furthering the views of Fate and of the bug——"

"My dear Legrand," I cried, interrupting him, "you are certainly unwell, and had better use some little precautions. You shall go to bed, and I will remain with you for a few days, until you get over this. You are feverish and——"

"Feel my pulse," said he.

I felt it, and to say the truth, found not the slightest indication of fever.

"But you may be ill and yet have no fever. Allow me this once to prescribe for you. In the first place go to bed. In the next——"

"You are mistaken," he interposed, "I am as well as I can expect to be under the excitement which I suffer. If you really wish me well you will relieve this excitement."

"And how is this to be done?"

"Very easily. Jupiter and myself are going upon an expedition into the hills, upon the mainland, and, in this expedition, we shall need the aid of some person in whom we can confide. You are the only one we can trust. Whether we succeed or fail, the excitement which you now perceive in me will be equally allayed."

"I am anxious to oblige you in any way," I replied; "but do you mean to say that this infernal beetle has any connexion with your expedition into the hills?"

"It has."

"Then, Legrand, I can become a party to no such absurd proceeding."

"I am sorry—very sorry—for we shall have to try it by ourselves."

"Try it by yourselves! The man is surely mad!—but stay!—how long do you propose to be absent?"

"Probably all night. We shall start immediately, and be back, at all events, by sunrise."

"And you will promise me, upon your honor, that when this freak of yours is over, and the bug business (good God!) settled to your satisfaction, you will then return home and follow my advice implicitly, as that of your physician?"

"Yes; I promise; and now let us be off, for we have no time to lose."

With a heavy heart I accompanied my friend. We started about four o'clock—Legrand, Jupiter, the dog, and myself. Jupiter had with him the scythe and spades—the whole of which he insisted upon carrying—more through fear, it seemed to me, of trusting either of the implements within reach of his master, than from any excess of industry or complaisance. His demeanor was dogged in the extreme, and "dat deuced bug" were the sole words which escaped his lips during the journey. For my own part, I had charge of a couple of dark lanterns, while Legrand contented himself with the scarabaeus, which he carried attached to the end of a bit of whipcord; twirling it to and fro, with the air of a conjurer, as he went. When I observed this last, plain evidence of my friend's aberration of mind, I could scarcely refrain from tears. I thought it best, however, to humor his fancy, at least for the present, or until I could adopt some more energetic measures with a chance of success. In the meantime, I endeavored, but all in vain, to sound him in regard to the object of the expedition. Having succeeded in inducing me to accompany him, he seemed unwilling to hold conversation upon any topic of minor importance, and to all my questions vouchsafed no other reply than "we shall see!"

We crossed the creek at the head of the island by means of a skiff, and, ascending the high grounds on the shore of the mainland, proceeded in a northwesterly direction, through a tract of country excessively wild and desolate, where no trace of a human footstep was to be seen. Legrand led the way with decision; pausing only for an instant, here and there, to consult what appeared to be certain landmarks of his own contrivance upon a former occasion.

In this manner we journeyed for about two hours, and the sun was just setting when we entered a region infinitely more dreary than any yet seen. It was a species of tableland, near the summit of an almost inaccessible hill, densely wooded from base to pinnacle, and interspersed with huge crags that appeared to lie loosely upon the soil, and in many cases were prevented from precipitating themselves into the valleys below, merely by the support of the trees against which they reclined. Deep ravines, in various directions, gave an air of still sterner solemnity to the scene.

The natural platform to which we had clambered was thickly overgrown with brambles, through which we soon discovered that it would have been impossible to force our way but for the scythe; and Jupiter, by direction of his master, proceeded to clear for us a path to the foot of an enormously tall tulip-tree, which stood, with some eight or ten oaks, upon the level, and far surpassed them all, and all other trees which I had then ever seen, in the beauty of its foliage and form, in the wide spread of its branches, and in the general majesty of its appearance. When we reached this tree, Legrand turned to Jupiter, and asked him if he thought he could climb it. The old man seemed a little staggered by the question, and for some moments made no reply. At length he approached the huge trunk, walked slowly around it, and examined it with minute attention. When he had completed his scrutiny, he merely said:

"Yes, massa, Jup climb any tree he ebber see in he life."

"Then up with you as soon as possible, for it will soon be too dark to see what we are about."

"How far mus' go up, massa?" inquired Jupiter.

"Get up the main trunk first, and then I will tell you which way to go—and here—stop! take this beetle with you."

"De bug, Massa Will!—de goole-bug!" cried the negro, drawing back in dismay—"what for mus' tote de bug way up de tree?—d——n if I do!"

"If you are afraid, Jup, a great big negro like you, to take hold of a harmless little dead beetle, why you can carry it up by this string—but if you do not take it up with you in some way, I shall be under the necessity of breaking your head with this shovel."

"What de matter now, massa?" said Jup, evidently shamed into compliance; "always want for to raise fuss wid old nigger. Was only funnin' anyhow. Me feered de bug! what I keer for de bug?" Here he took cautiously hold of the extreme end of the string, and, maintaining the insect as far from his person as circumstances would permit, prepared to ascend the tree.

In youth, the tulip-tree or *Liriodendron Tulipiferum*, the most magnificent of American foresters, has a trunk peculiarly smooth, and often rises to a great height without lateral branches; but, in its riper age, the bark becomes gnarled and uneven, while many short limbs make their appearance on the stem. Thus the difficulty of ascension, in the present case, lay more in semblance than in reality. Embracing the huge cylinder, as closely as possible, with his arms and knees, seizing with his hands some projections, and resting his naked toes upon others, Jupiter, after one or two narrow escapes from falling, at length wriggled himself into the first great fork, and seemed to consider the whole business as virtually accomplished. The risk of the achievement was, in fact, now over, although the climber was some sixty or seventy feet from the ground.

"Which way mus' go now, Massa Will?" he asked.

"Keep up the largest branch—the one on this side," said Legrand. The negro obeyed him promptly, and apparently with but little trouble; ascending higher and higher, until no glimpse of his squat figure could be obtained through the dense foliage which enveloped it. Presently his voice was heard in a sort of halloo.

"How much fudder is got for go?"

"How high up are you?" asked Legrand.

"Ebber so fur," replied the negro; "can see de sky fru de top ob de tree."

"Never mind the sky, but attend to what I say. Look down the trunk and count the limbs below you on this side. How many limbs have you passed?"

"One, two, tree, four, fibe—I done pass fibe big limb, massa, pon dis side."

"Then go one limb higher."

In a few minutes the voice was heard again, announcing that the seventh limb was attained.

"Now, Jup," cried Legrand, evidently much excited, "I want you to work your way out upon that limb as far as you can. If you see anything strange let me know."

By this time what little doubt I might have entertained of my poor friend's insanity was put finally at rest. I had no alternative but to conclude him stricken with lunacy, and I became seriously anxious about getting him home. While I was pondering upon what was best to be done, Jupiter's voice was again heard.

"Mos' feerd for to venture pon dis limb berry far—'tis dead limb putty much all de way."

"Did you say it was a dead limb, Jupiter?" cried Legrand in a quavering voice.

"Yes, massa, him dead as de door-nail—done up for sartain—done departed dis here life."

"What in the name of heaven shall I do?" asked Legrand, seemingly in the greatest distress.

"Do!" said I, glad of an opportunity to interpose a word, "why come home and go to bed. Come now!—that's a fine fellow. It's getting late, and, besides, you remember your promise."

"Jupiter," cried he, without heeding me in the least, "do you hear me?"

"Yes, Massa Will, hear you ebber so plain."

"Try the wood well, then, with your knife, and see if you think it very rotten."

"Him rotten, massa, sure nuff," replied the negro in a few moments, "but not so berry rotten as mought be. Mought venture out leetle way pon he limb by myself, dat's true."

"By yourself!—what do you mean?"

"Why, I mean de bug. 'Tis berry hebby bug. S'pose I drop him down fuss, and den de limb won't break wid just de weight ob one nigger."

"You infernal scoundrel!" cried Legrand, apparently much relieved, "what do you mean by telling me such nonsense as that? As sure as you drop that beetle I'll break your neck. Look here, Jupiter, do you hear me?"

"Yes, massa, needn't hollo at poor nigger dat style."

"Well! now listen!—if you will venture out on the limb as far as you think safe, and not let go the beetle, I'll make you a present of a silver dollar as soon as you get down."

"I'm gwine, Massa Will—deed I is," replied the negro very promptly—"mos' out to the end now."

"Out to the end!" here fairly screamed Legrand; "do you say you are out to the end of that limb?"

"Soon be to de end, massa—o-o-o-o-oh! Lor-gol-a-marcy! what is dis here pon de tree?"

"Well!" cried Legrand, highly delighted, "what is it?"

"Why, 'tain't noffin but a skull—somebody bin lef him head up de tree, and de crows done gobble ebery bit of de meat off."

"A skull, you say!—very well,—how is it fastened to the limb?—what holds it on?"

"Sure nuff, massa; mus' look. Why his berry curous sarcumstance, pon my word—dare's a great big nail in de skull, what fastens ob it on to de tree."

"Well now, Jupiter, do exactly as I tell you—do you hear?"

"Yes, massa."

"Pay attention, then—find the left eye of the skull."

"Hum! hoo! dat's good! why dey ain't no eye lef at all."

"Curse your stupidity! Do you know your right hand from your left?"

"Yes, I knows dat—knows all bout dat—'tis my lef hand what I chops de wood wid."

"To be sure! you are left-handed; and your left eye is on the same side as your left hand. Now, I suppose, you can find the left eye of the skull, or the place where the left eye has been. Have you found it?"

Here was a long pause. At length the negro asked:

"Is de lef eye of de skull pon de same side as de lef hand side of de skull too?—cause de skull ain't got not a bit ob a hand at all—never mind! I got de lef eye now—here de lef eye! what mus' do wid it?"

"Let the beetle drop through it, as far as the string will reach—but be careful and not let go your hold of the string."

"All dat done, Massa Will; mighty easy ting for to put de bug fru de hole—look out for him dare below!"

During this colloquy no portion of Jupiter's person could be seen; but the beetle, which he had suffered to descend, was now visible at the end of the string, and glistened, like a globe of burnished gold, in the last rays of the setting sun, some of which still faintly illumined the eminence upon which we stood. The scarabaeus hung quite clear of any branches, and, if allowed to fall, would have fallen at our feet. Legrand immediately took the scythe, and cleared with it a circular space, three or four yards in diameter, just beneath the insect, and, having accomplished this, ordered Jupiter to let go the string and come down from the tree.

Driving a peg, with great nicety, into the ground, at the precise spot where the beetle fell, my friend now produced from his pocket a tape-measure. Fastening one end of this at that point of the trunk of the tree which was nearest the peg, he unrolled it till it reached the peg and thence further unrolled it, in the direction already established by the two points of the tree and the peg, for the distance of fifty feet—Jupiter clearing away the brambles with the scythe. At the spot thus attained a second peg was driven, and about this, as a center, a rude circle, about four feet in diameter, described. Taking now a spade himself, and giving one to Jupiter and one to me, Legrand begged us to set about digging as quickly as possible.

To speak the truth, I had no especial relish for such amusement at any time, and, at that particular moment, would most willingly have declined it; for the night was coming on, and I felt much fatigued with the exercise already taken; but I saw no mode of escape, and was fearful of disturbing my poor friend's equanimity by a refusal. Could I have depended, indeed, upon Jupiter's aid, I would have had no hesitation in attempting to get the lunatic home by force; but I was too well assured of the old negro's disposition, to hope that he would assist me, under any circumstances, in a personal contest with his master. I made no doubt that the latter had been infected with some of the innumerable Southern superstitions about money buried, and that his phantasy had received confirmation by the finding of the scarabaeus, or, perhaps, by Jupiter's obstinacy in maintaining it to be "a bug of real gold." A mind disposed to lunacy would readily be led away by such suggestions—especially if chiming in with favorite preconceived ideas—and then I called to mind the poor fellow's speech about the beetle's being "the index of his fortune." Upon the whole, I was sadly vexed and puzzled, but, at length, I concluded to make a virtue of necessity—to dig with a good will, and thus the sooner to convince the visionary, by ocular demonstration, of the fallacy of the opinions he entertained.

The lanterns having been lit, we all fell to work with a zeal worthy a more rational cause; and, as the glare fell upon our persons and implements, I could not help thinking how picturesque a group we composed, and how strange and suspicious our labors must have appeared to any interloper who, by chance, might have stumbled upon our whereabouts.

We dug very steadily for two hours. Little was said; and our chief embarrassment lay in the yelpings of the dog, who took exceeding interest in our proceedings. He, at length, became so obstreperous that we grew fearful of his giving the alarm to some stragglers in the vicinity,—or, rather, this was the apprehension of Legrand;—for myself, I should have rejoiced at any interruption which might have enabled me to get the wanderer home. The noise was, at length, very effectually silenced by Jupiter, who, getting out of the hole with a dogged air of deliberation, tied the brute's mouth up with one of his suspenders, and then returned, with a grave chuckle, to his task.

When the time mentioned had expired, we had reached a depth of five feet, and yet no signs of any treasure became manifest. A general pause ensued, and I began to hope that the farce was at an end. Legrand, however, although evidently much disconcerted, wiped his brow thoughtfully and recommenced. We had excavated the entire circle of four feet diameter, and now we slightly enlarged the limit, and went to the farther depth of two feet. Still nothing appeared. The gold-seeker, whom I sincerely pitied, at length clambered from the pit, with the bitterest disappointment imprinted upon every feature, and proceeded, slowly and reluctantly, to put on his coat, which he had thrown off at the beginning of his labor. In the meantime I made no remark. Jupiter, at a signal from his master, began to gather up his tools. This done, and the dog having been unmuzzled, we turned in profound silence toward home.

We had taken, perhaps, a dozen steps in this direction, when, with a loud oath, Legrand strode up to Jupiter, and seized him by the collar. The astonished negro opened his eyes and mouth to the fullest extent, let fall the spades, and fell upon his knees.

"You scoundrel!" said Legrand, hissing out the syllables from between his clenched teeth—"you infernal black villain!—speak, I tell you!—answer me this instant, without prevarication!—which—which is your left eye?"

"Oh, my golly, Massa Will! ain't dis here my lef eye for sartain?" roared the terrified Jupiter, placing his hand upon his right organ of vision, and holding it there with a desperate pertinacity, as if in immediate dread of his master's attempt at a gouge.

"I thought so!—I knew it! hurrah!" vociferated Legrand, letting the negro go, and executing a series of curvets and caracols, much to the astonishment of his valet, who, arising from his knees, looked, mutely, from his master to myself, and then from myself to his master.

"Come! we must go back," said the latter, "the game's not up yet"; and he again led the way to the tulip-tree.

"Jupiter," said he, when we reached its foot, "come here! was the skull nailed to the limb with the face outward, or with the face to the limb?"

"De face was out, massa, so dat de crows could get at de eyes good, widout any trouble."

"Well, then, was it this eye or that through which you dropped the beetle?"—here Legrand touched each of Jupiter's eyes.

"'Twas dis eye, massa—de lef eye—jis as you tell me,"—and here it was his right eye that the negro indicated.

"That will do—we must try it again."

Here my friend, about whose madness I now saw, or fancied that I saw, certain indications of method, removed the peg which marked the spot where the beetle fell, to a spot about three inches to the westward of its former position. Taking, now, the tape measure from the nearest point of the trunk to the peg, as before, and continuing the extension in a straight line to the distance of fifty feet, a spot was indicated, removed, by several yards, from the point at which we had been digging.

Around the new position a circle, somewhat larger than in the former instance, was now described, and we again set to work with the spade. I was dreadfully weary, but, scarcely understanding what had occasioned the change in my thoughts, I felt no longer any great aversion from the labor imposed. I had become most unaccountably interested—nay, even excited. Perhaps there was something, amid all the extravagant demeanor of Legrand—some air of forethought, or of deliberation, which impressed me. I dug eagerly, and now and then caught myself actually looking, with something that very much resembled expectation, for the fancied treasure, the vision of which had demented my unfortunate companion. At a period when such vagaries of thought most fully possessed me, and when we had been at work perhaps an hour and a half, we were again interrupted by the violent howlings of the dog. His uneasiness, in the first instance, had been, evidently, but the result of playfulness or caprice, but he now assumed a bitter and serious tone. Upon Jupiter's again attempting to muzzle him, he made furious resistance, and, leaping into the hole, tore up the mold frantically with his claws. In a few seconds he had uncovered a mass of human bones, forming two complete skeletons, intermingled with several buttons of metal, and what appeared to be the dust of decayed woolen. One or two strokes of a spade upturned the blade of a large Spanish knife, and, as we dug farther, three or four loose pieces of gold and silver coin came to light.

At sight of these the joy of Jupiter could scarcely be restrained, but the countenance of his master wore an air of extreme disappointment. He urged us, however, to continue our exertions, and the words were hardly uttered when I stumbled and fell forward, having caught the toe of my boot in a large ring of iron that lay half buried in the loose earth.

We now worked in earnest, and never did I pass ten minutes of more intense excitement. During this interval we had fairly unearthed an oblong chest of wood, which, from its perfect preservation and wonderful hardness, had plainly been subjected to some mineralizing process—perhaps that of the bichloride of mercury. This box was three and a half feet long, three feet broad, and two and a half feet deep. It was firmly secured by bands of wrought iron, riveted, and forming a kind of open trellis-work over the whole. On each side of the chest, near the top, were three rings of iron—six in all—by means of which a firm hold could be obtained by six persons. Our utmost united endeavors served only to disturb the coffer very slightly in its bed. We at once saw the impossibility of removing so great a weight. Luckily, the sole fastenings of the lid consisted of two sliding bolts. These we drew back—trembling and panting with anxiety. In an instant, a treasure of incalculable value lay gleaming before us. As the rays of the lanterns fell within the pit, there flashed upward a glow and a glare, from a confused heap of gold and of jewels, that absolutely dazzled our eyes.

I shall not pretend to describe the feelings with which I gazed. Amazement was, of course, predominant. Legrand appeared exhausted with excitement, and spoke very few words. Jupiter's countenance wore, for some minutes, as deadly a pallor as it is possible, in the nature of things, for any negro's visage to assume. He seemed stupefied—thunderstricken. Presently he fell upon his knees in the pit, and burying his naked arms up to the elbows in gold, let them there remain, as if enjoying the luxury of a bath. At length with a deep sigh, he exclaimed, as if in a soliloquy;

"And dis all cum ob de goole-bug! de putty goole-bug! de poor little goole-bug, what I boosed in dat sabage kind ob style! Ain't you shamed ob yourself, nigger?—answer me dat!"

It became necessary, at last, that I should arouse both master and valet to the expediency of removing the treasure. It was growing late, and it behooved us to make exertion, that we might get everything housed before daylight. It was difficult to say what should be done, and much time was spent in deliberation—so confused were the ideas of all. We finally lightened the box by removing two-thirds of its contents, when we were enabled, with some trouble, to raise it from the hole. The articles taken out were deposited among the brambles, and the dog left to guard them, with strict orders from Jupiter, neither, upon any pretence, to stir from the spot, nor to open his mouth until our return. We then hurriedly made for home with the chest; reaching the hut in safety, but after excessive toil, at one o'clock in the morning. Worn out as we were, it was not in human nature to do more immediately. We rested until two, and had supper: starting for the hills immediately afterward, armed with three stout sacks, which, by good luck, were upon the premises. A little before four we arrived at the pit, divided the remainder of the booty, as equally as might be, among us, and, leaving the holes unfilled, again set out for the hut, at which, for the second time, we deposited our golden burdens, just as the first faint streaks of the dawn gleamed from over the tree-tops in the East.

We were now thoroughly broken down; but the intense excitement of the time denied us repose. After an unquiet slumber of some three or four hours' duration, we arose, as if by preconcert, to make examination of our treasure.

The chest had been full to the brim, and we spent the whole day, and the greater part of the next night, in a scrutiny of its contents. There had been nothing like order or arrangement. Everything had been heaped in promiscuously. Having assorted all with care, we found ourselves possessed of even vaster wealth than we had at first supposed. In coin there was rather more than four hundred and fifty thousand dollars—estimating the value of the pieces, as accurately as we could, by the tables of the period. There was not a particle of silver. All was gold of antique date and of great variety—French, Spanish, and German money, with a few English guineas, and some counters, of which we had never seen specimens before. There were several very large and heavy coins, so worn that we could make nothing of their inscriptions. There was no American money. The value of the jewels we found more difficult in estimating. There were diamonds—some of them exceedingly large and fine—a hundred and ten in all, and not one of them small; eighteen rubies of remarkable brilliancy;—three hundred and ten emeralds, all very beautiful; and twenty-one sapphires, with an opal. These stones had all been broken from their settings and thrown loose in the chest. The settings themselves, which we picked out from among the other gold, appeared to have been beaten up with hammers, as if to prevent identification. Besides all this, there was a vast quantity of solid gold ornaments: nearly two hundred massive finger- and ear-rings; rich chains—thirty of these, if I remember; eighty-three very large and heavy crucifixes; five gold censers of great value; a prodigious golden punch-bowl, ornamented with richly chased vine-leaves and Bacchanalian figures; with two sword-handles exquisitely embossed, and many other smaller articles which I cannot recollect. The weight of these valuables exceeded three hundred and fifty pounds avoirdupois; and in this estimate I have not included one hundred and ninety-seven superb gold watches; three of the number being worth each five hundred dollars, if one. Many of them were very old, and as timekeepers valueless; the works having suffered more or less from corrosion—but all were richly jeweled and in cases of great worth. We estimated the entire contents of the chest, that night, at a million and a half of dollars; and upon the subsequent disposal of the trinkets and jewels (a few being retained for our own use), it was found that we had greatly undervalued the treasure.

When, at length, we had concluded our examination, and the intense excitement of the time had, in some measure, subsided, Legrand, who saw that I was dying with impatience for a solution of this most extraordinary riddle, entered into a full detail of all the circumstances connected with it.

"You remember," said he, "the night when I handed you the rough sketch I had made of the scarabaeus. You recollect also, that I became quite vexed at you for insisting that my drawing resembled a death's head. When you first made this assertion, I thought you were jesting; but afterward I called to mind the peculiar spots on the back of the insect, and admitted to myself that your remark had some little foundation in fact. Still, the sneer at my graphic powers irritated me—for I am considered a good artist—and, therefore, when you handed me the scrap of parchment, I was about to crumple it up and throw it angrily into the fire."

"The scrap of paper, you mean?" said I.

'No; it had much of the appearance of paper, and at first I supposed it to be such, but when I came to draw upon it, I discovered it at once to be a piece of very thin parchment. It was quite dirty, you remember. Well, as I was in the very act of crumpling it up, my glance fell upon the sketch at which you had been looking, and you may imagine my astonishment when I perceived, in fact, the figure of a death's-head just where, it seemed to me, I had made the drawing of the beetle. For a moment I was too much amazed to think with accuracy. I knew that my design was very different in detail from this—although there was a certain similarity in general outline. Presently I took a candle, and seating myself at the other end of the room, proceeded to scrutinize the parchment more closely. Upon turning it over, I saw my own sketch upon the reverse, just as I had made it. My first idea, now, was mere surprise at the really remarkable similarity of outline—at the singular coincidence involved in the fact that, unknown to me, there should have been a skull upon the other side of the parchment, immediately beneath my figure of the scarabaeus, and that this skull, not only in outline, but in size, should so closely resemble my drawing. I say the singularity of this coincidence absolutely stupefied me for a time. This is the usual effect of such coincidences. The mind struggles to establish a connexion—a sequence of cause and effect—and, being unable to do so, suffers a species of temporary paralysis. But, when I recovered from this stupor, there dawned upon me gradually a conviction which startled me even far more than the coincidence. I began distinctly, positively, to remember that there had been no drawing upon the parchment when I made my sketch of the scarabaeus. I became perfectly certain of this; for I recollected turning up first one side and then the other, in search of the cleanest spot. Had the skull been then there, of course I could not have failed to notice it. Here was indeed a mystery which I felt it impossible to explain; but, even at that early moment, there seemed to glimmer, faintly, within the most remote and secret chambers of my intellect, a glow-worm-like conception of that truth which last night's adventure brought to so magnificent a demonstration. I arose at once, and putting the parchment securely away, dismissed all further reflection until I should be alone.

"When you had gone, and when Jupiter was fast asleep, I betook myself to a more methodical investigation of the affair. In the first place I considered the manner in which the parchment had come into my possession. The spot where we discovered the scarabaeus was on the coast of the mainland, about a mile eastward of the island, and but a short distance above high-water mark. Upon my taking hold of it, it gave me a sharp bite, which caused me to let it drop. Jupiter, with his accustomed caution, before seizing the insect, which had flown toward him, looked about him for a leaf, or something of that nature, by which to take hold of it. It was at this moment that his eyes, and mine also, fell upon the scrap of parchment, which I then supposed to be paper. It was lying half buried in the sand, a corner sticking up. Near the spot where we found it, I observed the remnants of the hull of what appeared to have been a ship's long-boat. The wreck seemed to have been there for a very great while; for the resemblance to boat timbers could scarcely be traced.

"Well, Jupiter picked up the parchment, wrapped the beetle in it, and gave it to me. Soon afterward we turned to go home, and on the way met Lieutenant G——. I showed him the insect, and he begged me to let him take it to the fort. Upon my consenting, he thrust it forthwith into his waistcoat pocket, without the parchment in which it had been wrapped, and which I had continued to hold in my hand during his inspection. Perhaps he dreaded my changing my mind, and thought it best to make sure of the prize at once—you know how enthusiastic he is on all subjects connected with Natural History. At the same time, without being conscious of it, I must have deposited the parchment in my own pocket.

"You remember that when I went to the table, for the purpose of making a sketch of the beetle, I found no paper where it was usually kept. I looked in the drawer, and found none there. I searched my pockets, hoping to find an old letter, when my hand fell upon the parchment. I thus detail the precise mode in which it came into my possession; for the circumstances impressed me with peculiar force.

"No doubt you will think me fanciful—but I had already established a kind of connexion. I had put together two links of a great chain. There was a boat lying upon a sea-coast, and not far from the boat was a parchment—not a paper—with a skull depicted upon it. You will, of course, ask, 'Where is the connexion?' I reply that the skull, or death's-head, is the well-known emblem of the pirate. The flag of the death's-head is hoisted in all engagements.

"I have said that the scrap was parchment, and not paper. Parchment is durable—almost imperishable. Matters of little moment are rarely consigned to parchment; since, for the mere ordinary purposes of drawing or writing, it is not nearly so well adapted as paper. This reflection suggested some meaning—some relevancy—in the death's-head. I did not fail to observe, also, the form of the parchment. Although one of its corners had been, by some accident, destroyed, it could be seen that the original form was oblong. It was just such a slip, indeed, as might have been chosen for a memorandum—for a record of something to be long remembered and carefully preserved."

"But," I interposed, "you say that the skull was not upon the parchment when you made the drawing of the beetle. How then do you trace any connexion between the boat and the skull—since this latter, according to your own admission, must have been designed (God only knows how or by whom) at some period subsequent to your sketching the scarabaeus."

"Ah, hereupon turns the whole mystery; although the secret, at this point, I had comparatively little difficulty in solving. My steps were sure, and could afford but a single result. I reasoned, for example, thus: When I drew the scarabaeus, there was no skull apparent upon the parchment. When I had completed the drawing I gave it to you, and observed you narrowly until you returned it. You, therefore, did not design the skull, and no one else was present to do it. Then it was not done by human agency. And nevertheless it was done.

"At this stage of my reflections I endeavored to remember, and did remember, with entire distinctness, every incident which occurred about the period in question. The weather was chilly (oh, rare and happy accident!), and a fire was blazing upon the hearth. I was heated with exercise, and sat near the table. You, however, had drawn a chair close to the chimney. Just as I had placed the parchment in your hand, and as you were in the act of inspecting it, Wolf, the Newfoundland, entered, and leaped upon your shoulders. With your left hand you caressed him and kept him off, while your right, holding the parchment, was permitted to fall listlessly between your knees, and in close proximity to the fire. At one moment I thought the blaze had caught it, and was about to caution you, but, before I could speak, you had withdrawn it, and were engaged in its examination. When I considered all these particulars, I doubted not for a moment that heat had been the agent in bringing to light, upon the parchment, the skull which I saw designed upon it. You are well aware that chemical preparations exist, and have existed time out of mind, by means of which it is possible to write upon either paper or vellum, so that the characters shall become visible only when subjected to the action of fire. Zaffre, digested in aqua regia, and diluted with four times its weight of water, is sometimes employed; a green tint results. The regulus of cobalt, dissolved in spirit of niter, gives a red. These colors disappear at longer or shorter intervals after the material written upon cools, but again become apparent upon the reapplication of heat.

"I now scrutinized the death's-head with care. Its outer edges—the edges of the drawing nearest the edge of the vellum—were far more distinct than the others. It was clear that the action of the caloric had been imperfect or unequal. I immediately kindled a fire, and subjected every portion of the parchment to a glowing heat. At first, the only effect was the strengthening of the faint lines in the skull; but, upon persevering in the experiment, there became visible, at the corner of the slip, diagonally opposite to the spot in which the death's-head was delineated, the figure of what I at first supposed to be a goat. A closer scrutiny, however, satisfied me that it was intended for a kid."

"Ha! ha!" said I, "to be sure I have no right to laugh at you—a million and a half of money is too serious a matter for mirth—but you are not about to establish a third link in your chain—you will not find any especial connexion between your pirates and a goat—pirates, you know, have nothing to do with goats; they appertain to the farming interest."

"But I have just said that the figure was not that of a goat."

"Well, a kid then—pretty much the same thing."

"Pretty much, but not altogether," said Legrand. "You may have heard of one Captain Kidd. I at once looked upon the figure of the animal as a kind of punning or hieroglyphical signature. I say signature; because its position upon the vellum suggested this idea. The death's-head at the corner diagonally opposite, had, in the same manner, the air of a stamp, or seal. But I was sorely put out by the absence of all else—of the body to my imagined instrument—of the text for my context."

"I presume you expected to find a letter between the stamp and the signature."

"Something of that kind. The fact is, I felt irresistibly impressed with a presentiment of some vast good fortune impending. I can scarcely say why. Perhaps, after all, it was rather a desire than an actual belief;—but do you know that Jupiter's silly words, about the bug being of solid gold, had a remarkable effect upon my fancy? And then the series of accidents and coincidences—these were so very extraordinary. Do you observe how mere an accident it was that these events should have occurred upon the sole day of all the year in which it has been, or may be sufficiently cool for fire, and that without the fire, or without the intervention of the dog at the precise moment in which he appeared, I should never have become aware of the death's-head, and so never the possessor of the treasure."

"But proceed—I am all impatience."

"Well; you have heard, of course, the many stories current—the thousand vague rumors afloat about money buried, somewhere upon the Atlantic coast, by Kidd and his associates. These rumors must have had some foundation in fact. And that the rumors have existed so long and so continuous, could have resulted, it appeared to me, only from the circumstance of the buried treasure still remaining entombed. Had Kidd concealed his plunder for a time, and afterward reclaimed it, the rumors would scarcely have reached us in their present unvarying form. You will observe that the stories told are all about money-seekers, not about money-finders. Had the pirate recovered his money, there the affair would have dropped. It seemed to me that some accident—say the loss of a memorandum indicating its locality—had deprived him of the means of recovering it, and that this accident had become known to his followers, who otherwise might never have heard that treasure had been concealed at all, and who, busying themselves in vain, because unguided, attempts to regain it, had first given birth, and then universal currency, to the reports which are now so common. Have you ever heard of any important treasure being unearthed along the coast?"

"Never."

"But that Kidd's accumulations were immense, is well known. I took it for granted, therefore, that the earth still held them; and you will scarcely be surprised when I tell you that I felt a hope, nearly amounting to certainty, that the parchment so strangely found involved a lost record of the place of deposit."

"But how did you proceed?"

"I held the vellum again to the fire, after increasing the heat, but nothing appeared. I now thought it possible that the coating of dirt might have something to do with the failure: so I carefully rinsed the parchment by pouring warm water over it, and, having done this, I placed it in a tin pan, with the skull downward, and put the pan upon a furnace of lighted charcoal. In a few minutes, the pan having become thoroughly heated, I removed the slip, and, to my inexpressible joy, found it spotted, in several places, with what appeared to be figures arranged in lines. Again I placed it in the pan, and suffered it to remain another minute. Upon taking it off, the whole was just as you see it now."

Here Legrand, having reheated the parchment, submitted it to my inspection. The following characters were rudely traced, in a red tint, between the death's-head and the goat:

53‡‡†305))6*;4826)4‡.)4‡) ;806*;48†8¶60))85;1‡(;:‡*8†83(88)
5*†;46(;88*96*?;8)*‡(;485) ;5*†2:*‡(;4956*2(5*—4)8¶8*;406928
5) ;)6†8)4‡‡;1(‡9;48081;8:8‡1;48†85;4)485†528806*81(‡9;48;(88;
4(‡?34;48)4‡;161;:188;‡?;

"But," said I, returning him the slip, "I am as much in the dark as ever. Were all the jewels of Golconda awaiting me upon my solution of this enigma, I am quite sure that I should be unable to earn them."

"And yet," said Legrand, "the solution is by no means so difficult as you might be led to imagine from the first hasty inspection of the characters. These characters, as any one might readily guess, form a cipher—that is to say they convey a meaning; but then from what is known of Kidd, I could not suppose him capable of constructing any of the more abstruse cryptographs. I made up my mind, at once, that this was of a simple species—such, however, as would appear, to the crude intellect of the sailor, absolutely insoluble without the key."

"And you really solved it?"

"Readily; I have solved others of an abstruseness ten thousand times greater. Circumstances, and a certain bias of mind, have led me to take interest in such riddles, and it may well be doubted whether human ingenuity can construct an enigma of the kind which human ingenuity may not, by proper application, resolve. In fact, having once established connected and legible characters, I scarcely gave a thought to the mere difficulty of developing their import.

"In the present case—indeed in all cases of secret writing—the first question regards the language of the cipher; for the principles of solution, so far, especially, as the more simple ciphers are concerned, depend upon, and are varied by, the genius of the particular idiom. In general, there is no alternative but experiment (directed by probabilities) of every tongue known to him who attempts the solution, until the true one be attained. But, with the cipher now before us all difficulty was removed by the signature. The pun upon the word 'Kidd' is appreciable in no other language than the English. But for this consideration I should have begun my attempts with the Spanish and French, as the tongues in which a secret of this kind would most naturally have been written by a pirate of the Spanish main. As it was, I assumed the cryptograph to be English.

"You observed there are no divisions between the words. Had there been divisions the task would have been comparatively easy. In such cases I should have commenced with a collation and analysis of the shorter words, and, had a word of a single letter occurred, as is most likely, (a or I, for example,) I should have considered the solution as assured. But, there being no division, my first step was to ascertain the predominant letters, as well as the least frequent. Counting all, I constructed a table thus:

Of the character	8	there are	33
	;	"	26
	4	"	19
	‡)	"	16
	*	"	13
	5	"	12
	6	"	11
	†1	"	8
	o	"	6
	92	"	5
	:3	"	4
	?	"	3
	¶	"	2
	—.	"	1

"Now, in English, the letter which most frequently occurs is *e*. Afterward, the succession runs thus: *a o i d h n r s t u y c f g l m w b k p q x z*. *E* predominates so remarkably, that an individual sentence of any length is rarely seen, in which it is not the prevailing character.

"Here, then, we have, in the very beginning, the groundwork for something more than a mere guess. The general use which may be made of the table is obvious—but, in this particular cipher, we shall only very partially require its aid. As our predominant character is 8, we will commence by assuming it as the *e* of the natural alphabet. To verify the supposition, let us observe if the 8 be seen often in couples—for *e* is doubled with great frequency in English—in such words, for example, as 'meet,' 'fleet,' 'speed,' 'seen,' 'been,' 'agree,' etc. In the present instance we see it doubled no less than five times, although the cryptograph is brief.

"Let us assume 8, then, as *e*. Now, of all *words* in the language, 'the' is most usual; let us see, therefore, whether there are not repetitions of any three characters, in the same order of collocation, the last of them being 8. If we discover repetitions of such letters, so arranged, they will most probably represent the word 'the.' Upon inspection, we find no less than seven such arrangements, the characters being ;48. We may, therefore assume that *;* represents *t*, 4 represents *h*, and 8 represents *e*—the last being now well confirmed. Thus a great step has been taken.

"But, having established a single word, we are enabled to establish a vastly important point; that is to say, several comments and terminations of other words. Let us refer, for example, to the last instance but one, in which the combination ;48 occurs—not far from the end of the cipher. We know that the immediately ensuing is the commencement of a word, and, of the six characters succeeding this 'the,' we are cognizant of no less than five. Let us set these characters down, thus, by the letters we know them to represent, leaving a space for the unknown—

t eeth

"Here we are enabled, at once, to discard the 'th,' as forming no portion of the word commencing with the first t; since, by experiment of the entire alphabet for a letter adapted to the vacancy, we perceive that no word can be formed of which this *th* can be a part. We are thus narrowed into t ee

and, going through the alphabet, if necessary, as before, we arrive at the word 'tree,' as the sole possible reading. We thus gain another letter, *r*, represented by (, with the words 'the tree' in juxtaposition.

"Looking beyond these words, for a short distance, we again see the combination ;48, and employ it by way of *termination* to what immediately precedes. We have thus this arrangement:

the tree ;4(‡?34 the

or, substituting the natural letters, where known, it reads thus:

the tree thr‡?3h the

"Now, if, in place of the unknown characters, we leave blank spaces, or substitute dots, we read thus:

the tree thr . . . h the

when the word 'through' makes itself evident at once. But this discovery gives us three new letters, *o*, *u*, and *g*, represented by ‡ ? and 3.

"Looking now, narrowly, through the cipher for combinations of known characters, we find, not very far from the beginning, this arrangement:

83(88, or egree

which, plainly, is the conclusion of the word 'degree,' and gives us another letter, *d*, represented by †.

"Four letters beyond the word 'degree,' we perceive the combination

;46(;88*

"Translating the known characters, and representing the unknown by dots, as before, we read thus:

th.rtee.

an arrangement immediately suggestive of the word 'thirteen,' and again furnishing us with two new characters, *i* and *n* represented by 6 and *.

"Referring, now, to the beginning of the cryptograph, we find the combination

53‡‡†

"Translating as before, we obtain

.good

which assures us that the first letter is A, and that the first two words are 'A good.'

"It is now time that we arrange our key, as far as discovered, in a tabular form, to avoid confusion. It will stand thus:

5 represents a

†	"	d
8	"	e
3	"	g
4	"	h
6	"	i
*	"	n
‡	represents	o
(	"	r
;	"	t
?	"	u

"We have, therefore, no less than eleven of the most important letters represented, and it will be unnecessary to proceed with the details of the solution. I have said enough to convince you that ciphers of this nature are readily soluble, and to give you some insight into the rationale of their development. But be assured the specimen before us appertains to the very simplest species of cryptograph. It now only remains to give you the full translation of the characters upon the parchment, as unriddled. Here it is:

> "A good glass in the bishop's hostel in the devil's seat forty-one degrees and thirteen minutes northeast and by north main branch seventh limb east side shoot from the left eye of the death's-head a bee-line from the tree through the shot fifty feet out."

"But," said I, "the enigma seems still in as bad a condition as ever. How is it possible to extort a meaning from all this jargon about 'devil's seats,' 'death's-head,' and 'bishop's hotels?'"

"I confess," replied Legrand, "that the matter still wears a serious aspect, when regarded with a casual glance. My first endeavor was to divide the sentence into the natural division intended by the cryptographist."

"You mean, to punctuate it?"

"Something of that kind."

"But how was it possible to effect this?"

"I reflected that it had been a point with the writer to run his words together without division, so as to increase the difficulty of solution. Now, a not overacute man, in pursuing such an object, would be nearly certain to overdo the matter. When, in the course of his composition, he arrived at a break in his subject which would naturally require a pause, or a point, he would be exceedingly apt to run his characters, at this place, more than usually close together. If you will observe the MS., in the present instance, you will easily detect five such cases of unusual crowding. Acting upon this hint, I made the division thus:

> "A good glass in the bishop's hostel in the devil's seat—forty-one degrees and thirteen minutes—northeast and by north—main branch seventh limb east side—shoot from the left eye of the death's-head—a bee-line from the tree through the shot fifty feet out."

"Even this division," said I, "leaves me still in the dark."

"It left me also in the dark," replied Legrand, "for a few days; during which I made diligent inquiry, in the neighborhood of Sullivan's Island, for any building which went by the name of the 'Bishop's Hotel'; for, of course, I dropped the obsolete word 'hostel.' Gaining no information on the subject, I was on the point of extending my sphere of search and proceeding in a more systematic manner, when, one morning, it entered into my head, quite suddenly, that this 'Bishop's Hostel' might have some reference to an old family, of the name of Bessop, which, time out of mind, had held possession of an ancient manor-house, about four miles to the northward of the island. I accordingly went over to the plantation, and reinstituted my inquiries among the older negroes of the place. At length, one of the most aged of the women said that she had heard of such a place as Bessop's Castle, and thought that she could guide me to it, but that it was not a castle, nor a tavern, but a high rock.

"I offered to pay her well for her trouble, and, after some demur, she consented to accompany me to the spot. We found it without much difficulty, when, dismissing her, I proceeded to examine the place. The 'castle' consisted of an irregular assemblage of cliffs and rocks—one of the latter being quite remarkable for its height as well as for its insulated and artificial appearance. I clambered to its apex, and then felt much at a loss as to what should be next done.

"While I was busied in reflection, my eyes fell upon a narrow ledge in the eastern face of the rock, perhaps a yard below the summit upon which I stood. This ledge projected about eighteen inches, and was not more than a foot wide, while a niche in the cliff just above it gave it a rude resemblance to one of the hollow-backed chairs used by our ancestors. I made no doubt that here was the 'devil's seat' alluded to in the MS., and now I seemed to grasp the full secret of the riddle.

"The 'good glass,' I knew, could have reference to nothing but a telescope; for the word 'glass' is rarely employed in any other sense by seamen. Now here, I at once saw, was a telescope to be used, and a definite point of view, admitting no variation, from which to use it. Nor did I hesitate to believe that the phrases, 'forty-one degrees and thirteen minutes,' and, 'northeast and by north,' were intended as directions for the leveling of the glass. Greatly excited by these discoveries, I hurried home, procured a telescope, and returned to the rock.

"I let myself down to the ledge, and found that it was impossible to retain a seat upon it except in one particular position. This fact confirmed my preconceived idea. I proceeded to use the glass. Of course, the 'forty-one degrees and thirteen minutes' could allude to nothing but elevation above the visible horizon, since the horizontal direction was clearly indicated by the words, 'northeast and by north.' This latter direction I at once established by means of a pocket-compass; then, pointing the glass as nearly at an angle of forty-one degrees of elevation as I could do it by guess, I moved it cautiously up or down, until my attention was arrested by a circular rift or opening in the foliage of a large tree that overtopped its fellows in the distance. In the center of this rift I perceived a white spot, but could not, at first, distinguish what it was. Adjusting the focus of the telescope, I again looked, and now made it out to be a human skull.

"Upon this discovery I was so sanguine as to consider the enigma solved; for the phrase 'main branch, seventh limb, east side,' could refer only to the position of the skull upon the tree, while 'shoot from the left eye of the death's-head' admitted, also, of but one interpretation, in regard to a search for buried treasure. I perceived that the design was to drop a bullet from the left eye of the skull, and that a bee-line, or, in other words, a straight line, drawn from the nearest point of the trunk through 'the shot' (or the spot where the bullet fell), and thence extended to a distance of fifty feet, would indicate a definite point—and beneath this point I thought it at least possible that a deposit of value lay concealed."

"All this," I said, "is exceedingly clear, and, although ingenious, still simple and explicit. When you left the Bishop's Hotel, what then?"

"Why, having carefully taken the bearings of the tree, I turned homeward. The instant that I left 'the devil's seat,' however, the circular rift vanished; nor could I get a glimpse of it afterward, turn as I would. What seems to me the chief ingenuity in this whole business, is the fact (for repeated experiment has convinced me it is a fact) that the circular opening in question is visible from no other attainable point of view than that afforded by the narrow ledge upon the face of the rock.

"In this expedition to the 'Bishop's Hotel' I had been attended by Jupiter, who had, no doubt, observed, for some weeks past, the abstraction of my demeanor, and took especial care not to leave me alone. But, on the next day, getting up very early, I contrived to give him the slip, and went into the hills in search of the tree. After much toil I found it. When I came home at night my valet proposed to give me a flogging.

With the rest of the adventure I believe you are as well acquainted as myself."

"I suppose," said I, "you missed the spot, in the first attempt at digging, through Jupiter's stupidity in letting the bug fall through the right instead of through the left eye of the skull."

"Precisely. This mistake made a difference of about two inches and a half in the 'shot'—that is to say, in the position of the peg nearest the tree; and had the treasure been *beneath* the 'shot' the error would have been of little moment; but the 'shot,' together with the nearest point of the tree, were merely two points for the establishment of a line of direction; of course the error, however trivial in the beginning, increased as we proceeded with the line, and by the time we had gone fifty feet threw us quite off the scent. But for my deep-seated impressions that treasure was here somewhere actually buried, we might have had all our labor in vain."

"But your grandiloquence, and your conduct in swinging the beetle—how excessively odd! I was sure you were made. And why did you insist upon letting fall the bug, instead of a bullet, from the skull?"

"Why, to be frank, I felt somewhat annoyed by your evident suspicions touching my sanity, and so resolved to punish you quietly, in my own way, by a little bit of sober mystification. For this reason I swung the beetle, and for this reason I let it fall from the tree. An observation of yours about its great weight suggested the latter idea."

"Yes, I perceive; and now there is only one point which puzzles me. What are we to make of the skeletons found in the hole?"

"That is a question I am no more able to answer than yourself. There seems, however, only one plausible way of accounting for them—and yet it is dreadful to believe in such atrocity as my suggestion would imply. It is clear that Kidd—if Kidd indeed secreted this treasure, which I doubt not—it is clear that me must have had assistance in the labor. But this labor concluded, he may have thought it expedient to remove all participants in his secret. Perhaps a couple of blows with a mattock were sufficient, while his coadjutors were busy in the pit; perhaps it required a dozen—who shall tell?"

THE BLACK CAT

FOR THE MOST wild, yet most homely narrative which I am about to pen, I neither expect nor solicit belief. Mad indeed would I be to expect it, in a case where my very senses reject their own evidence. Yet—mad am I not—and very surely do I not dream. But to-morrow I die, and to-day I would unburden my soul. My immediate purpose is to place before the world plainly, succinctly, and without comment, a series of mere household events. In their consequences these events have terrified—have tortured—have destroyed me. Yet I will not attempt to expound them. To me they have presented little but horror—to many they will seem less terrible than *barroques*. Hereafter, perhaps, some intellect may be found which will reduce my phantasm to the common-place—some intellect more calm, more logical, and far less excitable than my own, which will perceive in the circumstances I detail with awe, nothing more than an ordinary succession of very natural causes and effects.

From my infancy I was noted for the docility and humanity of my disposition. My tenderness of heart was even so conspicuous as to make me the jest of my companions. I was especially fond of animals, and was indulged by my parents with a great variety of pets. With these I spent most of my time, and never was so happy as when feeding and caressing them. This peculiarity of character grew with my growth, and in my manhood I derived from it one of my principal sources of pleasure. To those who have cherished an affection for a faithful and sagacious dog, I need hardly be at the trouble of explaining the nature or the intensity of the gratification thus derivable. There is something in the unselfish and self-sacrificing love of a brute which goes directly to the heart of him who has had frequent occasion to test the paltry friendship and gossamer fidelity of mere *Man*.

I married early, and was happy to find in my wife a disposition not uncongenial with my own. Observing my partiality for domestic pets, she lost no opportunity of procuring those of the most agreeable kind. We had birds, goldfish, a fine dog, rabbits, a small monkey, and a *cat*.

This latter was a remarkably large and beautiful animal, entirely black, and sagacious to an astonishing degree. In speaking of his intelligence, my wife, who at heart was not a little tinctured with superstition, made frequent allusion to the ancient popular notion which regarded all black cats as witches in disguise. Not that she was ever serious upon this point, and I mention the matter at all for no better reason than that it happens just now to be remembered.

Pluto—this was the cat's name—was my favorite pet and playmate. I alone fed him, and he attended me wherever I went about the house. It was even with difficulty that I could prevent him from following me through the streets.

Our friendship lasted in this manner for several years, during which my general temperament and character—through the instrumentality of the Fiend Intemperance—had (I blush to confess it) experienced a radical alteration for the worse. I grew, day by day, more moody, more irritable, more regardless of the feelings of others. I suffered myself to use intemperate language to my wife. At length, I even offered her personal violence. My pets of course were made to feel the change in my disposition. I not only neglected, but ill-used them. For Pluto, however, I still retained sufficient regard to restrain me from maltreating him, as I made no scruple of maltreating the rabbits, the monkey, or even the dog, when by accident, or through affection, they came in my way. But my disease grew upon me—for what disease is like Alcohol?—and at length even Pluto, who was now becoming old, and consequently somewhat peevish—even Pluto began to experience the effects of my ill-temper.

One night, returning home much intoxicated, from one of my haunts about town, I fancied that the cat avoided my presence. I seized him; when, in his fright at my violence, he inflicted a slight wound upon my hand with his teeth. The fury of a demon instantly possessed me. I knew myself no longer. My original soul seemed at once to take its flight from my body, and a more than fiendish malevolence, gin-nurtured, thrilled every fibre of my frame. I took from my waistcoat-pocket a penknife, opened it, grasped the poor beast by the throat, and deliberately cut one of its eyes from the socket! I blush, I burn, I shudder, while I pen the damnable atrocity.

When reason returned with the morning—when I had slept off the fumes of the night's debauch—I experienced a sentiment half of horror, half of remorse, for the crime of which I had been guilty; but it was, at best, a feeble and equivocal feeling, and the soul remained untouched. I again plunged into excess, and soon drowned in wine all memory of the deed.

In the meantime the cat slowly recovered. The socket of the lost eye presented, it is true, a frightful appearance, but he no longer appeared to suffer any pain. He went about the house as usual, but, as might be expected, fled in extreme terror at my approach. I had so much of my old heart left as to be at first grieved by this evident dislike on the part of a creature which had once so loved me. But this feeling soon gave place to irritation. And then came, as if to my final and irrevocable overthrow, the spirit of PERVERSENESS. Of this spirit philosophy takes no account. Yet I am not more sure that my soul lives, than I am that perverseness is one of the primitive impulses of the human heart—one of the indivisible primary faculties, or sentiments, which gives direction to the character of Man. Who has not, a hundred times, found himself committing a vile or a silly action for no other reason than because he knows he should not! Have we not a perpetual inclination, in the teeth of our best judgment, to violate that which is *Law*, merely because we understand it to be such? This spirit of perverseness, I say, came to my final overthrow. It was this unfathomable longing of the soul *to vex itself*—to offer violence to its own nature—to do wrong for the wrong's sake only—that urged me to continue and finally to consummate the injury I had inflicted upon the unoffending brute. One morning, in cold blood, I slipped a noose about its neck and hung it to the limb of a tree;—hung it with the tears streaming from my eyes; and with the bitterest remorse at my heart;—hung it *because* I knew that it had loved me, and *because* I felt it had given me no reason of offense;—hung it *because* I knew that in so doing I was committing a sin—a deadly sin that would so jeopardize my immortal soul as to place it, if such a thing were possible, even beyond the reach of the infinite mercy of the Most Merciful and Most Terrible God.

On the night of the day on which this cruel deed was done, I was aroused from sleep by the cry of fire. The curtains of my bed were in flames. The whole house was blazing. It was with great difficulty that my wife, a servant, and myself, made our escape from the conflagration. The destruction was complete. My entire worldly wealth was swallowed up, and I resigned myself thenceforward to despair.

I am above the weakness of seeking to establish a sequence of cause and effect, between the disaster and the atrocity. But I am detailing a chain of facts, and wish not to leave even a possible link imperfect. On the day succeeding the fire, I visited the ruins. The walls, with one exception, had fallen in. This exception was found in a compartment wall, not very thick, which stood about the middle of the house, and against which had rested the head of my bed. The plastering had here, in great measure, resisted the action of the fire, a fact which I attributed to its having been recently spread. About this wall a dense crowd were collected and many persons seemed to be examining a particular portion of it with very minute and eager attention. The words "strange!" "singular!" and other similar expressions, excited my curiosity. I approached, and saw, as if graven in bas-relief upon the white surface, the figure of a gigantic *cat*. The impression was given with an accuracy truly marvelous. There was a rope about the animal's neck.

When I first beheld this apparition—for I could scarcely regard it as less—my wonder and my terror were extreme. But at length reflection came to my aid. The cat, I remembered, had been hung in a garden adjacent to the house. Upon the alarm of fire, this garden had been immediately filled by the crowd, by some one of whom the animal must have been cut from the tree and thrown, through an open window, into my chamber. This had probably been done with the view of arousing me from sleep. The falling of the other walls had compressed the victim of my cruelty into the substance of the freshly spread plaster; the lime of which, with the flames and the *ammonia* from the carcass, had then accomplished the portraiture as I saw it.

Although I thus readily accounted to my reason, if not altogether to my conscience, for the startling fact just detailed, it did not the less fail to make a deep impression upon my fancy. For months I could not rid myself of the phantasm of the cat; and during this period there came back into my spirit a half-sentiment that seemed, but was not, remorse.

I went so far as to regret the loss of the animal, and to look about me, among the vile haunts which I now habitually frequented, for another pet of the same species, and of somewhat similar appearance, with which to supply its place.

One night as I sat half stupefied in a den of more than infamy, my attention was suddenly drawn to some black object reposing upon the head of one of the immense hogsheads of gin or of rum which constituted the chief furniture of the apartment. I had been looking steadily at the top of this hogshead for some minutes, and what now caused me surprise was the fact that I had not sooner perceived the object thereupon. I approached it, and touched it with my hand. It was a black cat, a very large one, fully as large as Pluto, and closely resembling him in every respect but one. Pluto had not a white hair upon any portion of his body; but this cat had a large, although indefinite, splotch of white, covering nearly the whole region of the breast.

Upon my touching him, he immediately arose, purred loudly, rubbed against my hand, and appeared delighted with my notice. This, then, was the very creature of which I was in search. I at once offered to purchase it of the landlord; but this person made no claim to it—knew nothing of it—had never seen it before.

I continued my caresses; and when I prepared to go home, the animal evinced a disposition to accompany me. I permitted it to do so, occasionally stooping and patting it as I proceeded. When it reached the house it domesticated itself at once, and became immediately a great favorite with my wife.

For my own part, I soon found a dislike to it arising within me. This was just the reverse of what I had anticipated; but—I know not how or why it was—its evident fondness for myself rather disgusted and annoyed. By slow degrees these feelings of disgust and annoyance rose into the bitterness of hatred. I avoided the creature; a certain sense of shame, and the remembrance of my former deed of cruelty, preventing me from physically abusing it. I did not for some weeks strike or otherwise violently ill-use it; but gradually—very gradually—I came to look upon it with unutterable loathing, and to flee silently from its odious presence, as from the breath of a pestilence.

What added, no doubt, to my hatred of the beast, was the discovery, on the morning after I brought it home, that, like Pluto, it also had been deprived of one of its eyes. This circumstance, however, only endeared it to my wife, who, as I have already said, possessed, in a high degree, that humanity of feeling which had once been my distinguishing trait, and the source of many of my simplest and purest pleasures.

With my aversion to this cat, however, its partiality for myself seemed to increase. It followed my footsteps with a pertinacity which it would be difficult to make the reader comprehend. Whenever I sat, it would crouch beneath my chair, or spring upon my knees, covering me with its loathsome caresses. If I arose to walk it would get between my feet, and thus nearly throw me down; or, fastening its long and sharp claws in my dress, clamber in this manner to my breast. At such times, although I longed to destroy it with a blow, I was yet withheld from so doing, partly by a memory of my former crime, but chiefly—let me confess it at once—by absolute dread of the beast.

This dread was not exactly a dread of physical evil—and yet I should be at a loss how otherwise to define it. I am almost ashamed to own—yes, even in this felon's cell I am almost ashamed to own—that the terror and horror with which the animal inspired me had been heightened by one of the merest chimeras it would be possible to conceive. My wife had called my attention more than once to the character of the mark of white hair of which I have spoken, and which constituted the sole visible difference between the strange beast and the one I had destroyed. The reader will remember that this mark, although large, had been originally very indefinite; but by slow degrees—degrees nearly imperceptible, and which for a long time my Reason struggled to reject as fanciful—it had at length assumed a rigorous distinctness of outline. It was now the representation of an object that I shudder to name—and for this, above all, I loathed and dreaded and would have rid myself of the monster *had I dared*—it was now, I say, the image of a hideous—of a ghastly thing—of the GALLOWS!—O mournful and terrible engine of Horror and of Crime—of Agony and of Death!

And now was I indeed wretched beyond the wretchedness of mere Humanity. And *a brute beast*—whose fellow I had contemptuously destroyed—*a brute beast* to work out for *me*—for me, a man fashioned in the image of the High God—so much of insufferable woe! Alas! neither by day nor by night knew I the blessing of rest any more! During the former the creature left me no moment alone; and, in the latter, I started hourly from dreams of unutterable fear, to find the hot breath of *the thing* upon my face, and its vast weight an incarnate Nightmare that I had no power to shake off—incumbent eternally upon my *heart*!

Beneath the pressure of torments such as these, the feeble remnant of the good within me succumbed. Evil thoughts became my sole intimates—the darkest and most evil of thoughts. The moodiness of my usual temper increased to hatred of all things and of all mankind; while, from the sudden, frequent, and ungovernable outbursts of a fury to which I now blindly abandoned myself, my uncomplaining wife, alas! was the most usual and the most patient of sufferers.

One day she accompanied me, upon some household errand, into the cellar of the old building which our poverty compelled us to inhabit. The cat followed me down the steep stairs, and, nearly throwing me headlong, exasperated me to madness. Uplifting an ax, and, forgetting in my wrath the childish dread which had hitherto stayed my mind, I aimed a blow at the animal, which of course would have proved instantly fatal had it descended as I wished. But this blow was arrested by the hand of my wife. Goaded, by the interference, into a rage more than demoniacal, I withdrew my arm from her grasp, and buried the ax in her brain. She fell dead upon the spot, without a groan.

This hideous murder accomplished, I set myself forthwith, and with entire deliberation, to the task of concealing the body. I knew that I could not remove it from the house, either by day or by night, without the risk of being observed by the neighbors. Many projects entered my mind. At one period I thought of cutting the corpse into minute fragments and destroying them by fire. At another, I resolved to dig a grave for it in the floor of the cellar. Again, I deliberated about casting it in the well in the yard—about packing it in a box, as if merchandise, with the usual arrangements, and so getting a porter to take it from the house. Finally I hit upon what I considered a far better expedient than either of these. I determined to wall it up in the cellar—as the monks of the Middle Ages are recorded to have walled up their victims.

For a purpose such as this the cellar was well adapted. Its walls were loosely constructed, and had lately been plastered throughout with rough plaster, which the dampness of the atmosphere had prevented from hardening. Moreover, in one of the walls was a projection, caused by a false chimney, or fireplace, that had been filled up, and made to resemble the rest of the cellar. I made no doubt that I could readily displace the bricks at this point, insert the corpse, and wall the whole up as before, so that no eye could detect anything suspicious.

And in this calculation I was not deceived. By means of a crowbar I easily dislodged the bricks; and, having carefully deposited the body against the inner wall, I propped it in that position, while with little trouble I relaid the whole structure as it originally stood. Having procured mortar, sand, and hair, with every possible precaution, I prepared a plaster which could not be distinguished from the old, and with this I very carefully went over the new brickwork. When I had finished, I felt satisfied that all was right. The wall did not present the slightest appearance of having been disturbed. The rubbish on the floor was picked up with the minutest care. I looked around triumphantly, and said to myself, "Here at last, then, my labor has not been in vain."

My next step was to look for the beast which had been the cause of so much wretchedness; for I had at length firmly resolved to put it to death. Had I been able to meet with it at the moment there could have been no doubt of its fate, but it appeared that the crafty animal had been alarmed at the violence of my previous anger, and forbore to present itself in my present mood. It is impossible to describe or to imagine the deep, the blissful sense of relief which the absence of the detested creature occasioned in my bosom. It did not make its appearance during the night; and thus for one night at least since its introduction into the house, I soundly and tranquilly slept—ay, slept even with the burden of murder upon my soul!

The second and third day passed, and still my tormentor came not. Once again I breathed as a free man. The monster, in terror, had fled the premises for ever! I should behold it no more! My happiness was supreme! The guilt of my dark deed disturbed me but little. Some few inquiries had been made, but these had been readily answered. Even a search had been instituted; but of course nothing was to be discovered. I looked upon my future felicity as secured.

Upon the fourth day of the assassination, a party of the police came over unexpectedly into the house, and proceeded again to make rigorous investigation of the premises. Secure, however, in the inscrutability of my place of concealment, I felt no embarrassment whatever. The officers bade me accompany them in their search. They left no nook or corner unexplored. At length, for the third or fourth time, they descended into the cellar. I quivered not in a muscle. My heart beat calmly as that of one who slumbers in innocence. I walked the cellar from end to end. I folded my arms upon my bosom, and roamed easily to and fro. The police were thoroughly satisfied, and prepared to depart. The glee of my heart was too strong to be restrained. I burned to say, if but one word, by way of triumph, and to render doubly sure their assurance of my guiltlessness.

"Gentlemen," I said at last, as the party ascended the steps, "I delight to have allayed your suspicions. I wish you all health, and a little more courtesy. By the by, gentlemen, this—this is a very well constructed house." (In the rabid desire to say something easily, I scarcely knew what I uttered at all.) "I may say an *excellently* well constructed house. These walls—are you going, gentlemen?—these walls are solidly put together"; and here, through the mere frenzy of bravado, I rapped heavily, with a cane which I held in my hand, upon that very portion of the brickwork behind which stood the corpse of the wife of my bosom.

But may God shield and deliver me from the fangs of the Arch-Fiend! No sooner had the reverberation of my blows sunk into silence than I was answered by a voice from within the tomb!—by a cry, at first muffled and broken, like the sobbing of a child, and then quickly swelling into one long, loud, and continuous scream, utterly anomalous and inhuman—a howl—a wailing shriek, half of horror and half of triumph, such as might have arisen only out of hell, conjointly from the throats of the damned in their agony and of the demons that exult in the damnation.

Of my own thoughts it is folly to speak. Swooning, I staggered to the opposite wall. For one instant the party upon the stairs remained motionless, through extremity of terror and of awe. In the next, a dozen stout arms were toiling at the wall. It fell bodily. The corpse, already greatly decayed and clotted with gore, stood erect before the eyes of the spectators. Upon its head, with red extended mouth and solitary eye of fire, sat the hideous beast whose craft had seduced me into murder, and whose informing voice had consigned me to the hangman. I had walled the monster up within the tomb!

THE SPECTACLES

MANY YEARS AGO, it was the fashion to ridicule the idea of "love at first sight"; but those who think, not less than those who feel deeply, have always advocated its existence. Modern discoveries, indeed, in what may be termed ethical magnetism or magneto-æsthetics, render it probable that the most natural, and, consequently, the truest and most intense of the human affections are those which arise in the heart as if by electric sympathy—in a word, that the brightest and most enduring of the psychal fetters are those which are riveted by a glance. The confession I am about to make will add another to the already almost innumerable instances of the truth of the position.

My story requires that I should be somewhat minute. I am still a very young man—not yet twenty-two years of age. My name, at present, is a very usual and rather plebeian one—Simpson. I say "at present"; for it is only lately that I have been so called—having legislatively adopted this surname within the last year, in order to receive a large inheritance left me by a distant male relative, Adolphus Simpson, Esq. The bequest was conditioned upon my taking the name of the testator—the family, not the Christian name; my Christian name is Napoleon Bonaparte—or, more properly, these are my first and middle appellations.

I assumed the same, Simpson, with some reluctance, as in my true patronym, Froissart, I felt a very pardonable pride—believing that I could trace a descent from the immortal author of the Chronicles. While on the subject of names, by the by, I may mention a singular coincidence of sound attending the names of some of my immediate predecessors. My father was a Monsieur Froissart, of Paris. His wife—my mother, whom he married at fifteen—was a Mademoiselle Croissart, eldest daughter of Croissart the banker; whose wife, again, being only sixteen when married, was the eldest daughter of one Victor Voissart. Monsieur

Voissart, very singularly, had married a lady of similar name—a Mademoiselle Moissart. She, too, was quite a child when married; and her mother, also, Madame Moissart, was only fourteen when led to the altar. These early marriages are usual in France. Here, however, are Moissart, Voissart, Croissart, and Froissart, all in the direct line of descent. My own name, though, as I say, became Simpson, by act of Legislature, and with so much repugnance on my part, that, at one period, I actually hesitated about accepting the legacy with the useless and annoying proviso attached.

As to personal endowments, I am by no means deficient. On the contrary, I believe that I am well made, and possess what nine-tenths of the world would call a handsome face. In height I am five feet eleven. My hair is black and curling. My nose is sufficiently good. My eyes are large and gray; and although, in fact, they are weak to a very inconvenient degree, still no defect in this regard would be suspected from their appearance. The weakness itself, however, has always much annoyed me, and I have resorted to every remedy—short of wearing glasses. Being youthful and good-looking, I naturally dislike these, and have absolutely refused to employ them. I know nothing, indeed, which so disfigures the countenance of a young person, or so impresses every feature with an air of demureness, if not altogether of sanctimoniousness and of age. An eye-glass, on the other hand, has a savor of downright foppery and affectation. I have hitherto managed as well as I could without either. But something too much of these merely personal details, which, after all, are of little importance. I will content myself with saying, in addition, that my temperament is sanguine, rash, ardent, enthusiastic—and that all my life I have been a devoted admirer of the women.

One night last winter I entered a box at the P—— Theater, in company with a friend, Mr. Talbot. It was an opera night, and the bills presented a very rare attraction, so that the house was excessively crowded. We were in time, however, to obtain the front seats which had been reserved for us, and into which, with some little difficulty, we elbowed our way.

For two hours my companion, who was a musical fanatico, gave his undivided attention to the stage; and, in the meantime, I amused myself by observing the audience, which consisted, in chief part, of the very élite of the city. Having satisfied myself upon this point, I was about turning my eyes to the prima donna, when they were arrested and riveted by a figure in one of the private boxes which had escaped my observation.

If I live a thousand years I can never forget the intense emotion with which I regarded this figure. It was that of a female, the most exquisite I had ever beheld. The face was so far turned toward the stage that, for some minutes, I could not obtain a view of it,—but the form was divine; no other word can sufficiently express its magnificent proportion—and even the term "divine" seems ridiculously feeble as I write it.

The magic of a lovely form in woman—the necromancy of female gracefulness—was always a power which I had found it impossible to resist; but there was grace personified, incarnate, the beau idéal of my wildest and most enthusiastic visions. The figure, almost all of which the construction of the box permitted to be seen, was somewhat above the medium height, and nearly approached, without positively reaching, the majestic. Its perfect fullness and tournure were delicious. The head, of which only the back was visible, rivaled in outline that of the Greek Psyche, and was rather displayed than concealed by an elegant cap of *gaze aérienne*, which put me in mind of the *ventum textilem* of Apuleius. The right arm hung over the balustrade of the box, and thrilled every nerve of my frame with its exquisite symmetry. Its upper portion was draperied by one of the loose open sleeves now in fashion. This extended but little below the elbow. Beneath it was worn an under one of some frail material, close-fitting, and terminated by a cuff of rich lace, which fell gracefully over the top of the hand revealing only the delicate fingers, upon one of which sparkled a diamond ring, which I at once saw was of extraordinary value. The admirable roundness of the wrist was well set off by a bracelet which encircled it, and which also was ornamented and clasped by a magnificent aigrette of jewels,—telling, in words that could not be mistaken, at once of the wealth and fastidious taste of the wearer.

I gazed at this queenly apparition for at least half an hour, as if I had been suddenly converted to stone; and, during this period, I felt the full force and truth of all that has been said or sung concerning "love at first sight." My feelings were totally different from any which I had hitherto experienced, in the presence of even the most celebrated specimens of female loveliness. An unaccountable, and what I am compelled to consider a magnetic, sympathy of soul for soul, seemed to rivet, not only my vision, but my whole powers of thought and feeling, upon the admirable object before me. I saw—I felt—I knew that I was deeply, madly, irrevocably in love—and this even before seeing the face of the person beloved. So intense, indeed, was the passion that consumed me, that I really believed it would have received little if any abatement had the features, yet unseen, proved of merely ordinary character; so anomalous is the nature of the only true love—of the love at first sight—and so little really dependent is it upon the external conditions which only seem to create and control it.

While I was thus wrapped in admiration of this lovely vision, a sudden disturbance among the audience caused her to turn her head partially toward me, so that I beheld the entire profile of the face. Its beauty even exceeded my anticipations—and yet there was something about it which disappointed me without my being able to tell exactly what it was. I said "disappointed," but this is not altogether the word. My sentiments were at once quieted and exalted. They partook less of transport and more of calm enthusiasm—of enthusiastic repose. This state of feeling arose, perhaps, from the Madonna-like and matronly air of the face; and yet I at once understood that it could not have arisen entirely from this. There was something else—some mystery which I could not develop—some expression about the countenance which slightly disturbed me while it greatly heightened my interest. In fact, I was just in that condition of mind which prepares a young and susceptible man for any act of extravagance. Had the lady been alone, I should undoubtedly have entered her box and accosted her at all hazards; but, fortunately, she was attended by two companions—a gentleman, and a strikingly beautiful woman, to all appearance a few years younger than herself.

I revolved in my mind a thousand schemes by which I might obtain, hereafter, an introduction to the elder lady, or, for the present, at all events, a more distinct view of her beauty. I would have removed my position to one nearer her own, but the crowded state of the theater rendered this impossible; and the stern decrees of Fashion had, of late, imperatively prohibited the use of the opera-glass, in a case such as this, even had I been so fortunate as to have one with me—but I had not—and was thus in despair.

At length I bethought me of applying to my companion.

"Talbot," I said, "you have an opera-glass. Let me have it."

"An opera-glass!—no!—what do you suppose I would be doing with an opera-glass?" Here he turned impatiently toward the stage.

"But, Talbot," I continued, pulling him by the shoulder, "listen to me, will you? Do you see the stage-box?—there!—no, the next.—Did you ever behold as lovely a woman?"

"She is very beautiful, no doubt," he said.

"I wonder who she can be?"

"Why, in the name of all that is angelic, don't you know who she is? 'Not to know her argues yourself unknown.' She is the celebrated Madame Lalande—the beauty of the day par excellence, and the talk of the whole town. Immensely wealthy, too—a widow—and a great match—has just arrived from Paris."

"Do you know her?"

"Yes—I have the honor."

"Will you introduce me?"

"Assuredly—with the greatest pleasure; when shall it be?"

"To-morrow, at one, I will call upon you at B——'s."

"Very good; and now do hold your tongue, if you can."

In this latter respect I was forced to take Talbot's advice; for he remained obstinately deaf to every further question or suggestion, and occupied himself exclusively for the rest of the evening with what was transacting upon the stage.

In the meantime I kept my eyes riveted on Madame Lalande, and at length had the good fortune to obtain a full front view of her face. It was exquisitely lovely: this, of course, my heart had told me before, even had not Talbot fully satisfied me upon the point—but still the unintelligible something disturbed me. I finally concluded that my senses were impressed by a certain air of gravity, sadness, or, still more properly, of weariness, which took something from the youth and freshness of the countenance, only to endow it with a seraphic tenderness and majesty, and thus, of course, to my enthusiastic and romantic temperament, with an interest tenfold.

While I thus feasted my eyes, I perceived, at last, to my great trepidation, by an almost imperceptible start on the part of the lady, that she had become suddenly aware of the intensity of my gaze. Still, I was absolutely fascinated, and could not withdraw it, even for an instant. She turned aside her face, and again I saw only the chiseled contour of the back portion of the head. After some minutes, as if urged by curiosity to see if I was still looking, she gradually brought her face again around and again encountered my burning gaze. Her large dark eyes fell instantly, and a deep blush mantled her cheek. But what was my astonishment at perceiving that she not only did not a second time avert her head, but that she actually took from her girdle a double eye-glass—elevated it—adjusted it—and then regarded me through it, intently and deliberately, for the space of several minutes.

Had a thunderbolt fallen at my feet I could not have been more thoroughly astounded—astounded only—not offended or disgusted in the slightest degree; although an action so bold in any other woman would have been likely to offend or disgust. But the whole thing was done with so much quietude—so much nonchalance—so much repose—with so evident an air of the highest breeding, in short—that nothing of mere effrontery was perceptible, and my sole sentiments were those of admiration and surprise.

I observed that, upon her first elevation of the glass, she had seemed satisfied with a momentary inspection of my person, and was withdrawing the instrument, when, as if struck by a second thought, she resumed it, and so continued to regard me with fixed attention for the space of several minutes—for five minutes, at the very least, I am sure.

This action, so remarkable in an American theater, attracted very general observation, and gave rise to an indefinite movement, or buzz, among the audience, which, for a moment, filled me with confusion, but produced no visible effect upon the countenance of Madame Lalande.

Having satisfied her curiosity—if such it was—she dropped the glass, and quietly gave her attention again to the stage; her profile now being turned toward myself, as before. I continued to watch her unremittingly, although I was fully conscious of my rudeness in so doing. Presently I saw the head slowly and slightly change its position; and soon I became convinced that the lady, while pretending to look at the stage was, in fact, attentively regarding myself. It is needless to say what effect this conduct, on the part of so fascinating a woman, had upon my excitable mind.

Having thus scrutinized me for perhaps a quarter of an hour, the fair object of my passion addressed the gentleman who attended her, and, while she spoke, I saw distinctly by the glances of both, that the conversation had reference to myself.

Upon its conclusion, Madame Lalande again turned toward the stage, and, for a few minutes, seemed absorbed in the performances. At the expiration of this period, however, I was thrown into an extremity of agitation by seeing her unfold, for the second time, the eye-glass which hung at her side, fully confront me as before, and, disregarding the renewed buzz of the audience, survey me, from head to foot, with the same miraculous composure which had previously so delighted and confounded my soul.

This extraordinary behavior, by throwing me into a perfect fever of excitement—into an absolute delirium of love—served rather to embolden than to disconcert me. In the mad intensity of my devotion, I forgot everything but the presence and the majestic loveliness of the vision which confronted my gaze. Watching my opportunity, when I thought the audience were fully engaged with the opera, I at length caught the eyes of Madame Lalande, and, upon the instant, made a slight but unmistakable bow.

She blushed very deeply—then averted her eyes—then slowly and cautiously looked around, apparently to see if my rash action had been noticed—then leaned over toward the gentleman who sat by her side.

I now felt a burning sense of the impropriety I had committed, and expected nothing less than instant exposure; while a vision of pistols upon the morrow floated rapidly and uncomfortably through my brain. I was greatly and immediately relieved, however, when I saw the lady merely hand the gentleman a play-bill, without speaking; but the reader may form some feeble conception of my astonishment—of my profound amazement—my delirious bewilderment of heart and soul—when, instantly afterward, having again glanced furtively around, she allowed her bright eyes to set fully and steadily upon my own, and then, with a faint smile, disclosing a bright line of her pearly teeth, made two distinct, pointed, and unequivocal affirmative inclinations of the head.

It is useless, of course, to dwell upon my joy—upon my transport—upon my illimitable ecstasy of heart. If ever man was mad with excess of happiness, it was myself at that moment. I loved. This was my first love—so I felt it to be. It was love supreme—indescribable. It was "love at first sight"; and at first sight, too, it had been appreciated and returned.

Yes, returned. How and why should I doubt it for an instant. What other construction could I possibly put upon such conduct, on the part of a lady so beautiful—so wealthy—evidently so accomplished—of so high breeding—of so lofty a position in society—in every regard so entirely respectable as I felt assured was Madame Lalande? Yes, she loved me—she returned the enthusiasm of my love, with an enthusiasm as blind—as uncompromising—as uncalculating—as abandoned—and as utterly unbounded as my own! These delicious fancies and reflections, however, were now interrupted by the falling of the drop-curtain. The audience arose; and the usual tumult immediately supervened. Quitting Talbot abruptly, I made every effort to force my way into closer proximity with Madame Lalande. Having failed in this, on account of the crowd, I at length gave up the chase, and bent my steps homeward; consoling myself for my disappointment in not having been able to touch even the hem of her robe, by the reflection that I should be introduced by Talbot, in due form, upon the morrow.

This morrow at last came; that is to say, a day finally dawned upon a long and weary night of impatience; and then the hours until "one" were snail-paced, dreary, and innumerable. But even Stamboul, it is said, shall have an end, and there came an end to this long delay. The clock struck. As the last echo ceased, I stepped into B——'s and inquired for Talbot.

"Out!" said the footman—Talbot's own.

"Out!" I replied, staggering back half a dozen paces—"let me tell you, my fine fellow, that this thing is thoroughly impossible and impracticable; Mr. Talbot is not out. What do you mean?"

"Nothing, sir; only Mr. Talbot is not in. That's all. He rode over to S——, immediately after breakfast, and left word that he would not be in town again for a week."

I stood petrified with horror and rage. I endeavored to reply, but my tongue refused its office. At length I turned on my heel, livid with wrath, and inwardly consigning the whole tribe of the Talbots to the inner-most regions of Erebus. It was evident that my considerate friend, *il fanatico*, had quite forgotten his appointment with myself—had forgotten it as soon as it was made. At no time was he a very scrupulous man of his word. There was no help for it; so, smothering my vexation as well as

I could, I strolled moodily up the street, propounding futile inquiries about Madame Lalande to every male acquaintance I met. By report she was known, I found, to all—to many by sight—but she had been in town only a few weeks, and there were very few, therefore, who claimed her personal acquaintance. These few, being still comparatively strangers, could not, or would not, take the liberty of introducing me through the formality of a morning call. While I stood thus, in despair, conversing with a trio of friends upon the all-absorbing subject of my heart, it so happened that the subject itself passed by.

"As I live, there she is!" cried one.

"Surprisingly beautiful!" exclaimed a second.

"An angel upon earth!" ejaculated a third.

I looked; and in an open carriage which approached us, passing slowly down the street, sat the enchanting vision of the opera, accompanied by the younger lady who had occupied a portion of her box.

"Her companion also wears remarkably well," said the one of my trio who had spoken first.

"Astonishingly," said the second; "still quite a brilliant air; but art will do wonders. Upon my word, she looks better than she did at Paris five years ago. A beautiful woman still;—don't you think so, Froissart?—Simpson, I mean."

"Still!" said I, "and why shouldn't she be? But compared with her friend she is as a rushlight to the evening star—a glow-worm to Antares."

"Ha! ha! ha!—why, Simpson, you have an astonishing tact at making discoveries—original ones, I mean." And here we separated, while one of the trio began humming a gay vaudeville, of which I caught only the lines—

Ninon, Ninon, Ninon à bas—
A bas Ninon de L'Enclos!

During this little scene, however, one thing had served greatly to console me, although it fed the passion by which I was consumed. As the carriage of Madame Lalande rolled by our group, I had observed that she recognized me; and more than this, she had blessed me, by the most seraphic of all imaginable smiles, with no equivocal mark of the recognition.

As for an introduction, I was obliged to abandon all hope of it, until such time as Talbot should think proper to return from the country. In the meantime I perseveringly frequented every reputable place of public amusement; and, at length, at the theater, where I first saw her, I had the supreme bliss of meeting her, and of exchanging glances with her once again. This did not occur, however, until the lapse of a fortnight. Every day, in the interim, I had inquired for Talbot at his hotel, and every day had been thrown into a spasm of wrath by the everlasting "Not come home yet" of his footman.

Upon the evening in question, therefore, I was in a condition little short of madness. Madame Lalande, I had been told, was a Parisian—had lately arrived from Paris—might she not suddenly return?—return before Talbot came back—and might she not be thus lost to me for ever? The thought was too terrible to bear. Since my future happiness was at issue, I resolved to act with a manly decision. In a word, upon the breaking up of the play, I traced the lady to her residence, noted the address, and the next morning sent her a full and elaborate letter, in which I poured out my whole heart.

I spoke boldly, freely—in a word, I spoke with passion. I concealed nothing—not even of my weakness. I alluded to the romantic circumstances of our first meeting—even to the glances which had passed between us. I went so far as to say that I felt assured of her love; while I offered this assurance, and my own intensity of devotion, as two excuses for my otherwise unpardonable conduct. As a third, I spoke of my fear that she might quit the city before I could have the opportunity of a formal introduction. I concluded the most wildly enthusiastic epistle ever penned, with a frank declaration of my worldly circumstances—of my affluence—and with an offer of my heart and of my hand.

In an agony of expectation I awaited the reply. After what seemed the lapse of a century it came.

Yes, actually came. Romantic as all this may appear, I really received a letter from Madame Lalande—the beautiful, the wealthy, the idolized Madame Lalande. Her eyes—her magnificent eyes, had not belied her noble heart. Like a true Frenchwoman, as she was, she had obeyed the frank dictates of her reason—the generous impulses of her nature—despising the conventional pruderies of the world. She had not scorned my proposals. She had not sheltered herself in silence. She had not returned my letter unopened. She had even sent me, in reply, one penned by her own exquisite fingers. It ran thus:

> Monsieur Simpson vill pardonne me for not compose de butefulle tong of his contrée so vell as might. It is only de late dat I am arrive, and not yet ave de opportunité for to—l'étudier. Vid dis apologie for the manière, I vill now say dat, hélas!—Monsieur Simpson ave guess but de too true. Need I say de more? Hélas! am I not ready speak de too moshe?
>
> Eugénie Lalande

This noble-spirited note I kissed a million times, and committed no doubt, on its account, a thousand other extravagances that have now escaped my memory. Still Talbot would not return. Alas! could he have formed even the vaguest idea of the suffering his absence had occasioned his friend, would not his sympathizing nature have flown immediately to my relief? Still, however, he came not. I wrote. He replied. He was detained by urgent business—but would shortly return. He begged me not to be impatient—to moderate my transports—to read soothing books—to drink nothing stronger than Hock—and to bring the consolations of philosophy in my aid. The fool! if he could not come himself, why, in the name of everything rational, could he not have enclosed me a letter of presentation? I wrote him again, entreating him to forward one forthwith. My letter was returned by that footman, with the following endorsement in pencil. The scoundrel had joined his master in the country:

> Left S—— yesterday, for parts unknown—did not say where—or when be back—so thought best to return letter, knowing your handwriting, and as how you is always, more or less, in a hurry.
>
> Yours sincerely,
> Stubbs

After this it is needless to say that I devoted to the infernal deities both master and valet:—but there was little use in anger, and no consolation at all in complaint.

But I had yet a resource left, in my constitutional audacity. Hitherto it had served me well, and I now resolved to make it avail me to the end. Besides, after the correspondence which had passed between us, what act of mere informality could I commit, within bounds, that ought to be regarded as indecorous by Madame Lalande? Since the affair of the letter, I had been in the habit of watching her house, and thus discovered that, about twilight, it was her custom to promenade, attended only by a negro in livery, in a public square overlooked by her windows. Here, amid the luxuriant and shadowing groves, in the gray gloom of a sweet midsummer evening, I observed my opportunity and accosted her.

The better to deceive the servant in attendance, I did this with the assured air of an old and familiar acquaintance. With a presence of mind truly Parisian, she took the cue at once, and, to greet me, held out the most bewitchingly little of hands. The valet at once fell into the rear, and now, with hearts full to overflowing, we discoursed long and unreservedly of our love.

As Madame Lalande spoke English even less fluently than she wrote it, our conversation was necessarily in French. In this sweet tongue, so adapted to passion, I gave loose rein to the impetuous enthusiasm of my nature, and, with all the eloquence I could command, besought her to consent to an immediate marriage.

At this impatience she smiled. She urged the old story of decorum—that bugbear which deters so many from bliss until the opportunity for bliss has for ever gone by. I had most imprudently made it known among my friends, she observed, that I desired her acquaintance—thus that I did not possess it—thus, again, there was no possibility of concealing the date of our first knowledge of each other. And then she adverted, with a blush, to the extreme recency of this date. To wed immediately would be improper—would be indecorous—would be outré. All this she said with a charming air of naïveté which enraptured while it grieved and convinced me. She went even so far as to accuse me, laughingly, of rashness—of imprudence. She bade me remember that I really even knew not who she was—what were her prospects, her connexions, her standing in society. She begged me, but with a sigh, to reconsider my proposal, and termed my love an infatuation—a will-o'-the-wisp—a fancy or phantasy of the moment, a baseless and unstable creation rather of the imagination than of the heart. These things she uttered as the shadows of the sweet twilight gathered darkly and more darkly around us—and then, with a gentle pressure of her fairy-like hand, overthrew in a single sweet instant, all the argumentative fabric she had reared.

I replied as best I could—as only as a true lover can. I spoke at length, and perseveringly of my devotion, of my passion—of her exceeding beauty, and of my own enthusiastic admiration. In conclusion, I dwelt, with a convincing energy, upon the perils that encompass the course of love—that course of true love that never did run smooth—and thus deduced the manifest danger of rendering that course unnecessarily long.

This latter argument seemed finally to soften the rigour of her determination. She relented; but there was yet an obstacle, she said, which she felt assured I had not properly considered. This was a delicate point—for a woman to urge, especially so; in mentioning it, she saw that she must make a sacrifice of her feelings; still, for me, every sacrifice should be made. She alluded to the topic of age. Was I aware—was I fully aware of this discrepancy between us? That the age of the husband should surpass by a few years—even by fifteen or twenty—the age of the wife, was regarded by the world as admissible, and indeed, as even proper: but she had always entertained the belief that the years of the wife should never exceed in number those of the husband. A discrepancy of this unnatural kind gave rise, too frequently, alas! to a life of unhappiness. Now she was aware that my own age did not exceed two and twenty; and I, on the contrary, perhaps was not aware that the years of my Eugénie extended very considerably beyond that number.

About all this there was a nobility of soul—a dignity of candor—which delighted—which enchanted me—which eternally riveted my chains. I could scarcely restrain the excessive transport which possessed me.

"My sweetest Eugénie," I cried, "what is all this about which you are discoursing? Your years surpass in some measure my own. But what then? The customs of the world are so many conventional follies. To those who love as ourselves, in what respect differs a year from an hour? I am twenty-two, you say; granted: indeed, you may as well call me, at once, twenty-three. Now you yourself, my dearest Eugénie, can have numbered no more than—can have numbered no more than—no more than—than—than—than——"

Here I paused for an instant, in the expectation that Madame Lalande would interrupt me by supplying her true age. But a Frenchwoman is seldom direct, and has always, by way of answering to an embarrassing query, some little practical reply of her own. In the present instance, Eugénie, who for a few moments past had seemed to be searching for something in her bosom, at length let fall upon the grass a miniature, which I immediately picked up and presented to her.

"Keep it!" she said, with one of her most ravishing smiles. "Keep it for my sake—for the sake of her whom it too flatteringly represents. Besides, upon the back of the trinket you may discover, perhaps, the very information you seem to desire. It is now, to be sure, growing rather dark—but you can examine it at your leisure in the morning. In the meantime, you shall be my escort home to-night. My friends are about holding a little musical levée. I can promise you, too, some good singing. We French are not nearly so punctilious as you Americans, and I shall have no difficulty in smuggling you in, in the character of an old acquaintance."

With this she took my arm, and I attended her home. The mansion was quite a fine one, and, I believe, furnished in good taste. Of this latter point, however, I am scarcely qualified to judge; for it was just dark as we arrived; and in American mansions of the better sort lights seldom, during the heat of summer, make their appearance at this, the most pleasant period of the day. In about an hour after my arrival, to be sure, a single shaded solar lamp was lit in the principal drawing-room; and this apartment, I could thus see, was arranged with unusual good taste and even splendor; but two other rooms of the suite, and in which the company chiefly assembled, remained, during the whole evening, in a very agreeable shadow. This is a well-conceived custom, giving the party at least a choice of light or shade, and one which our friends over the water could not do better than immediately adopt.

The evening thus spent was unquestionably the most delicious of my life. Madame Lalande had not overrated the musical abilities of her friends; and the singing I here heard I had never heard excelled in any private circle out of Vienna. The instrumental performers were many and of superior talents. The vocalists were chiefly ladies, and no individual sang less than well. At length, upon a peremptory call for "Madame Lalande," she arose at once, without affectation or demur, from the chaise longue upon which she had sat by my side, and, accompanied by one or two gentlemen and her female friend of the opera, repaired to the piano in the main drawing-room. I would have escorted her myself, but felt that, under the circumstances of my introduction to the house, I had better remain unobserved where I was. I was thus deprived of the pleasure of seeing, although not of hearing, her sing.

The impression she produced upon the company seemed electrical—but the effect upon myself was something even more. I know not how adequately to describe it. It arose in part, no doubt, from the sentiment of love with which I was imbued; but chiefly from my conviction of the extreme sensibility of the singer. It is beyond the reach of art to endow either air or recitative with more impassioned expression than was hers. Her utterance of the romance in *Otello*—the tone with which she gave the words "*sul mio sasso*," in the *Capuletti*—is ringing in my memory yet. Her lower tones were absolutely miraculous. Her voice embraced three complete octaves, extending from the contralto D to the D upper soprano, and, though sufficiently powerful to have filled the San Carlos, executed, with the minutest precision, every difficulty of vocal composition—ascending and descending scales, cadences, or fiorituri. In the finale of the *Sonnambula*, she brought about a most remarkable effect at the words:

Ah! non giunge uman pensiero
Al contento ond' io son piena.

Here, in imitation of Malibran, she modified the original phrase of Bellini, so as to let her voice descend to the tenor G, when, by a rapid transition, she struck the G above the treble stave, springing over an interval of two octaves.

Upon rising from the piano after these miracles of vocal execution, she resumed her seat by my side; when I expressed to her, in terms of the deepest enthusiasm, my delight at her performance. Of my surprise I said nothing, and yet was I most unfeignedly surprised; for a certain feebleness, or rather a certain tremulous indecision of voice in ordinary conversation, had prepared me to anticipate that, in singing, she would not acquit herself with any remarkable ability.

Our conversation was now long, earnest, uninterrupted, and totally unreserved. She made me relate many of the earlier passages of my life, and listened with breathless attention to every word of the narrative. I concealed nothing—felt that I had a right to conceal nothing—from her confiding affection. Encouraged by her candor upon the delicate point of her age, I entered, with perfect frankness, not only into a detail of my many minor vices, but made full confession of those moral and even of those physical infirmities, the disclosure of which, in demanding so much higher a degree of courage, is so much surer an evidence of love. I touched upon my college indiscretions—upon my extravagances—upon my carousals—upon my debts—upon my flirtations. I even went so far as to speak of a slightly hectic cough with which, at one time, I had been troubled—of a chronic rheumatism—of a twinge of hereditary gout—and, in conclusion, of the disagreeable and inconvenient, but hitherto carefully concealed weakness of my eyes.

"Upon this latter point," said Madame Lalande, laughingly, "you have been surely injudicious in coming to confession; for, without the confession, I take it for granted that no one would have accused you of the crime. By the by," she continued, "have you any recollection—" and here I fancied that a blush, even through the gloom of the apartment, became distinctly visible upon her cheek—"have you any recollection *mon cher ami*, of this little ocular assistant which now depends from my neck?"

As she spoke, she twirled in her fingers the identical double eye-glass, which had so overwhelmed me with confusion at the opera.

"Full well—alas! do I remember it," I exclaimed, pressing passionately the delicate hand which offered the glasses for my inspection. They formed a complex and magnificent toy, richly chased and filigreed, and gleaming with jewels which, even in the deficient light, I could not help perceiving were of high value.

"*Eh bien! mon ami*," she resumed with a certain empressement of manner that rather surprised me—"*Eh bien! mon ami*, you have earnestly besought of me a favor which you have been pleased to denominate priceless. You have demanded of me my hand upon the morrow. Should I yield to your entreaties—and, I may add, to the pleadings of my own bosom—would I not be entitled to demand of you a very—a very little boon in return?"

"Name it!" I exclaimed with an energy that had nearly drawn upon us the observation of the company, and restrained by their presence alone from throwing myself impetuously at her feet. "Name it, my beloved, my Eugénie, my own!—name it!—but, alas! it is already yielded ere named."

"You shall conquer, then, *mon ami*," said she, "for the sake of the Eugénie whom you love, this little weakness which you have at last confessed—this weakness more moral than physical—and which, let me assure you, is so unbecoming the nobility of your real nature—so inconsistent with the candor of your usual character—and which, if permitted further control, will assuredly involve you, sooner or later, in some very disagreeable scrape. You shall conquer, for my sake, this affectation which leads you, as you yourself acknowledge, to the tacit or implied denial of your infirmity of vision. For, this infirmity you virtually deny, in refusing to employ the customary means for its relief. You will understand me to say, then, that I wish you to wear spectacles:—ah, hush!—you have already consented to wear them, for my sake. You shall accept the little toy which I now hold in my hand, and which, though admirable as an aid to vision, is really of no very immense value as a gem. You perceive that, by a trifling modification thus—or thus—it can be adapted to the eyes in the form of spectacles, or worn in the waistcoat pocket as an eye-glass. It is in the former mode, however, and habitually, that you have already consented to wear it for my sake."

This request—must I confess it?—confused me in no little degree. But the condition with which it was coupled rendered hesitation, of course, a matter altogether out of the question.

"It is done!" I cried, with all the enthusiasm that I could muster at the moment. "It is done—it is most cheerfully agreed. I sacrifice every feeling for your sake. To-night I wear this dear eye-glass, as an eye-glass, and upon my heart; but with the earliest dawn of that morning which gives me the pleasure of calling you wife, I will place it upon my—upon my nose,—and there wear it ever afterward, in the less romantic, and less fashionable, but certainly in the more serviceable, form which you desire."

Our conversation now turned upon the details of our arrangements for the morrow. Talbot, I learned from my betrothed, had just arrived in town. I was to see him at once, and procure a carriage. The soirée would scarcely break up before two; and by this hour the vehicle was to be at the door; when, in the confusion occasioned by the departure of the company, Madame L. could easily enter it unobserved. We were then to call at the house of a clergyman who would be in waiting; there be married, drop Talbot, and proceed on a short tour to the East; leaving the fashionable world at home to make whatever comments upon the matter it thought best.

Having planned all this, I immediately took leave, and went in search of Talbot, but, on the way, I could not refrain from stepping into a hotel, for the purpose of inspecting the miniature, and this I did by the powerful aid of the glasses. The countenance was a surpassingly beautiful one! Those large luminous eyes!—that proud Grecian nose!—those dark luxuriant curls!—"Ah!" said I, exultantly to myself, "this is indeed the speaking image of my beloved!" I turned the reverse, and discovered the words—"Eugénie Lalande—aged twenty-seven years and seven months."

I found Talbot at home, and proceeded at once to acquaint him with my good fortune. He professed excessive astonishment, of course, but congratulated me most cordially, and proffered every assistance in his power. In a word, we carried out our arrangement to the letter; and at two in the morning, just ten minutes after the ceremony, I found myself in a close carriage with Madame Lalande—with Mrs. Simpson, I should say—and driving at a great rate out of town, in a direction northeast by north, half-north.

It had been determined for us by Talbot, that, as we were to be up all night, we should make our first stop at C——, a village about twenty miles from the city, and there get an early breakfast and some repose, before proceeding upon our route. At four, precisely, therefore, the carriage drew up at the door of the principal inn. I handed my adored wife out, and ordered breakfast forthwith. In the meantime we were shown into a small parlor, and sat down.

It was now nearly if not altogether daylight; and, as I gazed, enraptured, at the angel by my side, the singular idea came, all at once, into my head, that this was really the very first moment since my acquaintance with the celebrated loveliness of Madame Lalande, that I had enjoyed a near inspection of that loveliness by daylight at all.

"And now, *mon ami*," said she, taking my hand, and so interrupting this train of reflection, "and now, *mon cher ami*, since we are indissolubly one—since I have yielded to your passionate entreaties, and performed my portion of our agreement—I presume you have not forgotten that you also have a little favor to bestow—a little promise which it is your intention to keep. Ah! let me see! Let me remember! Yes; full easily do I call to mind the precise words of the dear promise you made to Eugénie last night. Listen! You spoke thus: 'It is done!—it is most cheerfully agreed! I sacrifice every feeling for your sake. To-night I wear this dear eye-glass, as an eye-glass, and upon my heart; but with the earliest dawn of that morning which gives me the privilege of calling you wife, I will place it upon my—upon my nose,—and there wear it ever afterward, in the less romantic, and less fashionable, but certainly in the more serviceable, form which you desire.' These were the exact words, my beloved husband, were they not?"

"They were," I said; "you have an excellent memory; and assuredly, my beautiful Eugénie, there is no disposition on my part to evade the performance of the trivial promise they imply. See! Behold! They are becoming—rather—are they not?" And here, having arranged the glasses in the ordinary form of spectacles, I applied them gingerly in their proper position; while Madame Simpson, adjusting her cap, and folding her arms, sat bolt upright in her chair, in a somewhat stiff and prim, and indeed, in a somewhat undignified position.

"Goodness gracious me!" I exclaimed, almost at the very instant that the rim of the spectacles had settled upon my nose. "My! goodness gracious me!—why what can be the matter with these glasses!" and taking them quickly off, I wiped them carefully with a silk handkerchief, and adjusted them again.

But if, in the first instance, there had occurred something which occasioned me surprise, in the second, this surprise became elevated into astonishment; and this astonishment was profound—was extreme—indeed I may say it was horrific. What, in the name of everything hideous, did this mean? Could I believe my eyes?—could I?—that was the question. Was that—was that—was that rouge! And were those—and were those—were those wrinkles; upon the visage of Eugénie Lalande? And oh! Jupiter, and every one of the gods and goddesses, little and big!—what—what—what—what had become of her teeth? I dashed the spectacles violently to the ground, and, leaping to my feet, stood erect in the middle of the floor, confronting Mrs. Simpson, with my arms set akimbo, and grinning and foaming, but, at the same time, utterly speechless with terror and with rage.

Now I have already said that Madame Eugénie Lalande—that is to say, Simpson—spoke the English language but very little better than she wrote it; and for this reason she very properly never attempted to speak it upon ordinary occasions. But rage will carry a lady to any extreme; and in the present case it carried Mrs. Simpson to the very extraordinary extreme of attempting to hold a conversation in a tongue that she did not altogether understand.

"Vell, monsieur," said she, after surveying me, in great apparent astonishment, for some moments—"Vell, monsieur!—and vat den?—vat de matter now? It is de dance of de Saint Vitusse dut you ave? If not like me, vat for vy buy de pig in de poke?"

"You wretch!" said I, catching my breath—"you—you—you villainous old hag!"

"Ag?—ole?—me not so ver ole, after all! me not one single day more dan de eighty-doo."

"Eighty-two!" I ejaculated, staggering to the wall—"eighty-two hundred thousand baboons! The miniature said twenty-seven years and seven months!"

"To be sure!—dat is so!—ver true! but den de portraite has been take for dese fifty-five year. Ven I go marry my segonde usbande, Monsieur Lalande, at dat time I had de portrait take for my daughter by my first usbande, Monsieur Moissart!"

"Moissart!" said I.

"Yes, Moissart," said she, mimicking my pronunciation, which, to speak the truth was none of the best; "and vat den? Vat you know about de Moissart?"

"Nothing, you old fright!—I know nothing about him at all; only I had an ancestor of that name, once upon a time."

"Dat name! and vat you ave for say to dat name? 'Tis ver goot name; and so is Voissart—dat is ver goot name too. My daughter, Mademoiselle Moissart, she marry von Monsieur Voissart; and de name is both ver respectaable name."

"Moissart?" I exclaimed, "and Voissart! why, what is it you mean?"

"Vat I mean?—I mean Moissart and Voissart; and for de matter of dat, I mean Croissart and Froissart, too, if I only tink proper to mean it. My daughter's daughter, Mademoiselle Voissart, she marry von Monsieur Croissart, and den agin, my daughter's grande-daughter, Mademoiselle Croissart, she marry von Monsieur Froissart; and I suppose you say dat dat is not von ver respectaable name."

"Froissart!" said I, beginning to faint, "why surely you don't say Moissart, and Voissart, and Croissart, and Froissart?"

"Yes," she replied, leaning fully back in her chair, and stretching out her lower limbs at great length; "yes, Moissart, and Voissart, and Croissart, and Froissart. But Monsieur Froissart, he vas von ver big vat you call fool—he vas von ver great big donce like yourself—for he left la belle France for come to dis stupide Amérique—and ven he get here he vent and ave von ver stupide, von ver, ver stupide sonn, so I hear, dough I not yet av ad de plaisir to meet vid him—neither me nor my companion, de Madame Stephanie Lalande. He is name de Napoleon Bonaparte Froissart, and I suppose you say dat dat, too, is not ver respectaable name."

Either the length or the nature of this speech, had the effect of working up Mrs. Simpson into a very extraordinary passion indeed: and as she made an end of it, with great labor, she jumped up from her chair like somebody bewitched, dropping upon the floor an entire universe of bustle as she jumped. Once upon her feet, she gnashed her gums, brandished her arms, rolled up her sleeves, shook her fist in my face, and concluded the performance by tearing the cap from her head, and with it an immense wig of the most valuable and beautiful black hair, the whole of which she dashed upon the ground with a yell, and there trampled and danced a fandango upon it, in an absolute ecstasy and agony of rage.

Meantime I sank aghast into the chair which she had vacated. "Moissart and Voissart!" I repeated thoughtfully, as she cut one of her pigeon-wings, "and Croissart and Froissart!" as she completed another—"Moissart and Voissart and Croissart and Napoleon Bonaparte Froissart! —why, you ineffable old serpent, that's me—that's me—d'ye hear?—that's me"—here I screamed at the top of my voice—"that's me-e-e! I am Napoleon Bonaparte Froissart! and if I haven't married my great, great, grandmother, I wish I may be everlastingly confounded!"

Madame Eugénie Lalande, quasi Simpson—formerly Moissart—was, in sober fact, my great, great, grandmother. In her youth she had been beautiful, and even at eighty-two, retained the majestic height, the sculptural contour of head, the fine eyes and the Grecian nose of her girlhood. By the aid of these, of pearl-powder, of rouge, of false hair, false teeth, and false tournure, as well as of the most skillful modistes of Paris, she contrived to hold a respectable footing among the beauties en peu passées of the French metropolis. In this respect, indeed, she might have been regarded as little less than the equal of the celebrated Ninon de L'Enclos.

She was immensely wealthy, and being left, for the second time, a widow without children, she bethought herself of my existence in America, and for the purpose of making me her heir, paid a visit to the United States, in company with a distant and exceedingly lovely relative of her second husband's—a Madame Stephanie Lalande.

At the opera, my great, great, grandmother's attention was arrested by my notice; and, upon surveying me through her eye-glass, she was struck with a certain family resemblance to herself. Thus interested, and knowing that the heir she sought was actually in the city, she made inquiries of her party respecting me. The gentleman who attended her knew my person, and told her who I was. The information thus obtained induced her to renew her scrutiny; and this scrutiny it was which so emboldened me that I behaved in the absurd manner already detailed. She returned my bow, however, under the impression that, by some odd accident, I had discovered her identity. When, deceived by my weakness of vision, and the arts of the toilet, in respect to the age and charms of the strange lady, I demanded so enthusiastically of Talbot who she was, he concluded that I meant the younger beauty, as a matter of course, and so informed me, with perfect truth, that she was "the celebrated widow, Madame Lalande."

In the street, next morning, my great, great, grandmother encountered Talbot, an old Parisian acquaintance; and the conversation very naturally turned upon myself. My deficiencies of vision were then explained; for these were notorious, although I was entirely ignorant of their notoriety; and my good old relative discovered, much to her chagrin, that she had been deceived in supposing me aware of her identity, and that I had been merely making a fool of myself in making open love, in a theater, to an old woman unknown. By way of punishing me for this imprudence, she concocted with Talbot a plot. He purposely kept out of my way to avoid giving me the introduction. My street inquiries about "the lovely widow, Madame Lalande," were supposed to refer to the younger lady, of course; and thus the conversation with the three gentlemen whom I encountered shortly after leaving Talbot's hotel will be easily explained, as also their allusion to Ninon de L'Enclos. I had no opportunity of seeing Madame Lalande closely during daylight, and, at her musical *soirée*, my silly weakness in refusing the aid of glasses effectually prevented me from making a discovery of her age. When "Madame Lalande" was called upon to sing, the younger lady was intended; and it was she who arose to obey the call; my great, great, grandmother, to further the deception, arising at the same moment and accompanying her to the piano in the main drawing-room. Had I decided upon escorting her thither, it had been her design to suggest the propriety of my remaining where I was; but my own prudential views rendered this unnecessary. The songs which I so much admired, and which so confirmed the impression of the youth of my mistress, were executed by Madame Stephanie Lalande. The eye-glass was presented by way of adding a reproof to the hoax—a sting to the epigram of the deception. Its presentation afforded an opportunity for the lecture upon affectation with which I was so especially edified. It is almost superfluous to add that the glasses of the instrument, as worn by the old lady, had been exchanged by her for a pair better adapted to my years. They suited me, in fact, to a T.

The clergyman, who merely pretended to tie the fatal knot, was a boon companion of Talbot's and no priest. He was an excellent "whip", however; and having doffed his cassock to put on a greatcoat, he drove the hack which conveyed the "happy couple" out of town. Talbot took a seat at his side. The two scoundrels were thus "in at the death," and through a half open window of the back parlor of the inn, amused themselves in grinning at the *dénouement* of the drama. I believe I shall be forced to call them both out.

Nevertheless, I am *not* the husband of my great, great, grandmother; and this is a reflection which affords me infinite relief;—but I *am* the husband of Madame Lalande—of Madame Stephanie Lalande—with whom my good old relative, besides making me her sole heir when she dies—if she ever does—has been at the trouble of concocting me a match. In conclusion: I am done for ever with *billets-doux*, and am never to be met without SPECTACLES.

THE PREMATURE BURIAL

THERE ARE CERTAIN themes of which the interest is all-absorbing but which are too entirely horrible for the purposes of legitimate fiction. These the mere romanticist must eschew, if he do not wish to offend, or to disgust. They are with propriety handled only when the severity and majesty of truth sanctify and sustain them. We thrill, for example, with the most intense of "pleasurable pain" over the accounts of the Passage of the Beresina, of the Earthquake at Lisbon, of the Plague at London, of the Massacre of St Bartholomew, or of the stifling of the hundred and twenty-three prisoners in the Black Hole at Calcutta. But, in these accounts, it is the fact—it is the reality—it is the history which excites. As inventions, we should regard them with simple abhorrence.

I have mentioned some few of the more prominent and august calamities on record; but in these it is extent, not less than the character of the calamity, which so vividly impresses the fancy. I need not remind the reader that, from the long and weird catalog of human miseries, I might have selected many individual instances more replete with essential suffering than any of these vast generalities of disaster. The true wretchedness, indeed,—the ultimate woe,—is particular, not diffuse. That the ghastly extremes of agony are endured by man the unit, and never by man the mass—for this let us thank a merciful God!

To be buried while alive is, beyond question, the most terrific of these extremes which has ever fallen to the lot of mere mortality. That it has frequently, very frequently, so fallen will scarcely be denied by those who think. The boundaries which divide Life from Death are at best shadowy and vague. Who shall say where the one ends, and where the other begins? We know that there are diseases in which occur total cessations of all the apparent functions of vitality, and yet in which these cessations are merely suspensions, properly so called. They are only temporary pauses in the incomprehensible mechanism. A certain period elapses, and some unseen mysterious principle again sets in motion the magic pinions and the wizard wheels. The silver cord was not for ever loosed, nor the golden bowl irreparably broken. But where, meantime, was the soul?

Apart, however, from the inevitable conclusion, a priori, that such causes must produce such effects,—that the well-known occurrence of such cases of suspended animation must naturally give rise, now and then, to premature interments,—apart from this consideration, we have the direct testimony of medical and ordinary experience to prove that a vast number of such interments have actually taken place. I might refer at once, if necessary, to a hundred well-authenticated instances. One of very remarkable character, and of which the circumstances may be fresh in the memory of some of my readers, occurred, not very long ago, in the neighboring city of Baltimore, where it occasioned a painful, intense, and widely extended excitement. The wife of one of the most respectable citizens—a lawyer of eminence and a member of Congress—was seized with a sudden and unaccountable illness, which completely baffled the skill of her physicians. After much suffering she died, or was supposed to die. No one suspected, indeed, or had reason to suspect; that she was not actually dead. She presented all the ordinary appearances of death. The face assumed the usual pinched and sunken outline. The lips were of the usual marble pallor. The eyes were lusterless. There was no warmth. Pulsation had ceased. For three days the body was preserved unburied, during which it had acquired a stony rigidity. The funeral, in short, was hastened, on account of the rapid advance of what was supposed to be decomposition.

The lady was deposited in her family vault, which, for three subsequent years, was undisturbed. At the expiration of this term it was opened for the reception of a sarcophagus;—but alas! how fearful a shock awaited the husband, who, personally, threw open the door! As its portals swung outwardly back, some white-appareled object fell rattling within his arms. It was the skeleton of his wife in her yet unmolded shroud.

A careful investigation rendered it evident that she had revived within two days after her entombment; that her struggles within the coffin had caused it to fall from a ledge, or shelf, to the floor, where it was so broken as to permit her escape. A lamp which had been accidentally left full of oil, within the tomb, was found empty; it might have been exhausted, however, by evaporation. On the uppermost of the steps which led down into the dread chamber was a large fragment of the coffin, with which it seemed that she had endeavored to arrest attention by striking the iron door. While thus occupied, she probably swooned, or possibly died, through sheer terror; and in falling, her shroud became entangled in some iron-work which projected interiorly. Thus she remained, and thus she rotted, erect.

In the year 1810, a case of living inhumation happened in France, attended with circumstances which go far to warrant the assertion that truth is, indeed, stranger than fiction. The heroine of the story was a Mademoiselle Victorine Lafourcade, a young girl of illustrious family, of wealth, and of great personal beauty. Among her numerous suitors was Julien Bossuet, a poor *littérateur*, or journalist, of Paris. His talents and general amiability had recommended him to the notice of the heiress, by whom he seems to have been truly beloved; but her pride of birth decided her, finally, to reject him, and to wed a Monsieur Renelle, a banker and a diplomatist of some eminence. After marriage, however, this gentleman neglected, and, perhaps, even more positively ill-treated her. Having passed with him some wretched years, she died—at least her condition so closely resembled death as to deceive everyone who saw her. She was buried—not in a vault, but in an ordinary grave in the village of her nativity. Filled with despair, and still inflamed by the memory of a profound attachment, the lover journeys from the capital to the remote province in which the village lies, with the romantic purpose of disinterring the corpse, and possessing himself of its luxuriant tresses. He reaches the grave. At midnight he unearths the coffin, opens it, and is in the act of detaching the hair, when he is arrested by the unclosing of the beloved eyes. In fact the lady had been buried alive. Vitality had not altogether departed, and she was aroused by the caresses of her lover from the lethargy which had been mistaken for death. He bore her frantically to his lodgings in the village. He employed certain powerful restoratives suggested by no little medical learning. In fine, she revived. She recognized her preserver. She remained with him until, by slow degrees, she fully recovered her original health. Her woman's heart was not adamant, and this last lesson of love sufficed to soften it. She bestowed it upon Bossuet. She returned no more to her husband, but, concealing from him her resurrection, fled with her lover to America. Twenty years afterward, the two returned to France, in the persuasion that time had so greatly altered the lady's appearance that her friends would be unable to recognize her. They were mistaken however; for at the first meeting, Monsieur Renelle did actually recognize and make claim to his wife. This claim she resisted, and a judicial tribunal sustained her in her resistance, deciding that the peculiar circumstances, with the long lapse of years, had extinguished, not only equitably, but legally, the authority of the husband.

The *Chirurgical Journal of Leipsic*, a periodical of high authority and merit, which some American booksellers would do well to translate and republish, records in a late number a very distressing event of the character in question.

An officer of artillery, a man of gigantic stature and of robust health, being thrown from an unmanageable horse, received a very severe contusion upon the head, which rendered him insensible at once; the skull was slightly fractured, but no immediate danger was apprehended. Trepanning was accomplished successfully. He was bled, and many other of the ordinary means of relief were adopted. Gradually, however, he fell into a more and more hopeless state of stupor, and, finally, it was thought that he died.

The weather was warm, and he was buried with indecent haste in one of the public cemeteries. His funeral took place on Thursday. On the Sunday following, the grounds of the cemetery were, as usual, much thronged with visitors, and about noon an intense excitement was created by the declaration of a peasant that, while sitting upon the grave of the officer, he had distinctly felt a commotion of the earth, as if occasioned by some one struggling beneath. At first little attention was paid to the man's asseveration; but his evident terror, and the dogged obstinacy with which he persisted in his story, had at length their natural effects upon the crowd. Spades were hurriedly procured, and the grave, which was shamefully shallow, was in a few minutes so far thrown open that the head of its occupant appeared. He was then seemingly dead; but he sat nearly erect within his coffin, the lid of which, in his furious struggles, he had partially uplifted.

He was forthwith conveyed to the nearest hospital, and there pronounced to be still living, although in an asphytic condition. After some hours he revived, recognized individuals of his acquaintance, and, in broken sentences, spoke of his agonies in the grave.

From what he related, it was clear that he must have been conscious of life for more than an hour, while inhumed, before lapsing into insensibility. The grave was carelessly and loosely filled with an exceedingly porous soil; and thus some air was necessarily admitted. He heard the footsteps of the crowd overhead, and endeavored to make himself heard in turn. It was the tumult within the grounds of the cemetery, he said, which appeared to awaken him from a deep sleep, but no sooner was he awake than he became fully aware of the awful horrors of his position.

This patient, it is recorded, was doing well, and seemed to be in a fair way of ultimate recovery, but fell a victim to the quackeries of medical experiment. The galvanic battery was applied, and he suddenly expired in one of those ecstatic paroxysms which, occasionally, it superinduces.

The mention of the galvanic battery, nevertheless, recalls to my memory a well-known and very extraordinary case in point, where its action proved the means of restoring to animation a young attorney of London, who had been interred for two days. This occurred in 1831, and created, at the time, a very profound sensation wherever it was made the subject of converse.

The patient, Mr. Edward Stapleton, had died, apparently, of typhus fever, accompanied with some anomalous symptoms which had excited the curiosity of his medical attendants. Upon his seeming decease, his friends were requested to sanction a post-mortem examination, but declined to permit it. As often happens, when such refusals are made, the practitioners resolve to disinter the body and dissect it at leisure, in private. Arrangements were easily effected with some of the numerous corps of body-snatchers with which London abounds; and, upon the third night after the funeral, the supposed corpse was unearthed from a grave eight feet deep, and deposited in the operating chamber of one of the private hospitals.

An incision of some extent had been actually made in the abdomen, when the fresh and undecayed appearance of the subject suggested an application of the battery. One experiment succeeded another, and the customary effects supervened, with nothing to characterize them in any respect, except, upon one or two occasions, a more than ordinary degree of life-likeness in the convulsive action.

It grew late. The day was about to dawn; and it was thought expedient, at length, to proceed at once to the dissection. A student, however, was especially desirous of testing a theory of his own, and insisted upon applying the battery to one of the pectoral muscles. A rough gash was made, and a wire hastily brought in contact; when the patient, with a hurried but quite unconvulsive movement, arose from the table, stepped into the middle of the floor, gazed about him uneasily for a few seconds, and then—spoke. What he said was unintelligible; but words were uttered; the syllabification was distinct. Having spoken, he fell heavily to the floor.

For some moments all were paralysed with awe—but the urgency of the case soon restored them their presence of mind. It was seen that Mr. Stapleton was alive, although in a swoon. Upon exhibition of ether he revived and was rapidly restored to health, and to the society of his friends—from whom, however, all knowledge of his resuscitation was withheld, until a relapse was no longer to be apprehended. Their wonder—their rapturous astonishment—may be conceived.

The most thrilling peculiarity of this incident, nevertheless, is involved in what Mr. S. himself asserts. He declares that at no period was he altogether insensible—that, dully and confusedly, he was aware of everything which happened to him, from the moment in which he was pronounced dead by his physicians, to that in which he fell swooning to the floor of the hospital. "I am alive," were the uncomprehended words which, upon recognizing the locality of the dissecting-room, he had endeavored, in his extremity, to utter.

It were an easy matter to multiply such histories as these—but I forbear—for, indeed, we have no need of such to establish the fact that premature interments occur. When we reflect how very rarely, from the nature of the case, we have it in our power to detect them, we must admit that they may frequently occur without our cognizance. Scarcely, in truth, is a graveyard ever encroached upon, for any purpose, to any great extent, that skeletons are not found in postures which suggest the most fearful of suspicions.

Fearful indeed the suspicion—but more fearful the doom! It may be asserted, without hesitation, that no event is so terribly well adapted to inspire the supremeness of bodily and of mental distress, as is burial before death. The unendurable oppression of the lungs—the stifling fumes of the damp earth—the clinging to the death garments—the rigid embrace of the narrow house—the blackness of the absolute Night—the silence like a sea that overwhelms—the unseen but palpable presence of the Conqueror Worm—these things, with the thoughts of the air and grass above, with memory of dear friends who would fly to save us if but informed of our fate, and with consciousness that of this fate they can never be informed—that our hopeless portion is that of the really dead—these considerations, I say, carry into the heart, which still palpitates, a degree of appalling and intolerable horror from which the most daring imagination must recoil. We know of nothing so agonizing upon Earth—we can dream of nothing half so hideous in the realms of the nethermost Hell. And thus all narratives upon this topic have an interest profound; an interest, nevertheless, which, through the sacred awe of the topic itself, very properly and very peculiarly depends upon our conviction of the truth of the matter narrated. What I have now to tell is of my own actual knowledge—of my own positive and personal experience.

For several years I had been subject to attacks of the singular disorder which physicians have agreed to term catalepsy, in default of a more definite title. Although both the immediate and the predisposing causes, and even the actual diagnosis of this disease are still mysterious, its obvious and apparent character is sufficiently well understood. Its variations seem to be chiefly of degree. Sometimes the patient lies, for a day only, or even for a shorter period, in a species of exaggerated lethargy. He is senseless and externally motionless; but the pulsation of the heart is still faintly perceptible; some traces of warmth remain; a slight color lingers within the center of the cheek; and, upon application of a mirror to the lips, we can detect a torpid, unequal, and vacillating action of the lungs. Then again the duration of the trance is for weeks—even for months; while the closest scrutiny, and the most rigorous medical tests, fail to establish any material distinction between the state of the sufferer and what we conceive of absolute death. Very usually he is saved from premature interment solely by the knowledge of his friends that he has been previously subject to catalepsy, by the consequent suspicion excited, and, above all, by the non-appearance of decay. The advances of the malady are luckily, gradual. The first manifestations, although marked, are unequivocal. The fits grow successively more and more distinctive, and endure each for a longer term than the preceding. In this lies the principal security from inhumation. The unfortunate whose first attack should be of the extreme character which is occasionally seen, would almost inevitably be consigned alive to the tomb.

My own case differed in no important particular from those mentioned in medical books. Sometimes, without any apparent cause, I sank, little by little, into a condition of semi-syncope, or half swoon; and, in this condition, without pain, without ability to stir, or, strictly speaking, to think, but with a dull lethargic consciousness of life and of the presence of those who surrounded my bed, I remained, until the crisis of the disease restored me, suddenly, to perfect sensation. At other times I was quickly and impetuously smitten. I grew sick, and numb, and chilly, and dizzy, and so fell prostrate at once. Then, for weeks, all was void, and black, and silent, and Nothing became the universe. Total annihilation could be no more. From these latter attacks I awoke, however, with a gradation slow in proportion to the suddenness of the seizure. Just as the day dawns to the friendless and houseless beggar who roams the streets throughout the long desolate winter night—just so tardily—just so wearily—just so cheerily came back the light of the Soul to me.

Apart from the tendency to trance, however, my general health appeared to be good; nor could I perceive that it was at all affected by the one prevalent malady—unless, indeed, an idiosyncrasy in my ordinary sleep may be looked upon as superinduced. Upon awakening from slumber, I could never gain, at once, thorough possession of my senses, and always remained, for many minutes, in much bewilderment and perplexity—the mental faculties in general, but the memory in especial, being in a condition of absolute abeyance.

In all that I endured there was no physical suffering, but of moral distress an infinitude. My fancy grew charnel. I talked "of worms, of tombs, of epitaphs." I was lost in reveries of death, and the idea of premature burial held continual possession of my brain. The ghastly Danger to which I was subjected haunted me day and night. In the former, the torture of meditation was excessive; in the latter, supreme. When the grim Darkness overspread the Earth, then, with every horror of thought, I shook—shook as the quivering plumes upon the hearse. When Nature could endure wakefulness no longer, it was with a struggle that I consented to sleep—for I shuddered to reflect that, upon awaking, I might find myself the tenant of a grave. And when, finally, I sank into slumber, it was only to rush at once into a world of phantasms, above which, with vast, sable, overshadowing wings, hovered, predominant, the one sepulchral Idea.

From the innumerable images of gloom which thus oppressed me in dreams, I select for record but a solitary vision. Methought I was immersed in a cataleptic trance of more than usual duration and profundity. Suddenly there came an icy hand upon my forehead, and an impatient, gibbering voice whispered "Arise!" within my ear.

I sat erect. The darkness was total. I could not see the figure of him who had aroused me. I could call to mind neither the period at which I had fallen into the trance, nor the locality in which I then lay. While I remained motionless, and busied in endeavors to collect my thoughts, the cold hand grasped me fiercely by the wrist, shaking it petulantly, while the gibbering voice said again:

"Arise! did I not bid thee arise?"

"And who," I demanded, "art thou?"

"I have no name in the regions which I inhabit," replied the voice, mournfully; "I was mortal, but am fiend. I am merciless, but am pitiful. Thou dost feel that I shudder. My teeth chatter as I speak, yet it is not with the chilliness of the night—of the night without end. But this hideousness is insufferable. How canst thou tranquilly sleep? I cannot rest for the cry of these great agonies. These sights are more than I can bear. Get thee up! Come with me into the outer Night, and let me unfold to thee the graves. Is not this a spectacle of woe?—Behold!"

I looked; and the unseen figure, which still grasped me by the wrist, had caused to be thrown open the graves of all mankind; and from each issued the faint phosphoric radiance of decay; so that I could see into the innermost recesses, and there view the shrouded bodies in their sad and solemn slumbers with the worm. But alas! the real sleepers were fewer, by many millions, than those who slumbered not at all; and there was a feeble struggling; and there was a general and sad unrest; and from out the depths of the countless pits there came a melancholy rustling from the garments of the buried. And of those who seemed tranquilly to repose, I saw that a vast number had changed, in a greater or less degree, the rigid and uneasy position in which they had originally been entombed. And the voice again said to me as I gazed:

"Is it not—oh! is it not a pitiful sight?" But, before I could find words to reply, the figure had ceased to grasp my wrist, the phosphoric lights expired, and the graves were closed with a sudden violence, while from out them arose a tumult of despairing cries, saying again: "Is it not—O God! is it not a very pitiful sight?"

Phantasies such as these, presenting themselves at night, extended their terrific influence far into my waking hours. My nerves became thoroughly unstrung, and I fell a prey to perpetual horror. I hesitated to ride, or to walk, or to indulge in any exercise that would carry me from home. In fact, I no longer dared trust myself out of the immediate presence of those who were aware of my proneness to catalepsy lest, falling into one of my usual fits, I should be buried before my real condition could be ascertained. I doubted the care, the fidelity of my dearest friends. I dreaded that, in some trance of more than customary duration, they might be prevailed upon to regard me as irrecoverable. I even went so far as to fear that, as I occasioned much trouble, they might be glad to consider any very protracted attack as sufficient excuse for getting rid of me altogether. It was in vain they endeavored to reassure me by the most solemn promises. I exacted the most sacred oaths, that under no circumstances they would bury me until decomposition had so materially advanced as to render further preservation impossible. And, even then, my mortal terrors would listen to no reason—would accept no consolation. I entered into a series of elaborate precautions. Among other things, I had the family vault so remodeled as to admit of being readily opened from within. The slightest pressure upon a long lever that extended far into the tomb would cause the iron portals to fly back. There were arrangements also for the free admission of air and light, and convenient receptacles for food and water, within immediate reach of the coffin intended for my reception. This coffin was warmly and softly padded, and was provided with a lid, fashioned upon the principle of the vault door, with the addition of springs so contrived that the feeblest movement of the body would be sufficient to set it at liberty. Besides all this, there was suspended from the roof of the tomb, a large bell, the rope of which, it was designed, should extend through a hole in the coffin, and so be fastened to one of the hands of the corpse. But, alas, what avails the vigilance against the Destiny of man? Not even these well-contrived securities sufficed to save from the uttermost agonies of living inhumation a wretch to these agonies foredoomed!

There arrived an epoch—as often before there had arrived—in which I found myself emerging from total unconsciousness into the first feeble and indefinite sense of existence. Slowly—with a tortoise gradation—approached the faint gray dawn of the psychal day. A torpid uneasiness. An apathetic endurance of dull pain. No care—no hope—no effort. Then, after a long interval, a ringing in the ears; then, after a lapse still longer, a pricking or tingling sensation in the extremities; then a seemingly eternal period of pleasurable quiescence, during which the awakening feelings are struggling into thought; then a brief re-sinking into non-entity; then a sudden recovery. At length the slight quivering of an eyelid, and immediately thereupon, an electric shock of a terror, deadly and indefinite, which sends the blood in torrents from the temples to the heart. And now the first positive effort to think. And now the first endeavor to remember. And now a partial and evanescent success. And now the memory has so far regained its dominion, that, in some measure, I am cognizant of my state. I feel that I am not awaking from ordinary sleep. I recollect that I have been subject to catalepsy. And now, at last, as if by the rush of an ocean, my shuddering spirit is overwhelmed by the one grim Danger—by the one spectral and ever-prevalent idea.

For some minutes after this fancy possessed me, I remained without motion. And why? I could not summon courage to move. I dared not make the effort which was to satisfy me of my fate—and yet there was something at my heart which whispered me it was sure. Despair—such as no other species of wretchedness ever calls into being—despair alone urged me, after long irresolution, to uplift the heavy lids of my eyes. I uplifted them. It was dark—all dark. I knew that the fit was over. I knew that the crisis of my disorder had long passed. I knew that I had now fully recovered the use of my visual faculties—and yet it was dark—all dark—the intense and utter raylessness of the Night that endureth for evermore.

I endeavored to shriek; and my lips and my parched tongue moved convulsively together in the attempt—but no voice issued from the cavernous lungs, which, oppressed as if by the weight of some incumbent mountain, gasped and palpitated, with the heart, at every elaborate and struggling inspiration.

The movement of the jaws, in this effort to cry aloud, showed me that they were bound up, as is usual with the dead. I felt, too, that I lay upon some hard substance; and by something similar my sides were, also, closely compressed. So far, I had not ventured to stir any of my limbs—but now I violently threw up my arms, which had been lying at length, with the wrists crossed. They struck a solid wooden substance, which extended above my person at an elevation of not more than six inches from my face. I could no longer doubt that I reposed within a coffin at last.

And now, amid all my infinite miseries, came sweetly the cherub Hope—for I thought of my precautions. I writhed, and made spasmodic exertions to force open the lid: it would not move. I felt my wrists for the bell-rope: it was not to be found. And now the Comforter fled for ever, and a still sterner Despair reigned triumphant; for I could not help perceiving the absence of the paddings which I had so carefully prepared—and then, too, there came suddenly to my nostrils the strong peculiar odor of moist earth. The conclusion was irresistible. I was not within the vault. I had fallen into a trance, while absent from home—while among strangers—when, or how, I could not remember—and it was they who had buried me as a dog—nailed up in some common coffin—and thrust, deep, deep, and for ever, into some ordinary and nameless grave.

As this awful conviction forced itself, thus, into the innermost chambers of my soul, I once again struggled to cry aloud. And in this second endeavor I succeeded. A long, wild, and continuous shriek, or yell of agony, resounded through the realms of the subterranean Night.

"Hillo! hillo, there!" said a gruff voice, in reply.

"What the devil's the matter now?" said a second.

"Get out o' that!" said a third.

"What do you mean by yowling in that ere kind of style, like a catty-mount?" said a fourth; and hereupon I was seized and shaken without ceremony, for several minutes, by a junto of very rough-looking individuals. They did not arouse me from my slumber— for I was wide-awake when I screamed—but they restored me to the full possession of my memory.

This adventure occurred near Richmond, in Virginia. Accompanied by a friend, I had proceeded, upon a gunning expedition, some miles down the banks of the James River. Night approached, and we were overtaken by a storm. The cabin of a small sloop lying at anchor in the stream, and laden with garden mold, afforded us the only available shelter. We made the best of it, and passed the night on board. I slept in one of the only two berths in the vessel—and the berths of a sloop of sixty or seventy tons need scarcely be described. That which I occupied had no bedding of any kind. Its extreme width was eighteen inches. The distance of its bottom from the deck overhead was precisely the same. I found it a matter of exceeding difficulty to squeeze myself in. Nevertheless, I slept soundly; and the whole of my vision— for it was no dream, and no nightmare—arose naturally from the circumstances of my position—from my ordinary bias of thought—and from the difficulty, to which I have alluded, of collecting my senses, and especially of regaining my memory, for a long time after awaking from slumber. The men who shook me were the crew of the sloop, and some laborers engaged to unload it. From the load itself came the earthy smell. The bandage about the jaws was a silk handkerchief in which I had bound up my head, in default of my customary nightcap.

The tortures endured, however, were indubitably quite equal, for the time, to those of actual sepulture. They were fearfully—they were inconceivably hideous; but out of Evil proceeded Good; for their very excess wrought in my spirit an inevitable revulsion. My soul acquired tone—acquired temper. I went abroad. I took vigorous exercise. I breathed the free air of Heaven. I thought upon other subjects than Death. I discarded my medical books. Buchan I burned. I read no Night Thoughts—no fustian about churchyards—no bugaboo tales—such as this. In short I became a new man, and lived a man's life. From that memorable night, I dismissed for ever my charnel apprehensions, and with them vanished the cataleptic disorder, of which, perhaps, they had been less the consequence than the cause.

There are moments when, even to the sober eye of Reason, the world of our sad Humanity may assume the semblance of a Hell—but the imagination of man is no Carathis, to explore with impunity its every cavern. Alas! the grim legion of sepulchral terrors cannot be regarded as altogether fanciful—but, like the Demons in whose company Afrasiab made his voyage down the Oxus, they must sleep, or they will devour us—they must be suffered to slumber, or we perish.

THE FACTS OF THE CASE OF M. VALDEMAR

OF COURSE I shall not pretend to consider it any matter for wonder, that the extraordinary case of M. Valdemar has excited discussion. It would have been a miracle had it not—especially under the circumstances. Through the desire of all parties concerned, to keep the affair from the public, at least for the present, or until we had further opportunities for investigation—through our endeavors to effect this—a garbled or exaggerated account made its way into society, and became the source of many unpleasant misrepresentations, and, very naturally, of a great deal of disbelief.

It is now rendered necessary that I give the facts—as far as I comprehend them myself. They are, succinctly, these:

My attention, for the last three years, had been repeatedly drawn to the subject of Mesmerism; and, about nine months ago, it occurred to me, quite suddenly, that in the series of experiments made hitherto, there had been a very remarkable and most unaccountable omission:—no person had as yet been mesmerized in *articulo mortis*. It remained to be seen, first, whether, in such condition, there existed in the patient any susceptibility to the magnetic influence; secondly, whether, if any existed, it was impaired or increased by the condition; thirdly, to what extent, or for how long a period, the encroachments of Death might be arrested by the process. There were other points to be ascertained, but these most excited my curiosity—the last in especial, from the immensely important character of its consequences.

In looking around me for some subject by whose means I might test these particulars, I was brought to think of my friend, M. Ernest Valdemar, the well-known compiler of the Bibliotheca Forensica, and author (under the nom de plume of Issachar Marx) of the Polish versions of Wallenstein and Gargantua. M. Valdemar, who has resided principally at Harlem, N.Y., since the year 1839, is (or was) particularly noticeable for the extreme spareness of his person—his lower limbs much resembling those of John Randolph; and, also, for the whiteness of his whiskers, in violent contrast to the blackness of his hair—the latter, in consequence, being very generally mistaken for a wig. His temperament was markedly nervous, and rendered him a good subject for mesmeric experiment. On two or three occasions I had put him to sleep with little difficulty, but was disappointed in other results which his peculiar constitution had naturally led me to anticipate. His will was at no period positively, or thoroughly, under my control, and in regard to clairvoyance, I could accomplish with him nothing to be relied upon. I always attributed my failure at these points to the disordered state of his health. For some months previous to my becoming acquainted with him, his physicians had declared him in a confirmed phthisis. It was his custom, indeed, to speak calmly of his approaching dissolution, as of a matter neither to be avoided nor regretted.

When the ideas to which I have alluded first occurred to me, it was of course very natural that I should think of M. Valdemar. I knew the steady philosophy of the man too well to apprehend any scruples from him; and he had no relatives in America who would be likely to interfere. I spoke to him frankly upon the subject; and, to my surprise, his interest seemed vividly excited. I say to my surprise; for, although he had always yielded his person freely to my experiments, he had never before given me any tokens of sympathy with what I did. His disease was of that character which would admit of exact calculation in respect to the epoch of its termination in death; and it was finally arranged between us that he would send for me about twenty-four hours before the period announced by his physicians as that of his decease.

It is now rather more than seven months since I received, from M. Valdemar himself, the subjoined note:

My Dear P——,

You may as well come now. D—— and F—— are agreed that I cannot hold out beyond to-morrow midnight; and I think they have hit the time very nearly.

Valdemar

I received this note within half an hour after it was written, and in fifteen minutes more I was in the dying man's chamber. I had not seen him for ten days, and was appalled by the fearful alteration which the brief interval had wrought in him. His face wore a leaden hue; the eyes were utterly lusterless; and the emaciation was so extreme that the skin had been broken through by the cheek-bones. His expectoration was excessive. The pulse was barely perceptible. He retained, nevertheless, in a very remarkable manner, both his mental power and a certain degree of physical strength. He spoke with distinctness—took some palliative medicines without aid—and, when I entered the room, was occupied in pencilling memoranda in a pocket-book. He was propped up in the bed by pillows. Doctors D—— and F—— were in attendance.

After pressing Valdemar's hand, I took these gentlemen aside, and obtained from them a minute account of the patient's condition. The left lung had been for eighteen months in a semi-osseous or cartilaginous state, and was, of course, entirely useless for all purposes of vitality. The right, in its upper portion, was also partially, if not thoroughly, ossified, while the lower region was merely a mass of purulent tubercles, running one into another. Several extensive perforations existed; and, at one point, permanent adhesion to the ribs had taken place. These appearances in the right lobe were of comparatively recent date. The ossification had proceeded with very unusual rapidity; no sign of it had been discovered a month before, and the adhesion had only been observed during the three previous days. Independently of the phthisis, the patient was suspected of aneurism of the aorta; but on this point the osseous symptoms rendered an exact diagnosis impossible. It was the opinion of both physicians that M. Valdemar would die about midnight on the morrow (Sunday). It was then seven o'clock on Saturday evening.

On quitting the invalid's bed-side to hold conversation with myself, Doctors D—— and F—— had bidden him a final farewell. It had not been their intention to return; but, at my request, they agreed to look in upon the patient about ten the next night.

When they had gone, I spoke freely with M. Valdemar on the subject of his approaching dissolution, as well as, more particularly, of the experiment proposed. He still professed himself quite willing and even anxious to have it made, and urged me to commence it at once. A male and a female nurse were in attendance; but I did not feel myself altogether at liberty to engage in a task of this character with no more reliable witnesses than these people, in case of sudden accident, might prove. I therefore postponed operations until about eight the next night, when the arrival of a medical student with whom I had some acquaintance (Mr. Theodore L——l), relieved me from further embarrassment. It had been my design, originally, to wait for the physicians; but I was induced to proceed, first, by the urgent entreaties of M. Valdemar, and secondly, by my conviction that I had not a moment to lose, as he was evidently sinking fast.

Mr. L——l was so kind as to accede to my desire that he would take notes of all that occurred; and it is from his memoranda that what I now have to relate is, for the most part, either condensed or copied verbatim.

It wanted about five minutes of eight when, taking the patient's hand, I begged him to state, as distinctly as he could, to Mr. L——l, whether he (M. Valdemar) was entirely willing that I should make the experiment of mesmerizing him in his then condition.

He replied feebly, yet quite audibly, "Yes, I wish to be mesmerized"—adding immediately afterward, "I fear you have deferred it too long."

While he spoke thus, I commenced the passes which I had already found most effectual in subduing him. He was evidently influenced with the first lateral stroke of my hand across his forehead; but although I exerted all my powers, no further perceptible effect was induced until some minutes after ten o'clock, when Doctors D—— and F—— called, according to appointment. I explained to them, in a few words, what I designed, and as they opposed no objection, saying that the patient was already in the death agony, I proceeded without hesitation—exchanging, however, the lateral passes for downward ones, and directing my gaze entirely into the right eye of the sufferer.

By this time his pulse was imperceptible and his breathing was stertorous, and at intervals of half a minute.

This condition was nearly unaltered for a quarter of an hour. At the expiration of this period, however, a natural although a very deep sigh escaped the bosom of the dying man, and the stertorous breathing ceased—that is to say, its stertorousness was no longer apparent; the intervals were undiminished. The patient's extremities were of an icy coldness.

At five minutes before eleven I perceived unequivocal signs of the mesmeric influence. The glassy roll of the eye was changed for that expression of uneasy inward examination which is never seen except in cases of sleep-waking, and which it is quite impossible to mistake. With a few rapid lateral passes I made the lids quiver, as in incipient sleep, and with a few more I closed them altogether. I was not satisfied, however, with this, but continued the manipulations vigorously, and with the fullest exertion of the will, until I had completely stiffened the limbs of the slumberer, after placing them in a seemingly easy position. The legs were at full length; the arms were nearly so, and reposed on the bed at a moderate distance from the loins. The head was very slightly elevated.

When I had accomplished this, it was fully midnight, and I requested the gentlemen present to examine M. Valdemar's condition. After a few experiments, they admitted him to be in an unusually perfect state of mesmeric trance. The curiosity of both the physicians was greatly excited. Dr. D—— resolved at once to remain with the patient all night, while Dr. F—— took leave with a promise to return at daybreak Mr. L——l and the nurses remained.

We left M. Valdemar entirely undisturbed until about three o'clock in the morning, when I approached him and found him in precisely the same condition as when Dr. F—— went away—that is to say, he lay in the same position; the pulse was imperceptible; the breathing was gentle (scarcely noticeable, unless through the application of a mirror to the lips); the eyes were closed naturally; and the limbs were as rigid and as cold as marble. Still, the general appearance was certainly not that of death.

As I approached M. Valdemar I made a kind of half effort to influence his right arm into pursuit of my own, as I passed the latter gently to and fro above his person. In such experiments with this patient. I had never perfectly succeeded before, and assuredly I had little thought of succeeding now; but to my astonishment, his arm very readily, although feebly, followed every direction I assigned it with mine. I determined to hazard a few words of conversation.

"M. Valdemar," I said, "are you asleep?" He made no answer, but I perceived a tremor about the lips, and was thus induced to repeat the question, again and again. At its third repetition, his whole frame was agitated by a very slight shivering; the eyelids unclosed themselves so far as to display a white line of the ball; the lips moved sluggishly, and from between them, in a barely audible whisper, issued the words:

"Yes;—asleep now. Do not wake me!—let me die so!"

I here felt the limbs and found them as rigid as ever. The right arm, as before, obeyed the direction of my hand. I questioned the sleepwaker again:

"Do you still feel pain in the breast, M. Valdemar?"

The answer now was immediate, but even less audible than before:

"No pain—I am dying."

I did not think it advisable to disturb him further just then, and nothing more was said or done until the arrival of Dr. F——, who came a little before sunrise, and expressed unbounded astonishment at finding the patient still alive. After feeling the pulse and applying a mirror to the lips, he requested me to speak to the sleep-waker again. I did so, saying:

"M. Valdemar, do you still sleep?"

As before, some minutes elapsed ere a reply was made; and during the interval the dying man seemed to be collecting his energies to speak. At my fourth repetition of the question, he said very faintly, almost inaudibly:

"Yes; still asleep—dying."

It was now the opinion, or rather the wish, of the physicians, that M. Valdemar should be suffered to remain undisturbed in his present apparently tranquil condition, until death should supervene—and this, it was generally agreed, must now take place within a few minutes. I concluded, however, to speak to him once more, and merely repeated my previous question.

While I spoke, there came a marked change over the countenance of the sleep-waker. The eyes rolled themselves slowly open, the pupils disappearing upwardly; the skin generally assumed a cadaverous hue, resembling not so much parchment as white paper; and the circular hectic spots which, hitherto, had been strongly defined in the center of each cheek, went out at once. I use this expression, because the suddenness of their departure put me in mind of nothing so much as the extinguishment of a candle by a puff of the breath. The upper lip, at the same time, writhed itself away from the teeth, which it had previously covered completely; while the lower jaw fell with an audible jerk, leaving the mouth widely extended, and disclosing in full view the swollen and blackened tongue. I presume that no member of the party then present had been unaccustomed to death-bed horrors; but so hideous beyond conception was the appearance of M. Valdemar at this moment, that there was a general shrinking back from the region of the bed.

I now feel that I have reached a point of this narrative at which every reader will be startled into positive disbelief. It is my business, however, simply to proceed.

There was no longer the faintest sign of vitality in M. Valdemar; and, concluding him to be dead, we were consigning him to the charge of the nurses, when a strong vibratory motion was observable in the tongue. This continued for perhaps a minute. At the expiration of this period, there issued from the distended and motionless jaws a voice—such as it would be madness in me to attempt describing. There are, indeed, two or three epithets which might be considered as applicable to it in parts; I might say, for example, that the sound was harsh, and broken, and hollow; but the hideous whole is indescribable, for the simple reason that no similar sounds have ever jarred upon the ear of humanity. There were two particulars, nevertheless, which I thought then, and still think, might fairly be stated as characteristic of the intonation—as well adapted to convey some idea of its unearthly peculiarity. In the first place, the voice seemed to reach our ears—at least mine—from a vast distance, or from some deep cavern within the earth. In the second place, it impressed me (I fear, indeed, that it will be impossible to make myself comprehended) as gelatinous or glutinous matters impress the sense of touch.

I have spoken both of "sound" and of "voice." I mean to say that the sound was one of distinct—of even wonderfully, thrillingly distinct—syllabification. M. Valdemar spoke—obviously in reply to the question

I had propounded to him a few minutes before. I had asked him, it will be remembered, if he still slept. He now said:

"Yes;—no;—I have been sleeping—and now—now—I am dead."

No person present even affected to deny, or attempted to repress, the unutterable, shuddering horror which these few words, thus uttered, were so well calculated to convey. Mr. L——l (the student) swooned. The nurses immediately left the chamber, and could not be induced to return. My own impressions I would not pretend to render intelligible to the reader. For nearly an hour, we busied ourselves, silently—without the utterance of a word—in endeavors to revive Mr. L——l. When he came to himself, we addressed ourselves again to an investigation of M. Valdemar's condition.

It remained in all respects as I have last described it, with the exception that the mirror no longer afforded evidence of respiration. An attempt to draw blood from the arm failed. I should mention, too, that this limb was no farther subject to my will. I endeavored in vain to make it follow the direction of my hand. The only real indication, indeed, of the mesmeric influence, was now found in the vibratory movement of the tongue, whenever I addressed M. Valdemar a question. He seemed to be making an effort to reply, but had no longer sufficient volition. To queries put to him by any other person than myself he seemed utterly insensible—although I endeavored to place each member of the company in mesmeric rapport with him. I believe that I have now related all that is necessary to an understanding of the sleep-waker's state at this epoch. Other nurses were procured; and at ten o'clock I left the house in company with the two physicians and Mr. L——l.

In the afternoon we all called again to see the patient. His condition remained precisely the same. We had now some discussion as to the propriety and feasibility of awakening him; but we had little difficulty in agreeing that no good purpose would be served by so doing. It was evident that, so far, death (or what is usually termed death) had been arrested by the mesmeric process. It seemed clear to us all that to awaken M. Valdemar would be merely to insure his instant, or at least his speedy dissolution.

From this period until the close of last week—an interval of nearly seven months— we continued to make daily calls at M. Valdemar's house, accompanied, now and then, by medical and other friends. All this time the sleep-waker remained exactly as I have last described him. The nurses' attentions were continual.

It was on Friday last that we finally resolved to make the experiment of awakening, or attempting to awaken him; and it is the (perhaps) unfortunate result of this latter experiment which has given rise to so much discussion in private circles—to so much of what I cannot help thinking unwarranted popular feeling.

For the purpose of relieving M. Valdemar from the mesmeric trance, I made use of the customary passes. These, for a time, were unsuccessful. The first indication of revival was afforded by a partial descent of the iris. It was observed, as especially remarkable, that this lowering of the pupil was accompanied by the profuse outflowing of a yellowish ichor (from beneath the lids) of a pungent and highly offensive odor.

It was now suggested that I should attempt to influence the patient's arm, as heretofore. I made the attempt and failed. Dr. F—— then intimated a desire to have me put a question. I did so, as follows:

"M. Valdemar, can you explain to us what are your feelings or wishes now?"

There was an instant return of the hectic circles on the cheeks, the tongue quivered, or rather rolled violently in the mouth (although the jaws and lips remained rigid as before); and at length the same hideous voice which I have already described, broke forth:

"For God's sake!—quick!—quick!—put me to sleep—or, quick!—waken me!—quick!—I say to you that I am dead!"

I was thoroughly unnerved, and for an instant remained undecided what to do. At first I made an endeavor to recompose the patient; but, failing in this through total abeyance of the will, I retraced my steps and as earnestly struggled to awaken him. In this attempt I soon saw that I should be successful—or at least I soon fancied that my success would be complete—and I am sure that all in the room were prepared to see the patient awaken.

For what really occurred, however, it is quite impossible that any human being could have been prepared.

As I rapidly made the mesmeric passes, amid ejaculations of "Dead! dead!" absolutely bursting from the tongue and not from the lips of the sufferer, his whole frame at once—within the space of a single minute, or even less, shrunk—crumbled—absolutely *bursting* from the tongue and not from the lips of the sufferer, his whole frame at once—within the space of a single minute, or even less, shrunk—crumbled—absolutely *rotted* away beneath my hands. Upon the bed, before that whole company, there lay a nearly liquid mass of loathsome—of detestable putridity.

THE OBLONG BOX

SOME YEARS AGO, I engaged passage from Charleston, S.C., to the city of New York, in the fine packet-ship *Independence*, Captain Hardy. We were to sail on the fifteenth of the month (June), weather permitting; and, on the fourteenth, I went on board to arrange some matters in my state-room.

I found that we were to have a great many passengers, including a more than usual number of ladies. On the list were several of my acquaintances; and among other names, I was rejoiced to see that of Mr. Cornelius Wyatt, a young artist, for whom I entertained feelings of warm friendship. He had been with me a fellow-student at C—— University, where we were very much together. He had the ordinary temperament of genius, and was a compound of misanthropy, sensibility, and enthusiasm. To these qualities he united the warmest and truest heart which ever beat in a human bosom.

I observed that his name was carded upon three state-rooms; and, upon again referring to the list of passengers, I found that he had engaged a passage for himself, wife, and two sisters—his own. The state-rooms were sufficiently roomy, and each had two berths, one above the other. These berths, to be sure, were so exceedingly narrow as to be insufficient for more than one person; still, I could not comprehend why there were three state-rooms for these four persons. I was, just at that epoch, in one of those moody frames of mind which makes a man abnormally inquisitive about trifles: and I confess, with shame, that I busied myself in a variety of ill-bred and preposterous conjectures about this matter of the supernumerary state-room. It was no business of mine, to be sure; but with none the less pertinacity did I occupy myself in attempts to solve the enigma. At last I reached a conclusion which wrought in me great wonder why I had not arrived at it before. "It is a servant, of course," I said; "what a fool I am, not sooner to have thought of so obvious a solution!" And then I again repaired to the list—but here I saw distinctly that no servant was to come with the party: although, in fact, it had been the original design to bring one—for the words "and servant" had been first written and then overscored. "Oh, extra baggage, to be sure," I now said to myself—"something he wishes not to be put in the hold—something to be kept under his own eye—ah, I have it—a painting or so—and this is what he has been bargaining about with Nicolino, the Italian Jew." This idea satisfied me, and I dismissed my curiosity for the nonce.

Wyatt's two sisters I knew very well, and most amiable and clever girls they were. His wife he had newly married, and I had never yet seen her. He had often talked about her in my presence, however, and in his usual style of enthusiasm. He described her as of surpassing beauty, wit, and accomplishment. I was, therefore, quite anxious to make her acquaintance.

On the day in which I visited the ship (the fourteenth), Wyatt and party were also to visit it—so the captain informed me,—and I waited on board an hour longer than I had designed, in hope of being presented to the bride; but then an apology came. "Mrs. W. was a little indisposed, and would decline coming on board until to-morrow, at the hour of sailing."

The morrow having arrived, I was going from my hotel to the wharf, when Captain Hardy met me and said that, "owing to circumstances" (a stupid but convenient phrase), "he rather thought the *Independence* would not sail for a day or two, and that when all was ready, he would send up and let me know." This I thought strange, for there was a stiff southerly breeze; but as "the circumstances" were not forthcoming, although I pumped for them with much perseverance, I had nothing to do but to return home and digest my impatience at leisure.

I did not receive the expected message from the captain for nearly a week. It came at length, however, and I immediately went on board. The ship was crowded with passengers, and everything was in the bustle attendant upon making sail. Wyatt's party arrived in about ten minutes after myself. There were the two sisters, the bride, and the artist—the latter in one of his customary fits of moody misanthropy. I was too well used to these, however, to pay them any special attention. He did not even introduce me to his wife;—this courtesy devolving, perforce, upon his sister Marian—a very sweet and intelligent girl, who, in a few hurried words, made us acquainted.

Mrs. Wyatt had been closely veiled; and when she raised her veil, in acknowledging my bow, I confess that I was very profoundly astonished. I should have been much more so, however, had not long experience advised me not to trust, with too implicit a reliance, the enthusiastic descriptions of my friend, the artist, when indulging in comments upon the loveliness of woman. When beauty was the theme, I well knew with what facility he soared into the regions of the purely ideal.

The truth is, I could not help regarding Mrs. Wyatt as a decidedly plain-looking woman. If not positively ugly, she was not, I think, very far from it. She was dressed, however, in exquisite taste—and then I had no doubt that she had captivated my friend's heart by the more enduring graces of the intellect and soul. She said very few words, and passed at once into her state-room with Mr. W.

My old inquisitiveness now returned. There was no servant—that was a settled point. I looked, therefore, for the extra baggage. After some delay, a cart arrived at the wharf, with an oblong pine box, which was everything that seemed to be expected. Immediately upon its arrival we made sail, and in a short time were safely over the bar and standing out to sea.

The box in question was, as I say, oblong. It was about six feet in length by two and a half in breadth:—I observed it attentively, and like to be precise. Now this shape was peculiar; and no sooner had I seen it than I took credit to myself for the accuracy of my guessing. I had reached the conclusion, it will be remembered, that the extra baggage of my friend, the artist, would prove to be pictures, or at least a picture; for I knew he had been for several weeks in conference with Nicolino:—and now here was a box, which, from its shape, could possibly contain nothing in the world but a copy of Leonardo's *Last Supper*; and a copy of this very *Last Supper*, done by Rubini the younger, at Florence, I had known, for some time, to be in the possession of

Nicolino. This point, therefore, I considered as sufficiently settled. I chuckled excessively when I thought of my acumen. It was the first time I had ever known Wyatt to keep from me any of his artistical secrets; but here he evidently intended to steal a march upon me, and smuggle a fine picture to New York, under my very nose; expecting me to know nothing of the matter. I resolved to quiz him well, now and hereafter.

One thing, however, annoyed me not a little. The box did not go into the extra state-room. It was deposited in Wyatt's own; and there, too, it remained, occupying very nearly the whole of the floor—no doubt to the exceeding discomfort of the artist and his wife;—this the more especially as the tar or paint with which it was lettered in sprawling capitals, emitted a strong, disagreeable, and, to my fancy, a peculiarly disgusting odor. On the lid were painted the words—"Mrs. Adelaide Curtis, Albany, New York, Charge of Cornelius Wyatt, Esq. This side up. To be handled with care."

Now, I was aware that Mrs. Adelaide Curtis, of Albany, was the artist's wife's mother;—but then I looked upon the whole address as a mystification, intended especially for myself. I made up my mind, of course, that the box and contents would never get farther north than the studio of my misanthropic friend, in Chambers Street, New York.

For the first three or four days we had fine weather, although the wind was dead ahead; having chopped round to the northward, immediately upon our losing sight of the coast. The passengers were, consequently, in high spirits and disposed to be social. I must except, however, Wyatt, and his sisters, who behaved stiffly, and I could not help thinking, uncourteously to the rest of the party. Wyatt's conduct I did not so much regard. He was gloomy, even beyond his usual habit—in fact he was morose—but in him I was prepared for eccentricity. For the sisters, however, I could make no excuse. They secluded themselves in their state-rooms during the greater part of the passage, and absolutely refused, although I repeatedly urged them, to hold communication with any person on board.

Mrs. Wyatt herself was far more agreeable. That is to say, she was chatty; and to be chatty is no slight recommendation at sea. She became excessively intimate with most of the ladies; and to my profound astonishment, evinced no equivocal disposition to coquet with the men. She amused us all very much. I say "amused"—and scarcely know how to explain myself. The truth is, I soon found that Mrs. W. was far oftener laughed at than with. The gentlemen said little about her; but the ladies, in a little while, pronounced her "a good-hearted thing, rather indifferent-looking, totally uneducated, and decidedly vulgar." The great wonder was, how Wyatt had been entrapped into such a match. Wealth was the general solution—but this I knew to be no solution at all; for Wyatt had told me that she neither brought him a dollar nor had any expectations from any source whatever. "He had married," he said, "for love, and for love only; and his bride was far more than worthy of his love." When I thought of these expressions, on the part of my friend, I confess that I felt indescribably puzzled. Could it be possible that he was taking leave of his senses? What else could I think? He, so refined, so intellectual, so fastidious, with so exquisite a perception of the faulty, and so keen an appreciation of the beautiful! To be sure, the lady seemed especially fond of him—particularly so in his absence—when she made herself ridiculous by frequent quotations of what had been said by her "beloved husband, Mr. Wyatt." The word "husband" seemed for ever—to use one of her own delicate expressions—for ever "on the tip of her tongue." In the meantime, it was observed by all on board, that he avoided her in the most pointed manner, and, for the most part, shut himself up alone in his state-room, where, in fact, he might have been said to live altogether, leaving his wife at full liberty to amuse herself as she thought best, in the public society of the main cabin.

My conclusion, from what I saw and heard, was, that the artist, by some unaccountable freak of fate, or perhaps in some fit of enthusiastic and fanciful passion, had been induced to unite himself with a person altogether beneath him, and that the natural result, entire and speedy disgust, had ensued. I pitied him from the bottom of my heart—but could not, for that reason, quite forgive his incommunicativeness in the matter of the *Last Supper*. For this I resolved to have my revenge.

One day he came upon deck, and, taking his arm as had been my wont, I sauntered with him backward and forward. His gloom, however (which I considered quite natural under the circumstances), seemed entirely unabated. He said little, and that moodily, and with evident effort. I ventured a jest or two, and he made a sickening attempt at a smile. Poor fellow!—as I thought of his wife, I wondered that he could have heart to put on even the semblance of mirth. At last I ventured a home thrust. I determined to commence a series of covert insinuations, or innuendoes, about the oblong box—just to let him perceive, gradually, that I was not altogether the butt, or victim, of his little bit of pleasant mystification. My first observation was by way of opening a masked battery. I said something about the "peculiar shape of that box"; and, as I spoke the words, I smiled knowingly, winked, and touched him gently with my forefinger in the ribs.

The manner in which Wyatt received this harmless pleasantry convinced me at once that he was mad. At first he stared at me as if he found it impossible to comprehend the witticism of my remark; but as its point seemed slowly to make its way into his brain, his eyes, in the same proportion, seemed protruding from their sockets. Then he grew very red—then hideously pale—then, as if highly amused with what I had insinuated, he began a loud and boisterous laugh, which, to my astonishment, he kept up, with gradually increasing vigor, for ten minutes or more. In conclusion, he fell flat and heavily upon the deck. When I ran to uplift him, to all appearance he was dead.

I called assistance, and, with much difficulty, we brought him to himself. Upon reviving he spoke incoherently for some time. At length we bled him and put him to bed. The next morning he was quite recovered, so far as regarded his mere bodily health. Of his mind I say nothing, of course. I avoided him during the rest of the passage, by advice of the captain, who seemed to coincide with me altogether in my views of his insanity, but cautioned me to say nothing on this head to any person on board.

Several circumstances occurred immediately after this fit of Wyatt's, which contributed to heighten the curiosity with which I was already possessed. Among other things, this: I had been nervous—drank too much strong green tea, and slept ill at night—in fact, for two nights I could not be properly said to sleep at all.

Now, my state-room opened into the main cabin, or dining-room, as did those of all the single men on board. Wyatt's three rooms were in the after-cabin, which was separated from the main one by a slight sliding-door, never locked even at night. As we were almost constantly on a wind, and the breeze was not a little stiff, the ship heeled to leeward very considerably; and whenever her starboard side was to leeward, the sliding door between the cabins slid open, and so remained, nobody taking the trouble to get up and shut it. But my berth was in such a position, that when my own state-room door was open, as well as the sliding door in question (and my own door was always open on account of the heat), I could see into the after-cabin, quite distinctly, and just at that portion of it, too, where were situated the state-rooms of Mr. Wyatt. Well, during two nights (not consecutive) while I lay awake, I clearly saw Mrs. W., about eleven o'clock upon each night, steal cautiously from the state-room of Mr. W., and enter the extra room, where she remained until daybreak, when she was called by her husband and went back. That they were virtually separated was clear. They had separate apartments—no doubt in contemplation of a more permanent divorce; and here, after all, I thought was the mystery of the extra state-room.

There was another circumstance, too, which interested me much. During the two wakeful nights in question, and immediately after the disappearance of Mrs. Wyatt into the extra state-room, I was attracted by certain singular, cautious, subdued noises in that of her husband. After listening to them for some time, with thoughtful attention, I at length succeeded perfectly in translating their import. They were sounds occasioned by the artist in prying open the oblong box, by means of a chisel and mallet—the latter being apparently muffled, or deadened, by some soft woolen or cotton substance in which its head was enveloped.

In this manner I fancied I could distinguish the precise moment when he fairly disengaged the lid—also, that I could determine when he removed it altogether, and when he deposited it upon the lower berth in his room; this latter point I knew, for example, by certain slight taps which the lid made in striking against the wooden edges of the berth, as he endeavored to lay it down very gently—

there being no room for it on the floor. After this there was a dead stillness, and I heard nothing more, upon either occasion, until nearly daybreak; unless, perhaps, I may mention a low sobbing, or murmuring sound, so very much suppressed as to be nearly inaudible—if, indeed, the whole of this latter noise were not rather produced by my own imagination. I say it seemed to resemble sobbing or sighing—but, of course, it could not have been either. I rather think it was a ringing in my own ears. Mr. Wyatt, no doubt according to custom, was merely giving the rein to one of his hobbies—indulging in one of his fits of artistic enthusiasm. He had opened his oblong box in order to feast his eyes on the pictorial treasure within. There was nothing in this, however, to make him sob. I repeat, therefore, that it must have been simply a freak of my own fancy, distempered by good Captain Hardy's green tea. Just before dawn, on each of the two nights of which I speak, I distinctly heard Mr. Wyatt replace the lid upon the oblong box, and force the nails into their old places by means of the muffled mallet. Having done this, he issued from his state-room, fully dressed, and proceeded to call Mrs. W. from hers.

We had been at sea seven days, and were now off Cape Hatteras, when there came a tremendously heavy blow from the southwest. We were, in a measure, prepared for it, however, as the weather had been holding out threats for some time. Everything was made snug, alow and aloft; and as the wind steadily freshened, we lay to, at length, under spanker and foretopsail, both double-reefed.

In this trim we rode safely enough for forty-eight hours—the ship proving herself an excellent sea-boat in many respects, and shipping no water of any consequence. At the end of this period, however, the gale had freshened into a hurricane, and our after-sail split into ribbons, bringing us so much in the trough of the water that we shipped several prodigious seas, one immediately after the other. By this accident we lost three men overboard with the caboose, and nearly the whole of the larboard bulwarks. Scarcely had we recovered our senses, before the foretopsail went into shreds, when we got up a storm stay-sail, and with this did pretty well for some hours, the ship heading the sea much more steadily than before.

The gale still held on, however, and we saw no signs of its

abating. The rigging was found to be ill-fitted, and greatly strained; and on the third day of the blow, about five in the afternoon, our mizzen-mast, in a heavy lurch to windward, went by the board. For an hour or more, we tried in vain to get rid of it, on account of the prodigious rolling of the ship; and, before we had succeeded, the carpenter came aft and announced four feet of water in the hold. To add to our dilemma, we found the pumps choked and nearly useless.

All was now confusion and despair—but an effort was made to lighten the ship by throwing overboard as much of her cargo as could be reached and by cutting away the two masts that remained. This we at last accomplished—but we were still unable to do anything at the pumps: and, in the meantime, the leak gained on us very fast.

At sundown, the gale had sensibly diminished in violence, and, as the sea went down with it, we still entertained faint hopes of saving ourselves in the boats. At eight p.m., the clouds broke away to windward, and we had the advantage of a full moon—a piece of good fortune which served wonderfully to cheer our drooping spirits.

After incredible labor we succeeded, at length, in getting the long-boat over the side without material accident, and into this we crowded the whole of the crew and most of the passengers. This party made off immediately, and, after undergoing much suffering, finally arrived, in safety, at Ocracoke Inlet, on the third day after the wreck.

Fourteen passengers, with the captain, remained on board, resolving to trust their fortunes to the jolly-boat at the stern. We lowered it without difficulty, although it was only by a miracle that we prevented it from swamping as it touched the water. It contained, when afloat, the captain and his wife, Mr. Wyatt, and party, a Mexican officer, wife, four children, and myself, with a negro valet.

We had no room, of course, for anything except a few positively necessary instruments, some provisions, and the clothes upon our backs. No one had thought of even attempting to save anything more. What must have been the astonishment of all, then, when, having proceeded a few fathoms from the ship, Mr. Wyatt stood up in the stern-sheets, and coolly demanded of Captain Hardy that the boat should be put back for the purpose of taking in his oblong box!

"Sit down, Mr. Wyatt," replied the captain, somewhat sternly, "you will capsize us if you do not sit quite still. Our gunwale is almost in the water now."

"The box!" vociferated Mr. Wyatt, still standing—"the box, I say! Captain Hardy, you cannot, you will not refuse me. Its weight will be but a trifle—it is nothing—mere nothing. By the mother who bore you—for the love of Heaven—by your hope of salvation, I implore you to put back for the box!"

The captain, for a moment, seemed touched by the earnest appeal of the artist, but he regained his stern composure, and merely said:

"Mr. Wyatt, you are mad. I cannot listen to you. Sit down, I say, or you will swamp the boat. Stay—hold him—seize him!—he is about to spring overboard! There—I knew it—he is over!"

As the captain said this, Mr. Wyatt, in fact, sprang from the boat, and, as we were yet in the lee of the wreck, succeeded, by almost superhuman exertion, in getting hold of a rope which hung from the fore-chains. In another moment he was on board, and rushing frantically down into the cabin.

In the meantime, we had been swept astern of the ship, and being quite out of her lee, were at the mercy of the tremendous sea which was still running. We made a determined effort to put back, but our little boat was like a feather in the breath of the tempest. We saw at a glance that the doom of the unfortunate artist was sealed.

As our distance from the wreck rapidly increased, the madman (for as such only could we regard him) was seen to emerge from the companion-way, up which by dint of strength that appeared gigantic, he dragged, bodily, the oblong box. While we gazed in the extremity of astonishment, he passed, rapidly, several turns of a three-inch rope, first around the box, and then around his body. In another instant both body and box were in the sea—disappearing suddenly, at once and for ever.

We lingered awhile sadly upon our oars, with our eyes riveted upon the spot. At length we pulled away. The silence remained unbroken for an hour. Finally, I hazarded a remark.

"Did you observe, captain, how suddenly they sank? Was not that an exceedingly singular thing? I confess that I entertained some feeble hope of his final deliverance, when I saw him lash himself to the box, and commit himself to the sea."

"They sank as a matter of course," replied the captain, "and that like a shot. They will soon rise again, however—but not till the salt melts."

"The salt!" I ejaculated.

"Hush!" said the captain, pointing to the wife and sisters of deceased. "We must talk of these things at some appropriate time."

We suffered much, and made a narrow escape; but fortune befriended us, as well as our mates in the long-boat. We landed, in fine, more dead than alive, after four days of intense distress, upon the beach opposite Roanoke Island. We remained here a week, were not ill-treated by the wreckers, and at length obtained a passage to New York.

About a month after the loss of the *Independence*, I happened to meet Captain Hardy on Broadway. Our conversation turned, naturally, upon the disaster, and especially upon the sad fate of poor Wyatt. I thus learned the following particulars.

The artist had engaged passage for himself, wife, two sisters, and a servant. His wife was, indeed, as she had been represented, a most lovely, and most accomplished woman. On the morning of the fourteenth of June (the day in which I first visited the ship), the lady suddenly sickened and died. The young husband was frantic with grief—but circumstances imperatively forbade the deferring his voyage to New York. It was necessary to take to her mother the corpse of his adored wife, and, on the other hand, the universal prejudice which would prevent his doing so openly was well known. Nine-tenths of the passengers would have abandoned the ship rather than take passage with a dead body.

In this dilemma, Captain Hardy arranged that the corpse, being first partially embalmed, and packed, with a large quantity of salt, in a box of suitable dimensions, should be conveyed on board as merchandise. Nothing was to be said of the lady's decease; and, as it was well understood that Mr. Wyatt had engaged passage for his wife, it became necessary that some person should personate her during the voyage. This the deceased lady's-maid was easily prevailed on to do. The extra state-room, originally engaged for this girl, during her mistress's life, was now merely retained. In this state-room the pseudo-wife slept, of course, every night. In the daytime she performed, to the best of her ability, the part of her mistress—whose person, it had been carefully ascertained, was unknown to any of the passengers on board.

My own mistake arose, naturally enough, through too careless, too inquisitive, and too impulsive a temperament. But of late, it is a rare thing that I sleep soundly at night. There is a countenance which haunts me, turn as I will. There is an hysterical laugh which will for ever ring within my ears.

THE CASK OF AMONTILLADO

THE THOUSAND INJURIES of Fortunato I had borne as I best could, but when he ventured upon insult I vowed revenge. You, who so well know the nature of my soul, will not suppose, however, that I gave utterance to a threat. At length I would be avenged; this was a point definitely settled—but the very definiteness with which it was resolved precluded the idea of risk. I must not only punish but punish with impunity. A wrong is unredressed when retribution overtakes its redresser. It is equally unredressed when the avenger fails to make himself felt as such to him who has done the wrong.

It must be understood that neither by word nor deed had I given Fortunato cause to doubt my good will. I continued, as was my wont, to smile in his face, and he did not perceive that my smile now was at the thought of his immolation.

He had a weak point—this Fortunato—although in other regards he was a man to be respected and even feared. He prided himself on his connoisseurship in wine. Few Italians have the true virtuoso spirit. For the most part their enthusiasm is adopted to suit the time and opportunity, to practice imposture upon the British and Austrian millionaires. In painting and gemmary, Fortunato, like his countrymen, was a quack, but in the matter of old wines he was sincere. In this respect I did not differ from him materially;—I was skillful in the Italian vintages myself, and bought largely whenever I could.

It was about dusk, one evening during the supreme madness of the carnival season, that I encountered my friend. He accosted me with excessive warmth, for he had been drinking much. The man wore motley. He had on a tight-fitting parti-striped dress, and his head was surmounted by the conical cap and bells. I was so pleased to see him that I thought I should never have done wringing his hand.

I said to him—"My dear Fortunato, you are luckily met. How remarkably well you are looking to-day. But I have received a pipe of what passes for Amontillado, and I have my doubts."

"How?" said he. "Amontillado? A pipe? Impossible! And in the middle of the carnival!"

"I have my doubts," I replied; "and I was silly enough to pay the full Amontillado price without consulting you in the matter. You were not to be found, and I was fearful of losing a bargain."

"Amontillado!"

"I have my doubts."

"Amontillado!"

"And I must satisfy them."

"Amontillado!"

"As you are engaged, I am on my way to Luchresi. If any one has a critical turn it is he. He will tell me——"

"Luchresi cannot tell Amontillado from Sherry."

"And yet some fools will have it that his taste is a match for your own."

"Come, let us go."

"Whither?"

"To your vaults."

"My friend, no; I will not impose upon your good nature. I perceive you have an engagement. Luchresi——"

"I have no engagement;—come."

"My friend, no. It is not the engagement, but the severe cold with which I perceive you are afflicted. The vaults are insufferably damp. They are encrusted with niter."

"Let us go, nevertheless. The cold is merely nothing. Amontillado! You have been imposed upon. And as for Luchresi, he cannot distinguish Sherry from Amontillado."

Thus speaking, Fortunato possessed himself of my arm; and putting on a mask of black silk and drawing a roquelaure closely about my person, I suffered him to hurry me to my palazzo.

There were no attendants at home; they had absconded to make merry in honor of the time. I had told them that I should not return until the morning, and had given them explicit orders not to stir from the house. These orders were sufficient, I knew well, to insure their immediate disappearance, one and all, as soon as my back was turned.

I took from their sconces two flambeaux, and giving one to Fortunato, bowed him through several suites of rooms to the archway that led into the vaults. I passed down a long and winding staircase, requesting him to be cautious as he followed. We came at length to the foot of the descent, and stood together upon the damp ground of the catacombs of the Montresors.

The gait of my friend was unsteady, and the bells upon his cap jingled as he strode.

"The pipe," he said.

"It is farther on," said I; "but observe the white web-work which gleams from these cavern walls."

He turned toward me, and looked into my eyes with two filmy orbs that distilled the rheum of intoxication.

"Niter?" he asked at length.

"Niter," I replied. "How long have you had that cough?"

"Ugh! ugh! ugh!—ugh! ugh! ugh!—ugh! ugh! ugh!—ugh! ugh! ugh!—ugh! ugh! ugh!"

My poor friend found it impossible to reply for many minutes.

"It is nothing," he said, at last.

"Come," I said, with decision, "we will go back; your health is precious. You are rich, respected, admired, beloved; you are happy, as once I was. You are a man to be missed. For me it is no matter. We will go back; you will be ill, and I cannot be responsible. Besides, there is Luchresi——"

"Enough," he said; "the cough is a mere nothing; it will not kill me. I shall not die of a cough."

"True—true," I replied; "and, indeed, I had no intention of alarming you unnecessarily—but you should use all proper caution. A draft of this Medoc will defend us from the damps."

Here I knocked off the neck of a bottle which I drew from a long row of its fellows that lay upon the mold.

"Drink," I said, presenting him the wine.

He raised it to his lips with a leer. He paused and nodded to me familiarly, while his bells jingled.

"I drink," he said, "to the buried that repose around us."

"And I to your long life."

He again took my arm, and we proceeded.

"These vaults," he said, "are extensive."

"The Montresors," I replied, "were a great and numerous family."

"I forget your arms."

"A huge human foot d'or, in a field azure; the foot crushes a serpent rampant whose fangs are imbedded in the heel."

"And the motto?"

"*Nemo me impune lacessit.*"

"Good!" he said.

The wine sparkled in his eyes and the bells jingled. My own fancy grew warm with the Medoc. We had passed through long walls of piled skeletons, with casks and puncheons intermingling, into the inmost recesses of catacombs. I paused again, and this time I made bold to seize Fortunato by an arm above the elbow.

"The niter!" I said; "see, it increases. It hangs like moss upon the vaults. We are below the river's bed. The drops of moisture trickle among the bones. Come, we will go back ere it is too late. Your cough——"

"It is nothing," he said; "let us go on. But first, another draft of the Medoc."

I broke and reached him a flagon of De Grâve. He emptied it at a breath. His eyes flashed with a fierce light. He laughed and threw the bottle upward with a gesticulation I did not understand.

I looked at him in surprise. He repeated the movement—a grotesque one.

"You do not comprehend?" he said.

"Not I," I replied.

"Then you are not of the brotherhood."

"How?"

"You are not of the masons."

"Yes, yes," I said; "yes, yes."

"You? Impossible! A mason?"

"A mason," I replied.

"A sign," he said, "a sign."

"It is this," I answered, producing from beneath the folds of my roquelaure a trowel.

"You jest," he exclaimed, recoiling a few paces. "But let us proceed to the Amontillado."

"Be it so," I said, replacing the tool beneath the cloak and again offering my arm. He leaned upon it heavily. We continued our route in search of the Amontillado. We passed through a range of low arches, descended, passed on, and descending again, arrived at a deep crypt, in which the foulness of the air caused our flambeaux rather to glow than flame.

At the most remote end of the crypt there appeared another less spacious. Its walls had been lined with human remains, piled to the vault overhead, in the fashion of the great catacombs of Paris. Three sides of this interior crypt were still ornamented in this manner. From the fourth side the bones had been thrown down, and lay promiscuously upon the earth, forming at one point a mound of some size. Within the wall thus exposed by the displacing of the bones, we perceived a still interior crypt or recess, in depth about four feet, in width three, in height six or seven. It seemed to have been constructed for no especial use within itself, but formed merely the interval between two of the colossal supports of the roof of the catacombs, and was backed by one of their circumscribing walls of solid granite.

It was in vain that Fortunato, uplifting his dull torch, endeavored to pry into the depth of the recess. Its termination the feeble light did not enable us to see.

"Proceed," I said; "herein is the Amontillado. As for Luchresi——"

"He is an ignoramus," interrupted my friend, as he stepped unsteadily forward, while I followed immediately at his heels. In an instant he had reached the extremity of the niche, and, finding his progress arrested by the rock, stood stupidly bewildered. A moment more and I had fettered him to the granite. In its surface were two iron staples, distant from each other about two feet, horizontally. From one of these depended a short chain, from the other a padlock.

Throwing the links about his waist, it was but the work of a few seconds to secure it. He was too much astounded to resist. Withdrawing the key I stepped back from the recess.

"Pass your hand," I said, "over the wall; you cannot help feeling the niter. Indeed, it is very damp. Once more let me implore you to return. No? Then I must positively leave you. But I must first render you all the little attentions in my power."

"The Amontillado!" ejaculated my friend, not yet recovered from his astonishment.

"True," I replied; "the Amontillado."

As I said these words I busied myself among the pile of bones of which I have before spoken. Throwing them aside, I soon uncovered a quantity of building stone and mortar. With these materials and with the aid of my trowel, I began vigorously to wall up the entrance of the niche.

I had scarcely laid the first tier of the masonry when I discovered that the intoxication of Fortunato had in a great measure worn off. The earliest indication I had of this was a low moaning cry from the depth of the recess. It was not the cry of a drunken man. There was then a long and obstinate silence. I laid the second tier, and the third, and the fourth, and then I heard the furious vibrations of the chain. The noise lasted for several minutes, during which, that I might hearken to it with the more satisfaction, I ceased my labors and sat down upon the bones. When at last the clanking subsided, I resumed the trowel, and finished without interruption the fifth, the sixth, and the seventh tier. The wall was now nearly upon a level with my breast. I again paused, and holding the flambeaux over the mason-work, threw a few feeble rays upon the figure within.

A succession of loud and shrill screams, bursting suddenly from the throat of the chained form, seemed to thrust me violently back. For a brief moment I hesitated, I trembled. Unsheathing my rapier, I began to grope with it about the recess; but the thought of an instant reassured me. I placed my hand upon the solid fabric of the catacombs, and felt satisfied. I reapproached the wall; I replied to the yells of him who clamoured. I re-echoed, I aided, I surpassed them in volume and in strength. I did this, and the clamourer grew still.

It was now midnight, and my task was drawing to a close. I had completed the eighth, the ninth, and the tenth tier. I had finished a portion of the last and the eleventh; there remained but a single stone to be fitted and plastered in. I struggled with its weight; I placed it partially in its destined position. But now there came from out the niche a low laugh that erected the hairs upon my head. It was succeeded by a sad voice, which I had difficulty in recognizing as that of the noble Fortunato. The voice said—

"Ha! ha! ha!—he! he! he!—a very good joke, indeed—an excellent jest. We shall have many a rich laugh about it at the palazzo—he! he! he!—over our wine—he! he! he!"

"The Amontillado!" I said.

"He! he! he!—he! he! he!—yes, the Amontillado. But is it not getting late? Will not they be awaiting us at the palazzo, the Lady Fortunato and the rest? Let us be gone."

"Yes," I said, "let us be gone."

"*For the love of God! Montresor!*"

"Yes," I said, "for the love of God!"

But to these words I hearkened in vain for a reply. I grew impatient. I called aloud—

"Fortunato!"

No answer. I called again,—

"Fortunato!"

No answer still. I thrust a torch through the remaining aperture and let it fall within. There came forth in return only a jingling of the bells. My heart grew sick; it was the dampness of the catacombs that made it so. I hastened to make an end of my labor. I forced the last stone into its position; I plastered it up. Against the new masonry I re-erected the old rampart of bones. For the half of a century no mortal has disturbed them. *In pace requiescat!*

LANDOR'S COTTAGE

DURING A PEDESTRIAN tour last summer, through one or two of the river counties of New York, I found myself, as the day declined, somewhat embarrassed about the road I was pursuing. The land undulated very remarkably; and my path, for the last hour, had wound about and about so confusedly, in its effort to keep in the valleys, that I no longer knew in what direction lay the sweet village of B——, where I had determined to stop for the night. The sun had scarcely shone—strictly speaking—during the day, which, nevertheless, had been unpleasantly warm. A smoky mist, resembling that of the Indian summer, enveloped all things, and, of course, added to my uncertainty. Not that I cared much about the matter. If I did not hit upon the village before sunset, or even before dark, it was more than possible that a little Dutch farmhouse, or something of that kind, would soon make its appearance—although, in fact, the neighborhood (perhaps on account of being more picturesque than fertile) was very sparsely inhabited. At all events, with my knapsack for a pillow, and my hound as a sentry, a bivouac in the open air was just the thing which would have amused me. I sauntered on, therefore, quite at ease—Ponto taking charge of my gun—until at length, just as I had begun to consider whether the numerous little glades that led hither and thither were intended to be paths at all, I was conducted by one of the most promising of them into an unquestionable carriage-track. There could be no mistaking it. The traces of light wheels were evident; and although the tall shrubberies and overgrown undergrowth met overhead, there was no obstruction whatever below, even to the passage of a Virginian mountain wagon—the most aspiring vehicle, I take it, of its kind. The road, however, except in being open through the wood—if wood be not too weighty a name for such an assemblage of light trees—and except in the particulars of evident wheeltracks—bore no resemblance to any road I had before seen. The tracks of which I speak were but faintly perceptible, having been impressed upon the firm, yet pleasantly moist surface of—what looked more like green Genoese velvet than anything else. It was grass, clearly—but grass such as we seldom see out of England—so short, so thick, so even, and so vivid in color. Not a single impediment lay in the wheel-route—not even a chip or dead twig. The stones that once obstructed the way had been carefully placed—not thrown—along the sides of the lane, so as to define its boundaries at bottom with a kind of half-precise, half-negligent, and wholly picturesque definition. Clumps of wild flowers grew everywhere, luxuriantly, in the interspaces.

What to make of all this, of course I knew not. Here was art undoubtedly—that did not surprise me—all roads, in the ordinary sense, are works of art; nor can I say that there was much to wonder at in the mere excess of art manifested; all that seemed to have been done, might have been done here—with such natural "capabilities" (as they have it in the books on Landscape Gardening)—with very little labor and expense. No; it was not the amount but the character of the art which caused me to take a seat on one of the blossomy stones and gaze up and down this fairylike avenue for half an hour or more in bewildered admiration. One thing became more and more evident the longer I gazed: an artist, and one with a most scrupulous eye for form, had superintended all these arrangements. The greatest care had been taken to preserve a due medium between the neat and graceful on the one hand, and the pittoresco, in the true sense of the Italian term, on the other. There were few straight, and no long uninterrupted lines. The same effect of curvature or of color, appeared twice, usually, but not oftener, at any one point of view. Everywhere was variety in uniformity. It was a piece of "composition," in which the most fastidiously critical taste could scarcely have suggested an emendation.

I had turned to the right as I entered this road, and now arising, I continued in the same direction. The path was so serpentine, that at no moment could I trace its course for more than two or three paces in advance. Its character did not undergo any material change.

Presently the murmur of water fell gently upon my ear—and in a few moments afterward, as I turned with the road somewhat more abruptly than hitherto, I became aware that a building of some kind lay at the foot of a gentle declivity just before me. I could see nothing distinctly on account of the mist which occupied all the little valley below. A gentle breeze, however, now arose, as the sun was about descending; and while I remained standing on the brow of the slope, the fog gradually became dissipated into wreaths, and so floated over the scene.

As it came fully into view—thus gradually as I describe it—piece by piece, here a tree, there a glimpse of water, and here again the summit of a chimney, I could scarcely help fancying that the whole was one of the ingenious illusions sometimes exhibited under the name of "vanishing pictures."

By the time, however, that the fog had thoroughly disappeared, the sun had made its way down behind the gentle hills, and thence, as if with a slight *chassez* to the south, had come again fully into sight; glaring with a purplish luster through a chasm that entered the valley from the west. Suddenly, therefore—and as if by the hand of magic—this whole valley and everything in it became brilliantly visible.

The first *coup d'œil*, as the sun slid into the position described, impressed me very much as I have been impressed when a boy, by the concluding scene of some well-arranged theatrical spectacle or melodrama. Not even the monstrosity of color was wanting; for the sunlight came out through the chasm, tinted all orange and purple; while the vivid green of the grass in the valley was reflected more or less upon all objects, from the curtain of vapor that still hung overhead, as if loth to take its total departure from a scene so enchantingly beautiful.

The little vale into which I thus peered down from under the fog-canopy, could not have been more than four hundred yards long; while in breadth it varied from fifty to one hundred and fifty, or perhaps two hundred. It was most narrow at its northern extremity, opening out as it tended southwardly, but with no very precise regularity. The widest portion was within eighty yards of the southern extreme. The slopes which encompassed the vale could not fairly be called hills, unless at their northern face. Here a precipitous ledge of granite arose to a height of some ninety feet; and, as I have mentioned, the valley at this point was not more than fifty feet wide; but as the visitor proceeded southwardly from this cliff, he found on his right hand and on his left, declivities at once less high, less precipitous, and less rocky. All, in a word, sloped and softened to the south; and yet the whole vale was engirdled by eminences, more or less high, except at two points. One of these I have already spoken of. It lay considerably to the north of west, and was where the setting sun made its way, as I have before described, into the amphitheater, through a cleanly cut natural cleft in the granite embankment: this fissure might have been ten yards wide at its widest point, so far as the eye could trace it. It seemed to lead up, up, like a natural causeway, into the recesses of unexplored mountains and forests. The other opening was directly at the southern end of the vale. Here, generally, the slopes were nothing more than gentle inclinations, extending from east to west about one hundred and fifty yards. In the middle of this extent was a depression, level with the ordinary floor of the valley. As regards vegetation, as well as in respect to everything else, the scene softened and sloped to the south. To the north—on the craggy precipice—a few paces from the verge—upsprang the magnificent trunks of numerous hickories, black walnuts, and chestnuts, interspersed with occasional oak; and the strong lateral branches thrown out by the walnuts especially, spread far over the edge of the cliff. Proceeding southwardly, the explorer saw, at first, the same class of trees, but less and less lofty and Salvatorish in character; then he saw the gentler elm, succeeded by the sassafras and locust—these again by the softer linden, red-bud, catalpa, and maple—these yet again by still more graceful and more modest varieties. The whole face of the southern declivity was covered with wild shrubbery alone—an occasional silver willow or white poplar excepted. In the bottom of the valley itself—(for it must be borne in mind that the vegetation hitherto mentioned grew only on the cliffs or hill-sides)—were to be seen three isolated trees. One was an elm of fine size and exquisite form; it stood guard over the southern gate of the vale. Another was a hickory, much larger than the elm, and altogether a much finer tree, although both were exceedingly beautiful: it seemed to have taken charge of the northwestern entrance, springing from a group of rocks in the very jaws of the ravine, and throwing its graceful body, at an angle of nearly forty-five degrees, far out into the sunshine of the amphitheater. About thirty yards east of this tree stood, however, the pride of the valley, and beyond all question the most magnificent tree I have ever seen, unless, perhaps, among the cypresses of the Itchiatuckanee. It was a triple-stemmed tulip-tree—the

Liriodendron Tulipiferum—one of the natural order of magnolias. Its three trunks separated from the parent at about three feet from the soil, and diverging very slightly and gradually, were not more than four feet apart at the point where the largest stem shot out into foliage: this was at an elevation of about eighty feet. The whole height of the principal division was one hundred and twenty feet. Nothing can surpass in beauty the form, or the glossy, vivid green of the leaves of the tulip-tree. In the present instance they were fully eight inches wide; but their glory was altogether eclipsed by the gorgeous splendor of the profuse blossoms. Conceive, closely congregated, a million of the largest and most resplendent tulips! Only thus can the reader get any idea of the picture I would convey. And then the stately grace of the clean, delicately-granulated columnar stems, the largest four feet in diameter, at twenty from the ground. The innumerable blossoms, mingling with those of other trees scarcely less beautiful, although infinitely less majestic, filled the valley with more than Arabian perfumes.

The general floor of the amphitheater was grass of the same character as that I had found in the road: if anything, more deliciously soft, thick, velvety, and miraculously green. It was hard to conceive how all this beauty had been attained.

I have spoken of the two openings into the vale. From the one to the northwest issued a rivulet, which came, gently murmuring and slightly foaming, down the ravine, until it dashed against the group of rocks out of which sprang the isolated hickory. Here, after encircling the tree, it passed on a little to the north of east, leaving the tulip-tree some twenty feet to the south, and making no decided alteration in its course until it came near the midway between the eastern and western boundaries of the valley. At this point, after a series of sweeps, it turned off at right angles and pursued a generally southern direction—meandering as it went—until it became lost in a small lake of irregular figure (although roughly oval), that lay gleaming near the lower extremity of the vale. This lakelet was, perhaps, a hundred yards in diameter at its widest part. No crystal could be clearer than its waters. Its bottom, which could be distinctly seen, consisted altogether of pebbles brilliantly white. Its banks, of the emerald grass already described, rounded, rather than sloped, off into the clear heaven below; and so clear was this heaven, so perfectly, at times, did it reflect all objects above it, that where the true bank ended and where the mimic one commenced, it was a point of no little difficulty to determine. The trout, and some other varieties of fish, with which this pond seemed to be almost inconveniently crowded, had all the appearance of veritable flying-fish. It was almost impossible to believe that they were not absolutely suspended in the air. A light birch canoe that lay placidly on the water, was reflected in its minutest fibres with a fidelity unsurpassed by the most exquisitely polished mirror. A small island, fairly laughing with flowers in full bloom, and affording little more space than just enough for a picturesque little building, seemingly a fowl-house—arose from the lake not far from its northern shore—to which it was connected by means of an inconceivably light-looking and yet very primitive bridge. It was formed of a single, broad and thick plank of the tulip wood. This was forty feet long, and spanned the interval between shore and shore with a slight but very perceptible arch, preventing all oscillation. From the southern extremity of the lake issued a continuation of the rivulet, which, after meandering for, perhaps, thirty yards, finally passed through the "depression" (already described) in the middle of the southern declivity, and tumbling down a sheer precipice of a hundred feet, made its devious and unnoticed way to the Hudson.

The lake was deep—at some points thirty feet—but the rivulet seldom exceeded three, while its greatest width was about eight. Its bottom and banks were as those of the pond—if a defect could have been attributed to them, in point of picturesqueness, it was that of excessive neatness.

The expanse of the green turf was relieved, here and there, by an occasional showy shrub, such as the hydrangea, or the common snow-ball, or the aromatic syringa; or, more frequently, by a clump of geraniums blossoming gorgeously in great varieties. These latter grew in pots which were carefully buried in the soil, so as to give the plants the appearance of being indigenous. Besides all this, the lawn's velvet was exquisitely spotted with sheep—a considerable flock of which roamed about the vale, in company with three tamed deer, and a vast number of brilliantly-plumed ducks. A very large mastiff seemed to be in vigilant attendance upon these animals, each and all.

Along the eastern and western cliffs—where, toward the upper portion of the amphitheater, the boundaries were more or less precipitous—grew ivy in great profusion—so that only here and there could even a glimpse of the naked rock be obtained. The northern precipice, in like manner, was almost entirely clothed by grape-vines of rare luxuriance; some springing from the soil at the base of the cliff, and others from ledges on its face.

The slight elevation which formed the lower boundary of this little domain, was crowned by a neat stone wall, of sufficient height to prevent the escape of the deer. Nothing of the fence kind was observable elsewhere; for nowhere else was an artificial enclosure needed:—any stray sheep, for example, which should attempt to make its way out of the vale by means of the ravine, would find its progress arrested, after a few yards' advance, by the precipitous ledge of rock over which tumbled the cascade that had arrested my attention as I first drew near the domain. In short, the only ingress or egress was through a gate occupying a rocky pass in the road, a few paces below the point at which I stopped to reconnoitre the scene.

I have described the brook as meandering very irregularly through the whole of its course. Its two general directions, as I have said, were first from west to east, and then from north to south. At the turn, the stream, sweeping backward, made an almost circular loop, so as to form a peninsula which was very nearly an island, and which included about the sixteenth of an acre. On this peninsula stood a dwelling-house—and when I say that this house, like the infernal terrace seen by Vathek, "*était d'une architecture inconnue dans les annales de la terre*," I mean, merely, that its tout ensemble struck me with the keenest sense of combined novelty and propriety—in a word, of poetry—(for, than in the words just employed, I could scarcely give, of poetry in the abstract, a more rigorous definition)—and I do not mean that the merely outré was perceptible in any respect.

In fact, nothing could well be more simple—more utterly unpretending than this cottage. Its marvelous effect lay altogether in its artistic arrangement as a picture. I could have fancied, while I looked at it, that some eminent landscape painter had built it with his brush.

The point of view from which I first saw the valley, was not altogether, although it was nearly, the best point from which to survey the house. I will therefore describe it as I afterward saw it—from a position on the stone wall at the southern extreme of the amphitheater.

The main building was about twenty-four feet long and sixteen broad—certainly not more. Its total height, from the ground to the apex of the roof, could not have exceeded eighteen feet. To the west end of this structure was attached one about a third smaller in all its proportions:—the line of its front standing back about two yards from that of the larger house; and the line of its roof, of course, being considerably depressed below that of the roof adjoining. At right angles to these buildings, and from the rear of the main one—not exactly in the middle—extended a third compartment, very small—being, in general, one third less than the western wing. The roofs of the two larger were very steep—sweeping down from the ridge-beam with a long concave curve, and extending at least four feet beyond the walls in front, so as to form the roofs of two piazzas. These latter roofs, of course, needed no support; but as they had the air of needing it, slight and perfectly plain pillars were inserted at the corners alone. The roof of the northern wing was merely an extension of a portion of the main roof. Between the chief building and western wing arose a very tall and rather slender square chimney of hard Dutch bricks, alternately black and red;—a slight cornice of projecting bricks at the top. Over the gables, the roofs also projected very much:—in the main building about four feet to the east and two to the west. The principal door was not exactly in the main division, being a little to the east—while the two windows were to the west. These latter did not extend to the floor, but were much longer and narrower than usual—they had single shutters like doors—the panes were of lozenge form, but quite large. The door itself had its upper half of glass, also in lozenge panes—a moveable shutter secured it at night. The door to the west wing was in its gable, and quite simple—a single window looked out to the south. There was no external door to the north wing, and it, also, had only one window to the east.

The blank wall of the eastern gable was relieved by stairs (with a balustrade) running diagonally across it—the ascent being from the south. Under cover of the widely-projecting eave these steps gave access to a door leading into the garret, or rather loft—for it was lighted only by a single window to the north, and seemed to have been intended as a storeroom.

The piazzas of the main building and western wing had no floors, as is usual; but at the doors and at each window, large, flat, irregular slabs of granite lay imbedded in the delicious turf, affording comfortable footing in all weather. Excellent paths of the same material—not nicely adapted, but with the velvety sod filling frequent intervals between the stones, led hither and thither from the house, to a crystal spring about five paces off, to the road, or to one or two outhouses that lay to the north, beyond the brook, and were thoroughly concealed by a few locusts and catalpas.

Not more than six steps from the main door of the cottage stood the dead trunk of a fantastic pear-tree, so clothed from head to foot in the gorgeous bignonia blossoms that one required no little scrutiny to determine what manner of sweet thing it could be. From various arms of this tree hung cages of different kinds. In one, a large wicker cylinder with a ring at top, reveled a mocking bird; in another, an oriole; in a third, the impudent bobolink—while three or four more delicate prisons were loudly vocal with canaries.

The pillars of the piazza were enwreathed in jasmine and sweet honeysuckle; while from the angle formed by the main structure and its west wing, in front, sprang a grape-vine of unexampled luxuriance. Scorning all restraint, it had clambered first to the lower roof—then to the higher; and along the ridge of this latter it continued to writhe on, throwing out tendrils to the right and left, until at length it fairly attained the east gable, and fell trailing over the stairs.

The whole house, with its wings, was constructed of the old-fashioned Dutch shingles—broad, and with unrounded corners. It is a peculiarity of this material to give houses built of it the appearance of being wider at bottom than at top—after the manner of Egyptian architecture; and in the present instance, this exceedingly picturesque effect was aided by numerous pots of gorgeous flowers that almost encompassed the base of the buildings.

The shingles were painted a dull gray; and the happiness with which this neutral tint melted into the vivid green of the tulip-tree leaves that partially overshadowed the cottage, can readily be conceived by an artist.

From the position near the stone wall, as described, the buildings were seen at great advantage—for the southeastern angle was thrown forward—so that the eye took in at once the whole of the two fronts, with the picturesque eastern gable, and at the same time obtained just a sufficient glimpse of the northern wing, with parts of a pretty roof to the spring-house, and nearly half of a light bridge that spanned the brook in the near vicinity of the main buildings.

I did not remain very long on the brow of the hill, although long enough to make a thorough survey of the scene at my feet. It was clear that I had wandered from the road to the village, and I had thus good traveler's excuse to open the gate before me, and inquire my way, at all events; so, without more ado, I proceeded.

The road, after passing the gate, seemed to lie upon a natural ledge, sloping gradually down along the face of the northeastern cliffs. It led me on to the foot of the northern precipice, and thence over the bridge, round by the eastern gable to the front door. In this progress, I took notice that no sight of the outhouses could be obtained.

As I turned the corner of the gable, the mastiff bounded toward me in stern silence, but with the eye and the whole air of a tiger. I held him out my hand, however, in token of amity—and I never yet knew the dog who was proof against such an appeal to his courtesy. He not only shut his mouth and wagged his tail, but absolutely offered me his paw— afterward extending his civilities to Ponto.

As no bell was discernible, I rapped with my stick against the door, which stood half open. Instantly a figure advanced to the threshold—that of a young woman about twenty-eight years of age—slender, or rather slight, and somewhat above the medium height. As she approached, with a certain modest decision of step altogether indescribable, I said to myself, "Surely here I have found the perfection of natural, in contra-distinction from artificial grace." The second impression which she made on me, but by far the more vivid of the two, was that of enthusiasm. So intense an expression of romance, perhaps I should call it, or of unworldliness, as that which gleamed from her deep-set eyes, had never so sunk into my heart of hearts before. I know not how it is, but this peculiar expression of the eye, wreathing itself occasionally into the lips, is the most powerful, if not absolutely the sole spell, which rivets my interest in woman. "Romance," provided my readers fully comprehend what I would here imply by the word—"romance" and "womanliness" seem to me convertible terms: and, after all, what man truly loves in woman is, simply, her womanhood. The eyes of Annie (I heard some one from the interior call her "Annie, darling!") were "spiritual gray"; her hair, a light chestnut: this is all I had time to observe of her.

At her most courteous of invitations, I entered—passing first into a tolerably wide vestibule. Having come mainly to observe, I took notice that to my right as I stepped in, was a window, such as those in front of the house; to the left, a door leading into the principal room; while, opposite me, an open door enabled me to see a small apartment, just the size of the vestibule, arranged as a study, and having a large bow window looking out to the north.

Passing into the parlor, I found myself with Mr. Landor—for this, I afterward found, was his name. He was civil, even cordial in his manner; but just then, I was more intent on observing the arrangements of the dwelling which had so much interested me, than the personal appearance of the tenant.

The north wing, I now saw, was a bedchamber: its door opened into the parlor. West of this door was a single window, looking toward the brook. At the west end of the parlor, were a fireplace, and a door leading into the west wing—probably a kitchen.

Nothing could be more rigorously simple than the furniture of the parlor. On the floor was an ingrain carpet, of excellent texture—a white ground, spotted with small circular green figures. At the windows were curtains of snowy white jaconet muslin: they were tolerably full, and hung decisively, perhaps rather formally, in sharp, parallel plaits to the floor—just to the floor. The walls were papered with a French paper of great delicacy—a silver ground, with a faint green cord running zigzag throughout. Its expanse was relieved merely by three of Julien's exquisite lithographs à trois crayons, fastened to the wall without frames. One of these drawings was a scene of Oriental luxury, or rather voluptuousness; another was a "carnival piece," spirited beyond compare; the third was a Greek female head—a face so divinely beautiful, and yet of an expression so provokingly indeterminate, never before arrested my attention.

The more substantial furniture consisted of a round table, a few chairs (including a large rocking-chair), and a sofa, or rather "settee": its material was plain maple painted a creamy white, slightly interstriped with green—the seat of cane. The chairs and table were "to match"; but the forms of all had evidently been designed by the same brain which planned "the grounds": it is impossible to conceive anything more graceful.

On the table were a few books; a large, square, crystal bottle of some novel perfume; a plain, ground-glass astral (not solar) lamp, with an

Italian shade; and a large vase of resplendently-blooming flowers. Flowers indeed of gorgeous colors and delicate odor, formed the sole mere decoration of the apartment. The fireplace was nearly filled with a vase of brilliant geranium. On a triangular shelf in each angle of the room stood also a similar vase, varied only as to its lovely contents. One or two smaller bouquets adorned the mantel; and late violets clustered about the open windows.

It is not the purpose of this work to do more than give, in detail, a picture of Mr. Landor's residence—*as I found it.*

"THOU ART THE MAN!"

I WILL NOW play the Œdipus to the Rattleborough enigma. I will expound to you—as I alone can—the secret of the enginery that effected the Rattleborough miracle—the one, the true, the admitted, the undisputed, the indisputable miracle which put a definite end to infidelity among the Rattleburghers, and converted to the orthodoxy of the grandames all the carnal-minded who had ventured to be skeptical before.

This event—which I should be sorry to discuss in a tone of unsuitable levity—occurred in the summer of 18—. Mr. Barnabas Shuttleworthy, one of the wealthiest and most respectable citizens of the borough, had been missing for several days under circumstances which gave rise to suspicion of foul play. Mr. Shuttleworthy had set out from Rattleborough very early one Saturday morning, on horseback, with the avowed intention of proceeding to the city of — — —, about fifteen miles distant, and of returning the night of the same day. Two hours after his departure, however, his horse returned without him, and without the saddle-bags which had been strapped on his back at starting. The animal was wounded, too, and covered with mud. These circumstances naturally gave rise to much alarm among the friends of the missing man, and when it was found, on Sunday morning, that he had not yet made his appearance, the whole borough arose *en masse* to go and look for his body.

The foremost and most energetic in instituting this search was the bosom friend of Mr. Shuttleworthy—a Mr. Charles Goodfellow, or, as he was universally called, "Charley Goodfellow," or "Old Charley Goodfellow." Now, whether it is a marvelous coincidence, or whether it is that the name itself has an imperceptible effect upon the character, I have never yet been able to ascertain; but the fact is unquestionable, that there never yet was any person named Charles who was not an open, manly, honest, good-natured and frank-hearted fellow, with a rich, clear voice, that did you good to hear it, and an eye that looked you always straight in the face, as much as to say "I have a clear conscience myself; am afraid of no man, and am altogether above doing a mean action." And thus all the hearty, careless, "walking gentlemen" of the stage are very certain to be called Charles.

Now "Old Charley Goodfellow," although he had been in Rattleborough not longer than six months or thereabouts, and although nobody knew anything about him before he came to settle in the neighborhood, had experienced no difficulty in the world in making the acquaintance of all the respectable people in the borough. Not a man of them but would have taken his bare word for a thousand at any moment; and as for the women, there is no saying what they would not have done to oblige him. And all this came of his having been christened Charles, and of his possessing, in consequence, that ingenuous face which is proverbially the very "best letter of recommendation."

I have already said that Mr. Shuttleworthy was one of the most respectable, and, undoubtedly, he was the most wealthy man in Rattleborough, while "Old Charley Goodfellow" was upon as intimate terms with him as if he had been his own brother. The two old gentlemen were next-door neighbors, and although Mr. Shuttleworthy seldom, if ever, visited "Old Charley," and never was known to take a meal in his house, still this did not prevent the two friends from being exceedingly intimate, as I have just observed; for "Old Charley" never let a day pass without stepping in three or four times to see how his neighbor came on, and very often he would stay to breakfast or tea, and almost always to dinner; and then the amount of wine that was made way with by the two cronies at a sitting, it would really be a difficult thing to ascertain. Old Charley's favorite beverage was *Château Margaux*, and it appeared to do Mr. Shuttleworthy's heart good to see the old fellow swallow it, as he did, quart after quart; so that, one day, when the wine was *in* and the wit, as a natural consequence, somewhat *out*, he said to his crony, as he slapped him upon the back—"I tell you what it is, Old Charley, you are, by all odds, the heartiest old fellow I ever came across in all my born days; and, since you love to guzzle the wine at that fashion, I'll be darned if I don't have to make thee a present of a big box of the Château Margaux. 'Od rot me,"—(Mr. Shuttleworthy had a sad habit of swearing, although he seldom went beyond "'Od rot me," or "By gosh," or "By the jolly golly.")—"'Od rot me," says he, "if I don't send an order to town this very afternoon for a double box of the best that can be got, and I'll make ye a present of it, I will—ye needn't say a word, now—I *will*, I tell ye, and there's an end of it; so look out for it—it will come to hand some of these fine days, precisely when ye are looking for it the least." I mention this little bit of liberality on the part of Mr. Shuttleworthy, just by way of showing you how *very* intimate an understanding existed between the two friends.

Well, on the Sunday morning in question, when it came to be fairly understood that Mr. Shuttleworthy had met with foul play, I never saw any one so profoundly affected as "Old Charley Goodfellow." When he first heard that the horse had come home without his master, and without his master's saddle-bags, and all bloody from a pistol shot that had gone clean through and through the poor animal's chest without quite killing him; when he heard all this, he turned as pale as if the missing man had been his own dear brother or father, and shivered and shook all over as if he had had a fit of the ague.

At first, he was too much overpowered with grief to be able to do any thing at all, or to concert upon any plan of action; so that for a long time he endeavored to dissuade Mr. Shuttleworthy's other friends from making a stir about the matter, thinking it best to wait awhile—say for a week or two, or a month or two, to see if something wouldn't turn up, or if Mr. Shuttleworthy wouldn't come in the natural way, and explain his reasons for sending his horse on before. I dare say you have often observed this disposition to temporize or to procrastinate in people who are laboring under any very poignant sorrow. Their powers of mind seem to be rendered torpid, so that they have a horror of any thing like action, and like nothing in the world so well as to lie quietly in bed and "nurse their grief," as the old ladies express it—that is to say, ruminate over their trouble.

The people of Rattleborough had, indeed, so high an opinion of the wisdom and discretion of "Old Charley," that the greater part of them felt disposed to agree with him, and not make a stir in the business "until something should turn up," as the honest old gentleman worded it; and I believe that, after all, this would have been the general determination but for the very suspicious interference of Mr. Shuttleworthy's nephew, a young man of very dissipated habits, and otherwise of rather bad character. This nephew, whose name was Pennifeather, would listen to nothing like reason in the matter of "lying quiet," but insisted upon making immediate search for the "corpse of the murdered man." This was the expression he employed; and Mr. Goodfellow acutely remarked at the time, that it was "a *singular* expression, to say no more." This remark of Old Charley's, too, had great effect upon the crowd; and one of the party was heard to ask, very impressively, "how it happened that young Mr. Pennifeather was so intimately cognizant of all the circumstances connected with his wealthy uncle's disappearance, as to feel authorized to assert, distinctly and unequivocally, that his uncle *was* 'a murdered man.'" Hereupon some little squibbing and bickering occurred among various members of the crowd, and especially between "Old Charley" and Mr. Pennifeather—although this latter occurrence was, indeed, by no means a novelty, for no good will had subsisted between the parties for the last three or four months; and matters had even gone so far that Mr. Pennifeather had actually knocked down his uncle's friend for some alleged excess of liberty that the latter had taken in the uncle's house, of which the nephew was an inmate. Upon this occasion, "Old Charley" is said to have behaved with exemplary moderation and Christian charity. He arose from the blow, adjusted his clothes, and made no attempt at retaliation at all—merely muttering a few words about "taking summary vengeance at the first convenient opportunity"—a natural and very justifiable ebullition of anger, which meant nothing, however, and, beyond doubt, was no sooner given vent to than forgotten.

However these matters may be (which have no reference to the point now at issue), it is quite certain that the people of Rattleborough, principally through the persuasion of Mr. Pennifeather, came at length to the determination of dispersing over the adjacent country in search of the missing Mr. Shuttleworthy. I say they came to this determination in the first instance. After it had been fully resolved that a search should be made, it was considered almost a matter of course that the seekers should disperse—that is to say, distribute themselves in parties—for the more thorough examination of the region round about. I forget, however, by what ingenious train of reasoning it was that "Old Charley" finally convinced the assembly that this was the most injudicious plan that could be pursued. Convince them, however, he did—all except Mr. Pennifeather;

and, in the end, it was arranged that a search should be instituted, carefully and very thoroughly, by the burghers *en masse*, "Old Charley" himself leading the way.

As for the matter of that, there could have been no better pioneer than "Old Charley," whom everybody knew to have the eye of a lynx; but, although he led them into all manner of out-of-the-way holes and corners, by routes that nobody had ever suspected of existing in the neighborhood, and although the search was incessantly kept up day and night for nearly a week, still no trace of Mr. Shuttleworthy could be discovered. When I say no trace, however, I must not be understood to speak literally; for trace, to some extent, there certainly was. The poor gentleman had been tracked, by his horse's shoes (which were peculiar), to a spot about three miles to the east of the borough, on the main road leading to the city. Here the track made off into a by-path through a piece of woodland—the path coming out again into the main road and cutting off about half a mile of the regular distance. Following the shoe-marks down this lane, the party came at length to a pool of stagnant water, half hidden by the brambles, to the right of the lane, and opposite this pool all vestige of the track was lost sight of. It appeared, however, that a struggle of some nature had here taken place, and it seemed as if some large and heavy body, much larger and heavier than a man, had been dragged from the by-path to the pool. This latter was carefully dragged twice, but nothing was found; and the party were upon the point of going away, in despair of coming to any result, when Providence suggested to Mr. Goodfellow the expediency of draining the water off altogether. This project was received with cheers and many high compliments to "Old Charley" upon his sagacity and consideration. As many of the burghers had brought spades with them, supposing that they might possibly be called upon to disinter a corpse, the drain was easily and speedily effected; and no sooner was the bottom visible than right in the middle of the mud that remained was discovered a black silk velvet waistcoat, which nearly everyone present immediately recognized as the property of Mr. Pennifeather. This waistcoat was much torn and stained with blood, and there were several persons among the party who had a distinct remembrance of its having been worn by its owner on the very morning of Mr. Shuttleworthy's departure for the city; while there were others, again, ready to testify upon oath, if required, that Mr. P. did *not* wear the garment in question at any period during the *remainder* of that memorable day; nor could anyone be found to say that he had seen it upon Mr. P.'s person at any period at all subsequent to Mr. Shuttleworthy's disappearance.

Matters now wore a very serious aspect for Mr. Pennifeather, and it was observed, as an indubitable confirmation of the suspicions which were excited against him, that he grew exceedingly pale, and when asked what he had to say for himself, was utterly incapable of saying a word. Hereupon, the few friends his riotous mode of living had left him deserted him at once to a man, and were even more clamorous than his ancient and avowed enemies for his instantaneous arrest. But, on the other hand, the magnanimity of Mr. Goodfellow shone forth with only the more brilliant luster through contrast. He made a warm and intensely eloquent defense of Mr. Pennifeather, in which he alluded more than once to his own sincere forgiveness of that wild young gentleman"the heir of the worthy Mr. Goodfellow"—for the insult which he (the young gentleman) had, no doubt in the heat of passion, thought proper to put upon him (Mr. Goodfellow). "He forgave him for it," he said, "from the very bottom of his heart; and for himself (Mr. Goodfellow), so far from pushing the suspicious circumstances to extremity, which, he was sorry to say, really *had* arisen against Mr. Pennifeather, he (Mr. Goodfellow) would make every exertion in his power, would employ all the little eloquence in his possession to—to—to—soften down, as much as he could conscientiously do so, the worst features of this really exceedingly perplexing piece of business."

Mr. Goodfellow went on for some half hour longer in this strain, very much to the credit both of his head and of his heart; but your warm-hearted people are seldom apposite in their observations—they run into all sorts of blunders, *contre-temps* and *malaproposisms*, in the hot-headedness of their zeal to serve a friend—thus, often with the kindest intentions in the world, doing infinitely more to prejudice his cause than to advance it.

So, in the present instance, it turned out with all the eloquence of "Old Charley;" for, although he labored earnestly in behalf of the suspected, yet it so happened, somehow or other, that every syllable he uttered of which the direct but unwitting tendency was not to exalt the speaker in the good opinion of his audience had the effect to deepen the suspicion already attached to the individual whose cause he pleaded, and to arouse against him the fury of the mob.

One of the most unaccountable errors committed by the orator was his allusion to the suspected as "the heir of the worthy old gentleman Mr. Shuttleworthy." The people had really never thought of this before. They had only remembered certain threats of disinheritance uttered a year or two previously by the uncle (who had no living relative except the nephew); and they had, therefore, always looked upon this disinheritance as a matter that was settled—so single-minded a race of beings were the Rattleburghers; but the remark of "Old Charley" brought them at once to a consideration of this point, and thus gave them to see the possibility of the threats having been nothing *more* than a threat. And straightway, hereupon, arose the natural question of *cui bono?*—a question that tended even more than the waistcoat to fasten the terrible crime upon the young man. And here, lest I be misunderstood, permit me to digress for one moment merely to observe that the exceedingly brief and simple Latin phrase which I have employed is invariably mistranslated and misconceived. "*Cui bono*," in all the crack novels and elsewhere—in those of Mrs. Gore, for example (the author of *Cecil*), a lady who quotes all tongues from the Chaldæan to Chickasaw, and is helped to her learning, "as needed," upon a systematic plan, by Mr. Beckford—in *all* the crack novels, I say, from those of Bulwer and Dickens to those of Turnapenny and Ainsworth, the two little Latin words *cui bono* are rendered "to what purpose," or (as if *quo bono*), "to what good." Their true meaning, nevertheless, is "for whose advantage." *Cui*, to whom; *bono*, is it for a benefit. It is a purely legal phrase, and applicable precisely in cases such as we have now under consideration, where the probability of the doer of a deed hinges upon the probability of the benefit accruing to this individual or to that from the deed's accomplishment. Now, in the present instance, the question *cui bono* very pointedly implicated Mr. Pennifeather. His uncle had threatened him, after making a will in his favor, with disinheritance. But the threat had not been actually kept; the original will, it appeared, had not been altered. *Had* it been altered, the only supposable motive for murder on the part of the suspected would have been the ordinary one of revenge; and even this would have been counteracted by the hope of reinstation into the good graces of the uncle. But the will being unaltered, while the threat to alter remained suspended over the nephew's head, there appears at once the very strongest possible inducement for the atrocity: and so concluded, very sagaciously, the worthy citizens of the borough of Rattle.

Mr. Pennifeather was, accordingly, arrested upon the spot, and the crowd, after some farther search, proceeded homeward, having him in custody. On the route, however, another circumstance occurred tending to confirm the suspicion entertained. Mr. Goodfellow, whose zeal led him to be always a little in advance of the party, was seen suddenly to run forward a few paces, stoop, and then apparently to pick up some small object from the grass. Having quickly examined it, he was observed, too, to make a sort of half attempt at concealing it in his coat pocket; but this action was noticed, as I say, and consequently prevented, when the object picked up was found to be a Spanish knife, which a dozen persons at once recognized as belonging to Mr. Pennifeather. Moreover, his initials were engraved upon the handle. The blade of this knife was open and bloody.

No doubt now remained of the guilt of the nephew, and immediately upon reaching Rattleborough he was taken before a magistrate for examination.

Here matters again took a most unfavorable turn. The prisoner, being questioned as to his whereabouts on the morning of Mr. Shuttleworthy's disappearance, had absolutely the audacity to acknowledge that on that very morning he had been out with his rifle deer-stalking, in the immediate neighborhood of the pool where the blood-stained waistcoat had been discovered through the sagacity of Mr. Goodfellow.

This latter now came forward, and, with tears in his eyes, asked permission to be examined. He said that a stern sense of the duty he owed to his Maker, not less than to his fellow men, would permit him no longer to remain silent. Hitherto, the sincerest affection for the young man (notwithstanding the latter's ill treatment of himself, Mr. Goodfellow) had induced him to make every hypothesis which imagination could suggest, by way of endeavoring to account for what appeared suspicious in the circumstances that told so seriously against Mr. Pennifeather; but these circumstances were now altogether *too* convincing—*too* damning; he would hesitate no longer—he would tell all he knew, although his heart (Mr. Goodfellow's) should absolutely burst asunder in the effort. He then went on to state that, on the afternoon of the day previous to Mr. Shuttleworthy's departure for the city, that worthy old gentleman had mentioned to his nephew, in *his* hearing (Mr. Goodfellow's), that his object in going to town on the morrow was to make a deposit of an unusually large sum of money in the "Farmers' and Mechanics' Bank," and that, then and there, the said Mr. Shuttleworthy had distinctly avowed to the said nephew his irrevocable determination of rescinding the will originally made, and of cutting him off with a shilling. He (the witness) now solemnly called upon the accused to state whether what he (the witness) had just stated was or was not the truth in every substantial particular. Much to the astonishment of every one present, Mr. Pennifeather frankly admitted that it *was*.

The magistrate now considered it his duty to send a couple of constables to search the chamber of the accused in the house of his uncle. From this search they almost immediately returned with the well known steel-bound, russet leather pocket-book which the old gentleman had been in the habit of carrying for years. Its valuable contents, however, had been abstracted, and the magistrate in vain endeavored to extort from the prisoner the use which had been made of them, or the place of their concealment. Indeed, he obstinately denied all knowledge of the matter. The constables also discovered, between the bed and sacking of the unhappy man, a shirt and neck-handkerchief both marked with the initials of his name, and both hideously besmeared with the blood of the victim.

At this juncture, it was announced that the horse of the murdered man had just expired in the stable from the effects of the wound he had received, and it was proposed by Mr. Goodfellow that a *post mortem* examination of the beast should be immediately made, with the view, if possible, of discovering the ball. This was accordingly done; and, as if to demonstrate beyond a question the guilt of the accused, Mr. Goodfellow, after considerable searching in the cavity of the chest, was enabled to detect and to pull forth a bullet of very extraordinary size, which, upon trial, was found to be exactly adapted to the bore of Mr. Pennifeather's rifle, while it was far too large for that of any other person in the borough or its vicinity. To render the matter even surer yet, however, this bullet was discovered to have a flaw or seam at right angles to the usual suture; and upon examination, this seam corresponded precisely with an accidental ridge or elevation in a pair of molds acknowledged by the accused himself to be his own property. Upon the finding of this bullet, the examining magistrate refused to listen to any farther testimony, and immediately committed the prisoner for trial—declining resolutely to take any bail in the case, although against this severity Mr. Goodfellow very warmly remonstrated, and offered to become surety in whatever amount might be required. This generosity on the part of "Old Charley" was only in accordance with the whole tenor of his amiable and chivalrous conduct during the entire period of his sojourn in the borough of Rattle. In the present instance, the worthy man was so entirely carried away by the excessive warmth of his sympathy, that he seemed to have quite forgotten, when he offered to go bail for his young friend, that he himself (Mr. Goodfellow) did not possess a single dollar's worth of property upon the face of the earth.

The result of the committal may be readily foreseen. Mr. Pennifeather, amid the loud execrations of all Rattleborough, was brought to trial at the next criminal sessions, when the chain of circumstantial evidence (strengthened as it was by some additional damning facts, which Mr. Goodfellow's sensitive conscientiousness forbade him to withhold from the court) was considered so unbroken and so thoroughly conclusive that the jury, without leaving their seats, returned an immediate verdict of "*Guilty of murder in the first degree.*" Soon afterward the unhappy wretch received sentence of death, and was remanded to the county jail to await the inexorable vengeance of the law.

In the mean time, the noble behavior of "Old Charley Goodfellow" had doubly endeared him to the honest citizens of the borough. He became ten times a greater favorite than ever; and, as a natural result of the hospitality with which he was treated, he relaxed, as it were, perforce, the extremely parsimonious habits which his poverty had hitherto impelled him to observe, and very frequently had little *réunions* at his own house, when wit and jollity reigned supreme—dampened a little, *of course*, by the occasional remembrance of the untoward and melancholy fate which impended over the nephew of the late lamented bosom friend of the generous host.

One fine day, this magnanimous old gentleman was agreeably surprised at the receipt of the following letter:—

Chat. Mar. A — No. 1. — *Charles Goodfellow, Esquire,* —
6 doz. bottles (1/2 Gross).
From H. F. B. & Co.
Charles Goodfellow, Esq.,
Rattleborough.

"*Dear Sir—In conformity with an order transmitted to our firm about two months since, by our esteemed correspondent, Mr. Barnabus Shuttleworthy, we have the honor of forwarding this morning, to your address, a double box of Château Margaux, of the antelope brand, violet seal. Box numbered and marked as per margin.*

"*We remain, Sir,*
Your most ob'nt ser'ts,

HOGGS, FROGS, BOGS & Co.

"*City of* —, *June* 21*st*, 18—.

"P.S.—*The box will reach you, by wagon, on the day after your receipt of this letter. Our respects to Mr. Shuttleworthy.*

H. F. B. & Co."

The fact is, that Mr. Goodfellow had, since the death of Mr. Shuttleworthy, given over all expectation of ever receiving the promised Château Margaux; and he, therefore, looked upon it *now* as a sort of especial dispensation of Providence in his behalf. He was highly delighted, of course, and, in the exuberance of his joy, invited a large party of friends to a *petit souper* on the morrow, for the purpose of broaching the good old Mr. Shuttleworthy's present. Not that he *said* any thing about "the good old Mr. Shuttleworthy" when he issued the invitations. The fact is, he thought much and concluded to say nothing at all. He did *not* mention to anyone—if I remember aright—that he had received a *present* of Château-Margaux. He merely asked his friends to come and help him to drink some, of a remarkably fine quality and rich flavor, that he had ordered up from the city a couple of months ago, and of which he would be in the receipt upon the morrow. I have often puzzled myself to imagine *why* it was that "Old Charley" came to the conclusion to say nothing about having received the wine from his old friend, but I could never precisely understand his reason for the silence, although he had *some* excellent and very magnanimous reason, no doubt.

The morrow at length arrived, and with it a very large and highly respectable company at Mr. Goodfellow's house. Indeed, half the borough was there—I myself among the number—but, much to the vexation of the host, the Château-Margaux did not arrive until a late hour, and when the sumptuous supper supplied by "Old Charley" had been done very ample justice by the guests. It came at length, however—a monstrously big box of it there was, too—and as the whole party were in excessively good humor, it was decided, *nem. con.*, that it should be lifted upon the table and its contents disemboweled forthwith.

No sooner said than done. I lent a helping hand; and, in a trice, we had the box upon the table, in the midst of all the bottles and glasses, not a few of which were demolished in the scuffle. "Old Charley," who was pretty much intoxicated, and excessively red in the face, now took a seat, with an air of mock dignity, at the head of the board, and thumped furiously upon it with a decanter, calling upon the company to keep order "during the ceremony of disinterring the treasure."

After some vociferation, quiet was at length fully restored, and, as very often happens in similar cases, a profound and remarkable silence ensued. Being then requested to force open the lid, I complied, of course, "with an infinite deal of pleasure." I inserted a chisel, and giving it a few slight taps with a hammer, the top of the box flew suddenly and violently off, and, at the same instant, there sprang up into a sitting position, directly facing the host, the bruised, bloody and nearly putrid corpse of the murdered Mr. Shuttleworthy himself. It gazed for a few moments, fixedly and sorrowfully, with its decaying and lack-luster eyes, full into the countenance of Mr. Goodfellow; uttered slowly, but clearly and impressively, the words—"Thou art the man!" and then, falling over the side of the chest as if thoroughly satisfied, stretched out its limbs quiveringly upon the table.

The scene that ensued is altogether beyond description. The rush for the doors and windows was terrific, and many of the most robust *men* in the room fainted outright through sheer horror. But after the first wild, shrieking burst of affright, all eyes were directed to Mr. Goodfellow. If I live a thousand years, I can never forget the more than mortal agony which was depicted in that ghastly face of his, so lately rubicund with triumph and wine. For several minutes, he sat rigidly as a statue of marble; his eyes seeming, in the intense vacancy of their gaze, to be turned inward and absorbed in the contemplation of his own miserable, murderous soul. At length, their expression appeared to flash suddenly out into the external world, when, with a quick leap, he sprang from his chair, and falling heavily with his head and shoulders upon the table, and in contact with the corpse, poured out rapidly and vehemently a detailed confession of the hideous crime for which Mr. Pennifeather was then imprisoned and doomed to die.

What he recounted was in substance this:—He followed his victim to the vicinity of the pool; there shot his horse with a pistol; despatched the rider with its butt end; possessed himself of the pocket-book; and, supposing the horse dead, dragged it with great labor to the brambles by the pond. Upon his own beast he slung the corpse of Mr. Shuttleworthy, and thus bore it to a secure place of concealment a long distance off through the woods.

The waistcoat, the knife, the pocket-book and the bullet had been placed by himself where found with the view of avenging himself upon Mr. Pennifeather. He had also contrived the discovery of the stained handkerchief and shirt.

Toward the end of the blood-chilling recital, the words of the guilty wretch faltered and grew hollow. When the record was finally exhausted, he arose, staggered backward from the table, and fell—*dead*.

The means by which this happily timed confession was extorted, although efficient, were simple indeed. Mr. Goodfellow's excess of frankness had disgusted me, and excited my suspicion from the first. I was present when Mr. Pennifeather had struck him, and the fiendish expression which then arose upon his countenance, although momentary, assured me that his threat of vengeance would, if possible, be rigidly fulfilled. I was thus prepared to view the *maneuvering* of "Old Charley" in a very different light from that in which it was regarded by the good citizens of Rattleborough. I saw at once that all the criminating discoveries arose, either directly or indirectly, from himself. But the fact which clearly opened my eyes to the true state of the case, was the affair of the bullet, *found* by Mr. G. in the carcass of the horse. *I* had not forgotten, although the Rattleburghers *had*, that there was a hole where the ball had entered the horse, and another where it *went out*. If it were found in the animal then, after having made its exit, I saw clearly that it must have been deposited by the person who found it. The bloody shirt and handkerchief confirmed the idea suggested by the bullet; for the blood upon examination proved to be capital claret, and no more. When I came to think of these things, and also of the late increase of liberality and expenditure on the part of Mr. Goodfellow, I entertained a suspicion which was none the less strong because I kept it altogether to myself.

In the mean time, I instituted a rigorous private search for the corpse of Mr. Shuttleworthy, and, for good reasons, searched in quarters as divergent as possible from those to which Mr. Goodfellow conducted his party. The result was that, after some days, I came across an old dry well, the mouth of which was nearly hidden by brambles; and here, at the bottom, I discovered what I sought.

Now it so happened that I had overheard the colloquy between the two cronies, when Mr. Goodfellow had contrived to cajole his host into the promise of a box of Château Margaux. Upon this hint I acted. I procured a stiff piece of whalebone, thrust it down the throat of the corpse, and deposited the latter in an old wine box—taking care so to double the body up as to double the whalebone with it. In this manner I had to press forcibly upon the lid to keep it down while I secured it with nails; and I anticipated, of course, that as soon as these latter were removed, the top would fly *off* and the body fly *up*.

Having thus arranged the box, I marked, numbered and addressed it as already told; and then writing a letter in the name of the wine merchants with whom Mr. Shuttleworthy dealt, I gave instructions to my servant to wheel the box to Mr. Goodfellow's door, in a barrow, at a given signal from myself. For the words which I intended the corpse to speak, I confidently depended upon my ventriloquial abilities; for their effect, I counted upon the conscience of the murderous wretch.

I believe there is nothing more to be explained. Mr. Pennifeather was released upon the spot, inherited the fortune of his uncle, profited by the lessons of experience, turned over a new leaf, and led happily ever afterward a new life.

THE PURLOINED LETTER

Nil sapientiae odiosius acumine nimio.
Seneca

AT PARIS, JUST after dark one gusty evening in the autumn of 18—, I was enjoying the twofold luxury of meditation and a meerschaum, in company with my friend C. Auguste Dupin, in his little back library, or book-closet, *au troisième*, *No.* 33, *Rue Dunôt, Faubourg St.-Germain*. For one hour at least we had maintained a profound silence; while each, to any casual observer, might have seemed intently and exclusively occupied with the curling eddies of smoke that oppressed the atmosphere of the chamber. For myself, however, I was mentally discussing certain topics which had formed matter for conversation between us at an earlier period of the evening; I mean the affair of the Rue Morgue, and the mystery attending the murder of Marie Rogêt. I looked upon it, therefore, as something of a coincidence, when the door of our apartment was thrown open and admitted our old acquaintance, Monsieur G — —, the Prefect of the Parisian police.

We gave him a hearty welcome; for there was nearly half as much of the entertaining as of the contemptible about the man, and we had not seen him for several years. We had been sitting in the dark, and Dupin now arose for the purpose of lighting a lamp, but sat down again, without doing so, upon G.'s saying that he had called to consult us, or rather to ask the opinion of my friend, about some official business which had occasioned a great deal of trouble.

"If it is any point requiring reflection," observed Dupin, as he forbore to enkindle the wick, "we shall examine it to better purpose in the dark."

"That is another of your odd notions," said the Prefect, who had a fashion of calling every thing "odd" that was beyond his comprehension, and thus lived amid an absolute legion of "oddities."

"Very true," said Dupin, as he supplied his visitor with a pipe, and rolled toward him a comfortable chair.

"And what is the difficulty now?" I asked. "Nothing more in the assassination way, I hope?"

"Oh no; nothing of that nature. The fact is, the business is *very* simple indeed, and I make no doubt that we can manage it sufficiently well ourselves; but then I thought Dupin would like to hear the details of it, because it is so excessively *odd*."

"Simple and odd," said Dupin.

"Why, yes; and not exactly that, either. The fact is, we have all been a good deal puzzled because the affair *is* so simple, and yet baffles us altogether."

"Perhaps it is the very simplicity of the thing which puts you at fault," said my friend.

"What nonsense you *do* talk!" replied the Prefect, laughing heartily.

"Perhaps the mystery is a little *too* plain," said Dupin.

"Oh, good heavens! who ever heard of such an idea?"

"A little *too* self-evident."

"Ha! Ha! Ha!—Ha! Ha! Ha!—Ho! Ho! Ho!" roared our visitor, profoundly amused, "Oh, Dupin, you will be the death of me yet!"

"And what, after all, *is* the matter on hand?" I asked.

"Why, I will tell you," replied the Prefect, as he gave a long, steady, and contemplative puff, and settled himself in his chair. "I will tell you in a few words; but, before I begin, let me caution you that this is an affair demanding the greatest secrecy, and that I should most probably lose the position I now hold, were it known that I confided it to any one."

"Proceed," said I.

"Or not," said Dupin.

"Well, then; I have received personal information, from a very high quarter, that a certain document of the last importance has been purloined from the royal apartments. The individual who purloined it is known; this beyond a doubt; he was seen to take it. It is known, also, that it still remains in his possession."

"How is this known?" asked Dupin.

"It is clearly inferred," replied the Prefect, "from the nature of the document, and from the non-appearance of certain results which would at once arise from its passing *out* of the robber's possession;—that is to say, from his employing it as he must design in the end to employ it."

"Be a little more explicit," I said.

"Well, I may venture so far as to say that the paper gives its holder a certain power in a certain quarter where such power is immensely valuable." The Prefect was fond of the cant of diplomacy.

"Still I do not quite understand," said Dupin.

"No? Well; the disclosure of the document to a third person, who shall be nameless, would bring in question the honor of a personage of most exalted station; and this fact gives the holder of the document an ascendancy over the illustrious personage whose honor and peace are so jeopardized."

"But this ascendancy," I interposed, "would depend upon the robber's knowledge of the loser's knowledge of the robber. Who would dare—"

"The thief," said G., "is the Minister D — — , who dares all things, those unbecoming as well as those becoming a man. The method of the theft was not less ingenious than bold. The document in question—a letter, to be frank—had been received by the personage robbed while alone in the royal *boudoir*. During its perusal she was suddenly interrupted by the entrance of the other exalted personage from whom especially it was her wish to conceal it. After a hurried and vain endeavor to thrust it in a drawer, she was forced to place it, open as it was, upon a table. The address, however, was uppermost, and, the contents thus unexposed, the letter escaped notice. At this juncture enters the Minister D — —. His lynx eye immediately perceives the paper, recognizes the handwriting of the address, observes the confusion of the personage addressed, and fathoms her secret. After some business transactions, hurried through in his ordinary manner, he produces a letter somewhat similar to the one in question, opens it, pretends to read it, and then places it in close juxtaposition to the other. Again he converses, for some fifteen minutes, upon the public affairs. At length, in taking leave, he takes also from the table the letter to which he had no claim. Its rightful owner saw, but, of course, dared not call attention to the act, in the presence of the third personage who stood at her elbow. The minister decamped; leaving his own letter—one of no importance—upon the table."

"Here, then," said Dupin to me, "you have precisely what you demand to make the ascendancy complete—the robber's knowledge of the loser's knowledge of the robber."

"Yes," replied the Prefect; "and the power thus attained has, for some months past, been wielded, for political purposes, to a very dangerous extent. The personage robbed is more thoroughly convinced, every day, of the necessity of reclaiming her letter. But this, of course, cannot be done openly. In fine, driven to despair, she has committed the matter to me."

"Than whom," said Dupin, amid a perfect whirlwind of smoke, "no more sagacious agent could, I suppose, be desired, or even imagined."

"You flatter me," replied the Prefect; "but it is possible that some such opinion may have been entertained."

"It is clear," said I, "as you observe, that the letter is still in possession of the minister; since it is this possession, and not any employment of the letter, which bestows the power. With the employment the power departs."

"True," said G.; "and upon this conviction I proceeded. My first care was to make thorough search of the minister's hotel; and here my chief embarrassment lay in the necessity of searching without his knowledge. Beyond all things, I have been warned of the danger which would result from giving him reason to suspect our design."

"But," said I, "you are quite *au fait* in these investigations. The Parisian police have done this thing often before."

"O yes; and for this reason I did not despair. The habits of the minister gave me, too, a great advantage. He is frequently absent from home all night. His servants are by no means numerous. They sleep at a distance from their master's apartment, and, being chiefly Neapolitans, are readily made drunk. I have keys, as you know, with which I can open any chamber or cabinet in Paris. For three months a night has not passed, during the greater part of which I have not been engaged, personally, in ransacking the D — — Hotel. My honor is interested, and, to mention a great secret, the reward is enormous. So I did not abandon the search until I had become fully satisfied that the thief is a more astute man than myself. I fancy that I have investigated every nook and corner of the premises in which it is possible that the paper can be concealed."

"But is it not possible," I suggested, "that although the letter may be in possession of the minister, as it unquestionably is, he may have concealed it elsewhere than upon his own premises?"

"This is barely possible," said Dupin. "The present peculiar condition of affairs at court, and especially of those intrigues in which D — — is known to be involved, would render the instant availability of the document—its susceptibility of being produced at a moment's notice—a point of nearly equal importance with its possession."

"Its susceptibility of being produced?" said I.

"That is to say, of being *destroyed*," said Dupin.

"True," I observed; "the paper is clearly then upon the premises. As for its being upon the person of the minister, we may consider that as out of the question."

"Entirely," said the Prefect. "He has been twice waylaid, as if by footpads, and his person rigorously searched under my own inspection."

"You might have spared yourself this trouble," said Dupin. "D — —, I presume, is not altogether a fool, and, if not, must have anticipated these waylayings, as a matter of course."

"Not *altogether* a fool," said G., "but then he's a poet, which I take to be only one remove from a fool."

"True," said Dupin, after a long and thoughtful whiff from his meerschaum, "although I have been guilty of certain doggerel myself."

"Suppose you detail," said I, "the particulars of your search."

"Why the fact is, we took our time, and we searched *everywhere*. I have had long experience in these affairs. I took the entire building, room by room; devoting the nights of a whole week to each. We examined, first, the furniture of each apartment. We opened every possible drawer; and I presume you know that, to a properly trained police agent, such a thing as a *secret* drawer is impossible. Any man is a dolt who permits a 'secret' drawer to escape him in a search of this kind. The thing is *so* plain. There is a certain amount of bulk—of space—to be accounted for in every cabinet. Then we have accurate rules. The fiftieth part of a line could not escape us. After the cabinets we took the chairs. The cushions we probed with the fine long needles you have seen me employ. From the tables we removed the tops."

"Why so?"

"Sometimes the top of a table, or other similarly arranged piece of furniture, is removed by the person wishing to conceal an article; then the leg is excavated, the article deposited within the cavity, and the top replaced. The bottoms and tops of bedposts are employed in the same way."

"But could not the cavity be detected by sounding?" I asked.

"By no means, if, when the article is deposited, a sufficient wadding of cotton be placed around it. Besides, in our case, we were obliged to proceed without noise."

"But you could not have removed—you could not have taken to pieces *all* articles of furniture in which it would have been possible to make a deposit in the manner you mention. A letter may be compressed into a thin spiral roll, not differing much in shape or bulk from a large knitting-needle, and in this form it might be inserted into the rung of a chair, for example. You did not take to pieces all the chairs?"

"Certainly not; but we did better—we examined the rungs of every chair in the hotel, and, indeed the jointings of every description of furniture, by the aid of a most powerful microscope. Had there been any traces of recent disturbance we should not have failed to detect it instanter. A single grain of gimlet-dust, or sawdust, for example, would have been as obvious as an apple. Any disorder in the glueing—any unusual gaping in the jointswould have sufficed to insure detection."

"Of course you looked to the mirrors, between the boards and the plates, and you probed the beds and the bed-clothes, as well as the curtains and carpets."

"That of course; and when we had absolutely completed every particle of the furniture in this way, then we examined the house itself. We divided its entire surface into compartments, which we numbered, so that none might be missed; then we scrutinized each individual square inch throughout the premises, including the two houses immediately adjoining, with the microscope, as before."

"The two houses adjoining!" I exclaimed; "you must have had a great deal of trouble."

"We had; but the reward offered is prodigious."

"You include the *grounds* about the houses?"

"All the grounds are paved with brick. They gave us comparatively little trouble. We examined the moss between the bricks, and found it undisturbed."

"You looked among D — — 's papers, of course, and into the books of the library?"

"Certainly; we opened every package and parcel; we not only opened every book, but we turned over every leaf in each volume, not contenting ourselves with a mere shake, according to the fashion of some of our police officers. We also measured the thickness of every book-*cover*, with the most accurate admeasurement, and applied to each the most jealous scrutiny of the microscope. Had any of the bindings been recently meddled with, it would have been utterly impossible that the fact should have escaped observation. Some five or six volumes, just from the hands of the binder, we carefully probed, longitudinally, with the needles."

"You explored the floors beneath the carpets?"

"Beyond doubt. We removed every carpet, and examined the boards with the microscope."

"And the paper on the walls?"

"Yes."

"You looked into the cellars?"

"We did."

"Then," I said, "you have been making a miscalculation, and the letter is *not* upon the premises, as you suppose."

"I fear you are right there," said the Prefect. "And now, Dupin, what would you advise me to do?"

"To make a thorough re-search of the premises."

"That is absolutely needless," replied G — —. "I am not more sure that I breathe than I am that the letter is not at the Hotel."

"I have no better advice to give you," said Dupin. "You have, of course, an accurate description of the letter?"

"Oh yes!"—And here the Prefect, producing a memorandum book proceeded to read aloud a minute account of the internal, and especially of the external appearance of the missing document. Soon after finishing the perusal of this description, he took his departure, more entirely depressed in spirits than I had ever known the good gentleman before.

In about a month afterward he paid us another visit, and found us occupied very nearly as before. He took a pipe and a chair and entered into some ordinary conversation. At length I said,—

"Well, but G — — , what of the purloined letter? I presume you have at last made up your mind that there is no such thing as overreaching the minister?"

"Confound him, say I—yes; I made the re-examination, however, as Dupin suggested—but it was all labor lost, as I knew it would be."

"How much was the reward offered, did you say?" asked Dupin.

"Why, a very great deal—a *very* liberal reward—I don't like to say how much, precisely; but one thing I *will* say, that I wouldn't mind giving my individual check for fifty thousand francs to anyone who could obtain me that letter. The fact is, it is becoming of more and more importance every day; and the reward has been lately doubled. If it were trebled, however, I could do no more than I have done."

"Why, yes," said Dupin, drawlingly, between the whiffs of his meerschaum, "I really—think, G — —, you have not exerted yourself—to the utmost in this matter. You might—do a little more, I think, eh?"

"How?—In what way?'

"Why—puff, puff—you might—puff, puff—employ counsel in the matter, eh?—Puff, puff, puff. Do you remember the story they tell of Abernethy?"

"No; hang Abernethy!"

"To be sure! Hang him and welcome. But, once upon a time, a certain rich miser conceived the design of sponging upon this Abernethy for a medical opinion. Getting up, for this purpose, an ordinary conversation in a private company, he insinuated his case to the physician, as that of an imaginary individual.

" 'We will suppose,' said the miser, 'that his symptoms are such and such; now, doctor, what would *you* have directed him to take?'

" 'Take!' said Abernethy 'Why, take *advice*, to be sure.' "

"But," said the Prefect, a little discomposed, "*I* am *perfectly* willing to take advice, and to pay for it. I would *really* give fifty thousand francs, every *centime* of it, to anyone who would aid me in the matter."

"In that case," replied Dupin, opening a drawer, and producing a check-book, "you may as well fill me up a check for the amount mentioned. When you have signed it, I will hand you the letter."

I was astounded. The Prefect appeared absolutely thunder-stricken. For some minutes he remained speechless and motionless, looking incredulously at my friend with open mouth, and eyes that seemed starting from their sockets; then, apparently recovering himself in some measure, he seized a pen, and after several pauses and vacant stares, finally filled up and signed a check for fifty thousand francs, and handed it across the table to Dupin. The latter examined it carefully and deposited it in his pocket-book; then, unlocking an *escritoire*, took thence a letter and gave it to the Prefect. This functionary grasped it in a perfect agony of joy, opened it with a trembling hand, cast a rapid glance at its contents, and then, scrambling and struggling to the door, rushed at length unceremoniously from the room and from the house, without having uttered a syllable since Dupin had requested him to fill up the check.

When he had gone, my friend entered into some explanations.

"The Parisian police," he said, "are exceedingly able in their way. They are persevering, ingenious, cunning, and thoroughly versed in the knowledge which their duties seem chiefly to demand. Thus, when G — — detailed to us his mode of searching the premises at the Hotel D — — , I felt entire confidence in his having made a satisfactory investigation — so far as his labors extended."

"So far as his labors extended?" said I.

"Yes," said Dupin. "The measures adopted were not only the best of their kind, but carried out to absolute perfection. Had the letter been deposited within the range of their search, these fellows would, beyond a question, have found it."

I merely laughed—but he seemed quite serious in all that he said.

"The measures, then," he continued, "were good in their kind, and well executed; their defect lay in their being inapplicable to the case, and to the man. A certain set of highly ingenious resources are, with the Prefect, a sort of Procrustean bed, to which he forcibly adapts his designs. But he perpetually errs by being too deep or too shallow, for the matter in hand; and many a schoolboy is a better reasoner than he. I knew one about eight years of age, whose success at guessing in the game of 'even and odd' attracted universal admiration. This game is simple, and is played with marbles. One player holds in his hand a number of these toys, and demands of another whether that number is even or odd. If the guess is right, the guesser wins one; if wrong, he loses one. The boy to whom I allude won all the marbles of the school. Of course he had some principle of guessing; and this lay in mere observation and admeasurement of the astuteness of his opponents. For example, an arrant simpleton is his opponent, and, holding up his closed hand, asks, 'are they even or odd?' Our schoolboy replies, 'odd,' and loses; but upon the second trial he wins, for he then says to himself, 'The simpleton had them even upon the first trial, and his amount of cunning is just sufficient to make him have them odd upon the second; I will therefore guess odd;'—he guesses odd, and wins. Now, with a simpleton a degree above the first, he would have reasoned thus: 'This fellow finds that in the first instance I guessed odd, and, in the second, he will propose to himself, upon the first impulse, a simple variation from even to odd, as did the first simpleton; but then a second thought will suggest that this is too simple a variation, and finally he will decide upon putting it even as before. I will therefore guess even;'—he guesses even, and wins. Now this mode of reasoning in the schoolboy, whom his fellows termed 'lucky,'—what, in its last analysis, is it?"

"It is merely," I said, "an identification of the reasoner's intellect with that of his opponent."

"It is," said Dupin; "and, upon inquiring of the boy by what means he effected the *thorough* identification in which his success consisted, I received answer as follows: 'When I wish to find out how wise, or how stupid, or how good, or how wicked is anyone, or what are his thoughts at the moment, I fashion the expression of my face, as accurately as possible, in accordance with the expression of his, and then wait to see what thoughts or sentiments arise in my mind or heart, as if to match or correspond with the expression.' This response of the schoolboy lies at the bottom of all the spurious profundity which has been attributed to Rochefoucault, to La Bougive, to Machiavelli, and to Campanella."

"And the identification," I said, "of the reasoner's intellect with that of his opponent, depends, if I understand you aright, upon the accuracy with which the opponent's intellect is admeasured."

"For its practical value it depends upon this," replied Dupin; "and the Prefect and his cohort fail so frequently, first, by default of this identification, and, secondly, by ill-admeasurement, or rather through non-admeasurement, of the intellect with which they are engaged. They consider only their *own* ideas of ingenuity; and, in searching for anything hidden, advert only to the modes in which *they* would have hidden it. They are right in this much—that their own ingenuity is a faithful representative of that of *the mass;* but when the cunning of the individual felon is diverse in character from their own, the felon foils them, of course. This always happens when it is above their own, and very usually when it is below. They have no variation of principle in their investigations; at best, when urged by some unusual emergency—by some extraordinary reward—they extend or exaggerate their old modes of *practice*, without touching their principles. What, for example, in this case of D — — , has been done to vary the principle of action? What is all this boring, and probing, and sounding, and scrutinizing with the microscope, and dividing the surface of the building into registered square inches—what is it all but an exaggeration *of the application* of the one principle or set of principles of search, which are based upon the one set of notions regarding human ingenuity, to which the Prefect, in the long routine of his duty, has been accustomed? Do you not see he has taken it for granted that *all* men proceed to conceal a letter—not exactly in a gimlet-hole bored in a chair-leg—but, at least, in *some* out-of-the-way hole or corner suggested by the same tenor of thought which would urge a man to secrete a letter in a gimlet-hole bored in a chair-leg? And do you not see also that such *recherché* nooks for concealment are adapted only for ordinary occasions, and would be adopted only by ordinary intellects; for, in all cases of concealment, a disposal of the article concealed—a disposal of it in this *recherché* manner—is, in the very first instance, presumable and presumed; and thus its discovery depends, not at all upon the acumen, but altogether upon the mere care, patience, and determination of the seekers; and where the case is of importance—or, what amounts to the same thing in the policial eyes, when the reward is of magnitude—the qualities in question have *never* been known to fail. You will now understand what I meant in suggesting that, had the purloined letter been hidden any where within the limits of the Prefect's examination—in other words, had the principle of its concealment been comprehended within the principles of the Prefect—its discovery would have been a matter altogether beyond question. This functionary, however, has been thoroughly mystified; and the remote source of his defeat lies in the supposition that the minister is a fool, because he has acquired renown as a poet. All fools are poets; this the Prefect *feels;* and he is merely guilty of a *non distributio medii* in thence inferring that all poets are fools."

"But is this really the poet?" I asked. "There are two brothers, I know; and both have attained reputation in letters. The minister I believe has written learnedly on the Differential Calculus. He is a mathematician, and no poet."

"You are mistaken; I know him well; he is both. As poet *and* mathematician, he would reason well; as mere mathematician, he could not have reasoned at all, and thus would have been at the mercy of the Prefect."

"You surprise me," I said, "by these opinions, which have been contradicted by the voice of the world. You do not mean to set at naught the well-digested idea of centuries? The mathematical reason has long been regarded as *the* reason *par excellence*."

"'*Il y a à parièr*,'" replied Dupin, quoting from Chamfort, "'*que toute idée publique, toute convention reçue est une sottise, car elle a convenue au plus grand nombre*.' The mathematicians, I grant you, have done their best to promulgate the popular error to which you allude, and which is none the less an error for its promulgation as truth. With an art worthy a better cause, for example, they have insinuated the term 'analysis' into application to algebra. The French are the originators of this particular deception; but if a term is of any importance—if words derive any value from applicability—then 'analysis' conveys 'algebra' about as much as, in Latin, '*ambitus*' implies 'ambition,' '*religio*' 'religion,' or '*homines honesti*,' a set of *honorable* men."

"You have a quarrel on hand, I see," said I, "with some of the algebraists of Paris; but proceed."

"I dispute the availability, and thus the value, of that reason which is cultivated in any especial form other than the abstractly logical. I dispute, in particular, the reason educed by mathematical study. The mathematics are the science of form and quantity; mathematical reasoning is merely logic applied to observation upon form and quantity. The great error lies in supposing that even the truths of what is called *pure* algebra are abstract or general truths. And this error is so egregious that I am confounded at the universality with which it has been received. Mathematical axioms are *not* axioms of general truth. What is true of *relation*—of form and quantity—is often grossly false in regard to morals, for example. In this latter science it is very usually *un*true that the aggregated parts are equal to the whole. In chemistry also the axiom fails. In the consideration of motive it fails; for two motives, each of a given value, have not, necessarily, a value when united equal to the sum of their values apart. There are numerous other mathematical truths which are only truths within the limits of *relation*. But the mathematician argues, from his *finite truths*, through habit, as if they were of an absolutely general applicability—as the world indeed imagines them to be. Bryant, in his very learned *Mythology*, mentions an analogous source of error, when he says that 'although the Pagan fables are not believed, yet we forget ourselves continually, and make inferences from them as existing realities.' With the algebraists, however, who are Pagans themselves, the 'Pagan fables' *are* believed, and the inferences are made, not so much through lapse of memory, as through an unaccountable addling of the brains. In short, I never yet encountered the mere mathematician who could be trusted out of equal roots, or one who did not clandestinely hold it as a point of his faith that $x^2 + px$ was absolutely and unconditionally equal to q. Say to one of these gentlemen, by way of experiment, if you please, that you believe occasions may occur where $x^2 + px$ is *not* altogether equal to q, and, having made him understand what you mean, get out of his reach as speedily as convenient, for, beyond doubt, he will endeavor to knock you down.

"I mean to say," continued Dupin, while I merely laughed at his last observations, "that if the minister had been no more than a mathematician, the Prefect would have been under no necessity of giving me this check. Had he been no more than a poet, I think it probable that he would have foiled us all. I knew him, however, as both mathematician and poet, and my measures were adapted to his capacity, with reference to the circumstances by which he was surrounded. I knew him as a courtier, too, and as a bold *intriguant*. Such a man, I considered, could not fail to be aware of the ordinary policial modes of action. He could not have failed to anticipate—and events have proved that he did not fail to anticipate—the waylayings to which he was subjected. He must have foreseen, I reflected, the secret investigations of his premises. His frequent absences from home at night, which were hailed by the Prefect as certain aids to his success, I regarded only as *ruses*, to afford opportunity for thorough search to the police, and thus the sooner to impress them with the conviction to which G — — , in fact, did finally arrive—the conviction that the letter was not upon the premises. I felt, also, that the whole train of thought, which I was at some pains in detailing to you just now, concerning the invariable principle of policial action in searches for articles concealed—I felt that this whole train of thought would necessarily pass through the mind of the minister. It would imperatively lead him to despise all the ordinary *nooks* of concealment. *He* could not, I reflected, be so weak as not to see that the most intricate and remote recess of his hotel would be as open as his commonest closets to the eyes, to the probes, to the gimlets, and to the microscopes of the Prefect. I saw, in fine, that he would be driven, as a matter of course, to *simplicity*, if not deliberately induced to it as a matter of choice. You will remember, perhaps, how desperately the Prefect laughed when I suggested, upon our first interview, that it was just possible this mystery troubled him so much on account of its being so *very* self-evident."

"Yes," said I, "I remember his merriment well. I really thought he would have fallen into convulsions."

"The material world," continued Dupin, "abounds with very strict analogies to the immaterial; and thus some color of truth has been given to the rhetorical dogma, that metaphor, or simile, may be made to strengthen an argument, as well as to embellish a description. The principle of the *vis inertiæ*, for example, seems to be identical in physics and metaphysics. It is not more true in the former that a large body is with more difficulty set in motion than a smaller one, and that its subsequent *impetus* is commensurate with this difficulty, than it is, in the latter, that intellects of the vaster capacity, while more forcible, more constant, and more eventful in their movements than those of inferior grade, are yet the less readily moved, and more embarrassed and full of hesitation in the first few steps of their progress. Again: have you ever noticed which of the street signs, over the shop-doors, are the most attractive of attention?"

"I have never given the matter a thought," I said.

"There is a game of puzzles," he resumed, "which is played upon a map. One party playing requires another to find a given word—the name of town, river, state or empire—any word, in short, upon the motley and perplexed surface of the chart. A novice in the game generally seeks to embarrass his opponents by giving them the most minutely lettered names; but the adept selects such words as stretch, in large characters, from one end of the chart to the other. These, like the overlargely lettered signs and placards of the street, escape observation by dint of being excessively obvious; and here the physical oversight is precisely analogous with the moral inapprehension by which the intellect suffers to pass unnoticed those considerations which are too obtrusively and too palpably self-evident. But this is a point, it appears, somewhat above or beneath the understanding of the Prefect. He never once thought it probable, or possible, that the minister had deposited the letter immediately beneath the nose of the whole world, by way of best preventing any portion of that world from perceiving it.

"But the more I reflected upon the daring, dashing, and discriminating ingenuity of D — — ; upon the fact that the document must always have been *at hand*, if he intended to use it to good purpose; and upon the decisive evidence, obtained by the Prefect, that it was not hidden within the limits of that dignitary's ordinary search—the more satisfied I became that, to conceal this letter, the minister had resorted to the comprehensive and sagacious expedient of not attempting to conceal it at all.

"Full of these ideas, I prepared myself with a pair of green spectacles, and called one fine morning, quite by accident, at the ministerial hotel. I found D — — at home, yawning, lounging, and dawdling, as usual, and pretending to be in the last extremity of *ennui*. He is, perhaps, the most really energetic human being now alive—but that is only when nobody sees him.

"To be even with him, I complained of my weak eyes, and lamented the necessity of the spectacles, under cover of which I cautiously and thoroughly surveyed the apartment, while seemingly intent only upon the conversation of my host.

"I paid especial attention to a large writing-table near which he sat, and upon which lay confusedly some miscellaneous letters and other papers, with one or two musical instruments and a few books. Here, however, after a long and very deliberate scrutiny, I saw nothing to excite particular suspicion.

"At length my eyes, in going the circuit of the room, fell upon a trumpery filigree card-rack of pasteboard, that hung dangling by a dirty blue ribbon, from a little brass knob just beneath the middle of the mantel-piece. In this rack, which had three or four compartments, were five or six visiting cards and a solitary letter. This last was much soiled and crumpled. It was torn nearly in two, across the middle—as if a design, in the first instance, to tear it entirely up as worthless, had been altered, or stayed, in the second. It had a large black seal, bearing the D — — cipher *very* conspicuously, and was addressed, in a diminutive female hand, to D — — , the minister, himself. It was thrust carelessly, and even, as it seemed, contemptuously, into one of the upper divisions of the rack.

"No sooner had I glanced at this letter, than I concluded it to be that of which I was in search. To be sure, it was, to all appearance, radically different from the one of which the Prefect had read us so minute a description. Here the seal was large and black, with the D — — cipher; there it was small and red, with the ducal arms of the S — — family. Here, the address, to the minister, was diminutive and feminine; there the superscription, to a certain royal personage, was markedly bold and decided; the size alone formed a point of correspondence. But, then, the *radicalness* of these differences, which was excessive; the dirt; the soiled and torn condition of the paper, so inconsistent with the *true* methodical habits of D — —, and so suggestive of a design to delude the beholder into an idea of the worthlessness of the document; these things, together with the hyper-obtrusive situation of this document, full in the view of every visitor, and thus exactly in accordance with the conclusions to which I had previously arrived; these things, I say, were strongly corroborative of suspicion, in one who came with the intention to suspect.

"I protracted my visit as long as possible, and, while I maintained a most animated discussion with the minister, upon a topic which I knew well had never failed to interest and excite him, I kept my attention really riveted upon the letter. In this examination, I committed to memory its external appearance and arrangement in the rack; and also fell, at length, upon a discovery which set at rest whatever trivial doubt I might have entertained. In scrutinizing the edges of the paper, I observed them to be more *chafed* than seemed necessary. They presented the *broken* appearance which is manifested when a stiff paper, having been once folded and pressed with a folder, is refolded in a reversed direction, in the same creases or edges which had formed the original fold. This discovery was sufficient. It was clear to me that the letter had been turned, as a glove, inside out, redirected, and resealed. I bade the minister good morning, and took my departure at once, leaving a gold snuff-box upon the table.

"The next morning I called for the snuff-box, when we resumed, quite eagerly, the conversation of the preceding day. While thus engaged, however, a loud report, as if of a pistol, was heard immediately beneath the windows of the hotel, and was succeeded by a series of fearful screams, and the shoutings of a mob. D — — rushed to a casement, threw it open, and looked out. In the meantime, I stepped to the card-rack, took the letter, put it in my pocket, and replaced it by a *facsimile*, (so far as regards externals), which I had carefully prepared at my lodgings—imitating the D — — cipher, very readily, by means of a seal formed of bread.

"The disturbance in the street had been occasioned by the frantic behavior of a man with a musket. He had fired it among a crowd of women and children. It proved, however, to have been without ball, and the fellow was suffered to go his way as a lunatic or a drunkard. When he had gone, D — — came from the window, whither I had followed him immediately upon securing the object in view. Soon afterward I bade him farewell. The pretended lunatic was a man in my own pay."

"But what purpose had you," I asked, "in replacing the letter by a *facsimile?* Would it not have been better, at the first visit, to have seized it openly, and departed?"

"D — —," replied Dupin, "is a desperate man, and a man of nerve. His hotel, too, is not without attendants devoted to his interests. Had I made the wild attempt you suggest, I might never have left the ministerial presence alive. The good people of Paris might have heard of me no more. But I had an object apart from these considerations. You know my political prepossessions. In this matter, I act as a partisan of the lady concerned. For eighteen months the minister has had her in his power. She has now him in hers—since, being unaware that the letter is not in his possession, he will proceed with his exactions as if it was. Thus will he inevitably commit himself, at once, to his political destruction. His downfall, too, will not be more precipitate than awkward. It is all very well to talk about the *facilis descensus Averni;* but in all kinds of climbing, as Catalani said of singing, it is far more easy to get up than to come down. In the present instance I have no sympathy—at least no pity—for him who descends. He is that *monstrum horrendum*, an unprincipled man of genius. I confess, however, that I should like very well to know the precise character of his thoughts, when, being defied by her whom the

Prefect terms 'a certain personage,' he is reduced to opening the letter which I left for him in the card-rack."

"How? Did you put any thing particular in it?"

"Why—it did not seem altogether right to leave the interior blank—that would have been insulting. D — —, at Vienna once, did me an evil turn, which I told him, quite good-humoredly, that I should remember. So, as I knew he would feel some curiosity in regard to the identity of the person who had outwitted him, I thought it a pity not to give him a clue. He is well acquainted with my MS., and I just copied into the middle of the blank sheet the words —

"'—— *Un dessein si funeste, S'il n'est digne d'Atrée, est digne de Thyeste. They are to be found in Crébillon's 'Atrée.'*"

THE UNPARALLELED ADVENTURE OF ONE HANS PFAALL

With a heart of furious fancies, Whereof I am commander, With a burning spear and a horse of air, To the wilderness I wander.

Tom O'Bedlam's Song

BY LATE ACCOUNTS from Rotterdam, that city seems to be in a high state of philosophical excitement. Indeed, phenomena have there occurred of a nature so completely unexpected—so entirely novel—so utterly at variance with preconceived opinions—as to leave no doubt on my mind that long ere this all Europe is in an uproar, all physics in a ferment, all reason and astronomy together by the ears.

It appears that on the ——— day of ———, (I am not positive about the date), a vast crowd of people, for purposes not specifically mentioned, were assembled in the great square of the Exchange in the well-conditioned city of Rotterdam. The day was warm—unusually so for the season—there was hardly a breath of air stirring; and the multitude were in no bad humor at being now and then besprinkled with friendly showers of momentary duration, that fell from large white masses of cloud profusely distributed about the blue vault of the firmament. Nevertheless, about noon, a slight but remarkable agitation became apparent in the assembly; the clattering of ten thousand tongues succeeded; and, in an instant afterward, ten thousand faces were upturned toward the heavens, ten thousand pipes descended simultaneously from the corners of ten thousand mouths, and a shout, which could be compared to nothing but the roaring of Niagara, resounded long, loudly and furiously, through all the city and through all the environs of Rotterdam.

The origin of this hubbub soon became sufficiently evident. From behind the huge bulk of one of those sharply defined masses of cloud already mentioned, was seen slowly to emerge into an open area of blue space a queer, heterogeneous, but apparently solid substance, so oddly shaped, so whimsically put together as not to be in any manner comprehended, and never to be sufficiently admired, by the host of sturdy burghers who stood open-mouthed below. What could it be? In the name of all the devils in Rotterdam, what could it possibly portend? No one knew; no one could imagine; no one—not even the burgomaster Mynheer Superbus Von Underduk—had the slightest clew by which to unravel the mystery; so, as nothing more reasonable could be done, everyone to a man replaced his pipe carefully in the corner of his mouth, and maintaining an eye steadily upon the phenomenon, puffed, paused, waddled about, and grunted significantly—then waddled back, grunted, paused, and finally—puffed again.

In the meantime, however, lower and still lower toward the goodly city came the object of so much curiosity, and the cause of so much smoke. In a very few minutes it arrived near enough to be accurately discerned. It appeared to be—yes! It *was* undoubtedly a species of balloon; but surely no *such* balloon had ever been seen in Rotterdam before. For who, let me ask, ever heard of a balloon manufactured entirely of dirty newspapers? No man in Holland certainly; yet here, under the very noses of the people, or rather at some distance *above* their noses, was the identical thing in question, and composed, I have it on the best authority, of the precise material which no one had ever before known to be used for a similar purpose.—It was an egregious insult to the good sense of the burghers of Rotterdam. As to the shape of the phenomenon, it was even still more reprehensible. Being little or nothing better than a huge fool's-cap turned upside down. And this similitude was regarded as by no means lessened, when upon nearer inspection, the crowd saw a large tassel depending from its apex, and, around the upper rim or base of the cone, a circle of little instruments, resembling sheep-bells, which kept up a continual tinkling to the tune of "Betty Martin".—But still worse. Suspended by blue ribbons to the end of this fantastic machine, there hung, by way of car, an enormous drab beaver hat, with a brim superlatively broad, and a hemispherical crown with a black band and a silver buckle. It is, however, somewhat remarkable that many citizens of Rotterdam swore to having seen the same hat repeatedly before; and indeed the whole assembly seemed to regard it with eyes of familiarity; while the *vrow* Grettel Pfaall, upon sight of it, uttered an exclamation of joyful surprise, and declared it to be the identical hat of her good man himself. Now this was a circumstance the more to be observed, as Pfaall, with three companions, had actually disappeared from Rotterdam about five years before, in a very sudden and unaccountable manner, and up to the date of this narrative all attempts at obtaining intelligence concerning them had failed. To be sure, some bones which were thought to be human, mixed up with a quantity of odd-looking rubbish, had been lately discovered in a retired situation to the east of the city; and some people went so far as to imagine that in this spot a foul murder had been committed, and that the sufferers were in all probability Hans Pfaall and his associates.—But to return.

The balloon (for such no doubt it was) had now descended to within a hundred feet of the earth, allowing the crowd below a sufficiently distinct view of the person of its occupant. This was in truth a very singular somebody. He could not have been more than two feet in height; but this altitude, little as it was, would have been sufficient to destroy his *equilibrium*, and tilt him over the edge of his tiny car, but for the intervention of a circular rim reaching as high as the breast, and rigged on to the cords of the balloon. The body of the little man was more than proportionally broad, giving to his entire figure a rotundity highly absurd. His feet, of course, could not be seen at all. His hands were enormously large. His hair was gray, and collected into a *queue* behind. His nose was prodigiously long, crooked and inflammatory; his eyes full, brilliant, and acute; his chin and cheeks, although wrinkled with age, were broad, puffy, and double; but of ears of any kind there was not a semblance to be discovered upon any portion of his head. This odd little gentleman was dressed in a loose surtout of sky-blue satin, with tight breeches to match, fastened with silver buckles at the knees. His vest was of some bright yellow material; a white taffeta cap was set jauntily on one side of his head; and, to complete his equipment, a blood-red silk handkerchief enveloped his throat, and fell down, in a dainty manner, upon his bosom, in a fantastic bow-knot of super-eminent dimensions.

Having descended, as I said before, to about one hundred feet from the surface of the earth, the little old gentleman was suddenly seized with a fit of trepidation, and appeared disinclined to make any nearer approach to *terra firma*. Throwing out, therefore, a quantity of sand from a canvass bag, which he lifted with great difficulty, he became stationary in an instant. He then proceeded, in a hurried and agitated manner, to extract from a side-pocket in his surtout a large morocco pocket-book. This he poised suspiciously in his hand; then eyed it with an air of extreme surprise, and was evidently astonished at its weight. He at length opened it, and, drawing therefrom a huge letter sealed with red sealing-wax and tied carefully with red tape, let it fall precisely at the feet of the burgomaster Superbus Von Underduk. His Excellency stooped to take it up. But the æronaut, still greatly discomposed, and having apparently no further business to detain him in Rotterdam, began at this moment to make busy preparations for departure; and, it being necessary to discharge a portion of ballast to enable him to reascend, the half dozen bags which he threw out, one after another, without taking the trouble to empty their contents, tumbled, every one of them, most unfortunately, upon the back of the burgomaster, and rolled him over and over no less than half a dozen times, in the face of every individual in Rotterdam. It is not to be supposed, however, that the great Underduk suffered this impertinence on the part of the little old man to pass off with impunity. It is said, on the contrary, that during each of his half dozen circumvolutions, he emitted no less than half a dozen distinct and furious whiffs from his pipe, to which he held fast the whole time with all his might, and to which he intends holding fast, (God willing), until the day of his decease.

In the meantime the balloon arose like a lark, and, soaring far away above the city, at length drifted quietly behind a cloud similar to that from which it had so oddly emerged, and was thus lost forever to the wondering eyes of the good citizens of Rotterdam. All attention was now directed to the letter, the descent of which, and the consequences attending thereupon, had proved so fatally subversive of both person and personal dignity to his Excellency, Von Underduk. That functionary, however, had not failed, during his circumgyratory movements, to bestow a thought upon the important object of securing the epistle, which was seen, upon inspection, to have fallen into the most proper hands, being actually addressed to himself and Professor Rubadub, in their official capacities of President and Vice-President of the Rotterdam College of Astronomy. It was accordingly opened by those dignitaries upon the spot, and found to contain the following extraordinary, and indeed very serious, communication:—*To their Excellencies Von Underduk and Rubadub, President and Vice-President of the States' College of Astronomers, in the city of Rotterdam.*

> Your Excellencies may perhaps be able to remember an humble artisan, by name Hans Pfaall, and by occupation a mender of bellows, who, with three others, disappeared from Rotterdam, about five years ago, in a manner which must have been considered unaccountable. If, however, it so please your Excellencies, I, the writer of this communication, am the identical Hans Pfaall himself. It is well known to most of my fellow-citizens, that for the period of forty years I continued to occupy the little square brick building, at the head of the alley called Sauerkraut, in which I resided at the time of my disappearance. My ancestors have also resided therein time out of mind—they, as well as myself, steadily following the respectable and indeed lucrative profession of mending of bellows: for, to speak the truth, until of late years, that the heads of all the people have been set agog with politics, no better business than my own could an honest citizen of Rotterdam either desire or deserve. Credit was good, employment was never wanting, and there was no lack of either money or good will. But, as I was saying, we soon began to feel the effects of liberty, and long speeches, and radicalism, and all that sort of thing. People who were formerly the very best customers in the world had now not a moment of time to think of us at all. They had as much as they could do to read about the revolutions, and keep up with the march of intellect and the spirit of the age. If a fire wanted fanning, it could readily be fanned with a newspaper; and as the government grew weaker, I have no doubt that leather and iron acquired durability in proportion—for, in a very short time, there was not a pair of bellows in all Rotterdam that ever stood in need of a stitch or

required the assistance of a hammer. This was a state of things not to be endured. I soon grew as poor as a rat, and, having a wife and children to provide for, my burdens at length became intolerable, and I spent hour after hour in reflecting upon the most convenient method of putting an end to my life. Duns, in the meantime, left me little leisure for contemplation. My house was literally besieged from morning till night. There were three fellows in particular, who worried me beyond endurance, keeping watch continually about my door, and threatening me with the law. Upon these three I vowed the bitterest revenge, if ever I should be so happy as to get them within my clutches; and I believe nothing in the world but the pleasure of this anticipation prevented me from putting my plan of suicide into immediate execution, by blowing my brains out with a blunderbuss. I thought it best, however, to dissemble my wrath, and to treat them with promises and fair words, until, by some good turn of fate, an opportunity of vengeance should be afforded me.

One day, having given them the slip, and feeling more than usually dejected, I continued for a long time to wander about the most obscure streets without object, until at length I chanced to stumble against the corner of a bookseller's stall. Seeing a chair close at hand, for the use of customers, I threw myself doggedly into it, and, hardly knowing why, opened the pages of the first volume which came within my reach. It proved to be a small pamphlet treatise on Speculative Astronomy, written either by Professor Encke of Berlin, or by a Frenchman of somewhat similar name. I had some little tincture of information on matters of this nature, and soon became more and more absorbed in the contents of the book—reading it actually through twice before I awoke to a recollection of what was passing around me. By this time it began to grow dark, and I directed my steps toward home. But the treatise (in conjunction with a discovery in pneumatics, lately communicated to me as an important secret, by a cousin from Nantz), had made an indelible impression on my mind, and, as I sauntered along the dusky streets, I revolved carefully over in my memory the wild and sometimes unintelligible reasonings of the writer. There were some particular passages which affected my imagination in an extraordinary manner. The longer I meditated upon these, the more intense grew the interest which had been excited within me. The limited nature of my education in general, and more especially my ignorance on subjects connected with natural philosophy, so far from rendering me diffident of my own ability to comprehend what I had read, or inducing me to mistrust the many vague notions which had arisen in consequence, merely served as a farther stimulus to imagination; and I was vain enough, or perhaps reasonable enough, to doubt whether those crude ideas which, arising in ill-regulated minds, have all the appearance, may not often in effect possess all the force, the reality, and other inherent properties of instinct or intuition.

It was late when I reached home, and I went immediately to bed. My mind, however, was too much occupied to sleep, and I lay the whole night buried in meditation. Arising early in the morning, I repaired eagerly to the bookseller's stall, and laid out what little ready money I possessed, in the purchase of some volumes of Mechanics and Practical Astronomy. Having arrived at home safely with these, I devoted every spare moment to their perusal, and soon made such proficiency in studies of this nature as I thought sufficient for the execution of a certain design with which either the devil or my better genius had inspired me. In the intervals of this period, I made every endeavor to conciliate the three creditors who had given me so much annoyance. In this I finally succeeded—partly by selling enough of my household furniture to satisfy a moiety of their claim, and partly by a promise of paying the balance upon completion of a little project which I told them I had in view, and for assistance in which I solicited their services. By these means (for they were ignorant men) I found little difficulty in gaining them over to my purpose.

Matters being thus arranged, I contrived, by the aid of my wife, and with the greatest secrecy and caution, to dispose of what property I had remaining, and to borrow, in small sums, under various pretences, and without giving any attention (I am ashamed to say) to my future means of repayment, no inconsiderable quantity of ready money. With the means thus accruing I proceeded to procure at intervals, cambric muslin, very fine, in pieces of twelve yards each; twine; a lot of the varnish of caoutchouc; a large and deep basket of wickerwork, made to order; and several other articles necessary in the construction and equipment of a balloon of extraordinary dimensions. This I directed my wife to make up as soon as possible, and gave her all requisite information as to the particular method of proceeding. In the meantime I worked up the twine into net-work of sufficient dimensions; rigged it with a hoop and the necessary cords; and made purchase of numerous instruments and materials for experiment in the upper regions of the upper atmosphere. I then took opportunities of conveying by night, to a retired situation east of Rotterdam, five iron-bound casks, to contain about fifty gallons each, and one of a larger size; six tin tubes, three inches in diameter, properly shaped, and ten feet in length; a quantity of a *particular metallic substance, or semi-metal* which I shall not name, and a dozen demijohns of *a very common acid*. The gas to be formed from these latter materials is a gas never yet generated by any other person than myself—or at least never applied to any similar purpose. I can only venture to say here that it is *a constituent of azote*, so long considered irreducible, and that its density is about 37.4 times *less than that of hydrogen*. It is tasteless, but not odorless; burns, when pure, with a greenish flame, and is instantaneously fatal to animal life. Its full secret I would make no difficulty in disclosing, but that it of right belongs (as I have before hinted) to a citizen of Nantz, in France, by whom it was conditionally communicated to myself. The same individual submitted to me, without being at all aware of my intentions, a method of constructing balloons from the membrane of a certain animal, through which substance any escape of gas was nearly an impossibility. I found it, however, altogether too expensive, and was not sure, upon the whole, whether cambric muslin with a coating of gum caoutchouc was not equally as good. I mention this circumstance, because I think it probable that hereafter the individual in question may attempt a balloon ascension with the novel gas and material I have spoken of, and I do not wish to deprive him of the honor of a very singular invention.

On the spot which I intended each of the smaller casks to occupy respectively during the inflation of the balloon, I privately dug a small hole; the holes forming in this manner a circle twenty-five feet in diameter. In the center of this circle, being the station designed for the large cask, I also dug a hole of greater depth. In each of the five smaller holes, I deposited a canister containing fifty pounds, and in the larger one a keg holding one hundred and fifty pounds of cannon powder. These—the keg and the canisters—I connected in a proper manner with covered trains; and having let into one of the canisters the end of about four feet of slow-match, I covered up the hole, and placed the cask over it, leaving the other end of the match protruding about an inch, and barely visible beyond the cask. I then filled up the remaining holes, and placed the barrels over them in their destined situation!

Besides the articles above enumerated, I conveyed to the *dépôt*, and there secreted, one of M. Grimm's improvements upon the apparatus for condensation of the atmospheric air. I found this machine, however, to require considerable alteration before it could be adapted to the purposes to which I intended making it applicable. But, with severe labor and unremitting perseverance, I at length met with entire success in all my preparations. My balloon was soon completed. It would contain more than forty thousand cubic feet of gas; would take me up easily, I calculated, with all my implements, and, if I managed rightly, with one hundred and seventy-five pounds of ballast into the bargain. It had received three coats of varnish, and I found the cambric muslin to answer all the purposes of silk itself, being quite as strong and a good deal less expensive.

Everything being now ready, I exacted from my wife an oath of secrecy in relation to all my actions from the day of my first visit to the bookseller's stall; and promising, on my part, to return as soon as circumstances would permit, I gave her what little money I had left, and bade her farewell. Indeed I had no fear on her account. She was what people call a notable woman, and could manage matters in the world without my assistance. I believe, to tell the truth, she always looked upon me as an idle body—a mere make-weight—good for nothing but building castles in the air—and was rather glad to get rid of me. It was a dark night when I bade her good bye, and taking with me, as *aides-de-camp*, the three creditors who had given me so much trouble, we carried the balloon, with the car and accoutrements, by a roundabout way, to the station where the other articles were deposited. We there found them all unmolested, and I proceeded immediately to business.

It was the first of April. The night, as I said before, was dark; there was not a star to be seen; and a drizzling rain, falling at intervals, rendered us very uncomfortable. But my chief anxiety was concerning the balloon, which, in spite of the varnish with which it was defended, began to grow rather heavy with the moisture; the powder also was liable to damage. I therefore kept my three duns working with great diligence, pounding down ice around the central cask, and stirring the acid in the others. They did not cease, however, importuning me with questions as to what I intended to do with all this apparatus, and expressed much dissatisfaction at the terrible labor I made them undergo. They could not perceive (so they said) what good was likely to result from their getting wet to the skin, merely to take a part in such horrible incantations. I began to get uneasy, and worked away with all my might; for I verily believe the idiots supposed that I had entered into a compact with the devil, and that, in short, what I was now doing was nothing better than it should be. I was, therefore, in great fear of their leaving me altogether. I contrived, however, to pacify them by promises of payment of all scores in full, as soon as I could bring the present business to a termination. To these speeches they gave of course their own interpretation; fancying, no doubt, that at all events I should come into possession of vast quantities of ready money; and provided I paid them all I owed, and a trifle more, in consideration of their services, I dare say they cared very little what became of either my soul or my carcass.

In about four hours and a half I found the balloon sufficiently inflated. I attached the car, therefore, and put all my implements in it—a telescope; a barometer, with some important modifications; a thermometer; an electrometer; a compass; a magnetic needle; a seconds watch; a bell; a speaking trumpet, etc., etc., etc.—also a globe of glass, exhausted of air, and carefully closed with a stopper—not forgetting the condensing apparatus, some unslacked lime, a stick of sealing wax, a copious supply of water, and a large quantity of provisions, such as pemmican, in which much nutriment is contained in comparatively little bulk. I also secured in the car a pair of pigeons and a cat.

It was now nearly daybreak, and I thought it high time to take my departure. Dropping a lighted cigar on the ground, as if by accident, I took the opportunity, in stooping to pick it up, of igniting privately the piece of slow match, the end of which, as I said before, protruded a little beyond the lower rim of one of the smaller casks. This maneuver was totally unperceived on the part of the three duns; and, jumping into the car, I immediately cut the single cord which held me to the earth, and was pleased to find that I shot upward with inconceivable rapidity, carrying with all ease one hundred and seventy-five pounds of leaden ballast, and able to have carried up as many more. As I left the earth, the barometer stood at thirty inches, and the centigrade thermometer at nineteen degrees.

Scarcely, however, had I attained the height of fifty yards, when, roaring and rumbling up after me in the most tumultuous and terrible manner, came so dense a hurricane of fire, and gravel, and burning wood, and blazing metal, and mangled limbs, that my very heart sunk within me, and I fell down in the bottom of the car, trembling with terror. Indeed, I now perceived that I had entirely overdone the business, and that the main consequences of the shock were yet to be experienced. Accordingly, in less than a second, I felt all the blood in my body rushing to my temples, and, immediately thereupon, a concussion, which I shall never forget, burst abruptly through the night, and seemed to rip the very firmament asunder. When I afterward had time for reflection, I did not fail to attribute the extreme violence of the explosion, as regarded myself, to its proper cause—my situation directly above it, and in the line of its greatest power. But at the time, I thought only of preserving my life. The balloon at first collapsed, then furiously expanded, then whirled round and round with sickening velocity, and finally, reeling and staggering like a drunken man, hurled me over the rim of the car, and left me dangling, at a terrific height, with my head downward, and my face outward, by a piece of slender cord about three feet in length, which hung accidentally through a crevice near the bottom of the wickerwork, and in which, as I fell, my left foot became most providentially entangled. It is impossible—utterly impossible—to form any adequate idea of the horror of my situation. I gasped convulsively for breath—a shudder resembling a fit of the ague agitated every nerve and muscle in my frame—I felt my eyes starting from their sockets—a horrible nausea overwhelmed me—and at length I lost all consciousness in a swoon.

How long I remained in this state it is impossible to say. It must, however, have been no inconsiderable time, for when I partially recovered the sense of existence, I found the day breaking, the balloon at a prodigious height over a wilderness of ocean, and not a trace of land to be discovered far and wide within the limits of the vast horizon. My sensations, however, upon thus recovering, were by no means so replete with agony as might have been anticipated. Indeed, there was much of madness in the calm survey which I began to take of my situation. I drew up to my eyes each of my hands, one after the other, and wondered what occurrence could have given rise to the swelling of the veins, and the horrible blackness of the finger nails. I afterward carefully examined my head, shaking it repeatedly, and feeling it with minute attention, until I succeeded in satisfying myself that it was not, as I had more than half suspected, larger than my balloon. Then, in a knowing manner, I felt in both my breeches pockets, and, missing therefrom a set of tablets and a tooth-pick case, endeavored to account for their disappearance, and, not being able to do so, felt inexpressibly chagrined. It now occurred to me that I suffered great uneasiness in the joint of my left ankle, and a dim consciousness of my situation began to glimmer through my mind. But, strange to say! I was neither astonished nor horror-stricken. If I felt any emotion at all, it was a kind of chuckling satisfaction at the cleverness I was about to display in extricating myself from this dilemma; and never, for a moment, did I look upon my ultimate safety as a question susceptible of doubt. For a few minutes I remained wrapped in the profoundest meditation. I have a distinct recollection of frequently compressing my lips, putting my forefinger to the side of my nose, and making use of other gesticulations and grimaces common to men who, at ease in their arm-chairs, meditate upon matters of intricacy or importance. Having, as I thought, sufficiently collected my ideas, I now, with great caution and deliberation, put my hands behind my back, and unfastened the large iron buckle which belonged to the waist-band of my pantaloons. This buckle had three teeth, which, being somewhat rusty, turned with great difficulty on their axis. I brought them, however, after some trouble, at right angles to the body of the buckle, and was glad to find them remain firm in that position. Holding within my teeth the instrument thus obtained, I now proceeded to untie the knot of my cravat. I had to rest several times before I could accomplish this manœuvre; but it was at length accomplished. To one end of the cravat I then made fast the buckle, and the other end I tied, for greater security, tightly around my wrist. Drawing now my body upward, with a prodigious exertion of muscular force, I succeeded, at the very first trial, in throwing the buckle over the car, and entangling it, as I had anticipated, in the circular rim of the wickerwork.

My body was now inclined toward the side of the car, at an angle of about forty-five degrees; but it must not be understood that I was therefore only forty-five degrees below the perpendicular. So far from it, I still lay nearly level with the plane of the horizon; for the change of situation which I had acquired, had forced the bottom of the car considerably outward from my position, which was accordingly one of the most imminent peril. It should be remembered, however, that when I fell, in the first instance, from the car, if I had fallen with my face turned toward the balloon, instead of turned outwardly from it as it actually was—or if, in the second place, the cord by which I was suspended had chanced to hang over the upper edge, instead of through a crevice near the bottom of the car—I say it may readily be conceived that, in either of these supposed cases, I should have been unable to accomplish even as much as I had now accomplished, and the disclosures now made would have been utterly lost to posterity. I had therefore every reason to be grateful; although, in point of fact, I was still too stupid to be any thing at all, and hung for, perhaps, a quarter of an hour, in that extraordinary manner, without making the slightest farther exertion, and in a singularly tranquil state of idiotic enjoyment. But this feeling did not fail to die rapidly away, and thereunto succeeded horror, and dismay, and a sense of utter helplessness and ruin. In fact, the blood so long accumulating in the vessels of my head and throat, and which had hitherto buoyed up my spirits with delirium, had now begun to retire within their proper channels, and the distinctness which was thus added to my perception of the danger merely served to deprive me of the self-possession and courage to encounter it. But this weakness was, luckily for me, of no very long duration. In good time came to my rescue the spirit of despair, and, with frantic cries and struggles, I jerked my way bodily upward, till, at length, clutching with a vice-like grip the long-desired rim, I writhed my person over it, and fell headlong and shuddering within the car.

It was not until some time afterward that I recovered myself sufficiently to attend to the ordinary cares of the balloon. I then, however, examined it with attention, and found it, to my great relief, uninjured. My implements were all safe, and, fortunately, I had lost neither ballast nor provisions. Indeed, I had so well secured them in their places, that such an accident was entirely out of the question. Looking at my watch, I found it six o'clock. I was still rapidly ascending, and the barometer gave a present altitude of three and three-quarter miles. Immediately beneath me in the ocean lay a small black object, slightly oblong in shape, seemingly about the size of a domino, and in every respect bearing a great resemblance to one of those toys. Bringing my telescope to bear upon it, I plainly discerned it to be a British ninety-four-gun ship, close-hauled, and pitching heavily in the sea with her head to the W.S.W. Besides this ship, I saw nothing but the ocean and the sky, and the sun, which had long arisen.

It is now high time that I should explain to your Excellencies the object of my voyage. Your Excellencies will bear in mind that distressed circumstances in Rotterdam had at length driven me to the resolution of committing suicide. It was not, however, that to life itself I had any positive disgust, but that I was harassed beyond endurance by the adventitious miseries attending my situation. In this state of mind, wishing to live, yet wearied with life, the treatise at the stall of the bookseller, backed by the opportune discovery of my cousin of Nantz, opened a resource to my imagination. I then finally made up my mind. I determined to depart, yet live—to leave the world, yet continue to exist—in short, to drop enigmas,

I resolved, let what would ensue, to force a passage, if I could, *to the moon*. Now, lest I should be supposed more of a madman than I actually am, I will detail, as well as I am able, the considerations which led me to believe that an achievement of this nature, although without doubt difficult, and full of danger, was not absolutely, to a bold spirit, beyond the confines of the possible.

The moon's actual distance from the earth was the first thing to be attended to. Now, the mean or average interval between the *centers* of the two planets is 59.9643 of the earth's equatorial *radii*, or only about 237,000 miles. I say the mean or average interval;—but it must be borne in mind that the form of the moon's orbit being an ellipse of eccentricity amounting to no less than 0.05484 of the major semi-axis of the ellipse itself, and the earth's center being situated in its focus, if I could, in any manner, contrive to meet the moon in its perigee, the above-mentioned distance would be materially diminished. But to say nothing, at present, of this possibility, it was very certain that, at all events, from the 237,000 miles I would have to deduct the *radius* of the earth, say 4000, and the radius of the moon, say 1080, in all 5080, leaving an actual interval to be traversed, under average circumstances, of 231,920 miles. Now this, I reflected, was no very extraordinary distance. Traveling on the land has been repeatedly accomplished at the rate of sixty miles per hour; and indeed a much greater speed may be anticipated. But even at this velocity, it would take me no more than 161 days to reach the surface of the moon. There were, however, many particulars inducing me to believe that my average rate of traveling might possibly very much exceed that of sixty miles per hour, and, as these considerations did not fail to make a deep impression upon my mind, I will mention them more fully hereafter.

The next point to be regarded was one of far greater importance. From indications afforded by the barometer, we find that, in ascensions from the surface of the earth we have, at the height of a 1000 feet, left below us about one-thirtieth of the entire mass of atmospheric air; that at 10,600, we have ascended through nearly one-third; and that at 18,000, which is not far from the elevation of Cotopaxi, we have surmounted one-half the material, or, at all events, one-half the *ponderable* body of air incumbent upon our globe. It is also calculated that at an altitude not exceeding the hundredth part of the earth's diameter—that is, not exceeding eighty miles—the rarefaction would be so excessive that animal life could in no manner be sustained, and, moreover, that the most delicate means we possess of ascertaining the presence of the atmosphere would be inadequate to assure us of its existence. But I did not fail to perceive that these latter calculations are founded altogether on our experimental knowledge of the properties of air, and the mechanical laws regulating its dilation and compression, in what may be called, comparatively speaking, *the immediate vicinity* of the earth itself; and, at the same time, it is taken for granted that animal life is and must be essentially *incapable of modification* at any given unattainable distance from the surface. Now, all such reasoning and from such *data*, must of course be simply analogical. The greatest height ever reached by man was that of 25,000 feet, attained in the æronautic expedition of Messieurs Gay-Lussac and Biot. This is a moderate altitude, even when compared with the eighty miles in question; and I could not help thinking that the subject admitted room for doubt, and great latitude for speculation.

But, in point of fact, an ascension being made to any given altitude, the ponderable quantity of air surmounted in any *farther ascension* is by no means in proportion to the additional height ascended (as may be plainly seen from what has been stated before), but in a *ratio* constantly decreasing. It is therefore evident that, ascend as high as we may, we cannot, literally speaking, arrive at a limit beyond which *no* atmosphere is to be found. It *must exist*, I argued; although it *may* exist in a state of infinite rarefaction.

On the other hand, I was aware that arguments have not been wanting to prove the existence of a real and definite limit to the atmosphere, beyond which there is absolutely no air whatsoever. But a circumstance which has been left out of view by those who contend for such a limit seemed to me, although no positive refutation of their creed, still a point worthy of very serious investigation. On comparing the intervals between the successive arrivals of Encke's comet at its perihelion, after giving credit, in the most exact manner, for all the disturbances due to the attractions of the planets, it appears that the periods are gradually diminishing;

that is to say, the major axis of the comet's ellipse is growing shorter, in a slow but perfectly regular decrease. Now, this is precisely what ought to be the case, if we suppose a resistance experienced from the comet from an extremely *rare ethereal medium* pervading the regions of its orbit. For it is evident that such a medium must, in retarding the comet's velocity, increase its centripetal, by weakening its centrifugal force. In other words, the sun's attraction would be constantly attaining greater power, and the comet would be drawn nearer at every revolution. Indeed, there is no other way of accounting for the variation in question. But again:—The real diameter of the same comet's nebulosity is observed to contract rapidly as it approaches the sun, and dilate with equal rapidity in its departure toward its aphelion. Was I not justifiable in supposing, with M. Valz, that this apparent condensation of volume has its origin in the compression of the same ethereal medium I have spoken of before, and which is dense in proportion to its vicinity to the sun? The lenticular-shaped phenomenon, also, called the zodiacal light, was a matter worthy of attention. This radiance, so apparent in the tropics, and which cannot be mistaken for any meteoric luster, extends from the horizon obliquely upward, and follows generally the direction of the sun's equator. It appeared to me evidently in the nature of a rare atmosphere extending from the sun outward, beyond the orbit of Venus at least, and I believed indefinitely farther. Indeed, this medium I could not suppose confined to the path of the comet's ellipse, or to the immediate neighborhood of the sun. It was easy, on the contrary, to imagine it pervading the entire regions of our planetary system, condensed into what we call atmosphere at the planets themselves, and perhaps at some of them modified by considerations purely geological; that is to say, modified, or varied in its proportions (or absolute nature) by matters volatilized from the respective orbs.

Having adopted this view of the subject, I had little further hesitation. Granting that on my passage I should meet with atmosphere *essentially* the same as at the surface of the earth, I conceived that, by means of the very ingenious apparatus of M. Grimm, I should readily be enabled to condense it in sufficient quantity for the purposes of respiration. This would remove the chief obstacle in a journey to the moon. I had indeed spent some money and great labor in adapting the apparatus to the object intended, and confidently looked forward to its successful application, if I could manage to complete the voyage within any reasonable period.—This brings me back to the *rate* at which it would be possible to travel.

It is true that balloons, in the first stage of their ascensions from the earth, are known to rise with a velocity comparatively moderate. Now, the power of elevation lies altogether in the superior gravity of the atmospheric air compared with the gas in the balloon; and, at first sight, it does not appear probable that, as the balloon acquires altitude, and consequently arrives successively in atmospheric *strata* of densities rapidly diminishing—I say, it does not appear at all reasonable that, in this its progress upward, the original velocity should be accelerated. On the other hand, I was not aware that, in any recorded ascension, a *diminution* had been proved to be apparent in the absolute rate of ascent; although such should have been the case, if on account of nothing else, on account of the escape of gas through balloons ill-constructed, and varnished with no better material than the ordinary varnish. It seemed, therefore, that the effect of such escape was only sufficient to counterbalance the effect of the acceleration attained in the diminishing of the balloon's distance from the gravitating center. I now considered that, provided in my passage I found the *medium* I had imagined, and provided it should prove to be *essentially* what we denominate atmospheric air, it could make comparatively little difference at what extreme state of rarefaction I should discover it—that is to say, in regard to my power of ascending—for the gas in the balloon would not only be itself subject to similar rarefaction (in proportion to the occurrence of which, I could suffer an escape of so much as would be requisite to prevent explosion), but, *being what it was*, would, at all events, continue specifically lighter than any compound whatever of mere nitrogen and oxygen. Thus there was a chance—in fact, there was a strong probability—that, *at no epoch of my ascent, I should reach a point where the united weights of my immense balloon, the inconceivably rare gas within it, the car, and its contents, should equal the weight of the mass of the surrounding atmosphere displaced;* and this will be readily understood as the sole condition upon which my upward flight would be arrested. But, if this point were even attained, I could dispense with ballast and other weight to the amount of nearly 300 pounds. In the meantime, the force of gravitation would be constantly diminishing, in proportion to the squares of the distances, and so, with a velocity prodigiously accelerating, I should at length arrive in those distant regions where the force of the earth's attraction would be superseded by that of the moon.

There was another difficulty, however, which occasioned me some little disquietude. It has been observed, that, in balloon ascensions to any considerable height, besides the pain attending respiration, great uneasiness is experienced about the head and body, often accompanied with bleeding at the nose, and other symptoms of an alarming kind, and growing more and more inconvenient in proportion to the altitude attained. This was a reflection of a nature somewhat startling. Was it not probable that these symptoms would increase until terminated by death itself? I finally thought not. Their origin was to be looked for in the progressive removal of the *customary* atmospheric pressure upon the surface of the body, and consequent distention of the superficial blood-vessels—not in any positive disorganization of the animal system, as in the case of difficulty in breathing, where the atmospheric density is *chemically insufficient* for the due renovation of blood in a ventricle of the heart. Unless for default of this renovation, I could see no reason, therefore, why life could not be sustained even in a *vacuum;* for the expansion and compression of chest, commonly called breathing, is action purely muscular, and the *cause*, not the *effect*, of respiration. In a word, I conceived that, as the body should become habituated to the want of atmospheric pressure, these sensations of pain would gradually diminish—and to endure them while they continued, I relied with confidence upon the iron hardihood of my constitution.

Thus, may it please your Excellencies, I have detailed some, though by no means all, the considerations which led me to form the project of a lunar voyage. I shall now proceed to lay before you the result of an attempt so apparently audacious in conception, and, at all events, so utterly unparalleled in the annals of mankind.

Having attained the altitude before mentioned—that is to say, three miles and three quarters—I threw out from the car a quantity of feathers, and found that I still ascended with sufficient rapidity; there was, therefore, no necessity for discharging any ballast. I was glad of this, for I wished to retain with me as much weight as I could carry, for the obvious reason that I could not be *positive* either about the gravitation or the atmospheric density of the moon. I as yet suffered no bodily inconvenience, breathing with great freedom, and feeling no pain whatever in the head. The cat was lying very demurely upon my coat, which I had taken off, and eyeing the pigeons with an air of *nonchalance*. These latter being tied by the leg, to prevent their escape, were busily employed in picking up some grains of rice scattered for them in the bottom of the car.

At twenty minutes past six o'clock, the barometer showed an elevation of 26,400 feet, or five miles to a fraction. The prospect seemed unbounded. Indeed, it is very easily calculated by means of spherical geometry, how great an extent of the earth's area I beheld. The convex surface of any segment of a sphere is, to the entire surface of the sphere itself, as the versed sine of the segment to the diameter of the sphere. Now, in my case, the versed sine—that is to say, the *thickness* of the segment beneath me—was about equal to my elevation, or the elevation of the point of sight above the surface. "As five miles, then, to eight thousand," would express the proportion of the earth's area seen by me. In other words, I beheld as much as a sixteen-hundredth part of the whole surface of the globe. The sea appeared unruffled as a mirror, although, by means of the telescope, I could perceive it to be in a state of violent agitation. The ship was no longer visible, having drifted away, apparently, to the eastward. I now began to experience, at intervals, severe pain in the head, especially about the ears—still, however, breathing with tolerable freedom. The cat and pigeons seemed to suffer no inconvenience whatsoever.

At twenty minutes before seven, the balloon entered a long series of dense cloud, which put me to great trouble, by damaging my condensing apparatus, and wetting me to the skin. This was, to be sure, a singular *rencontre*, for I had not believed it possible that a cloud of this nature could be sustained at so great an elevation. I thought it best, however, to throw out two five-pound pieces of ballast, reserving still a weight of one hundred and sixty-five pounds. Upon so doing, I soon rose above the difficulty, and perceived immediately that I had obtained a great increase in my rate of ascent. In a few seconds after my leaving the cloud, a flash of vivid lightning shot from one end of it to the other, and caused it to kindle up, throughout its vast extent, like a mass of ignited charcoal. This, it must be remembered, was in the broad light of day. No fancy may picture the sublimity which might have been exhibited by a similar phenomenon taking place amid the darkness of the night. Hell itself might then have found a fitting image. Even as it was, my hair stood on end, while I gazed afar down within the yawning abysses, letting imagination descend, and stalk about in the strange vaulted halls, and ruddy gulfs, and red ghastly chasms of the hideous and unfathomable fire. I had indeed made a narrow escape. Had the balloon remained a very short while longer within the cloud—that is to say, had not the inconvenience of getting wet determined me to discharge the ballast—my destruction might, and probably would, have been the consequence. Such perils, although little considered, are perhaps the greatest which must be encountered in balloons. I had by this time, however, attained too great an elevation to be any longer uneasy on this head.

I was now rising rapidly, and by seven o'clock the barometer indicated an altitude of no less than nine miles and a half. I began to find great difficulty in drawing my breath. My head, too, was excessively painful; and, having felt for some time a moisture about my cheeks, I at length discovered it to be blood, which was oozing quite fast from the drums of my ears. My eyes, also, gave me great uneasiness. Upon passing the hand over them they seemed to have protruded from their sockets in no inconsiderable degree; and all objects in the car, and even the balloon itself, appeared distorted to my vision. These symptoms were more than I had expected, and occasioned me some alarm. At this juncture, very imprudently, and without consideration, I threw out from the car three five-pound pieces of ballast. The accelerated rate of ascent thus obtained, carried me too rapidly, and without sufficient gradation, into a highly rarefied *stratum* of the atmosphere, and the result had nearly proved fatal to my expedition and to myself. I was suddenly seized with a spasm which lasted for more than five minutes, and even when this, in a measure, ceased, I could catch my breath only at long intervals, and in a gasping manner—bleeding all the while copiously at the nose and ears, and even slightly at the eyes. The pigeons appeared distressed in the extreme, and struggled to escape; while the cat mewed piteously, and, with her tongue hanging out of her mouth, staggered to and fro in the car as if under the influence of poison. I now too late discovered the great rashness of which I had been guilty in discharging the ballast, and my agitation was excessive. I anticipated nothing less than death, and death in a few minutes. The physical suffering I underwent contributed also to render me nearly incapable of making any exertion for the preservation of my life. I had, indeed, little power of reflection left, and the violence of the pain in my head seemed to be greatly on the increase. Thus I found that my senses would shortly give way altogether, and I had already clutched one of the valve ropes with the view of attempting a descent, when the recollection of the trick I had played the three creditors, and the possible consequences to myself, should I return, operated to deter me for the moment. I lay down in the bottom of the car, and endeavored to collect my faculties. In this I so far succeeded as to determine upon the experiment of losing blood. Having no lancet, however, I was constrained to perform the operation in the best manner I was able, and finally succeeded in opening a vein in my left arm, with the blade of my penknife. The blood had hardly commenced flowing when I experienced a sensible relief, and by the time I had lost about half a moderate basin-full, most of the worst symptoms had abandoned me entirely. I nevertheless did not think it expedient to attempt getting on my feet immediately; but, having tied up my arm as well as I could, I lay still for about a quarter of an hour. At the end of this time I arose, and found myself freer from absolute *pain* of any kind than I had been during the last hour and a quarter of my ascension. The difficulty of breathing, however, was diminished in a very slight degree, and I found that it would soon be positively necessary to make use of my condenser. In the meantime, looking toward the cat, who was again snugly stowed away upon my coat, I discovered, to my infinite surprise, that she had taken the opportunity of my indisposition to bring into light a litter of three little kittens. This was an addition to the number of passengers on my part altogether unexpected; but I was pleased at the occurrence. It would afford me a chance of bringing to a kind of test the truth of a surmise, which, more than any thing else, had influenced me in attempting this ascension. I had imagined that the *habitual* endurance of the atmospheric pressure at the surface of the earth was the cause, or nearly so, of the pain attending animal existence at a distance above the surface. Should the kittens be found to suffer uneasiness *in an equal degree with their mother*, I must consider my theory in fault, but a failure to do so I should look upon as a strong confirmation of my idea.

By eight o'clock I had actually attained an elevation of seventeen miles above the surface of the earth. Thus it seemed to me evident that my rate of ascent was not only on the increase, but that the progression would have been apparent in a slight degree even had I not discharged the ballast which I did. The pains in my head and ears returned, at intervals, with violence, and I still continued to bleed occasionally at the nose: but, upon the whole, I suffered much less than might have been expected. I breathed, however, at every moment, with more and more difficulty, and each inhalation was attended with a troublesome spasmodic action of the chest. I now unpacked the condensing apparatus, and got it ready for immediate use.

The view of the earth, at this period of my ascension, was beautiful indeed. To the westward, the northward, and the southward, as far as I could see, lay a boundless sheet of apparently unruffled ocean, which every moment gained a deeper and deeper tint of blue. At a vast distance to the eastward, although perfectly discernible, extended the islands of Great Britain, the entire Atlantic coasts of France and Spain, with a small portion of the northern part of the continent of Africa. Of individual edifices not a trace could be discovered, and the proudest cities of mankind had utterly faded away from the face of the earth.

What mainly astonished me, in the appearance of things below, was the seeming concavity of the surface of the globe. I had, thoughtlessly enough, expected to see its real *convexity* become evident as I ascended; but a very little reflection sufficed to explain the discrepancy. A line, dropped from my position perpendicularly to the earth, would have formed the perpendicular of a right-angled triangle, of which the base would have extended from the right-angle to the horizon, and the hypothenuse from the horizon to my position. But my height was little or nothing in comparison with my prospect. In other words, the base and hypothenuse of the supposed triangle would, in my case, have been so long, when compared to the perpendicular, that the two former might have been regarded as nearly parallel. In this manner the horizon of the æronaut appears always to be *upon a level* with the car. But as the point immediately beneath him seems, and is, at a great distance below him, it seems, of course, also at a great distance below the horizon. Hence the impression of concavity; and this impression must remain, until the elevation shall bear so great a proportion to the prospect that the apparent parallelism of the base and hypothenuse disappears.

The pigeons about this time seeming to undergo much suffering, I determined upon giving them their liberty. I first untied one of them, a beautiful gray-mottled pigeon, and placed him upon the rim of the wickerwork. He appeared extremely uneasy, looking anxiously around him, fluttering his wings, and making a loud cooing noise, but could not be persuaded to trust himself from the car. I took him up at last, and threw him to about half-a-dozen yards from the balloon. He made, however, no attempt to descend as I had expected, but struggled with great vehemence to get back, uttering at the same time very shrill and piercing cries. He at length succeeded in regaining his former station on the rim, but had hardly done so when his head dropped upon his breast, and he fell dead within the car. The other one did not prove so unfortunate. To prevent his following the example of his companion, and accomplishing a return, I threw him downward with all my force, and was pleased to find him continue his descent, with great velocity, making use of his wings with ease, and in a perfectly natural manner. In a very short time he was out of sight, and I have no doubt he reached home in safety. Puss, who seemed in a great measure recovered from her illness, now made a hearty meal of the dead bird, and then went to sleep with much apparent satisfaction. Her kittens were quite lively, and so far evinced not the slightest sign of any uneasiness.

At a quarter-past eight, being able no longer to draw breath without the most intolerable pain, I proceeded, forthwith, to adjust around the car the apparatus belonging to the condenser. This apparatus will require some little explanation, and your Excellencies will please to bear in mind that my object, in the first place, was to surround myself and car entirely with a barricade against the highly rarefied atmosphere in which I was existing, with the intention of introducing within this barricade, by means of my condenser, a quantity of this same atmosphere sufficiently condensed for the purposes of respiration. With this object in view I had prepared a very strong, perfectly air-tight, but flexible gum-elastic bag. In this bag, which was of sufficient dimensions, the entire car was in a manner placed. That is to say, it (the bag) was drawn over the whole bottom of the car, up its sides, and so on, along the outside of the ropes, to the upper rim or hoop where the net-work is attached. Having pulled the bag up in this way, and formed a complete enclosure on all sides, and at bottom, it was now necessary to fasten up its top or mouth, by passing its material over the hoop of the net-work—in other words, between the net-work and the hoop. But if the net-work were separated from the hoop to admit this passage, what was to sustain the car in the meantime? Now the net-work was not permanently fastened to the hoop, but attached by a series of running loops or nooses. I therefore undid only a few of these loops at one time, leaving the car suspended by the remainder. Having thus inserted a portion of the cloth forming the upper part of the bag, I refastened the loops—not to the hoop, for that would have been impossible, since the cloth now intervened—but to a series of large buttons, affixed to the cloth itself, about three feet below the mouth of the bag; the intervals between the buttons having been made to correspond to the intervals between the loops. This done, a few more of the loops were unfastened from the rim, a farther portion of the cloth introduced, and the disengaged loops then connected with their proper buttons. In this way it was possible to insert the whole upper part of the bag between the net-work and the hoop. It is evident that the hoop would now drop down within the car, while the whole weight of the car itself, with all its contents, would be held up merely by the strength of the buttons. This, at first sight, would seem an inadequate dependence; but it was by no means so, for the buttons were not only very strong in themselves, but so close together that a very slight portion of the whole weight was supported by any one of them. Indeed, had the car and contents been three times heavier than they were, I should not have been at all uneasy. I now raised up the hoop again within the covering of gum-elastic, and propped it at nearly its former height by means of three light poles prepared for the occasion. This was done, of course, to keep the bag distended at the top, and to preserve the lower part of the net-work in its proper situation. All that now remained was to fasten up the mouth of the enclosure; and this was readily accomplished by gathering the folds of the material together, and twisting them up very tightly on the inside by means of a kind of stationary *tourniquet*.

In the sides of the covering thus adjusted round the car had been inserted three circular panes of thick but clear glass, through which I could see without difficulty around me in every horizontal direction. In that portion of the cloth forming the bottom was likewise a fourth window, of the same kind, and corresponding with a small aperture in the floor of the car itself. This enabled me to see perpendicularly down, but having found it impossible to place any similar contrivance overhead, on account of the peculiar manner of closing up the opening there, and the consequent wrinkles in the cloth, I could expect to see no objects situated directly in my zenith. This, of course, was a matter of little consequence; for, had I even been able to place a window at top, the balloon itself would have prevented my making any use of it.

About a foot below one of the side windows was a circular opening, three inches in diameter, and fitted with a brass rim adapted in its inner edge to the windings of a screw. In this rim was screwed the large tube of the condenser, the body of the machine being, of course, within the chamber of gum-elastic. Through this tube a quantity of the rare atmosphere circumjacent being drawn by means of a *vacuum* created in the body of the machine was thence discharged, in a state of condensation, to mingle with the thin air already in the chamber. This operation, being repeated several times, at length filled the chamber with atmosphere proper for all the purposes of respir-ation. But in so confined a space it would, in a short time, necessarily become foul, and unfit for use from frequent contact with the lungs. It was then ejected by a small valve at the bottom of the car—the dense air readily sinking into the thinner atmosphere below. To avoid the inconvenience of making a total *vacuum* at any moment within the chamber, this purification was never accomplished all at once, but in a gradual manner—the valve being opened only for a few seconds, then closed again, until one or two strokes from the pump of the condenser had supplied the place of the atmosphere ejected. For the sake of experiment I had put the cat and kittens in a small basket, and suspended it outside the car to a button at the bottom, close by the valve, through which I could feed them at any moment when necessary. I did this at some little risk, and before closing the mouth of the chamber, by reaching under the car with one of the poles before mentioned to which a hook had been attached. As soon as dense air was admitted in the chamber, the hoop and poles became unnecessary; the expansion of the enclosed atmosphere powerfully distending the gum-elastic.

By the time I had fully completed these arrangements and filled the chamber as explained, it wanted only ten minutes of nine o'clock. During the whole period of my being thus employed, I endured the most terrible distress from difficulty of respiration; and bitterly did I repent the negligence, or rather fool-hardiness, of which I had been guilty, of putting off to the last moment a matter of so much importance. But having at length accomplished it, I soon began to reap the benefit of my invention. Once again I breathed with perfect freedom and ease—and indeed why should I not? I was also agreeably surprised to find myself, in a great measure, relieved from the violent pains which had hitherto tormented me. A slight headache, accompanied with a sensation of fulness or distention about the wrists, the ankles, and the throat, was nearly all of which I had now to complain. Thus it seemed evident that a greater part of the uneasiness attending the removal of atmospheric pressure had actually *worn off*, as I had expected, and that much of the pain endured for the last two hours should have been attributed altogether to the effects of a deficient respiration.

At twenty minutes before nine o'clock—that is to say, a short time prior to my closing up the mouth of the chamber, the mercury attained its limit, or ran down, in the barometer, which, as I mentioned before, was one of an extended construction. It then indicated an altitude on my part of 132,000 feet, or five-and-twenty miles, and I consequently surveyed at that time an extent of the earth's area amounting to no less than the three-hundred-and-twentieth part of its entire superficies. At nine o'clock I had again lost sight of land to the eastward, but not before I became aware that the balloon was drifting rapidly to the N.N.W. The ocean beneath me still retained its apparent concavity, although my view was often interrupted by the masses of cloud which floated to and fro.

At half past nine I tried the experiment of throwing out a handful of feathers through the valve. They did not float as I had expected; but dropped down perpendicularly, like a bullet, *en masse*, and with the greatest velocity—being out of sight in a very few seconds. I did not at first know what to make of this extraordinary phenomenon; not being able to believe that my rate of ascent had, of a sudden, met with so prodigious an acceleration. But it soon occurred to me that the atmosphere was now far too rare to sustain even the feathers; that they actually fell, as they appeared to do, with great rapidity; and that I had been surprised by the united velocities of their descent and my own elevation.

By ten o'clock I found that I had very little to occupy my immediate attention. Affairs went on swimmingly, and I believed the balloon to be going upward with a speed increasing momently, although I had no longer any means of ascertaining the progression of the increase. I suffered no pain or uneasiness of any kind, and enjoyed better spirits than I had at any period since my departure from Rotterdam; busying myself now in examining the state of my various apparatus, and now in regenerating the atmosphere within the chamber. This latter point I determined to attend to at regular intervals of forty minutes, more on account of the preservation of my health, than from so frequent a renovation being absolutely necessary. In the meanwhile I could not help making anticipations. Fancy reveled in the wild and dreamy regions of the moon. Imagination, feeling herself for once unshackled, roamed at will among the ever-changing wonders of a shadowy and unstable land. Now there were hoary and time-honored forests, and craggy precipices, and waterfalls tumbling with a loud noise into abysses without a bottom. Then I came suddenly into still noonday solitudes, where no wind of heaven ever intruded, and where vast meadows of poppies, and slender, lily-looking flowers spread themselves out a weary distance, all silent and motionless for ever. Then again I journeyed far down away into another country where it was all one dim and vague lake, with a boundary-line of clouds. But fancies such as these were not the sole possessors of my brain. Horrors of a nature most stern and most appalling would too frequently obtrude themselves upon my mind, and shake the innermost depths of my soul with the bare supposition of their possibility. Yet I would not suffer my thoughts for any length of time to dwell upon these latter speculations, rightly judging the real and palpable dangers of the voyage sufficient for my undivided attention.

At five o'clock, p.m., being engaged in regenerating the atmosphere within the chamber, I took that opportunity of observing the cat and kittens through the valve. The cat herself appeared to suffer again very much, and I had no hesitation in attributing her uneasiness chiefly to a difficulty in breathing; but my experiment with the kittens had resulted very strangely. I had expected, of course, to see them betray a sense of pain, although in a less degree than their mother; and this would have been sufficient to confirm my opinion concerning the habitual endurance of atmospheric pressure. But I was not prepared to find them, upon close examination, evidently enjoying a high degree of health, breathing with the greatest ease and perfect regularity, and evincing not the slightest sign of any uneasiness. I could only account for all this by extending my theory, and supposing that the highly rarefied atmosphere around, might perhaps not be, as I had taken for granted, chemically insufficient for the purposes of life, and that a person born in such a *medium* might, possibly, be unaware of any inconvenience attending its inhalation, while, upon removal to the denser *strata* near the earth, he might endure tortures of a similar nature to those I had so lately experienced. It has since been to me a matter of deep regret that an awkward accident, at this time, occasioned me the loss of my little family of cats, and deprived me of the insight into this matter which a continued experiment might have afforded. In passing my hand through the valve, with a cup of water for the old puss, the sleeve of my shirt became entangled in the loop which sustained the basket, and thus, in a moment, loosened it from the button. Had the whole actually vanished into air, it could not have shot from my sight in a more abrupt and instantaneous manner. Positively, there could not have intervened the tenth part of a second between the disengagement of the basket and its absolute disappearance with all that it contained. My good wishes followed it to the earth, but, of course, I had no hope that either cat or kittens would ever live to tell the tale of their misfortune.

At six o'clock, I perceived a great portion of the earth's visible area to the eastward involved in thick shadow, which continued to advance with great rapidity, until, at five minutes before seven, the whole surface in view was enveloped in the darkness of night. It was not, however, until long after this time that the rays of the setting sun ceased to illumine the balloon; and this circumstance, although of course fully anticipated, did not fail to give me an infinite deal of pleasure. It was evident that, in the morning, I should behold the rising luminary many hours at least before the citizens of Rotterdam, in spite of their situation so much farther to the eastward, and thus, day after day, in proportion to the height ascended, would I enjoy the light of the sun for a longer and a longer period. I now determined to keep a journal of my passage, reckoning the days from one to twenty-four hours continuously, without taking into consideration the intervals of darkness.

At ten o'clock, feeling sleepy, I determined to lie down for the rest of the night; but here a difficulty presented itself, which, obvious as it may appear, had escaped my attention up to the very moment of which I am now speaking. If I went to sleep as I proposed, how could the atmosphere in the chamber be regenerated in the *interim?* To breathe it for more than an hour, at the farthest, would be a matter of impossibility; or, if even this term could be extended to an hour and a quarter, the most ruinous consequences might ensue. The consideration of this dilemma gave me no little disquietude; and it will hardly be believed, that, after the dangers I had undergone, I should look upon this business in so serious a light, as to give up all hope of accomplishing my ultimate design, and finally make up my mind to the necessity of a descent. But this hesitation was only momentary. I reflected that man is the veriest slave of custom, and that many points in the routine of his existence are deemed *essentially* important, which are only so *at all* by his having rendered them habitual. It was very certain that I could not do without sleep; but I might easily bring myself to feel no inconvenience from being awakened at intervals of an hour during the whole period of my repose. It would require but five minutes at most, to regenerate the atmosphere in the fullest manner—and the only real difficulty was to contrive a method of arousing myself at the proper moment for so doing. But this was a question which, I am willing to confess, occasioned me no little trouble in its solution. To be sure, I had heard of the student who, to prevent his falling asleep over his books, held in one hand a ball of copper, the din of whose descent into a basin of the same metal on the floor beside his chair served effectually to startle him up, if, at any moment, he should be overcome with drowsiness. My own case, however, was very different indeed, and left me no room for any similar idea; for I did not wish to keep awake, but to be aroused from slumber at regular intervals of time. I at length hit upon the following expedient, which, simple as it may seem, was hailed by me, at the moment of discovery, as an invention fully equal to that of the telescope, the steam-engine, or the art of printing itself.

It is necessary to premise that the balloon, at the elevation now attained, continued its course upward with an even and undeviating ascent, and the car consequently followed with a steadiness so perfect that it would have been impossible to detect in it the slightest vacillation. This circumstance favored me greatly in the project I now determined to adopt. My supply of water had been put on board in kegs containing five gallons each, and ranged very securely around the interior of the car. I unfastened one of these, and taking two ropes, tied them tightly across the rim of the wickerwork from one side to the other; placing them about a foot apart and parallel, so as to form a kind of shelf, upon which I placed the keg, and steadied it in a horizontal position. About eight inches immediately below these ropes, and four feet from the bottom of the car, I fastened another shelf—but made of thin plank, being the only similar piece of wood I had. Upon this latter shelf, and exactly beneath one of the rims of the keg, a small earthen pitcher was deposited. I now bored a hole in the end of the keg over the pitcher, and fitted in a plug of soft wood, cut in a tapering or conical shape. This plug I pushed in or pulled out, as might happen, until, after a few experiments, it arrived at that exact degree of tightness, at which the water, oozing from the hole, and falling into the pitcher below, would fill the latter to the brim in the period of sixty minutes. This, of course, was a matter briefly and easily ascertained, by noticing the proportion of the pitcher filled in any given time. Having arranged all this, the rest of the plan is obvious. My bed was so contrived upon the floor of the car, as to bring my head, in lying down, immediately below the mouth of the pitcher. It was evident, that, at the expiration of an hour, the pitcher, getting full, would be forced to run over, and to run over at the mouth, which was somewhat lower than the rim. It was also evident, that the water, thus falling from a height of more than four feet, could not do otherwise than fall upon my face, and that the sure consequence would be, to waken me up instantaneously, even from the soundest slumber in the world.

It was fully eleven by the time I had completed these arrangements, and I immediately betook myself to bed, with full confidence in the efficiency of my invention. Nor in this matter was I disappointed. Punctually every sixty minutes was I aroused by my trusty chronometer, when, having emptied the pitcher into the bung-hole of the keg, and performed the duties of the condenser, I retired again to bed. These regular interruptions to my slumber caused me even less discomfort than I had anticipated; and when I finally arose for the day, it was seven o'clock, and the sun had attained many degrees above the line of my horizon.

April 3rd. I found the balloon at an immense height indeed, and the earth's convexity had now become strikingly manifest. Below me in the ocean lay a cluster of black specks, which undoubtedly were islands. Overhead, the sky was of a jetty black, and the stars were brilliantly visible; indeed they had been so constantly since the first day of ascent. Far away to the northward I perceived a thin, white, and exceedingly brilliant line, or streak, on the edge of the horizon, and I had no hesitation in supposing it to be the southern disc of the ices of the Polar sea. My curiosity was greatly excited, for I had hopes of passing on much farther to the north, and might possibly, at some period, find myself placed directly above the Pole itself. I now lamented that my great elevation would, in this case, prevent my taking as accurate a survey as I could wish. Much, however, might be ascertained.

Nothing else of an extraordinary nature occurred during the day. My apparatus all continued in good order, and the balloon still ascended without any perceptible vacillation. The cold was intense, and obliged me to wrap up closely in an overcoat. When darkness came over the earth, I betook myself to bed, although it was for many hours afterward broad daylight all around my immediate situation. The water-clock was punctual in its duty, and I slept until next morning soundly, with the exception of the periodical interruption.

April 4th. Arose in good health and spirits, and was astonished at the singular change which had taken place in the appearance of the sea. It had lost, in a great measure, the deep tint of blue it had hitherto worn, being now of a grayish-white, and of a luster dazzling to the eye. The convexity of the ocean had become so evident that the entire mass of the distant water seemed to be tumbling headlong over the abyss of the horizon, and I found myself listening on tiptoe for the echoes of the mighty cataract. The islands were no longer visible; whether they had passed down the horizon to the southeast, or whether my increasing elevation had left them out of sight, it is impossible to say. I was inclined, however, to the latter opinion. The rim of ice to the northward was growing more and more apparent. Cold by no means so intense. Nothing of importance occurred, and I passed the day in reading, having taken care to supply myself with books.

April 5th. Beheld the singular phenomenon of the sun rising while nearly the whole visible surface of the earth continued to be involved in darkness. In time, however, the light spread itself over all, and I again saw the line of ice to the northward. It was now very distinct, and appeared of a much darker hue than the waters of the ocean. I was evidently approaching it, and with great rapidity. Fancied I could again distinguish a strip of land to the eastward, and one also to the westward, but could not be certain. Weather moderate. Nothing of any consequence happened during the day. Went early to bed.

April 6th. Was surprised at finding the rim of ice at a very moderate distance, and an immense field of the same material stretching away off to the horizon in the north. It was evident that if the balloon held its present course, it would soon arrive above the Frozen Ocean, and I had now little doubt of ultimately seeing the Pole. During the whole of the day I continued to near the ice. Toward night the limits of my horizon very suddenly and materially increased, owing undoubtedly to the earth's form being that of an oblate spheroid, and my arriving above the flattened regions in the vicinity of the Arctic circle. When darkness at length overtook me, I went to bed in great anxiety, fearing to pass over the object of so much curiosity when I should have no opportunity of observing it.

April 7th. Arose early, and, to my great joy, at length beheld what there could be no hesitation in supposing the northern Pole itself. It was there, beyond a doubt, and immediately beneath my feet; but, alas! I had now ascended to so vast a distance that nothing could with accuracy be discerned. Indeed, to judge from the progression of the numbers indicating my various altitudes, respectively, at different periods, between six a.m. on the second of April, and twenty minutes before nine a.m., of the same day, (at which time the barometer ran down), it might be fairly inferred that the balloon had now, at four o'clock in the morning of April the seventh, reached a height of *not less*, certainly, than 7254 miles above the surface of the sea. This elevation may appear immense, but the estimate upon which it is calculated gave a result in all probability far inferior to the truth. At all events I undoubtedly beheld the whole of the earth's major diameter; the entire northern hemisphere lay beneath me like a chart orthographically projected; and the great circle of the equator itself formed the boundary line of my horizon. Your Excellencies may, however, readily imagine that the confined regions hitherto unexplored within the limits of the Arctic circle, although situated directly beneath me, and therefore seen without any appearance of being foreshortened, were still, in themselves, comparatively too diminutive, and at too great a distance from the point of sight, to admit of any very accurate examination. Nevertheless, what could be seen was of a nature singular and exciting. Northwardly from that huge rim before mentioned, and which, with slight qualification, may be called the limit of human discovery in these regions, one unbroken, or nearly unbroken sheet of ice continues to extend. In the first few degrees of this its progress, its surface is very sensibly flattened, farther on depressed into a plane, and finally, becoming *not a little concave*, it terminates, at the Pole itself, in a circular center, sharply defined, whose apparent diameter subtended at the balloon an angle of about sixty-five seconds, and whose dusky hue, varying in intensity, was at all times darker than any other spot upon the visible hemisphere, and occasionally deepened into the most absolute blackness. Farther than this, little could be ascertained. By twelve o'clock the circular center had materially decreased in circumference, and by seven p.m., I lost sight of it entirely; the balloon passing over the western limb of the ice, and floating away rapidly in the direction of the equator.

April 8th. Found a sensible diminution in the earth's apparent diameter, besides a material alteration in its general color and appearance. The whole visible area partook in different degrees of a tint of pale yellow, and in some portions had acquired a brilliancy even painful to the eye. My view downward was also considerably impeded by the dense atmosphere in the vicinity of the surface being loaded with clouds, between whose masses I could only now and then obtain a glimpse of the earth itself. This difficulty of direct vision had troubled me more or less for the last forty-eight hours; but my present enormous elevation brought closer together, as it were, the floating bodies of vapor, and the inconvenience became, of course, more and more palpable in proportion to my ascent. Nevertheless, I could easily perceive that the balloon now hovered above the range of great lakes in the continent of North America, and was holding a course, due south, which would soon bring me to the tropics. This circumstance did not fail to give me the most heartfelt satisfaction, and I hailed it as a happy omen of ultimate success. Indeed, the direction I had hitherto taken had filled me with uneasiness; for it was evident that, had I continued it much longer, there would have been no possibility of my arriving at the moon at all, whose orbit is inclined to the ecliptic at only the small angle of 5° 8' 48". Strange as it may seem, it was only at this late period that I began to understand the great error I had committed, in not taking my departure from earth at some point *in the plane of the lunar ellipse.*

April 9th. Today, the earth's diameter was greatly diminished, and the color of the surface assumed hourly a deeper tint of yellow. The balloon kept steadily on her course to the southward, and arrived, at nine p.m., over the northern edge of the Mexican Gulf.

April 10th. I was suddenly aroused from slumber, about five o'clock this morning, by a loud, crackling, and terrific sound, for which I could in no manner account. It was of very brief duration, but, while it lasted, resembled nothing in the world of which I had any previous experience. It is needless to say that I became excessively alarmed, having, in the first instance, attributed the noise to the bursting of the balloon. I examined all my apparatus, however, with great attention, and could discover nothing out of order. Spent a great part of the day in meditating upon an occurrence so extraordinary, but could find no means whatever of accounting for it. Went to bed dissatisfied, and in a state of great anxiety and agitation.

April 11th. Found a startling diminution in the apparent diameter of the earth, and a considerable increase, now observable for the first time, in that of the moon itself, which wanted only a few days of being full. It now required long and excessive labor to condense within the chamber sufficient atmospheric air for the sustenance of life.

April 12th. A singular alteration took place in regard to the direction of the balloon, and although fully anticipated, afforded me the most unequivocal delight. Having reached, in its former course, about the twentieth parallel of southern latitude, it turned off suddenly, at an acute angle, to the eastward, and thus proceeded throughout the day, keeping nearly, if not altogether, *in the exact plane of the lunar ellipse*. What was worthy of remark, a very perceptible vacillation in the car was a consequence of this change of route—a vacillation which prevailed, in a more or less degree, for a period of many hours.

April 13th. Was again very much alarmed by a repetition of the loud crackling noise which terrified me on the tenth. Thought long upon the subject, but was unable to form any satisfactory conclusion. Great decrease in the earth's apparent diameter, which now subtended from the balloon an angle of very little more than twenty-five degrees. The moon could not be seen at all, being nearly in my zenith. I still continued in the plane of the ellipse, but made little progress to the eastward.

April 14th. Extremely rapid decrease in the diameter of the earth. Today I became strongly impressed with the idea that the balloon was now actually running up the line of apsides to the point of perigee—in other words, holding the direct course which would bring it immediately to the moon in that part of its orbit the nearest to the earth. The moon itself was directly overhead, and consequently hidden from my view. Great and long continued labor necessary for the condensation of the atmosphere.

April 15th. Not even the outlines of continents and seas could now be traced upon the earth with distinctness. About twelve o'clock I became aware, for the third time, of that appalling sound which had so astonished me before. It now, however, continued for some moments, and gathered intensity as it continued. At length, while, stupified and terror-stricken, I stood in expectation of I knew not what hideous destruction, the car vibrated with excessive violence, and a gigantic and flaming mass of some material which I could not distinguish came with a voice of a thousand thunders, roaring and booming by the balloon. When my fears and astonishment had in some degree subsided, I had little difficulty in supposing it to be some mighty volcanic fragment ejected from that world to which I was so rapidly approaching, and, in all probability, one of that singular class of substances occasionally picked up on the earth, and termed meteoric stones for want of a better appellation.

April 16th. Today, looking upward as well as I could, through each of the side windows alternately, I beheld, to my great delight, a very small portion of the moon's disk protruding, as it were, on all sides beyond the huge circumference of the balloon. My agitation was extreme; for I had now little doubt of soon reaching the end of my perilous voyage. Indeed, the labor now required by the condenser had increased to a most oppressive degree, and allowed me scarcely any respite from exertion. Sleep was a matter nearly out of the question. I became quite ill, and my frame trembled with exhaustion. It was impossible that human nature could endure this state of intense suffering much longer. During the now brief interval of darkness a meteoric stone again passed in my vicinity, and the frequency of these phenomena began to occasion me much apprehension.

April 17th. This morning proved an epoch in my voyage. It will be remembered, that, on the thirteenth, the earth subtended an angular breadth of twenty-five degrees. On the fourteenth, this had greatly diminished; on the fifteenth, a still more rapid decrease was observable; and, on retiring for the night of the sixteenth, I had noticed an angle of no more than about seven degrees and fifteen minutes. What, therefore, must have been my amazement, on awakening from a brief and disturbed slumber, on the morning of this day, the seventeenth, at finding the surface beneath me so suddenly and wonderfully *augmented* in volume, as to subtend no less than thirty-nine degrees in apparent angular diameter! I was thunderstruck! No words can give any adequate idea of the extreme, the absolute horror and astonishment, with which I was seized, possessed, and altogether overwhelmed. My knees tottered beneath me—my teeth chattered—my hair started up on end. "The balloon, then, had actually burst!" These were the first tumultuous ideas which hurried through my mind: "The balloon had positively burst!—I was falling—falling with the most impetuous, the most unparalleled velocity! To judge from the immense distance already so quickly passed over, it could not be more than ten minutes, at the farthest, before I should meet the surface of the earth, and be hurled into annihilation!" But at length reflection came to my relief. I paused; I considered; and I began to doubt. The matter was impossible. I could not in any reason have so rapidly come down. Besides, although I was evidently approaching the surface below me, it was with a speed by no means commensurate with the velocity I had at first conceived. This consideration served to calm the perturbation of my mind, and I finally succeeded in regarding the phenomenon in its proper point of view. In fact, amazement must have fairly deprived me of my senses, when I could not see the vast difference, in appearance, between the surface below me, and the surface of my mother earth. The latter was indeed over my head, and completely hidden by the balloon, while the moon—the moon itself in all its glory—lay beneath me, and at my feet.

The stupor and surprise produced in my mind by this extraordinary change in the posture of affairs, was perhaps, after all, that part of the adventure least susceptible of explanation. For the *bouleversement* in itself was not only natural and inevitable, but had been long actually anticipated, as a circumstance to be expected whenever I should arrive at that exact point of my voyage where the attraction of the planet should be superseded by the attraction of the satellite—or, more precisely, where the gravitation of the balloon toward the earth should be less powerful than its gravitation toward the moon. To be sure I arose from a sound slumber, with all my senses in confusion, to the contemplation of a very startling phenomenon, and one which, although expected, was not expected at the moment. The revolution itself must, of course, have taken place in an easy and gradual manner, and it is by no means clear that, had I even been awake at the time of the occurrence, I should have been made aware of it by any *internal* evidence of an inversion—that is to say, by any inconvenience or disarrangement, either about my person or about my apparatus.

It is almost needless to say, that, upon coming to a due sense of my situation, and emerging from the terror which had absorbed every faculty of my soul, my attention was, in the first place, wholly directed to the contemplation of the general physical appearance of the moon. It lay beneath me like a chart—and although I judged it to be still at no inconsiderable distance, the indentures of its surface were defined to my vision with a most striking and altogether unaccountable distinctness. The entire absence of ocean or sea, and indeed of any lake or river, or body of water whatsoever, struck me, at the first glance, as the most extraordinary feature in its geological condition. Yet, strange to say, I beheld vast level regions of a character decidedly alluvial, although by far the greater portion of the hemisphere in sight was covered with innumerable volcanic mountains, conical in shape, and having more the appearance of artificial than of natural protuberances. The highest among them does not exceed three and three-quarter miles in perpendicular elevation; but a map of the volcanic districts of the Campi Phlegræi would afford to your Excellencies a better idea of their general surface than any unworthy description I might think proper to attempt. The greater part of them were in a state of evident eruption, and gave me fearfully to understand their fury and their power, by the repeated thunders of the mis-called meteoric stones, which now rushed upward by the balloon with a frequency more and more appalling.

April 18th. Today I found an enormous increase in the moon's apparent bulk—and the evidently accelerated velocity of my descent began to fill me with alarm. It will be remembered that, in the earliest stage of my speculations upon the possibility of a passage to the moon, the existence, in its vicinity, of an atmosphere dense in proportion to the bulk of the planet, had entered largely into my calculations; this too in spite of many theories to the contrary, and, it may be added, in spite of a general disbelief in the existence of any lunar atmosphere at all. But, in addition to what I have already urged in regard to Encke's comet and the zodiacal light, I had been strengthened in my opinion by certain observations of Mr. Schroeter, of Lilienthal. He observed the moon, when two days and a half old, in the evening soon after sunset, before the dark part was visible, and continued to watch it until it became visible. The two cusps appeared tapering in a very sharp faint prolongation, each exhibiting its farthest extremity faintly illuminated by the solar rays, before any part of the dark hemisphere was visible. Soon afterward, the whole dark limb became illuminated. This prolongation of the cusps beyond the semicircle, I thought, must have arisen from the refraction of the sun's rays by the moon's atmosphere. I computed, also, the height of the atmosphere (which could refract light enough into its dark hemisphere, to produce a twilight more luminous than the light reflected from the earth when the moon is about 32° from the new) to be 1356 Paris feet; in this view, I supposed the greatest height capable of refracting the solar ray, to be 5376 feet. My ideas upon this topic had also received confirmation by a passage in the eighty-second volume of the *Philosophical Transactions*, in which it is stated that, at an occultation of Jupiter's satellites, the third disappeared after having been about one or two minutes of time indistinct, and the fourth became indiscernible near the limb.

Upon the resistance, or more properly, upon the support of an atmosphere, existing in the state of density imagined, I had, of course, entirely depended for the safety of my ultimate descent. Should I then, after all, prove to have been mistaken, I had in consequence nothing better to expect, as a *finale* to my adventure, than being dashed into atoms against the rugged surface of the satellite. And, indeed, I had now every reason to be terrified. My distance from the moon was comparatively trifling, while the labor required by the condenser was diminished not at all, and I could discover no indication whatever of a decreasing rarity in the air.

April 19th. This morning, to my great joy, about nine o'clock, the surface of the moon being frightfully near, and my apprehensions excited to the utmost, the pump of my condenser at length gave evident tokens of an alteration in the atmosphere. By ten, I had reason to believe its density considerably increased. By eleven, very little labor was necessary at the apparatus; and at twelve o'clock, with some hesitation, I ventured to unscrew the *tourniquet*, when, finding no inconvenience from having done so, I finally threw open the gum-elastic chamber, and unrigged it from around the car. As might have been expected, spasms and violent headache were the immediate consequences of an experiment so precipitate and full of danger. But these and other difficulties attending respiration, as they were by no means so great as to put me in peril of my life, I determined to endure as I best could, in consideration of my leaving them behind me momently in my approach to the denser *strata* near the moon. This approach, however, was still impetuous in the extreme; and it soon became alarmingly certain that, although I had probably not been deceived in the expectation of an atmosphere dense in proportion to the mass of the satellite, still I had been wrong in supposing this density, even at the surface, at all adequate to the support of the great weight contained in the car of my balloon. Yet this *should* have been the case, and in an equal degree as at the surface of the earth, the actual gravity of bodies at either planet supposed in the ratio of the atmospheric condensation. That it *was not* the case, however, my precipitous downfall gave testimony enough; *why* it was not so can only be explained by a reference to those possible geological disturbances to which I have formerly alluded. At all events I was now close upon the planet, and coming down with the most terrible impetuosity. I lost not a moment, accordingly, in throwing overboard first my ballast, then my water-kegs, then my condensing apparatus and gum-elastic chamber, and finally every article within the car. But it was all to no purpose. I still fell with horrible rapidity, and was now not more than half a mile from the surface. As a last resource, therefore, having got rid of my coat, hat, and boots, I cut loose from the balloon *the car itself*, which was of no inconsiderable weight, and thus, clinging with both hands to the net-work, I had barely time to observe that the whole country, as far as the eye could reach, was thickly interspersed with diminutive habitations, ere I tumbled headlong into the very heart of a fantastical-looking city, and into the middle of a vast crowd of ugly little people, who none of them uttered a single syllable, or gave themselves the least trouble to render me assistance, but stood, like a parcel of idiots, grinning in a ludicrous manner, and eyeing me and my balloon askant, with their arms set a-kimbo. I turned from them in contempt, and, gazing upward at the earth so lately left, and left perhaps for ever, beheld it like a huge, dull, copper shield, about two degrees in diameter, fixed immovably in the heavens overhead, and tipped on one of its edges with a crescent border of the most brilliant gold. No traces of land or water could be discovered, and the whole was clouded with variable spots, and belted with tropical and equatorial zones.

Thus, may it please your Excellencies, after a series of great anxieties, unheard-of dangers, and unparalleled escapes, I had, at length, on the nineteenth day of my departure from Rotterdam, arrived in safety at the conclusion of a voyage undoubtedly the most extraordinary, and the most momentous, ever accomplished, undertaken, or conceived by any denizen of earth. But my adventures yet remain to be related. And indeed your Excellencies may well imagine that, after a residence of five years upon a planet not only deeply interesting in its own peculiar character, but rendered doubly so by its intimate connection, in capacity of satellite, with the world inhabited by man, I may have intelligence for the private ear of the States' College of Astronomers of far more importance than the details, however wonderful, of the mere *voyage* which so happily concluded. This is, in fact, the case. I have much—very much—which it would give me the greatest pleasure to communicate. I have much to say of the climate of the planet; of its wonderful alternations of heat and cold; of unmitigated and burning sunshine for one fortnight, and more than polar frigidity for the next; of a constant transfer of moisture, by distillation like that *in vacuo*, from the point beneath the sun to the point the farthest from it; of a variable zone of running water; of the people themselves; of their manners, customs, and political institutions; of their peculiar physical construction; of their ugliness; of their want of ears, those useless appendages in an atmosphere so peculiarly modified; of their consequent ignorance of the use and properties of speech; of their substitute for speech in a singular method of inter-communication; of the incomprehensible connection between each particular individual in the moon with some particular individual on the earth—a connection analogous with, and depending upon that of the orbs of the planet and the satellite, and by means of which the lives and destinies of the inhabitants of the one are interwoven with the lives and destinies of the inhabitants of the other; and above all, if it so please your Excellencies—above all of those dark and hideous mysteries which lie in the outer regions of the moon—regions which, owing to the almost miraculous accordance of the satellite's rotation on its own axis with its sidereal revolution about the earth, have never yet been turned, and, by God's mercy, never shall be turned, to the scrutiny of the telescopes of man. All this, and more—much more—would I most willingly detail. But, to be brief, I must have my reward. I am pining for a return to my family and to my home: and as the price of any farther communications on my part—in consideration of the light which I have it in my power to throw upon many very important branches of physical and metaphysical science—I must solicit, through the influence of your honorable body, a pardon for the crime of which I have been guilty in the death of the creditors upon my departure from Rotterdam. This, then, is the object of the present paper. Its bearer, an inhabitant of the moon, whom I have prevailed upon, and properly instructed, to be my messenger to the earth, will await your Excellencies' pleasure, and return to me with the pardon in question, if it can, in any manner, be obtained.

I have the honor to be, &c., your Excellencies' very humble servant,

Hans Pfaall

Upon finishing the perusal of this very extraordinary document, Professor Rubadub, it is said, dropped his pipe upon the ground in the extremity of his surprise, and Mynheer Superbus Von Underduk having taken off his spectacles, wiped them, and deposited them in his pocket, so far forgot both himself and his dignity as to turn round three times upon his heel in the quintessence of astonishment and admiration. There was no doubt about the matter—the pardon should be obtained. So at least swore, with a round oath, Professor Rubadub, and so finally thought the illustrious Von Underduk, as he took the arm of his brother in science, and without saying a word, began to make the best of his way home to deliberate upon the measures to be adopted. Having reached the door, however, of the burgomaster's dwelling, the professor ventured to suggest that as the messenger had thought proper to disappear—no doubt frightened to death by the savage appearance of the burghers of Rotterdam—the pardon would be of little use, as no one but a man of the moon would undertake a voyage to so vast a distance. To the truth of this observation the burgomaster assented, and the matter was therefore at an end. Not so, however, rumors and speculations. The letter, having been published, gave rise to a variety of gossip and opinion. Some of the over-wise even made themselves ridiculous by decrying the whole business as nothing better than a hoax. But hoax, with these sort of people, is, I believe, a general term for all matters above their comprehension. For my part, I cannot conceive upon what data they have founded such an accusation. Let us see what they say:

Imprimis. That certain wags in Rotterdam have certain especial antipathies to certain burgomasters and astronomers.

Secondly. That an odd little dwarf and bottle conjurer, both of whose ears, for some misdemeanor, have been cut off close to his head, has been missing for several days from the neighboring city of Bruges.

Thirdly. That the newspapers which were stuck all over the little balloon were newspapers of Holland, and therefore could not have been made in the moon. They were dirty papers—very dirty—and Gluck, the printer, would take his bible oath to their having been printed in Rotterdam.

Fourthly. That Hans Pfaall himself, the drunken villain, and the three very idle gentlemen styled his creditors, were all seen, no longer than two or three days ago, in a tippling house in the suburbs, having just returned, with money in their pockets, from a trip beyond the sea.

Lastly. That it is an opinion very generally received, or which ought to be generally received, that the College of Astronomers in the city of Rotterdam, as well as all other colleges in all other parts of the world—not to mention colleges and astronomers in general—are, to say the least of the matter, not a whit better, nor greater, nor wiser than they ought to be.

NOTE—Strictly speaking, there is but little similarity between the above sketchy trifle, and the celebrated "Moon-Story" of Mr. Locke; but as both have the character of *hoaxes*, (although the one is in a tone of banter, the other of downright earnest), and as both hoaxes are on the same subject, the moon—moreover, as both attempt to give plausibility by scientific detail—the author of "Hans Pfaall" thinks it necessary to say, *in self-defense*, that his own *jeu d'esprit* was published, in the *Southern Literary Messenger*, about three weeks before the commencement of Mr. L's in the *New York Sun*. Fancying a likeness which, perhaps, does not exist, some of the New York papers copied "Hans Pfaall," and collated it with the "Moon-Hoax," by way of detecting the writer of the one in the writer of the other.

As many more persons were actually gulled by the "Moon-Hoax" than would be willing to acknowledge the fact, it may here afford some little amusement to show why no one should have been deceived—to point out those particulars of the story which should have been sufficient to establish its real character. Indeed, however rich the imagination displayed in this ingenious fiction, it wanted much of the force which might have been given it by a more scrupulous attention to facts and to general analogy. That the public were misled, even for an instant, merely proves the gross ignorance which is so generally prevalent upon subjects of an astronomical nature.

The moon's distance from the earth is, in round numbers, 240,000 miles. If we desire to ascertain how near, apparently, a lens would bring the satellite (or any distant object), we, of course, have but to divide the distance by the magnifying, or more strictly, by the space-penetrating power of the glass. Mr. L. makes his lens have a power of 42,000 times. By this divide 240,000 (the moon's real distance), and we have five miles and five-sevenths, as the apparent distance. No animal at all could be seen so far; much less the minute points particularized in the story. Mr. L. speaks about Sir John Herschel's perceiving flowers (the Papaver rhoeas, &c.,) and even detecting the color and the shape of the eyes of small birds. Shortly before, too, he has himself observed that the lens would not render perceptible objects of less than eighteen inches in diameter; but even this, as I have said, is giving the glass by far too great power. It may be observed, in passing, that this prodigious glass is said to have been molded at the glass-house of Messrs. Hartley and Grant, in Dumbarton; but Messrs. H. and G.'s establishment had ceased operations for many years previous to the publication of the hoax.

On page 13, pamphlet edition, speaking of "a hairy veil" over the eyes of a species of bison, the author says—"It immediately occurred to the acute mind of Dr. Herschel that this was a providential contrivance to protect the eyes of the animal from the great extremes of light and darkness to which all the inhabitants of our side of the moon are periodically subjected." But this cannot be thought a very "acute" observation of the Doctor's. The inhabitants of our side of the moon have, evidently, no darkness at all; so there can be nothing of the "extremes" mentioned. In the absence of the sun they have a light from the earth equal to that of thirteen full unclouded moons.

The topography throughout, even when professing to accord with Blunt's Lunar Chart, is entirely at variance with that or any other lunar chart, and even grossly at variance with itself. The points of the compass, too, are in inextricable confusion; the writer appearing to be ignorant that, on a lunar map, these are not in accordance with terrestrial points; the east being to the left, &c.

Deceived, perhaps, by the vague titles, *Mare Nubium*, *Mare Tranquillitatis*, *Mare Fæcunditatis*, &c., given to the dark spots by former astronomers, Mr. L. has entered into details regarding oceans and other large bodies of water in the moon; whereas there is no astronomical point more positively ascertained than that no such bodies exist there. In examining the boundary between light and darkness (in the crescent or gibbous moon) where this boundary crosses any of the dark places, the line of division is found to be rough and jagged; but, were these dark places liquid, it would evidently be even.

The description of the wings of the man-bat, on page 21, is but a literal copy of Peter Wilkins's account of the wings of his flying islanders. This simple fact should have induced suspicion, at least, it might be thought.

On page 23, we have the following: "What a prodigious influence must our thirteen times larger globe have exercised upon this satellite when an embryo in the womb of time, the passive subject of chemical affinity!" This is very fine; but it should be observed that no astronomer would have made such remark, especially to any *Journal of Science*; for the earth, in the sense intended, is not only thirteen, but forty-nine times *larger* than the moon. A similar objection applies to the whole of the concluding pages, where, by way of introduction to some discoveries in Saturn, the philosophical correspondent enters into a minute schoolboy account of that planet:—this to the *Edinburgh Journal of Science*!

But there is one point, in particular, which should have betrayed the fiction. Let us imagine the power actually possessed of seeing animals upon the moon's surface;—what would *first* arrest the attention of an observer from the earth? Certainly neither their shape, size, nor any other such peculiarity, so soon as their remarkable *situation*. They would appear to be walking, with heels up and head down, in the manner of flies on a ceiling. The *real* observer would have uttered an instant ejaculation of surprise (however prepared by previous knowledge) at the singularity of their position; the *fictitious* observer has not even mentioned the subject, but speaks of seeing the entire bodies of such creatures, when it is demonstrable that he could have seen only the diameter of their heads!

It might as well be remarked, in conclusion, that the size, and particularly the powers of the man-bats (for example, their ability to fly in so rare an atmosphere—if, indeed, the moon have any)—with most of the other fancies in regard to animal and vegetable existence, are at variance, generally, with all analogical reasoning on these themes; and that analogy here will often amount to conclusive demonstration. It is, perhaps, scarcely necessary to add, that all the suggestions attributed to Brewster and Herschel, in the beginning of the article, about "a transfusion of artificial light through the focal object of vision," &c., &c., belong to that species of figurative writing which comes, most properly, under the denomination of rigmarole.

There is a real and very definite limit to optical discovery among the stars—a limit whose nature need only be stated to be understood. If, indeed, the casting of large lenses were all that is required, man's ingenuity would ultimately prove equal to the task, and we might have them of any size demanded. But, unhappily, in proportion to the increase of size in the lens, and, consequently, of space-penetrating power, is the diminution of light from the object, by diffusion of its rays. And for this evil there is no remedy within human ability; for an object is seen by means of that light alone which proceeds from itself, whether direct or reflected. Thus the only "*artificial*" light which could avail Mr. Locke would be some artificial light which he should be able to throw—not upon the "focal object of vision," but upon the real object to be viewed—to wit: *upon the moon*. It has been easily calculated that, when the light proceeding from a star becomes so diffused as to be as weak as the natural light proceeding from the whole of the stars, in a clear and moonless night, then the star is no longer visible for any practical purpose.

The Earl of Ross telescope, lately constructed in England, has a *speculum* with a reflecting surface of 4071 square inches; the Herschel telescope having one of only 1811. The metal of the Earl of Ross's is 6 feet diameter; it is 5½ inches thick at the edges, and 5 at the center. The weight is 3 tons. The focal length is 50 feet.

I have lately read a singular and somewhat ingenious little book, whose title page runs thus:—"*L'Homme dans la lvne, ou le Voyage Chimerique fait au Monde de la Lvne, nouuellement decouuert par Dominique Gonzales, Aduanturier Espagnol, autremèt dit le Courier volant. Mis en notre langve par J. B. D. A. Paris, chez Francois Piot, pres la Fontaine de Saint Benoist. Et chez J. Goignard, au premier pilier de la grand' salle du Palais, proche les Consultations, MDCXLVIII.*" pp. 176.

The writer professes to have translated his work from the English of one Mr. D'Avisson (Davidson?) although there is a terrible ambiguity in the statement. "*J'en ai eu,*" says he, "*l'original de Monsieur D'Avisson, medecin des mieux versez qui soient aujourd'hui dans la conaissance des Belles Lettres, et sur tout de la Philosophie Naturelle. Je lui ai cette obligation entre les autres, de m'avoir non seulement mis en main ce Livre en anglais, mais encore le Manuscrit du Sieur Thomas D'Anan, gentilhomme Eccossois, recommandable pour sa vertu, sur la version duquel j'advoue que j'ay tiré le plan de la mienne.*"

After some irrelevant adventures, much in the manner of Gil Blas, and which occupy the first thirty pages, the author relates that, being ill during a sea voyage, the crew abandoned him, together with a negro servant, on the island of St. Helena. To increase the chances of obtaining food, the two separate, and live as far apart as possible. This brings about a training of birds, to serve the purpose of carrier -pigeons between them. By and by these are taught to carry parcels of some weight—and this weight is gradually increased. At length the idea is entertained of uniting the force of a great number of the birds, with a view to raising the author himself. A machine is contrived for the purpose, and we have a minute description of it, which is materially helped out by a steel engraving. Here we perceive the Signor Gonzales, with point ruffles and a huge periwig, seated astride something which resembles very closely a broomstick, and borne aloft by a multitude of wild swans (*ganzas*) who had strings reaching from their tails to the machine.

The main event detailed in the signor's narrative depends upon a very important fact, of which the reader is kept in ignorance until near the end of the book. The *ganzas*, with whom he had become so familiar, were not really denizens of St. Helena, but of the moon. Thence it had been their custom, time out of mind, to migrate annually to some portion of the earth. In proper season, of course they would return home; and the author, happening, one day, to require their services for a short voyage, is unexpectedly carried straight up, and in a very brief period arrives at the satellite. Here he finds, among other odd things, that the people enjoy extreme happiness; that they have no *law;* that they die without pain; that they are from ten to thirty feet in height; that they live five thousand years; that they have an emperor called Irdonozur; and that they can jump sixty feet high, when, being out of the gravitating influence, they fly about with fans.

I cannot forbear giving a specimen of the general *philosophy* of the volume.

"I must now declare to you," says the Signor Gonzales, "the nature of the place in which I found myself. All the clouds were beneath my feet, or, if you please, spread between me and the earth. As to the stars, *since there was no night where I was, they always had the same appearance; not brilliant, as usual, but pale, and very nearly like the moon of a morning.* But few of them were visible, and these ten times larger (as well as I could judge) than they seem to the inhabitants of the earth. The moon which wanted two days of being full, was of a terrible bigness.

"I must not forget here that the stars appeared only on that side of the globe turned towards the moon, and that the closer they were to it the larger they seemed. I have also to inform you that, whether it was calm weather or stormy, I found myself *always immediately between the moon and the earth.* I was convinced of this for two reasons—because my birds always flew in a straight line; and because whenever we attempted to rest, *we were carried insensibly around the globe of the earth.* For I admit the opinion of Copernicus, who maintains that it never ceases to revolve *from the east to the west*, not upon the poles of the Equinoctial, commonly called the poles of the world, but upon those of the Zodiac, a question of which I propose to speak more at length hereafter, when I shall have leisure to refresh my memory in regard to the astrology which I learned at Salamanca when young, and have since forgotten."

Notwithstanding the blunders italicized, the book is not without some claim to attention, as affording a naïve specimen of the current astronomical notions of the time. One of these assumed that the "gravitating power" extended but a short distance from the earth's surface, and, accordingly, we find our voyager "carried insensibly around the globe," &c.

There have been other "voyages to the moon," but none of higher merit than the one just mentioned. That of Bergerac is utterly meaningless. In the third volume of the *American Quarterly Review* will be found quite an elaborate criticism upon a certain "Journey" of the kind in question—a criticism in which it is difficult to say whether the critic most exposes the stupidity of the book, or his own absurd ignorance of astronomy. I forget the title of the work; but the *means* of the voyage are more deplorably ill conceived than are even the *ganzas* of our friend the Signor Gonzales. The adventurer, in digging the earth, happens to discover a peculiar metal for which the moon has a strong attraction, and straightway constructs of it a box, which, when cast loose from its terrestrial fastenings, flies with him, forthwith, to the satellite. The *Flight of Thomas O'Rourke* is a *jeu d'esprit* not altogether contemptible, and has been translated into German. Thomas, the hero, was, in fact, the gamekeeper of an Irish peer, whose eccentricities gave rise to the tale. The "flight" is made on an eagle's back, from Hungry Hill, a lofty mountain at the end of Bantry Bay.

In these various *brochures* the aim is always satirical; the theme being a description of Lunarian customs as compared with ours. In none, is there any effort at *plausibility* in the details of the voyage itself. The writers seem, in each instance, to be utterly uninformed in respect to astronomy. In "Hans Pfaall" the design is original, inasmuch as regards an attempt at *verisimilitude*, in the application of scientific principles (so far as the whimsical nature of the subject would permit) to the actual passage between the earth and the moon.

SHADOW—A PARABLE

"Yea! Though I walk through the valley of the Shadow"
Psalm of David [XXIII]

YE WHO READ are still among the living: but I who write shall have long since gone my way into the region of shadows. For indeed strange things shall happen, and secret things be known, and many centuries shall pass away, ere these memorials be seen of men. And, when seen, there will be some to disbelieve, and some to doubt, and yet a few who will find much to ponder upon in the characters here graven with a stylus of iron.

The year had been a year of terror, and of feelings more intense than terror for which there is no name upon the earth. For many prodigies and signs had taken place, and far and wide, over sea and land, the black wings of the Pestilence were spread abroad. To those, nevertheless, cunning in the stars, it was not unknown that the heavens wore an aspect of ill; and to me, the Greek Oinos, among others, it was evident that now had arrived the alternation of that seven hundred and ninety-fourth year when, at the entrance of Aries, the planet Jupiter is conjoined with the red ring of the terrible Saturnus. The peculiar spirit of the skies, if I mistake not greatly, made itself manifest, not only in the physical orb of the earth, but in the souls, imaginations, and meditations of mankind.

Over some flasks of the red Chian wine, within the walls of a noble hall, in a dim city called Ptolemais, we sat, at night, a company of seven. And to our chamber there was no entrance save by a lofty door of brass: and the door was fashioned by the artisan Corinnos, and, being of rare workmanship, was fastened from within. Black draperies, likewise, in the gloomy room, shut out from our view the moon, the lurid stars, and the peopleless streets—but the boding and the memory of Evil, they would not be so excluded. There were things around us and about of which I can render no distinct account—things material and spiritual—heaviness in the atmosphere—a sense of suffocation—anxiety—and, above all, that terrible state of existence which the nervous experience when the senses are keenly living and awake, and meanwhile the powers of thought lie dormant. A dead weight hung upon us. It hung upon our limbs—upon the household furniture—upon the goblets from which we drank; and all things were depressed, and borne down thereby—all things save only the flames of the seven iron lamps which illumined our revel. Uprearing themselves in tall slender lines of light, they thus remained burning all pallid and motionless; and in the mirror which their luster formed upon the round table of ebony at which we sat, each of us there assembled beheld the pallor of his own countenance, and the unquiet glare in the downcast eyes of his companions. Yet we laughed and were merry in our proper way—which was hysterical; and sang the songs of Anacreon—which are madness; and drank deeply—although the purple wine reminded us of blood. For there was yet another tenant of our chamber in the person of young Zoilus. Dead, and at full length he lay, enshrouded—the genius and the demon of the scene. Alas! He bore no portion in our mirth, save that his countenance, distorted with the plague, and his eyes in which Death had but half extinguished the fire of the pestilence, seemed to take such interest in our merriment as the dead may haply take in the merriment of those who are to die. But although I, Oinos, felt that the eyes of the departed were upon me, still I forced myself not to perceive the bitterness of their expression, and, gazing down steadily into the depths of the ebony mirror, sang with a loud and sonorous voice the songs of the son of Teios. But gradually my songs they ceased, and their echoes, rolling afar off among the sable draperies of the chamber, became weak, and undistinguishable, and so faded away. And lo! From among those sable draperies where the sounds of the song departed, there came forth a dark and undefined shadow—a shadow such as the moon, when low in heaven, might fashion from the figure of a man:

but it was the shadow neither of man nor of God, nor of any familiar thing. And, quivering awhile among the draperies of the room, it at length rested in full view upon the surface of the door of brass. But the shadow was vague, and formless, and indefinite, and was the shadow neither of man nor of God—neither God of Greece, nor God of Chaldæa, nor any Egyptian God. And the shadow rested upon the brazen doorway, and under the arch of the entablature of the door, and moved not, nor spoke any word, but there became stationary and remained. And the door whereupon the shadow rested was, if I remember aright, over against the feet of the young Zoilus enshrouded. But we, the seven there assembled, having seen the shadow as it came out from among the draperies, dared not steadily behold it, but cast down our eyes, and gazed continually into the depths of the mirror of ebony. And at length I, Oinos, speaking some low words, demanded of the shadow its dwelling and its appellation. And the shadow answered, "I am SHADOW, and my dwelling is near to the Catacombs of Ptolemais, and hard by those dim plains of Helusion which border upon the foul Charonian canal." And then did we, the seven, start from our seats in horror, and stand trembling, and shuddering, and aghast: for the tones in the voice of the shadow were not the tones of any one being, but of a multitude of beings, and, varying in their cadences from syllable to syllable, fell duskily upon our ears in the well remembered and familiar accents of many thousand departed friends.

THE OVAL PORTRAIT

THE CHATEAU INTO which my valet had ventured to make forcible entrance, rather than permit me, in my desperately wounded condition, to pass a night in the open air, was one of those piles of commingled gloom and grandeur which have so long frowned among the Apennines, not less in fact than in the fancy of Mrs. Radcliffe. To all appearance it had been temporarily and very lately abandoned. We established ourselves in one of the smallest and least sumptuously furnished apartments. It lay in a remote turret of the building. Its decorations were rich, yet tattered and antique. Its walls were hung with tapestry and bedecked with manifold and multiform armorial trophies, together with an unusually great number of very spirited modern paintings in frames of rich golden arabesque. In these paintings, which depended from the walls not only in their main surfaces, but in very many nooks which the bizarre architecture of the chateau rendered necessary—in these paintings my incipient delirium, perhaps, had caused me to take deep interest; so that I bade Pedro to close the heavy shutters of the room—since it was already night—to light the tongues of a tall candelabrum which stood by the head of my bed—and to throw open far and wide the fringed curtains of black velvet which enveloped the bed itself. I wished all this done that I might resign myself, if not to sleep, at least alternately to the contemplation of these pictures, and the perusal of a small volume which had been found upon the pillow, and which purported to criticize and describe them.

Long—long I read—and devoutly, devotedly I gazed. Rapidly and gloriously the hours flew by, and the deep midnight came. The position of the candelabrum displeased me, and outreaching my hand with difficulty, rather than disturb my slumbering valet, I placed it so as to throw its rays more fully upon the book.

But the action produced an effect altogether unanticipated. The rays of the numerous candles (for there were many) now fell within a niche of the room which had hitherto been thrown into deep shade by one of the bed-posts. I thus saw in vivid light a picture all unnoticed before. It was the portrait of a young girl just ripening into womanhood. I glanced at the painting hurriedly, and then closed my eyes. Why I did this was not at first apparent even to my own perception. But while my lids remained thus shut, I ran over in my mind my reason for so shutting them. It was an impulsive movement to gain time for thought—to make sure that my vision had not deceived me—to calm and subdue my fancy for a more sober and more certain gaze. In a very few moments I again looked fixedly at the painting.

That I now saw aright I could not and would not doubt; for the first flashing of the candles upon that canvas had seemed to dissipate the dreamy stupor which was stealing over my senses, and to startle me at once into waking life.

The portrait, I have already said, was that of a young girl. It was a mere head and shoulders, done in what is technically termed a *vignette* manner; much in the style of the favorite heads of Sully. The arms, the bosom and even the ends of the radiant hair, melted imperceptibly into the vague yet deep shadow which formed the background of the whole. The frame was oval, richly gilded and filigreed in *Moresque*. As a thing of art nothing could be more admirable than the painting itself. But it could have been neither the execution of the work, nor the immortal beauty of the countenance, which had so suddenly and so vehemently moved me. Least of all, could it have been that my fancy, shaken from its half slumber, had mistaken the head for that of a living person. I saw at once that the peculiarities of the design, of the *vignetting*, and of the frame, must have instantly dispelled such idea—must have prevented even its momentary entertainment. Thinking earnestly upon these points, I remained, for an hour perhaps, half sitting, half reclining, with my vision riveted upon the portrait. At length, satisfied with the true secret of its effect, I fell back within the bed. I had found the spell of the picture in an absolute *life-likeliness* of expression, which, at first startling, finally confounded, subdued and appalled me. With deep and reverent awe I replaced the candelabrum in its former position. The cause of my deep agitation being thus shut from view, I sought eagerly the volume which discussed the paintings and their histories. Turning to the number which designated the oval portrait, I there read the vague and quaint words which follow:

"She was a maiden of rarest beauty, and not more lovely than full of glee. And evil was the hour when she saw, and loved, and wedded the painter. He, passionate, studious, austere, and having already a bride in his Art: she a maiden of rarest beauty, and not more lovely than full of glee: all light and smiles, and frolicsome as the young fawn: loving and cherishing all things: hating only the Art which was her rival: dreading only the pallet and brushes and other untoward instruments which deprived her of the countenance of her lover. It was thus a terrible thing for this lady to hear the painter speak of his desire to portray even his young bride. But she was humble and obedient, and sat meekly for many weeks in the dark high turret-chamber where the light dripped upon the pale canvas only from overhead. But he, the painter, took glory in his work, which went on from hour to hour and from day to day. And he was a passionate, and wild and moody man, who became lost in reveries; so that he *would* not see that the light which fell so ghastly in that lone turret withered the health and the spirits of his bride, who pined visibly to all but him. Yet she smiled on and still on, uncomplainingly, because she saw that the painter (who had high renown) took a fervid and burning pleasure in his task, and wrought day and night to depict her who so loved him, yet who grew daily more dispirited and weak. And in sooth some who beheld the portrait spoke of its resemblance in low words, as of a mighty marvel, and a proof not less of the power of the painter than of his deep love for her whom he depicted so surpassingly well.

But at length, as the labor drew nearer to its conclusion, there were admitted none into the turret; for the painter had grown wild with the ardor of his work, and turned his eyes from the canvas rarely, even to regard the countenance of his wife. And he *would* not see that the tints which he spread upon the canvas were drawn from the cheeks of her who sat beside him. And when many weeks had passed, and but little remained to do, save one brush upon the mouth and one tint upon the eye, the spirit of the lady again flickered up as the flame within the socket of the lamp. And then the brush was given, and then the tint was placed; and, for one moment, the painter stood entranced before the work which he had wrought; but in the next, while he yet gazed, he grew tremulous and very pallid, and aghast, and crying with a loud voice "This is indeed *Life* itself!" turned suddenly to regard his beloved: *She was dead.*

THE IMP OF THE PERVERSE

IN THE CONSIDERATION of the faculties and impulses—of the *prima mobilia* of the human soul, the phrenologists have failed to make room for a propensity which, although obviously existing as a radical, primitive, irreducible sentiment, has been equally overlooked by all the moralists who have preceded them. In the pure arrogance of the reason, we have all overlooked it. We have suffered its existence to escape our senses, solely through want of belief—of faith; whether it be faith in Revelation, or faith in the Kabbala. The idea of it has never occurred to us, simply because of its supererogation. We saw no *need* of the impulse—for the propensity. We could not perceive its necessity. We could not understand, that is to say, we could not have understood, had the notion of this *primum mobile* ever obtruded itself; we could not have understood in what manner it might be made to further the objects of humanity, either temporal or eternal. It cannot be denied that phrenology and, in great measure, all metaphysicianism, have been concocted *a priori*. The intellectual or logical man, rather than the understanding or observant man, set himself to imagine designs—to dictate purposes to God. Having thus fathomed, to his satisfaction, the intentions of Jehovah, out of these intentions he built his innumerable systems of mind. In the matter of phrenology, for example, we first determined, naturally enough, that it was the design of the Deity that man should eat. We then assigned to man an organ of alimentiveness, and this organ is the scourge with which the Deity compels man, will-I nill-I, into eating. Secondly, having settled it to be God's will that man should continue his species, we discovered an organ of amativeness, forthwith.

And so with combativeness, with ideality, with causality, with constructiveness—so, in short, with every organ, whether representing a propensity, a moral sentiment, or a faculty of the pure intellect. And in these arrangements of the *principia* of human action, the Spurzheimites, whether right or wrong, in part, or upon the whole, have but followed, in principle, the footsteps of their predecessors; deducing and establishing every thing from the preconceived destiny of man, and upon the ground of the objects of his Creator.

It would have been wiser, it would have been safer to classify (if classify we must) upon the basis of what man usually or occasionally did, and was always occasionally doing, rather than upon the basis of what we took it for granted the Deity intended him to do. If we cannot comprehend God in his visible works, how then in his inconceivable thoughts, that call the works into being? If we cannot understand him in his objective creatures, how then in his substantive moods and phases of creation?

Induction, *a posteriori*, would have brought phrenology to admit, as an innate and primitive principle of human action, a paradoxical something, which we may call *perverseness*, for want of a more characteristic term. In the sense I intend, it is, in fact, a *mobile* without motive, a motive not *motivirt*. Through its promptings we act without comprehensible object; or, if this shall be understood as a contradiction in terms, we may so far modify the proposition as to say, that through its promptings we act, for the reason that we should *not*. In theory, no reason can be more unreasonable; but, in fact, there is none more strong. With certain minds, under certain conditions, it becomes absolutely irresistible. I am not more certain that I breathe, than that the assurance of the wrong or error of any action is often the one unconquerable *force* which impels us, and alone impels us to its prosecution. Nor will this overwhelming tendency to do wrong for the wrong's sake, admit of analysis, or resolution into ulterior elements. It is a radical, a primitive impulse—elementary. It will be said, I am aware, that when we persist in acts because we feel we should *not* persist in them, our conduct is but a modification of that which ordinarily springs from the combativeness of phrenology. But a glance will show the fallacy of this idea. The phrenological *combativeness* has for its essence the necessity of self-defense. It is our safeguard against injury. Its principle regards our well-being; and thus the desire to be well is excited simultaneously with its development. It follows, that the desire to be well must be excited simultaneously with any principle which shall be merely a modification of combativeness, but in the case of that something which I term *perverseness*, the desire to be well is not only not aroused, but a strongly antagonistical sentiment exists.

An appeal to one's own heart is, after all, the best reply to the sophistry just noticed. No one who trustingly consults and thoroughly questions his own soul will be disposed to deny the entire radicalness of the propensity in question. It is not more incomprehensible than distinctive. There lives no man who, at some period, has not been tormented, for example, by an earnest desire to tantalize a listener by circumlocution. The speaker is aware that he displeases; he has every intention to please; he is usually curt, precise, and clear; the most laconic and luminous language is struggling for utterance upon his tongue; it is only with difficulty that he restrains himself from giving it flow; he dreads and deprecates the anger of him whom he addresses; yet, the thought strikes him, that by certain involutions and parentheses, this anger may be engendered. That single thought is enough. The impulse increases to a wish, the wish to a desire, the desire to an uncontrollable longing, and the longing (to the deep regret and mortification of the speaker, and in defiance of all consequences) is indulged.

We have a task before us which must be speedily performed. We know that it will be ruinous to make delay. The most important crisis of our life calls, trumpet-tongued, for immediate energy and action. We glow, we are consumed with eagerness to commence the work, with the anticipation of whose glorious result our whole souls are on fire. It must, it shall be undertaken today, and yet we put it off until tomorrow, and why? There is no answer, except that we feel *perverse*, using the word with no comprehension of the principle. Tomorrow arrives; and with it a more impatient anxiety to do our duty, but with this very increase of anxiety arrives, also, a nameless, a positively fearful, because unfathomable craving for delay. This craving gathers strength as the moments fly. The last hour for action is at hand. We tremble with the violence of the conflict within us—of the definite with the indefinite—of the substance with the shadow. But, if the contest has proceeded thus far, it is the shadow which prevails—we struggle in vain. The clock strikes, and is the knell of our welfare. At the same time, it is the chanticleer-note to the ghost that has so long overawed us. It flies—it disappears—we are free. The old energy returns. We will labor *now*. Alas, it is *too late!*

We stand upon the brink of a precipice. We peer into the abyss—we grow sick and dizzy. Our first impulse is to shrink from the danger. Unaccountably we remain. By slow degrees our sickness and dizziness, and horror become merged in a cloud of unnamable feeling. By gradations, still more imperceptible, this cloud assumes shape, as did the vapor from the bottle out of which arose the genius in the Arabian Nights. But out of this *our* cloud upon the precipice's edge, there grows into palpability, a shape, far more terrible than any genius, or any demon of a tale, and yet it is but a thought, although a fearful one, and one which chills the very marrow of our bones with the fierceness of the delight of its horror. It is merely the idea of what would be our sensations during the sweeping precipitancy of a fall from such a height. And this fall—this rushing annihilation—for the very reason that it involves that one most ghastly and loathsome of all the most ghastly and loathsome images of death and suffering which have ever presented themselves to our imagination—for this very cause do we now the most vividly desire it. And because our reason violently deters us from the brink, *therefore*, do we the most impetuously approach it. There is no passion in nature so demoniacally impatient, as that of him, who shuddering upon the edge of a precipice, thus meditates a plunge. To indulge for a moment in any attempt *at thought*, is to be inevitably lost; for reflection but urges us to forbear, and *therefore* it is, I say, that we *cannot*. If there be no friendly arm to check us, or if we fail in a sudden effort to prostrate ourselves backward from the abyss, we plunge, and are destroyed.

Examine these similar actions as we will, we shall find them resulting solely from the spirit of the *Perverse*. We perpetrate them because we feel that we should *not*. Beyond or behind this, there is no intelligible principle: and we might, indeed, deem this perverseness a direct instigation of the arch-fiend, were it not occasionally known to operate in furtherance of good.

I have said thus much, that in some measure I may answer your question—that I may explain to you why I am here—that I may assign to you something that shall have at least the faint aspect of a cause for my wearing these fetters, and for my tenanting this cell of the condemned.

Had I not been thus prolix, you might either have misunderstood me altogether, or, with the rabble, have fancied me mad. As it is, you will easily perceive that I am one of the many uncounted victims of the Imp of the Perverse.

It is impossible that any deed could have been wrought with a more thorough deliberation. For weeks, for months, I pondered upon the means of the murder. I rejected a thousand schemes, because their accomplishment involved a *chance* of detection. At length, in reading some French memoirs, I found an account of a nearly fatal illness that occurred to Madame Pilau, through the agency of a candle accidentally poisoned. The idea struck my fancy at once. I knew my victim's habit of reading in bed. I knew, too, that his apartment was narrow and ill-ventilated. But I need not vex you with impertinent details. I need not describe the easy artifices by which I substituted, in his bedroom candle-stand, a wax-light of my own making, for the one which I there found. The next morning he was discovered dead in his bed, and the Coroner's verdict was—"Death by the visitation of God."

Having inherited his estate, all went well with me for years. The idea of detection never once entered my brain. Of the remains of the fatal taper, I had myself carefully disposed. I had left no shadow of a clue by which it would be possible to convict, or even to suspect me of the crime. It is inconceivable how rich a sentiment of satisfaction arose in my bosom as I reflected upon my absolute security. For a very long period of time, I was accustomed to revel in this sentiment. It afforded me more real delight than all the mere worldly advantages accruing from my sin. But there arrived at length an epoch, from which the pleasurable feeling grew, by scarcely perceptible gradations, into a haunting and harassing thought. It harassed because it haunted. I could scarcely get rid of it for an instant. It is quite a common thing to be thus annoyed with the ringing in our ears, or rather in our memories, of the burthen of some ordinary song, or some unimpressive snatches from an opera. Nor will we be the less tormented if the song in itself be good, or the opera air meritorious. In this manner, at last, I would perpetually catch myself pondering upon my security, and repeating, in a low, under-tone, the phrase, "I am safe."

One day, whilst sauntering along the streets, I arrested myself in the act of murmuring, half aloud, these customary syllables. In a fit of petulance, I remodeled them thus:—"I am safe—I am safe—yes—if I be not fool enough to make open confession!"

No sooner had I spoken these words, than I felt an icy chill creep to my heart. I had had some experience in these fits of perversity (whose nature I have been at some trouble to explain) and I remembered well, that in no instance I had successfully resisted their attacks. And now my own casual self-suggestion, that I might possibly be fool enough to confess the murder of which I had been guilty, confronted me, as if the very ghost of him whom I had murdered—and beckoned me on to death.

At first, I made an effort to shake off this nightmare of the soul. I walked vigorously—faster—still faster—at length I ran. I felt a maddening desire to shriek aloud. Every succeeding wave of thought overwhelmed me with new terror, for, alas! I well, too well understood that, to *think*, in my situation, was to be lost. I still quickened my pace. I bounded like a madman through the crowded thoroughfares. At length, the populace took the alarm, and pursued me. I felt then the consummation of my fate. Could I have torn out my tongue, I would have done it—but a rough voice resounded in my ears—a rougher grasp seized me by the shoulder. I turned—I gasped for breath. For a moment I experienced all the pangs of suffocation; I became blind, and deaf, and giddy; and then some invisible fiend, I thought, struck me with his broad palm upon the back. The long-imprisoned secret burst forth from my soul.

They say that I spoke with a distinct enunciation, but with marked emphasis and passionate hurry, as if in dread of interruption before concluding the brief but pregnant sentences that consigned me to the hangman and to hell.

Having related all that was necessary for the fullest judicial conviction, I fell prostrate in a swoon.

But why shall I say more? Today I wear these chains, and am *here!* Tomorrow I shall be fetterless!—*But where?*

HOP-FROG

I NEVER KNEW any one so keenly alive to a joke as the king was. He seemed to live only for joking. To tell a good story of the joke kind, and to tell it well, was the surest road to his favor. Thus it happened that his seven ministers were all noted for their accomplishments as jokers. They all took after the king, too, in being large, corpulent, oily men, as well as inimitable jokers. Whether people grow fat by joking, or whether there is something in fat itself which predisposes to a joke, I have never been quite able to determine; but certain it is that a lean joker is a *rara avis in terris*.

About the refinements, or, as he called them, the "ghosts" of wit, the king troubled himself very little. He had an especial admiration for *breadth* in a jest, and would often put up with *length*, for the sake of it. Overniceties wearied him. He would have preferred Rabelais's *Gargantua* to the *Zadig* of Voltaire: and, upon the whole, practical jokes suited his taste far better than verbal ones.

At the date of my narrative, professing jesters had not altogether gone out of fashion at court. Several of the great continental "powers" still retained their "fools," who wore motley, with caps and bells, and who were expected to be always ready with sharp witticisms, at a moment's notice, in consideration of the crumbs that fell from the royal table.

Our king, as a matter of course, retained his "fool." The fact is, he *required* something in the way of folly—if only to counterbalance the heavy wisdom of the seven wise men who were his ministers—not to mention himself.

His fool, or professional jester, was not *only* a fool, however. His value was trebled in the eyes of the king, by the fact of his being also a dwarf and a cripple. Dwarfs were as common at court, in those days, as fools; and many monarchs would have found it difficult to get through their days (days are rather longer at court than elsewhere) without both a jester to laugh *with* and a dwarf to laugh *at*. But, as I have already observed, your jesters, in ninety-nine cases out of a hundred, are fat, round and unwieldy—so that it was no small source of self-gratulation with our king that in Hop-Frog (this was the fool's name) he possessed a triplicate treasure in one person.

I believe the name "Hop-Frog" was *not* that given to the dwarf by his sponsors at baptism, but it was conferred upon him, by general consent of the several ministers, on account of his inability to walk as other men do. In fact, Hop-Frog could only get along by a sort of interjectional gait—something between a leap and a wriggle—a movement that afforded illimitable amusement, and of course consolation, to the king, for (notwithstanding the protuberance of his stomach and a constitutional swelling of the head) the king, by his whole court, was accounted a capital figure.

But although Hop-Frog, through the distortion of his legs, could move only with great pain and difficulty along a road or floor, the prodigious muscular power which nature seemed to have bestowed upon his arms, by way of compensation for deficiency in the lower limbs, enabled him to perform many feats of wonderful dexterity, where trees or ropes were in question, or anything else to climb. At such exercises he certainly much more resembled a squirrel, or a small monkey, than a frog.

I am not able to say, with precision, from what country Hop-Frog originally came. It was from some barbarous region, however, that no person ever heard of—a vast distance from the court of our king. Hop-Frog, and a young girl very little less dwarfish than himself (although of exquisite proportions, and a marvelous dancer), had been forcibly carried off from their respective homes in adjoining provinces, and sent as presents to the king, by one of his ever--victorious generals.

Under these circumstances, it is not to be wondered at that a close intimacy arose between the two little captives. Indeed, they soon became sworn friends. Hop-Frog, who, although he made a great deal of sport, was by no means popular, had it not in his power to render Trippetta many services; but she, on account of her grace and exquisite beauty (although a dwarf), was universally admired and petted: so she possessed much influence; and never failed to use it, whenever she could, for the benefit of Hop-Frog.

On some grand state occasion—I forgot what—the king determined to have a masquerade, and whenever a masquerade or anything of that kind, occurred at our court, then the talents both of Hop-Frog and Trippetta were sure to be called in play. Hop-Frog, in especial, was so inventive in the way of getting up pageants, suggesting novel characters, and arranging costume, for masked balls, that nothing could be done, it seems, without his assistance.

The night appointed for the *fête* had arrived. A gorgeous hall had been fitted up, under Trippetta's eye, with every kind of device which could possibly give *éclat* to a masquerade. The whole court was in a fever of expectation. As for costumes and characters, it might well be supposed that everybody had come to a decision on such points. Many had made up their minds (as to what roles they should assume) a week, or even a month, in advance; and, in fact, there was not a particle of indecision anywhere—except in the case of the king and his seven minsters. Why *they* hesitated I never could tell, unless they did it by way of a joke. More probably, they found it difficult, on account of being so fat, to make up their minds. At all events, time flew; and, as a last resource, they sent for Trippetta and Hop-Frog.

When the two little friends obeyed the summons of the king, they found him sitting at his wine with the seven members of his cabinet council; but the monarch appeared to be in a very ill humor. He knew that Hop-Frog was not fond of wine; for it excited the poor cripple almost to madness; and madness is no comfortable feeling. But the king loved his practical jokes, and took pleasure in forcing Hop-Frog to drink and (as the king called it) "to be merry."

"Come here, Hop-Frog," said he, as the jester and his friend entered the room: "swallow this bumper to the health of your absent friends [here Hop-Frog sighed], and then let us have the benefit of your invention. We want characters—*characters*, man—something novel—out of the way. We are wearied with this everlasting sameness. Come, drink! The wine will brighten your wits."

Hop-Frog endeavored, as usual, to get up a jest in reply to these advances from the king; but the effort was too much. It happened to be the poor dwarf's birthday, and the command to drink to his "absent friends" forced the tears to his eyes. Many large, bitter drops fell into the goblet as he took it, humbly, from the hand of the tyrant.

"Ah! Ha! ha! ha!" roared the latter, as the dwarf reluctantly drained the beaker. "See what a glass of good wine can do! Why, your eyes are shining already!"

Poor fellow! His large eyes *gleamed*, rather than shone; for the effect of wine on his excitable brain was not more powerful than instantaneous. He placed the goblet nervously on the table, and looked round upon the company with a half-insane stare. They all seemed highly amused at the success of the king's "*joke*."

"And now to business," said the prime minister, a *very* fat man.

"Yes," said the King; "come, Hop-Frog, lend us your assistance. Characters, my fine fellow; we stand in need of characters—all of us—ha! ha! ha!" And as this was seriously meant for a joke, his laugh was chorused by the seven.

Hop-Frog also laughed, although feebly and somewhat vacantly.

"Come, come," said the king, impatiently, "have you nothing to suggest?"

"I am endeavoring to think of something *novel*," replied the dwarf, abstractedly, for he was quite bewildered by the wine.

"Endeavoring!" cried the tyrant, fiercely; "what do you mean by *that?* Ah, I perceive. You are sulky, and want more wine. Here, drink this!" And he poured out another goblet full and offered it to the cripple, who merely gazed at it, gasping for breath.

"Drink, I say!" shouted the monster. "Or by the fiends —"

The dwarf hesitated. The king grew purple with rage. The courtiers smirked. Trippetta, pale as a corpse, advanced to the monarch's seat, and, falling on her knees before him, implored him to spare her friend.

The tyrant regarded her, for some moments, in evident wonder at her audacity. He seemed quite at a loss what to do or say—how most becomingly to express his indignation. At last, without uttering a syllable, he pushed her violently from him, and threw the contents of the brimming goblet in her face.

The poor girl got up as best she could, and, not daring even to sigh, resumed her position at the foot of the table.

There was a dead silence for about half a minute, during which the falling of a leaf, or of a feather, might have been heard. It was interrupted by a low, but harsh and protracted *grating* sound which seemed to come at once from every corner of the room.

"What—what—*what* are you making that noise for?" demanded the king, turning furiously to the dwarf.

The latter seemed to have recovered, in great measure, from his intoxication, and looking fixedly but quietly into the tyrant's face, merely ejaculated:

"I—I? How could it have been me?"

"The sound appeared to come from without," observed one of the courtiers. "I fancy it was the parrot at the window, whetting his bill upon his cage-wires."

"True," replied the monarch, as if much relieved by the suggestion. "But, on the honor of a knight, I could have sworn that it was the gritting of this vagabond's teeth."

Hereupon the dwarf laughed (the king was too confirmed a joker to object to any one's laughing), and displayed a set of large, powerful, and very repulsive teeth. Moreover, he avowed his perfect willingness to swallow as much wine as desired. The monarch was pacified; and having drained another bumper with no very perceptible ill effect, Hop-Frog entered at once, and with spirit, into the plans for the masquerade.

"I cannot tell what was the association of idea," observed he, very tranquilly, and as if he had never tasted wine in his life, "but just after your majesty had struck the girl and thrown the wine in her face—*just after* your majesty had done this, and while the parrot was making that odd noise outside the window, there came into my mind a capital diversion—one of my own country frolics—often enacted among us, at our masquerades: but here it will be new altogether. Unfortunately, however, it requires a company of eight persons, and —"

"Here we *are!* " cried the king, laughing at his acute discovery of the coincidence; "Eight to a fraction—I and my seven ministers. Come! What is the diversion?"

"We call it," replied the cripple, "the Eight Chained Orang-utans, and it really is excellent sport if well enacted."

"*We* will enact it," remarked the king, drawing himself up, and lowering his eyelids.

"The beauty of the game," continued Hop-Frog, "lies in the fright it occasions among the women."

"Capital!" roared in chorus the monarch and his ministry.

"*I* will equip you as orang-utans," proceeded the dwarf; "leave all that to me. The resemblance shall be so striking, that the company of masqueraders will take you for real beasts—and of course, they will be as much terrified as astonished."

"Oh, this is exquisite!" exclaimed the king. "Hop-Frog! I will make a man of you."

"The chains are for the purpose of increasing the confusion by their jangling. You are supposed to have escaped, *en masse*, from your keepers. Your majesty cannot conceive the *effect* produced, at a masquerade, by eight chained orang-utans, imagined to be real ones by most of the company; and rushing in with savage cries, among the crowd of delicately and gorgeously habited men and women. The *contrast* is inimitable."

"It *must* be," said the king: and the council arose hurriedly (as it was growing late), to put in execution the scheme of Hop-Frog.

His mode of equipping the party as orang-utans was very simple, but effective enough for his purposes. The animals in question had, at the epoch of my story, very rarely been seen in any part of the civilized world; and as the imitations made by the dwarf were sufficiently beast-like and more than sufficiently hideous, their truthfulness to nature was thus thought to be secured.

The king and his ministers were first encased in tight-fitting stockinet shirts and drawers. They were then saturated with tar. At this stage of the process, some one of the party suggested feathers; but the suggestion was at once overruled by the dwarf, who soon convinced the eight, by ocular demonstration, that the hair of such a brute as the orang-utan was much more efficiently represented by *flax*. A thick coating of the latter was accordingly plastered upon the coating of tar. A long chain was now procured. First, it was passed about the waist of the king, *and tied*; then about another of the party, and also tied;

then about all successively, in the same manner. When this chaining arrangement was complete, and the party stood as far apart from each other as possible, they formed a circle; and to make all things appear natural, Hop-Frog passed the residue of the chain, in two diameters, at right angles, across the circle, after the fashion adopted, at the present day, by those who capture chimpanzees, or other large apes, in Borneo.

The grand saloon in which the masquerade was to take place was a circular room, very lofty, and receiving the light of the sun only through a single window at top. At night (the season for which the apartment was especially designed) it was illuminated principally by a large chandelier, depending by a chain from the center of the sky-light, and lowered, or elevated, by means of a counter-balance as usual; but (in order not to look unsightly) this latter passed outside the cupola and over the roof.

The arrangements of the room had been left to Trippetta's superintendence; but, in some particulars, it seems, she had been guided by the calmer judgment of her friend the dwarf. At his suggestion it was that, on this occasion, the chandelier was removed. Its waxen drippings (which, in weather so warm, it was quite impossible to prevent) would have been seriously detrimental to the rich dresses of the guests, who, on account of the crowded state of the saloon, could not *all* be expected to keep from out its center—that is to say, from under the chandelier. Additional sconces were set in various parts of the hall, out of the way; and a flambeau, emitting sweet odor, was placed in the right hand of each of the Caryatids that stood against the wall—some fifty or sixty altogether.

The eight orang-utans, taking Hop-Frog's advice, waited patiently until midnight (when the room was thoroughly filled with masqueraders) before making their appearance. No sooner had the clock ceased striking, however, than they rushed, or rather rolled in, all together—for the impediment of their chains caused most of the party to fall, and all to stumble as they entered.

The excitement among the masqueraders was prodigious, and filled the heart of the king with glee. As had been anticipated, there were not a few of the guests who supposed the ferocious-looking creatures to be beasts of *some* kind in reality, if not precisely orang-utans. Many of the women swooned with affright; and had not the king taken the precaution to exclude all weapons from the saloon, his party might soon have expiated their frolic in their blood. As it was, a general rush was made for the doors; but the king had ordered them to be locked immediately upon his entrance; and, at the dwarf's suggestion, the keys had been deposited with *him*.

While the tumult was at its height, and each masquerader attentive only to his own safety—(for, in fact, there was much *real* danger from the pressure of the excited crowd)—the chain by which the chandelier ordinarily hung, and which had been drawn up on its removal, might have been seen very gradually to descend, until its hooked extremity came within three feet of the floor.

Soon after this, the king and his seven friends, having reeled about the hall in all directions, found themselves, at length, in its center, and, of course, in immediate contact with the chain. While they were thus situated, the dwarf, who had followed closely at their heels, inciting them to keep up the commotion, took hold of their own chain at the intersection of the two portions which crossed the circle diametrically and at right angles. Here, with the rapidity of thought, he inserted the hook from which the chandelier had been wont to depend; and, in an instant, by some unseen agency, the chandelier-chain was drawn so far upward as to take the hook out of reach, and, as an inevitable consequence, to drag the orang-utans together in close connection, and face to face.

The masqueraders, by this time, had recovered, in some measure, from their alarm; and, beginning to regard the whole matter as a well-contrived pleasantry, set up a loud shout of laughter at the predicament of the apes.

"Leave them to *me!* " now screamed Hop-Frog, his shrill voice making itself easily heard through all the din. "Leave them to *me*. I fancy *I* know them. If I can only get a good look at them, I can soon tell who they are."

Here, scrambling over the heads of the crowd, he managed to get to the wall; when, seizing a flambeau from one of the Caryatids, he returned, as he went, to the center of the room—leaped, with the agility of a monkey, upon the kings head—and thence clambered a few feet up the chain—holding down the torch to examine the group of orang-utans, and still screaming, "*I* shall soon find out who they are!"

And now, while the whole assembly (the apes included) were convulsed with laughter, the jester suddenly uttered a shrill whistle; when the chain flew violently up for about thirty feet—dragging with it the dismayed and struggling orang-utans, and leaving them suspended in mid-air between the sky-light and the floor. Hop-Frog, clinging to the chain as it rose, still maintained his relative position in respect to the eight maskers, and still (as if nothing were the matter) continued to thrust his torch down toward them, as though endeavoring to discover who they were.

So thoroughly astonished was the whole company at this ascent, that a dead silence, of about a minute's duration, ensued. It was broken by just such a low, harsh, *grating* sound, as had before attracted the attention of the king and his councillors, when the former threw the wine in the face of Trippetta. But, on the present occasion, there could be no question as to *whence* the sound issued. It came from the fang-like teeth of the dwarf, who ground them and gnashed them as he foamed at the mouth, and glared, with an expression of maniacal rage, into the upturned countenances of the king and his seven companions.

"Aha!" said at length the infuriated jester. "Aha! I begin to see who these people are, now!" Here, pretending to scrutinize the king more closely, he held the flambeau to the flaxen coat which enveloped him, and which instantly burst into a sheet of vivid flame. In less than half a minute the whole eight orang-utans were blazing fiercely, amid the shrieks of the multitude who gazed at them from below, horror-stricken, and without the power to render them the slightest assistance.

At length the flames, suddenly increasing in virulence, forced the jester to climb higher up the chain, to be out of their reach; and, as he made this movement, the crowd again sank, for a brief instant, into silence. The dwarf seized his opportunity, and once more spoke:

"I now see *distinctly*," he said, "what manner of people these maskers are. They are a great king and his seven privy-councillors—a king who does not scruple to strike a defenseless girl, and his seven councillors who abet him in the outrage. As for myself, I am simply Hop-Frog, the jester—and *this is my last jest.*"

Owing to the high combustibility of both the flax and the tar to which it adhered, the dwarf had scarcely made an end of his brief speech before the work of vengeance was complete. The eight corpses swung in their chains, a fetid, blackened, hideous, and indistinguishable mass. The cripple hurled his torch at them, clambered leisurely to the ceiling, and disappeared through the sky-light.

It is supposed that Trippetta, stationed on the roof of the saloon, had been the accomplice of her friend in his fiery revenge, and that, together, they effected their escape to their own country: for neither was seen again.

THE BALLOON-HOAX

[Astounding News by Express, via *Norfolk!—The Atlantic crossed in Three Days! Signal Triumph of Mr. Monck Mason's Flying Machine!— Arrival at Sullivan›s Island, near Charleston, S.C., of Mr. Mason, Mr. Robert Holland, Mr. Henson, Mr. Harrison Ainsworth, and four others, in the Steering Balloon, "Victoria," after a passage of Seventy-five Hours from Land to Land! Full Particulars of the Voyage!*

The subjoined jeu d'esprit *with the preceding heading in magnificent capitals, well interspersed with notes of admiration, was originally published, as matter of fact, in the "New-York Sun," a daily newspaper, and therein fully subserved the purpose of creating indigestible aliment for the quid-nuncs during the few hours intervening between a couple of the Charleston mails. The rush for the "sole paper which had the news," was something beyond even the prodigious; and, in fact, if (as some assert) the "Victoria" did* not *absolutely accomplish the voyage recorded, it will be difficult to assign a reason why she* should *not have accomplished it.]*

THE GREAT PROBLEM is at length solved! The air, as well as the earth and the ocean, has been subdued by science, and will become a common and convenient highway for mankind. *The Atlantic has been actually crossed in a Balloon!* and this too without difficulty—without any great apparent danger—with thorough control of the machine—and in the inconceivably brief period of seventy-five hours from shore to shore! By the energy of an agent at Charleston, S.C., we are enabled to be the first to furnish the public with a detailed account of this most extraordinary voyage, which was performed between Saturday, the 6th instant, at 11, A.M., and 2, P.M., on Tuesday, the 9th instant, by Sir Everard Bringhurst; Mr. Osborne, a nephew of Lord Bentinck›s; Mr. Monck Mason and Mr. Robert Holland, the well-known æronauts; Mr. Harrison Ainsworth, author of *Jack Sheppard*, &c.; and Mr. Henson, the projector of the late unsuccessful flying machine—with two seamen from Woolwich—in all, eight persons. The particulars furnished below may be relied on as authentic and accurate in every respect, as, with a slight exception, they are copied *verbatim* from the joint diaries of Mr. Monck Mason and Mr. Harrison Ainsworth, to whose politeness our agent is also indebted for much verbal information respecting the balloon itself, its construction, and other matters of interest. The only alteration in the MS. received, has been made for the purpose of throwing the hurried account of our agent, Mr. Forsyth, in a connected and intelligible form.

The BALLOON

TWO VERY DECIDED failures, of late—those of Mr. Henson and Sir George Cayley—had much weakened the public interest in the subject of aerial navigation. Mr. Henson's scheme (which at first was considered very feasible even by men of science,) was founded upon the principle of an inclined plane, started from an eminence by an extrinsic force, applied and continued by the revolution of impinging vanes, in form and number resembling the vanes of a windmill. But, in all the experiments made with models at the Adelaide Gallery, it was found that the operation of these fans not only did not propel the machine, but actually impeded its flight. The only propelling force it ever exhibited, was the mere *impetus* acquired from the descent of the inclined plane; and this *impetus* carried the machine farther when the vanes were at rest, than when they were in motion—a fact which sufficiently demonstrates their inutility; and in the absence of the propelling, which was also the *sustaining* power, the whole fabric would necessarily descend. This consideration led Sir George Cayley to think only of adapting a propeller to some machine having of itself an independent power of support—in a word, to a balloon; the idea, however, being novel, or original, with Sir George, only so far as regards the mode of its application to practice. He exhibited a model of his invention at the Polytechnic Institution. The propelling principle, or power, was here, also, applied to interrupted surfaces, or vanes, put in revolution. These vanes were four in number, but were found entirely ineffectual in moving the balloon, or in aiding its ascending power. The whole project was thus a complete failure.

It was at this juncture that Mr. Monck Mason (whose voyage from Dover to Weilburg in the balloon, "Nassau," occasioned so much excitement in 1837,) conceived the idea of employing the principle of the Archimedean screw for the purpose of propulsion through the air—rightly attributing the failure of Mr. Henson's scheme, and of Sir George Cayley's, to the interruption of surface in the independent vanes. He made the first public experiment at Willis's Rooms, but afterward removed his model to the Adelaide Gallery.

Like Sir George Cayley's balloon, his own was an ellipsoid. Its length was thirteen feet six inches—height, six feet eight inches. It contained about three hundred and twenty cubic feet of gas, which, if pure hydrogen, would support twenty-one pounds upon its first inflation, before the gas has time to deteriorate or escape. The weight of the whole machine and apparatus was seventeen pounds—leaving about four pounds to spare. Beneath the center of the balloon, was a frame of light wood, about nine feet long, and rigged on to the balloon itself with a network in the customary manner. From this framework was suspended a wicker basket or car.

The screw consists of an axis of hollow brass tube, eighteen inches in length, through which, upon a semi-spiral inclined at fifteen degrees, pass a series of a steel wire radii, two feet long, and thus projecting a foot on either side. These radii are connected at the outer extremities by two bands of flattened wire—the whole in this manner forming the framework of the screw, which is completed by a covering of oiled silk cut into gores, and tightened so as to present a tolerably uniform surface. At each end of its axis this screw is supported by pillars of hollow brass tube descending from the hoop. In the lower ends of these tubes are holes in which the pivots of the axis revolve. From the end of the axis which is next the car, proceeds a shaft of steel, connecting the screw with the pinion of a piece of spring machinery fixed in the car. By the operation of this spring, the screw is made to revolve with great rapidity, communicating a progressive motion to the whole. By means of the rudder, the machine was readily turned in any direction. The spring was of great power, compared with its dimensions, being capable of raising forty-five pounds upon a barrel of four inches diameter, after the first turn, and gradually increasing as it was wound up. It weighed, altogether, eight pounds six ounces. The rudder was a light frame of cane covered with silk, shaped somewhat like a battledoor, and was about three feet long, and at the widest, one foot. Its weight was about two ounces. It could be turned *flat*, and directed upward or downward, as well as to the right or left; and thus enabled the æronaut to transfer the resistance of the air which in an inclined position it must generate in its passage, to any side upon which he might desire to act; thus determining the balloon in the opposite direction.

This model (which, through want of time, we have necessarily described in an imperfect manner,) was put in action at the Adelaide Gallery, where it accomplished a velocity of five miles per hour; although, strange to say, it excited very little interest in comparison with the previous complex machine of Mr. Henson—so resolute is the world to despise anything which carries with it an air of simplicity. To accomplish the great desideratum of ærial navigation, it was very generally supposed that some exceedingly complicated application must be made of some unusually profound principle in dynamics.

So well satisfied, however, was Mr. Mason of the ultimate success of his invention, that he determined to construct immediately, if possible, a balloon of sufficient capacity to test the question by a voyage of some extent—the original design being to cross the British Channel, as before, in the Nassau balloon. To carry out his views, he solicited and obtained the patronage of Sir Everard Bringhurst and Mr. Osborne, two gentlemen well known for scientific acquirement, and especially for the interest they have exhibited in the progress of ærostation. The project, at the desire of Mr. Osborne, was kept a profound secret from the public—the only persons entrusted with the design being those actually engaged in the construction of the machine, which was built (under the superintendence of Mr. Mason, Mr. Holland, Sir Everard Bringhurst, and Mr. Osborne,) at the seat of the latter gentleman near Penstruthal, in Wales. Mr. Henson, accompanied by his friend Mr. Ainsworth, was admitted to a private view of the balloon, on Saturday last—when the two gentlemen made final arrangements to be included in the adventure. We are not informed for what reason the two seamen were also included in the party—but, in the course of a day or two, we shall put our readers in possession of the minutest particulars respecting this extraordinary voyage.

The balloon is composed of silk, varnished with the liquid gum caoutchouc. It is of vast dimensions, containing more than 40,000 cubic feet of gas; but as coal gas was employed in place of the more expensive and inconvenient hydrogen, the supporting power of the machine, when fully inflated, and immediately after inflation, is not more than about 2500 pounds. The coal gas is not only much less costly, but is easily procured and managed.

For its introduction into common use for purposes of aerostation, we are indebted to Mr. Charles Green. Up to his discovery, the process of inflation was not only exceedingly expensive, but uncertain. Two, and even three days, have frequently been wasted in futile attempts to procure a sufficiency of hydrogen to fill a balloon, from which it had great tendency to escape owing to its extreme subtlety, and its affinity for the surrounding atmosphere. In a balloon sufficiently perfect to retain its contents of coal-gas unaltered, in quality or amount, for six months, an equal quantity of hydrogen could not be maintained in equal purity for six weeks.

The supporting power being estimated at 2500 pounds, and the united weights of the party amounting only to about 1200, there was left a surplus of 1300, of which again 1200 was exhausted by ballast, arranged in bags of different sizes, with their respective weights marked upon them—by cordage, barometers, telescopes, barrels containing provision for a fortnight, water-casks, cloaks, carpet-bags, and various other indispensable matters, including a coffee-warmer, contrived for warming coffee by means of slack-lime, so as to dispense altogether with fire, if it should be judged prudent to do so. All these articles, with the exception of the ballast, and a few trifles, were suspended from the hoop over head. The car is much smaller and lighter, in proportion, than the one appended to the model. It is formed of a light wicker, and is wonderfully strong, for so frail looking a machine. Its rim is about four feet deep. The rudder is also very much larger, in proportion, than that of the model; and the screw is considerably smaller. The balloon is furnished besides, with a grapnel, and a guide-rope; which latter is of the most indispensable importance. A few words, in explanation, will here be necessary for such of our readers as are not conversant with the details of aerostation.

As soon as the balloon quits the earth, it is subjected to the influence of many circumstances tending to create a difference in its weight; augmenting or dimishing its ascending power. For example, there may be a disposition of dew upon the silk, to the extent, even, of several hundred pounds; ballast has then to be thrown out, or the machine may descend. This ballast being discarded, and a clear sunshine evaporating the dew, and at the same time expanding the gas in the silk, the whole will again rapidly ascend. To check this ascent, the only resource is, (or rather *was*, until Mr. Green's invention of the guide-rope,) the permission of the escape of gas from the valve; but, in the loss of gas, is a proportionate general loss of ascending power; so that, in a comparatively brief period, the best constructed balloon must necessarily exhaust all its resources, and come to the earth. This was the great obstacle to voyages of length.

The guide-rope remedies the difficulty in the simplest manner conceivable. It is merely a very long rope which is suffered to trail from the car, and the effect of which is to prevent the balloon from changing its level in any material degree. If, for example, there should be a deposition of moisture upon the silk, and the machine begins to descend in consequence, there will be no neccesity for discharging ballast to remedy the increase of weight, for it is remedied, or counteracted, in an exactly just proportion, by the deposit on the ground of just so much of the end of the rope as is necessary. If, on the other hand, any circumstances should cause undue levity, and consequent ascent, this levity is immediately counteracted by the additional weight of rope upraised from the earth. Thus, the balloon can neither ascend or descend, except within very narrow limits, and its resources, either in gas or ballast, remain comparatively unimpaired. When passing over an expanse of water, it becomes necessary to employ small kegs of copper or wood, filled with liquid ballast of a lighter nature than water. These float, and serve all the purposes of a mere rope on land. Another most important office of the guide-rope, is to point out the *direction* of the balloon. The rope *drags*, either on land or sea, while the balloon is free; the latter, consequently, is always in advance, when any progress whatever is made: a comparison, therefore, by means of the compass, of the relative positions of the two objects, will always indicate the *course*. In the same way, the angle formed by the rope with the vertical axis of the machine, indicates the *velocity*. When there is *no* angle—in other words, when the rope hangs perpendicularly, the whole apparatus is stationary; but the larger the angle, that is to say, the farther the balloon precedes the end of the rope, the greater the velocity; and the converse.

As the original design was to cross the British Channel, and alight as near Paris as possible, the voyagers had taken the precaution to prepare themselves with passports directed to all parts of the Continent, specifying the nature of the expedition, as in the case of the Nassau voyage, and entitling the adventurers to exemption from the usual formalities of office: unexpected events, however, rendered these passports superfluous.

The inflation was commenced very quietly at daybreak, on Saturday morning, the 6th instant, in the Court-Yard of Weal-Vor House, Mr. Osborne's seat, about a mile from Penstruthal, in North Wales; and at 7 minutes past 11, every thing being ready for departure, the balloon was set free, rising gently but steadily, in a direction nearly South; no use being made, for the first half hour, of either the screw or the rudder. We proceed now with the journal, as transcribed by Mr. Forsyth from the joint MSS. of Mr. Monck Mason, and Mr. Ainsworth. The body of the journal, as given, is in the hand-writing of Mr. Mason, and a P.S. is appended, each day, by Mr. Ainsworth, who has in preparation, and will shortly give the public a more minute, and no doubt, a thrillingly interesting account of the voyage.

The JOURNAL

SATURDAY, APRIL THE 6th.—Every preparation likely to embarrass us, having been made over night, we commenced the inflation this morning at daybreak; but owing to a thick fog, which encumbered the folds of the silk and rendered it unmanageable, we did not get through before nearly eleven o'clock. Cut loose, then, in high spirits, and rose gently but steadily, with a light breeze at North, which bore us in the direction of the British Channel. Found the ascending force greater than we had expected; and as we arose higher and so got clear of the cliffs, and more in the sun's rays, our ascent became very rapid. I did not wish, however, to lose gas at so early a period of the adventure, and so concluded to ascend for the present. We soon ran out our guide-rope; but even when we had raised it clear of the earth, we still went up very rapidly. The balloon was unusually steady, and looked beautifully. In about ten minutes after starting, the barometer indicated an altitude of 15,000 feet. The weather was remarkably fine, and the view of the subjacent country—a most romantic one when seen from any point,—was now especially sublime. The numerous deep gorges presented the appearance of lakes, on account of the dense vapors with which they were filled, and the pinnacles and crags to the South East, piled in inextricable confusion, resembled nothing so much as the giant cities of eastern fable. We were rapidly approaching the mountains in the South; but our elevation was more than sufficient to enable us to pass them in safety. In a few minutes we soared over them in fine style; and Mr. Ainsworth, with the seamen, were surprised at their apparent want of altitude when viewed from the car, the tendency of great elevation in a balloon being to reduce inequalities of the surface below, to nearly a dead level. At half-past eleven still proceeding nearly South, we obtained our first view of the Bristol Channel; and, in fifteen minutes afterward, the line of breakers on the coast appeared immediately beneath us, and we were fairly out at sea. We now resolved to let off enough gas to bring our guide-rope, with the buoys affixed, into the water. This was immediately done, and we commenced a gradual descent. In about twenty minutes our first buoy dipped, and at the touch of the second soon afterward, we remained stationary as to elevation. We were all now anxious to test the efficiency of the rudder and screw, and we put them both into requisition forthwith, for the purpose of altering our direction more to the eastward, and in a line for Paris. By means of the rudder we instantly effected the necessary change of direction, and our course was brought nearly at right angles to that of the wind; when we set in motion the spring of the screw, and were rejoiced to find it propel us readily as desired. Upon this we gave nine hearty cheers, and dropped in the sea a bottle, enclosing a slip of parchment with a brief account of the principle of the invention. Hardly, however, had we done with our rejoicings, when an unforeseen accident occurred which discouraged us in no little degree. The steel rod connecting the spring with the propeller was suddenly jerked out of place, at the car end, (by a swaying of the car through some movement of one of the two seamen we had taken up,) and in an instant hung dangling out of reach, from the pivot of the axis of the screw. While we were endeavoring to regain it, our attention being completely absorbed, we became involved in a strong current of wind from the East, which bore us, with rapidly increasing force, toward the Atlantic. We soon found ourselves driving out to sea at the rate of not less, certainly, than fifty or sixty miles an hour, so that we came up with Cape Clear, at some forty miles to our North, before we had secured the rod, and had time to think what we were about. It was now that Mr. Ainsworth made an extraordinary, but to my fancy, a by no means unreasonable or chimerical proposition, in which he was instantly seconded by Mr. Holland—viz.: that we should take advantage of the strong gale which bore us on, and in place of beating back to Paris, make an attempt to reach the coast of North America. After slight reflection I gave a willing assent to this bold proposition, which (strange to say) met with objection from the two seamen only. As the stronger party, however, we overruled their fears, and kept resolutely upon our course. We steered due West; but as the trailing of the buoys materially impeded our progress, and we had the balloon abundantly at command, either for ascent or descent, we first threw out fifty pounds of ballast, and then wound up (by means of a windlass) so much of a rope as brought it quite clear of the sea. We perceived the effect of this manœuvre immediately, in a vastly increased rate of progress; and, as the gale freshened, we flew with a velocity nearly inconceivable; the guide-rope flying out behind the car, like a streamer from a vessel. It is needless to say that a very short time sufficed us to lose sight of the coast. We passed over innumerable vessels of all kinds, a few of which were endeavoring to beat up, but the most of them lying to. We occasioned the greatest excitement on board all—an excitement greatly relished by ourselves, and especially by our two men, who, now under the influence of a dram of Geneva, seemed resolved to give all scruple, or fear, to the wind. Many of the vessels fired signal guns; and in all we were saluted with loud cheers (which we heard with surprising distinctness) and the waving of caps and handkerchiefs. We kept on in this manner throughout the day, with no material incident, and, as the shades of night closed around us, we made a rough estimate of the distance traversed. It could not have been less than five hundred miles, and was probably much more. The propeller was kept in constant operation, and, no doubt, aided our progress materially. As the sun went down, the gale freshened into an absolute hurricane, and the ocean beneath was clearly visible on account of its phosphorescence. The wind was from the East all night, and gave us the brightest omen of success. We suffered no little from cold, and the dampness of the atmosphere was most unpleasant; but the ample space in the car enabled us to lie down, and by means of cloaks and a few blankets, we did sufficiently well.

P.S. (by Mr. Ainsworth). The last nine hours have been unquestionably the most exciting of my life. I can conceive nothing more sublimating than the strange peril and novelty of an adventure such as this. May God grant that we succeed! I ask not success for mere safety to my insignificant person, but for the sake of human knowledge and—for the vastness of the triumph. And yet the feat is only so evidently feasible that the sole wonder is why men have scrupled to attempt it before. One single gale such as now befriends us—let such a tempest whirl forward a balloon for four or five days (these gales often last longer) and the voyager will be easily borne, in that period, from coast to coast. In view of such a gale the broad Atlantic becomes a mere lake. I am more struck, just now, with the supreme silence which reigns in the sea beneath us, notwithstanding its agitation, than with any other phenomenon presenting itself. The waters give up no voice to the heavens. The immense flaming ocean writhes and is tortured uncomplainingly. The mountainous surges suggest the idea of innumerable dumb gigantic fiends struggling in impotent agony. In a night such as is this to me, a man *lives*—lives a whole century of ordinary life—nor would I forego this rapturous delight for that of a whole century of ordinary existence.

Sunday, the 7th. [Mr. Mason's MS.] This morning the gale, by 10, had subsided to an eight or nine knot breeze, (for a vessel at sea,) and bears us, perhaps, thirty miles per hour, or more. It has veered however, very considerably to the north; and now, at sundown, we are holding our course due west, principally by the screw and rudder, which answer their purposes to admiration. I regard the project as thoroughly successful, and the easy navigation of the air in any direction (not exactly in the teeth of a gale) as no longer problematical. We could not have made head against the strong wind of yesterday; but, by ascending, we might have got out of its influence, if requisite. Against a pretty stiff breeze, I feel convinced, we can make our way with the propeller. At noon, to-day, ascended to an elevation of nearly 25,000 feet, by discharging ballast. Did this to search for a more direct current, but found none so favorable as the one we are now in. We have an abundance of gas to take us across this small pond, even should the voyage last three weeks. I have not the slightest fear for the result. The difficulty has been strangely exaggerated and misapprehended. I can choose my current, and should I find *all* currents against me, I can make very tolerable headway with the propeller. We have had no incidents worth recording. The night promises fair.

P.S. [By Mr. Ainsworth.] I have little to record, except the fact (to me quite a surprising one) that, at an elevation equal to that of Cotopaxi, I experienced neither very intense cold, nor headache, nor difficulty of breathing; neither, I find, did Mr. Mason, nor Mr. Holland, nor Sir Everard. Mr. Osborne complained of constriction of the chest—but this soon wore off. We have flown at a great rate during the day, and we must be more than half way across the Atlantic. We have passed over some twenty or thirty vessels of various kinds, and all seem to be delightfully astonished. Crossing the ocean in a balloon is not so difficult a feat after all. *Omne ignotum pro magnifico. Mem:* at 25,000 feet elevation the sky appears nearly black, and the stars are distinctly visible; while the sea does not seem convex (as one might suppose) but absolutely and most unequivocally *concave.*[1]

1 Note.—Mr. Ainsworth has not attempted to account for this phenomena, which, however, is quite susceptible of explanation. A line dropped from an elevation of 25,000 feet, perpendicularly to the surface of the earth (or sea), would form the perpendicular of a right-angled triangle, of which the base would extend from the right angle to the horizon, and the hypothenuse from the horizon to the balloon. But the 25,000 feet of altitude is little or nothing, in comparison with the extent of the prospect. In other words, the base and hypothenuse of the supposed triangle would be so long when compared with the perpendicular, that the two former may be regarded as nearly parallel. In this manner the horizon of the æronaut would appear to be *on a level* with the car. But, as the point immediately beneath him seems, and is, at a great distance below him, it seems, of course, also, at a great distance below the horizon. Hence the impression of *concavity;* and this impression must remain, until he elevation shall bear so great a proportion to the extent of prospect, that the apparet parallelism of the base and hypothenuse disappears—when the earth's real convexity must become apparent.

Monday, the 8th. [Mr. Mason's MS.] This morning we had again some little trouble with the rod of the propeller, which must be entirely remodeled, for fear of serious accident—I mean the steel rod—not the vanes. The latter could not be improved. The wind has been blowing steadily and strongly from the northeast all day; and so far fortune seems bent upon favoring us. Just before day, we were all somewhat alarmed at some odd noises and concussions in the balloon, accompanied with the apparent rapid subsidence of the whole machine. These phenomena were occasioned by the expansion of the gas, through increase of heat in the atmosphere, and the consequent disruption of the minute particles of ice with which the network had become encrusted during the night. Threw down several bottles to the vessels below. Saw one of them picked up by a large ship—seemingly one of the New York line packets. Endeavored to make out her name, but could not be sure of it. Mr. Osborne's telescope made it out something like "Atalanta." It is now 12, at night, and we are still going nearly west, at a rapid pace. The sea is peculiarly phosphorescent.

P.S. [By Mr. Ainsworth.] It is now 2, A. M., and nearly calm, as well as I can judge—but it is very difficult to determine this point, since we move *with* the air so completely. I have not slept since quitting Wheal-Vor, but can stand it no longer, and must take a nap. We cannot be far from the American coast.

Tuesday, the 9th. [Mr. Ainsworth's M. S.] *One, P.M. We are in full view of the low coast of South Carolina.* The great problem is accomplished. We have crossed the Atlantic—fairly and *easily* crossed it in a balloon! God be praised! Who shall say that anything is impossible hereafter?

The Journal here ceases. Some particulars of the descent were communicated, however, by Mr. Ainsworth to Mr. Forsyth. It was nearly dead calm when the voyagers first came in view of the coast, which was immediately recognized by both the seamen, and by Mr. Osborne. The latter gentleman having acquaintances at Fort Moultrie, it was immediately resolved to descend in its vicinity. The balloon was brought over the beach (the tide being out and the sand hard, smooth, and admirably adapted for a descent,) and the grapnel let go, which took firm hold at once. The inhabitants of the island, and of the fort, thronged out, of course, to see the balloon; but it was with the greatest difficulty that any one could be made to credit the actual voyage—*the crossing of the Atlantic*. The grapnel caught at 2, P.M., precisely; and thus the whole voyage was completed in seventy-five hours; or rather less, counting from shore to shore. No serious accident occurred. No real danger was at any time apprehended. The balloon was exhausted and secured without trouble; and when the MS. from which this narrative is compiled was despatched from Charleston, the party were still at Fort Moultrie. Their farther intentions were not ascertained; but we can safely promise our readers some additional information either on Monday or in the course of the next day, at farthest.

This is unquestionably the most stupendous, the most interesting, and the most important undertaking, ever accomplished or even attempted by man. What magnificent events may ensue, it would be useless now to think of determining.

ELEONORA

Sub conservatione formae specificae salva anima.
Raymond Lully

I AM COME of a race noted for vigor of fancy and ardor of passion. Men have called me mad; but the question is not yet settled, whether madness is or is not the loftiest intelligence—whether much that is glorious—whether all that is profound—does not spring from disease of thought—from *moods* of mind exalted at the expense of the general intellect. They who dream by day are cognizant of many things which escape those who dream only by night. In their gray visions they obtain glimpses of eternity, and thrill, in waking, to find that they have been upon the verge of the great secret. In snatches, they learn something of the wisdom which is of good, and more of the mere knowledge which is of evil. They penetrate, however rudderless or compassless, into the vast ocean of the "light ineffable"; and again, like the adventures of the Nubian geographer, "*agressi sunt mare tenebrarum, quid in eo esset exploraturi.*"

We will say, then, that I am mad. I grant, at least, that there are two distinct conditions of my mental existence—the condition of a lucid reason, not to be disputed, and belonging to the memory of events forming the first epoch of my life—and a condition of shadow and doubt, appertaining to the present, and to the recollection of what constitutes the second great era of my being. Therefore, what I shall tell of the earlier period, believe; and to what I may relate of the later time, give only such credit as may seem due; or doubt it altogether; or, if doubt it ye cannot, then play unto its riddle the Oedipus.

She whom I loved in youth, and of whom I now pen calmly and

distinctly these remembrances, was the sole daughter of the only sister of my mother long departed. Eleonora was the name of my cousin. We had always dwelled together, beneath a tropical sun, in the Valley of the Many-Colored Grass. No unguided footstep ever came upon that vale; for it lay far away up among a range of giant hills that hung beetling around about it, shutting out the sunlight from its sweetest recesses. No path was trodden in its vicinity; and, to reach our happy home, there was need of putting back, with force, the foliage of many thousands of forest trees, and of crushing to death the glories of many millions of fragrant flowers. Thus it was that we lived all alone, knowing nothing of the world without the valley,—I, and my cousin, and her mother.

From the dim regions beyond the mountains at the upper end of our encircled domain, there crept out a narrow and deep river, brighter than all save the eyes of Eleonora; and, winding stealthily about in mazy courses, it passed away, at length, through a shadowy gorge, among hills still dimmer than those whence it had issued. We called it the "River of Silence;" for there seemed to be a hushing influence in its flow. No murmur arose from its bed, and so gently it wandered along, that the pearly pebbles upon which we loved to gaze, far down within its bosom, stirred not at all, but lay in a motionless content, each in its own old station, shining on gloriously forever.

The margin of the river, and of the many dazzling rivulets that glided through devious ways into its channel, as well as the spaces that extended from the margins away down into the depths of the streams until they reached the bed of pebbles at the bottom,—these spots, not less than the whole surface of the valley, from the river to the mountains that girdled it in, were carpeted all by a soft green grass, thick, short, perfectly even, and vanilla-perfumed, but so besprinkled throughout with the yellow buttercup, the white daisy, the purple violet, and the ruby-red asphodel, that its exceeding beauty spoke to our hearts in loud tones, of the love and of the glory of God.

And, here and there, in groves about this grass, like wildernesses of dreams, sprang up fantastic trees, whose tall slender stems stood not upright, but slanted gracefully toward the light that peered at noon-day into the center of the valley. Their bark was speckled with the vivid alternate splendor of ebony and silver, and was smoother than all save the cheeks of Eleonora; so, that but for the brilliant green of the huge leaves that spread from their summits in long, tremulous lines, dallying with the Zephyrs, one might have fancied them giant serpents of Syria doing homage to their Sovereign the Sun.

Hand in hand about this valley, for fifteen years, roamed I with Eleonora before Love entered within our hearts. It was one evening at the close of the third lustrum of her life, and of the fourth of my own, that we sat, locked in each other's embrace, beneath the serpent-like trees, and looked down within the waters of the River of Silence at our images therein. We spoke no words during the rest of that sweet day; and our words even upon the morrow were tremulous and few. We had drawn the god Eros from that wave, and now we felt that he had enkindled within us the fiery souls of our forefathers. The passions which had for centuries distinguished our race, came thronging with the fancies for which they had been equally noted, and together breathed a delirious bliss over the Valley of the Many-Colored Grass. A change fell upon all things. Strange, brilliant flowers, star-shaped, burst out upon the trees where no flowers had been known before. The tints of the green carpet deepened; and when, one by one, the white daisies shrank away, there sprang up in place of them, ten by ten of the ruby-red asphodel. And life arose in our paths; for the tall flamingo, hitherto unseen, with all gay glowing birds, flaunted his scarlet plumage before us. The golden and silver fish haunted the river, out of the bosom of which issued, little by little, a murmur that swelled, at length, into a lulling melody more divine than that of the harp of Æolus—sweeter than all save the voice of Eleonora. And now, too, a voluminous cloud, which we had long watched in the regions of Hesper, floated out thence, all gorgeous in crimson and gold, and settling in peace above us, sank, day by day, lower and lower, until its edges rested upon the tops of the mountains, turning all their dimness into magnificence, and shutting us up, as if forever, within a magic prison-house of grandeur and of glory.

The loveliness of Eleonora was that of the Seraphim; but she was a maiden artless and innocent as the brief life she had led among the flowers. No guile disguised the fervor of love which animated her heart, and she examined with me its inmost recesses as we walked together in the Valley of the Many-Colored Grass, and discoursed of the mighty changes which had lately taken place therein.

At length, having spoken one day, in tears, of the last sad change which must befall Humanity, she thenceforward dwelt only upon this one sorrowful theme, interweaving it into all our converse, as, in the songs of the bard of Schiraz, the same images are found occurring, again and again, in every impressive variation of phrase.

She had seen that the finger of Death was upon her bosom—that, like the ephemeron, she had been made perfect in loveliness only to die; but the terrors of the grave to her, lay solely in a consideration which she revealed to me, one evening at twilight, by the banks of the River of Silence. She grieved to think that, having entombed her in the Valley of the Many-Colored Grass, I would quit forever its happy recesses, transferring the love which now was so passionately her own to some maiden of the outer and every-day world. And, then and there, I threw myself hurriedly at the feet of Eleonora, and offered up a vow, to herself and to Heaven, that I would never bind myself in marriage to any daughter of Earth—that I would in no manner prove recreant to her dear memory, or to the memory of the devout affection with which she had blessed me. And I called the Mighty Ruler of the Universe to witness the pious solemnity of my vow. And the curse which I invoked of *Him* and of her, a saint in Helusion, should I prove traitorous to that promise, involved a penalty the exceeding great horror of which will not permit me to make record of it here. And the bright eyes of Eleonora grew brighter at my words; and she sighed as if a deadly burthen had been taken from her breast; and she trembled and very bitterly wept; but she made acceptance of the vow, (for what was she but a child?) and it made easy to her the bed of her death. And she said to me, not many days afterward, tranquilly dying, that, because of what I had done for the comfort of her spirit, she would watch over me in that spirit when departed, and, if so it were permitted her, return to me visibly in the watches of the night; but, if this thing were, indeed, beyond the power of the souls in Paradise, that she would, at least, give me frequent indications of her presence; sighing upon me in the evening winds, or filling the air which I breathed with perfume from the censers of the angels. And, with these words upon her lips, she yielded up her innocent life, putting an end to the first epoch of my own.

Thus far I have faithfully said. But as I pass the barrier in Time's path, formed by the death of my beloved, and proceed with the second era of my existence, I feel that a shadow gathers over my brain, and I mistrust the perfect sanity of the record. But let me on.—Years dragged themselves along heavily, and still I dwelled within the Valley of the Many-Colored Grass; but a second change had come upon all things. The star-shaped flowers shrank into the stems of the trees, and appeared no more. The tints of the green carpet faded; and, one by one, the ruby-red asphodels withered away; and there sprang up, in place of them, ten by ten, dark, eye-like violets, that writhed uneasily and were ever encumbered with dew. And Life departed from our paths; for the tall flamingo flaunted no longer his scarlet plumage before us, but flew sadly from the vale into the hills, with all the gay glowing birds that had arrived in his company. And the golden and silver fish swam down through the gorge at the lower end of our domain and bedecked the sweet river never again. And the lulling melody that had ben softer than the wind-harp of Æolus, and more divine than all save the voice of Eleonor, it died little by little away, in murmurs growing lower and lower, until the stream returned, at length, utterly, into the solemnity of its original silence. And then, lastly, the voluminous cloud uprose, and, abandoning the tops of the mountains to the dimness of old, fell back into the regions of Hesper, and took away all its manifold golden and gorgeous glories from the Valley of the Many-Colored Grass.

Yet the promises of Eleonora were not forgotten; for I heard the sounds of the swinging of the censers of the angels; and streams of a holy perfume floated ever and ever about the valley; and at lone hours, when my heart beat heavily, the winds that bathed my brow came unto me laden with soft sighs; and indistinct murmurs filled often the night air; and once—oh, but once only! I was awakened from a slumber, like the slumber of death, by the pressing of spiritual lips upon my own.

But the void within my heart refused, even thus, to be filled. I longed for the love which had before filled it to overflowing. At length the valley *pained* me through its memories of Eleonora, and I left it forever for the vanities and the turbulent triumphs of the world.

I found myself within a strange city, where all things might have served to blot from recollection the sweet dreams I had dreamed so long in the Valley of the Many-Colored Grass. The pomps and pageantries of a stately court, and the mad clangor of arms, and the radiant loveliness of woman, bewildered and intoxicated my brain. But as yet my soul had proved true to its vows, and the indications of the presence of Eleonora were still given me in the silent hours of the night. Suddenly, these manifestations they ceased; and the world grew dark before mine eyes; and I stood aghast at the burning thoughts which possessed—at the terrible temptations which beset me; for there came from some far, far distant and unknown land, into the gay court of the king I served, a maiden to whose beauty my whole recreant heart yielded at once—at whose footstool I bowed down without a struggle, in the most ardent, in the most abject worship of love. What indeed was my passion for the young girl of the valley in comparison with the fervor, and the delirium, and the spirit-lifting ecstasy of adoration with which I poured out my whole soul in tears at the feet of the ethereal Ermengarde?—Oh, bright was the seraph Ermengarde! and in that knowledge I had room for none other.—Oh, divine was the angel Ermengarde! and as I looked down into the depths of her memorial eyes, I thought only of them—and *of her*.

I wedded;—nor dreaded the curse I had invoked; and its bitterness was not visited upon me. And once—but once again in the silence of the night, there came through my lattice the soft sighs which had forsaken me; and they modeled themselves into familiar and sweet voice, saying—

"Sleep in peace!—for the Spirit of Love reigneth and ruleth, and, in taking to thy passionate heart her who is Ermengarde, thou art absolved, for reasons which shall be made known to thee in Heaven, of thy vows unto Eleonora."

THE SYSTEM OF DOCTOR TARR AND PROFESSOR FETHER

DURING THE AUTUMN of 18—, while on a tour through the extreme southern provinces of France, my route led me within a few miles of a certain Maison de Santé or private mad-house, about which I had heard much in Paris from my medical friends. As I had never visited a place of the kind, I thought the opportunity too good to be lost; and so proposed to my traveling companion (a gentleman with whom I had made casual acquaintance a few days before) that we should turn aside, for an hour or so, and look through the establishment. To this he objected—pleading haste in the first place, and, in the second, a very usual horror at the sight of a lunatic. He begged me, however, not to let any mere courtesy toward himself interfere with the gratification of my curiosity, and said that he would ride on leisurely, so that I might overtake him during the day, or, at all events, during the next. As he bade me good-bye, I bethought me that there might be some difficulty in obtaining access to the premises, and mentioned my fears on this point. He replied that, in fact, unless I had personal knowledge of the superintendent, Monsieur Maillard, or some credential in the way of a letter, a difficulty might be found to exist, as the regulations of these private mad-houses were more rigid than the public hospital laws. For himself, he added, he had, some years since, made the acquaintance of Maillard, and would so far assist me as to ride up to the door and introduce me; although his feelings on the subject of lunacy would not permit of his entering the house.

I thanked him, and, turning from the main road, we entered a grass-grown by-path, which, in half an hour, nearly lost itself in a dense forest, clothing the base of a mountain. Through this dank and gloomy wood we rode some two miles, when the Maison de Santé came in view. It was a fantastic chateau, much dilapidated, and indeed scarcely tenantable through age and neglect. Its aspect inspired me with absolute dread, and, checking my horse, I half resolved to turn back. I soon, however, grew ashamed of my weakness, and proceeded.

As we rode up to the gate-way, I perceived it slightly open, and the visage of a man peering through. In an instant afterward, this man came forth, accosted my companion by name, shook him cordially by the hand, and begged him to alight. It was Monsieur Maillard himself. He was a portly, fine-looking gentleman of the old school, with a polished manner, and a certain air of gravity, dignity, and authority which was very impressive.

My friend, having presented me, mentioned my desire to inspect the establishment, and received Monsieur Maillard's assurance that he would show me all attention, now took leave, and I saw him no more. When he had gone, the superintendent ushered me into a small and exceedingly neat parlor, containing, among other indications of refined taste, many books, drawings, pots of flowers, and musical instruments. A cheerful fire blazed upon the hearth. At a piano, singing an aria from Bellini, sat a young and very beautiful woman, who, at my entrance, paused in her song, and received me with graceful courtesy. Her voice was low, and her whole manner subdued. I thought, too, that I perceived the traces of sorrow in her countenance, which was excessively, although to my taste, not unpleasingly, pale. She was attired in deep mourning, and excited in my bosom a feeling of mingled respect, interest, and admiration.

I had heard, at Paris, that the institution of Monsieur Maillard was managed upon what is vulgarly termed the "system of soothing"—that all punishments were avoided—that even confinement was seldom resorted to—that the patients, while secretly watched, were left much apparent liberty, and that most of them were permitted to roam about the house and grounds in the ordinary apparel of persons in right mind. Keeping these impressions in view, I was cautious in what I said before the young lady; for I could not be sure that she was sane; and, in fact, there was a certain restless brilliancy about her eyes which half led me to imagine she was not. I confined my remarks, therefore, to general topics, and to such as I thought would not be displeasing or exciting even to a lunatic. She replied in a perfectly rational manner to all that I said; and even her original observations were marked with the soundest good sense, but a long acquaintance with the metaphysics of mania, had taught me to put no faith in such evidence of sanity, and I continued to practice, throughout the interview, the caution with which I commenced it.

Presently a smart footman in livery brought in a tray with fruit, wine, and other refreshments, of which I partook, the lady soon afterward leaving the room. As she departed I turned my eyes in an inquiring manner toward my host.

"No," he said, "oh, no—a member of my family—my niece, and a most accomplished woman." "I beg a thousand pardons for the suspicion," I replied, "but of course you will know how to excuse me. The excellent administration of your affairs here is well understood in Paris, and I thought it just possible, you know—

"Yes, yes—say no more—or rather it is myself who should thank you for the commendable prudence you have displayed. We seldom find so much of forethought in young men; and, more than once, some unhappy *contre-temps* has occurred in consequence of thoughtlessness on the part of our visitors. While my former system was in operation, and my patients were permitted the privilege of roaming to and fro at will, they were often aroused to a dangerous frenzy by injudicious persons who called to inspect the house. Hence I was obliged to enforce a rigid system of exclusion; and none obtained access to the premises upon whose discretion I could not rely."

"While your former system was in operation!" I said, repeating his words—"do I understand you, then, to say that the 'soothing system' of which I have heard so much is no longer in force?"

"It is now," he replied, "several weeks since we have concluded to renounce it forever."

"Indeed! you astonish me!"

"We found it, sir," he said, with a sigh, "absolutely necessary to return to the old usages. The danger of the soothing system was, at all times, appalling; and its advantages have been much overrated. I believe, sir, that in this house it has been given a fair trial, if ever in any. We did every thing that rational humanity could suggest. I am sorry that you could not have paid us a visit at an earlier period, that you might have judged for yourself. But I presume you are conversant with the soothing practice—with its details."

"Not altogether. What I have heard has been at third or fourth hand."

"I may state the system, then, in general terms, as one in which the patients were menages-humored. We contradicted no fancies which entered the brains of the mad. On the contrary, we not only indulged but encouraged them; and many of our most permanent cures have been thus effected. There is no argument which so touches the feeble reason of the madman as the *argumentum ad absurdum*. We have had men, for example, who fancied themselves chickens. The cure was, to insist upon the thing as a fact—to accuse the patient of stupidity in not sufficiently perceiving it to be a fact—and thus to refuse him any other diet for a week than that which properly appertains to a chicken. In this manner a little corn and gravel were made to perform wonders."

"But was this species of acquiescence all?"

"By no means. We put much faith in amusements of a simple kind, such as music, dancing, gymnastic exercises generally, cards, certain classes of books, and so forth. We affected to treat each individual as if for some ordinary physical disorder, and the word 'lunacy' was never employed. A great point was to set each lunatic to guard the actions of all the others. To repose confidence in the understanding or discretion of a madman, is to gain him body and soul. In this way we were enabled to dispense with an expensive body of keepers."

"And you had no punishments of any kind?"

"None."

"And you never confined your patients?"

"Very rarely. Now and then, the malady of some individual growing to a crisis, or taking a sudden turn of fury, we conveyed him to a secret cell, lest his disorder should infect the rest, and there kept him until we could dismiss him to his friends—for with the raging maniac we have nothing to do. He is usually removed to the public hospitals."

"And you have now changed all this—and you think for the better?"

"Decidedly. The system had its disadvantages, and even its dangers. It is now, happily, exploded throughout all the Maisons de Santé of France."

"I am very much surprised," I said, "at what you tell me; for I made sure that, at this moment, no other method of treatment for mania existed in any portion of the country."

"You are young yet, my friend," replied my host, "but the time will arrive when you will learn to judge for yourself of what is going on in the world, without trusting to the gossip of others. Believe nothing you hear, and only one-half that you see. Now about our Maisons de Santé, it is clear that some ignoramus has misled you. After dinner, however, when you have sufficiently recovered from the fatigue of your ride, I will be happy to take you over the house, and introduce to you a system which, in my opinion, and in that of every one who has witnessed its operation, is incomparably the most effectual as yet devised."

"Your own?" I inquired—"one of your own invention?"

"I am proud," he replied, "to acknowledge that it is—at least in some measure."

In this manner I conversed with Monsieur Maillard for an hour or two, during which he showed me the gardens and conservatories of the place.

"I cannot let you see my patients," he said, "just at present. To a sensitive mind there is always more or less of the shocking in such exhibitions; and I do not wish to spoil your appetite for dinner. We will dine. I can give you some veal à la Menehoult, with cauliflowers in velouté sauce—after that a glass of *Clos de Vougeot*—then your nerves will be sufficiently steadied."

At six, dinner was announced; and my host conducted me into a large salle a manger, where a very numerous company were assembled—twenty-five or thirty in all. They were, apparently, people of rank-certainly of high breeding—although their habiliments, I thought, were extravagantly rich, partaking somewhat too much of the ostentatious finery of the *vielle cour*. I noticed that at least two-thirds of these guests were ladies; and some of the latter were by no means accoutred in what a Parisian would consider good taste at the present day. Many females, for example, whose age could not have been less than seventy were bedecked with a profusion of jewelry, such as rings, bracelets, and earrings, and wore their bosoms and arms shamefully bare. I observed, too, that very few of the dresses were well made—or, at least, that very few of them fitted the wearers. In looking about, I discovered the interesting girl to whom Monsieur Maillard had presented me in the little parlor; but my surprise was great to see her wearing a hoop and farthingale, with high-heeled shoes, and a dirty cap of Brussels lace, so much too large for her that it gave her face a ridiculously diminutive expression. When I had first seen her, she was attired, most becomingly, in deep mourning. There was an air of oddity, in short, about the dress of the whole party, which, at first, caused me to recur to my original idea of the "soothing system," and to fancy that Monsieur Maillard had been willing to deceive me until after dinner, that I might experience no uncomfortable feelings during the repast, at finding myself dining with lunatics; but I remembered having been informed, in Paris, that the southern provincialists were a peculiarly eccentric people, with a vast number of antiquated notions; and then, too, upon conversing with several members of the company, my apprehensions were immediately and fully dispelled.

The dining-room itself, although perhaps sufficiently comfortable and of good dimensions, had nothing too much of elegance about it. For example, the floor was uncarpeted; in France, however, a carpet is frequently dispensed with. The windows, too, were without curtains; the shutters, being shut, were securely fastened with iron bars, applied diagonally, after the fashion of our ordinary shop-shutters. The apartment, I observed, formed, in itself, a wing of the chateau, and thus the windows were on three sides of the parallelogram, the door being at the other. There were no less than ten windows in all.

The table was superbly set out. It was loaded with plate, and more than loaded with delicacies. The profusion was absolutely barbaric. There were meats enough to have feasted the Anakim. Never, in all my life, had I witnessed so lavish, so wasteful an expenditure of the good things of life. There seemed very little taste, however, in the arrangements; and my eyes, accustomed to quiet lights, were sadly offended by the prodigious glare of a multitude of wax candles, which, in silver candelabra, were deposited upon the table, and all about the room, wherever it was possible to find a place. There were several active servants in attendance; and, upon a large table, at the farther end of the apartment, were seated seven or eight people with fiddles, fifes, trombones, and a drum. These fellows annoyed me very much, at intervals, during the repast, by an infinite variety of noises, which were intended for music, and which appeared to afford much entertainment to all present, with the exception of myself.

Upon the whole, I could not help thinking that there was much of the bizarre about every thing I saw—but then the world is made up of all kinds of persons, with all modes of thought, and all sorts of conventional customs. I had traveled, too, so much, as to be quite an adept at the *nil admirari*; so I took my seat very coolly at the right hand of my host, and, having an excellent appetite, did justice to the good cheer set before me.

The conversation, in the meantime, was spirited and general. The ladies, as usual, talked a great deal. I soon found that nearly all the company were well educated; and my host was a world of good-humored anecdote in himself. He seemed quite willing to speak of his position as superintendent of a Maison de Santé; and, indeed, the topic of lunacy was, much to my surprise, a favorite one with all present. A great many amusing stories were told, having reference to the whims of the patients.

"We had a fellow here once," said a fat little gentleman, who sat at my right,—"a fellow that fancied himself a tea-pot; and by the way, is it not especially singular how often this particular crotchet has entered the brain of the lunatic? There is scarcely an insane asylum in France which cannot supply a human tea-pot. Our gentleman was a Britannia — ware tea-pot, and was careful to polish himself every morning with buckskin and whiting."

"And then," said a tall man just opposite, "we had here, not long ago, a person who had taken it into his head that he was a donkey— which allegorically speaking, you will say, was quite true. He was a troublesome patient; and we had much ado to keep him within bounds. For a long time he would eat nothing but thistles; but of this idea we soon cured him by insisting upon his eating nothing else. Then he was perpetually kicking out his heels-so-so-"

"Mr. De Kock! I will thank you to behave yourself!" here interrupted an old lady, who sat next to the speaker. "Please keep your feet to yourself! You have spoiled my brocade! Is it necessary, pray, to illustrate a remark in so practical a style? Our friend here can surely comprehend you without all this. Upon my word, you are nearly as great a donkey as the poor unfortunate imagined himself. Your acting is very natural, as I live."

"*Mille pardons! Ma'm'selle!*" replied Monsieur De Kock, thus addressed—"a thousand pardons! I had no intention of offending. Ma'm'selle Laplace—Monsieur De Kock will do himself the honor of taking wine with you."

Here Monsieur De Kock bowed low, kissed his hand with much ceremony, and took wine with Ma'm'selle Laplace.

"Allow me, *mon ami*," now said Monsieur Maillard, addressing myself, "allow me to send you a morsel of this veal *à la* St. Menhoult—you will find it particularly fine."

At this instant three sturdy waiters had just succeeded in depositing safely upon the table an enormous dish, or trencher, containing what I supposed to be the "*monstrum horrendum, informe, ingens, cui lumen ademptum.*" A closer scrutiny assured me, however, that it was only a small calf roasted whole, and set upon its knees, with an apple in its mouth, as is the English fashion of dressing a hare.

"Thank you, no," I replied; "to say the truth, I am not particularly partial to veal *à la* St.—what is it?—for I do not find that it altogether agrees with me. I will change my plate, however, and try some of the rabbit."

There were several side-dishes on the table, containing what appeared to be the ordinary French rabbit—a very delicious morceau, which I can recommend.

"Pierre," cried the host, "change this gentleman's plate, and give him a side-piece of this rabbit *au-chat*."

"This what?" said I.

"This rabbit *au-chat*."

"Why, thank you—upon second thoughts, no. I will just help myself to some of the ham."

There is no knowing what one eats, thought I to myself, at the tables of these people of the province. I will have none of their rabbit *au-chat*—and, for the matter of that, none of their cat-au-rabbit either. "And then," said a cadaverous looking personage, near the foot of the table, taking up the thread of the conversation where it had been broken off,—"and then, among other oddities, we had a patient, once upon a time, who very pertinaciously maintained himself to be a Cordova cheese, and went about, with a knife in his hand, soliciting his friends to try a small slice from the middle of his leg."

"He was a great fool, beyond doubt," interposed some one, "but not to be compared with a certain individual whom we all know, with the exception of this strange gentleman. I mean the man who took himself for a bottle of champagne, and always went off with a pop and a fizz, in this fashion."

Here the speaker, very rudely, as I thought, put his right thumb in his left cheek, withdrew it with a sound resembling the popping of a cork, and then, by a dexterous movement of the tongue upon the teeth, created a sharp hissing and fizzing, which lasted for several minutes, in imitation of the frothing of champagne. This behavior, I saw plainly, was not very pleasing to Monsieur Maillard; but that gentleman said nothing, and the conversation was resumed by a very lean little man in a big wig.

"And then there was an ignoramus," said he, "who mistook himself for a frog, which, by the way, he resembled in no little degree. I wish you could have seen him, sir,"—here the speaker addressed myself—"it would have done your heart good to see the natural airs that he put on. Sir, if that man was not a frog, I can only observe that it is a pity he was not. His croak thus—*o-o-o-o-gh—o-o-o-o-gh!* was the finest note in the world—B flat; and when he put his elbows upon the table thus—after taking a glass or two of wine—and distended his mouth, thus, and rolled up his eyes, thus, and winked them with excessive rapidity, thus, why then, sir, I take it upon myself to say, positively, that you would have been lost in admiration of the genius of the man."

"I have no doubt of it," I said.

"And then," said somebody else, "then there was Petit Gaillard, who thought himself a pinch of snuff, and was truly distressed because he could not take himself between his own finger and thumb."

"And then there was Jules Desoulieres, who was a very singular genius, indeed, and went mad with the idea that he was a pumpkin. He persecuted the cook to make him up into pies—a thing which the cook indignantly refused to do. For my part, I am by no means sure that a pumpkin pie *à la* Desoulieres would not have been very capital eating indeed!"

"You astonish me!" said I; and I looked inquisitively at Monsieur Maillard.

"Ha! ha! ha!" said that gentleman—"he! he! he!—hi! hi! hi!—ho! ho!

ho!—hu! hu! hu! hu!—very good indeed! You must not be astonished, *mon ami*; our friend here is a wit—a drole—you must not understand him to the letter."

"And then," said some other one of the party,—"then there was Bouffon Le Grand—another extraordinary personage in his way. He grew deranged through love, and fancied himself possessed of two heads. One of these he maintained to be the head of Cicero; the other he imagined a composite one, being Demosthenes' from the top of the forehead to the mouth, and Lord Brougham's from the mouth to the chin. It is not impossible that he was wrong; but he would have convinced you of his being in the right; for he was a man of great eloquence. He had an absolute passion for oratory, and could not refrain from display. For example, he used to leap upon the dinner-table thus, and—and—"

Here a friend, at the side of the speaker, put a hand upon his shoulder and whispered a few words in his ear, upon which he ceased talking with great suddenness, and sank back within his chair.

"And then," said the friend who had whispered, "there was Boullard, the tee-totum. I call him the tee-totum because, in fact, he was seized with the droll but not altogether irrational crotchet, that he had been converted into a tee-totum. You would have roared with laughter to see him spin. He would turn round upon one heel by the hour, in this manner—so-

Here the friend whom he had just interrupted by a whisper, performed an exactly similar office for himself.

"But then," cried the old lady, at the top of her voice, "your Monsieur Boullard was a madman, and a very silly madman at best; for who, allow me to ask you, ever heard of a human tee-totum? The thing is absurd. Madame Joyeuse was a more sensible person, as you know. She had a crotchet, but it was instinct with common sense, and gave pleasure to all who had the honor of her acquaintance. She found, upon mature deliberation, that, by some accident, she had been turned into a chicken-cock; but, as such, she behaved with propriety. She flapped her wings with prodigious effect—so—so—and, as for her crow, it was delicious! Cock-a-doodle-doo!—cock-a-doodle-doo!—cock-a-doodle-de-doo-dooo-do-o-o-o-o-o-o!"

"Madame Joyeuse, I will thank you to behave yourself!" here interrupted our host, very angrily. "You can either conduct yourself as a lady should do, or you can quit the table forthwith—take your choice."

The lady (whom I was much astonished to hear addressed as Madame Joyeuse, after the description of Madame Joyeuse she had just given) blushed up to the eyebrows, and seemed exceedingly abashed at the reproof. She hung down her head, and said not a syllable in reply. But another and younger lady resumed the theme. It was my beautiful girl of the little parlor.

"Oh, Madame Joyeuse was a fool!" she exclaimed, "but there was really much sound sense, after all, in the opinion of Eugenie Salsafette. She was a very beautiful and painfully modest young lady, who thought the ordinary mode of habiliment indecent, and wished to dress herself, always, by getting outside instead of inside of her clothes. It is a thing very easily done, after all. You have only to do so—and then so—so—so—and then so—so—so—and then so—so—and then—

"*Mon dieu!* Ma'm'selle Salsafette!" here cried a dozen voices at once. "What are you about?—forbear!—that is sufficient!—we see, very plainly, how it is done!—hold! hold!" and several persons were already leaping from their seats to withhold Ma'm'selle Salsafette from putting herself upon a par with the Medicean Venus, when the point was very effectually and suddenly accomplished by a series of loud screams, or yells, from some portion of the main body of the chateau.

My nerves were very much affected, indeed, by these yells; but the rest of the company I really pitied. I never saw any set of reasonable people so thoroughly frightened in my life. They all grew as pale as so many corpses, and, shrinking within their seats, sat quivering and gibbering with terror, and listening for a repetition of the sound. It came again—louder and seemingly nearer—and then a third time very loud, and then a fourth time with a vigor evidently diminished. At this apparent dying away of the noise, the spirits of the company were immediately regained, and all was life and anecdote as before. I now ventured to inquire the cause of the disturbance.

"A mere bagtelle," said Monsieur Maillard. "We are used to these things, and care really very little about them. The lunatics, every now and then, get up a howl in concert; one starting another, as is sometimes the case with a bevy of dogs at night. It occasionally happens, however, that the concerto yells are succeeded by a simultaneous effort at breaking loose, when, of course, some little danger is to be apprehended."

"And how many have you in charge?"

"At present we have not more than ten, altogether."

"Principally females, I presume?"

"Oh, no—every one of them men, and stout fellows, too, I can tell you."

"Indeed! I have always understood that the majority of lunatics were of the gentler sex."

"It is generally so, but not always. Some time ago, there were about twenty-seven patients here; and, of that number, no less than eighteen were women; but, lately, matters have changed very much, as you see."

"Yes—have changed very much, as you see," here interrupted the gentleman who had broken the shins of Ma'm'selle Laplace.

"Yes—have changed very much, as you see!" chimed in the whole company at once.

"Hold your tongues, every one of you!" said my host, in a great rage. Whereupon the whole company maintained a dead silence for nearly a minute. As for one lady, she obeyed Monsieur Maillard to the letter, and thrusting out her tongue, which was an excessively long one, held it very resignedly, with both hands, until the end of the entertainment.

"And this gentlewoman," said I, to Monsieur Maillard, bending over and addressing him in a whisper—"this good lady who has just spoken, and who gives us the cock-a-doodle-de-doo—she, I presume, is harmless—quite harmless, eh?"

"Harmless!" ejaculated he, in unfeigned surprise, "why—why, what can you mean?"

"Only slightly touched?" said I, touching my head. "I take it for granted that she is not particularly not dangerously affected, eh?"

"*Mon dieu!* what is it you imagine? This lady, my particular old friend Madame Joyeuse, is as absolutely sane as myself. She has her little eccentricities, to be sure—but then, you know, all old women—all very old women—are more or less eccentric!"

"To be sure," said I,—"to be sure—and then the rest of these ladies and gentlemen—"

"Are my friends and keepers," interupted Monsieur Maillard, drawing himself up with hauteur,—"my very good friends and assistants."

"What! all of them?" I asked,—"the women and all?"

"Assuredly," he said,—"we could not do at all without the women; they are the best lunatic nurses in the world; they have a way of their own, you know; their bright eyes have a marvelous effect;—something like the fascination of the snake, you know."

"To be sure," said I,—"to be sure! They behave a little odd, eh?—they are a little queer, eh?—don't you think so?"

"Odd!—queer!—why, do you really think so? We are not very prudish, to be sure, here in the South—do pretty much as we please—enjoy life, and all that sort of thing, you know—"

"To be sure," said I,—"to be sure."

And then, perhaps, this Clos de Vougeot is a little heady, you know—a little strong—you understand, eh?"

"To be sure," said I,—"to be sure. By the bye, Monsieur, did I understand you to say that the system you have adopted, in place of the celebrated soothing system, was one of very rigorous severity?"

"By no means. Our confinement is necessarily close; but the treatment—the medical treatment, I mean—is rather agreeable to the patients than otherwise."

"And the new system is one of your own invention?"

"Not altogether. Some portions of it are referable to Professor Tarr, of whom you have, necessarily, heard; and, again, there are modifications in my plan which I am happy to acknowledge as belonging of right to the celebrated Fether, with whom, if I mistake not, you have the honor of an intimate acquaintance."

"I am quite ashamed to confess," I replied, "that I have never even heard the names of either gentleman before."

"Good heavens!" ejaculated my host, drawing back his chair abruptly, and uplifting his hands. "I surely do not hear you aright! You did not intend to say, eh? that you had never heard either of the learned Doctor Tarr, or of the celebrated Professor Fether?"

"I am forced to acknowledge my ignorance," I replied; "but the truth should be held inviolate above all things. Nevertheless, I feel humbled to the dust, not to be acquainted with the works of these, no doubt, extraordinary men. I will seek out their writings forthwith, and peruse them with deliberate care. Monsieur Maillard, you have really—I must confess it—you have really—made me ashamed of myself!" And this was the fact.

"Say no more, my good young friend," he said kindly, pressing my hand,—"join me now in a glass of Sauterne."

We drank. The company followed our example without stint. They chatted—they jested—they laughed—they perpetrated a thousand absurdities—the fiddles shrieked—the drum row-de-dowed—the trombones bellowed like so many brazen bulls of Phalaris—and the whole scene, growing gradually worse and worse, as the wines gained the ascendancy, became at length a sort of *pandemonium in petto*. In the meantime, Monsieur Maillard and myself, with some bottles of Sauterne and Vougeot between us, continued our conversation at the top of the voice. A word spoken in an ordinary key stood no more chance of being heard than the voice of a fish from the bottom of Niagra Falls.

"And, sir," said I, screaming in his ear, "you mentioned something before dinner about the danger incurred in the old system of soothing. How is that?"

"Yes," he replied, "there was, occasionally, very great danger indeed. There is no accounting for the caprices of madmen; and, in my opinion as well as in that of Dr. Tarr and Professor Fether, it is never safe to permit them to run at large unattended. A lunatic may be 'soothed,' as it is called, for a time, but, in the end, he is very apt to become obstreperous. His cunning, too, is proverbial and great. If he has a project in view, he conceals his design with a marvelous wisdom; and the dexterity with which he counterfeits sanity, presents, to the metaphysician, one of the most singular problems in the study of mind. When a madman appears thoroughly sane, indeed, it is high time to put him in a strait-jacket."

"But the danger, my dear sir, of which you were speaking, in your own experience—during your control of this house—have you had practical reason to think liberty hazardous in the case of a lunatic?"

"Here?—in my own experience?—why, I may say, yes. For example:—no very long while ago, a singular circumstance occurred in this very house. The 'soothing system,' you know, was then in operation, and the patients were at large. They behaved remarkably well—especially so, any one of sense might have known that some devilish scheme was brewing from that particular fact, that the fellows behaved so remarkably well. And, sure enough, one fine morning the keepers found themselves pinioned hand and foot, and thrown into the cells, where they were attended, as if they were the lunatics, by the lunatics themselves, who had usurped the offices of the keepers."

"You don't tell me so! I never heard of any thing so absurd in my life!"

"Fact—it all came to pass by means of a stupid fellow—a lunatic—who, by some means, had taken it into his head that he had invented a better system of government than any ever heard of before—of lunatic government, I mean. He wished to give his invention a trial, I suppose, and so he persuaded the rest of the patients to join him in a conspiracy for the overthrow of the reigning powers."

"And he really succeeded?"

"No doubt of it. The keepers and kept were soon made to exchange places. Not that exactly either—for the madmen had been free, but the keepers were shut up in cells forthwith, and treated, I am sorry to say, in a very cavalier manner."

"But I presume a counter-revolution was soon effected. This condition of things could not have long existed. The country people in the neighborhood-visitors coming to see the establishment—would have given the alarm."

"There you are out. The head rebel was too cunning for that. He admitted no visitors at all—with the exception, one day, of a very stupid-looking young gentleman of whom he had no reason to be afraid. He let him in to see the place—just by way of variety,—to have a little fun with him. As soon as he had gammoned him sufficiently, he let him out, and sent him about his business."

"And how long, then, did the madmen reign?"

"Oh, a very long time, indeed—a month certainly—how much longer I can't precisely say. In the meantime, the lunatics had a jolly season of it—that you may swear. They doffed their own shabby clothes, and made free with the family wardrobe and jewels. The cellars of the chateau were well stocked with wine; and these madmen are just the devils that know how to drink it. They lived well, I can tell you."

"And the treatment—what was the particular species of treatment which the leader of the rebels put into operation?"

"Why, as for that, a madman is not necessarily a fool, as I have already observed; and it is my honest opinion that his treatment was a much better treatment than that which it superseded. It was a very capital system indeed—simple—neat—no trouble at all—in fact it was delicious." It was here my host's observations were cut short by another series of yells, of the same character as those which had previously disconcerted us. This time, however, they seemed to proceed from persons rapidly approaching.

"Gracious heavens!" I ejaculated—"the lunatics have most undoubtedly broken loose."

"I very much fear it is so," replied Monsieur Maillard, now becoming excessively pale. He had scarcely finished the sentence, before loud shouts and imprecations were heard beneath the windows; and, immediately afterward, it became evident that some persons outside were endeavoring to gain entrance into the room. The door was beaten with what appeared to be a sledge-hammer, and the shutters were wrenched and shaken with prodigious violence.

A scene of the most terrible confusion ensued. Monsieur Maillard, to my excessive astonishment threw himself under the side-board. I had expected more resolution at his hands. The members of the orchestra, who, for the last fifteen minutes, had been seemingly too much intoxicated to do duty, now sprang all at once to their feet and to their instruments, and, scrambling upon their table, broke out, with one accord, into, *Yankee Doodle*, which they performed, if not exactly in tune, at least with an energy superhuman, during the whole of the uproar.

Meantime, upon the main dining-table, among the bottles and glasses, leaped the gentleman who, with such difficulty, had been restrained from leaping there before. As soon as he fairly settled himself, he commenced an oration, which, no doubt, was a very capital one, if it could only have been heard. At the same moment, the man with the tee-totum predilection, set himself to spinning around the apartment, with immense energy, and with arms outstretched at right angles with his body; so that he had all the air of a tee-totum in fact, and knocked everybody down that happened to get in his way. And now, too, hearing an incredible popping and fizzing of champagne, I discovered at length, that it proceeded from the person who performed the bottle of that delicate drink during dinner. And then, again, the frog-man croaked away as if the salvation of his soul depended upon every note that he uttered. And, in the midst of all this, the continuous braying of a donkey arose over all. As for my old friend, Madame Joyeuse, I really could have wept for the poor lady, she appeared so terribly perplexed. All she did, however, was to stand up in a corner, by the fireplace, and sing out incessantly at the top of her voice, "Cock-a-doodle-de-dooooooh!"

And now came the climax—the catastrophe of the drama. As no resistance, beyond whooping and yelling and cock-a-doodling, was offered to the encroachments of the party without, the ten windows were very speedily, and almost simultaneously, broken in. But I shall never forget the emotions of wonder and horror with which I gazed, when, leaping through these windows, and down among us pele-mele, fighting, stamping, scratching, and howling, there rushed a perfect army of what I took to be Chimpanzees, Ourang-Outangs, or big black baboons of the Cape of Good Hope.

I received a terrible beating—after which I rolled under a sofa and lay still. After lying there some fifteen minutes, during which time I listened with all my ears to what was going on in the room, I came to same satisfactory denouement of this tragedy. Monsieur Maillard, it appeared, in giving me the account of the lunatic who had excited his fellows to rebellion, had been merely relating his own exploits. This gentleman had, indeed, some two or three years before, been the superintendent of the establishment, but grew crazy himself, and so became a patient. This fact was unknown to the traveling companion who introduced me. The keepers, ten in number, having been suddenly overpowered, were first well tarred, then—carefully feathered, and then shut up in underground cells. They had been so imprisoned for more than a month, during which period Monsieur Maillard had generously allowed them not only the tar and feathers (which constituted his "system"), but some bread and abundance of water. The latter was pumped on them daily. At length, one escaping through a sewer, gave freedom to all the rest.

The "soothing system," with important modifications, has been resumed at the chateau; yet I cannot help agreeing with Monsieur Maillard, that his own "treatment" was a very capital one of its kind. As he justly observed, it was "simple—neat—and gave no trouble at all—not the least."

I have only to add that, although I have searched every library in Europe for the works of Doctor Tarr and Professor Fether, I have, up to the present day, utterly failed in my endeavors at procuring an edition.

NEVER BET THE DEVIL YOUR HEAD

"*CON TAL QUE las costumbres de un autor,*" says Don Thomas de las Torres, in the preface to his "Amatory Poems" "*sean puras y castas, importa muy poco que no sean igualmente severas sus obras*"—meaning, in plain English, that, provided the morals of an author are pure personally, it signifies nothing what are the morals of his books. We presume that Don Thomas is now in Purgatory for the assertion. It would be a clever thing, too, in the way of poetical justice, to keep him there until his "Amatory Poems" get out of print, or are laid definitely upo`n the shelf through lack of readers. Every fiction *should have* a moral; and, what is more to the purpose, the critics have discovered that every fiction *has*. Philip Melanchthon, some time ago, wrote a commentary upon the "Batrachomyomachia," and proved that the poet's object was to excite a distaste for sedition. Pierre la Seine, going a step farther, shows that the intention was to recommend to young men temperance in eating and drinking. Just so, too, Jacobus Hugo has satisfied himself that, by Euenis, Homer meant to insinuate John Calvin; by Antinous, Martin Luther; by the Lotophagi, Protestants in general; and, by the Harpies, the Dutch. Our more modern Scholiasts are equally acute. These fellows demonstrate a hidden meaning in "The Antediluvians," a parable in Powhatan," new views in "Cock Robin," and transcendentalism in "Hop O' My Thumb." In short, it has been shown that no man can sit down to write without a very profound design. Thus to authors in general much trouble is spared. A novelist, for example, need have no care of his moral. It is there—that is to say, it is somewhere—and the moral and the critics can take care of themselves. When the proper time arrives, all that the gentleman intended, and all that he did not intend, will be brought to light, in the *Dial*" or the *Down-Easter*, together with all that he ought to have intended, and the rest that he clearly meant to intend:—so that it will all come very straight in the end.

There is no just ground, therefore, for the charge brought against me by certain ignoramuses—that I have never written a moral tale, or, in more precise words, a tale with a moral. They are not the critics predestined to bring me out, and develop my morals:—that is the secret. By and by the *North American Quarterly Humdrum* will make them ashamed of their stupidity. In the meantime, by way of staying execution—by way of mitigating the accusations against me—I offer the sad history appended,—a history about whose obvious moral there can be no question whatever, since he who runs may read it in the large capitals which form the title of the tale. I should have credit for this arrangement—a far wiser one than that of La Fontaine and others, who reserve the impression to be conveyed until the last moment, and thus sneak it in at the fag end of their fables.

Defuncti injuria ne afficiantur was a law of the twelve tables, and *De mortuis nil nisi bonum* is an excellent injunction—even if the dead in question be nothing but dead small beer. It is not my design, therefore, to vituperate my deceased friend, Toby Dammit. He was a sad dog, it is true, and a dog's death it was that he died; but he himself was not to blame for his vices. They grew out of a personal defect in his mother. She did her best in the way of flogging him while an infant—for duties to her well—regulated mind were always pleasures, and babies, like tough steaks, or the modern Greek olive trees, are invariably the better for beating—but, poor woman! she had the misfortune to be left-handed, and a child flogged left-handedly had better be left unflogged. The world revolves from right to left. It will not do to whip a baby from left to right. If each blow in the proper direction drives an evil propensity out, it follows that every thump in an opposite one knocks its quota of wickedness in. I was often present at Toby's chastisements, and, even by the way in which he kicked, I could perceive that he was getting worse and worse every day. At last I saw, through the tears in my eyes, that there was no hope of the villain at all, and one day when he had been cuffed until he grew so black in the face that one might have mistaken him for a little African, and no effect had been produced beyond that of making him wriggle himself into a fit, I could stand it no longer, but went down upon my knees forthwith, and, uplifting my voice, made prophecy of his ruin.

The fact is that his precocity in vice was awful. At five months of age he used to get into such passions that he was unable to articulate. At six months, I caught him gnawing a pack of cards. At seven months he was in the constant habit of catching and kissing the female babies. At eight months he peremptorily refused to put his signature to the Temperance pledge. Thus he went on increasing in iniquity, month after month, until, at the close of the first year, he not only insisted upon wearing moustaches, but had contracted a propensity for cursing and swearing, and for backing his assertions by bets.

Through this latter most ungentlemanly practice, the ruin which I had predicted to Toby Dammit overtook him at last. The fashion had "grown with his growth and strengthened with his strength," so that, when he came to be a man, he could scarcely utter a sentence without interlarding it with a proposition to gamble. Not that he actually laid wagers—no. I will do my friend the justice to say that he would as soon have laid eggs. With him the thing was a mere formula—nothing more. His expressions on this head had no meaning attached to them whatever. They were simple if not altogether innocent expletives—imaginative phrases wherewith to round off a sentence. When he said "I'll bet you so and so," nobody ever thought of taking him up; but still I could not help thinking it my duty to put him down. The habit was an immoral one, and so I told him. It was a vulgar one—this I begged him to believe. It was discountenanced by society—here I said nothing but the truth. It was forbidden by act of Congress—here I had not the slightest intention of telling a lie. I remonstrated—but to no purpose. I demonstrated—in vain. I entreated—he smiled. I implored—he laughed. I preached—he sneered. I threatened—he swore. I kicked him—he called for the police. I pulled his nose—he blew it, and offered to bet the Devil his head that I would not venture to try that experiment again.

Poverty was another vice which the peculiar physical deficiency of Dammit's mother had entailed upon her son. He was detestably poor, and this was the reason, no doubt, that his expletive expressions about betting, seldom took a pecuniary turn. I will not be bound to say that I ever heard him make use of such a figure of speech as "I'll bet you a dollar." It was usually "I'll bet you what you please," or "I'll bet you what you dare," or "I'll bet you a trifle," or else, more significantly still, "*I'll bet the Devil my head.*"

This latter form seemed to please him best;—perhaps because it involved the least risk; for Dammit had become excessively parsimonious. Had any one taken him up, his head was small, and thus his loss would have been small too. But these are my own reflections and I am by no means sure that I am right in attributing them to him. At all events the phrase in question grew daily in favor, notwithstanding the gross impropriety of a man betting his brains like bank-notes:—but this was a point which my friend's perversity of disposition would not permit him to comprehend. In the end, he abandoned all other forms of wager, and gave himself up to "I'll bet the Devil my head," with a pertinacity and exclusiveness of devotion that displeased not less than it surprised me. I am always displeased by circumstances for which I cannot account. Mysteries force a man to think, and so injure his health. The truth is, there was something in the air with which Mr. Dammit was wont to give utterance to his offensive expression—something in his *manner* of enunciation—which at first interested, and afterward made me very uneasy—something which, for want of a more definite term at present, I must be permitted to call *queer*; but which Mr. Coleridge would have called mystical, Mr. Kant pantheistical, Mr. Carlyle twistical, and Mr. Emerson hyperquizzitistical. I began not to like it at all. Mr. Dammit's soul was in a perilous state. I resolved to bring all my eloquence into play to save it. I vowed to serve him as St. Patrick, in the Irish chronicle, is said to have served the toad,—that is to say, "awaken him to a sense of his situation." I addressed myself to the task forthwith. Once more I betook myself to remonstrance. Again I collected my energies for a final attempt at expostulation.

When I had made an end of my lecture, Mr. Dammit indulged himself in some very equivocal behavior. For some moments he remained silent, merely looking me inquisitively in the face. But presently he threw his head to one side, and elevated his eyebrows to a great extent. Then he spread out the palms of his hands and shrugged up his shoulders. Then he winked with the right eye. Then he repeated the operation with the left. Then he shut them both up very tight. Then he opened them both so very wide that I became seriously alarmed for the consequences.

Then, applying his thumb to his nose, he thought proper to make an indescribable movement with the rest of his fingers. Finally, setting his arms a-kimbo, he condescended to reply.

I can call to mind only the beads of his discourse. He would be obliged to me if I would hold my tongue. He wished none of my advice. He despised all my insinuations. He was old enough to take care of himself. Did I still think him baby Dammit? Did I mean to say any thing against his character? Did I intend to insult him? Was I a fool? Was my maternal parent aware, in a word, of my absence from the domiciliary residence? He would put this latter question to me as to a man of veracity, and he would bind himself to abide by my reply. Once more he would demand explicitly if my mother knew that I was out. My confusion, he said, betrayed me, and he would be willing to bet the Devil his head that she did not.

Mr. Dammit did not pause for my rejoinder. Turning upon his heel, he left my presence with undignified precipitation. It was well for him that he did so. My feelings had been wounded. Even my anger had been aroused. For once I would have taken him up upon his insulting wager. I would have won for the Arch-Enemy Mr. Dammit's little head—for the fact is, my mamma *was* very well aware of my merely temporary absence from home.

But *Khoda shefa midêhed*—Heaven gives relief—as the Mussulmans say when you tread upon their toes. It was in pursuance of my duty that I had been insulted, and I bore the insult like a man. It now seemed to me, however, that I had done all that could be required of me, in the case of this miserable individual, and I resolved to trouble him no longer with my counsel, but to leave him to his conscience and himself. But although I forebore to intrude with my advice, I could not bring myself to give up his society altogether. I even went so far as to humor some of his less reprehensible propensities; and there were times when I found myself lauding his wicked jokes, as epicures do mustard, with tears in my eyes:—so profoundly did it grieve me to hear his evil talk.

One fine day, having strolled out together, arm in arm, our route led us in the direction of a river. There was a bridge, and we resolved to cross it. It was roofed over, by way of protection from the weather, and the archway, having but few windows, was thus very uncomfortably dark. As we entered the passage, the contrast between the external glare and the interior gloom struck heavily upon my spirits. Not so upon those of the unhappy Dammit, who offered to bet the Devil his head that I was hipped. He seemed to be in an unusual good humor. He was excessively lively—so much so that I entertained I know not what of uneasy suspicion. It is not impossible that he was affected with the transcendentals. I am not well enough versed, however, in the diagnosis of this disease to speak with decision upon the point; and unhappily there were none of my friends of the *Dial* present. I suggest the idea, nevertheless, because of a certain species of austere Merry-Andrewism which seemed to beset my poor friend, and caused him to make quite a Tom-Fool of himself. Nothing would serve him but wriggling and skipping about under and over every thing that came in his way; now shouting out, and now lisping out, all manner of odd little and big words, yet preserving the gravest face in the world all the time. I really could not make up my mind whether to kick or to pity him. At length, having passed nearly across the bridge, we approached the termination of the footway, when our progress was impeded by a turnstile of some height. Through this I made my way quietly, pushing it around as usual. But this turn would not serve the turn of Mr. Dammit. He insisted upon leaping the stile, and said he could cut a pigeon-wing over it in the air. Now this, conscientiously speaking, I did not think he could do. The best pigeon-winger over all kinds of style was my friend Mr. Carlyle, and as I knew *he* could not do it, I would not believe that it could be done by Toby Dammit. I therefore told him, in so many words, that he was a braggadocio, and could not do what he said. For this I had reason to be sorry afterward;—for he straightway offered to *bet the Devil his head* that he could.

I was about to reply, notwithstanding my previous resolutions, with some remonstrance against his impiety, when I heard, close at my elbow, a slight cough, which sounded very much like the ejaculation "*ahem!*" I started, and looked about me in surprise. My glance at length fell into a nook of the frame—work of the bridge, and upon the figure of a little lame old gentleman of venerable aspect. Nothing could be more reverend than his whole appearance; for he not only had on a full suit of black, but his shirt was perfectly clean and the collar turned very neatly down over a white cravat, while his hair was parted in front like a girl's. His hands were clasped pensively together over his stomach, and his two eyes were carefully rolled up into the top of his head.

Upon observing him more closely, I perceived that he wore a black silk apron over his small-clothes; and this was a thing which I thought very odd. Before I had time to make any remark, however, upon so singular a circumstance, he interrupted me with a second "*ahem!*"

To this observation I was not immediately prepared to reply. The fact is, remarks of this laconic nature are nearly unanswerable. I have known a *Quarterly Review nonplussed by* the word "*Fudge!*" I am not ashamed to say, therefore, that I turned to Mr. Dammit for assistance.

"Dammit," said I, "what are you about? don't you hear?—the gentleman says 'ahem!'" I looked sternly at my friend while I thus addressed him; for, to say the truth, I felt particularly puzzled, and when a man is particularly puzzled he must knit his brows and look savage, or else he is pretty sure to look like a fool.

"Dammit," observed I—although this sounded very much like an oath, than which nothing was further from my thoughts—"Dammit," I suggested—"the gentleman says '*ahem!*'"

I do not attempt to defend my remark on the score of profundity; I did not think it profound myself; but I have noticed that the effect of our speeches is not always proportionate with their importance in our own eyes; and if I had shot Mr. D. through and through with a Paixhan bomb, or knocked him in the head with the *Poets and Poetry of America*, he could hardly have been more discomfited than when I addressed him with those simple words: "Dammit, what are you about?—don't you hear?—the gentleman says '*ahem!*'"

"You don't say *so*?" gasped he at length, after turning more colors than a pirate runs up, one after the other, when chased by a man-of-war. "Are you quite sure he said that? Well, at all events I am in for it now, and may as well put a bold face upon the matter. Here goes, then—*ahem!*"

At this the little old gentleman seemed pleased—God only knows why. He left his station at the nook of the bridge, limped forward with a gracious air, took Dammit by the hand and shook it cordially, looking all the while straight up in his face with an air of the most unadulterated benignity which it is possible for the mind of man to imagine.

"I am quite sure you will win it, Dammit," said he, with the frankest of all smiles, "but we are obliged to have a trial, you know, for the sake of mere form."

"Ahem!" replied my friend, taking off his coat, with a deep sigh, tying a pocket-handkerchief around his waist, and producing an unaccountable alteration in his countenance by twisting up his eyes and bringing down the corners of his mouth—"ahem!" And "ahem!" said he again, after a pause; and not another word more than "ahem!" did I ever know him to say after that. "Aha!" thought I, without expressing myself aloud—"this is quite a remarkable silence on the part of Toby Dammit, and is no doubt a consequence of his verbosity upon a previous occasion. One extreme induces another. I wonder if he has forgotten the many unanswerable questions which he propounded to me so fluently on the day when I gave him my last lecture? At all events, he is cured of the transcendentals."

"Ahem!" here replied Toby, just as if he had been reading my thoughts, and looking like a very old sheep in a revery.

The old gentleman now took him by the arm, and led him more into the shade of the bridge—a few paces back from the turnstile. "My good fellow," said he, "I make it a point of conscience to allow you this much run. Wait here, till I take my place by the stile, so that I may see whether you go over it handsomely, and transcendentally, and don't omit any flourishes of the pigeon-wing. A mere form, you know. I will say 'one, two, three, and away.' Mind you, start at the word 'away'" Here he took his position by the stile, paused a moment as if in profound reflection, then *looked up* and, I thought, smiled very slightly, then tightened the strings of his apron, then took a long look at Dammit, and finally gave the word as agreed upon—

One—two—three—and—away!

Punctually at the word "away," my poor friend set off in a strong gallop. The stile was not very high, like Mr. Lord's—nor yet very low, like that of Mr. Lord's reviewers, but upon the whole I made sure that he would clear it. And then what if he did not?—ah, that was the question—what if he did not? "What right," said I, "had the old gentleman to make any other gentleman jump? The little old dot-and-carry-one! who is he? If he asks me to jump, I won't do it, that's flat, and I don't care who the devil he is." The bridge, as I say, was arched and covered in, in a very ridiculous manner, and there was a most uncomfortable echo about it at all times—an echo which I never before so particularly observed as when I uttered the four last words of my remark.

But what I said, or what I thought, or what I heard, occupied only an instant. In less than five seconds from his starting, my poor Toby had taken the leap. I saw him run nimbly, and spring grandly from the floor of the bridge, cutting the most awful flourishes with his legs as he went up. I saw him high in the air, pigeon-winging it to admiration just over the top of the stile; and of course I thought it an unusually singular thing that he did not continue to go over. But the whole leap was the affair of a moment, and, before I had a chance to make any profound reflections, down came Mr. Dammit on the flat of his back, on the same side of the stile from which he had started. At the same instant I saw the old gentleman limping off at the top of his speed, having caught and wrapt up in his apron something that fell heavily into it from the darkness of the arch just over the turnstile. At all this I was much astonished; but I had no leisure to think, for Dammit lay particularly still, and I concluded that his feelings had been hurt, and that he stood in need of my assistance. I hurried up to him and found that he had received what might be termed a serious injury. The truth is, he had been deprived of his head, which after a close search I could not find anywhere; so I determined to take him home and send for the homoeopathists. In the meantime a thought struck me, and I threw open an adjacent window of the bridge, when the sad truth flashed upon me at once. About five feet just above the top of the turnstile, and crossing the arch of the foot-path so as to constitute a brace, there extended a flat iron bar, lying with its breadth horizontally, and forming one of a series that served to strengthen the structure throughout its extent. With the edge of this brace it appeared evident that the neck of my unfortunate friend had come precisely in contact.

He did not long survive his terrible loss. The homoeopathists did not give him little enough physic, and what little they did give him he hesitated to take. So in the end he grew worse, and at length died, a lesson to all riotous livers. I bedewed his grave with my tears, worked a bar sinister on his family escutcheon, and, for the general expenses of his funeral, sent in my very moderate bill to the transcendentalists. The scoundrels refused to pay it, so I had Mr. Dammit dug up at once, and sold him for dog's meat.

THE SPHINX

DURING THE DREAD reign of the Cholera in New York, I had accepted the invitation of a relative to spend a fortnight with him in the retirement of his cottage ornee on the banks of the Hudson. We had here around us all the ordinary means of summer amusement; and what with rambling in the woods, sketching, boating, fishing, bathing, music, and books, we should have passed the time pleasantly enough, but for the fearful intelligence which reached us every morning from the populous city. Not a day elapsed which did not bring us news of the decease of some acquaintance. Then as the fatality increased, we learned to expect daily the loss of some friend. At length we trembled at the approach of every messenger. The very air from the South seemed to us redolent with death. That palsying thought, indeed, took entire posession of my soul. I could neither speak, think, nor dream of any thing else. My host was of a less excitable temperament, and, although greatly depressed in spirits, exerted himself to sustain my own. His richly philosophical intellect was not at any time affected by unrealities. To the substances of terror he was sufficiently alive, but of its shadows he had no apprehension.

His endeavors to arouse me from the condition of abnormal gloom into which I had fallen, were frustrated, in great measure, by certain volumes which I had found in his library. These were of a character to force into germination whatever seeds of hereditary superstition lay latent in my bosom. I had been reading these books without his knowledge, and thus he was often at a loss to account for the forcible impressions which had been made upon my fancy.

A favorite topic with me was the popular belief in omens—a belief which, at this one epoch of my life, I was almost seriously disposed to defend. On this subject we had long and animated discussions; he maintaining the utter groundlessness of faith in such matters, I contending that a popular sentiment arising with absolute spontaneity—that is to say, without apparent traces of suggestion—had in itself the unmistakable elements of truth, and was entitled to as much respect as that intuition which is the idiosyncrasy of the individual man of genius.

The fact is, that soon after my arrival at the cottage there had occurred to myself an incident so entirely inexplicable, and which had in it so much of the portentous character, that I might well have been excused for regarding it as an omen. It appalled, and at the same time so confounded and bewildered me, that many days elapsed before I could make up my mind to communicate the circumstances to my friend.

Near the close of an exceedingly warm day, I was sitting, book in hand, at an open window, commanding, through a long vista of the river banks, a view of a distant hill, the face of which nearest my position had been denuded, by what is termed a land-slide, of the principal portion of its trees. My thoughts had been long wandering from the volume before me to the gloom and desolation of the neighboring city. Uplifting my eyes from the page, they fell upon the naked face of the hill, and upon an object—upon some living monster of hideous conformation, which very rapidly made its way from the summit to the bottom, disappearing finally in the dense forest below. As this creature first came in sight, I doubted my own sanity—or at least the evidence of my own eyes—and many minutes passed before I succeeded in convincing myself that I was neither mad nor in a dream. Yet when I described the monster (which I distinctly saw, and calmly surveyed through the whole period of its progress), my readers, I fear, will feel more difficulty in being convinced of these points than even I did myself.

Estimating the size of the creature by comparison with the diameter of the large trees near which it passed—the few giants of the forest which had escaped the fury of the land-slide—I concluded it to be far larger than any ship of the line in existence. I say ship of the line, because the shape of the monster suggested the idea—the hull of one of our seventy-fours might convey a very tolerable conception of the general outline. The mouth of the animal was situated at the extremity of a proboscis some sixty or seventy feet in length, and about as thick as the body of an ordinary elephant. Near the root of this trunk was an immense quantity of black shaggy hair—more than could have been supplied by the coats of a score of buffaloes; and projecting from this hair downwardly and laterally, sprang two gleaming tusks not unlike those of the wild boar, but of infinitely greater dimensions. Extending forward, parallel with the proboscis, and on each side of it, was a gigantic staff, thirty or forty feet in length, formed seemingly of pure crystal and in shape a perfect prism—it reflected in the most gorgeous manner the rays of the declining sun. The trunk was fashioned like a wedge with the apex to the earth. From it there were outspread two pairs of wings—each wing nearly one hundred yards in length—one pair being placed above the other, and all thickly covered with metal scales; each scale apparently some ten or twelve feet in diameter. I observed that the upper and lower tiers of wings were connected by a strong chain. But the chief peculiarity of this horrible thing was the representation of a *Death's Head*, which covered nearly the whole surface of its breast, and which was as accurately traced in glaring white, upon the dark ground of the body, as if it had been there carefully designed by an artist. While I regarded the terrific animal, and more especially the appearance on its breast, with a feeling or horror and awe—with a sentiment of forthcoming evil, which I found it impossible to quell by any effort of the reason, I perceived the huge jaws at the extremity of the proboscis suddenly expand themselves, and from them there proceeded a sound so loud and so expressive of woe, that it struck upon my nerves like a knell and as the monster disappeared at the foot of the hill, I fell at once, fainting, to the floor.

Upon recovering, my first impulse, of course, was to inform my friend of what I had seen and heard—and I can scarcely explain what feeling of repugnance it was which, in the end, operated to prevent me.

At length, one evening, some three or four days after the occurrence, we were sitting together in the room in which I had seen the apparition—I occupying the same seat at the same window, and he lounging on a sofa near at hand. The association of the place and time impelled me to give him an account of the phenomenon. He heard me to the end—at first laughed heartily—and then lapsed into an excessively grave demeanor, as if my insanity was a thing beyond suspicion. At this instant I again had a distinct view of the monster—to which, with a shout of absolute terror, I now directed his attention. He looked eagerly—but maintained that he saw nothing—although I designated minutely the course of the creature, as it made its way down the naked face of the hill.

I was now immeasurably alarmed, for I considered the vision either as an omen of my death, or, worse, as the forerunner of an attack of mania. I threw myself passionately back in my chair, and for some moments buried my face in my hands. When I uncovered my eyes, the apparition was no longer apparent.

My host, however, had in some degree resumed the calmness of his demeanor, and questioned me very rigorously in respect to the conformation of the visionary creature. When I had fully satisfied him on this head, he sighed deeply, as if relieved of some intolerable burden, and went on to talk, with what I thought a cruel calmness, of various points of speculative philosophy, which had heretofore formed subject of discussion between us. I remember his insisting very especially (among other things) upon the idea that the principle source of error in all human investigations lay in the liability of the understanding to under-rate or to overvalue the importance of an object, through mere mis-admeasurement of its propinquity. "To estimate properly, for example," he said, "the influence to be exercised on mankind at large by the thorough diffusion of Democracy, the distance of the epoch at which such diffusion may possibly be accomplished should not fail to form an item in the estimate. Yet can you tell me one writer on the subject of government who has ever thought this particular branch of the subject worthy of discussion at all?"

He here paused for a moment, stepped to a book-case, and brought forth one of the ordinary synopses of Natural History. Requesting me then to exchange seats with him, that he might the better distinguish the fine print of the volume, he took my armchair at the window, and, opening the book, resumed his discourse very much in the same tone as before.

"But for your exceeding minuteness," he said, "in describing the monster, I might never have had it in my power to demonstrate to you what it was. In the first place, let me read to you a schoolboy account of the genus *Sphinx*, of the family *Crepuscularia* of the order *Lepidoptera*, of the class of *Insecta*—or insects. The account runs thus:

"'Four membranous wings covered with little colored scales of metallic appearance; mouth forming a rolled proboscis, produced by an elongation of the jaws, upon the sides of which are found the rudiments of mandibles and downy palpi; the inferior wings retained to the superior by a stiff hair; antennae in the form of an elongated club, prismatic; abdomen pointed, The Death's-headed Sphinx has occasioned much terror among the vulgar, at times, by the melancholy kind of cry which it utters, and the insignia of death which it wears upon its corslet.'"

He here closed the book and leaned forward in the chair, placing himself accurately in the position which I had occupied at the moment of beholding "the monster."

"Ah, here it is," he presently exclaimed—"it is reascending the face of the hill, and a very remarkable looking creature I admit it to be. Still, it is by no means so large or so distant as you imagined it; for the fact is that, as it wriggles its way up this thread, which some spider has wrought along the window-sash, I find it to be about the sixteenth of an inch in its extreme length, and also about the sixteenth of an inch distant from the pupil of my eye."

THE MAN THAT WAS USED UP

Pleurez, pleurez, mes yeux, et fondez vous en eau!
La moitie de ma vie a mis l'autre au tombeau.
Corneille

I CANNOT JUST now remember when or where I first made the acquaintance of that truly fine-looking fellow, Brevet Brigadier General John A. B. C. Smith. Some one *did* introduce me to the gentleman, I am sure—at some public meeting, I know very well—held about something of great importance, no doubt—at some place or other, I feel convinced, whose name I have unaccountably forgotten. The truth is—that the introduction was attended, upon my part, with a degree of anxious embarrassment which operated to prevent any definite impressions of either time or place. I am constitutionally nervous—this, with me, is a family failing, and I can't help it. In especial, the slightest appearance of mystery—of any point I cannot exactly comprehend—puts me at once into a pitiable state of agitation.

There was something, as it were, *remarkable*—yes, remarkable, although this is but a feeble term to express my full meaning—about the entire individuality of the personage in question. He was, perhaps, six feet in height, and of a presence singularly commanding. There was an *air distingué* pervading the whole man, which spoke of high breeding, and hinted at high birth. Upon this topic—the topic of Smith's personal appearance—I have a kind of melancholy satisfaction in being minute. His head of hair would have done honor to a Brutus,—nothing could be more richly flowing, or possess a brighter gloss. It was of a jetty black,—which was also the color, or more properly the no-color of his unimaginable whiskers. You perceive I cannot speak of these latter without enthusiasm; it is not too much to say that they were the handsomest pair of whiskers under the sun. At all events, they encircled, and at times partially overshadowed, a mouth utterly unequaled. Here were the most entirely even, and the most brilliantly white of all conceivable teeth. From between them, upon every proper occasion, issued a voice of surpassing clearness, melody, and strength. In the matter of eyes, also, my acquaintance was pre-eminently endowed. Either one of such a pair was worth a couple of the ordinary ocular organs. They were of a deep hazel exceedingly large and lustrous; and there was perceptible about them, ever and anon, just that amount of interesting obliquity which gives pregnancy to expression.

The bust of the General was unquestionably the finest bust I ever saw. For your life you could not have found a fault with its wonderful proportion. This rare peculiarity set off to great advantage a pair of shoulders which would have called up a blush of conscious inferiority into the countenance of the marble Apollo. I have a passion for fine shoulders, and may say that I never beheld them in perfection before. The arms altogether were admirably modeled. Nor were the lower limbs less superb. These were, indeed, the *ne plus ultra* of good legs. Every connoisseur in such matters admitted the legs to be good. There was neither too much flesh nor too little,—neither rudeness nor fragility. I could not imagine a more graceful curve than that of the *os femoris*, and there was just that due gentle prominence in the rear of the *fibula* which goes to the conformation of a properly proportioned calf. I wish to God my young and talented friend Chiponchipino, the sculptor, had but seen the legs of Brevet Brigadier General John A. B. C. Smith.

But although men so absolutely fine-looking are neither as plenty as reasons or blackberries, still I could not bring myself to believe that *the remarkable* something to which I alluded just now,—that the odd air of *je ne sais quoi* which hung about my new acquaintance,—lay altogether, or indeed at all, in the supreme excellence of his bodily endowments. Perhaps it might be traced to the *manner*;—yet here again I could not pretend to be positive. There *was* a primness, not to say stiffness, in his carriage—a degree of measured and, if I may so express it, of rectangular precision attending his every movement, which, observed in a more diminutive figure, would have had the least little savor in the world of affectation, pomposity, or constraint, but which, noticed in a gentleman of his undoubted dimensions, was readily placed to the account of reserve, *hauteur*—of a commendable sense, in short, of what is due to the dignity of colossal proportion.

The kind friend who presented me to General Smith whispered in my ear some few words of comment upon the man. He was a *remarkable* man—a *very* remarkable man—indeed one of the most remarkable men of the age. He was an especial favorite, too, with the ladies—chiefly on account of his high reputation for courage.

"In *that* point he is unrivaled—indeed he is a perfect desperado—a downright fire-eater, and no mistake," said my friend, here dropping his voice excessively low, and thrilling me with the mystery of his tone.

"A downright fire-eater, and *no* mistake. Showed *that*, I should say, to some purpose, in the late tremendous swamp-fight, away down South, with the Bugaboo and Kickapoo Indians." [Here my friend opened his eyes to some extent.] "Bless my soul!—blood and thunder, and all that!—*prodigies* of valor!—heard of him of course?—you know he's the man—"

"Man alive, how *do* you do? why, how *are* ye? *very* glad to see ye, indeed!" here interrupted the General himself, seizing my companion by the hand as he drew near, and bowing stiffly but profoundly, as I was presented. I then thought (and I think so still) that I never heard a clearer nor a stronger voice, nor beheld a finer set of teeth: but I must say that I was sorry for the interruption just at that moment, as, owing to the whispers and insinuations aforesaid, my interest had been greatly excited in the hero of the Bugaboo and Kickapoo campaign.

However, the delightfully luminous conversation of Brevet Brigadier General John A. B. C. Smith soon completely dissipated this chagrin. My friend leaving us immediately, we had quite a long *tête-à-tête*, and I was not only pleased but *really*—instructed. I never heard a more fluent talker, or a man of greater general information. With becoming modesty, he forebore, nevertheless, to touch upon the theme I had just then most at heart—I mean the mysterious circumstances attending the Bugaboo war—and, on my own part, what I conceive to be a proper sense of delicacy forbade me to broach the subject; although, in truth, I was exceedingly tempted to do so. I perceived, too, that the gallant soldier preferred topics of philosophical interest, and that he delighted, especially, in commenting upon the rapid march of mechanical invention. Indeed, lead him where I would, this was a point to which he invariably came back.

"There is nothing at all like it," he would say, "we are a wonderful people, and live in a wonderful age. Parachutes and rail-roads-mantraps and spring-guns! Our steam-boats are upon every sea, and the Nassau balloon packet is about to run regular trips (fare either way only twenty pounds sterling) between London and Timbuctoo. And who shall calculate the immense influence upon social life—upon arts—upon commerce—upon literature—which will be the immediate result of the great principles of electro-magnetics! Nor, is this all, let me assure you! There is really no end to the march of invention. The most wonderful—the most ingenious—and let me add, Mr.—Mr.—Thompson, I believe, is your name—let me add, I say the most *useful*—the most truly *useful*—mechanical contrivances are daily springing up like mushrooms, if I may so express myself, or, more figuratively, like—ah—grasshoppers—like grasshoppers, Mr. Thompson—about us and ah—ah—ah—around us!"

Thompson, to be sure, is not my name; but it is needless to say that I left General Smith with a heightened interest in the man, with an exalted opinion of his conversational powers, and a deep sense of the valuable privileges we enjoy in living in this age of mechanical invention. My curiosity, however, had not been altogether satisfied, and I resolved to prosecute immediate inquiry among my acquaintances, touching the Brevet Brigadier General himself, and particularly respecting the tremendous events *quorum pars magna fuit*, during the Bugaboo and Kickapoo campaign.

The first opportunity which presented opportunity which presented itself, and which (*horresco referens*) I did not in the least scruple to seize, occurred at the Church of the Reverend Doctor Drummummupp, where I found myself established, one Sunday, just at sermon time, not only in the pew, but by the side of that worthy and communicative little friend of mine, Miss Tabitha T. Thus seated, I congratulated myself, and with much reason, upon the very flattering state of affairs. If any person knew any thing about Brevet Brigadier General John A. B. C. Smith, that person it was clear to me, was Miss Tabitha T. We telegraphed a few signals and then commenced, *sotto voce*, a brisk *tête-à-téte*.

"Smith!" said she in reply to my very earnest inquiry: "Smith!—why, not General John A. B. C.? Bless me, I thought you *knew* all about *him*! This is a wonderfully inventive age! Horrid affair that!—a bloody set of wretches, those Kickapoos!—fought like a hero—prodigies of valor—immortal renown. Smith!—Brevet Brigadier General John A. B. C.! Why, you know he's the man—

"Man," here broke in Doctor Drummummupp, at the top of his voice, and with a thump that came near knocking the pulpit about our ears; "man that is born of a woman hath but a short time to live; he cometh up and is cut down like a flower!" I started to the extremity of the pew, and perceived by the animated looks of the divine, that the wrath which had nearly proved fatal to the pulpit had been excited by the whispers of the lady and myself. There was no help for it; so I submitted with a good grace, and listened, in all the martyrdom of dignified silence, to the balance of that very capital discourse.

Next evening found me a somewhat late visitor at the Rantipole Theater, where I felt sure of satisfying my curiosity at once, by merely stepping into the box of those exquisite specimens of affability and omniscience, the Misses Arabella and Miranda Cognoscenti. That fine tragedian, Climax, was doing Iago to a very crowded house, and I experienced some little difficulty in making my wishes understood; especially as our box was next the slips, and completely overlooked the stage.

"Smith!" said Miss Arabella, as she at comprehended the purport of my query; "Smith?—why, not General John A. B. C.?"

"Smith!" inquired Miranda, musingly. "God bless me, did you ever behold a finer figure?"

"Never, madam, but *do* tell me—"

"Or so inimitable grace?"

"Never, upon my word!—But pray, inform me—"

"Or so just an appreciation of stage effect?"

"Madam!"

"Or a more delicate sense of the true beauties of Shakespeare? Be so good as to look at that leg!"

"The devil!" and I turned again to her sister.

"Smith!" said she, "why, not General John A. B. C.? Horrid affair that, wasn't it?—great wretches, those Bugaboos—savage and so on—but we live in a wonderfully inventive age!—Smith!—O yes! great man!—

perfect desperado—immortal renown—prodigies of valor! *Never heard!*" [This was given in a scream.] "Bless my soul! why, he's the man—"

"—mandragora
Nor all the drowsy syrups of the world
Shall ever medicine thee to that sweet sleep
Which thou ow'dst yesterday!"

here roared our Climax just in my ear, and shaking his fist in my face all the time, in a way that I *couldn't* stand, and I *wouldn't*. I left the Misses Cognoscenti immediately, went behind the scenes forthwith, and gave the beggarly scoundrel such a thrashing as I trust he will remember till the day of his death.

At the *soirée* of the lovely widow, Mrs. Kathleen O'Trump, I was confident that I should meet with no similar disappointment. Accordingly, I was no sooner seated at the card-table, with my pretty hostess for a vis-a-vis, than I propounded those questions the solution of which had become a matter so essential to my peace.

"Smith!" said my partner, "why, not General John A. B. C.? Horrid affair that, wasn't it?—diamonds did you say?—terrible wretches those Kickapoos!—we are playing *whist*, if you please, Mr. Tattle—however, this is the age of invention, most certainly the age, one may say—*the* age *par excellence*—speak French?—oh, quite a hero—perfect desperado!—*no hearts*, Mr. Tattle? I don't believe it!—Immortal renown and all that!—prodigies of valor! *Never heard!!*—why, bless me, he's the man—"

"Mann?—*Captain* Mann!" here screamed some little feminine interloper from the farthest corner of the room. "Are you talking about Captain Mann and the duel?—oh, I must hear—do tell—go on, Mrs. O'Trump!—do now go on!" And go on Mrs. O'Trump did—all about a certain Captain Mann, who was either shot or hung, or should have been both shot and hung. Yes! Mrs. O'Trump, she went on, and I—I went off. There was no chance of hearing any thing farther that evening in regard to Brevet Brigadier General John A. B. C. Smith.

Still I consoled myself with the reflection that the tide of ill-luck would not run against me forever, and so determined to make a bold push for information at the rout of that bewitching little angel, the graceful Mrs. Pirouette.

"Smith!" said Mrs. P., as we twirled about together in a *pas de zephyr*, "Smith?—why, not General John A. B. C.? Dreadful business that of the Bugaboos, wasn't it?—dreadful creatures, those Indians!—do turn out your toes! I really am ashamed of you—man of great courage, poor fellow!—but this is a wonderful age for invention—O dear me, I'm out of breath—quite a desperado—prodigies of valor—*never heard!!*—can't believe it—I shall have to sit down and enlighten you—Smith! why, he's the man—"

"Man-*Fred*, I tell you!" here bawled out Miss Bas-Bleu, as I led Mrs. Pirouette to a seat. "Did ever anybody hear the like? It's Man-*Fred*, I say, and not at all by any means Man-*Friday*." Here Miss Bas-Bleu beckoned to me in a very peremptory manner; and I was obliged, willy-nilly, to leave Mrs. P. for the purpose of deciding a dispute touching the title of a certain poetical drama of Lord Byron's. Although I pronounced, with great promptness, that the true title was Man-*Friday*, and not by any means Man-*Fred* yet when I returned to seek Mrs. Pirouette she was not to be discovered, and I made my retreat from the house in a very bitter spirit of animosity against the whole race of the Bas-Bleus.

Matters had now assumed a really serious aspect, and I resolved to call at once upon my particular friend, Mr. Theodore Sinivate; for I knew that here at least I should get something like definite information.

"Smith!" said he, in his well known peculiar way of drawling out his syllables; "Smith!—why, not General John A. B. C.? Savage affair that with the Kickapo-o-o-os, wasn't it? Say, don't you think so?—perfect despera-a-ado—great pity, 'pon my honor!—wonderfully inventive age!—pro-o-digies of valor! By the by, did you ever hear about Captain Ma-a-a-a-n?"

"Captain Mann be d-d!" said I; "please to go on with your story."

"Hem!—oh well!—quite *la même cho-o-ose*, as we say in France. Smith, eh? Brigadier-General John A. B. C.? I say"—[here Mr. S. thought proper to put his finger to the side of his nose]—"I say, you don't mean to insinuate now, really and truly, and conscientiously, that you don't know all about that affair of Smith's, as well as I do, eh? Smith? John A-B-C.? Why, bless me, he's the ma-a-an-"

"*Mr.* Sinivate," said I, imploringly, "*is* he the man in the mask?"

"No-o-o!" said he, looking wise, "nor the man in the mo-o-on."

This reply I considered a pointed and positive insult, and so left the house at once in high dudgeon, with a firm resolve to call my friend, Mr. Sinivate, to a speedy account for his ungentlemanly conduct and ill breeding.

In the meantime, however, I had no notion of being thwarted touching the information I desired. There was one resource left me yet. I would go to the fountain head. I would call forthwith upon the General himself, and demand, in explicit terms, a solution of this abominable piece of mystery. Here, at least, there should be no chance for equivocation. I would be plain, positive, peremptory—as short as pie-crust—as concise as Tacitus or Montesquieu.

It was early when I called, and the General was dressing, but I pleaded urgent business, and was shown at once into his bedroom by an old negro valet, who remained in attendance during my visit. As I entered the chamber, I looked about, of course, for the occupant, but did not immediately perceive him. There was a large and exceedingly odd looking bundle of something which lay close by my feet on the floor, and, as I was not in the best humor in the world, I gave it a kick out of the way.

"Hem! ahem! rather civil that, I should say!" said the bundle, in one of the smallest, and altogether the funniest little voices, between a squeak and a whistle, that I ever heard in all the days of my existence.

"Ahem! rather civil that I should observe."

I fairly shouted with terror, and made off, at a tangent, into the farthest extremity of the room.

"God bless me, my dear fellow!" here again whistled the bundle, "what—what—what—why, what is the matter? I really believe you don't know me at all."

What *could* I say to all this—what *could* I? I staggered into an armchair, and, with staring eyes and open mouth, awaited the solution of the wonder.

"Strange you shouldn't know me though, isn't it?" presently resqueaked the nondescript, which I now perceived was performing upon the floor some inexplicable evolution, very analogous to the drawing on of a stocking. There was only a single leg, however, apparent.

"Strange you shouldn't know me though, isn't it? Pompey, bring me that leg!" Here Pompey handed the bundle a very capital cork leg, already dressed, which it screwed on in a trice; and then it stood upright before my eyes.

"And a bloody action it *was*," continued the thing, as if in a soliloquy; "but then one mustn't fight with the Bugaboos and Kickapoos, and think of coming off with a mere scratch. Pompey, I'll thank you now for that arm. Thomas" [turning to me] "is decidedly the best hand at a cork leg; but if you should ever want an arm, my dear fellow, you must really let me recommend you to Bishop." Here Pompey screwed on an arm.

"We had rather hot work of it, that you may say. Now, you dog, slip on my shoulders and bosom. Pettit makes the best shoulders, but for a bosom you will have to go to Ducrow."

"Bosom!" said I.

"Pompey, will you *never* be ready with that wig? Scalping is a rough process, after all; but then you can procure such a capital scratch at De L'Orme's."

"Scratch!"

"Now, you nigger, my teeth! For a good set of these you had better go to Parmly's at once; high prices, but excellent work. I swallowed some very capital articles, though, when the big Bugaboo rammed me down with the butt end of his rifle."

"Butt end! ram down!! my eye!!"

"O yes, by the way, my eye—here, Pompey, you scamp, screw it in! Those Kickapoos are not so very slow at a gouge; but he's a belied man, that Dr. Williams, after all; you can't imagine how well I see with the eyes of his make."

I now began very clearly to perceive that the object before me was nothing more nor less than my new acquaintance, Brevet Brigadier General John A. B. C. Smith. The manipulations of Pompey had made, I must confess, a very striking difference in the appearance of the personal man. The voice, however, still puzzled me no little; but even this apparent mystery was speedily cleared up.

"Pompey, you black rascal," squeaked the General, "I really do believe you would let me go out without my palate."

Hereupon, the negro, grumbling out an apology, went up to his master, opened his mouth with the knowing air of a horse-jockey, and adjusted therein a somewhat singular-looking machine, in a very dexterous manner, that I could not altogether comprehend. The alteration, however, in the entire expression of the General's countenance was instantaneous and surprising. When he again spoke, his voice had resumed all that rich melody and strength which I had noticed upon our original introduction.

"D-n the vagabonds!" said he, in so clear a tone that I positively started at the change, "D-n the vagabonds! they not only knocked in the roof of my mouth, but took the trouble to cut off at least seven-eighths of my tongue. There isn't Bonfanti's equal, however, in America, for really good articles of this description. I can recommend you to him with confidence," [here the General bowed,] "and assure you that I have the greatest pleasure in so doing."

I acknowledged his kindness in my best manner, and took leave of him at once, with a perfect understanding of the true state of affairs—with a full comprehension of the mystery which had troubled me so long. It was evident. It was a clear case. Brevet Brigadier General John A. B. C. Smith was the man—*the man that was used up*.

A TALE OF THE RAGGED MOUNTAINS

DURING THE FALL of the year 1827, while residing near Charlottesville, Virginia, I casually made the acquaintance of Mr. Augustus Bedloe. This young gentleman was remarkable in every respect, and excited in me a profound interest and curiosity. I found it impossible to comprehend him either in his moral or his physical relations. Of his family I could obtain no satisfactory account. Whence he came, I never ascertained. Even about his age—although I call him a young gentleman—there was something which perplexed me in no little degree. He certainly *seemed* young—and he made a point of speaking about his youth—yet there were moments when I should have had little trouble in imagining him a hundred years of age. But in no regard was he more peculiar than in his personal appearance. He was singularly tall and thin. He stooped much. His limbs were exceedingly long and emaciated. His forehead was broad and low. His complexion was absolutely bloodless. His mouth was large and flexible, and his teeth were more widely uneven, although sound, than I had ever before seen teeth in a human head. The expression of his smile, however, was by no means unpleasing, as might be supposed; but it had no variation whatever. It was one of profound melancholy—of a phaseless and unceasing gloom. His eyes were abnormally large, and round like those of a cat. The pupils, too, upon any accession or dimunition of light, underwent contraction or dilation, just such as is observed in the feline tribe. In moments of excitement the orbs grew bright to a degree almost inconceivable; seeming to emit luminous rays, not of a reflected, but of an intrinsic luster, as does a candle or the sun; yet their ordinary condition was so totally vapid, filmy, and dull, as to convey the idea of the eyes of a long-interred corpse.

These peculiarities of person appeared to cause him much annoyance, and he was continually alluding to them in a sort of half explanatory, half apologetic strain, which, when I first heard it, impressed me very painfully. I soon, however, grew accustomed to it, and my uneasiness wore off. It seemed to be his design rather to insinuate, than directly to assert that, physically, he had not always been what he was—that a long series of neuralgic attacks had reduced him from a condition of more than usual personal beauty, to that which I saw. For many years past he had been attended by a physician, named Templeton—an old gentleman, perhaps seventy years of age—whom he had first encountered at Saratoga, and from whose attention, while there, he either received, or fancied that he received, great benefit. The result was that Bedloe, who was wealthy, had made an arrangement with Doctor Templeton, by which the latter, in consideration of a liberal annual allowance, had consented to devote his time and medical experience exclusively to the care of the invalid.

Doctor Templeton had been a traveler in his younger days, and, at Paris, had become a convert, in great measure, to the doctrines of Mesmer. It was altogether by means of magnetic remedies that he had succeeded in alleviating the acute pains of his patient; and this success had very naturally inspired the latter with a certain degree of confidence in the opinions from which the remedies had been educed. The Doctor, however, like all enthusiasts, had struggled hard to make a thorough convert of his pupil, and finally so far gained his point as to induce the sufferer to submit to numerous experiments.—By a frequent repetition of these, a result had arisen, which of late days has become so common as to attract little or no attention, but which, at the period of which I write, had very rarely been known in America. I mean to say, that between Doctor Templeton and Bedloe there had grown up, little by little, a very distinct and strongly-marked *rapport*, or magnetic relation. I am not prepared to assert, however, that this *rapport* extended beyond the limits of the simple sleep-producing power; but this power itself had attained great intensity. At the first attempt to induce the magnetic somnolency, the mesmerist entirely failed. In the fifth or sixth he succeeded very partially, and after long continued effort. Only at the twelfth was the triumph complete. After this the will of the patient succumbed rapidly to that of the physician, so that, when I first became acquainted with the two, sleep was brought about almost instantaneously, by the mere volition of the operator, even when the invalid was unaware of his presence. It is only now in the year 1845, when similar miracles are witnessed daily by thousands, that I dare venture to record this apparent impossibility as a matter of serious fact.

The temperament of Bedloe was, in the highest degree, sensitive, excitable, enthusiastic. His imagination was singularly vigorous and creative; and no doubt it derived additional force from the habitual use of morphine, which he swallowed in great quantity, and without which he would have found it impossible to exist. It was his practice to take a very large dose of it immediately after breakfast, each morning—or rather immediately after a cup of strong coffee, for he ate nothing in the forenoon—and then set forth alone, or attended only by a dog, upon a long ramble among the chain of wild and dreary hills that lie westward and southward of Charlottesville, and are there dignified by the title of the Ragged Mountains.

Upon a dim, warm, misty day, toward the close of November, and during the strange *interregnum* of the seasons which in America is termed the Indian Summer, Mr. Bedloe departed as usual for the hills. The day passed, and still he did not return.

About eight o'clock at night, having become seriously alarmed at his protracted absence, we were about setting out in search of him, when he unexpectedly made his appearance, in health no worse than usual, and in rather more than ordinary spirits. The account which he gave of his expedition, and of the events which had detained him, was a singular one indeed.

"You will remember," said he, "that it was about nine in the morning when I left Charlottesville. I bent my steps immediately to the mountains, and, about ten, entered a gorge which was entirely new to me. I followed the windings of this pass with much interest. The scenery which presented itself on all sides, although scarcely entitled to be called grand, had about it an indescribable, and to me, a delicious aspect of dreary desolation. The solitude seemed absolutely virgin. I could not help believing that the green sods and the gray rocks upon which I trod, had never before been trodden by the foot of a human being. So entirely secluded, and in fact inaccessible, except through a series of accidents, is the entrance of the ravine, that it is by no means impossible that I was indeed the first adventurer—the very first and sole adventurer—who had ever penetrated its recesses.

"The thick and peculiar mist or smoke which distinguishes the Indian Summer, and which now hung heavily over all objects, served no doubt to deepen the vague impressions which these objects created. So dense was this pleasant fog that I could at no time see more than a dozen yards of the path before me. This path was excessively sinuous, and as the sun could not be seen, I soon lost all idea of the direction in which I journeyed. In the meantime the morphine had its customary effect—that of enduing all the external world with an intensity of interest. In the quivering of a leaf—in the hue of a blade of grass—in the shape of a trefoil—in the humming of a bee—in the gleaming of a dew-drop—in the breathing of the wind—in the faint odors that came from the forest—there came a whole universe of suggestion—a gay and motley train of rhapsodical and immethodical thought.

"Busied in this, I walked on for several hours, during which the mist deepened around me to so great an extent that at length I was reduced to an absolute groping of the way. And now an indescribable uneasiness possessed me—a species of nervous hesitation and tremor,—I feared to tread, lest I should be precipitated into some abyss. I remembered, too, strange stories told about these Ragged Hills, and of the uncouth and fierce races of men who tenanted their groves and caverns. A thousand vague fancies oppressed and disconcerted me—fancies the more distressing because vague. Very suddenly my attention was arrested by the loud beating of a drum.

"My amazement was, of course, extreme. A drum in these hills was a thing unknown. I could not have been more surprised at the sound of the trump of the Archangel. But a new and still more astounding source of interest and perplexity arose. There came a wild rattling or jingling sound, as if of a bunch of large keys—and upon the instant a dusky-visaged and half-naked man rushed past me with a shriek. He came so close to my person that I felt his hot breath upon my face. He bore in one hand an instrument composed of an assemblage of steel rings, and shook them vigorously as he ran. Scarcely had he disappeared in the mist, before, panting after him, with open mouth and glaring eyes, there darted a huge beast. I could not be mistaken in its character. It was a hyena.

"The sight of this monster rather relieved than heightened my terrors—for I now made sure that I dreamed, and endeavored to arouse myself to waking consciousness. I stepped boldly and briskly forward. I rubbed my eyes. I called aloud. I pinched my limbs. A small spring of water presented itself to my view, and here stooping, I bathed my hands and my head and neck. This seemed to dissipate the equivocal sensations which had hitherto annoyed me. I arose, as I thought, a new man, and proceeded steadily and complacently on my unknown way.

"At length, quite overcome by exertion, and by a certain oppressive closeness of the atmosphere, I seated myself beneath a tree. Presently there came a feeble gleam of sunshine, and the shadow of the leaves of the tree fell faintly but definitely upon the grass. At this shadow I gazed wonderingly for many minutes. Its character stupefied me with astonishment. I looked upward. The tree was a palm.

"I now arose hurriedly, and in a state of fearful agitation—for the fancy that I dreamed would serve me no longer. I saw—I felt that I had perfect command of my senses—and these senses now brought to my soul a world of novel and singular sensation. The heat became all at once intolerable. A strange odor loaded the breeze.—A low continuous murmur, like that arising from a full, but gently flowing river, came to my ears, intermingled with the peculiar hum of multitudinous human voices.

"While I listened in an extremity of astonishment which I need not attempt to describe, a strong and brief gust of wind bore off the incumbent fog as if by the wand of an enchanter.

"I found myself at the foot of a high mountain, and looking down into a vast plain, through which wound a majestic river. On the margin of this river stood an Eastern-looking city, such as we read of in the Arabian Tales, but of a character even more singular than any there described. From my position, which was far above the level of the town, I could perceive its every nook and corner, as if delineated on a map. The streets seemed innumerable, and crossed each other irregularly in all directions, but were rather long winding alleys than streets, and absolutely swarmed with inhabitants. The houses were wildly picturesque. On every hand was a wilderness of balconies, of verandahs, of minarets, of shrines, and fantastically carved oriels. Bazaars abounded; and in these were displayed rich wares in infinite variety and profusion—silks, muslins, the most dazzling cutlery, the most magnificent jewels and gems. Besides these things, were seen on all sides, banners and palanquins, litters with stately dames close veiled, elephants gorgeously caparisoned, idols grotesquely hewn, drums, banners and gongs, spears, silver and gilded maces. And amid the crowd, and the clamour, and the general intricacy and confusion—amid the million of black and yellow men, turbaned and robed, and of flowing beard, there roamed a countless multitude of holy filleted bulls, while vast legions of the filthy but sacred ape clambered, chattering and shrieking, about the cornices of the mosques, or clung to the minarets and oriels. From the swarming streets to the banks of the river there descended innumerable flights of steps leading to bathing places, while the river itself seemed to force a passage with difficulty through the vast fleets of deeply-burthened ships that far and wide encumbered its surface. Beyond the limits of the city arose, in frequent majestic groups, the palm and the cocoa, with other gigantic and weird trees, of vast age; and here and there might be seen a field of rice, the thatched hut of a peasant, a tank, a stray temple, a gipsy camp, or a solitary graceful maiden taking her way, with a pitcher upon her head, to the banks of the magnificent river.

"You will say now, of course, that I dreamed; but not so. What I saw—what I heard—what I felt—what I thought—had about it nothing of the unmistakeable idiosyncrasy of the dream. All was rigorously self-consistent. At first doubting that I was really awake, I entered into a series of tests which soon convinced me that I really was. Now, when one dreams, and in the dream suspects that he dreams, the suspicion *never fails to confirm itself*, and the sleeper is almost immediately aroused. Thus Novalis errs not in saying that 'we are near waking when we dream that we dream.' Had the vision occurred to me as I describe it, without my suspecting it as a dream, then a dream it might absolutely have been, but occurring as it did, and suspected and tested as it was, I am forced to class it among other phenomena."

"In this I am not sure that you are wrong," observed Dr. Templeton, "but proceed. You arose and descended into the city."

"I arose," continued Bedloe, regarding the Doctor with an air of profound astonishment, "I arose, as you say, and descended into the city.

On my way, I fell in with an immense populace, crowding through every avenue, all in the same direction, and exhibiting in every action the wildest excitement. Very suddenly, and by some inconceivable impulse, I became intensely imbued with personal interest in what was going on. I seemed to feel that I had an important part to play, without exactly understanding what it was. Against the crowd which environed me, however, I experienced a deep sentiment of animosity. I shrank from amid them, and, swiftly, by a circuitous path, reached and entered the city. Here all was the wildest tumult and contention. A small party of men, clad in garments half Indian, half European, and officered by a gentleman in a uniform partly British, were engaged, at great odds, with the swarming rabble of the alleys. I joined the weaker party, arming myself with the weapons of a fallen officer, and fighting I knew not whom with the nervous ferocity of despair. We were soon overpowered by numbers, and driven to seek refuge in a species of kiosk. Here we barricaded ourselves, and, for the present, were secure. From a loop-hole near the summit of the kiosk, I perceived a vast crowd, in furious agitation, surrounding and assaulting a gay palace that overhung the river. Presently from an upper window of this palace, there descended an effeminate-looking person, by means of a string made of the turbans of his attendants. A boat was at hand, in which he escaped to the opposite bank of the river.

"And now a new object took possession of my soul. I spoke a few hurried but energetic words to my companions, and, having succeeded in gaining over a few of them to my purpose, made a frantic sally from the kiosk. We rushed amid the crowd that surrounded it. They retreated at first before us. They rallied, fought madly, and retreated again. In the meantime we were borne far from the kiosk, and became bewildered and entangled among the narrow streets of tall overhanging houses, into the recesses of which the sun had never been able to shine. The rabble pressed impetuously upon us, harassing us with their spears, and overwhelming us with flights of arrows. These latter were very remarkable, and resembled in some respects the writhing creese of the Malay. They were made to imitate the body of the creeping serpent, and were long and black, with a poisoned barb. One of them struck me upon the right temple. I reeled and fell. An instantaneous and dreadful sickness seized me. I struggled—I gasped—I died."

"You will hardly persist *now*," said I, smiling, "that the whole of your adventure was not a dream. You are not prepared to maintain that you are dead?"

When I said these words, I of course expected some lively sally from Bedloe in reply; but, to my astonishment, he hesitated, trembled, became fearfully pallid, and remained silent. I looked toward Templeton. He sat erect and rigid in his chair—his teeth chattered, and his eyes were starting from their sockets. "Proceed!" he at length said hoarsely to Bedloe.

"For many minutes," continued the latter, "my sole sentiment—my sole feeling—was that of darkness and nonentity, with the consciousness of death. At length, there seemed to pass a violent and sudden shock through my soul, as if of electricity. With it came the sense of elasticity and of light. This latter I felt—not saw. In an instant I seemed to rise from the ground. But I had no bodily, no visible, audible, or palpable presence. The crowd had departed. The tumult had ceased. The city was in comparative repose. Beneath me lay my corpse, with the arrow in my temple, the whole head greatly swollen and disfigured. But all these things I felt—not saw. I took interest in nothing. Even the corpse seemed a matter in which I had no concern. Volition I had none, but appeared to be impelled into motion, and flitted buoyantly out of the city, retracing the circuitous path by which I had entered it. When I had attained that point of the ravine in the mountains at which I had encountered the hyena, I again experienced a shock as of a galvanic battery; the sense of weight, of volition, of substance, returned. I became my original self, and bent my steps eagerly homeward—but the past had not lost the vividness of the real—and not now, even for an instant, can I compel my understanding to regard it as a dream."

"Nor was it," said Templeton, with an air of deep solemnity, "yet it would be difficult to say how otherwise it should be termed. Let us suppose only, that the soul of the man of to-day is upon the verge of some stupendous psychal discoveries. Let us content ourselves with this supposition. For the rest I have some explanation to make. Here is a water-color drawing, which I should have shown you before, but which an unaccountable sentiment of horror has hitherto prevented me from showing."

We looked at the picture which he presented. I saw nothing in it of an extraordinary character; but its effect upon Bedloe was prodigious. He nearly fainted as he gazed. And yet it was but a miniature portrait—a miraculously accurate one, to be sure—of his own very remarkable features. At least this was my thought as I regarded it.

"You will perceive," said Templeton, "the date of this picture—it is here, scarcely visible, in this corner—1780. In this year was the portrait taken. It is the likeness of a dead friend—a Mr. Oldeb—to whom I became much attached at Calcutta, during the administration of Warren Hastings. I was then only twenty years old. When I first saw you, Mr. Bedloe, at Saratoga, it was the miraculous similarity which existed between yourself and the painting which induced me to accost you, to seek your friendship, and to bring about those arrangements which resulted in my becoming your constant companion. In accomplishing this point I was urged partly, and perhaps principally, by a regretful memory of the deceased, but also, in part, by an uneasy and not altogether horrorless curiosity respecting yourself.

"In your detail of the vision which presented itself to you amid the hills, you have described with the minutest accuracy, the Indian city of Benares upon the holy river. The riots, the combats, the massacre, were the actual events of the insurrection of Cheyte Sing, which took place in 1780, when Hastings was put in imminent peril of his life. The man escaping by the string of turbans was Cheyte Sing himself. The party in the kiosk were sepoys and British officers headed by Hastings. Of this party I was one, and did all I could to prevent the rash and fatal sally of the officer who fell, in the crowded alleys, by the poisoned arrow of a Bengalee. That officer was my dearest friend. It was Oldeb. You will perceive by these manuscripts" (here the speaker produced a notebook in which several pages appeared to have been, freshly written) "that at the very period in which you fancied these things amid the hills, I was engaged in detailing them upon paper here at home."

In about a week after this conversation, the following paragraphs appeared in a Charlottesville paper:

"We have the painful duty of announcing the death of MR. AUGUSTUS BEDLO, a gentleman whose amiable manners and many virtues have long endeared him to the citizens of Charlottesville.

"Mr. B., for some years past, has been subject to neuralgia, which has often threatened to terminate fatally; but this can be regarded only as the mediate cause of his decease. The approximate cause was one of especial singularity. In an excursion to the Ragged Mountains, a few days since, a slight cold and fever were contracted, attended with great determination of blood to the head. To relieve this, Dr. Tempieton resorted to topical bleeding. Leeches were applied to the temples. In a fearfully brief period the patient died, when it appeared that, in the jar containing the leeches, had been introduced, by accident, one of the venomous vermicular sangsues which are now and then found in the neighboring ponds. This creature fastened itself upon a small artery in the right temple. Its close resemblance to the medicinal leech caused the mistake to be overlooked until too late.

"*N. B.*—The poisonous sangsue of Charlottesville may always be distinguished from the medicinal leech by its blackness, and especially by its writhing or vermicular motions which very nearly resembles those of a snake."

I was speaking with the editor of the paper in question, upon the topic of this remarkable accident, when it occurred to me to ask how it happened that the name of the deceased had been given as Bedlo.

"I presume," said I, "you have authority for this spelling, but I have always supposed the name to be written with an *e* at the end."

"Authority?—no," he replied. "It is a mere typographical error. The name is Bedlo with an *e*, all the world over, and I never knew it to be spelt otherwise in my life."

"Then," said I mutteringly, as I turned upon my heel, "then indeed has it come to pass that one truth is stranger than any fiction—for Bedlo without the *e*, what is it but Oldeb conversed? And this man tells me it is a typographical error."

THE DEVIL IN THE BELFRY

What o'clock is it?—Old saying

EVERYBODY KNOWS, IN a general way, that the finest place in the world is—or, alas, *was*—the Dutch borough of Vondervotteimittiss. Yet as it lies some distance from any of the main roads, being in a somewhat out-of-the-way situation, there are perhaps a few of my readers who have ever paid it a visit. For the benefit of those who have *not*, therefore, it will be only proper that I should enter into some account of it. And this is indeed the more necessary, as with the hope of enlisting public sympathy in behalf of the inhabitants, I design here to give a history of the calamitous events which have so lately occurred within its limits. No one who knows me will doubt that the duty thus self-imposed will be executed to the best of my ability, with all that rigid impartiality, all that cautious examination into facts, and diligent collation of authorities, which should ever distinguish him who aspires to the title of historian.

By the united aid of medals, manuscripts, and inscriptions, I am enabled to say, positively, that the borough of Vondervotteimittiss has existed, from its origin, in precisely the same condition which it at present preserves. Of the date of this origin, however, I grieve that I can only speak with that species of indefinite definiteness which mathematicians are at times forced to put up with in certain algebraic formulæ. The date, I may thus say, in regard to the remoteness of its antiquity, cannot be less than any assignable quantity whatsoever.

Touching the derivation of the name Vondervotteimittiss, I confess myself with sorrow equally at fault. Among a multitude of opinions upon this delicate point—some acute, some learned, some sufficiently the reverse—I am able to select nothing which ought to be considered satisfactory. Perhaps the idea of Grogswigg—nearly coincident with that of Kroutaplenttey—is to be cautiously preferred:—It runs:—"*Vondervotteimittiss—Vonder, lege Donder—Votteimittiss, quasi und Bleitziz—Bleitziz, obsol: pro Blitzen.*" This derivation, to say the truth, is still countenanced by some traces of the electric fluid evident on the summit of the steeple of the House of the Town-Council. I do not choose, however, to commit myself on a theme of such importance, and must refer the reader desirous of information to the *Oratiunculæ de Rebus Præteritis*, of Dundergutz. See also Blunderbuzzard *De Derivationibus*, pp. 27 to 5010, Folio, Gothic edit., Red and Black character, Catchword and No Cypher;—wherein consult also marginal notes in the autograph of Stuffundpuff, with the Sub-Commentaries of Gruntundguzzel.

Notwithstanding the obscurity which thus envelops the date of the foundation of Vondervotteimittiss, and the derivation of its name, there can be no doubt, as I said before, that it has always existed as we find it at this epoch. The oldest man in the borough can remember not the slightest difference in the appearance of any portion of it; and indeed the very suggestion of such a possibility is considered an insult. The site of the village is in a perfectly circular valley, about a quarter of a mile in circumference, and entirely surrounded by gentle hills, over whose summit the people have never yet ventured to pass. For this they assign the very good reason that they do not believe there is anything at all on the other side.

Round the skirts of the valley (which is quite level, and paved throughout with flat tiles), extends a continuous row of sixty little houses. These, having their backs on the hills, must look of course, to the center of the plain, which is just sixty yards from the front door of each dwelling. Every house has a small garden before it, with a circular path, a sun-dial, and twenty-four cabbages. The buildings themselves are so precisely alike that one can in no manner be distinguished from the other. Owing to the vast antiquity, the style of architecture is somewhat odd, but it is not for that reason the less strikingly picturesque. They are fashioned of hard-burned little bricks, red, with black ends, so that the walls look like a chess-board upon a great scale. The gables are turned to the front, and there are cornices as big as all the rest of the house over the eaves and over the main doors. The windows are narrow and deep, with very tiny panes and a great deal of sash. On the roof is a vast quantity of tiles with long curly ears. The woodwork throughout is of a dark hue, and there is much carving about it, with but a trifling variety of pattern; for time out of mind, the carvers of Vondervotteimittiss have never been able to carve more than two objects—a time-piece and a cabbage But these they do exceedingly well, and intersperse them, with singular ingenuity, wherever they find room for the chisel.

The dwellings are as much alike inside as out, and the furniture is all upon one plan. The floors are of square tiles, the chairs and tables of black-looking wood with thin crooked legs and puppy feet. The mantel-pieces are wide and high, and have not only time-pieces and cabbages sculptured over the front, but a real time-piece, which makes a prodigious ticking, on the top in the middle, with a flower-pot containing a cabbage standing on each extremity by way of outrider. Between each cabbage and the time-piece, again, is a little China man having a large stomach with a great round hole in it, through which is seen the dial-plate of a watch.

The fireplaces are large and deep, with fierce crooked-looking fire-dogs. There is constantly a rousing fire, and a huge pot over it, full of sauer-kraut and pork, to which the good woman of the house is always busy in attending. She is a little fat old lady, with blue eyes and a red face, and wears a huge cap like a sugar-loaf, ornamented with purple and yellow ribbons. Her dress is of orange-colored linsey-woolsey, made very full behind and very short in the waist, and indeed very short in other respects, not reaching below the middle of her leg. This is somewhat thick, and so are her ankles, but she has a fine pair of green stockings to cover them. Her shoes—of pink leather—are fastened each with a bunch of yellow ribbons puckered up in the shape of a cabbage. In her left hand she has a little heavy Dutch watch; in her right she wields a ladle for the sauer-kraut and pork. By her side there stands a fat tabby cat, with a gilt toy repeater tied to its tail, which "the boys" have fastened there by way of a quiz.

The boys themselves are, all three of them, in the garden attending the pig. They are each two feet in height. They have three-cornered cocked hats, purple waistcoats reaching down to their thighs, buckskin knee-breeches, red woolen stockings, heavy shoes with big silver buckles, and long surtout coats with large buttons of mother-of-pearl. Each, too, has a pipe in his mouth, and a little dumpy watch in his right hand. He takes a puff and a look, and then a look and a puff. The pig—which is corpulent and lazy—is occupied now in picking up the stray leaves that fall from the cabbages, and now in giving a kick behind at the gilt repeater, which the urchins have also tied to *his* tail in order to make him look as handsome as the cat.

Right at the front door, in a high-backed leather-bottomed arm chair, with crooked legs and puppy feet like the tables, is seated the old man of the house himself. He is an exceedingly puffy little old gentleman, with big circular eyes and a huge double chin. His dress resembles that of the boys, and I need say nothing farther about it. All the difference is, that his pipe is somewhat bigger than theirs, and he can make a greater smoke. Like them, he has a watch, but he carries his watch in his pocket. To say the truth, he has something of more importance than a watch to attend to, and what that is I shall presently explain. He sits with his right leg upon his left knee, wears a grave countenance, and always keeps one of his eyes at least resolutely bent upon a certain remarkable object in the center of the plain.

This object is situated in the steeple of the House of the Town-Council. The Town-Council are all very little, round, oily, intelligent men, with big saucer eyes and fat double chins, and have their coats much longer and their shoe-buckles much bigger than the ordinary inhabitants of Vondervotteimittiss. Since my sojourn in the borough they have had several special meetings, and have adopted these three important resolutions:—

> "That it is wrong to alter the good old course of things";
> "That there is nothing tolerable out of Vondervotteimittiss"; and—
> "That we will stick by our clocks and our cabbages."

Above the session-room of the Council is the steeple, and in the steeple is the belfry, where exists, and has existed time out of mind, the pride and wonder of the village—the great clock of the borough of Vondervotteimittiss. And this is the object to which the eyes of the old gentlemen are turned who sit in the leather-bottomed arm-chairs.

The great clock has seven faces—one in each of the seven sides of the steeple—so that it can be readily seen from all quarters. Its faces are large and white, and its hands heavy and black. There is a belfry-man whose sole duty is to attend to it; but this duty is the most perfect of sinecures—for the clock of Vondervotteimittiss was never yet known to have anything the matter with it. Until lately, the bare supposition of such a thing was considered heretical. From the remotest period of antiquity to which the archives have reference, the hours have been regularly struck by the big bell. And, indeed, the case was just the same with all the other clocks and watches in the borough. Never was such a place for keeping the true time. When the large clapper thought proper to say "Twelve o'clock!" all its obedient followers opened their throats simultaneously and responded like a very echo. In short, the good burghers were fond of their sauer-kraut, but then they were proud of their clocks.

All people who hold sinecure offices are held in more or less respect, and as the belfry-man of Vondervotteimittiss has the most perfect of sinecures, he is the most perfectly respected of any man in the world. He is the chief dignitary of the borough, and the very pigs look at him with a sentiment of reverence. His coat-tail is *very* far longer—his pipe, his shoe-buckles, his eyes, and his stomach, *very* far bigger—than those of any other old gentleman in the village; and as to his chin, it is not only double, but triple.

I have thus painted the happy estate of Vondervotteimittiss: alas, that so fair a picture should ever experience a reverse!

There has been long a saying among the wisest inhabitants, that "no good can come from over the hills;" and it really seemed that the words had in them something of the spirit of prophecy. It wanted five minutes of noon, on the day before yesterday, when there appeared a very odd-looking object on the summit of the ridge to the eastward. Such an occurrence of course attracted universal attention, and every little old gentleman who sat in a leather-bottomed arm-chair turned one of his eyes with a stare of dismay upon the phenomenon, still keeping the other upon the clock in the steeple.

By the time that it wanted only three minutes to noon the droll object in question was perceived to be a very diminutive foreign-looking young man. He descended the hills at a great rate, so that everybody had soon a good look at him. He was really the most finnicky little personage that had ever been seen in Vondervotteimittiss. His countenance was of a dark snuff-color, and he had a long hooked nose, pea eyes, a wide mouth, and an excellent set of teeth, which latter he seemed anxious of displaying, as he was grinning from ear to ear. What with mustachios and whiskers, there was none of the rest of his face to be seen. His head was uncovered, and his hair neatly done up in *papillotes*. His dress was a tight-fitting swallow-tailed black coat (from one of whose pockets dangled a vast length of white handkerchief), black kerseymere knee-breeches, black stockings, and stumpy-looking pumps, with huge bunches of black satin ribbon for bows. Under one arm he carried a huge *chapeau-de-bras*, and under the other a fiddle nearly five times as big as himself. In his left hand was a gold snuff-box, from which, as he capered down the hill, cutting all manner of fantastical steps, he took snuff incessantly with an air of the greatest possible self-satisfaction. God bless me!—here was a sight for the honest burghers of Vondervotteimittiss.

To speak plainly, the fellow had, in spite of his grinning, an audacious and sinister kind of face; and as he curvetted right into the village, the odd stumpy appearance of his pumps excited no little suspicion; and many a burgher who beheld him that day would have given a trifle for a peep beneath the white cambric handkerchief which hung so obtrusively from the pocket of his swallow-tailed coat. But what mainly occasioned a righteous indignation was that the scoundrelly popinjay, while he cut a fandango here and a whirligig there, did not seem to have the remotest idea in the world of such a thing as *keeping time* in his steps.

The good people of the borough had scarcely a chance, however, to get their eyes thoroughly open, when, just as it wanted half-a-minute of noon, the rascal bounced, as I say, right into the midst of them; gave a *chassez* here, and a *balancez* there; and then, after a *pirouette* and a *pas-de-zéphyr*, pigeon-winged himself right up into the belfry of the House of the Town-Council, where the wonder-stricken belfry-man sat smoking in a state of dignity and dismay. But the little chap seized him at once by the nose; gave it a swing and a pull; clapped the big *chapeau-de-bras* upon his head; knocked it down over his eyes and mouth; and then, lifting up the big fiddle, beat him with it so long and so soundly that, what with the belfry-man being so fat and the fiddle being so hollow, you would have sworn that there was a regiment of double-bass drummers all beating the devil's tattoo up in the belfry of the steeple of Vondervotteimittiss.

There is no knowing to what desperate act of vengeance this unprincipled attack might have aroused the inhabitants but for the important fact that it now wanted only half-a-second of noon. The bell was about to strike, and it was a matter of absolute and preeminent necessity that everybody should look well at his watch. It was evident however, that just at this moment the fellow in the steeple was doing something that he had no business to do with the clock. But as it now began to strike nobody had any time to attend to his manœuvres, for they had all to count the strokes of the bell as it sounded.

"One!" said the clock.

"Von!" echoed every little old gentleman in every leather-bottomed arm-chair in Vondervotteimittiss. "Von!" said his watch also; "von!" said the watch of his *vrow*, and "von!" said the watches of the boys, and the little gilt repeaters on the tails of the cat and pig.

"Two!" continued the big bell; and

"Doo!" repeated all the repeaters.

"Three! Four! Five! Six! Seven! Eight! Nine! Ten!" said the bell.

"Dree! Vour! Fibe! Sax! Seben! Aight! Noin! Den!" answered the others.

"Eleven!" said the big one.

"Eleben!" assented the little fellows.

"Twelve!" said the bell.

"Dvelf!" they replied, perfectly satisfied, and dropping their voices.

"Und dvelf it iss!" said all the little old gentlemen, putting up their watches. But the big bell had not done with them yet.

"*Thirteen!*" said he.

"Der Teufel!" gasped the little old gentlemen, turning pale, dropping their pipes, and putting down all their right legs from over their left knees.

"Der Teufel!" groaned they, "Dirteen! Dirteen! !—*Mein Gott*, it is Dirteen o'clock! !"

Why attempt to describe the terrible scene which ensued? All Vondervotteimittiss flew at once into a lamentable state of uproar.

"Vot is cum'd to mein pelly?" roared all the boys,—"I've been ongry for dis hour!"

"Vot is cum'd to mein kraut?" screamed all the vrows, "It has been done to rags for dis hour!"

"Vot is cum'd to mein pipe?" swore all the little old gentlemen, "Donder and Blitzen! it has been smoked out for dis hour!"—and they filled them up again in a great rage, and, sinking back in their arm-chairs, puffed away so fast and so fiercely that the whole valley was immediately filled with impenetrable smoke.

Meantime the cabbages all turned very red in the face, and it seemed as if Old Nick himself had taken possession of everything in the shape of a timepiece. The clocks carved upon the furniture took to dancing as if bewitched, while those upon the mantelpieces could scarcely contain themselves for fury, and kept such a continual striking of thirteen, and such a frisking and wriggling of their pendulums as was really horrible to see. But, worse than all, neither the cats nor the pigs could put up any longer with the behavior of the little repeaters tied to their tails, and resented it by scampering all over the place, scratching and poking, and squeaking and screeching, and caterwauling and squalling, and flying into the faces, and running under the petticoats of the people, and creating altogether the most abominable din and confusion which it is possible for a reasonable person to conceive. And to make matters still more distressing, the rascally little scapegrace in the steeple was evidently exerting himself to the utmost. Every now and then one might catch a glimpse of the scoundrel through the smoke. There he sat in the belfry upon the belfry-man, who was lying flat upon his back. In his teeth the villain held the bell-rope, which he kept jerking about with his head, raising such a clatter that my ears ring again even to think of it. On his lap lay the big fiddle at which he was scraping out of all time and tune with both hands, making a great show, the nincompoop! of playing "Judy O'Flannagan and Paddy O'Rafferty."

Affairs being thus miserably situated I left the place in disgust, and now appeal for aid to all lovers of correct time and fine kraut. Let us proceed in a body to the borough, and restore the ancient order of things in Vondervotteimittiss by ejecting that little fellow from the steeple.

THE ANGEL OF THE ODD

IT WAS A chilly November afternoon. I had just consummated an unusually hearty dinner, of which the dyspeptic truffe formed not the least important item, and was sitting alone in the dining-room, with my feet upon the fender, and at my elbow a small table which I had rolled up to the fire, and upon which were some apologies for dessert, with some miscellaneous bottles of wine, spirit, and *liqueur*. In the morning I had been reading Glover's *Leonidas*, Wilkies *Epigoniad*, Lamartine's *Pilgrimage*, Barlow's *Columbiad*, Tuckermann's *Sicily*, and Griswold's *Curiosities*; I am willing to confess, therefore, that I now felt a little stupid. I made effort to arouse myself by aid of frequent Lafitte, and, all failing, I betook myself to a stray newspaper in despair. Having carefully perused the column of "houses to let," and the column of "dogs lost," and then the two columns of "wives and apprentices runaway," I attacked with great resolution the editorial matter, and, reading it from beginning to end without understanding a syllable, conceived the possibility of its being Chinese, and so reread it from the end to the beginning, but with no more satisfactory result. I was about throwing away, in disgust,

> This folio of four pages, happy work
> Which not even poets criticise,

when I felt my attention somewhat aroused by the paragraph which follows:

> "The avenues to death are numerous and strange. A London paper mentions the decease of a person from a singular cause. He was playing at 'puff the dart,' which is played with a long needle inserted

> in some worsted, and blown at a target through a tin tube. He placed the needle at the wrong end of the tube, and drawing his breath strongly to puff the dart forward with force, drew the needle into his throat. It entered the lungs, and in a few days killed him."

Upon seeing this I fell into a great rage, without exactly knowing why. "This thing," I exclaimed, "is a contemptible falsehood—a poor hoax—the lees of the invention of some pitiable penny-a-liner—of some wretched concocter of accidents in Cocaigne. These fellows, knowing the extravagant gullibility of the age, set their wits to work in the imagination of improbable possibilities—of odd accidents, as they term them; but to a reflecting intellect (like mine," I added, in parenthesis, putting my forefinger unconsciously to the side of my nose), "to a contemplative understanding such as I myself possess, it seems evident at once that the marvelous increase of late in these 'odd accidents' is by far the oddest accident of all. For my own part, I intend to believe nothing henceforward that has anything of the 'singular' about it.

"*Mein Gott*, den, vat a vool you bees for dat!" replied one of the most remarkable voices I ever heard. At first I took it for a rumbling in my ears—such as man sometimes experiences when getting very drunk—but, upon second thought, I considered the sound as more nearly resembling that which proceeds from an empty barrel beaten with a big stick; and, in fact, this I should have concluded it to be, but for the articulation of the syllables and words. I am by no means naturally nervous, and the very few glasses of Lafitte which I had sipped served to embolden me a little, so that I felt nothing of trepidation, but merely uplifted my eyes with a leisurely movement, and looked carefully around the room for the intruder. I could not, however, perceive any one at all.

"Humph!" resumed the voice, as I continued my survey, "you mus pe so dronk as de pig, den, for not zee me as I zit here at your zide."

Hereupon I bethought me of looking immediately before my nose, and there, sure enough, confronting me at the table sat a personage nondescript, although not altogether indescribable. His body was a wine-pipe, or a rum-puncheon, or something of that character, and had a truly Falstaffian air. In its nether extremity were inserted two kegs, which seemed to answer all the purposes of legs. For arms there dangled from the upper portion of the carcass two tolerably long bottles, with the necks outward for hands. All the head that I saw the monster possessed of was one of those Hessian canteens which resemble a large snuff-box with a hole in the middle of the lid. This canteen (with a funnel on its top, like a cavalier cap slouched over the eyes) was set on edge upon the puncheon, with the hole toward myself; and through this hole, which seemed puckered up like the mouth of a very precise old maid, the creature was emitting certain rumbling and grumbling noises which he evidently intended for intelligible talk.

"I zay," said he, "you mos pe dronk as de pig, vor zit dare and not zee me zit ere; and I zay, doo, you most pe pigger vool as de goose, vor to dispelief vat iz print in de print. 'Tiz de troof-dat it iz—eberry vord ob it."

"Who are you, pray?" said I, with much dignity, although somewhat puzzled; "how did you get here? and what is it you are talking about?"

"Az vor ow I com'd ere," replied the figure, "dat iz none of your pizzness; and as vor vat I be talking apout, I be talk apout vot I tink proper; and as vor who I be, vy dat is de very ting I com'd here for to let you zee for yourzelf."

"You are a drunken vagabond," said I, "and I shall ring the bell and order my footman to kick you into the street."

"He! he! he!" said the fellow, "hu! hu! hu! dat you can't do."

"Can't do!" said I, "what do you mean?—can't do what?"

"Ring de pell," he replied, attempting a grin with his little villainous mouth.

Upon this I made an effort to get up, in order to put my threat into execution; but the ruffian just reached across the table very deliberately, and hitting me a tap on the forehead with the neck of one of the long bottles, knocked me back into the arm-chair from which I had half arisen. I was utterly astounded; and, for a moment, was quite at a loss what to do. In the meantime, he continued his talk.

"You zee," said he, "it iz te bess vor zit still; and now you shall know who I pe. Look at me! zee! I am te *Angel ov te Odd*!"

"And odd enough, too," I ventured to reply; "but I was always under the impression that an angel had wings."

"Te wing!" he cried, highly incensed, "vat I pe do mit te wing? *Mein Gott!* do you take me vor a shicken?"

"No—oh, no!" I replied, much alarmed, "you are no chicken—certainly not."

"Well, den, zit still and pehabe yourself, or I'll rap you again mid me vist. It iz te shicken ab te wing, und te owl ab te wing, und te imp ab te wing, und te headteuffel ab te wing. Te angel ab not te wing, and I am te Angel ov te Odd."

"And your business with me at present is—is—"

"My pizzness!" ejaculated the thing, "vy vot a low bred puppy you mos pe vor to ask a gentleman und an angel apout his pizzness!"

This language was rather more than I could bear, even from an angel; so, plucking up courage, I seized a salt-cellar which lay within reach, and hurled it at the head of the intruder. Either he dodged, however, or my aim was inaccurate; for all I accomplished was the demolition of the crystal which protected the dial of the clock upon the mantelpiece. As for the Angel, he evinced his sense of my assault by giving me two or three hard consecutive raps upon the forehead as before. These reduced me at once to submission, and I am almost ashamed to confess that, either through pain or vexation, there came a few tears into my eyes.

"*Mein Gott!*" said the Angel of the Odd, apparently much softened at my distress; "*Mein Gott*, te man is eder ferry dronck or ferry sorry. You mos not trink it so strong—you mos put de water in te wine. Here, trink dis, like a goot veller, und don't gry now—don't!"

Hereupon the Angel of the Odd replenished my goblet (which was about a third full of Port) with a colorless fluid that he poured from one of his hand bottles. I observed that these bottles had labels about their necks, and that these labels were inscribed "*Kirschenwasser.*"

The considerate kindness of the Angel mollified me in no little measure; and, aided by the water with which he diluted my Port more than once, I at length regained sufficient temper to listen to his very extraordinary discourse. I cannot pretend to recount all that he told me, but I gleaned from what he said that he was the genius who presided over the *contre-temps* of mankind, and whose business it was to bring about the *odd accidents* which are continually astonishing the skeptic. Once or twice, upon my venturing to express my total incredulity in respect to his pretensions, he grew very angry indeed, so that at length I considered it the wiser policy to say nothing at all, and let him have his own way. He talked on, therefore, at great length, while I merely leaned back in my chair with my eyes shut, and amused myself with munching raisins and flipping the stems about the room. But, by and bye, the Angel suddenly construed this behavior of mine into contempt. He arose in a terrible passion, slouched his funnel down over his eyes, swore a vast oath, uttered a threat of some character which I did not precisely comprehend, and finally made me a low bow and departed, wishing me, in the language of the archbishop in Gil-Blas, "*beaucoup de bonheur et un peu plus de bon sens.*"

His departure afforded me relief. The very few glasses of Lafitte that I had sipped had the effect of rendering me drowsy, and I felt inclined to take a nap of some fifteen or twenty minutes, as is my custom after dinner. At six I had an appointment of consequence, which it was quite indispensable that I should keep. The policy of insurance for my dwelling house had expired the day before; and, some dispute having arisen, it was agreed that, at six, I should meet the board of directors of the company and settle the terms of a renewal. Glancing upward at the clock on the mantel-piece (for I felt too drowsy to take out my watch), I had the pleasure to find that I had still twenty-five minutes to spare. It was half past five; I could easily walk to the insurance office in five minutes; and my usual post prandian siestas had never been known to exceed five and twenty. I felt sufficiently safe, therefore, and composed myself to my slumbers forthwith.

Having completed them to my satisfaction, I again looked toward the time-piece, and was half inclined to believe in the possibility of odd accidents when I found that, instead of my ordinary fifteen or twenty minutes, I had been dozing only three; for it still wanted seven and twenty of the appointed hour. I betook myself again to my nap, and at length a second time awoke, when, to my utter amazement, it still wanted twenty-seven minutes of six. I jumped up to examine the clock, and found that it had ceased running. My watch informed me that it was half past seven; and, of course, having slept two hours, I was too late for my appointment "It will make no difference," I said; "I can call at the office in the morning and apologize; in the meantime what can be the matter with the clock?" Upon examining it I discovered that one of the raisin-stems which I had been flipping about the room during the discourse of the Angel of the Odd had flown through the fractured crystal, and lodging, singularly enough, in the key-hole, with an end projecting outward, had thus arrested the revolution of the minute-hand.

"Ah!" said I; "I see how it is. This thing speaks for itself. A natural accident, such as will happen now and then!"

I gave the matter no further consideration, and at my usual hour retired to bed. Here, having placed a candle upon a reading-stand at the bed-head, and having made an attempt to peruse some pages of the *Omnipresence of the Deity*, I unfortunately fell asleep in less than twenty seconds, leaving the light burning as it was.

My dreams were terrifically disturbed by visions of the Angel of the Odd. Methought he stood at the foot of the couch, drew aside the curtains, and, in the hollow, detestable tones of a rum-puncheon, menaced me with the bitterest vengeance for the contempt with which I had treated him. He concluded a long harrangue by taking off his funnelcap, inserting the tube into my gullet, and thus deluging me with an ocean of Kirschenwasser, which he poured, in a continuous flood, from one of the long-necked bottles that stood him instead of an arm. My agony was at length insufferable, and I awoke just in time to perceive that a rat had ran off with the lighted candle from the stand, but not in season to prevent his making his escape with it through the hole. Very soon, a strong suffocating odor assailed my nostrils; the house, I clearly perceived, was on fire. In a few minutes the blaze broke forth with violence, and in an incredibly brief period the entire building was wrapped in flames. All egress from my chamber, except through a window, was cut off. The crowd, however, quickly procured and raised a long ladder. By means of this I was descending rapidly, and in apparent safety, when a huge hog, about whose rotund stomach, and indeed about whose whole air and physiognomy, there was something which reminded me of the Angel of the Odd,—when this hog, I say, which hitherto had been quietly slumbering in the mud, took it suddenly into his head that his left shoulder needed scratching, and could find no more convenient rubbing post than that afforded by the foot of the ladder. In an instant I was precipitated, and had the misfortune to fracture my arm.

This accident, with the loss of my insurance, and with the more serious loss of my hair, the whole of which had been singed off by the fire, predisposed me to serious impressions, so that, finally, I made up my mind to take a wife. There was a rich widow disconsolate for the loss of her seventh husband, and to her wounded spirit I offered the balm of my vows. She yielded a reluctant consent to my prayers. I knelt at her feet in gratitude and adoration. She blushed, and bowed her luxuriant tresse into close contact with those supplied me, temporarily, by Grandjean. I know not how the entanglement took place, but so it was. I arose with a shining pate, wigless, she in disdain and wrath, half buried in alien hair. Thus ended my hopes of the widow by an accident which could not have been anticipated, to be sure, but which the natural sequence of events had brought about.

Without despairing, however, I undertook the siege of a less implacable heart. The fates were again propitious for a brief period; but again a trivial incident interfered. Meeting my betrothed in an avenue thronged with the elite of the city, I was hastening to greet her with one of my best considered bows, when a small particle of some foreign matter lodging in the corner of my eye, rendered me, for the moment, completely blind. Before I could recover my sight, the lady of my love had disappeared—irreparably affronted at what she chose to consider my premeditated rudeness in passing her by ungreeted. While I stood bewildered at the suddenness of this accident (which might have happened, nevertheless, to any one under the sun), and while I still continued incapable of sight, I was accosted by the Angel of the Odd, who proffered me his aid with a civility which I had no reason to expect. He examined my disordered eye with much gentleness and skill, informed me that I had a drop in it, and (whatever a "drop" was) took it out, and afforded me relief.

I now considered it time to die, (since fortune had so determined to persecute me,) and accordingly made my way to the nearest river. Here, divesting myself of my clothes, (for there is no reason why we cannot die as we were born,) I threw myself headlong into the current; the sole witness of my fate being a solitary crow that had been seduced into the eating of brandy-saturated corn, and so had staggered away from his fellows. No sooner had I entered the water than this bird took it into its head to fly away with the most indispensable portion of my apparel. Postponing, therefore, for the present, my suicidal design, I just slipped my nether extremities into the sleeves of my coat, and betook myself to a pursuit of the felon with all the nimbleness which the case required and its circumstances would admit. But my evil destiny attended me still. As I ran at full speed, with my nose up in the atmosphere, and intent only upon the purloiner of my property, I suddenly perceived that my feet rested no longer upon *terra firma*; the fact is, I had thrown myself over a precipice, and should inevitably have been dashed to pieces, but for my good fortune in grasping the end of a long guide-rope, which descended from a passing balloon.

As soon as I sufficiently recovered my senses to comprehend the terrific predicament in which I stood or rather hung, I exerted all the power of my lungs to make that predicament known to the aeronaut overhead. But for a long time I exerted myself in vain. Either the fool could not, or the villain would not perceive me. Meantime the machine rapidly soared, while my strength even more rapidly failed. I was soon upon the point of resigning myself to my fate, and dropping quietly into the sea, when my spirits were suddenly revived by hearing a hollow voice from above, which seemed to be lazily humming an opera air. Looking up, I perceived the Angel of the Odd. He was leaning with his arms folded, over the rim of the car, and with a pipe in his mouth, at which he puffed leisurely, seemed to be upon excellent terms with himself and the universe. I was too much exhausted to speak, so I merely regarded him with an imploring air.

For several minutes, although he looked me full in the face, he said nothing. At length removing carefully his meerschaum from the right to the left corner of his mouth, he condescended to speak.

"Who pe you?" he asked, "und what der teuffel you pe do dare?"

To this piece of impudence, cruelty, and affectation, I could reply only by ejaculating the monosyllable "Help!"

"Elp!" echoed the ruffian— "not I. Dare iz te pottle—elp yourself, und pe tam'd!"

With these words he let fall a heavy bottle of Kirschenwasser which, dropping precisely upon the crown of my head, caused me to imagine that my brains were entirely knocked out. Impressed with this idea, I was about to relinquish my hold and give up the ghost with a good grace, when I was arrested by the cry of the Angel, who bade me hold on.

"Old on!" he said; "don't pe in te urry—don't. Will you pe take de odder pottle, or ave you pe got zober yet and come to your zenzes?"

I made haste, hereupon, to nod my head twice—once in the negative, meaning thereby that I would prefer not taking the other bottle at present—and once in the affirmative, intending thus to imply that I was sober and had positively come to my senses. By these means I somewhat softened the Angel.

"Und you pelief, ten," he inquired, "at te last? You pelief, ten, in te possibilty of te odd?"

I again nodded my head in assent.

"Und you ave pelief in me, te Angel of te Odd?"

I nodded again.

"Und you acknowledge tat you pe te blind dronk and te vool?"

I nodded once more.

"Put your right hand into your left hand preeches pocket, ten, in token oy your vull zubmission unto te Angel ov te Odd."

This thing, for very obvious reasons, I found it quite impossible to do. In the first place, my left arm had been broken in my fall from the ladder, and, therefore, had I let go my hold with the right hand, I must have let go altogether. In the second place, I could have no breeches until I came across the crow. I was therefore obliged, much to my regret, to shake my head in the negative—intending thus to give the Angel to understand that I found it inconvenient, just at that moment, to comply with his very reasonable demand! No sooner, however, had I ceased shaking my head than-

"Go to der teuffel ten!" roared the Angel of the Odd.

In pronouncing these words, he drew a sharp knife across the guide rope by which I was suspended, and as we then happened to be precisely over my own house, (which, during my peregrinations, had been handsomely rebuilt,) it so occurred that I tumbled headlong down the ample chimney and alit upon the dining-room hearth.

Upon coming to my senses, (for the fall had very thoroughly stunned me,) I found it about four o'clock in the morning. I lay outstretched where I had fallen from the balloon. My head grovelled in the ashes of an extinguished fire, while my feet reposed upon the wreck of a small table, overthrown, and amid the fragments of a miscellaneous dessert, intermingled with a newspaper, some broken glass and shattered bottles, and an empty jug of the Schiedam Kirschenwasser. Thus revenged himself the Angel of the Odd.

THE ISLAND OF THE FAY

Nullus enim locus sine genio est.—Servius

"*LA MUSIQUE*," SAYS Marmontel, in those "Contes Moraux"[1] which, in all our translations, we have insisted upon calling "Moral Tales," as if in mockery of their spirit—"*la musique est le seul des talents qui jouissent de lui même; tous les autres veulent des temoins.*" He here confounds the pleasure derivable from sweet sounds with the capacity for creating them. No more than any other *talent*, is that for music susceptible of complete enjoyment, where there is no second party to appreciate its exercise. And it is only in common with other talents that it produces *effects* which may be fully enjoyed in solitude. The idea which the *raconteur* has either failed to entertain clearly, or has sacrificed in its expression to his national love of *point*, is, doubtless, the very tenable one that the higher order of music is the most thoroughly estimated when we are exclusively alone. The proposition, in this form, will be admitted at once by those who love the lyre for its own sake, and for its spiritual uses. But there is one pleasure still within the reach of fallen mortality—and perhaps only one—which owes even more than does music to the accessory sentiment of seclusion. I mean the happiness experienced in the contemplation of natural scenery. In truth, the man who would behold aright the glory of God upon earth must in solitude behold that glory. To me, at least, the presence—not of human life only—but of life in any other form than that of the green things which grow upon the soil and are voiceless—is a stain upon the land-

1 Moraux is here derived from *mœurs*, and its meaning is "*fashionable*," or, more strictly, "of manners."

scape—is at war with the genius of the scene. I love, indeed, to regard the dark valleys, and the gray rocks, and the waters that silently smile, and the forests that sigh in uneasy slumbers, and the proud watchful mountains that look down upon all—I love to regard these as themselves but the colossal members of one vast animate and sentient whole—a whole whose form (that of the sphere) is the most perfect and most inclusive of all; whose path is among associate planets; whose meek handmaiden is the moon; whose mediate sovereign is the sun; whose life is eternity; whose thought is that of a God; whose enjoyment is knowledge; whose destinies are lost in immensity; whose cognizance of ourselves is akin with our own cognizance of the *animalculæ* which infest the brain—a being which we, in consequence, regard as purely inanimate and material, much in the same manner as these *animalculæ* must thus regard us.

Our telescopes, and our mathematical investigations assure us on every hand—notwithstanding the cant of the more ignorant of the priesthood—that space, and therefore that bulk, is an important consideration in the eyes of the Almighty. The cycles in which the stars move are those best adapted for the evolution, without collision, of the greatest possible number of bodies. The forms of those bodies are accurately such as, within a given surface, to include the greatest possible amount of matter;—while the surfaces themselves are so disposed as to accommodate a denser population than could be accommodated on the same surfaces otherwise arranged. Nor is it any argument against bulk being an object with God, that space itself is infinite; for there may be an infinity of matter to fill it. And since we see clearly that the endowment of matter with vitality is a principle—indeed, as far as our judgments extend, the *leading* principle in the operations of Deity—it is scarcely logical to imagine it confined to the regions of the minute, where we daily trace it, and not extending to those of the august. As we find cycle within cycle without end—yet all revolving around one far-distant center which is the Godhead, may we not analogically suppose, in the same manner, life within life, the less within the greater, and all within the Spirit Divine? In short, we are madly erring, through self-esteem, in believing man, in either his temporal or future destinies, to be of more moment in the universe than that vast "clod of the valley" which he tills and contemns, and to which he denies a soul for no more profound reason than that he does not behold it in operation.[1]

These fancies, and such as these, have always given to my meditations among the mountains, and the forests, by the rivers and the ocean, a tinge of what the every-day world would not fail to term the fantastic. My wanderings amid such scenes have been many, and far-searching, and often solitary; and the interest with which I have strayed through many a dim deep valley, or gazed into the reflected Heaven of many a bright lake, has been an interest greatly deepened by the thought that I have strayed and gazed *alone*. What flippant Frenchman[2] was it who said, in allusion to the well-known work of Zimmerman, that, "*la solitude est une belle chose; mais il faut quelqu 'un pour vous dire que la solitude est une belle chose?*" The epigram cannot be gainsayed; but the necessity is a thing that does not exist.

It was during one of my lonely journeyings, amid a far-distant region of mountain locked within mountain, and sad rivers and melancholy tarns writhing or sleeping within all—that I chanced upon a certain rivulet and island. I came upon them suddenly in the leafy June, and threw myself upon the turf, beneath the branches of an unknown odorous shrub, that I might doze as I contemplated the scene. I felt that thus only should I look upon it such was the character of phantasm which it wore.

On all sides—save to the west, where the sun was about sinking—arose the verdant walls of the forest. The little river which turned sharply in its course, and was thus immediately lost to sight, seemed to have no exit from its prison, but to be absorbed by the deep green foliage of the trees to the east—while in the opposite quarter (so it appeared to me as I lay at length and glanced upward) there poured down noiselessly and continuously into the valley, a rich golden and crimson water-fall from the sunset fountains of the sky.

About midway in th short vista which my dreamy vision took in, one small circular island, profusely verdured, reposed upon the bosom of the stream.

1 Speaking of the tides, Pomponius Mela, in his treatise *De Sitú Orbis*, says "either the world is a great animal, or" &c.

2 Balzac—in substance—I do not remember the words.

So blended bank and shadow there,
That each seemed pendulous in air—

so mirror-like was the glassy water, that it was scarcely possible to say at what point upon the slope of the emerald turf its crystal dominion began.

My position enabled me to include in a single view both the eastern and western extremities of the islet; and I observed a singularly-marked difference in their aspects. The latter was all one radiant harem of garden beauties. It glowed and blushed beneath the eye of the slant sunlight, and fairly laughed with flowers. The grass was short, springy, sweet-scented, and Asphodel-interspersed. The trees were lithe, mirthful, erect—bright, slender and graceful—of eastern figure and foliage, with bark smooth, glossy, and parti-colored. There seemed a deep sense of life and joy about all; and although no airs blew from out the Heavens, yet every thing had motion through the gentle sweepings to and fro of innumerable butterflies, that might have been mistaken for tulips with wings.[1]

The other or eastern end of the isle was whelmed in the blackest shade. A somber, yet beautiful and peaceful gloom here pervaded all things. The trees were dark in color and mournful in form and attitude—wreathing themselves into sad, solemn, and spectral shapes, that conveyed ideas of mortal sorrow and untimely death. The grass wore the deep tint of the cypress, and the heads of its blades hung droopingly, and, hither and thither among it, were many small unsightly hillocks, low, and narrow, and not very long, that had the aspect of graves, but were not; although over and all about them the rue and the rosemary clambered. The shade of the trees fell heavily upon the water, and seemed to bury itself therein, impregnating the depths of the element with darkness. I fancied that each shadow, as the sun descended lower and lower, separated itself sullenly from the trunk that gave it birth, and thus became absorbed by the stream; while other shadows issued momently from the trees, taking the place of their predecessors thus entombed.

This idea, having once seized upon my fancy, greatly excited it, and

1 *Florem putares nare per liquidum æthera*—P. Commire.

I lost myself forthwith in revery. "If ever island were enchanted," said I to myself, "this is it. This is the haunt of the few gentle Fays who remain from the wreck of the race. Are these green tombs theirs?—or do they yield up their sweet lives as mankind yield up their own? In dying, do they not rather waste away mournfully; rendering unto God little by little their existence, as these trees render up shadow after shadow, exhausting their substance unto dissolution? What the wasting tree is to the water that imbibes its shade, growing thus blacker by what it preys upon, may not the life of the Fay be to the death which ingulfs it?"

As I thus mused, with half-shut eyes, while the sun sank rapidly to rest, and eddying currents careered round and round the island, bearing upon their bosom large, dazzling, white flakes, of the bark of the sycamore—flakes which, in their multiform positions upon the water, a quick imagination might have converted into any thing it pleased—while I thus mused, it appeared to me that the form of one of those very Fays about whom I had been pondering, made its way slowly into the darkness from out the light at the western end of the island. She stood erect in a singularly fragile canoe, and urged it with the mere phantom of an oar. While within the influence of the lingering sunbeams, her attitude seemed indicative of joy—but sorrow deformed it as she passed within the shade. Slowly she glided along, and at length rounded the islet and re-entered the region of light. "The revolution which has just been made by the Fay," continued I, musingly, "is the cycle of the brief year of her life. She has floated through her winter and through her summer. She is a year nearer unto Death: for I did not fail to see that as she came into the shade, her shadow fell from her, and was swallowed up in the dark water, making its blackness more black."

And again the boat appeared, and the Fay; but about the attitude of the latter there was more of care and uncertainty, and less of elastic joy. She floated again from out the light, and into the gloom (which deepened momently) and again her shadow fell from her into the ebony water, and became absorbed into its blackness. And again and again she made the circuit of the island, (while the sun rushed down to his slumbers) and at each issuing into the light, there was more sorrow about her person, while it grew feebler, and far fainter, and more indistinct; and at each passage into the gloom, there fell from her a darker shade, which became whelmed in a shadow more black. But at length, when the sun had utterly departed, the Fay, now the mere ghost of her former self, went disconsolately with her boat into the region of the ebony flood—and that she issued thence at all I cannot say,—for darkness fell over all things, and I beheld her magical figure no more.

SOME WORDS WITH A MUMMY

THE SYMPOSIUM OF the preceding evening had been a little too much for my nerves. I had a wretched headache, and was desperately drowsy. Instead of going out therefore to spend the evening as I had proposed, it occurred to me that I could not do a wiser thing than just eat a mouthful of supper and go immediately to bed.

A *light* supper of course. I am exceedingly fond of Welsh rabbit. More than a pound at once, however, may not at all times be advisable. Still, there can be no material objection to two. And really between two and three, there is merely a single unit of difference. I ventured, perhaps, upon four. My wife will have it five;—but, clearly, she has confounded two very distinct affairs. The abstract number, five, I am willing to admit; but, concretely, it has reference to bottles of Brown Stout, without which, in the way of condiment, Welsh rabbit is to be eschewed.

Having thus concluded a frugal meal, and donned my night-cap, with the serene hope of enjoying it till noon the next day, I placed my head upon the pillow, and, through the aid of a capital conscience, fell into a profound slumber forthwith.

But when were the hopes of humanity fulfilled? I could not have completed my third snore when there came a furious ringing at the street-door bell, and then an impatient thumping at the knocker, which awakened me at once. In a minute afterward, and while I was still rubbing my eyes, my wife thrust in my face a note, from my old friend, Doctor Ponnonner. It ran thus:

Come to me, by all means, my dear good friend, as soon as you receive this. Come and help us to rejoice. At last, by long persevering diplomacy, I have gained the assent of the Directors of the City Museum, to my examination of the Mummy—you know the one I mean. I have permission to unswathe it and open it, if desirable. A few friends only will be present—you, of course. The Mummy is now at my house, and we shall begin to unroll it at eleven to-night.

Yours, ever, PONNONNER.

By the time I had reached the "PONNONNER," it struck me that I was as wide awake as a man need be. I leaped out of bed in an ecstacy, overthrowing all in my way; dressed myself with a rapidity truly marvelous; and set off, at the top of my speed, for the doctor's.

There I found a very eager company assembled. They had been awaiting me with much impatience; the Mummy was extended upon the dining-table; and the moment I entered its examination was commenced.

It was one of a pair brought, several years previously, by Captain Arthur Sabretash, a cousin of Ponnonner's from a tomb near Eleithias, in the Lybian mountains, a considerable distance above Thebes on the Nile. The grottoes at this point, although less magnificent than the Theban sepulchres, are of higher interest, on account of affording more numerous illustrations of the private life of the Egyptians. The chamber from which our specimen was taken, was said to be very rich in such illustrations; the walls being completely covered with fresco paintings and bas-reliefs, while statues, vases, and Mosaic work of rich patterns, indicated the vast wealth of the deceased.

The treasure had been deposited in the Museum precisely in the same condition in which Captain Sabretash had found it;—that is to say, the coffin had not been disturbed. For eight years it had thus stood, subject only externally to public inspection. We had now, therefore, the complete Mummy at our disposal; and to those who are aware how very rarely the unransacked antique reaches our shores, it will be evident, at once that we had great reason to congratulate ourselves upon our good fortune.

Approaching the table, I saw on it a large box, or case, nearly seven feet long, and perhaps three feet wide, by two feet and a half deep. It was oblong—not coffin-shaped. The material was at first supposed to be the wood of the sycamore (*platanus*), but, upon cutting into it, we found it to be pasteboard, or, more properly, *papier mâché*, composed of papyrus. It was thickly ornamented with paintings, representing funeral scenes, and other mournful subjects—interspersed among which, in every variety of position, were certain series of hieroglyphical characters, intended, no doubt, for the name of the departed. By good luck, Mr. Gliddon formed one of our party; and he had no difficulty in translating the letters, which were simply phonetic, and represented the word *Allamistakeo*.

We had some difficulty in getting this case open without injury; but having at length accomplished the task, we came to a second, coffin-shaped, and very considerably less in size than the exterior one, but resembling it precisely in every other respect. The interval between the two was filled with resin, which had, in some degree, defaced the colors of the interior box.

Upon opening this latter (which we did quite easily), we arrived at a third case, also coffin-shaped, and varying from the second one in no particular, except in that of its material, which was cedar, and still emitted the peculiar and highly aromatic odor of that wood. Between the second and the third case there was no interval—the one fitting accurately within the other.

Removing the third case, we discovered and took out the body itself. We had expected to find it, as usual, enveloped in frequent rolls, or bandages, of linen; but, in place of these, we found a sort of sheath, made of papyrus, and coated with a layer of plaster, thickly gilt and painted. The paintings represented subjects connected with the various supposed duties of the soul, and its presentation to different divinities, with numerous identical human figures, intended, very probably, as portraits of the persons embalmed. Extending from head to foot was a columnar, or perpendicular, inscription, in phonetic hieroglyphics, giving again his name and titles, and the names and titles of his relations.

Around the neck thus ensheathed, was a collar of cylindrical glass beads, diverse in color, and so arranged as to form images of deities, of the scarabaeus, etc, with the winged globe. Around the small of the waist was a similar collar or belt.

Stripping off the papyrus, we found the flesh in excellent preservation, with no perceptible odor. The color was reddish. The skin was hard, smooth, and glossy. The teeth and hair were in good condition. The eyes (it seemed) had been removed, and glass ones substituted, which were very beautiful and wonderfully life-like, with the exception of somewhat too determined a stare. The fingers and the nails were brilliantly gilded.

Mr. Gliddon was of opinion, from the redness of the epidermis, that the embalmment had been effected altogether by asphaltum; but, on scraping the surface with a steel instrument, and throwing into the fire some of the powder thus obtained, the flavor of camphor and other sweet-scented gums became apparent.

We searched the corpse very carefully for the usual openings through which the entrails are extracted, but, to our surprise, we could discover none. No member of the party was at that period aware that entire or unopened mummies are not infrequently met. The brain it was customary to withdraw through the nose; the intestines through an incision in the side; the body was then shaved, washed, and salted; then laid aside for several weeks, when the operation of embalming, properly so called, began.

As no trace of an opening could be found, Doctor Ponnonner was preparing his instruments for dissection, when I observed that it was then past two o'clock. Hereupon it was agreed to postpone the internal examination until the next evening; and we were about to separate for the present, when some one suggested an experiment or two with the Voltaic pile.

The application of electricity to a mummy three or four thousand years old at the least, was an idea, if not very sage, still sufficiently original, and we all caught it at once. About one-tenth in earnest and nine-tenths in jest, we arranged a battery in the Doctor's study, and conveyed thither the Egyptian.

It was only after much trouble that we succeeded in laying bare some portions of the temporal muscle which appeared of less stony rigidity than other parts of the frame, but which, as we had anticipated, of course, gave no indication of galvanic susceptibility when brought in contact with the wire. This, the first trial, indeed, seemed decisive, and, with a hearty laugh at our own absurdity, we were bidding each other good night, when my eyes, happening to fall upon those of the Mummy, were there immediately riveted in amazement. My brief glance, in fact, had sufficed to assure me that the orbs which we had all supposed to be glass, and which were originally noticeable for a certain wild stare, were now so far covered by the lids, that only a small portion of the *tunica albuginea* remained visible.

With a shout I called attention to the fact, and it became immediately obvious to all.

I cannot say that I was alarmed at the phenomenon, because "alarmed" is, in my case, not exactly the word. It is possible, however, that, but for the Brown Stout, I might have been a little nervous. As for the rest of the company, they really made no attempt at concealing the downright fright which possessed them. Doctor Ponnonner was a man to be pitied. Mr. Gliddon, by some peculiar process, rendered himself invisible. Mr. Silk Buckingham, I fancy, will scarcely be so bold as to deny that he made his way, upon all fours, under the table.

After the first shock of astonishment, however, we resolved, as a matter of course, upon further experiment forthwith. Our operations were now directed against the great toe of the right foot. We made an incision over the outside of the exterior *os sesamoideum pollicis pedis*, and thus got at the root of the *abductor* muscle. Readjusting the battery, we now applied the fluid to the bisected nerves—when, with a movement of exceeding life-likeness, the Mummy first drew up its right knee so as to bring it nearly in contact with the abdomen, and then, straightening the limb with inconceivable force, bestowed a kick upon Doctor Ponnonner, which had the effect of discharging that gentleman, like an arrow from a catapult, through a window into the street below.

We rushed out *en masse* to bring in the mangled remains of the victim, but had the happiness to meet him upon the staircase, coming up in an unaccountable hurry, brimful of the most ardent philosophy, and more than ever impressed with the necessity of prosecuting our experiment with vigor and with zeal.

It was by his advice, accordingly, that we made, upon the spot, a profound incision into the tip of the subject's nose, while the Doctor himself, laying violent hands upon it, pulled it into vehement contact with the wire.

Morally and physically—figuratively and literally—was the effect electric. In the first place, the corpse opened its eyes and winked very rapidly for several minutes, as does Mr. Barnes in the pantomime, in the second place, it sneezed; in the third, it sat upon end; in the fourth, it shook its fist in Doctor Ponnonner's face; in the fifth, turning to Messieurs Gliddon and Buckingham, it addressed them, in very capital Egyptian, thus:

"I must say, gentlemen, that I am as much surprised as I am mortified at your behavior. Of Doctor Ponnonner nothing better was to be expected. He is a poor little fat fool who knows no better. I pity and forgive him. But you, Mr. Gliddon—and you, Silk—who have traveled and resided in Egypt until one might imagine you to the manner born—you, I say who have been so much among us that you speak Egyptian fully as well, I think, as you write your mother tongue—you, whom I have always been led to regard as the firm friend of the mummies—I really did anticipate more gentlemanly conduct from you. What am I to think of your standing quietly by and seeing me thus unhandsomely used? What am I to suppose by your permitting Tom, Dick, and Harry to strip me of my coffins, and my clothes, in this wretchedly cold climate? In what light (to come to the point) am I to regard your aiding and abetting that miserable little villain, Doctor Ponnonner, in pulling me by the nose?"

It will be taken for granted, no doubt, that upon hearing this speech under the circumstances, we all either made for the door, or fell into violent hysterics, or went off in a general swoon. One of these three things was, I say, to be expected. Indeed each and all of these lines of conduct might have been very plausibly pursued. And, upon my word, I am at a loss to know how or why it was that we pursued neither the one nor the other. But, perhaps, the true reason is to be sought in the spirit of the age, which proceeds by the rule of contraries altogether, and is now usually admitted as the solution of every thing in the way of paradox and impossibility. Or, perhaps, after all, it was only the Mummy's exceedingly natural and matter-of-course air that divested his words of the terrible. However this may be, the facts are clear, and no member of our party betrayed any very particular trepidation, or seemed to consider that any thing had gone very especially wrong.

For my part I was convinced it was all right, and merely stepped aside, out of the range of the Egyptian's fist. Doctor Ponnonner thrust his hands into his breeches' pockets, looked hard at the Mummy, and grew excessively red in the face. Mr. Glidden stroked his whiskers and drew up the collar of his shirt. Mr. Buckingham hung down his head, and put his right thumb into the left corner of his mouth.

The Egyptian regarded him with a severe countenance for some minutes and at length, with a sneer, said:

"Why don't you speak, Mr. Buckingham? Did you hear what I asked you, or not? *Do* take your thumb out of your mouth!"

Mr. Buckingham, hereupon, gave a slight start, took his right thumb out of the left corner of his mouth, and, by way of indemnification inserted his left thumb in the right corner of the aperture above-mentioned.

Not being able to get an answer from Mr. B., the figure turned peevishly to Mr. Gliddon, and, in a peremptory tone, demanded in general terms what we all meant.

Mr. Gliddon replied at great length, in phonetics; and but for the deficiency of American printing-offices in hieroglyphical type, it would afford me much pleasure to record here, in the original, the whole of his very excellent speech.

I may as well take this occasion to remark, that all the subsequent conversation in which the Mummy took a part, was carried on in primitive Egyptian, through the medium (so far as concerned myself and other untraveled members of the company)—through the medium, I say, of Messieurs Gliddon and Buckingham, as interpreters. These gentlemen spoke the mother tongue of the Mummy with inimitable fluency and grace; but I could not help observing that (owing, no doubt, to the introduction of images entirely modern, and, of course, entirely novel to the stranger) the two travelers were reduced, occasionally, to the employment of sensible forms for the purpose of conveying a particular meaning. Mr. Gliddon, at one period, for example, could not make the Egyptian comprehend the term "politics," until he sketched upon the wall, with a bit of charcoal a little carbuncle-nosed gentleman, out at elbows, standing upon a stump, with his left leg drawn back, right arm thrown forward, with his fist shut, the eyes rolled up toward Heaven, and the mouth open at an angle of ninety degrees. Just in the same way Mr. Buckingham failed to convey the absolutely modern idea "wig," until (at Doctor Ponnonner's suggestion) he grew very pale in the face, and consented to take off his own.

It will be readily understood that Mr. Gliddon's discourse turned chiefly upon the vast benefits accruing to science from the unrolling and disemboweling of mummies; apologizing, upon this score, for any disturbance that might have been occasioned him, in particular, the individual Mummy called Allamistakeo; and concluding with a mere hint (for it could scarcely be considered more) that, as these little matters were now explained, it might be as well to proceed with the investigation intended. Here Doctor Ponnonner made ready his instruments.

In regard to the latter suggestions of the orator, it appears that Allamistakeo had certain scruples of conscience, the nature of which I did not distinctly learn; but he expressed himself satisfied with the apologies tendered, and, getting down from the table, shook hands with the company all round.

When this ceremony was at an end, we immediately busied ourselves in repairing the damages which our subject had sustained from the scalpel. We sewed up the wound in his temple, bandaged his foot, and applied a square inch of black plaster to the tip of his nose.

It was now observed that the Count (this was the title, it seems, of Allamistakeo) had a slight fit of shivering—no doubt from the cold. The doctor immediately repaired to his wardrobe, and soon returned with a black dress coat, made in Jennings' best manner, a pair of sky-blue plaid pantaloons with straps, a pink gingham chemise, a flapped vest of brocade, a white sack overcoat, a walking cane with a hook, a hat with no brim, patent-leather boots, straw-colored kid gloves, an eye-glass, a pair of whiskers, and a waterfall cravat. Owing to the disparity of size between the Count and the doctor (the proportion being as two to one), there was some little difficulty in adjusting these habiliments upon the person of the Egyptian; but when all was arranged, he might have been said to be dressed. Mr. Gliddon, therefore, gave him his arm, and led him to a comfortable chair by the fire, while the doctor rang the bell upon the spot and ordered a supply of cigars and wine.

The conversation soon grew animated. Much curiosity was, of course, expressed in regard to the somewhat remarkable fact of Allamistakeo's still remaining alive.

"I should have thought," observed Mr. Buckingham, "that it is high time you were dead."

"Why," replied the Count, very much astonished, "I am little more than seven hundred years old! My father lived a thousand, and was by no means in his dotage when he died."

Here ensued a brisk series of questions and computations, by means of which it became evident that the antiquity of the Mummy had been grossly misjudged. It had been five thousand and fifty years and some months since he had been consigned to the catacombs at Eleithias.

"But my remark," resumed Mr. Buckingham, "had no reference to your age at the period of interment (I am willing to grant, in fact, that you are still a young man), and my illusion was to the immensity of time during which, by your own showing, you must have been done up in asphaltum."

"In what?" said the Count.

"In asphaltum," persisted Mr. B.

"Ah, yes; I have some faint notion of what you mean; it might be made to answer, no doubt—but in my time we employed scarcely any thing else than the Bichloride of Mercury."

"But what we are especially at a loss to understand," said Doctor Ponnonner, "is how it happens that, having been dead and buried in Egypt five thousand years ago, you are here to-day all alive and looking so delightfully well."

"Had I been, as you say, *dead*," replied the Count, "it is more than probable that dead, I should still be; for I perceive you are yet in the infancy of Calvanism, and cannot accomplish with it what was a common thing among us in the old days. But the fact is, I fell into catalepsy, and it was considered by my best friends that I was either dead or should be; they accordingly embalmed me at once—I presume you are aware of the chief principle of the embalming process?"

"Why not altogether."

"Why, I perceive—a deplorable condition of ignorance! Well I cannot enter into details just now: but it is necessary to explain that to embalm (properly speaking), in Egypt, was to arrest indefinitely *all* the animal functions subjected to the process. I use the word 'animal' in its widest sense, as including the physical not more than the moral and *vital* being. I repeat that the leading principle of embalmment consisted, with us, in the immediately arresting, and holding in perpetual *abeyance*, all the animal functions subjected to the process. To be brief, in whatever condition the individual was, at the period of embalmment, in that condition he remained. Now, as it is my good fortune to be of the blood of the Scarabaeus, I was embalmed *alive*, as you see me at present."

"The blood of the Scarabaeus!" exclaimed Doctor Ponnonner.

"Yes. The Scarabaeus was the *insignium* or the 'arms,' of a very distinguished and very rare patrician family. To be 'of the blood of the Scarabaeus,' is merely to be one of that family of which the Scarabaeus is the *insignium*. I speak figuratively."

"But what has this to do with you being alive?"

"Why, it is the general custom in Egypt to deprive a corpse, before embalmment, of its bowels and brains; the race of the Scarabaei alone did not coincide with the custom. Had I not been a Scarabeus, therefore, I should have been without bowels and brains; and without either it is inconvenient to live."

"I perceive that," said Mr. Buckingham, "and I presume that all the *entire* mummies that come to hand are of the race of Scarabaei."

"Beyond doubt."

"I thought," said Mr. Gliddon, very meekly, "that the Scarabaeus was one of the Egyptian gods."

"One of the Egyptian what?" exclaimed the Mummy, starting to its feet.

"Gods!" repeated the traveler.

"Mr. Gliddon, I really am astonished to hear you talk in this style," said the Count, resuming his chair. "No nation upon the face of the earth has ever acknowledged more than *one god*. The Scarabaeus, the Ibis, etc., were with us (as similar creatures have been with others) the symbols, or *media*, through which we offered worship to the Creator too august to be more directly approached."

There was here a pause. At length the colloquy was renewed by Doctor Ponnonner.

"It is not improbable, then, from what you have explained," said he, "that among the catacombs near the Nile there may exist other mummies of the Scarabaeus tribe, in a condition of vitality?"

"There can be no question of it," replied the Count; "all the Scarabaei embalmed accidentally while alive, are alive now. Even some of those purposely so embalmed, may have been overlooked by their executors, and still remain in the tomb."

"Will you be kind enough to explain," I said, "what you mean by 'purposely so embalmed'?"

"With great pleasure!" answered the Mummy, after surveying me leisurely through his eye-glass—for it was the first time I had ventured to address him a direct question.

"With great pleasure," he said. "The usual duration of man's life, in my time, was about eight hundred years. Few men died, unless by most extraordinary accident, before the age of six hundred; few lived longer than a decade of centuries; but eight were considered the natural term. After the discovery of the embalming principle, as I have already described it to you, it occurred to our philosophers that a laudable curiosity might be gratified, and, at the same time, the interests of science much advanced, by living this natural term in installments. In the case of history, indeed, experience demonstrated that something of this kind was indispensable. An historian, for example, having attained the age of five hundred, would write a book with great labor and then get himself carefully embalmed; leaving instructions to his executors pro tem., that they should cause him to be revivified after the lapse of a certain period—say five or six hundred years. Resuming existence at the expiration of this time, he would invariably find his great work converted into a species of hap-hazard note-book—that is to say, into a kind of literary arena for the conflicting guesses, riddles, and personal squabbles of whole herds of exasperated commentators. These guesses, etc., which passed under the name of annotations, or emendations, were found so completely to have enveloped, distorted, and overwhelmed the text, that the author had to go about with a lantern to discover his own book. When discovered, it was never worth the trouble of the search. After rewriting it throughout, it was regarded as the bounden duty of the historian to set himself to work immediately in correcting, from his own private knowledge and experience, the traditions of the day concerning the epoch at which he had originally lived. Now this process of rescription and personal rectification, pursued by various individual sages from time to time, had the effect of preventing our history from degenerating into absolute fable."

"I beg your pardon," said Doctor Ponnonner at this point, laying his hand gently upon the arm of the Egyptian—"I beg your pardon, sir, but may I presume to interrupt you for one moment?"

"By all means, *sir*," replied the Count, drawing up.

"I merely wished to ask you a question," said the doctor. "You mentioned the historian's personal correction of traditions respecting his own epoch. Pray, sir, upon an average what proportion of these Kabbala were usually found to be right?"

"The Kabbala, as you properly term them, sir, were generally discovered to be precisely on a par with the facts recorded in the un-rewritten histories themselves;—that is to say, not one individual iota of either was ever known, under any circumstances, to be not totally and radically wrong."

"But since it is quite clear," resumed the Doctor, "that at least five thousand years have elapsed since your entombment, I take it for granted that your histories at that period, if not your traditions were sufficiently explicit on that one topic of universal interest, the Creation, which took place, as I presume you are aware, only about ten centuries before."

"Sir!" said the Count Allamistakeo.

The Doctor repeated his remarks, but it was only after much additional explanation that the foreigner could be made to comprehend them. The latter at length said, hesitatingly:

"The ideas you have suggested are to me, I confess, utterly novel. During my time I never knew any one to entertain so singular a fancy as that the universe (or this world if you will have it so) ever had a beginning at all. I remember once, and once only, hearing something remotely hinted, by a man of many speculations, concerning the origin *of the human race*; and by this individual, the very word Adam (or Red Earth), which you make use of, was employed. He employed it, however, in a generical sense, with reference to the spontaneous germination from rank soil (just as a thousand of the lower genera of creatures are germinated)—the spontaneous germination, I say, of five vast hordes of men, simultaneously upspringing in five distinct and nearly equal divisions of the globe."

Here, in general, the company shrugged their shoulders, and one or two of us touched our foreheads with a very significant air. Mr. Silk Buckingham, first glancing slightly at the occiput and then at the sinciput of Allamistakeo, spoke as follows:

"The long duration of human life in your time, together with the occasional practice of passing it, as you have explained, in installments, must have had, indeed, a strong tendency to the general development and conglomeration of knowledge. I presume, therefore, that we are to attribute the marked inferiority of the old Egyptians in all particulars of science, when compared with the moderns, and more especially with the Yankees, altogether to the superior solidity of the Egyptian skull."

"I confess again," replied the Count, with much suavity, "that I am somewhat at a loss to comprehend you; pray, to what particulars of science do you allude?"

Here our whole party, joining voices, detailed, at great length, the assumptions of phrenology and the marvels of animal magnetism.

Having heard us to an end, the Count proceeded to relate a few anecdotes, which rendered it evident that prototypes of Gall and Spurzheim had flourished and faded in Egypt so long ago as to have been nearly forgotten, and that the maneuvers of Mesmer were really very contemptible tricks when put in collation with the positive miracles of the Theban savans, who created lice and a great many other similar things.

I here asked the Count if his people were able to calculate eclipses. He smiled rather contemptuously, and said they were.

This put me a little out, but I began to make other inquiries in regard to his astronomical knowledge, when a member of the company, who had never as yet opened his mouth, whispered in my ear, that for information on this head, I had better consult Ptolemy (whoever Ptolemy is), as well as one Plutarch *de facie lunae*.

I then questioned the Mummy about burning-glasses and lenses, and, in general, about the manufacture of glass; but I had not made an end of my queries before the silent member again touched me quietly on the elbow, and begged me for God's sake to take a peep at Diodorus Siculus. As for the Count, he merely asked me, in the way of reply, if we moderns possessed any such microscopes as would enable us to cut cameos in the style of the Egyptians. While I was thinking how I should answer this question, little Doctor Ponnonner committed himself in a very extraordinary way.

"Look at our architecture!" he exclaimed, greatly to the indignation of both the travelers, who pinched him black and blue to no purpose.

"Look," he cried with enthusiasm, "at the Bowling-Green Fountain in New York! or if this be too vast a contemplation, regard for a moment the Capitol at Washington, D. C.!"—and the good little medical man went on to detail very minutely, the proportions of the fabric to which he referred. He explained that the portico alone was adorned with no less than four and twenty columns, five feet in diameter, and ten feet apart.

The Count said that he regretted not being able to remember, just at that moment, the precise dimensions of any one of the principal buildings of the city of Aznac, whose foundations were laid in the night of Time, but the ruins of which were still standing, at the epoch of his entombment, in a vast plain of sand to the westward of Thebes. He recollected, however, (talking of the porticoes,) that one affixed to an inferior palace in a kind of suburb called Carnac, consisted of a hundred and forty-four columns, thirty-seven feet in circumference, and twenty-five feet apart. The approach to this portico, from the Nile, was through an avenue two miles long, composed of sphynxes, statues, and obelisks, twenty, sixty, and a hundred feet in height. The palace itself (as well as he could remember) was, in one direction, two miles long, and might have been altogether about seven in circuit. Its walls were richly painted all over, within and without, with hieroglyphics. He would not pretend to assert that even fifty or sixty of the doctor's Capitols might have been built within these walls, but he was by no means sure that two or three hundred of them might not have been squeezed in with some trouble. That palace at Carnac was an insignificant little building after all. He (the Count), however, could not conscientiously refuse to admit the ingenuity, magnificence, and superiority of the Fountain at the Bowling Green, as described by the doctor. Nothing like it, he was forced to allow, had ever been seen in Egypt or elsewhere.

I here asked the Count what he had to say to our railroads.

"Nothing," he replied, "in particular." They were rather slight, rather ill-conceived, and clumsily put together. They could not be compared, of course, with the vast, level, direct, iron-grooved causeways upon which the Egyptians conveyed entire temples and solid obelisks of a hundred and fifty feet in altitude.

I spoke of our gigantic mechanical forces.

He agreed that we knew something in that way, but inquired how I should have gone to work in getting up the imposts on the lintels of even the little palace at Carnac.

This question I concluded not to hear, and demanded if he had any idea of Artesian wells; but he simply raised his eyebrows; while Mr. Gliddon winked at me very hard and said, in a low tone, that one had been recently discovered by the engineers employed to bore for water in the Great Oasis.

I then mentioned our steel; but the foreigner elevated his nose, and asked me if our steel could have executed the sharp carved work seen on the obelisks, and which was wrought altogether by edge-tools of copper.

This disconcerted us so greatly that we thought it advisable to vary the attack to Metaphysics. We sent for a copy of a book called the *Dial*, and read out of it a chapter or two about something that is not very clear, but which the Bostonians call the Great Movement of Progress.

The Count merely said that Great Movements were awfully common things in his day, and as for Progress, it was at one time quite a nuisance, but it never progressed.

We then spoke of the great beauty and importance of Democracy, and were at much trouble in impressing the Count with a due sense of the advantages we enjoyed in living where there was suffrage *ad libitum*, and no king.

He listened with marked interest, and in fact seemed not a little amused. When we had done, he said that, a great while ago, there had occurred something of a very similar sort. Thirteen Egyptian provinces determined all at once to be free, and to set a magnificent example to the rest of mankind. They assembled their wise men, and concocted the most ingenious constitution it is possible to conceive. For a while they managed remarkably well; only their habit of bragging was prodigious. The thing ended, however, in the consolidation of the thirteen states, with some fifteen or twenty others, in the most odious and insupportable despotism that was ever heard of upon the face of the Earth.

I asked what was the name of the usurping tyrant.

As well as the Count could recollect, it was Mob.

Not knowing what to say to this, I raised my voice, and deplored the Egyptian ignorance of steam.

The Count looked at me with much astonishment, but made no answer. The silent gentleman, however, gave me a violent nudge in the ribs with his elbows—told me I had sufficiently exposed myself for once—and demanded if I was really such a fool as not to know that the modern steam-engine is derived from the invention of Hero, through Solomon de Caus.

We were now in imminent danger of being discomfited; but, as good luck would have it, Doctor Ponnonner, having rallied, returned to our rescue, and inquired if the people of Egypt would seriously pretend to rival the moderns in the all—important particular of dress.

The Count, at this, glanced downward to the straps of his pantaloons, and then taking hold of the end of one of his coat-tails, held it up close to his eyes for some minutes. Letting it fall, at last, his mouth extended itself very gradually from ear to ear; but I do not remember that he said any thing in the way of reply.

Hereupon we recovered our spirits, and the doctor, approaching the Mummy with great dignity, desired it to say candidly, upon its honor as a gentleman, if the Egyptians had comprehended, at any period, the manufacture of either Ponnonner's lozenges or Brandreth's pills.

We looked, with profound anxiety, for an answer—but in vain. It was not forthcoming. The Egyptian blushed and hung down his head. Never was triumph more consummate; never was defeat borne with so ill a grace. Indeed, I could not endure the spectacle of the poor Mummy's mortification. I reached my hat, bowed to him stiffly, and took leave.

Upon getting home I found it past four o'clock, and went immediately to bed. It is now ten A.M. I have been up since seven, penning these memoranda for the benefit of my family and of mankind. The former I shall behold no more. My wife is a shrew. The truth is, I am heartily sick of this life and of the nineteenth century in general. I am convinced that every thing is going wrong. Besides, I am anxious to know who will be President in 2045. As soon, therefore, as I shave and swallow a cup of coffee, I shall just step over to Ponnonner's and get embalmed for a couple of hundred years.

THE NARRATIVE OF ARTHUR GORDON PYM OF NANTUCKET

CONTENTS

PREFACE

UPON MY RETURN to the United States a few months ago, after the extraordinary series of adventure in the South Seas and elsewhere, of which an account is given in the following pages, accident threw me into the society of several gentlemen in Richmond, Va., who felt deep interest in all matters relating to the regions I had visited, and who were constantly urging it upon me, as a duty, to give my narrative to the public. I had several reasons, however, for declining to do so, some of which were of a nature altogether private, and concern no person but myself; others not so much so. One consideration which deterred me was, that, having kept no journal during a greater portion of the time in which I was absent, I feared I should not be able to write, from mere memory, a statement so minute and connected as to have the *appearance* of that truth it would really possess, barring only the natural and unavoidable exaggeration to which all of us are prone when detailing events which have had powerful influence in exciting the imaginative faculties. Another reason was, that the incidents to be narrated were of a nature so positively marvelous, that, unsupported as my assertions must necessarily be (except by the evidence of a single individual, and he a half-breed Indian), I could only hope for belief among my family, and those of my friends who have had reason, through life, to put faith in my veracity—the probability being that the public at large would regard what I should put forth as merely an impudent and ingenious fiction. A distrust in my own abilities as a writer was, nevertheless, one of the principal causes which prevented me from complying with the suggestions of my advisers.

Among those gentlemen in Virginia who expressed the greatest interest in my statement, more particularly in regard to that portion of it which related to the Antarctic Ocean, was Mr. Poe, lately editor of the *Southern Literary Messenger*, a monthly magazine, published by Mr. Thomas W. White, in the city of Richmond. He strongly advised me, among others, to prepare at once a full account of what I had seen and undergone, and trust to the shrewdness and common sense of the public—insisting, with great plausibility, that however roughly, as regards mere authorship, my book should be got up, its very uncouthness, if there were any, would give it all the better chance of being received as truth.

Notwithstanding this representation, I did not make up my mind to do as he suggested. He afterward proposed (finding that I would not stir in the matter) that I should allow him to draw up, in his own words, a narrative of the earlier portion of my adventures, from facts afforded by myself, publishing it in the *Southern Messenger*, *under the garb of fiction*. To this, perceiving no objection, I consented, stipulating only that my real name should be retained. Two numbers of the pretended fiction appeared, consequently, in the *Messenger* for January and February (1837), and, in order that it might certainly be regarded as fiction, the name of Mr. Poe was affixed to the articles in the table of contents of the magazine.

The manner in which this *ruse* was received has induced me at length to undertake a regular compilation and publication of the adventures in question; for I found that, in spite of the air of fable which had been so ingeniously thrown around that portion of my statement which appeared in the *Messenger* (without altering or distorting a single fact), the public were still not at all disposed to receive it as fable, and several letters were sent to Mr. P.'s address distinctly expressing a conviction to the contrary. I thence concluded that the facts of my narrative would prove of such a nature as to carry with them sufficient evidence of their own authenticity, and that I had consequently little to fear on the score of popular incredulity.

This *exposé* being made, it will be seen at once how much of what follows I claim to be my own writing; and it will also be understood that no fact is misrepresented in the first few pages which were written by Mr. Poe. Even to those readers who have not seen the *Messenger*, it will be unnecessary to point out where his portion ends and my own commences; the difference in point of style will be readily perceived.

NEW-YORK, JULY, 1838. A. G. PYM.

CHAPTER 1

MY NAME IS Arthur Gordon Pym. My father was a respectable trader in sea-stores at Nantucket, where I was born. My maternal grandfather was an attorney in good practice. He was fortunate in every thing, and had speculated very successfully in stocks of the Edgarton New Bank, as it was formerly called. By these and other means he had managed to lay by a tolerable sum of money. He was more attached to myself, I believe, than to any other person in the world, and I expected to inherit the most of his property at his death. He sent me, at six years of age, to the school of old Mr. Ricketts, a gentleman with only one arm and of eccentric manners—he is well known to almost every person who has visited New Bedford. I stayed at his school until I was sixteen, when I left him for Mr. E. Ronald's academy on the hill. Here I became intimate with the son of Mr. Barnard, a sea-captain, who generally sailed in the employ of Lloyd and Vredenburgh—Mr. Barnard is also very well known in New Bedford, and has many relations, I am certain, in Edgarton. His son was named Augustus, and he was nearly two years older than myself. He had been on a whaling voyage with his father in the John Donaldson, and was always talking to me of his adventures in the South Pacific Ocean. I used frequently to go home with him, and remain all day, and sometimes all night. We occupied the same bed, and he would be sure to keep me awake until almost light, telling me stories of the natives of the Island of Tinian, and other places he had visited in his travels. At last I could not help being interested in what he said, and by degrees I felt the greatest desire to go to sea. I owned a sailboat called the *Ariel*, and worth about seventy-five dollars. She had a half-deck or cuddy, and was rigged sloop-fashion—I forget her tonnage, but she would hold ten persons without much crowding. In this boat we were in the habit of going on some of the maddest freaks in the world; and, when I now think of them, it appears to me a thousand wonders that I am alive today.

I will relate one of these adventures by way of introduction to a longer and more momentous narrative. One night there was a party at Mr. Barnard's, and both Augustus and myself were not a little intoxicated toward the close of it. As usual, in such cases, I took part of his bed in preference to going home. He went to sleep, as I thought, very quietly (it being near one when the party broke up), and without saying a word on his favorite topic. It might have been half an hour from the time of our getting in bed, and I was just about falling into a doze, when he suddenly started up, and swore with a terrible oath that he would not go to sleep for any Arthur Pym in Christendom, when there was so glorious a breeze from the southwest. I never was so astonished in my life, not knowing what he intended, and thinking that the wines and liquors he had drunk had set him entirely beside himself. He proceeded to talk very coolly, however, saying he knew that I supposed him intoxicated, but that he was never more sober in his life. He was only tired, he added, of lying in bed on such a fine night like a dog, and was determined to get up and dress, and go out on a frolic with the boat. I can hardly tell what possessed me, but the words were no sooner out of his mouth than I felt a thrill of the greatest excitement and pleasure, and thought his mad idea one of the most delightful and most reasonable things in the world. It was blowing almost a gale, and the weather was very cold—it being late in October. I sprang out of bed, nevertheless, in a kind of ecstasy, and told him I was quite as brave as himself, and quite as tired as he was of lying in bed like a dog, and quite as ready for any fun or frolic as any Augustus Barnard in Nantucket.

We lost no time in getting on our clothes and hurrying down to the boat. She was lying at the old decayed wharf by the lumber-yard of Pankey & Co., and almost thumping her side out against the rough logs. Augustus got into her and bailed her, for she was nearly half full of water. This being done, we hoisted jib and mainsail, kept full, and started boldly out to sea.

The wind, as I before said, blew freshly from the southwest. The night was very clear and cold. Augustus had taken the helm, and I stationed myself by the mast, on the deck of the cuddy. We flew along at a great rate—neither of us having said a word since casting loose from the wharf. I now asked my companion what course he intended to steer, and what time he thought it probable we should get back. He whistled for a few minutes, and then said crustily: "*I* am going to sea—*you* may go home if you think proper." Turning my eyes upon him, I perceived at once that, in spite of his assumed *nonchalance*, he was greatly agitated. I could see him distinctly by the light of the moon—his face was paler than any marble, and his hand shook so excessively that he could scarcely retain hold of the tiller. I found that something had gone wrong, and became seriously alarmed. At this period I knew little about the management of a boat, and was now depending entirely upon the nautical skill of my friend. The wind, too, had suddenly increased, as we were fast getting out of the lee of the land—still I was ashamed to betray any trepidation, and for almost half an hour maintained a resolute silence. I could stand it no longer, however, and spoke to Augustus about the propriety of turning back. As before, it was nearly a minute before he made answer, or took any notice of my suggestion. "By-and-by," said he at length—"time enough—home by-and-by." I had expected a similar reply, but there was something in the tone of these words which filled me with an indescribable feeling of dread. I again looked at the speaker attentively. His lips were perfectly livid, and his knees shook so violently together that he seemed scarcely able to stand. "For God's sake, Augustus," I screamed, now heartily frightened, "what ails you?—what is the matter?—what *are* you going to do?" "Matter!" he stammered, in the greatest apparent surprise, letting go the tiller at the same moment, and falling forward into the bottom of the boat—"matter—why, nothing is the—matter—going home—d—d—don't you see?" The whole truth now flashed upon me. I flew to him and raised him up. He was drunk—beastly drunk—he could no longer either stand, speak, or see. His eyes were perfectly glazed; and as I let him go in the extremity of my despair, he rolled like a mere log into the bilge-water, from which I had lifted him. It was evident that, during the evening, he had drunk far more than I suspected, and that his conduct in bed had been the result of a highly-concentrated state of intoxication—a state which, like madness, frequently enables the victim to imitate the outward demeanor of one in perfect possession of his senses. The coolness of the night air, however, had had its usual effect—the mental energy began to yield before its influence—and the confused perception which he no doubt then had of his perilous situation had assisted in hastening the catastrophe. He was now thoroughly insensible, and there was no probability that he would be otherwise for many hours.

It is hardly possible to conceive the extremity of my terror. The fumes of the wine lately taken had evaporated, leaving me doubly timid and irresolute. I knew that I was altogether incapable of managing the boat, and that a fierce wind and strong ebb tide were hurrying us to destruction. A storm was evidently gathering behind us; we had neither compass nor provisions; and it was clear that, if we held our present course, we should be out of sight of land before daybreak. These thoughts, with a crowd of others equally fearful, flashed through my mind with a bewildering rapidity, and for some moments paralyzed me beyond the possibility of making any exertion. The boat was going through the water at a terrible rate—full before the wind—no reef in either jib or mainsail—running her bows completely under the foam. It was a thousand wonders she did not broach to—Augustus having let go the tiller, as I said before, and I being too much agitated to think of taking it myself. By good luck, however, she kept steady, and gradually I recovered some degree of presence of mind. Still the wind was increasing fearfully, and whenever we rose from a plunge forward, the sea behind fell combing over our counter, and deluged us with water. I was so utterly benumbed, too, in every limb, as to be nearly unconscious of sensation. At length I summoned up the resolution of despair, and rushing to the mainsail let it go by the run. As might have been expected, it flew over the bows, and, getting drenched with water, carried away the mast short off by the board. This latter accident alone saved me from instant destruction. Under the jib only, I now boomed along before the wind, shipping heavy seas occasionally over the counter, but relieved from the terror of immediate death. I took the helm, and breathed with greater freedom as I found that there yet remained to us a chance of ultimate escape. Augustus still lay senseless in the bottom of the boat; and as there was imminent danger of his drowning (the water being nearly a foot deep just where he fell), I contrived to raise him partially up, and keep him in a sitting position, by passing a rope round his waist, and lashing it to a ringbolt in the deck of the cuddy. Having thus arranged every thing as well as I could in my chilled and agitated condition, I recommended myself to God, and made up my mind to bear whatever might happen with all the fortitude in my power.

Hardly had I come to this resolution, when, suddenly, a loud and long scream or yell, as if from the throats of a thousand demons, seemed to pervade the whole atmosphere around and above the boat. Never while I live shall I forget the intense agony of terror I experienced at that moment. My hair stood erect on my head—I felt the blood congealing in my veins—my heart ceased utterly to beat, and without having once raised my eyes to learn the source of my alarm, I tumbled headlong and insensible upon the body of my fallen companion.

I found myself, upon reviving, in the cabin of a large whaling-ship (the *Penguin*) bound to Nantucket. Several persons were standing over me, and Augustus, paler than death, was busily occupied in chafing my hands. Upon seeing me open my eyes, his exclamations of gratitude and joy excited alternate laughter and tears from the rough-looking personages who were present. The mystery of our being in existence was now soon explained. We had been run down by the whaling-ship, which was close-hauled, beating up to Nantucket with every sail she could venture to set, and consequently running almost at right angles to our own course. Several men were on the look-out forward, but did not perceive our boat until it was an impossibility to avoid coming in contact—their shouts of warning upon seeing us were what so terribly alarmed me. The huge ship, I was told, rode immediately over us with as much ease as our own little vessel would have passed over a feather, and without the least perceptible impediment to her progress. Not a scream arose from the deck of the victim—there was a slight grating sound to be heard mingling with the roar of wind and water, as the frail bark which was swallowed up rubbed for a moment along the keel of her destroyer—but this was all. Thinking our boat (which it will be remembered was dismasted) some mere shell cut adrift as useless, the captain (Captain E. T. V. Block, of New London) was for proceeding on his course without troubling himself further about the matter. Luckily, there were two of the look-out who swore positively to having seen some person at our helm, and represented the possibility of yet saving him. A discussion ensued, when Block grew angry, and, after a while, said that "it was no business of his to be eternally watching for egg-shells; that the ship should *not* put about for any such nonsense; and if there was a man run down, it was nobody's fault" but Henderson, the first mate, now took the matter up, being justly indignant, as well as the whole ship's crew, at a speech evincing so base a degree of heartless atrocity. He spoke plainly, seeing himself upheld by the men, told the captain he considered him a fit subject for the gallows, and that he would disobey his orders if he were hanged for it the moment he set his foot on shore. He strode aft, jostling Block (who turned pale and made no answer) on one side, and seizing the helm, gave the word, in a firm voice, *Hard-a-lee!* The men flew to their posts, and the ship went cleverly about. All this had occupied nearly five minutes, and it was supposed to be hardly within the bounds of possibility that any individual could be saved—allowing any to have been on board the boat. Yet, as the reader has seen, both Augustus and myself were rescued; and our deliverance seemed to have been brought about by two of those almost inconceivable pieces of good fortune which are attributed by the wise and pious to the special interference of Providence.

While the ship was yet in stays, the mate lowered the jolly-boat and jumped into her with the very two men, I believe, who spoke up as having seen me at the helm. They had just left the lee of the vessel (the moon still shining brightly) when she made a long and heavy roll to windward, and Henderson, at the same moment, starting up in his seat bawled out to his crew to *back water*. He would say nothing else—repeating his cry impatiently, *back water! black water!* The men put back as speedily as possible, but by this time the ship had gone round, and gotten fully under headway, although all hands on board were making great exertions to take in sail. In despite of the danger of the attempt, the mate clung to the main-chains as soon as they came within his reach. Another huge lurch now brought the starboard side of the vessel out of water nearly as far as her keel, when the cause of his anxiety was rendered obvious enough. The body of a man was seen to be affixed in the most singular manner to the smooth and shining bottom (the *Penguin* was coppered and copper-fastened), and beating violently against it with every movement of the hull. After several ineffectual efforts, made during the lurches of the ship, and at the imminent risk of swamping the boat I was finally disengaged from my perilous situation and taken on board—for the body proved to be my own. It appeared that one of the timber-bolts having started and broken a passage through the copper, it had arrested my progress as I passed under the ship, and fastened me in so extraordinary a manner to her bottom. The head of the bolt had made its way through the collar of the green baize jacket I had on, and through the back part of my neck, forcing itself out between two sinews and just below the right ear. I was immediately put to bed—although life seemed to be totally extinct. There was no surgeon on board. The captain, however, treated me with every attention—to make amends, I presume, in the eyes of his crew, for his atrocious behavior in the previous portion of the adventure.

In the meantime, Henderson had again put off from the ship, although the wind was now blowing almost a hurricane. He had not been gone many minutes when he fell in with some fragments of our boat, and shortly afterward one of the men with him asserted that he could distinguish a cry for help at intervals amid the roaring of the tempest. This induced the hardy seamen to persevere in their search for more than half an hour, although repeated signals to return were made them by Captain Block, and although every moment on the water in so frail a boat was fraught to them with the most imminent and deadly peril. Indeed, it is nearly impossible to conceive how the small jolly they were in could have escaped destruction for a single instant. She was built, however, for the whaling service, and was fitted, as I have since had reason to believe, with air-boxes, in the manner of some life-boats used on the coast of Wales.

After searching in vain for about the period of time just mentioned, it was determined to get back to the ship. They had scarcely made this resolve when a feeble cry arose from a dark object that floated rapidly by. They pursued and soon overtook it. It proved to be the entire deck of the *Ariel*'s cuddy. Augustus was struggling near it, apparently in the last agonies. Upon getting hold of him it was found that he was attached by a rope to the floating timber. This rope, it will be remembered, I had myself tied around his waist, and made fast to a ringbolt, for the purpose of keeping him in an upright position, and my so doing, it appeared, had been ultimately the means of preserving his life. The *Ariel* was slightly put together, and in going down her frame naturally went to pieces; the deck of the cuddy, as might have been expected, was lifted, by the force of the water rushing in, entirely from the main timbers, and floated (with other fragments, no doubt) to the surface—Augustus was buoyed up with it, and thus escaped a terrible death.

It was more than an hour after being taken on board the *Penguin* before he could give any account of himself, or be made to comprehend the nature of the accident which had befallen our boat. At length he became thoroughly aroused, and spoke much of his sensations while in the water. Upon his first attaining any degree of consciousness, he found himself beneath the surface, whirling round and round with inconceivable rapidity, and with a rope wrapped in three or four folds tightly about his neck. In an instant afterward he felt himself going rapidly upward, when, his head striking violently against a hard substance, he again relapsed into insensibility. Upon once more reviving he was in fuller possession of his reason—this was still, however, in the greatest degree clouded and confused. He now knew that some accident had occurred, and that he was in the water, although his mouth was above the surface, and he could breathe with some freedom. Possibly, at this period the deck was drifting rapidly before the wind, and drawing him after it, as he floated upon his back. Of course, as long as he could have retained this position, it would have been nearly impossible that he should be drowned. Presently a surge threw him directly athwart the deck, and this post he endeavored to maintain, screaming at intervals for help. Just before he was discovered by Mr. Henderson, he had been obliged to relax his hold through exhaustion, and, falling into the sea, had given himself up for lost. During the whole period of his struggles he had not the faintest recollection of the *Ariel*, nor of the matters in connexion with the source of his disaster. A vague feeling of terror and despair had taken entire possession of his faculties. When he was finally picked up, every power of his mind had failed him; and, as before said, it was nearly an hour after getting on board the *Penguin* before he became fully aware of his condition. In regard to myself—I was resuscitated from a state bordering very nearly upon death (and after every other means had been tried in vain for three hours and a half) by vigorous friction with flannels bathed in hot oil—a proceeding suggested by Augustus. The wound in my neck, although of an ugly appearance, proved of little real consequence, and I soon recovered from its effects.

The Penguin got into port about nine o'clock in the morning, after encountering one of the severest gales ever experienced off Nantucket. Both Augustus and myself managed to appear at Mr. Barnard's in time for breakfast—which, luckily, was somewhat late, owing to the party over night. I suppose all at the table were too much fatigued themselves to notice our jaded appearance—of course, it would not have borne a very rigid scrutiny. Schoolboys, however, can accomplish wonders in the way of deception, and I verily believe not one of our friends in Nantucket had the slightest suspicion that the terrible story told by some sailors in town of their having run down a vessel at sea and drowned some thirty or forty poor devils, had reference either to the *Ariel*, my companion, or myself. We two have since very frequently talked the matter over—but never without a shudder. In one of our conversations Augustus frankly confessed to me, that in his whole life he had at no time experienced so excruciating a sense of dismay, as when on board our little boat he first discovered the extent of his intoxication, and felt himself sinking beneath its influence.

CHAPTER 2

IN NO AFFAIRS of mere prejudice, pro or con, do we deduce inferences with entire certainty, even from the most simple data. It might be supposed that a catastrophe such as I have just related would have effectually cooled my incipient passion for the sea. On the contrary, I never experienced a more ardent longing for the wild adventures incident to the life of a navigator than within a week after our miraculous deliverance. This short period proved amply long enough to erase from my memory the shadows, and bring out in vivid light all the pleasurably exciting points of color, all the picturesqueness, of the late perilous accident. My conversations with Augustus grew daily more frequent and more intensely full of interest. He had a manner of relating his stories of the ocean (more than one half of which I now suspect to have been sheer fabrications) well adapted to have weight with one of my enthusiastic temperament and somewhat gloomy although glowing imagination. It is strange, too, that he most strongly enlisted my feelings in behalf of the life of a seaman, when he depicted his more terrible moments of suffering and despair. For the bright side of the painting I had a limited sympathy. My visions were of shipwreck and famine; of death or captivity among barbarian hordes; of a lifetime dragged out in sorrow and tears, upon some gray and desolate rock, in an ocean unapproachable and unknown. Such visions or desires—for they amounted to desires—are common, I have since been assured, to the whole numerous race of the melancholy among men—at the time of which I speak I regarded them only as prophetic glimpses of a destiny which I felt myself in a measure bound to fulfill. Augustus thoroughly entered into my state of mind. It is probable, indeed, that our intimate communion had resulted in a partial interchange of character.

About eighteen months after the period of the *Ariel*'s disaster, the firm of Lloyd and Vredenburgh (a house connected in some manner with the Messieurs Enderby, I believe, of Liverpool) were engaged in repairing and fitting out the brig *Grampus* for a whaling voyage. She was an old hulk, and scarcely seaworthy when all was done to her that could be done. I hardly know why she was chosen in preference to other good vessels belonging to the same owners—but so it was. Mr. Barnard was appointed to command her, and Augustus was going with him.

While the brig was getting ready, he frequently urged upon me the excellency of the opportunity now offered for indulging my desire of travel. He found me by no means an unwilling listener—yet the matter could not be so easily arranged. My father made no direct opposition; but my mother went into hysterics at the bare mention of the design; and, more than all, my grandfather, from whom I expected much, vowed to cut me off with a shilling if I should ever broach the subject to him again. These difficulties, however, so far from abating my desire, only added fuel to the flame. I determined to go at all hazards; and, having made known my intentions to Augustus, we set about arranging a plan by which it might be accomplished. In the meantime I forbore speaking to any of my relations in regard to the voyage, and, as I busied myself ostensibly with my usual studies, it was supposed that I had abandoned the design. I have since frequently examined my conduct on this occasion with sentiments of displeasure as well as of surprise. The intense hypocrisy I made use of for the furtherance of my project—an hypocrisy pervading every word and action of my life for so long a period of time—could only have been rendered tolerable to myself by the wild and burning expectation with which I looked forward to the fulfillment of my long-cherished visions of travel.

In pursuance of my scheme of deception, I was necessarily obliged to leave much to the management of Augustus, who was employed for the greater part of every day on board the *Grampus*, attending to some arrangements for his father in the cabin and cabin hold. At night, however, we were sure to have a conference and talk over our hopes. After nearly a month passed in this manner, without our hitting upon any plan we thought likely to succeed, he told me at last that he had determined upon everything necessary. I had a relation living in New Bedford, a Mr. Ross, at whose house I was in the habit of spending occasionally two or three weeks at a time. The brig was to sail about the middle of June (June, 1827), and it was agreed that, a day or two before her putting to sea, my father was to receive a note, as usual, from Mr. Ross, asking me to come over and spend a fortnight with Robert and Emmet (his sons). Augustus charged himself with the inditing of this note and getting it delivered. Having set out as supposed, for New Bedford, I was then to report myself to my companion, who would contrive a hiding-place for me in the *Grampus*. This hiding-place, he assured me, would be rendered sufficiently comfortable for a residence of many days, during which I was not to make my appearance. When the brig had proceeded so far on her course as to make any turning back a matter out of question, I should then, he said, be formally installed in all the comforts of the cabin; and as to his father, he would only laugh heartily at the joke. Vessels enough would be met with by which a letter might be sent home explaining the adventure to my parents.

The middle of June at length arrived, and every thing had been matured. The note was written and delivered, and on a Monday morning I left the house for the New Bedford packet, as supposed. I went, however, straight to Augustus, who was waiting for me at the corner of a street. It had been our original plan that I should keep out of the way until dark, and then slip on board the brig; but, as there was now a thick fog in our favor, it was agreed to lose no time in secreting me. Augustus led the way to the wharf, and I followed at a little distance, enveloped in a thick seaman's cloak, which he had brought with him, so that my person might not be easily recognized. just as we turned the second corner, after passing Mr. Edmund's well, who should appear, standing right in front of me, and looking me full in the face, but old Mr. Peterson, my grandfather. "Why, bless my soul, Gordon," said he, after a long pause, "why, why,—*whose* dirty cloak is that you have on?" "Sir!" I replied, assuming, as well as I could, in the exigency of the moment, an air of offended surprise, and talking in the gruffest of all imaginable tones—"sir! you are a sum'mat mistaken—my name, in the first place, bee'nt nothing at all like Goddin, and I'd want you for to know better, you blackguard, than to call my new obercoat a darty one." For my life I could hardly refrain from screaming with laughter at the odd manner in which the old gentleman received this handsome rebuke. He started back two or three steps, turned first pale and then excessively red, threw up his spectacles, then, putting them down, ran full tilt at me, with his umbrella uplifted. He stopped short, however, in his career, as if struck with a sudden recollection; and presently, turning round, hobbled off down the street, shaking all the while with rage, and muttering between his teeth: "Won't do—new glasses—thought it was Gordon—d–d good-for-nothing salt water Long Tom."

After this narrow escape we proceeded with greater caution, and arrived at our point of destination in safety. There were only one or two of the hands on board, and these were busy forward, doing something to the forecastle combings. Captain Barnard, we knew very well, was engaged at Lloyd and Vredenburgh's, and would remain there until late in the evening, so we had little to apprehend on his account. Augustus went first up the vessel's side, and in a short while I followed him, without being noticed by the men at work. We proceeded at once into the cabin, and found no person there. It was fitted up in the most comfortable style—a thing somewhat unusual in a whaling-vessel. There were four very excellent staterooms, with wide and convenient berths. There was also a large stove, I took notice, and a remarkably thick and valuable carpet covering the floor of both the cabin and staterooms. The ceiling was full seven feet high, and, in short, every thing appeared of a more roomy and agreeable nature than I had anticipated. Augustus, however, would allow me but little time for observation, insisting upon the necessity of my concealing myself as soon as possible. He led the way into his own stateroom, which was on the starboard side of the brig, and next to the bulkheads. Upon entering, he closed the door and bolted it. I thought I had never seen a nicer little room than the one in which I now found myself. It was about ten feet long, and had only one berth, which, as I said before, was wide and convenient. In that portion of the closet nearest the bulkheads there was a space of four feet square, containing a table, a chair, and a set of hanging shelves full of books, chiefly books of voyages and travels. There were many other little comforts in the room, among which I ought not to forget a kind of safe or refrigerator, in which Augustus pointed out to me a host of delicacies, both in the eating and drinking department.

He now pressed with his knuckles upon a certain spot of the carpet in one corner of the space just mentioned, letting me know that a portion of the flooring, about sixteen inches square, had been neatly cut out and again adjusted. As he pressed, this portion rose up at one end sufficiently to allow the passage of his finger beneath. In this manner he raised the mouth of the trap (to which the carpet was still fastened by tacks), and I found that it led into the after hold. He next lit a small taper by means of a phosphorous match, and, placing the light in a dark lantern, descended with it through the opening, bidding me follow. I did so, and he then pulled the cover upon the hole, by means of a nail driven into the under side—the carpet, of course, resuming its original position on the floor of the stateroom, and all traces of the aperture being concealed.

The taper gave out so feeble a ray that it was with the greatest difficulty I could grope my way through the confused mass of lumber among which I now found myself. By degrees, however, my eyes became accustomed to the gloom, and I proceeded with less trouble, holding on to the skirts of my friend's coat. He brought me, at length, after creeping and winding through innumerable narrow passages, to an iron-bound box, such as is used sometimes for packing fine earthenware. It was nearly four feet high, and full six long, but very narrow. Two large empty oil-casks lay on the top of it, and above these, again, a vast quantity of straw matting, piled up as high as the floor of the cabin. In every other direction around was wedged as closely as possible, even up to the ceiling, a complete chaos of almost every species of ship-furniture, together with a heterogeneous medley of crates, hampers, barrels, and bales, so that it seemed a matter no less than miraculous that we had discovered any passage at all to the box. I afterward found that Augustus had purposely arranged the stowage in this hold with a view to affording me a thorough concealment, having had only one assistant in the labor, a man not going out in the brig.

My companion now showed me that one of the ends of the box could be removed at pleasure. He slipped it aside and displayed the interior, at which I was excessively amused. A mattress from one of the cabin berths covered the whole of its bottom, and it contained almost every article of mere comfort which could be crowded into so small a space, allowing me, at the same time, sufficient room for my accommodation, either in a sitting position or lying at full length. Among other things, there were some books, pen, ink, and paper, three blankets, a large jug full of water, a keg of sea-biscuit, three or four immense Bologna sausages, an enormous ham, a cold leg of roast mutton, and half a dozen bottles of cordials and liqueurs. I proceeded immediately to take possession of my little apartment, and this with feelings of higher satisfaction, I am sure, than any monarch ever experienced upon entering a new palace. Augustus now pointed out to me the method of fastening the open end of the box, and then, holding the taper close to the deck, showed me a piece of dark whipcord lying along it. This, he said, extended from my hiding-place throughout an the necessary windings among the lumber, to a nail which was driven into the deck of the hold, immediately beneath the trap-door leading into his stateroom. By means of this cord I should be enabled readily to trace my way out without his guidance, provided any unlooked-for accident should render such a step necessary. He now took his departure, leaving with me the lantern, together with a copious supply of tapers and phosphorous, and promising to pay me a visit as often as he could contrive to do so without observation. This was on the seventeenth of June.

I remained three days and nights (as nearly as I could guess) in my hiding-place without getting out of it at all, except twice for the purpose of stretching my limbs by standing erect between two crates just opposite the opening. During the whole period I saw nothing of Augustus; but this occasioned me little uneasiness, as I knew the brig was expected to put to sea every hour, and in the bustle he would not easily find opportunities of coming down to me. At length I heard the trap open and shut. and presently he called in a low voice, asking if all was well, and if there was any thing I wanted. "Nothing," I replied; "I am as comfortable as can be; when will the brig sail?" "She will be under weigh in less than half an hour," he answered. "I came to let you know, and for fear you should be uneasy at my absence. I shall not have a chance of coming down again for some time—perhaps for three or four days more. All is going on right aboveboard. After I go up and close the trap, do you creep along by the whipcord to where the nail is driven in. You will find my watch there—it may be useful to you, as you have no daylight to keep time by. I suppose you can't tell how long you have been buried—only three days—this is the twentieth. I would bring the watch to your box, but am afraid of being missed." With this he went up.

In about an hour after he had gone I distinctly felt the brig in motion, and congratulated myself upon having at length fairly commenced a voyage. Satisfied with this idea, I determined to make my mind as easy as possible, and await the course of events until I should be permitted to exchange the box for the more roomy, although hardly more comfortable, accommodations of the cabin. My first care was to get the watch. Leaving the taper burning, I groped along in the dark, following the cord through windings innumerable, in some of which I discovered that, after toiling a long distance, I was brought back within a foot or two of a former position. At length I reached the nail, and securing the object of my journey, returned with it in safety. I now looked over the books which had been so thoughtfully provided, and selected the expedition of Lewis and Clarke to the mouth of the Columbia. With this I amused myself for some time, when, growing sleepy, I extinguished the light with great care, and soon fell into a sound slumber.

Upon awakening I felt strangely confused in mind, and some time elapsed before I could bring to recollection all the various circumstances of my situation. By degrees, however, I remembered all. Striking a light, I looked at the watch; but it was run down, and there were, consequently, no means of determining how long I slept. My limbs were greatly cramped, and I was forced to relieve them by standing between the crates. Presently feeling an almost ravenous appetite, I bethought myself of the cold mutton, some of which I had eaten just before going to sleep, and found excellent. What was my astonishment in discovering it to be in a state of absolute putrefaction! This circumstance occasioned me great disquietude; for, connecting it with the disorder of mind I experienced upon awakening, I began to suppose that I must have slept for an inordinately long period of time. The close atmosphere of the hold might have had something to do with this, and might, in the end, be productive of the most serious results. My head ached excessively; I fancied that I drew every breath with difficulty; and, in short, I was oppressed with a multitude of gloomy feelings. Still I could not venture to make any disturbance by opening the trap or otherwise, and, having wound up the watch, contented myself as well as possible.

Throughout the whole of the next tedious twenty-four hours no person came to my relief, and I could not help accusing Augustus of the grossest inattention. What alarmed me chiefly was, that the water in my jug was reduced to about half a pint, and I was suffering much from thirst, having eaten freely of the Bologna sausages after the loss of my mutton. I became very uneasy, and could no longer take any interest in my books. I was overpowered, too, with a desire to sleep, yet trembled at the thought of indulging it, lest there might exist some pernicious influence, like that of burning charcoal, in the confined air of the hold. In the meantime the roll of the brig told me that we were far in the main ocean, and a dull humming sound, which reached my ears as if from an immense distance, convinced me no ordinary gale was blowing. I could not imagine a reason for the absence of Augustus. We were surely far enough advanced on our voyage to allow of my going up. Some accident might have happened to him—but I could think of none which would account for his suffering me to remain so long a prisoner, except, indeed, his having suddenly died or fallen overboard, and upon this idea I could not dwell with any degree of patience. It was possible that we had been baffled by head winds, and were still in the near vicinity of Nantucket. This notion, however, I was forced to abandon; for such being the case, the brig must have frequently gone about; and I was entirely satisfied, from her continual inclination to the larboard, that she had been sailing all along with a steady breeze on her starboard quarter. Besides, granting that we were still in the neighborhood of the island, why should not Augustus have visited me and informed me of the circumstance? Pondering in this manner upon the difficulties of my solitary and cheerless condition, I resolved to wait yet another twenty-four hours, when, if no relief were obtained, I would make my way to the trap, and endeavor either to hold a parley with my friend, or get at least a little fresh air through the opening, and a further supply of water from the stateroom. While occupied with this thought, however, I fell in spite of every exertion to the contrary, into a state of profound sleep, or rather stupor. My dreams were of the most terrific description. Every species of calamity and horror befell me. Among other miseries I was smothered to death between huge pillows, by demons of the most ghastly and ferocious aspect. Immense serpents held me in their embrace, and looked earnestly in my face with their fearfully shining eyes. Then deserts, limitless, and of the most forlorn and awe-inspiring character, spread themselves out before me. Immensely tall trunks of trees, gray and leafless, rose up in endless succession as far as the eye could reach. Their roots were concealed in wide-spreading morasses, whose dreary water lay intensely black, still, and altogether terrible, beneath. And the strange trees seemed endowed with a human vitality, and waving to and fro their skeleton arms, were crying to the silent waters for mercy, in the shrill and piercing accents of the most acute agony and despair. The scene changed; and I stood, naked and alone, amidst the burning sand-plains of Sahara. At my feet lay crouched a fierce lion of the tropics. Suddenly his wild eyes opened and fell upon me. With a conculsive bound he sprang to his feet, and laid bare his horrible teeth. In another instant there burst from his red throat a roar like the thunder of the firmament, and I fell impetuously to the earth. Stifling in a paroxysm of terror, I at last found myself partially awake. My dream, then, was not all a dream. Now, at least, I was in possession of my senses. The paws of some huge and real monster were pressing heavily upon my bosom—his hot breath was in my ear—and his white and ghastly fangs were gleaming upon me through the gloom.

Had a thousand lives hung upon the movement of a limb or the utterance of a syllable, I could have neither stirred nor spoken. The beast, whatever it was, retained his position without attempting any immediate violence, while I lay in an utterly helpless, and, I fancied, a dying condition beneath him. I felt that my powers of body and mind were fast leaving me—in a word, that I was perishing, and perishing of sheer fright. My brain swam—I grew deadly sick—my vision failed—even the glaring eyeballs above me grew dim. Making a last strong effort, I at length breathed a faint ejaculation to God, and resigned myself to die. The sound of my voice seemed to arouse all the latent fury of the animal. He precipitated himself at full length upon my body; but what was my astonishment, when, with a long and low whine, he commenced licking my face and hands with the greatest eagerness, and with the most extravagant demonstration of affection and joy! I was bewildered, utterly lost in amazement—but I could not forget the peculiar whine of my Newfoundland dog Tiger, and the odd manner of his caresses I well knew. It was he. I experienced a sudden rush of blood to my temples—a giddy and overpowering sense of deliverance and reanimation. I rose hurriedly from the mattress upon which I had been lying, and, throwing myself upon the neck of my faithful follower and friend, relieved the long oppression of my bosom in a flood of the most passionate tears.

As upon a former occasion my conceptions were in a state of the greatest indistinctness and confusion after leaving the mattress. For a long time I found it nearly impossible to connect any ideas; but, by very slow degrees, my thinking faculties returned, and I again called to memory the several incidents of my condition. For the presence of Tiger I tried in vain to account; and after busying myself with a thousand different conjectures respecting him, was forced to content myself with rejoicing that he was with me to share my dreary solitude, and render me comfort by his caresses. Most people love their dogs—but for Tiger I had an affection far more ardent than common; and never, certainly, did any creature more truly deserve it. For seven years he had been my inseparable companion, and in a multitude of instances had given evidence of all the noble qualities for which we value the animal. I had rescued him, when a puppy, from the clutches of a malignant little villain in Nantucket who was leading him, with a rope around his neck, to the water; and the grown dog repaid the obligation, about three years afterward, by saving me from the bludgeon of a street robber.

Getting now hold of the watch, I found, upon applying it to my ear, that it had again run down; but at this I was not at all surprised, being convinced, from the peculiar state of my feelings, that I had slept, as before, for a very long period of time, how long, it was of course impossible to say. I was burning up with fever, and my thirst was almost intolerable. I felt about the box for my little remaining supply of water, for I had no light, the taper having burnt to the socket of the lantern, and the phosphorus-box not coming readily to hand. Upon finding the jug, however, I discovered it to be empty—Tiger, no doubt, having been tempted to drink it, as well as to devour the remnant of mutton, the bone of which lay, well picked, by the opening of the box. The spoiled meat I could well spare, but my heart sank as I thought of the water. I was feeble in the extreme—so much so that I shook all over, as with an ague, at the slightest movement or exertion. To add to my troubles, the brig was pitching and rolling with great violence, and the oil-casks which lay upon my box were in momentary danger of falling down, so as to block up the only way of ingress or egress. I felt, also, terrible sufferings from sea-sickness. These considerations determined me to make my way, at all hazards, to the trap, and obtain immediate relief, before I should be incapacitated from doing so altogether. Having come to this resolve, I again felt about for the phosphorus-box and tapers. The former I found after some little trouble; but, not discovering the tapers as soon as I had expected (for I remembered very nearly the spot in which I had placed them), I gave up the search for the present, and bidding Tiger lie quiet, began at once my journey toward the trap.

In this attempt my great feebleness became more than ever apparent. It was with the utmost difficulty I could crawl along at all, and very frequently my limbs sank suddenly from beneath me; when, falling prostrate on my face, I would remain for some minutes in a state bordering on insensibility. Still I struggled forward by slow degrees, dreading every moment that I should swoon amid the narrow and intricate windings of the lumber, in which event I had nothing but death to expect as the result. At length, upon making a push forward with all the energy I could command, I struck my forehead violently against the sharp corner of an iron-bound crate. The accident only stunned me for a few moments; but I found, to my inexpressible grief, that the quick and violent roll of the vessel had thrown the crate entirely across my path, so as effectually to block up the passage. With my utmost exertions I could not move it a single inch from its position, it being closely wedged in among the surrounding boxes and ship-furniture. It became necessary, therefore, enfeebled as I was, either to leave the guidance of the whipcord and seek out a new passage, or to climb over the obstacle, and resume the path on the other side. The former alternative presented too many difficulties and dangers to be thought of without a shudder. In my present weak state of both mind and body, I should infallibly lose my way if I attempted it, and perish miserably amid the dismal and disgusting labyrinths of the hold. I proceeded, therefore, without hesitation, to summon up all my remaining strength and fortitude, and endeavor, as I best might, to clamber over the crate.

Upon standing erect, with this end in view, I found the undertaking even a more serious task than my fears had led me to imagine. On each side of the narrow passage arose a complete wall of various heavy lumber, which the least blunder on my part might be the means of bringing down upon my head; or, if this accident did not occur, the path might be effectually blocked up against my return by the descending mass, as it was in front by the obstacle there. The crate itself was a long and unwieldy box, upon which no foothold could be obtained. In vain I attempted, by every means in my power, to reach the top, with the hope of being thus enabled to draw myself up. Had I succeeded in reaching it, it is certain that my strength would have proved utterly inadequate to the task of getting over, and it was better in every respect that I failed. At length, in a desperate effort to force the crate from its ground, I felt a strong vibration in the side next me. I thrust my hand eagerly to the edge of the planks, and found that a very large one was loose. With my pocket-knife, which, luckily, I had with me, I succeeded, after great labor, in prying it entirely off; and getting it through the aperture, discovered, to my exceeding joy, that there were no boards on the opposite side—in other words, that the top was wanting, it being the bottom through which I had forced my way. I now met with no important difficulty in proceeding along the line until I finally reached the nail. With a beating heart I stood erect, and with a gentle touch pressed against the cover of the trap. It did not rise as soon as I had expected, and I pressed it with somewhat more determination, still dreading lest some other person than Augustus might be in his state-room. The door, however, to my astonishment, remained steady, and I became somewhat uneasy, for I knew that it had formerly required but little or no effort to remove it. I pushed it strongly—it was nevertheless firm: with all my strength—it still did not give way: with rage, with fury, with despair—it set at defiance my utmost efforts; and it was evident, from the unyielding nature of the resistance, that the hole had either been discovered and effectually nailed up, or that some immense weight had been placed upon it, which it was useless to think of removing.

My sensations were those of extreme horror and dismay. In vain I attempted to reason on the probable cause of my being thus entombed. I could summon up no connected chain of reflection, and, sinking on the floor, gave way, unresistingly, to the most gloomy imaginings, in which the dreadful deaths of thirst, famine, suffocation, and premature interment crowded upon me as the prominent disasters to be encountered. At length there returned to me some portion of presence of mind. I arose, and felt with my fingers for the seams or cracks of the aperture. Having found them, I examined them closely to ascertain if they emitted any light from the state-room; but none was visible. I then forced the blade of my pen-knife through them, until I met with some hard obstacle. Scraping against it, I discovered it to be a solid mass of iron, which, from its peculiar wavy feel as I passed the blade along it, I concluded to be a chain-cable. The only course now left me was to retrace my way to the box, and there either yield to my sad fate, or try so to tranquilize my mind as to admit of my arranging some plan of escape. I immediately set about the attempt, and succeeded, after innumerable difficulties, in getting back. As I sank, utterly exhausted, upon the mattress, Tiger threw himself at full length by my side, and seemed as if desirous, by his caresses, of consoling me in my troubles, and urging me to bear them with fortitude.

The singularity of his behavior at length forcibly arrested my attention. After licking my face and hands for some minutes, he would suddenly cease doing so, and utter a low whine. Upon reaching out my hand toward him, I then invariably found him lying on his back, with his paws uplifted. This conduct, so frequently repeated, appeared strange, and I could in no manner account for it. As the dog seemed distressed, I concluded that he had received some injury; and, taking his paws in my hands, I examined them one by one, but found no sign of any hurt. I then supposed him hungry, and gave him a large piece of ham, which he devoured with avidity—afterward, however, resuming his extraordinary maneuvers. I now imagined that he was suffering, like myself, the torments of thirst, and was about adopting this conclusion as the true one, when the idea occurred to me that I had as yet only examined his paws, and that there might possibly be a wound upon some portion of his body or head. The latter I felt carefully over, but found nothing. On passing my hand, however, along his back, I perceived a slight erection of the hair extending completely across it. Probing this with my finger, I discovered a string, and tracing it up, found that it encircled the whole body. Upon a closer scrutiny, I came across a small slip of what had the feeling of letter paper, through which the string had been fastened in such a manner as to bring it immediately beneath the left shoulder of the animal.

CHAPTER 3

THE THOUGHT INSTANTLY occurred to me that the paper was a note from Augustus, and that some unaccountable accident having happened to prevent his relieving me from my dungeon, he had devised this method of acquainting me with the true state of affairs. Trembling with eagerness, I now commenced another search for my phosphorus matches and tapers. I had a confused recollection of having put them carefully away just before falling asleep; and, indeed, previously to my last journey to the trap, I had been able to remember the exact spot where I had deposited them. But now I endeavored in vain to call it to mind, and busied myself for a full hour in a fruitless and vexatious search for the missing articles; never, surely, was there a more tantalizing state of anxiety and suspense. At length, while groping about, with my head close to the ballast, near the opening of the box, and outside of it, I perceived a faint glimmering of light in the direction of the steerage. Greatly surprised, I endeavored to make my way toward it, as it appeared to be but a few feet from my position. Scarcely had I moved with this intention, when I lost sight of the glimmer entirely, and, before I could bring it into view again, was obliged to feel along by the box until I had exactly resumed my original situation. Now, moving my head with caution to and fro, I found that, by proceeding slowly, with great care, in an opposite direction to that in which I had at first started, I was enabled to draw near the light, still keeping it in view. Presently I came directly upon it (having squeezed my way through innumerable narrow windings), and found that it proceeded from some fragments of my matches lying in an empty barrel turned upon its side. I was wondering how they came in such a place, when my hand fell upon two or three pieces of taper wax, which had been evidently mumbled by the dog. I concluded at once that he had devoured the whole of my supply of candles, and I felt hopeless of being ever able to read the note of Augustus. The small remnants of the wax were so mashed up among other rubbish in the barrel, that I despaired of deriving any service from them, and left them as they were. The phosphorus, of which there was only a speck or two, I gathered up as well as I could, and returned with it, after much difficulty, to my box, where Tiger had all the while remained.

What to do next I could not tell. The hold was so intensely dark that I could not see my hand, however close I would hold it to my face. The white slip of paper could barely be discerned, and not even that when I looked at it directly; by turning the exterior portions of the retina toward it—that is to say, by surveying it slightly askance, I found that it became in some measure perceptible. Thus the gloom of my prison may be imagined, and the note of my friend, if indeed it were a note from him, seemed only likely to throw me into further trouble, by disquieting to no purpose my already enfeebled and agitated mind. In vain I revolved in my brain a multitude of absurd expedients for procuring light—such expedients precisely as a man in the perturbed sleep occasioned by opium would be apt to fall upon for a similar purpose—each and all of which appear by turns to the dreamer the most reasonable and the most preposterous of conceptions, just as the reasoning or imaginative faculties flicker, alternately, one above the other. At last an idea occurred to me which seemed rational, and which gave me cause to wonder, very justly, that I had not entertained it before. I placed the slip of paper on the back of a book, and, collecting the fragments of the phosphorus matches which I had brought from the barrel, laid them together upon the paper. I then, with the palm of my hand, rubbed the whole over quickly, yet steadily. A clear light diffused itself immediately throughout the whole surface; and had there been any writing upon it, I should not have experienced the least difficulty, I am sure, in reading it. Not a syllable was there, however—nothing but a dreary and unsatisfactory blank; the illumination died away in a few seconds, and my heart died away within me as it went.

I have before stated more than once that my intellect, for some period prior to this, had been in a condition nearly bordering on idiocy. There were, to be sure, momentary intervals of perfect sanity, and, now and then, even of energy; but these were few. It must be remembered that I had been, for many days certainly, inhaling the almost pestilential atmosphere of a close hold in a whaling vessel, and for a long portion of that time but scantily supplied with water. For the last fourteen or fifteen hours I had none—nor had I slept during that time. Salt provisions of the most exciting kind had been my chief, and, indeed, since the loss of the mutton, my only supply of food, with the exception of the sea-biscuit; and these latter were utterly useless to me, as they were too dry and hard to be swallowed in the swollen and parched condition of my throat. I was now in a high state of fever, and in every respect exceedingly ill. This will account for the fact that many miserable hours of despondency elapsed after my last adventure with the phosphorus, before the thought suggested itself that I had examined only one side of the paper. I shall not attempt to describe my feelings of rage (for I believe I was more angry than any thing else) when the egregious oversight I had committed flashed suddenly upon my perception. The blunder itself would have been unimportant, had not my own folly and impetuosity rendered it otherwise—in my disappointment at not finding some words upon the slip, I had childishly torn it in pieces and thrown it away, it was impossible to say where.

From the worst part of this dilemma I was relieved by the sagacity of Tiger. Having got, after a long search, a small piece of the note, I put it to the dog's nose, and endeavored to make him understand that he must bring me the rest of it. To my astonishment, (for I had taught him none of the usual tricks for which his breed are famous,) he seemed to enter at once into my meaning, and, rummaging about for a few moments, soon found another considerable portion. Bringing me this, he paused awhile, and, rubbing his nose against my hand, appeared to be waiting for my approval of what he had done. I patted him on the head, when he immediately made off again. It was now some minutes before he came back—but when he did come, he brought with him a large slip, which proved to be all the paper missing—it having been torn, it seems, only into three pieces. Luckily, I had no trouble in finding what few fragments of the phosphorus were left—being guided by the indistinct glow one or two of the particles still emitted. My difficulties had taught me the necessity of caution, and I now took time to reflect upon what I was about to do. It was very probable, I considered, that some words were written upon that side of the paper which had not been examined—but which side was that? Fitting the pieces together gave me no clew in this respect, although it assured me that the words (if there were any) would be found all on one side, and connected in a proper manner, as written. There was the greater necessity of ascertaining the point in question beyond a doubt, as the phosphorus remaining would be altogether insufficient for a third attempt, should I fail in the one I was now about to make. I placed the paper on a book as before, and sat for some minutes thoughtfully revolving the matter over in my mind. At last I thought it barely possible that the written side might have some unevenness on its surface, which a delicate sense of feeling might enable me to detect. I determined to make the experiment and passed my finger very carefully over the side which first presented itself. Nothing, however, was perceptible, and I turned the paper, adjusting it on the book. I now again carried my forefinger cautiously along, when I was aware of an exceedingly slight, but still discernable glow, which followed as it proceeded. This, I knew, must arise from some very minute remaining particles of the phosphorus with which I had covered the paper in my previous attempt. The other, or under side, then, was that on which lay the writing, if writing there should finally prove to be. Again I turned the note, and went to work as I had previously done. Having rubbed in the phosphorus, a brilliancy ensued as before—but this time several lines of MS. in a large hand, and apparently in red ink, became distinctly visible. The glimmer, although sufficiently bright, was but momentary. Still, had I not been too greatly excited, there would have been ample time enough for me to peruse the whole three sentences before me—for I saw there were three. In my anxiety, however, to read all at once, I succeeded only in reading the seven concluding words, which thus appeared—"*blood—your life depends upon lying close.*"

Had I been able to ascertain the entire contents of the note— the full meaning of the admonition which my friend had thus attempted to convey, that admonition, even although it should have revealed a story of disaster the most unspeakable, could not, I am firmly convinced, have imbued my mind with one tithe of the harrowing and yet indefinable horror with which I was inspired by the fragmentary warning thus received. And "*blood*," too, that word of all words—so rife at all times with mystery, and suffering, and terror—how trebly full of import did it now appear—how chilly and heavily (disjointed, as it thus was, from any foregoing words to qualify or render it distinct) did its vague syllables fall, amid the deep gloom of my prison, into the innermost recesses of my soul!

Augustus had, undoubtedly, good reasons for wishing me to remain concealed, and I formed a thousand surmises as to what they could be—but I could think of nothing affording a satisfactory solution of the mystery. Just after returning from my last journey to the trap, and before my attention had been otherwise directed by the singular conduct of

Tiger, I had come to the resolution of making myself heard at all events by those on board, or, if I could not succeed in this directly, of trying to cut my way through the orlop deck. The half certainty which I felt of being able to accomplish one of these two purposes in the last emergency, had given me courage (which I should not otherwise have had) to endure the evils of my situation. The few words I had been able to read, however, had cut me off from these final resources, and I now, for the first time, felt all the misery of my fate. In a paroxysm of despair I threw myself again upon the mattress, where, for about the period of a day and night, I lay in a kind of stupor, relieved only by momentary intervals of reason and recollection.

At length I once more arose, and busied myself in reflection upon the horrors which encompassed me. For another twenty-four hours it was barely possible that I might exist without water—for a longer time I could not do so. During the first portion of my imprisonment I had made free use of the cordials with which Augustus had supplied me, but they only served to excite fever, without in the least degree assuaging thirst. I had now only about a gill left, and this was of a species of strong peach liqueur at which my stomach revolted. The sausages were entirely consumed; of the ham nothing remained but a small piece of the skin; and all the biscuit, except a few fragments of one, had been eaten by Tiger. To add to my troubles, I found that my headache was increasing momentarily, and with it the species of delirium which had distressed me more or less since my first falling asleep. For some hours past it had been with the greatest difficulty I could breathe at all, and now each attempt at so doing was attended with the most depressing spasmodic action of the chest. But there was still another and very different source of disquietude, and one, indeed, whose harassing terrors had been the chief means of arousing me to exertion from my stupor on the mattress. It arose from the demeanor of the dog.

I first observed an alteration in his conduct while rubbing in the phosphorus on the paper in my last attempt. As I rubbed, he ran his nose against my hand with a slight snarl; but I was too greatly excited at the time to pay much attention to the circumstance. Soon afterward, it will be remembered, I threw myself on the mattress, and fell into a species of lethargy. Presently I became aware of a singular hissing sound close at my ears, and discovered it to proceed from Tiger, who was panting and wheezing in a state of the greatest apparent excitement, his eyeballs flashing fiercely through the gloom. I spoke to him, when he replied with a low growl, and then remained quiet. Presently I relapsed into my stupor, from which I was again awakened in a similar manner. This was repeated three or four times, until finally his behavior inspired me with so great a degree of fear, that I became fully aroused. He was now lying close by the door of the box, snarling fearfully, although in a kind of undertone, and grinding his teeth as if strongly convulsed. I had no doubt whatever that the want of water or the confined atmosphere of the hold had driven him mad, and I was at a loss what course to pursue. I could not endure the thought of killing him, yet it seemed absolutely necessary for my own safety. I could distinctly perceive his eyes fastened upon me with an expression of the most deadly animosity, and I expected every instant that he would attack me. At last I could endure my terrible situation no longer, and determined to make my way from the box at all hazards, and dispatch him, if his opposition should render it necessary for me to do so. To get out, I had to pass directly over his body, and he already seemed to anticipate my design—missing himself upon his forelegs (as I perceived by the altered position of his eyes), and displayed the whole of his white fangs, which were easily discernible. I took the remains of the ham-skin, and the bottle containing the liqueur, and secured them about my person, together with a large carving-knife which Augustus had left me—then, folding my cloak around me as closely as possible, I made a movement toward the mouth of the box. No sooner did I do this, than the dog sprang with a loud growl toward my throat. The whole weight of his body struck me on the right shoulder, and I fell violently to the left, while the enraged animal passed entirely over me. I had fallen upon my knees, with my head buried among the blankets, and these protected me from a second furious assault, during which I felt the sharp teeth pressing vigorously upon the woolen which enveloped my neck—yet, luckily, without being able to penetrate all the folds. I was now beneath the dog, and a few moments would place me completely in his power. Despair gave me strength, and I rose boldly up, shaking him from me by main force, and dragging with me the blankets from the mattress. These I now threw over him, and before he could extricate himself, I had got through the door and closed it effectually against his pursuit. In this struggle, however, I had been forced to drop the morsel of ham-skin, and I now found my whole stock of provisions reduced to a single gill of liqueur, As this reflection crossed my mind, I felt myself actuated by one of those fits of perverseness which might be supposed to influence a spoiled child in similar circumstances, and, raising the bottle to my lips, I drained it to the last drop, and dashed it furiously upon the floor.

Scarcely had the echo of the crash died away, when I heard my name pronounced in an eager but subdued voice, issuing from the direction of the steerage. So unexpected was anything of the kind, and so intense was the emotion excited within me by the sound, that I endeavored in vain to reply. My powers of speech totally failed, and in an agony of terror lest my friend should conclude me dead, and return without attempting to reach me, I stood up between the crates near the door of the box, trembling convulsively, and gasping and struggling for utterance. Had a thousand words depended upon a syllable, I could not have spoken it. There was a slight movement now audible among the lumber somewhere forward of my station. The sound presently grew less distinct, then again less so, and still less. Shall I ever forget my feelings at this moment? He was going—my friend, my companion, from whom I had a right to expect so much—he was going—he would abandon me—he was gone! He would leave me to perish miserably, to expire in the most horrible and loathesome of dungeons—and one word, one little syllable, would save me—yet that single syllable I could not utter! I felt, I am sure, more than ten thousand times the agonies of death itself. My brain reeled, and I fell, deadly sick, against the end of the box.

As I fell the carving-knife was shaken out from the waist-band of my pantaloons, and dropped with a rattling sound to the floor. Never did any strain of the richest melody come so sweetly to my ears! With the intensest anxiety I listened to ascertain the effect of the noise upon Augustus—for I knew that the person who called my name could be no one but himself. All was silent for some moments. At length I again heard the word "*Arthur!*" repeated in a low tone, and one full of hesitation. Reviving hope loosened at once my powers of speech, and I now screamed at the top of my voice, "*Augustus! oh, Augustus!*" "Hush! for God's sake be silent!" he replied, in a voice trembling with agitation; "I will be with you immediately—as soon as I can make my way through the hold." For a long time I heard him moving among the lumber, and every moment seemed to me an age. At length I felt his hand upon my shoulder, and he placed, at the same moment, a bottle of water to my lips. Those only who have been suddenly redeemed from the jaws of the tomb, or who have known the insufferable torments of thirst under circumstances as aggravated as those which encompassed me in my dreary prison, can form any idea of the unutterable transports which that one long draft of the richest of all physical luxuries afforded.

When I had in some degree satisfied my thirst, Augustus produced from his pocket three or four boiled potatoes, which I devoured with the greatest avidity. He had brought with him a light in a dark lantern, and the grateful rays afforded me scarcely less comfort than the food and drink. But I was impatient to learn the cause of his protracted absence, and he proceeded to recount what had happened on board during my incarceration.

CHAPTER 4

THE BRIG PUT to sea, as I had supposed, in about an hour after he had left the watch. This was on the twentieth of June. It will be remembered that I had then been in the hold for three days; and, during this period, there was so constant a bustle on board, and so much running to and fro, especially in the cabin and staterooms, that he had had no chance of visiting me without the risk of having the secret of the trap discovered. When at length he did come, I had assured him that I was doing as well as possible; and, therefore, for the two next days be felt but little uneasiness on my account—still, however, watching an opportunity of going down. It was not *until the fourth day* that he found one. Several times during this interval he had made up his mind to let his father know of the adventure, and have me come up at once; but we were still within reaching distance of Nantucket, and it was doubtful, from some expressions which had escaped Captain Barnard, whether he would not immediately put back if he discovered me to be on board. Besides, upon thinking the matter over, Augustus, so he told me, could not imagine that I was in immediate want, or that I would hesitate, in such case, to make myself heard at the trap. When, therefore, he considered everything he concluded to let me stay until he could meet with an opportunity of visiting me unobserved. This, as I said before, did not occur until the fourth day after his bringing me the watch, and the seventh since I had first entered the hold. He then went down without taking with him any water or provisions, intending in the first place merely to call my attention, and get me to come from the box to the trap,—when he would go up to the stateroom and thence hand me down a supply. When he descended for this purpose he found that I was asleep, for it seems that I was snoring very loudly. From all the calculations I can make on the subject, this must have been the slumber into which I fell just after my return from the trap with the watch, and which, consequently, must have lasted *for more than three entire days and nights* at the very least. Latterly, I have had reason both from my own experience and the assurance of others, to be acquainted with the strong soporific effects of the stench arising from old fish-oil when closely confined; and when I think of the condition of the hold in which I was imprisoned, and the long period during which the brig had been used as a whaling vessel, I am more inclined to wonder that I awoke at all, after once falling asleep, than that I should have slept uninterruptedly for the period specified above.

Augustus called to me at first in a low voice and without closing the trap—but I made him no reply. He then shut the trap, and spoke to me in a louder, and finally in a very loud tone—still I continued to snore. He was now at a loss what to do. It would take him some time to make his way through the lumber to my box, and in the meanwhile his absence would be noticed by Captain Barnard, who had occasion for his services every minute, in arranging and copying papers connected with the business of the voyage. He determined, therefore, upon reflection, to ascend, and await another opportunity of visiting me. He was the more easily induced to this resolve, as my slumber appeared to be of the most tranquil nature, and he could not suppose that I had undergone any inconvenience from my incarceration. He had just made up his mind on these points when his attention was arrested by an unusual bustle, the sound of which proceeded apparently from the cabin. He sprang through the trap as quickly as possible, closed it, and threw open the door of his stateroom. No sooner had he put his foot over the threshold than a pistol flashed in his face, and he was knocked down, at the same moment, by a blow from a handspike.

A strong hand held him on the cabin floor, with a tight grasp upon his throat; still he was able to see what was going on around him. His father was tied hand and foot, and lying along the steps of the companion-way, with his head down, and a deep wound in the forehead, from which the blood was flowing in a continued stream. He spoke not a word, and was apparently dying. Over him stood the first mate, eyeing him with an expression of fiendish derision, and deliberately searching his pockets, from which he presently drew forth a large wallet and a chronometer. Seven of the crew (among whom was the cook, a negro) were rummaging the staterooms on the larboard for arms, where they soon equipped themselves with muskets and ammunition. Besides Augustus and Captain Barnard, there were nine men altogether in the cabin, and these among the most ruffianly of the brig's company. The villains now went upon deck, taking my friend with them after having secured his arms behind his back. They proceeded straight to the forecastle, which was fastened down—two of the mutineers standing by it with axes—two also at the main hatch. The mate called out in a loud voice: "Do you hear there below? tumble up with you, one by one—now, mark that—and no grumbling!" It was some minutes before any one appeared:—at last an Englishman, who had shipped as a raw hand, came up, weeping piteously, and entreating the mate, in the most humble manner, to spare his life. The only reply was a blow on the forehead from an ax. The poor fellow fell to the deck without a groan, and the black cook lifted him up in his arms as he would a child, and tossed him deliberately into the sea. Hearing the blow and the plunge of the body, the men below could now be induced to venture on deck neither by threats nor promises, until a proposition was made to smoke them out. A general rush then ensued, and for a moment it seemed possible that the brig might be retaken. The mutineers, however, succeeded at last in closing the forecastle effectually before more than six of their opponents could get up. These six, finding themselves so greatly outnumbered and without arms, submitted after a brief struggle. The mate gave them fair words—no doubt with a view of inducing those below to yield, for they had no difficulty in hearing all that was said on deck. The result proved his sagacity, no less than his diabolical villainy. All in the forecastle presently signified their intention of submitting, and, ascending one by one, were pinioned and then thrown on their backs, together with the first six—there being in all, of the crew who were not concerned in the mutiny, twenty-seven.

A scene of the most horrible butchery ensued. The bound seamen were dragged to the gangway. Here the cook stood with an ax, striking each victim on the head as he was forced over the side of the vessel by the other mutineers. In this manner twenty-two perished, and Augustus had given himself up for lost, expecting every moment his own turn to come next. But it seemed that the villains were now either weary, or in some measure disgusted with their bloody labor; for the four remaining prisoners, together with my friend, who had been thrown on the deck with the rest, were respited while the mate sent below for rum, and the whole murderous party held a drunken carouse, which lasted until sunset. They now fell to disputing in regard to the fate of the survivors, who lay not more than four paces off, and could distinguish every word said. Upon some of the mutineers the liquor appeared to have a softening effect, for several voices were heard in favor of releasing the captives altogether, on condition of joining the mutiny and sharing the profits. The black cook, however (who in all respects was a perfect demon, and who seemed to exert as much influence, if not more, than the mate himself), would listen to no proposition of the kind, and rose repeatedly for the purpose of resuming his work at the gangway. Fortunately he was so far overcome by intoxication as to be easily restrained by the less bloodthirsty of the party, among whom was a line-manager, who went by the name of Dirk Peters. This man was the son of an Indian squaw of the tribe of Upsarokas, who live among the fastnesses of the Black Hills, near the source of the Missouri. His father was a fur-trader, I believe, or at least connected in some manner with the Indian trading-posts on Lewis river. Peters himself was one of the most ferocious-looking men I ever beheld. He was short in stature, not more than four feet eight inches high, but his limbs were of Herculean mold. His hands, especially, were so enormously thick and broad as hardly to retain a human shape. His arms, as well as legs, were *bowed* in the most singular manner, and appeared to possess no flexibility whatever. His head was equally deformed, being of immense size, with an indentation on the crown (like that on the head of most negroes), and entirely bald. To conceal this latter deficiency, which did not proceed from old age, he usually wore a wig formed of any hair-like material which presented itself—occasionally the skin of a Spanish dog or American grizzly bear. At the time spoken of, he had on a portion of one of these bearskins; and it added no little to the natural ferocity of his countenance, which betook of the Upsaroka character. The mouth extended nearly from ear to ear, the lips were thin, and seemed, like some other portions of his frame, to be devoid of natural pliancy, so that the ruling expression never varied under the influence of any emotion whatever. This ruling expression may be conceived when it is considered that the teeth were exceedingly long and protruding, and never even partially covered, in any instance, by the lips. To pass this man with a casual glance, one might imagine him to be convulsed with laughter, but a second look would induce a shuddering acknowledgment, that if such an expression were indicative of merriment, the merriment must be that of a demon. Of this singular being many anecdotes were prevalent among the seafaring men of Nantucket. These anecdotes went to prove his prodigious strength when under excitement, and some of them had given rise to a doubt of his sanity. But on board the *Grampus*, it seems, he was regarded, at the time of the mutiny, with feelings more of derision than of anything else. I have been thus particular in speaking of Dirk Peters, because, ferocious as he appeared, he proved the main instrument in preserving the life of Augustus, and because I shall have frequent occasion to mention him hereafter in the course of my narrative—a narrative, let me here say, which, in its latter portions, will be found to include incidents of a nature so entirely out of the range of human experience, and for this reason so far beyond the limits of human credulity, that I proceed in utter hopelessness of obtaining credence for all that I shall tell, yet confidently trusting in time and progressing science to verify some of the most important and most improbable of my statements.

After much indecision and two or three violent quarrels, it was determined at last that all the prisoners (with the exception of Augustus, whom Peters insisted in a jocular manner upon keeping as his clerk) should be set adrift in one of the smallest whaleboats. The mate went down into the cabin to see if Captain Barnard was still living—for, it will be remembered, he was left below when the mutineers came up. Presently the two made their appearance, the captain pale as death, but somewhat recovered from the effects of his wound. He spoke to the men in a voice hardly articulate, entreated them not to set him adrift, but to return to their duty, and promising to land them wherever they chose, and to take no steps for bringing them to justice. He might as well have spoken to the winds. Two of the ruffians seized him by the arms and hurled him over the brig's side into the boat, which had been lowered while the mate went below. The four men who were lying on the deck were then untied and ordered to follow, which they did without attempting any resistance—Augustus being still left in his painful position, although he struggled and prayed only for the poor satisfaction of being permitted to bid his father farewell. A handful of sea-biscuit and a jug of water were now handed down; but neither mast, sail, oar, nor compass. The boat was towed astern for a few minutes, during which the mutineers held another consultation—it was then finally cut adrift. By this time night had come on—there were neither moon nor stars visible—and a short and ugly sea was running, although there was no great deal of wind. The boat was instantly out of sight, and little hope could be entertained for the unfortunate sufferers who were in it. This event happened, however, in latitude 35° 30' north, longitude 61° 20' west, and consequently at no very great distance from the Bermuda Islands. Augustus therefore endeavored to console himself with the idea that the boat might either succeed in reaching the land, or come sufficiently near to be fallen in with by vessels off the coast.

All sail was now put upon the brig, and she continued her original course to the southwest—the mutineers being bent upon some piratical expedition, in which, from all that could be understood, a ship was to be intercepted on her way from the Cape Verd Islands to Porto Rico. No attention was paid to Augustus, who was untied and suffered to go about anywhere forward of the cabin companion-way. Dirk Peters treated him with some degree of kindness, and on one occasion saved him from the brutality of the cook. His situation was still one of the most precarious, as the men were continually intoxicated, and there was no relying upon their continued good-humor or carelessness in regard to himself. His anxiety on my account he represented, however, as the most distressing result of his condition; and, indeed, I had never reason to doubt the sincerity of his friendship. More than once he had resolved to acquaint the mutineers with the secret of my being on board, but was restrained from so doing, partly through recollection of the atrocities he had already beheld, and partly through a hope of being able soon to bring me relief. For the latter purpose he was constantly on the watch; but, in spite of the most constant vigilance, three days elapsed after the boat was cut adrift before any chance occurred. At length, on the night of the third day, there came on a heavy blow from the eastward, and all hands were called up to take in sail. During the confusion which ensued, he made his way below unobserved, and into the stateroom. What was his grief and horror in discovering that the latter had been rendered a place of deposit for a variety of sea-stores and ship-furniture, and that several fathoms of old chain-cable, which had been stowed away beneath the companion-ladder, had been dragged thence to make room for a chest, and were now lying immediately upon the trap! To remove it without discovery was impossible, and he returned on deck as quickly as he could. As he came up, the mate seized him by the throat, and demanding what he had been doing in the cabin, was about flinging him over the larboard bulwark, when his life was again preserved through the interference of Dirk Peters. Augustus was now put in handcuffs (of which there were several pairs on board), and his feet lashed tightly together. He was then taken into the steerage, and thrown into a lower berth next to the forecastle bulkheads, with the assurance that he should never put his foot on deck again "until the brig was no longer a brig." This was the expression of the cook, who threw him into the berth—it is hardly possible to say what precise meaning intended by the phrase. The whole affair, however, proved the ultimate means of my relief, as will presently appear.

CHAPTER 5

FOR SOME MINUTES after the cook had left the forecastle, Augustus abandoned himself to despair, never hoping to leave the berth alive. He now came to the resolution of acquainting the first of the men who should come down with my situation, thinking it better to let me take my chance with the mutineers than perish of thirst in the hold,—for it had been ten days since I was first imprisoned, and my jug of water was not a plentiful supply even for four. As he was thinking on this subject, the idea came all at once into his head that it might be possible to communicate with me by the way of the main hold. In any other circumstances, the difficulty and hazard of the undertaking would have prevented him from attempting it; but now he had, at all events, little prospect of life, and consequently little to lose, he bent his whole mind, therefore, upon the task.

His handcuffs were the first consideration. At first he saw no method of removing them, and feared that he should thus be baffled in the very outset; but upon a closer scrutiny he discovered that the irons could be slipped off and on at pleasure, with very little effort or inconvenience, merely by squeezing his hands through them,—this species of manacle being altogether ineffectual in confining young persons, in whom the smaller bones readily yield to pressure. He now untied his feet, and, leaving the cord in such a manner that it could easily be readjusted in the event of any person's coming down, proceeded to examine the bulkhead where it joined the berth. The partition here was of soft pine board, an inch thick, and he saw that he should have little trouble in cutting his way through. A voice was now heard at the forecastle companion-way, and he had just time to put his right hand into its handcuff (the left had not been removed) and to draw the rope in a slipknot around his ankle, when Dirk Peters came below, followed by Tiger, who immediately leaped into the berth and lay down. The dog had been brought on board by Augustus, who knew my attachment to the animal, and thought it would give me pleasure to have him with me during the voyage. He went up to our house for him immediately after first taking me into the hold, but did not think of mentioning the circumstance upon his bringing the watch. Since the mutiny, Augustus had not seen him before his appearance with Dirk Peters, and had given him up for lost, supposing him to have been thrown overboard by some of the malignant villains belonging to the mate's gang. It appeared afterward that he had crawled into a hole beneath a whale-boat, from which, not having room to turn round, he could not extricate himself. Peters at last let him out, and, with a species of good feeling which my friend knew well how to appreciate, had now brought him to him in the forecastle as a companion, leaving at the same time some salt junk and potatoes, with a can of water, he then went on deck, promising to come down with something more to eat on the next day.

When he had gone, Augustus freed both hands from the manacles and unfastened his feet. He then turned down the head of the mattress on which he had been lying, and with his penknife (for the ruffians had not thought it worth while to search him) commenced cutting vigorously across one of the partition planks, as closely as possible to the floor of the berth. He chose to cut here, because, if suddenly interrupted, he would be able to conceal what had been done by letting the head of the mattress fall into its proper position. For the remainder of the day, however, no disturbance occurred, and by night he had completely divided the plank. It should here be observed that none of the crew occupied the forecastle as a sleeping-place, living altogether in the cabin since the mutiny, drinking the wines and feasting on the sea-stores of Captain Barnard, and giving no more heed than was absolutely necessary to the navigation of the brig. These circumstances proved fortunate both for myself and Augustus; for, had matters been otherwise, he would have found it impossible to reach me. As it was, he proceeded with confidence in his design. It was near daybreak, however, before he completed the second division of the board (which was about a foot above the first cut), thus making an aperture quite large enough to admit his passage through with facility to the main orlop deck. Having got here, he made his way with but little trouble to the lower main hatch, although in so doing he had to scramble over tiers of oil-casks piled nearly as high as the upper deck, there being barely room enough left for his body. Upon reaching the hatch he found that Tiger had followed him below, squeezing between two rows of the casks. It was now too late, however, to attempt getting to me before dawn, as the chief difficulty lay in passing through the close stowage in the lower hold. He therefore resolved to return, and wait till the next night. With this design, he proceeded to loosen the hatch, so that he might have as little detention as possible when he should come again. No sooner had he loosened it than Tiger sprang eagerly to the small opening produced, snuffed for a moment, and then uttered a long whine, scratching at the same time, as if anxious to remove the covering with his paws. There could be no doubt, from his behavior, that he was aware of my being in the hold, and Augustus thought it possible that he would be able to get to me if he put him down. He now hit upon the expedient of sending the note, as it was especially desirable that I should make no attempt at forcing my way out at least under existing circumstances, and there could be no certainty of his getting to me himself on the morrow as he intended. After-events proved how fortunate it was that the idea occurred to him as it did; for, had it not been for the receipt of the note, I should undoubtedly have fallen upon some plan, however desperate, of alarming the crew, and both our lives would most probably have been sacrificed in consequence.

Having concluded to write, the difficulty was now to procure the materials for so doing. An old toothpick was soon made into a pen; and this by means of feeling altogether, for the between-decks was as dark as pitch. Paper enough was obtained from the back of a letter—a duplicate of the forged letter from Mr. Ross. This had been the original draft; but the handwriting not being sufficiently well imitated, Augustus had written another, thrusting the first, by good fortune, into his coat-pocket, where it was now most opportunely discovered. Ink alone was thus wanting, and a substitute was immediately found for this by means of a slight incision with the pen-knife on the back of a finger just above the nail—a copious flow of blood ensuing, as usual, from wounds in that vicinity. The note was now written, as well as it could be in the dark and under the circumstances. It briefly explained that a mutiny had taken place; that Captain Barnard was set adrift; and that I might expect immediate relief as far as provisions were concerned, but must not venture upon making any disturbance. It concluded with these words: "*I have scrawled this with blood—your life depends upon lying close.*"

This slip of paper being tied upon the dog, he was now put down the hatchway, and Augustus made the best of his way back to the forecastle, where be found no reason to believe that any of the crew had been in his absence. To conceal the hole in the partition, he drove his knife in just above it, and hung up a pea-jacket which he found in the berth. His handcuffs were then replaced, and also the rope around his ankles.

These arrangements were scarcely completed when Dirk Peters came below, very drunk, but in excellent humor, and bringing with him my friend's allowance of provision for the day. This consisted of a dozen large Irish potatoes roasted, and a pitcher of water. He sat for some time on a chest by the berth, and talked freely about the mate and the general concerns of the brig. His demeanor was exceedingly capricious, and even grotesque. At one time Augustus was much alarmed by odd conduct. At last, however, he went on deck, muttering a promise to bring his prisoner a good dinner on the morrow. During the day two of the crew (harpooners) came down, accompanied by the cook, all three in nearly the last stage of intoxication. Like Peters, they made no scruple of talking unreservedly about their plans. It appeared that they were much divided among themselves as to their ultimate course, agreeing in no point, except the attack on the ship from the Cape Verd Islands, with which they were in hourly expectation of meeting. As far as could be ascertained, the mutiny had not been brought about altogether for the sake of booty; a private pique of the chief mate's against Captain Barnard having been the main instigation. There now seemed to be two principal factions among the crew—one headed by the mate, the other by the cook. The former party were for seizing the first suitable vessel which should present itself, and equipping it at some of the West India Islands for a piratical cruise. The latter division, however, which was the stronger, and included Dirk Peters among its partisans, were bent upon pursuing the course originally laid out for the brig into the South Pacific; there either to take whale, or act otherwise, as circumstances should suggest. The representations of Peters, who had frequently visited these regions, had great weight, apparently, with the mutineers, wavering, as they were, between half-engendered notions of profit and pleasure. He dwelt on the world of novelty and amusement to be found among the innumerable islands of the Pacific, on the perfect security and freedom from all restraint to be enjoyed, but, more particularly, on the deliciousness of the climate, on the abundant means of good living, and on the voluptuous beauty of the women. As yet, nothing had been absolutely determined upon; but the pictures of the hybrid line-manager were taking strong hold upon the ardent imaginations of the seamen, and there was every possibility that his intentions would be finally carried into effect.

The three men went away in about an hour, and no one else entered the forecastle all day. Augustus lay quiet until nearly night. He then freed himself from the rope and irons, and prepared for his attempt. A bottle was found in one of the berths, and this he filled with water from the pitcher left by Peters, storing his pockets at the same time with cold potatoes. To his great joy he also came across a lantern, with a small piece of tallow candle in it. This he could light at any moment, as be had in his possession a box of phosphorus matches. When it was quite dark, he got through the hole in the bulkhead, having taken the precaution to arrange the bedclothes in the berth so as to convey the idea of a person covered up. When through, he hung up the pea-jacket on his knife, as before, to conceal the aperture—this maneuver being easily effected, as he did not readjust the piece of plank taken out until afterward. He was now on the main orlop deck, and proceeded to make his way, as before, between the upper deck and the oil-casks to the main hatchway. Having reached this, he lit the piece of candle, and descended, groping with extreme difficulty among the compact stowage of the hold. In a few moments he became alarmed at the insufferable stench and the closeness of the atmosphere. He could not think it possible that I had survived my confinement for so long a period breathing so oppressive an air. He called my name repeatedly, but I made him no reply, and his apprehensions seemed thus to be confirmed. The brig was rolling violently, and there was so much noise in consequence, that it was useless to listen for any weak sound, such as those of my breathing or snoring. He threw open the lantern, and held it as high as possible, whenever an opportunity occurred, in order that, by observing the light, I might, if alive, be aware that succor was approaching. Still nothing was heard from me, and the supposition of my death began to assume the character of certainty. He determined, nevertheless, to force a passage, if possible, to the box, and at least ascertain beyond a doubt the truth of his surmises. He pushed on for some time in a most pitiable state of anxiety, until, at length, he found the pathway utterly blocked up, and that there was no possibility of making any farther way by the course in which he had set out. Overcome now by his feelings, he threw himself among the lumber in despair, and wept like a child. It was at this period that he heard the crash occasioned by the bottle which I had thrown down. Fortunate, indeed, was it that the incident occurred—for, upon this incident, trivial as it appears, the thread of my destiny depended. Many years elapsed, however, before I was aware of this fact. A natural shame and regret for his weakness and indecision prevented Augustus from confiding to me at once what a more intimate and unreserved communion afterward induced him to reveal. Upon finding his further progress in the hold impeded by obstacles which he could not overcome, he had resolved to abandon his attempt at reaching me, and return at once to the forecastle. Before condemning him entirely on this head, the harassing circumstances which embarrassed him should be taken into consideration. The night was fast wearing away, and his absence from the forecastle might be discovered; and indeed would necessarily be so, if be should fail to get back to the berth by daybreak. His candle was expiring in the socket, and there would be the greatest difficulty in retracing his way to the hatchway in the dark. It must be allowed, too, that he had every good reason to believe me dead; in which event no benefit could result to me from his reaching the box, and a world of danger would be encountered to no purpose by himself. He had repeatedly called, and I had made him no answer. I had been now eleven days and nights with no more water than that contained in the jug which he had left with me—a supply which it was not at all probable I had boarded in the beginning of my confinement, as I had every cause to expect a speedy release. The atmosphere of the hold, too, must have appeared to him, coming from the comparatively open air of the steerage, of a nature absolutely poisonous, and by far more intolerable than it had seemed to me upon my first taking up my quarters in the box—the hatchways at that time having been constantly open for many months previous. Add to these considerations that of the scene of bloodshed and terror so lately witnessed by my friend; his confinement, privations, and narrow escapes from death, together with the frail and equivocal tenure by which he still existed—circumstances all so well calculated to prostrate every energy of mind—and the reader will be easily brought, as I have been, to regard his apparent falling off in friendship and in faith with sentiments rather of sorrow than of anger.

The crash of the bottle was distinctly heard, yet Augustus was not sure that it proceeded from the hold. The doubt, however, was sufficient inducement to persevere. He clambered up nearly to the orlop deck by means of the stowage, and then, watching for a lull in the pitchings of the vessel, he called out to me in as loud a tone as he could command, regardless, for the moment, of being overheard by the crew. It will be remembered that on this occasion the voice reached me, but I was so entirely overcome by violent agitation as to be incapable of reply. Confident, now, that his worst apprehensions were well founded, be descended, with a view of getting back to the forecastle without loss of time. In his haste some small boxes were thrown down, the noise occasioned by which I heard, as will be recollected. He had made considerable progress on his return when the fall of the knife again caused him to hesitate. He retraced his steps immediately, and, clambering up the stowage a second time, called out my name, loudly as before, having watched for a lull. This time I found voice to answer. Overjoyed at discovering me to be still alive, he now resolved to brave every difficulty and danger in reaching me. Having extricated himself as quickly as possible from the labyrinth of lumber by which he was hemmed in, he at length struck into an opening which promised better, and finally, after a series of struggles, arrived at the box in a state of utter exhaustion.

CHAPTER 6

THE LEADING PARTICULARS of this narration were all that Augustus communicated to me while we remained near the box. It was not until afterward that he entered fully into all the details. He was apprehensive of being missed, and I was wild with impatience to leave my detested place of confinement. We resolved to make our way at once to the hole in the bulkhead, near which I was to remain for the present, while he went through to reconnoiter. To leave Tiger in the box was what neither of us could endure to think of, yet, how to act otherwise was the question. He now seemed to be perfectly quiet, and we could not even distinguish the sound of his breathing upon applying our ears closely to the box. I was convinced that he was dead, and determined to open the door. We found him lying at full length, apparently in a deep stupor, yet still alive. No time was to be lost, yet I could not bring myself to abandon an animal who had now been twice instrumental in saving my life, without some attempt at preserving him. We therefore dragged him along with us as well as we could, although with the greatest difficulty and fatigue; Augustus, during part of the time, being forced to clamber over the impediments in our way with the huge dog in his arms—a feat to which the feebleness of my frame rendered me totally inadequate. At length we succeeded in reaching the hole, when Augustus got through, and Tiger was pushed in afterward. All was found to be safe, and we did not fail to return sincere thanks to God for our deliverance from the imminent danger we had escaped. For the present, it was agreed that I should remain near the opening, through which my companion could readily supply me with a part of his daily provision, and where I could have the advantages of breathing an atmosphere comparatively pure.

In explanation of some portions of this narrative, wherein I have spoken of the stowage of the brig, and which may appear ambiguous to some of my readers who may have seen a proper or regular stowage, I must here state that the manner in which this most important duty had been performed on board the *Grampus* was a most shameful piece of neglect on the part of Captain Barnard, who was by no means as careful or as experienced a seaman as the hazardous nature of the service on which he was employed would seem necessarily to demand. A proper stowage cannot be accomplished in a careless manner, and many most disastrous accidents, even within the limits of my own experience, have arisen from neglect or ignorance in this particular. Coasting vessels, in the frequent hurry and bustle attendant upon taking in or discharging cargo, are the most liable to mishap from the want of a proper attention to stowage. The great point is to allow no possibility of the cargo or ballast shifting position even in the most violent rollings of the vessel. With this end, great attention must be paid, not only to the bulk taken in, but to the nature of the bulk, and whether there be a full or only a partial cargo. In most kinds of freight the stowage is accomplished by means of a screw. Thus, in a load of tobacco or flour, the whole is screwed so tightly into the hold of the vessel that the barrels or hogsheads, upon discharging, are found to be completely flattened, and take some time to regain their original shape. This screwing, however, is resorted to principally with a view of obtaining more room in the hold; for in a *full* load of any such commodities as flour or tobacco, there can be no danger of any shifting whatever, at least none from which inconvenience can result. There have been instances, indeed, where this method of screwing has resulted in the most lamentable consequences, arising from a cause altogether distinct from the danger attendant upon a shifting of cargo. A load of cotton, for example, tightly screwed while in certain conditions, has been known, through the expansion of its bulk, to rend a vessel asunder at sea. There can be no doubt either that the same result would ensue in the case of tobacco, while undergoing its usual course of fermentation, were it not for the interstices consequent upon the rotundity of the hogsheads.

It is when a partial cargo is received that danger is chiefly to be apprehended from shifting, and that precautions should be always taken to guard against such misfortune. Only those who have encountered a violent gale of wind, or rather who have experienced the rolling of a vessel in a sudden calm after the gale, can form an idea of the tremendous force of the plunges, and of the consequent terrible impetus given to all loose articles in the vessel. It is then that the necessity of a cautious stowage, when there is a partial cargo, becomes obvious. When lying-to (especially with a small bead sail), a vessel which is not properly modeled in the bows is frequently thrown upon her beam-ends; this occurring even every fifteen or twenty minutes upon an average, yet without any serious consequences resulting, *provided there be a proper stowage*. If this, however, has not been strictly attended to, in the first of these heavy lurches the whole of the cargo tumbles over to the side of the vessel which lies upon the water, and, being thus prevented from regaining her equilibrium, as she would otherwise necessarily do, she is certain to fill in a few seconds and go down. It is not too much to say that at least one-half of the instances in which vessels have foundered in heavy gales at sea may be attributed to a shifting of cargo or of ballast.

When a partial cargo of any kind is taken on board, the whole, after being first stowed as compactly as may be, should be covered with a layer of stout shifting-boards, extending completely across the vessel. Upon these boards strong temporary stanchions should be erected, reaching to the timbers above, and thus securing every thing in its place. In cargoes consisting of grain, or any similar matter, additional precautions are requisite. A hold filled entirely with grain upon leaving port will be found not more than three fourths full upon reaching its destination—this, too, although the freight, when measured bushel by bushel by the consignee, will overrun by a vast deal (on account of the swelling of the grain) the quantity consigned. This result is occasioned by *settling* during the voyage, and is the more perceptible in proportion to the roughness of the weather experienced. If grain loosely thrown in a vessel, then, is ever so well secured by shifting-boards and stanchions, it will be liable to shift in a long passage so greatly as to bring about the most distressing calamities. To prevent these, every method should be employed before leaving port to *settle* the cargo as much as possible; and for this there are many contrivances, among which may be mentioned the driving of wedges into the grain. Even after all this is done, and unusual pains taken to secure the shifting-boards, no seaman who knows what he is about will feel altogether secure in a gale of any violence with a cargo of grain on board, and, least of all, with a partial cargo. Yet there are hundreds of our coasting vessels, and, it is likely, many more from the ports of Europe, which sail daily with partial cargoes, even of the most dangerous species, and without any precaution whatever. The wonder is that no more accidents occur than do actually happen. A lamentable instance of this heedlessness occurred to my knowledge in the case of Captain Joel Rice of the schooner *Firefly*, which sailed from Richmond, Virginia, to Madeira, with a cargo of corn, in the year

1825. The captain had gone many voyages without serious accident, although he was in the habit of paying no attention whatever to his stowage, more than to secure it in the ordinary manner. He had never before sailed with a cargo of grain, and on this occasion had the corn thrown on board loosely, when it did not much more than half fill the vessel. For the first portion of the voyage he met with nothing more than light breezes; but when within a day's sail of Madeira there came on a strong gale from the N. N. E. which forced him to lie-to. He brought the schooner to the wind under a double-reefed foresail alone, when she rode as well as any vessel could be expected to do, and shipped not a drop of water. Toward night the gale somewhat abated, and she rolled with more unsteadiness than before, but still did very well, until a heavy lurch threw her upon her beam-ends to starboard. The corn was then heard to shift bodily, the force of the movement bursting open the main hatchway. The vessel went down like a shot. This happened within hail of a small sloop from Madeira, which picked up one of the crew (the only person saved), and which rode out the gale in perfect security, as indeed a jolly boat might have done under proper management.

The stowage on board the *Grampus* was most clumsily done, if stowage that could be called which was little better than a promiscuous huddling together of oil-casks[1] and ship furniture. I have already spoken of the condition of articles in the hold. On the orlop deck there was space enough for my body (as I have stated) between the oil-casks and the upper deck; a space was left open around the main hatchway; and several other large spaces were left in the stowage. Near the hole cut through the bulkhead by Augustus there was room enough for an entire cask, and in this space I found myself comfortably situated for the present.

By the time my friend had got safely into the berth, and readjusted his handcuffs and the rope, it was broad daylight. We had made a narrow escape indeed; for scarcely had he arranged all matters, when the mate came below, with Dirk Peters and the cook. They talked for some time about the vessel from the Cape Verds, and seemed to be excessively anxious for her appearance. At length the cook came to the berth in

1 Whaling ships are usually fitted with iron oil-tanks—why the *Grampus* was not I have never been able to ascertain..

which Augustus was lying, and seated himself in it near the head. I could see and hear every thing from my hiding-place, for the piece cut out had not been put back, and I was in momentary expectation that the negro would fall against the pea-jacket, which was hung up to conceal the aperture, in which case all would have been discovered, and our lives would, no doubt, have been instantly sacrificed. Our good fortune prevailed, however; and although he frequently touched it as the vessel rolled, he never pressed against it sufficiently to bring about a discovery. The bottom of the jacket had been carefully fastened to the bulkhead, so that the hole might not be seen by its swinging to one side. All this time Tiger was lying in the foot of the berth, and appeared to have recovered in some measure his faculties, for I could see him occasionally open his eyes and draw a long breath.

After a few minutes the mate and cook went above, leaving Dirk Peters behind, who, as soon as they were gone, came and sat himself down in the place just occupied by the mate. He began to talk very sociably with Augustus, and we could now see that the greater part of his apparent intoxication, while the two others were with him, was a feint. He answered all my companion's questions with perfect freedom; told him that he had no doubt of his father's having been picked up, as there were no less than five sail in sight just before sundown on the day he was cut adrift; and used other language of a consolatory nature, which occasioned me no less surprise than pleasure. Indeed, I began to entertain hopes, that through the instrumentality of Peters we might be finally enabled to regain possession of the brig, and this idea I mentioned to Augustus as soon as I found an opportunity. He thought the matter possible, but urged the necessity of the greatest caution in making the attempt, as the conduct of the hybrid appeared to be instigated by the most arbitrary caprice alone; and, indeed, it was difficult to say if he was at any moment of sound mind. Peters went upon deck in about an hour, and did not return again until noon, when he brought Augustus a plentiful supply of junk beef and pudding. Of this, when we were left alone, I partook heartily, without returning through the hole. No one else came down into the forecastle during the day, and at night, I got into Augustus' berth, where I slept soundly and sweetly until nearly daybreak, when he awakened me upon hearing a stir upon deck, and I regained my hiding-place as quickly as possible. When the day was fully broke, we found that Tiger had recovered his strength almost entirely, and gave no indications of hydrophobia, drinking a little water that was offered him with great apparent eagerness. During the day he regained all his former vigor and appetite. His strange conduct had been brought on, no doubt, by the deleterious quality of the air of the hold, and had no connexion with canine madness. I could not sufficiently rejoice that I had persisted in bringing him with me from the box. This day was the thirtieth of June, and the thirteenth since the *Grampus* made sail from Nantucket.

On the second of July the mate came below drunk as usual, and in an excessively good-humor. He came to Augustus's berth, and, giving him a slap on the back, asked him if he thought he could behave himself if he let him loose, and whether he would promise not to be going into the cabin again. To this, of course, my friend answered in the affirmative, when the ruffian set him at liberty, after making him drink from a flask of rum which he drew from his coat-pocket. Both now went on deck, and I did not see Augustus for about three hours. He then came below with the good news that he had obtained permission to go about the brig as he pleased anywhere forward of the mainmast, and that he had been ordered to sleep, as usual, in the forecastle. He brought me, too, a good dinner, and a plentiful supply of water. The brig was still cruising for the vessel from the Cape Verds, and a sail was now in sight, which was thought to be the one in question. As the events of the ensuing eight days were of little importance, and had no direct bearing upon the main incidents of my narrative, I will here throw them into the form of a journal, as I do not wish to omit them altogether.

July 3rd. Augustus furnished me with three blankets, with which I contrived a comfortable bed in my hiding-place. No one came below, except my companion, during the day. Tiger took his station in the berth just by the aperture, and slept heavily, as if not yet entirely recovered from the effects of his sickness. Toward night a flaw of wind struck the brig before sail could be taken in, and very nearly capsized her. The puff died away immediately, however, and no damage was done beyond the splitting of the foretopsail. Dirk Peters treated Augustus all this day with great kindness and entered into a long conversation with him respecting the Pacific Ocean, and the islands he had visited in that region. He asked him whether he would not like to go with the mutineers on a kind of exploring and pleasure voyage in those quarters, and said that the men were gradually coming over to the mate's views. To this Augustus thought it best to reply that he would be glad to go on such an adventure, since nothing better could be done, and that any thing was preferable to a piratical life.

July 4th. The vessel in sight proved to be a small brig from Liverpool, and was allowed to pass unmolested. Augustus spent most of his time on deck, with a view of obtaining all the information in his power respecting the intentions of the mutineers. They had frequent and violent quarrels among themselves, in one of which a harpooner, Jim Bonner, was thrown overboard. The party of the mate was gaining ground. Jim Bonner belonged to the cook's gang, of which Peters was a partisan.

July 5th. About daybreak there came on a stiff breeze from the west, which at noon freshened into a gale, so that the brig could carry nothing more than her trysail and foresail. In taking in the foretopsail, Simms, one of the common hands, and belonging also to the cook's gang, fell overboard, being very much in liquor, and was drowned—no attempt being made to save him. The whole number of persons on board was now thirteen, to wit: Dirk Peters; Seymour, the black cook; Jones, Greely, Hartman Rogers and William Allen, all of the cook's party; the mate, whose name I never learned; Absalom Hicks;—Wilson; John Hunt; and Richard Parker, of the mate's party;—besides Augustus and myself.

July 6th. The gale lasted all this day, blowing in heavy squalls, accompanied with rain. The brig took in a good deal of water through her seams, and one of the pumps was kept continually going, Augustus being forced to take his turn. just at twilight a large ship passed close by us, without having been discovered until within hail. The ship was supposed to be the one for which the mutineers were on the lookout. The mate hailed her, but the reply was drowned in the roaring of the gale. At eleven, a sea was shipped amidships, which tore away a great portion of the larboard bulwarks, and did some other slight damage. Toward morning the weather moderated, and at sunrise there was very little wind.

July 7th. There was a heavy swell running all this day, during which the brig, being light, rolled excessively, and many articles broke loose in the hold, as I could hear distinctly from my hiding-place. I suffered a great deal from sea-sickness. Peters had a long conversation this day with Augustus, and told him that two of his gang, Greely and Allen, had gone over to the mate, and were resolved to turn pirates. He put several questions to Augustus which he did not then exactly understand. During a part of this evening the leak gained upon the vessel; and little could be done to remedy it, as it was occasioned by the brigs straining, and taking in the water through her seams. A sail was thrummed, and got under the bows, which aided us in some measure, so that we began to gain upon the leak.

July 8th. A light breeze sprang up at sunrise from the eastward, when the mate headed the brig to the southwest, with the intention of making some of the West India islands in pursuance of his piratical designs. No opposition was made by Peters or the cook—at least none in the hearing of Augustus. All idea of taking the vessel from the Cape Verds was abandoned. The leak was now easily kept under by one pump going every three quarters of an hour. The sail was drawn from beneath the bows. Spoke two small schooners during the day.

July 9th. Fine weather. All hands employed in repairing bulwarks. Peters had again a long conversation with Augustus, and spoke more plainly than he had done heretofore. He said nothing should induce him to come into the mate's views, and even hinted his intention of taking the brig out of his hands. He asked my friend if he could depend upon his aid in such case, to which Augustus said, "Yes," without hesitation. Peters then said he would sound the others of his party upon the subject, and went away. During the remainder of the day Augustus had no opportunity of speaking with him privately.

CHAPTER 7

JULY 10. *SPOKE* a brig from Rio, bound to Norfolk. Weather hazy, with a light baffling wind from the eastward. To-day Hartman Rogers died, having been attacked on the eighth with spasms after drinking a glass of grog. This man was of the cook's party, and one upon whom Peters placed his main reliance. He told Augustus that he believed the mate had poisoned him, and that he expected, if he did not be on the look-out, his own turn would come shortly. There were now only himself, Jones, and the cook belonging to his own gang—on the other side there were five. He had spoken to Jones about taking the command from the mate; but the project having been coolly received, he had been deterred from pressing the matter any further, or from saying any thing to the cook. It was well, as it happened, that he was so prudent, for in the afternoon the cook expressed his determination of siding with the mate, and went over formally to that party; while Jones took an opportunity of quarreling with Peters, and hinted that he would let the mate know of the plan in agitation. There was now, evidently, no time to be lost, and Peters expressed his determination of attempting to take the vessel at all hazards, provided Augustus would lend him his aid. My friend at once assured him of his willingness to enter into any plan for that purpose, and, thinking the opportunity a favorable one, made known the fact of my being on board. At this the hybrid was not more astonished than delighted, as he had no reliance whatever upon Jones, whom he already considered as belonging to the party of the mate. They went below immediately, when Augustus called to me by name, and Peters and myself were soon made acquainted. It was agreed that we should attempt to retake the vessel upon the first good opportunity, leaving Jones altogether out of our councils. In the event of success, we were to run the brig into the first port that offered, and deliver her up. The desertion of his party had frustrated Peters' design of going into the Pacific—an adventure which could not be accomplished without a crew, and he depended upon either getting acquitted upon trial, on the score of insanity (which he solemnly avowed had actuated him in lending his aid to the mutiny), or upon obtaining a pardon, if found guilty, through the representations of Augustus and myself. Our deliberations were interrupted for the present by the cry of, "All hands take in sail," and Peters and Augustus ran up on deck.

As usual, the crew were nearly all drunk; and, before sail could be properly taken in, a violent squall laid the brig on her beam-ends. By keeping her away, however, she righted, having shipped a good deal of water. Scarcely was everything secure, when another squall took the vessel, and immediately afterward another—no damage being done. There was every appearance of a gale of wind, which, indeed, shortly came on, with great fury, from the northward and westward. All was made as snug as possible, and we laid-to, as usual, under a close-reefed foresail. As night drew on, the wind increased in violence, with a remarkably heavy sea. Peters now came into the forecastle with Augustus, and we resumed our deliberations.

We agreed that no opportunity could be more favorable than the present for carrying our designs into effect, as an attempt at such a moment would never be anticipated. As the brig was snugly laid-to, there would be no necessity of maneuvering her until good weather, when, if we succeeded in our attempt, we might liberate one, or perhaps two of the men, to aid us in taking her into port. The main difficulty was the great disproportion in our forces. There were only three of us, and in the cabin there were nine. All the arms on board, too, were in their possession, with the exception of a pair of small pistols which Peters had concealed about his person, and the large seaman's knife which he always wore in the waistband of his pantaloons. From certain indications, too—such, for example, as there being no such thing as an ax or a handspike lying in their customary places—we began to fear that the mate had his suspicions, at least in regard to Peters, and that he would let slip no opportunity of getting rid of him. It was clear, indeed, that what we should determine to do could not be done too soon. Still the odds were too much against us to allow of our proceeding without the greatest caution.

Peters proposed that he should go up on deck, and enter into conversation with the watch (Allen), when he would be able to throw him into the sea without trouble, and without making any disturbance, by seizing a good opportunity, that Augustus and myself should then come up, and endeavor to provide ourselves with some kind of weapons from the deck, and that we should then make a rush together, and secure the companion-way before any opposition could be offered. I objected to this, because I could not believe that the mate (who was a cunning fellow in all matters which did not affect his superstitious prejudices) would suffer himself to be so easily entrapped. The very fact of there being a watch on deck at all was sufficient proof that he was upon the alert,—it not being usual except in vessels where discipline is most rigidly enforced, to station a watch on deck when a vessel is lying-to in a gale of wind. As I address myself principally, if not altogether, to persons who have never been to sea, it may be as well to state the exact condition of a vessel under such circumstances. Lying-to, or, in sea-parlance, "laying-to," is a measure resorted to for various purposes, and effected in various manners. In moderate weather it is frequently done with a view of merely bringing the vessel to a stand-still, to wait for another vessel or any similar object. If the vessel which lies-to is under full sail, the maneuver is usually accomplished by throwing round some portion of her sails, so as to let the wind take them aback, when she becomes stationary. But we are now speaking of lying-to in a gale of wind. This is done when the wind is ahead, and too violent to admit of carrying sail without danger of capsizing; and sometimes even when the wind is fair, but the sea too heavy for the vessel to be put before it. If a vessel be suffered to scud before the wind in a very heavy sea, much damage is usually done her by the shipping of water over her stern, and sometimes by the violent plunges she makes forward. This maneuver, then, is seldom resorted to in such case, unless through necessity. When the vessel is in a leaky condition she is often put before the wind even in the heaviest seas; for, when lying-to, her seams are sure to be greatly opened by her violent straining, and it is not so much the case when scudding. Often, too, it becomes necessary to scud a vessel, either when the blast is so exceedingly furious as to tear in pieces the sail which is employed with a view of bringing her head to the wind, or when, through the false modeling of the frame or other causes, this main object cannot be effected.

Vessels in a gale of wind are laid-to in different manners, according to their peculiar construction. Some lie-to best under a foresail, and this, I believe, is the sail most usually employed. Large square-rigged vessels have sails for the express purpose, called storm-staysails. But the jib is occasionally employed by itself,—sometimes the jib and foresail, or a double-reefed foresail, and not unfrequently the after-sails, are made use of. Foretopsails are very often found to answer the purpose better than any other species of sail. The *Grampus* was generally laid-to under a close-reefed foresail.

When a vessel is to be laid-to, her head is brought up to the wind just so nearly as to fill the sail under which she lies when hauled flat aft, that is, when brought diagonally across the vessel. This being done, the bows point within a few degrees of the direction from which the wind issues, and the windward bow of course receives the shock of the waves. In this situation a good vessel will ride out a very heavy gale of wind without shipping a drop of water, and without any further attention being requisite on the part of the crew. The helm is usually lashed down, but this is altogether unnecessary (except on account of the noise it makes when loose), for the rudder has no effect upon the vessel when lying-to. Indeed, the helm had far better be left loose than lashed very fast, for the rudder is apt to be torn off by heavy seas if there be no room for the helm to play. As long as the sail holds, a well modeled vessel will maintain her situation, and ride every sea, as if instinct with life and reason. If the violence of the wind, however, should tear the sail into pieces (a feat which it requires a perfect hurricane to accomplish under ordinary circumstances), there is then imminent danger. The vessel falls off from the wind, and, coming broadside to the sea, is completely at its mercy: the only resource in this case is to put her quietly before the wind, letting her scud until some other sail can be set. Some vessels will lie-to under no sail whatever, but such are not to be trusted at sea.

But to return from this digression. It had never been customary with the mate to have any watch on deck when lying-to in a gale of wind, and the fact that he had now one, coupled with the circumstance of the missing axes and handspikes, fully convinced us that the crew were too well on the watch to be taken by surprise in the manner Peters had suggested. Something, however, was to be done, and that with as little delay as practicable, for there could be no doubt that a suspicion having been once entertained against Peters, he would be sacrificed upon the earliest occasion, and one would certainly be either found or made upon the breaking of the gale.

Augustus now suggested that if Peters could contrive to remove, under any pretext, the piece of chain-cable which lay over the trap in the stateroom, we might possibly be able to come upon them unawares by means of the hold; but a little reflection convinced us that the vessel rolled and pitched too violently for any attempt of that nature.

By good fortune I at length hit upon the idea of working upon the superstitious terrors and guilty conscience of the mate. It will be remembered that one of the crew, Hartman Rogers, had died during the morning, having been attacked two days before with spasms after drinking some spirits and water. Peters had expressed to us his opinion that this man had been poisoned by the mate, and for this belief he had reasons, so he said, which were incontrovertible, but which he could not be prevailed upon to explain to us—this wayward refusal being only in keeping with other points of his singular character. But whether or not he had any better grounds for suspecting the mate than we had ourselves, we were easily led to fall in with his suspicion, and determined to act accordingly.

Rogers had died about eleven in the forenoon, in violent convulsions; and the corpse presented in a few minutes after death one of the most horrid and loathsome spectacles I ever remember to have seen. The stomach was swollen immensely, like that of a man who has been drowned and lain under water for many weeks. The hands were in the same condition, while the face was shrunken, shriveled, and of a chalky whiteness, except where relieved by two or three glaring red blotches like those occasioned by the erysipelas: one of these blotches extended diagonally across the face, completely covering up an eye as if with a band of red velvet. In this disgusting condition the body had been brought up from the cabin at noon to be thrown overboard, when the mate getting a glimpse of it (for he now saw it for the first time), and being either touched with remorse for his crime or struck with terror at so horrible a sight, ordered the men to sew the body up in its hammock, and allow it the usual rites of sea-burial. Having given these directions, he went below, as if to avoid any further sight of his victim. While preparations were making to obey his orders, the gale came on with great fury, and the design was abandoned for the present. The corpse, left to itself, was washed into the larboard scuppers, where it still lay at the time of which I speak, floundering about with the furious lurches of the brig.

Having arranged our plan, we set about putting it in execution as speedily as possible. Peters went upon deck, and, as he had anticipated, was immediately accosted by Allen, who appeared to be stationed more as a watch upon the forecastle than for any other purpose. The fate of this villain, however, was speedily and silently decided; for Peters, approaching him in a careless manner, as if about to address him, seized him by the throat, and, before he could utter a single cry, tossed him over the bulwarks. He then called to us, and we came up. Our first precaution was to look about for something with which to arm ourselves, and in doing this we had to proceed with great care, for it was impossible to stand on deck an instant without holding fast, and violent seas broke over the vessel at every plunge forward. It was indispensable, too, that we should be quick in our operations, for every minute we expected the mate to be up to set the pumps going, as it was evident the brig must be taking in water very fast. After searching about for some time, we could find nothing more fit for our purpose than the two pump-handles, one of which Augustus took, and I the other. Having secured these, we stripped off the shirt of the corpse and dropped the body overboard. Peters and myself then went below, leaving Augustus to watch upon deck, where he took his station just where Allen had been placed, and with his back to the cabin companionway, so that, if any of the mates gang should come up, he might suppose it was the watch.

As soon as I got below I commenced disguising myself so as to represent the corpse of Rogers. The shirt which we had taken from the body aided us very much, for it was of singular form and character, and easily recognizable—a kind of smock, which the deceased wore over his other clothing. It was a blue stockinett, with large white stripes running across. Having put this on, I proceeded to equip myself with a false stomach, in imitation of the horrible deformity of the swollen corpse. This was soon effected by means of stuffing with some bedclothes. I then gave the same appearance to my hands by drawing on a pair of white woolen mittens, and filling them in with any kind of rags that offered themselves. Peters then arranged my face, first rubbing it well over with white chalk, and afterward blotching it with blood, which he took from a cut in his finger. The streak across the eye was not forgotten and presented a most shocking appearance.

CHAPTER 8

AS I VIEWED myself in a fragment of looking-glass which hung up in the cabin, and by the dim light of a kind of battle-lantern, I was so impressed with a sense of vague awe at my appearance, and at the recollection of the terrific reality which I was thus representing, that I was seized with a violent tremour, and could scarcely summon resolution to go on with my part. It was necessary, however, to act with decision, and Peters and myself went upon deck.

We there found everything safe, and, keeping close to the bulwarks, the three of us crept to the cabin companion-way. It was only partially closed, precautions having been taken to prevent its being suddenly pushed to from without, by means of placing billets of wood on the upper step so as to interfere with the shutting. We found no difficulty in getting a full view of the interior of the cabin through the cracks where the hinges were placed. It now proved to have been very fortunate for us that we had not attempted to take them by surprise, for they were evidently on the alert. Only one was asleep, and he lying just at the foot of the companion-ladder, with a musket by his side. The rest were seated on several mattresses, which had been taken from the berths and thrown on the floor. They were engaged in earnest conversation; and although they had been carousing, as appeared from two empty jugs, with some tin tumblers which lay about, they were not as much intoxicated as usual. All had knives, one or two of them pistols, and a great many muskets were lying in a berth close at hand.

We listened to their conversation for some time before we could make up our minds how to act, having as yet resolved on nothing determinate, except that we would attempt to paralyze their exertions, when we should attack them, by means of the apparition of Rogers. They were discussing their piratical plans, in which all we could hear distinctly was, that they would unite with the crew of a schooner *Hornet*, and, if possible, get the schooner herself into their possession preparatory to some attempt on a large scale, the particulars of which could not be made out by either of us.

One of the men spoke of Peters, when the mate replied to him in a low voice which could not be distinguished, and afterward added more loudly, that "he could not understand his being so much forward with the captain's brat in the forecastle, and he thought the sooner both of them were overboard the better." To this no answer was made, but we could easily perceive that the hint was well received by the whole party, and more particularly by Jones. At this period I was excessively agitated, the more so as I could see that neither Augustus nor Peters could determine how to act. I made up my mind, however, to sell my life as dearly as possible, and not to suffer myself to be overcome by any feelings of trepidation.

The tremendous noise made by the roaring of the wind in the rigging, and the washing of the sea over the deck, prevented us from hearing what was said, except during momentary lulls. In one of these, we all distinctly heard the mate tell one of the men to "go forward, and order the d—d lubbers to come into the cabin, where he could have an eye upon them, for he wanted no such secret doings on board the brig." It was well for us that the pitching of the vessel at this moment was so violent as to prevent this order from being carried into instant execution. The cook got up from his mattress to go for us, when a tremendous lurch, which I thought would carry away the masts, threw him headlong against one of the larboard stateroom doors, bursting it open, and creating a good deal of other confusion. Luckily, neither of our party was thrown from his position, and we had time to make a precipitate retreat to the forecastle, and arrange a hurried plan of action before the messenger made his appearance, or rather before he put his head out of the companion-hatch, for he did not come on deck. From this station he could not notice the absence of Allen, and he accordingly bawled out, as if to him, repeating the orders of the mate. Peters cried out, "Ay, ay," in a disguised voice, and the cook immediately went below, without entertaining a suspicion that all was not right.

My two companions now proceeded boldly aft and down into the cabin, Peters closing the door after him in the same manner he had found it. The mate received them with feigned cordiality, and told Augustus that, since he had behaved himself so well of late, he might take up his quarters in the cabin and be one of them for the future. He then poured him out a tumbler half full of rum, and made him drink it. All this I saw and heard, for I followed my friends to the cabin as soon as the door was shut, and took up my old point of observation. I had brought with me the two pump-handles, one of which I secured near the companion-way, to be ready for use when required.

I now steadied myself as well as possible so as to have a good view of all that was passing within, and endeavored to nerve myself to the task of descending among the mutineers when Peters should make a signal to me, as agreed upon. Presently he contrived to turn the conversation upon the bloody deeds of the mutiny, and by degrees led the men to talk of the thousand superstitions which are so universally current among seamen. I could not make out all that was said, but I could plainly see the effects of the conversation in the countenances of those present. The mate was evidently much agitated, and presently, when some one mentioned the terrific appearance of Rogers' corpse, I thought he was upon the point of swooning. Peters now asked him if he did not think it would be better to have the body thrown overboard at once as it was too horrible a sight to see it floundering about in the scuppers. At this the villain absolutely gasped for breath, and turned his head slowly round upon his companions, as if imploring some one to go up and perform the task. No one, however, stirred, and it was quite evident that the whole party were wound up to the highest pitch of nervous excitement. Peters now made me the signal. I immediately threw open the door of the companion-way, and, descending, without uttering a syllable, stood erect in the midst of the party.

The intense effect produced by this sudden apparition is not at all to be wondered at when the various circumstances are taken into consideration. Usually, in cases of a similar nature, there is left in the mind of the spectator some glimmering of doubt as to the reality of the vision before his eyes; a degree of hope, however feeble, that he is the victim of chicanery, and that the apparition is not actually a visitant from the old world of shadows. It is not too much to say that such remnants of doubt have been at the bottom of almost every such visitation, and that the appalling horror which has sometimes been brought about, is to be attributed, even in the cases most in point, and where most suffering has been experienced, more to a kind of anticipative horror, lest the apparition *might possibly be* real, than to an unwavering belief in its reality. But, in the present instance, it will be seen immediately, that in the minds of the mutineers there was not even the shadow of a basis upon which to rest a doubt that the apparition of Rogers was indeed a revivification of his disgusting corpse, or at least its spiritual image. The isolated situation of the brig, with its entire inaccessibility on account of the gale, confined the apparently possible means of deception within such narrow and definite limits, that they must have thought themselves enabled to survey them all at a glance. They had now been at sea twenty-four days, without holding more than a speaking communication with any vessel whatever. The whole of the crew, too—at least all whom they had the most remote reason for suspecting to be on board—were assembled in the cabin, with the exception of Allen, the watch; and his gigantic stature (he was six feet six inches high) was too familiar in their eyes to permit the notion that he was the apparition before them to enter their minds even for an instant. Add to these considerations the awe-inspiring nature of the tempest, and that of the conversation brought about by Peters; the deep impression which the loathsomeness of the actual corpse had made in the morning upon the imaginations of the men; the excellence of the imitation in my person, and the uncertain and wavering light in which they beheld me, as the glare of the cabin lantern, swinging violently to and fro, fell dubiously and fitfully upon my figure, and there will be no reason to wonder that the deception had even more than the entire effect which we had anticipated. The mate sprang up from the mattress on which he was lying, and, without uttering a syllable, fell back, stone dead, upon the cabin floor, and was hurled to the leeward like a log by a heavy roll of the brig. Of the remaining seven, there were but three who had at first any degree of presence of mind. The four others sat for some time rooted apparently to the floor, the most pitiable objects of horror and utter despair my eyes ever encountered. The only opposition we experienced at all was from the cook, John Hunt, and Richard Parker; but they made but a feeble and irresolute defense. The two former were shot instantly by Peters, and I felled Parker with a blow on the head from the pump-handle which I had brought with me. In the meantime, Augustus seized one of the muskets lying on the floor now but three remaining; but by this time they had become aroused from their lethargy, and perhaps began to see that a deception had been practiced upon them, for they fought with great resolution and fury, and, but for the immense muscular strength of Peters, might have ultimately got the better of us. These three men were—Jones,—Greely, and Absolom Hicks. Jones had thrown Augustus to the floor, stabbed him in several places along the right arm, and would no doubt have soon dispatched him (as neither Peters nor myself could immediately get rid of our own antagonists), had it not been for the timely aid of a friend, upon whose assistance we, surely, had never depended. This friend was no other than Tiger. With a low growl, he bounded into the cabin, at a most critical moment for Augustus, and throwing himself upon Jones, pinned him to the floor in an instant. My friend, however, was now too much injured to render us any aid whatever, and I was so encumbered with my disguise that I could do but little. The dog would not leave his hold upon the throat of Jones—Peters, nevertheless, was far more than a match for the two men who remained, and would, no doubt, have dispatched them sooner, had it not been for the narrow space in which he had to act, and the tremendous lurches of the vessel. Presently he was enabled to get hold of a heavy stool, several of which lay about the floor. With this he beat out the brains of Greely as he was in the act of discharging a musket at me, and immediately afterward a roll of the brig throwing him in contact with Hicks, he seized him by the throat, and, by dint of sheer strength, strangled him instantaneously. Thus, in far less time than I have taken to tell it, we found ourselves masters of the brig.

The only person of our opponents who was left alive was Richard Parker. This man, it will be remembered, I had knocked down with a blow from the pump-handle at the commencement of the attack. He now lay motionless by the door of the shattered stateroom; but, upon Peters touching him with his foot, he spoke, and entreated for mercy. His head was only slightly cut, and otherwise he had received no injury, having been merely stunned by the blow. He now got up, and, for the present, we secured his hands behind his back. The dog was still growling over Jones; but, upon examination, we found him completely dead, the blood issuing in a stream from a deep wound in the throat, inflicted, no doubt, by the sharp teeth of the animal.

It was now about one o'clock in the morning, and the wind was still blowing tremendously. The brig evidently labored much more than usual, and it became absolutely necessary that something should be done with a view of easing her in some measure. At almost every roll to leeward she shipped a sea, several of which came partially down into the cabin during our scuffle, the hatchway having been left open by myself when I descended. The entire range of bulwarks to larboard had been swept away, as well as the caboose, together with the jollyboat from the counter. The creaking and working of the mainmast, too, gave indication that it was nearly sprung. To make room for more stowage in the afterhold, the heel of this mast had been stepped between decks (a very reprehensible practice, occasionally resorted to by ignorant ship-builders), so that it was in imminent danger of working from its step. But, to crown all our difficulties, we plummed the well, and found no less than seven feet of water.

Leaving the bodies of the crew lying in the cabin, we got to work immediately at the pumps—Parker, of course, being set at liberty to assist us in the labor. Augustus's arm was bound up as well as we could effect it, and he did what he could, but that was not much. However, we found that we could just manage to keep the leak from gaining upon us by having one pump constantly going. As there were only four of us, this was severe labor; but we endeavored to keep up our spirits, and looked anxiously for daybreak, when we hoped to lighten the brig by cutting away the mainmast.

In this manner we passed a night of terrible anxiety and fatigue, and, when the day at length broke, the gale had neither abated in the least, nor were there any signs of its abating. We now dragged the bodies on deck and threw them overboard. Our next care was to get rid of the mainmast. The necessary preparations having been made, Peters cut away at the mast (having found axes in the cabin), while the rest of us stood by the stays and lanyards. As the brig gave a tremendous lee-lurch, the word was given to cut away the weather-lanyards, which being done, the whole mass of wood and rigging plunged into the sea, clear of the brig, and without doing any material injury. We now found that the vessel did not labor quite as much as before, but our situation was still exceedingly precarious, and in spite of the utmost exertions, we could not gain upon the leak without the aid of both pumps. The little assistance which Augustus could render us was not really of any importance. To add to our distress, a heavy sea, striking the brig to the windward, threw her off several points from the wind, and, before she could regain her position, another broke completely over her, and hurled her full upon her beam-ends. The ballast now shifted in a mass to leeward (the stowage had been knocking about perfectly at random for some time), and for a few moments we thought nothing could save us from capsizing. Presently, however, we partially righted; but the ballast still retaining its place to larboard, we lay so much along that it was useless to think of working the pumps, which indeed we could not have done much longer in any case, as our hands were entirely raw with the excessive labor we had undergone, and were bleeding in the most horrible manner.

Contrary to Parker's advice, we now proceeded to cut away the foremast, and at length accomplished it after much difficulty, owing to the position in which we lay. In going overboard the wreck took with it the bowsprit, and left us a complete hulk.

So far we had had reason to rejoice in the escape of our longboat, which had received no damage from any of the huge seas which had come on board. But we had not long to congratulate ourselves; for the foremast having gone, and, of course, the foresail with it, by which the brig had been steadied, every sea now made a complete breach over us, and in five minutes our deck was swept from stern to stern, the longboat and starboard bulwarks torn off, and even the windlass shattered into fragments. It was, indeed, hardly possible for us to be in a more pitiable condition.

At noon there seemed to be some slight appearance of the gale's abating, but in this we were sadly disappointed, for it only lulled for a few minutes to blow with redoubled fury. About four in the afternoon it was utterly impossible to stand up against the violence of the blast; and, as the night closed in upon us, I had not a shadow of hope that the vessel would hold together until morning.

By midnight we had settled very deep in the water, which was now up to the orlop deck. The rudder went soon afterward, the sea which tore it away lifting the after portion of the brig entirely from the water, against which she thumped in her descent with such a concussion as would be occasioned by going ashore. We had all calculated that the rudder would hold its own to the last, as it was unusually strong, being rigged as I have never seen one rigged either before or since. Down its main timber there ran a succession of stout iron hooks, and others in the same manner down the stern-post. Through these hooks there extended a very thick wrought-iron rod, the rudder being thus held to the stern-post and swinging freely on the rod. The tremendous force of the sea which tore it off may be estimated by the fact, that the hooks in the stern-post, which ran entirely through it, being clinched on the inside, were drawn every one of them completely out of the solid wood.

We had scarcely time to draw breath after the violence of this shock, when one of the most tremendous waves I had then ever known broke right on board of us, sweeping the companion-way clear off, bursting in the hatchways, and firing every inch of the vessel with water.

CHAPTER 9

LUCKILY, JUST BEFORE night, all four of us had lashed ourselves firmly to the fragments of the windlass, lying in this manner as flat upon the deck as possible. This precaution alone saved us from destruction. As it was, we were all more or less stunned by the immense weight of water which tumbled upon us, and which did not roll from above us until we were nearly exhausted. As soon as I could recover breath, I called aloud to my companions. Augustus alone replied, saying: "It is all over with us, and may God have mercy upon our souls!" By-and-by both the others were enabled to speak, when they exhorted us to take courage, as there was still hope; it being impossible, from the nature of the cargo, that the brig could go down, and there being every chance that the gale would blow over by the morning. These words inspired me with new life; for, strange as it may seem, although it was obvious that a vessel with a cargo of empty oil-casks would not sink, I had been hitherto so confused in mind as to have overlooked this consideration altogether; and the danger which I had for some time regarded as the most imminent was that of foundering. As hope revived within me, I made use of every opportunity to strengthen the lashings which held me to the remains of the windlass, and in this occupation I soon discovered that my companions were also busy. The night was as dark as it could possibly be, and the horrible shrieking din and confusion which surrounded us it is useless to attempt describing. Our deck lay level with the sea, or rather we were encircled with a towering ridge of foam, a portion of which swept over us even instant. It is not too much to say that our heads were not fairly out of the water more than one second in three. Although we lay close together, no one of us could see the other, or, indeed, any portion of the brig itself, upon which we were so tempestuously hurled about. At intervals we called one to the other, thus endeavoring to keep alive hope, and render consolation and encouragement to such of us as stood most in need of it. The feeble condition of Augustus made him an object of solicitude with us all; and as, from the lacerated condition of his right arm, it must have been impossible for him to secure his lashings with any degree of firmness, we were in momentary expectation of finding that he had gone overboard—yet to render him aid was a thing altogether out of the question. Fortunately, his station was more secure than that of any of the rest of us; for the upper part of his body lying just beneath a portion of the shattered windlass, the seas, as they tumbled in upon him, were greatly broken in their violence. In any other situation than this (into which he had been accidentally thrown after having lashed himself in a very exposed spot) he must inevitably have perished before morning. Owing to the brig's lying so much along, we were all less liable to be washed off than otherwise would have been the case. The heel, as I have before stated, was to larboard, about one half of the deck being constantly under water. The seas, therefore, which struck us to starboard were much broken, by the vessel's side, only reaching us in fragments as we lay flat on our faces; while those which came from larboard being what are called back-water seas, and obtaining little hold upon us on account of our posture, had not sufficient force to drag us from our fastenings.

In this frightful situation we lay until the day broke so as to show us more fully the horrors which surrounded us. The brig was a mere log, rolling about at the mercy of every wave; the gale was upon the increase, if any thing, blowing indeed a complete hurricane, and there appeared to us no earthly prospect of deliverance. For several hours we held on in silence, expecting every moment that our lashings would either give way, that the remains of the windlass would go by the board, or that some of the huge seas, which roared in every direction around us and above us, would drive the hulk so far beneath the water that we should be drowned before it could regain the surface. By the mercy of God, however, we were preserved from these imminent dangers, and about midday were cheered by the light of the blessed sun. Shortly afterward we could perceive a sensible diminution in the force of the wind, when, now for the first time since the latter part of the evening before, Augustus spoke, asking Peters, who lay closest to him, if he thought there was any possibility of our being saved. As no reply was at first made to this question, we all concluded that the hybrid had been drowned where he lay; but presently, to our great joy, he spoke, although very feebly, saying that he was in great pain, being so cut by the tightness of his lashings across the stomach, that he must either find means of loosening them or perish, as it was impossible that he could endure his misery much longer. This occasioned us great distress, as it was altogether useless to think of aiding him in any manner while the sea continued washing over us as it did. We exhorted him to bear his sufferings with fortitude, and promised to seize the first opportunity which should offer itself to relieve him. He replied that it would soon be too late; that it would be all over with him before we could help him; and then, after moaning for some minutes, lay silent, when we concluded that he had perished.

As the evening drew on, the sea had fallen so much that scarcely more than one wave broke over the hulk from windward in the course of five minutes, and the wind had abated a great deal, although still blowing a severe gale. I had not heard any of my companions speak for hours, and now called to Augustus. He replied, although very feebly, so that I could not distinguish what he said. I then spoke to Peters and to Parker, neither of whom returned any answer.

Shortly after this period I fell into a state of partial insensibility, during which the most pleasing images floated in my imagination; such as green trees, waving meadows of ripe grain, processions of dancing girls, troops of cavalry, and other phantasies. I now remember that, in all which passed before my mind's eye, *motion* was a predominant idea. Thus, I never fancied any stationary object, such as a house, a mountain, or any thing of that kind; but windmills, ships, large birds, balloons, people on horseback, carriages driving furiously, and similar moving objects, presented themselves in endless succession. When I recovered from this state, the sun was, as near as I could guess, an hour high. I had the greatest difficulty in bringing to recollection the various circumstances connected with my situation, and for some time remained firmly convinced that I was still in the hold of the brig, near the box, and that the body of Parker was that of Tiger.

When I at length completely came to my senses, I found that the wind blew no more than a moderate breeze, and that the sea was comparatively calm; so much so that it only washed over the brig amidships. My left arm had broken loose from its lashings, and was much cut about the elbow; my right was entirely benumbed, and the hand and wrist swollen prodigiously by the pressure of the rope, which had worked from the shoulder downward. I was also in great pain from another rope which went about my waist, and had been drawn to an insufferable degree of tightness. Looking round upon my companions, I saw that Peters still lived, although a thick line was pulled so forcibly around his loins as to give him the appearance of being cut nearly in two; as I stiffed, he made a feeble motion to me with his hand, pointing to the rope. Augustus gave no indication of life whatever, and was bent nearly double across a splinter of the windlass. Parker spoke to me when he saw me moving, and asked me if I had not sufficient strength to release him from his situation, saying that if I would summon up what spirits I could, and contrive to untie him, we might yet save our lives; but that otherwise we must all perish. I told him to take courage, and I would endeavor to free him. Feeling in my pantaloons' pocket, I got hold of my penknife, and, after several ineffectual attempts, at length succeeded in opening it. I then, with my left hand, managed to free my right from its fastenings, and afterward cut the other ropes which held me. Upon attempting, however, to move from my position, I found that my legs failed me altogether, and that I could not get up; neither could I move my right arm in any direction. Upon mentioning this to Parker, he advised me to lie quiet for a few minutes, holding on to the windlass with my left hand, so as to allow time for the blood to circulate. Doing this, the numbness presently began to die away so that I could move first one of my legs, and then the other, and, shortly afterward I regained the partial use of my right arm. I now crawled with great caution toward Parker, without getting on my legs, and soon cut loose all the lashings about him, when, after a short delay, he also recovered the partial use of his limbs. We now lost no time in getting loose the rope from Peters. It had cut a deep gash through the waistband of his woolen pantaloons, and through two shirts, and made its way into his groin, from which the blood flowed out copiously as we removed the cordage. No sooner had we removed it, however, than he spoke, and seemed to experience instant relief—being able to move with much greater ease than either Parker or myself—this was no doubt owing to the discharge of blood.

We had little hopes that Augustus would recover, as he evinced no signs of life; but, upon getting to him, we discovered that he had merely swooned from the loss of blood, the bandages we had placed around his wounded arm having been torn off by the water; none of the ropes which held him to the windlass were drawn sufficiently tight to occasion his death. Having relieved him from the fastenings, and got him clear of the broken wood about the windlass, we secured him in a dry place to windward, with his head somewhat lower than his body, and all three of us busied ourselves in chafing his limbs. In about half an hour he came to himself, although it was not until the next morning that he gave signs of recognizing any of us, or had sufficient strength to speak. By the time we had thus got clear of our lashings it was quite dark, and it began to cloud up, so that we were again in the greatest agony lest it should come on to blow hard, in which event nothing could have saved us from perishing, exhausted as we were. By good fortune it continued very moderate during the night, the sea subsiding every minute, which gave us great hopes of ultimate preservation. A gentle breeze still blew from the N. W., but the weather was not at all cold. Augustus was lashed carefully to windward in such a manner as to prevent him from slipping overboard with the rolls of the vessel, as he was still too weak to hold on at all. For ourselves there was no such necessity. We sat close together, supporting each other with the aid of the broken ropes about the windlass, and devising methods of escape from our frightful situation. We derived much comfort from taking off our clothes and wringing the water from them. When we put them on after this, they felt remarkably warm and pleasant, and served to invigorate us in no little degree. We helped Augustus off with his, and wrung them for him, when he experienced the same comfort.

Our chief sufferings were now those of hunger and thirst, and when we looked forward to the means of relief in this respect, our hearts sunk within us, and we were induced to regret that we had escaped the less dreadful perils of the sea. We endeavored, however, to console ourselves with the hope of being speedily picked up by some vessel and encouraged each other to bear with fortitude the evils that might happen.

The morning of the fourteenth at length dawned, and the weather still continued clear and pleasant, with a steady but very light breeze from the N. W. The sea was now quite smooth, and as, from some cause which we could not determine, the brig did not he so much along as she had done before, the deck was comparatively dry, and we could move about with freedom. We had now been better than three entire days and nights without either food or drink, and it became absolutely necessary that we should make an attempt to get up something from below. As the brig was completely full of water, we went to this work despondently, and with but little expectation of being able to obtain anything. We made a kind of drag by driving some nails which we broke out from the remains of the companion-hatch into two pieces of wood. Tying these across each other, and fastening them to the end of a rope, we threw them into the cabin, and dragged them to and fro, in the faint hope of being thus able to entangle some article which might be of use to us for food, or which might at least render us assistance in getting it. We spent the greater part of the morning in this labor without effect, fishing up nothing more than a few bedclothes, which were readily caught by the nails. Indeed, our contrivance was so very clumsy that any greater success was hardly to be anticipated.

We now tried the forecastle, but equally in vain, and were upon the brink of despair, when Peters proposed that we should fasten a rope to his body, and let him make an attempt to get up something by diving into the cabin. This proposition we hailed with all the delight which reviving hope could inspire. He proceeded immediately to strip off his clothes with the exception of his pantaloons; and a strong rope was then carefully fastened around his middle, being brought up over his shoulders in such a manner that there was no possibility of its slipping. The undertaking was one of great difficulty and danger; for, as we could hardly expect to find much, if any, provision in the cabin itself, it was necessary that the diver, after letting himself down, should make a turn to the right, and proceed under water a distance of ten or twelve feet, in a narrow passage, to the storeroom, and return, without drawing breath.

Everything being ready, Peters now descended in the cabin, going down the companion-ladder until the water reached his chin. He then plunged in, head first, turning to the right as he plunged, and endeavoring to make his way to the storeroom. In this first attempt, however, he was altogether unsuccessful. In less than half a minute after his going down we felt the rope jerked violently (the signal we had agreed upon when he desired to be drawn up). We accordingly drew him up instantly, but so incautiously as to bruise him badly against the ladder. He had brought nothing with him, and had been unable to penetrate more than a very little way into the passage, owing to the constant exertions he found it necessary to make in order to keep himself from floating up against the deck. Upon getting out he was very much exhausted, and had to rest full fifteen minutes before he could again venture to descend.

The second attempt met with even worse success; for he remained so long under water without giving the signal, that, becoming alarmed for his safety, we drew him out without it, and found that he was almost at the last gasp, having, as he said, repeatedly jerked at the rope without our feeling it. This was probably owing to a portion of it having become entangled in the balustrade at the foot of the ladder. This balustrade was, indeed, so much in the way, that we determined to remove it, if possible, before proceeding with our design. As we had no means of getting it away except by main force, we all descended into the water as far as we could on the ladder, and giving a pull against it with our united strength, succeeded in breaking it down.

The third attempt was equally unsuccessful with the two first, and it now became evident that nothing could be done in this manner without the aid of some weight with which the diver might steady himself, and keep to the floor of the cabin while making his search. For a long time we looked about in vain for something which might answer this purpose; but at length, to our great joy, we discovered one of the weather-forechains so loose that we had not the least difficulty in wrenching it off. Having fastened this securely to one of his ankles, Peters now made his fourth descent into the cabin, and this time succeeded in making his way to the door of the steward's room. To his inexpressible grief, however, he found it locked, and was obliged to return without effecting an entrance, as, with the greatest exertion, he could remain under water not more, at the utmost extent, than a single minute. Our affairs now looked gloomy indeed, and neither Augustus nor myself could refrain from bursting into tears, as we thought of the host of difficulties which encompassed us, and the slight probability which existed of our finally making an escape. But this weakness was not of long duration. Throwing ourselves on our knees to God, we implored His aid in the many dangers which beset us; and arose with renewed hope and vigor to think what could yet be done by mortal means toward accomplishing our deliverance.

CHAPTER 10

SHORTLY AFTERWARD AN incident occurred which I am induced to look upon as more intensely productive of emotion, as far more replete with the extremes first of delight and then of horror, than even any of the thousand chances which afterward befell me in nine long years, crowded with events of the most startling and, in many cases, of the most unconceived and unconceivable character. We were lying on the deck near the companion-way, and debating the possibility of yet making our way into the storeroom, when, looking toward Augustus, who lay fronting myself, I perceived that he had become all at once deadly pale, and that his lips were quivering in the most singular and unaccountable manner. Greatly alarmed, I spoke to him, but he made me no reply, and I was beginning to think that he was suddenly taken ill, when I took notice of his eyes, which were glaring apparently at some object behind me. I turned my head, and shall never forget the ecstatic joy which thrilled through every particle of my frame, when I perceived a large brig bearing down upon us, and not more than a couple of miles off. I sprung to my feet as if a musket bullet had suddenly struck me to the heart; and, stretching out my arms in the direction of the vessel, stood in this manner, motionless, and unable to articulate a syllable. Peters and Parker were equally affected, although in different ways. The former danced about the deck like a madman, uttering the most extravagant rhodomontades, intermingled with howls and imprecations, while the latter burst into tears, and continued for many minutes weeping like a child.

The vessel in sight was a large hermaphrodite brig, of a Dutch build, and painted black, with a tawdry gilt figurehead. She had evidently seen a good deal of rough weather, and, we supposed, had suffered much in the gale which had proved so disastrous to ourselves; for her foretopmast was gone, and some of her starboard bulwarks. When we first saw her, she was, as I have already said, about two miles off and to windward, bearing down upon us. The breeze was very gentle, and what astonished us chiefly was, that she had no other sails set than her foremast and mainsail, with a flying jib—of course she came down but slowly, and our impatience amounted nearly to phrensy. The awkward manner in which she steered, too, was remarked by all of us, even excited as we were. She yawed about so considerably, that once or twice we thought it impossible she could see us, or imagined that, having seen us, and discovered no person on board, she was about to tack and make off in another direction. Upon each of these occasions we screamed and shouted at the top of our voices, when the stranger would appear to change for a moment her intention, and again hold on toward us—this singular conduct being repeated two or three times, so that at last we could think of no other manner of accounting for it than by supposing the helmsman to be in liquor.

No person was seen upon her decks until she arrived within about a quarter of a mile of us. We then saw three seamen, whom by their dress we took to be Hollanders. Two of these were lying on some old sails near the forecastle, and the third, who appeared to be looking at us with great curiosity, was leaning over the starboard bow near the bowsprit. This last was a stout and tall man, with a very dark skin. He seemed by his manner to be encouraging us to have patience, nodding to us in a cheerful although rather odd way, and smiling constantly, so as to display a set of the most brilliantly white teeth. As his vessel drew nearer, we saw a red flannel cap which he had on fall from his head into the water; but of this he took little or no notice, continuing his odd smiles and gesticulations. I relate these things and circumstances minutely, and I relate them, it must be understood, precisely as they *appeared* to us.

The brig came on slowly, and now more steadily than before, and—I cannot speak calmly of this event—our hearts leaped up wildly within us, and we poured out our whole souls in shouts and thanksgiving to God for the complete, unexpected, and glorious deliverance that was so palpably at hand. Of a sudden, and all at once, there came wafted over the ocean from the strange vessel (which was now close upon us) a smell, a stench, such as the whole world has no name for—no conception of—hellish—utterly suffocating—insufferable, inconceivable. I gasped for breath, and turning to my companions, perceived that they were paler than marble. But we had now no time left for question or surmise—the brig was within fifty feet of us, and it seemed to be her intention to run under our counter, that we might board her without putting out a boat. We rushed aft, when, suddenly, a wide yaw threw her off full five or six points from the course she had been running, and, as she passed under our stern at the distance of about twenty feet, we had a full view of her decks. Shall I ever forget the triple horror of that spectacle? Twenty-five or thirty human bodies, among whom were several females, lay scattered about between the counter and the galley in the last and most loathsome state of putrefaction. We plainly saw that not a soul lived in that fated vessel! Yet we could not help shouting to the dead for help! Yes, long and loudly did we beg, in the agony of the moment, that those silent and disgusting images would stay for us, would not abandon us to become like them, would receive us among their goodly company! We were raving with horror and despair—thoroughly mad through the anguish of our grievous disappointment.

As our first loud yell of terror broke forth, it was replied to by something, from near the bowsprit of the stranger, so closely resembling the scream of a human voice that the nicest ear might have been startled and deceived. At this instant another sudden yaw brought the region of the forecastle for a moment into view, and we beheld at once the origin of the sound. We saw the tall stout figure still leaning on the bulwark, and still nodding his head to and fro, but his face was now turned from us so that we could not behold it. His arms were extended over the rail, and the palms of his hands fell outward. His knees were lodged upon a stout rope, tightly stretched, and reaching from the heel of the bowsprit to a cathead. On his back, from which a portion of the shirt had been torn, leaving it bare, there sat a huge sea-gull, busily gorging itself with the horrible flesh, its bill and talons deep buried, and its white plumage spattered all over with blood. As the brig moved farther round so as to bring us close in view, the bird, with much apparent difficulty, drew out its crimsoned head, and, after eyeing us for a moment as if stupefied, arose lazily from the body upon which it had been feasting, and, flying directly above our deck, hovered there a while with a portion of clotted and liver-like substance in its beak. The horrid morsel dropped at length with a sullen splash immediately at the feet of Parker. May God forgive me, but now, for the first time, there flashed through my mind a thought, a thought which I will not mention, and I felt myself making a step toward the ensanguined spot. I looked upward, and the eyes of Augustus met my own with a degree of intense and eager meaning which immediately brought me to my senses. I sprang forward quickly, and, with a deep shudder, threw the frightful thing into the sea.

The body from which it had been taken, resting as it did upon the rope, had been easily swayed to and fro by the exertions of the carnivorous bird, and it was this motion which had at first impressed us with the belief of its being alive. As the gull relieved it of its weight, it swung round and fell partially over, so that the face was fully discovered. Never, surely, was any object so terribly full of awe! The eyes were gone, and the whole flesh around the mouth, leaving the teeth utterly naked. This, then, was the smile which had cheered us on to hope! this the—but I forbear. The brig, as I have already told, passed under our stern, and made its way slowly but steadily to leeward. With her and with her terrible crew went all our gay visions of deliverance and joy. Deliberately as she went by, we might possibly have found means of boarding her, had not our sudden disappointment and the appalling nature of the discovery which accompanied it laid entirely prostrate every active faculty of mind and body. We had seen and felt, but we could neither think nor act, until, alas! too late. How much our intellects had been weakened by this incident may be estimated by the fact, that when the vessel had proceeded so far that we could perceive no more than the half of her hull, the proposition was seriously entertained of attempting to overtake her by swimming!

I have, since this period, vainly endeavored to obtain some clew to the hideous uncertainty which enveloped the fate of the stranger. Her build and general appearance, as I have before stated, led us to the belief that she was a Dutch trader, and the dresses of the crew also sustained this opinion. We might have easily seen the name upon her stern, and, indeed, taken other observations, which would have guided us in making out her character; but the intense excitement of the moment blinded us to every thing of that nature. From the saffron-like hue of such of the corpses as were not entirely decayed, we concluded that the whole of her company had perished by the yellow fever, or some other virulent disease of the same fearful kind. If such were the case (and I know not what else to imagine), death, to judge from the positions of the bodies, must have come upon them in a manner awfully sudden and overwhelming, in a way totally distinct from that which generally characterizes even the most deadly pestilences with which mankind are acquainted. It is possible, indeed, that poison, accidentally introduced into some of their sea-stores, may have brought about the disaster, or that the eating of some unknown venomous species of fish, or other marine animal, or oceanic bird, might have induced it—but it is utterly useless to form conjectures where all is involved, and will, no doubt, remain for ever involved, in the most appalling and unfathomable mystery.

CHAPTER 11

WE SPENT THE remainder of the day in a condition of stupid lethargy, gazing after the retreating vessel until the darkness, hiding her from our sight, recalled us in some measure to our senses. The pangs of hunger and thirst then returned, absorbing all other cares and considerations. Nothing, however, could be done until the morning, and, securing ourselves as well as possible, we endeavored to snatch a little repose. In this I succeeded beyond my expectations, sleeping until my companions, who had not been so fortunate, aroused me at daybreak to renew our attempts at getting up provisions from the hull.

It was now a dead calm, with the sea as smooth as have ever known it,—the weather warm and pleasant. The brig was out of sight. We commenced our operations by wrenching off, with some trouble, another of the forechains; and having fastened both to Peters' feet, he again made an endeavor to reach the door of the storeroom, thinking it possible that he might be able to force it open, provided he could get at it in sufficient time; and this he hoped to do, as the hulk lay much more steadily than before.

He succeeded very quickly in reaching the door, when, loosening one of the chains from his ankle, be made every exertion to force the passage with it, but in vain, the framework of the room being far stronger than was anticipated. He was quite exhausted with his long stay under water, and it became absolutely necessary that some other one of us should take his place. For this service Parker immediately volunteered; but, after making three ineffectual efforts, found that he could never even succeed in getting near the door. The condition of Augustus's wounded arm rendered it useless for him to attempt going down, as he would be unable to force the room open should be reach it, and it accordingly now devolved upon me to exert myself for our common deliverance.

Peters had left one of the chains in the passage, and I found, upon plunging in, that I had not sufficient balance to keep me firmly down. I determined, therefore, to attempt no more, in my first effort, than merely to recover the other chain. In groping along the floor of the passage for this, I felt a hard substance, which I immediately grasped, not having time to ascertain what it was, but returning and ascending instantly to the surface. The prize proved to be a bottle, and our joy may be conceived when I say that it was found to be full of port wine. Giving thanks to God for this timely and cheering assistance, we immediately drew the cork with my penknife, and, each taking a moderate sup, felt the most indescribable comfort from the warmth, strength, and spirits with which it inspired us. We then carefully recorked the bottle, and, by means of a handkerchief, swung it in such a manner that there was no possibility of its getting broken.

Having rested a while after this fortunate discovery, I again descended, and now recovered the chain, with which I instantly came up. I then fastened it on and went down for the third time, when I became fully satisfied that no exertions whatever, in that situation, would enable me to force open the door of the storeroom. I therefore returned in despair.

There seemed now to be no longer any room for hope, and I could perceive in the countenances of my companions that they had made up their minds to perish. The wine had evidently produced in them a species of delirium, which, perhaps, I had been prevented from feeling by the immersion I had undergone since drinking it. They talked incoherently, and about matters unconnected with our condition, Peters repeatedly asking me questions about Nantucket. Augustus, too, I remember, approached me with a serious air, and requested me to lend him a pocket-comb, as his hair was full of fish-scales, and he wished to get them out before going on shore. Parker appeared somewhat less affected, and urged me to dive at random into the cabin, and bring up any article which might come to hand. To this I consented, and, in the first attempt, after staying under a full minute, brought up a small leather trunk belonging to Captain Barnard. This was immediately opened in the faint hope that it might contain something to eat or drink. We found nothing, however, except a box of razors and two linen shirts. I now went down again, and returned without any success. As my head came above water I heard a crash on deck, and, upon getting up, saw that my companions had ungratefully taken advantage of my absence to drink the remainder of the wine, having let the bottle fall in the endeavor to replace it before I saw them. I remonstrated with them on the heartlessness of their conduct, when Augustus burst into tears. The other two endeavored to laugh the matter off as a joke, but I hope never again to behold laughter of such a species: the distortion of countenance was absolutely frightful.

Indeed, it was apparent that the stimulus, in the empty state of their stomachs, had taken instant and violent effect, and that they were all exceedingly intoxicated. With great difficulty I prevailed upon them to lie down, when they fell very soon into a heavy slumber, accompanied with loud stertorous breathing.

I now found myself, as it were, alone in the brig, and my reflections, to be sure, were of the most fearful and gloomy nature. No prospect offered itself to my view but a lingering death by famine, or, at the best, by being overwhelmed in the first gale which should spring up, for in our present exhausted condition we could have no hope of living through another.

The gnawing hunger which I now experienced was nearly insupportable, and I felt myself capable of going to any lengths in order to appease it. With my knife I cut off a small portion of the leather trunk, and endeavored to eat it, but found it utterly impossible to swallow a single morsel, although I fancied that some little alleviation of my suffering was obtained by chewing small pieces of it and spitting them out. Toward night my companions awoke, one by one, each in an indescribable state of weakness and horror, brought on by the wine, whose fumes had now evaporated. They shook as if with a violent ague, and uttered the most lamentable cries for water. Their condition affected me in the most lively degree, at the same time causing me to rejoice in the fortunate train of circumstances which had prevented me from indulging in the wine, and consequently from sharing their melancholy and most distressing sensations. Their conduct, however, gave me great uneasiness and alarm; for it was evident that, unless some favorable change took place, they could afford me no assistance in providing for our common safety. I had not yet abandoned all idea being able to get up something from below; but the attempt could not possibly be resumed until some one of them was sufficiently master of himself to aid me by holding the end of the rope while I went down. Parker appeared to be somewhat more in possession of his senses than the others, and I endeavored, by every means in my power, to rouse him. Thinking that a plunge in the sea-water might have a beneficial effect, I contrived to fasten the end of a rope around his body, and then, leading him to the companion-way (he remaining quite passive all the while), pushed him in, and immediately drew him out. I had good reason to congratulate myself upon having made this experiment; for he appeared much revived and invigorated, and, upon getting out, asked me, in a rational manner, why I had so served him. Having explained my object, he expressed himself indebted to me, and said that he felt greatly better from the immersion, afterward conversing sensibly upon our situation. We then resolved to treat Augustus and Peters in the same way, which we immediately did, when they both experienced much benefit from the shock. This idea of sudden immersion had been suggested to me by reading in some medical work the good effect of the shower-bath in a case where the patient was suffering from *mania a potu.*

Finding that I could now trust my companions to hold the end of the rope, I again made three or four plunges into the cabin, although it was now quite dark, and a gentle but long swell from the northward rendered the hulk somewhat unsteady. In the course of these attempts I succeeded in bringing up two case-knives, a three-gallon jug, empty, and a blanket, but nothing which could serve us for food. I continued my efforts, after getting these articles, until I was completely exhausted, but brought up nothing else. During the night Parker and Peters occupied themselves by turns in the same manner; but nothing coming to hand, we now gave up this attempt in despair, concluding that we were exhausting ourselves in vain.

We passed the remainder of this night in a state of the most intense mental and bodily anguish that can possibly be imagined. The morning of the sixteenth at length dawned, and we looked eagerly around the horizon for relief, but to no purpose. The sea was still smooth, with only a long swell from the northward, as on yesterday. This was the sixth day since we had tasted either food or drink, with the exception of the bottle of port wine, and it was clear that we could hold out but a very little while longer unless something could be obtained. I never saw before, nor wish to see again, human beings so utterly emaciated as Peters and Augustus. Had I met them on shore in their present condition I should not have had the slightest suspicion that I had ever beheld them. Their countenances were totally changed in character, so that I could not bring myself to believe them really the same individuals with whom I had been in company but a few days before. Parker, although sadly reduced, and so feeble that he could not raise his head from his bosom, was not so far gone as the other two. He suffered with great patience, making no complaint, and endeavoring to inspire us with hope in every manner he could devise. For myself, although at the commencement of the voyage I had been in bad health, and was at all times of a delicate constitution, I suffered less than any of us, being much less reduced in frame, and retaining my powers of mind in a surprising degree, while the rest were completely prostrated in intellect, and seemed to be brought to a species of second childhood, generally simpering in their expressions, with idiotic smiles, and uttering the most absurd platitudes. At intervals, however, they would appear to revive suddenly, as if inspired all at once with a consciousness of their condition, when they would spring upon their feet in a momentary flash of vigor, and speak, for a short period, of their prospects, in a manner altogether rational, although full of the most intense despair. It is possible, however, that my companions may have entertained the same opinion of their own condition as I did of mine, and that I may have unwittingly been guilty of the same extravagances and imbecilities as themselves—this is a matter which cannot be determined.

About noon Parker declared that he saw land off the larboard quarter, and it was with the utmost difficulty I could restrain him from plunging into the sea with the view of swimming toward it. Peters and Augustus took little notice of what he said, being apparently wrapped up in moody contemplation. Upon looking in the direction pointed out, I could not perceive the faintest appearance of the shore—indeed, I was too well aware that we were far from any land to indulge in a hope of that nature. It was a long time, nevertheless, before I could convince Parker of his mistake. He then burst into a flood of tears, weeping like a child, with loud cries and sobs, for two or three hours, when becoming exhausted, he fell asleep.

Peters and Augustus now made several ineffectual efforts to swallow portions of the leather. I advised them to chew it and spit it out; but they were too excessively debilitated to be able to follow my advice. I continued to chew pieces of it at intervals, and found some relief from so doing; my chief distress was for water, and I was only prevented from taking a draft from the sea by remembering the horrible consequences which thus have resulted to others who were similarly situated with ourselves.

The day wore on in this manner, when I suddenly discovered a sail to the eastward, and on our larboard bow. She appeared to be a large ship, and was coming nearly athwart us, being probably twelve or fifteen miles distant. None of my companions had as yet discovered her, and I forbore to tell them of her for the present, lest we might again be disappointed of relief. At length upon her getting nearer, I saw distinctly that she was heading immediately for us, with her light sails filled. I could now contain myself no longer, and pointed her out to my fellow-sufferers. They immediately sprang to their feet, again indulging in the most extravagant demonstrations of joy, weeping, laughing in an idiotic manner, jumping, stamping upon the deck, tearing their hair, and praying and cursing by turns. I was so affected by their conduct, as well as by what I considered a sure prospect of deliverance, that I could not refrain from joining in with their madness, and gave way to the impulses of my gratitude and ecstasy by lying and rolling on the deck, clapping my hands, shouting, and other similar acts, until I was suddenly called to my recollection, and once more to the extreme human misery and despair, by perceiving the ship all at once with her stern fully presented toward us, and steering in a direction nearly opposite to that in which I had at first perceived her.

It was some time before I could induce my poor companions to believe that this sad reverse in our prospects had actually taken place. They replied to all my assertions with a stare and a gesture implying that they were not to be deceived by such misrepresentations. The conduct of Augustus most sensibly affected me. In spite of all I could say or do to the contrary, he persisted in saying that the ship was rapidly nearing us, and in making preparations to go on board of her. Some seaweed floating by the brig, he maintained that it was the ship's boat, and endeavored to throw himself upon it, howling and shrieking in the most heartrending manner, when I forcibly restrained him from thus casting himself into the sea.

Having become in some degree pacified, we continued to watch the ship until we finally lost sight of her, the weather becoming hazy, with a light breeze springing up. As soon as she was entirely gone, Parker turned suddenly toward me with an expression of countenance which made me shudder. There was about him an air of self-possession which I had not noticed in him until now, and before he opened his lips my heart told me what he would say. He proposed, in a few words, that one of us should die to preserve the existence of the others.

CHAPTER 12

I HAD FOR some time past, dwelt upon the prospect of our being reduced to this last horrible extremity, and had secretly made up my mind to suffer death in any shape or under any circumstances rather than resort to such a course. Nor was this resolution in any degree weakened by the present intensity of hunger under which I labored. The proposition had not been heard by either Peters or Augustus. I therefore took Parker aside; and mentally praying to God for power to dissuade him from the horrible purpose he entertained, I expostulated with him for a long time, and in the most supplicating manner, begging him in the name of every thing which he held sacred, and urging him by every species of argument which the extremity of the case suggested, to abandon the idea, and not to mention it to either of the other two.

He heard all I said without attempting to controvert any of my arguments, and I had begun to hope that he would be prevailed upon to do as I desired. But when I had ceased speaking, he said that he knew very well all I had said was true, and that to resort to such a course was the most horrible alternative which could enter into the mind of man; but that he had now held out as long as human nature could be sustained; that it was unnecessary for all to perish, when, by the death of one, it was possible, and even probable, that the rest might be finally preserved; adding that I might save myself the trouble of trying to turn him from his purpose, his mind having been thoroughly made up on the subject even before the appearance of the ship, and that only her heaving in sight had prevented him from mentioning his intention at an earlier period.

I now begged him, if he would not be prevailed upon to abandon his design, at least to defer it for another day, when some vessel might come to our relief; again reiterating every argument I could devise, and which I thought likely to have influence with one of his rough nature. He said, in reply, that he had not spoken until the very last possible moment, that he could exist no longer without sustenance of some kind, and that therefore in another day his suggestion would be too late, as regarded himself at least.

Finding that he was not to be moved by anything I could say in a mild tone, I now assumed a different demeanor, and told him that he must be aware I had suffered less than any of us from our calamities; that my health and strength, consequently, were at that moment far better than his own, or than that either of Peters or Augustus; in short, that I was in a condition to have my own way by force if I found it necessary; and that if he attempted in any manner to acquaint the others with his bloody and cannibal designs, I would not hesitate to throw him into the sea. Upon this he immediately seized me by the throat, and drawing a knife, made several ineffectual efforts to stab me in the stomach; an atrocity which his excessive debility alone prevented him from accomplishing. In the meantime, being roused to a high pitch of anger, I forced him to the vessel's side, with the full intention of throwing him overboard. He was saved from his fate, however, by the interference of Peters, who now approached and separated us, asking the cause of the disturbance. This Parker told before I could find means in any manner to prevent him.

The effect of his words was even more terrible than what I had anticipated. Both Augustus and Peters, who, it seems, had long secretly entertained the same fearful idea which Parker had been merely the first to broach, joined with him in his design and insisted upon its immediately being carried into effect. I had calculated that one at least of the two former would be found still possessed of sufficient strength of mind to side with myself in resisting any attempt to execute so dreadful a purpose, and, with the aid of either one of them, I had no fear of being able to prevent its accomplishment. Being disappointed in this expectation, it became absolutely necessary that I should attend to my own safety, as a further resistance on my part might possibly be considered by men in their frightful condition a sufficient excuse for refusing me fair play in the tragedy that I knew would speedily be enacted.

I now told them I was willing to submit to the proposal, merely requesting a delay of about one hour, in order that the fog which had gathered around us might have an opportunity of lifting, when it was possible that the ship we had seen might be again in sight. After great difficulty I obtained from them a promise to wait thus long; and, as I had anticipated (a breeze rapidly coming in), the fog lifted before the hour had expired, when, no vessel appearing in sight, we prepared to draw lots.

It is with extreme reluctance that I dwell upon the appalling scene which ensued; a scene which, with its minutest details, no after events have been able to efface in the slightest degree from my memory, and whose stern recollection will embitter every future moment of my existence. Let me run over this portion of my narrative with as much haste as the nature of the events to be spoken of will permit. The only method we could devise for the terrific lottery, in which we were to take each a chance, was that of drawing straws. Small splinters of wood were made to answer our purpose, and it was agreed that I should be the holder. I retired to one end of the hulk, while my poor companions silently took up their station in the other with their backs turned toward me. The bitterest anxiety which I endured at any period of this fearful drama was while I occupied myself in the arrangement of the lots. There are few conditions into which man can possibly fall where he will not feel a deep interest in the preservation of his existence; an interest momentarily increasing with the frailness of the tenure by which that existence may be held. But now that the silent, definite, and stern nature of the business in which I was engaged (so different from the tumultuous dangers of the storm or the gradually approaching horrors of famine) allowed me to reflect on the few chances I had of escaping the most appalling of deaths—a death for the most appalling of purposes—every particle of that energy which had so long buoyed me up departed like feathers before the wind, leaving me a helpless prey to the most abject and pitiable terror. I could not, at first, even summon up sufficient strength to tear and fit together the small splinters of wood, my fingers absolutely refusing their office, and my knees knocking violently against each other. My mind ran over rapidly a thousand absurd projects by which to avoid becoming a partner in the awful speculation. I thought of falling on my knees to my companions, and entreating them to let me escape this necessity; of suddenly rushing upon them, and, by putting one of them to death, of rendering the decision by lot useless—in short, of every thing but of going through with the matter I had in hand. At last, after wasting a long time in this imbecile conduct, I was recalled to my senses by the voice of Parker, who urged me to relieve them at once from the terrible anxiety they were enduring. Even then I could not bring myself to arrange the splinters upon the spot, but thought over every species of finesse by which I could trick some one of my fellow-sufferers to draw the short straw, as it had been agreed that whoever drew the shortest of four splinters from my hand was to die for the preservation of the rest. Before any one condemn me for this apparent heartlessness, let him be placed in a situation precisely similar to my own.

At length delay was no longer possible, and, with a heart almost bursting from my bosom, I advanced to the region of the forecastle, where my companions were awaiting me. I held out my hand with the splinters, and Peters immediately drew. He was free—*his*, at least, was not the shortest; and there was now another chance against my escape. I summoned up all my strength, and passed the lots to Augustus. He also drew immediately, and he also was free; and now, whether I should live or die, the chances were no more than precisely even. At this moment all the fierceness of the tiger possessed my bosom, and I felt toward my poor fellow-creature, Parker, the most intense, the most diabolical hatred. But the feeling did not last; and, at length, with a convulsive shudder and closed eyes, I held out the two remaining splinters toward him. It was fully five minutes before he could summon resolution to draw, during which period of heartrending suspense I never once opened my eyes. Presently one of the two lots was quickly drawn from my hand. The decision was then over, yet I knew not whether it was for me or against me. No one spoke, and still I dared not satisfy myself by looking at the splinter I held. Peters at length took me by the hand, and I forced myself to look up, when I immediately saw by the countenance of Parker that I was safe, and that he it was who had been doomed to suffer. Gasping for breath, I fell senseless to the deck.

I recovered from my swoon in time to behold the consummation of the tragedy in the death of him who had been chiefly instrumental in bringing it about. He made no resistance whatever, and was stabbed in the back by Peters, when he fell instantly dead. I must not dwell upon the fearful repast which immediately ensued. Such things may be imagined, but words have no power to impress the mind with the exquisite horror of their reality. Let it suffice to say that, having in some measure appeased the raging thirst which consumed us by the blood of the victim, and having by common consent taken off the hands, feet, and head, throwing them together with the entrails, into the sea, we devoured the rest of the body, piecemeal, during the four ever memorable days of the seventeenth, eighteenth, nineteenth, and twentieth of the month.

On the nineteenth, there coming on a smart shower which lasted fifteen or twenty minutes, we contrived to catch some water by means of a sheet which had been fished up from the cabin by our drag just after the gale. The quantity we took in all did not amount to more than half a gallon; but even this scanty allowance supplied us with comparative strength and hope.

On the twenty-first we were again reduced to the last necessity. The weather still remained warm and pleasant, with occasional fogs and light breezes, most usually from N. to W.

On the twenty-second, as we were sitting close huddled together, gloomily revolving over our lamentable condition, there flashed through my mind all at once an idea which inspired me with a bright gleam of hope. I remembered that, when the foremast had been cut away, Peters, being in the windward chains, passed one of the axes into my hand, requesting me to put it, if possible, in a place of security, and that a few minutes before the last heavy sea struck the brig and filled her I had taken this ax into the forecastle and laid it in one of the larboard berths. I now thought it possible that, by getting at this ax, we might cut through the deck over the storeroom, and thus readily supply ourselves with provisions.

When I communicated this object to my companions, they uttered a feeble shout of joy, and we all proceeded forthwith to the forecastle. The difficulty of descending here was greater than that of going down in the cabin, the opening being much smaller, for it will be remembered that the whole framework about the cabin companion-hatch had been carried away, whereas the forecastle-way, being a simple hatch of only about three feet square, had remained uninjured. I did not hesitate, however, to attempt the descent; and a rope being fastened round my body as before, I plunged boldly in, feet foremost, made my way quickly to the berth, and at the first attempt brought up the ax. It was hailed with the most ecstatic joy and triumph, and the ease with which it had been obtained was regarded as an omen of our ultimate preservation.

We now commenced cutting at the deck with all the energy of rekindled hope, Peters and myself taking the ax by turns, Augustus's wounded arm not permitting him to aid us in any degree. As we were still so feeble as to be scarcely able to stand unsupported, and could consequently work but a minute or two without resting, it soon became evident that many long hours would be necessary to accomplish our task—that is, to cut an opening sufficiently large to admit of a free access to the storeroom. This consideration, however, did not discourage us; and, working all night by the light of the moon, we succeeded in effecting our purpose by daybreak on the morning of the twenty-third.

Peters now volunteered to go down; and, having made all arrangements as before, he descended, and soon returned bringing up with him a small jar, which, to our great joy, proved to be full of olives. Having shared these among us, and devoured them with the greatest avidity, we proceeded to let him down again. This time he succeeded beyond our utmost expectations, returning instantly with a large ham and a bottle of Madeira wine. Of the latter we each took a moderate sup, having learned by experience the pernicious consequences of indulging too freely. The ham, except about two pounds near the bone, was not in a condition to be eaten, having been entirely spoiled by the salt water. The sound part was divided among us. Peters and Augustus, not being able to restrain their appetite, swallowed theirs upon the instant; but I was more cautious, and ate but a small portion of mine, dreading the thirst which I knew would ensue. We now rested a while from our labors, which had been intolerably severe.

By noon, feeling somewhat strengthened and refreshed, we again renewed our attempt at getting up provisions, Peters and myself going down alternately, and always with more or less success, until sundown. During this interval we had the good fortune to bring up, altogether, four more small jars of olives, another ham, a carboy containing nearly three gallons of excellent Cape Madeira wine, and, what gave us still more delight, a small tortoise of the Gallipago breed, several of which had been taken on board by Captain Barnard, as the *Grampus* was leaving port, from the schooner *Mary Pitts*, just returned from a sealing voyage in the Pacific.

In a subsequent portion of this narrative I shall have frequent occasion to mention this species of tortoise. It is found principally, as most of my readers may know, in the group of islands called the Gallipagos, which, indeed, derive their name from the animal—the Spanish word Gallipago meaning a fresh-water terrapin. From the peculiarity of their shape and action they have been sometimes called the elephant tortoise. They are frequently found of an enormous size. I have myself seen several which would weigh from twelve to fifteen hundred pounds, although I do not remember that any navigator speaks of having seen them weighing more than eight hundred. Their appearance is singular, and even disgusting. Their steps are very slow, measured, and heavy, their bodies being carried about a foot from the ground. Their neck is long, and exceedingly slender, from eighteen inches to two feet is a very common length, and I killed one where the distance from the shoulder to the extremity of the head was no less than three feet ten inches. The head has a striking resemblance to that of a serpent. They can exist without food for an almost incredible length of time, instances having been known where they have been thrown into the hold of a vessel and lain two years without nourishment of any kind—being as fat, and, in every respect, in as good order at the expiration of the time as when they were first put in. In one particular these extraordinary animals bear a resemblance to the dromedary, or camel of the desert. In a bag at the root of the neck they carry with them a constant supply of water. In some instances, upon killing them after a full year's deprivation of all nourishment, as much as three gallons of perfectly sweet and fresh water have been found in their bags. Their food is chiefly wild parsley and celery, with purslain, sea-kelp, and prickly pears, upon which latter vegetable they thrive wonderfully, a great quantity of it being usually found on the hillsides near the shore wherever the animal itself is discovered. They are excellent and highly nutritious food, and have, no doubt, been the means of preserving the lives of thousands of seamen employed in the whale-fishery and other pursuits in the Pacific.

The one which we had the good fortune to bring up from the store-room was not of a large size, weighing probably sixty-five or seventy pounds. It was a female, and in excellent condition, being exceedingly fat, and having more than a quart of limpid and sweet water in its bag. This was indeed a treasure; and, falling on our knees with one accord, we returned fervent thanks to God for so seasonable a relief.

We had great difficulty in getting the animal up through the opening, as its struggles were fierce and its strength prodigious. It was upon the point of making its escape from Peter's grasp, and slipping back into the water, when Augustus, throwing a rope with a slipknot around its throat, held it up in this manner until I jumped into the hole by the side of Peters, and assisted him in lifting it out.

The water we drew carefully from the bag into the jug; which, it will be remembered, had been brought up before from the cabin. Having done this, we broke off the neck of a bottle so as to form, with the cork, a kind of glass, holding not quite half a gill. We then each drank one of these measures full, and resolved to limit ourselves to this quantity per day as long as it should hold out.

During the last two or three days, the weather having been dry and pleasant, the bedding we had obtained from the cabin, as well as our clothing, had become thoroughly dry, so that we passed this night (that of the twenty-third) in comparative comfort, enjoying a tranquil repose, after having supped plentifully on olives and ham, with a small allowance of the wine. Being afraid of losing some of our stores overboard during the night, in the event of a breeze springing up, we secured them as well as possible with cordage to the fragments of the windlass. Our tortoise, which we were anxious to preserve alive as long as we could, we threw on its back, and otherwise carefully fastened.

CHAPTER 13

JULY 24. THIS morning saw us wonderfully recruited in spirits and strength. Notwithstanding the perilous situation in which we were still placed, ignorant of our position, although certainly at a great distance from land, without more food than would last us for a fortnight even with great care, almost entirely without water, and floating about at the mercy of every wind and wave on the merest wreck in the world, still the infinitely more terrible distresses and dangers from which we had so lately and so providentially been delivered caused us to regard what we now endured as but little more than an ordinary evil—so strictly comparative is either good or ill.

At sunrise we were preparing to renew our attempts at getting up something from the storeroom, when, a smart shower coming on, with some lightning, we turn our attention to the catching of water by means of the sheet we had used before for this purpose. We had no other means of collecting the rain than by holding the sheet spread out with one of the forechain-plates in the middle of it. The water, thus conducted to the center, was drained through into our jug. We had nearly filled it in this manner, when, a heavy squall coming on from the northward, obliged us to desist, as the hulk began once more to roll so violently that we could no longer keep our feet. We now went forward, and, lashing ourselves securely to the remnant of the windlass as before, awaited the event with far more calmness than could have been anticipated or would have been imagined possible under the circumstances. At noon the wind had freshened into a two-reef breeze, and by night into a stiff gale, accompanied with a tremendously heavy swell. Experience having taught us, however, the best method of arranging our lashings, we weathered this dreary night in tolerable security, although thoroughly drenched at almost every instant by the sea, and in momentary dread of being washed off. Fortunately, the weather was so warm as to render the water rather grateful than otherwise.

July 25. This morning the gale had diminished to a mere ten-knot breeze, and the sea had gone down with it so considerably that we were able to keep ourselves dry upon the deck. To our great grief, however, we found that two jars of our olives, as well as the whole of our ham, had been washed overboard, in spite of the careful manner in which they had been fastened. We determined not to kill the tortoise as yet, and contented ourselves for the present with a breakfast on a few of the olives, and a measure of water each, which latter we mixed half and half, with wine, finding great relief and strength from the mixture, without the distressing intoxication which had ensued upon drinking the port. The sea was still far too rough for the renewal of our efforts at getting up provision from the storeroom. Several articles, of no importance to us in our present situation, floated up through the opening during the day, and were immediately washed overboard. We also now observed that the hulk lay more along than ever, so that we could not stand an instant without lashing ourselves. On this account we passed a gloomy and uncomfortable day. At noon the sun appeared to be nearly vertical, and we had no doubt that we had been driven down by the long succession of northward and northwesterly winds into the near vicinity of the equator. Toward evening saw several sharks, and were somewhat alarmed by the audacious manner in which an enormously large one approached us. At one time, a lurch throwing the deck very far beneath the water, the monster actually swam in upon us, floundering for some moments just over the companion-hatch, and striking Peters violently with his tail. A heavy sea at length hurled him overboard, much to our relief. In moderate weather we might have easily captured him.

July 26. This morning, the wind having greatly abated, and the sea not being very rough, we determined to renew our exertions in the storeroom. After a great deal of hard labor during the whole day, we found that nothing further was to be expected from this quarter, the partitions of the room having been stove during the night, and its contents swept into the hold. This discovery, as may be supposed, filled us with despair.

July 27. The sea nearly smooth, with a light wind, and still from the northward and westward. The sun coming out hotly in the afternoon, we occupied ourselves in drying our clothes. Found great relief from thirst, and much comfort otherwise, by bathing in the sea; in this, however, we were forced to use great caution, being afraid of sharks, several of which were seen swimming around the brig during the day.

July 28. Good weather still. The brig now began to lie along so alarmingly that we feared she would eventually roll bottom up. Prepared ourselves as well as we could for this emergency, lashing our tortoise, waterjug, and two remaining jars of olives as far as possible over to the windward, placing them outside the hull below the main-chains. The sea very smooth all day, with little or no wind.

July 29. A continuance of the same weather. Augustus's wounded arm began to evince symptoms of mortification. He complained of drowsiness and excessive thirst, but no acute pain. Nothing could be done for his relief beyond rubbing his wounds with a little of the vinegar from the olives, and from this no benefit seemed to be experienced. We did every thing in our power for his comfort, and trebled his allowance of water.

July 30. An excessively hot day, with no wind. An enormous shark kept close by the hulk during the whole of the forenoon. We made several unsuccessful attempts to capture him by means of a noose. Augustus much worse, and evidently sinking as much from want of proper nourishment as from the effect of his wounds. He constantly prayed to be relieved from his sufferings, wishing for nothing but death. This evening we ate the last of our olives, and found the water in our jug so putrid that we could not swallow it at all without the addition of wine. Determined to kill our tortoise in the morning.

July 31. After a night of excessive anxiety and fatigue, owing to the position of the hulk, we set about killing and cutting up our tortoise. He proved to be much smaller than we had supposed, although in good condition,—the whole meat about him not amounting to more than ten pounds. With a view of preserving a portion of this as long as possible, we cut it into fine pieces, and filled with them our three remaining olive jars and the wine-bottle (all of which had been kept), pouring in afterward the vinegar from the olives. In this manner we put away about three pounds of the tortoise, intending not to touch it until we had consumed the rest. We concluded to restrict ourselves to about four ounces of the meat per day; the whole would thus last us thirteen days. A brisk shower, with severe thunder and lightning, came on about dusk, but lasted so short a time that we only succeeded in catching about half a pint of water. The whole of this, by common consent, was given to Augustus, who now appeared to be in the last extremity. He drank the water from the sheet as we caught it (we holding it above him as he lay so as to let it run into his mouth), for we had now nothing left capable of holding water, unless we had chosen to empty out our wine from the carboy, or the stale water from the jug. Either of these expedients would have been resorted to had the shower lasted.

The sufferer seemed to derive but little benefit from the draft. His arm was completely black from the wrist to the shoulder, and his feet were like ice. We expected every moment to see him breathe his last. He was frightfully emaciated; so much so that, although he weighed a hundred and twenty-seven pounds upon his leaving Nantucket, he now did not weigh more than *forty or fifty at the farthest*. His eyes were sunk far in his head, being scarcely perceptible, and the skin of his cheeks hung so loosely as to prevent his masticating any food, or even swallowing any liquid, without great difficulty.

August 1. A continuance of the same calm weather, with an oppressively hot sun. Suffered exceedingly from thirst, the water in the jug being absolutely putrid and swarming with vermin. We contrived, nevertheless, to swallow a portion of it by mixing it with wine; our thirst, however, was but little abated. We found more relief by bathing in the sea, but could not avail ourselves of this expedient except at long intervals, on account of the continual presence of sharks. We now saw clearly that Augustus could not be saved; that he was evidently dying. We could do nothing to relieve his sufferings, which appeared to be great. About twelve o'clock he expired in strong convulsions, and without having spoken for several days. His death filled us with the most gloomy forebodings, and had so great an effect upon our spirits that we sat motionless by the corpse during the whole day, and never addressed each other except in a whisper. It was not until some time after dark that we took courage to get up and throw the body overboard. It was then loathsome beyond expression, and so far decayed that, as Peters attempted to lift it, an entire leg came off in his grasp. As the mass of putrefaction slipped over the vessel's side into the water, the glare of phosphoric light with which it was surrounded plainly discovered to us seven or eight large sharks, the clashing of whose horrible teeth, as their prey was torn to pieces among them, might have been heard at the distance of a mile. We shrunk within ourselves in the extremity of horror at the sound.

August 2. The same fearfully calm and hot weather. The dawn found us in a state of pitiable dejection as well as bodily exhaustion. The water in the jug was now absolutely useless, being a thick gelatinous mass; nothing but frightful-looking worms mingled with slime. We threw it out, and washed the jug well in the sea, afterward pouring a little vinegar in it from our bottles of pickled tortoise. Our thirst could now scarcely be endured, and we tried in vain to relieve it by wine, which seemed only to add fuel to the flame, and excited us to a high degree of intoxication. We afterward endeavored to relieve our sufferings by mixing the wine with seawater; but this instantly brought about the most violent retchings, so that we never again attempted it. During the whole day we anxiously sought an opportunity of bathing, but to no purpose; for the hulk was now entirely besieged on all sides with sharks—no doubt the identical monsters who had devoured our poor companion on the evening before, and who were in momentary expectation of another similar feast. This circumstance occasioned us the most bitter regret and filled us with the most depressing and melancholy forebodings. We had experienced indescribable relief in bathing, and to have this resource cut off in so frightful a manner was more than we could bear. Nor, indeed, were we altogether free from the apprehension of immediate danger, for the least slip or false movement would have thrown us at once within reach of those voracious fish, who frequently thrust themselves directly upon us, swimming up to leeward. No shouts or exertions on our part seemed to alarm them. Even when one of the largest was struck with an ax by Peters and much wounded, he persisted in his attempts to push in where we were. A cloud came up at dusk, but, to our extreme anguish, passed over without discharging itself. It is quite impossible to conceive our sufferings from thirst at this period. We passed a sleepless night, both on this account and through dread of the sharks.

August 3. No prospect of relief, and the brig lying still more and more along, so that now we could not maintain a footing upon deck at all. Busied ourselves in securing our wine and tortoise-meat, so that we might not lose them in the event of our rolling over. Got out two stout spikes from the forechains, and, by means of the ax, drove them into the hull to windward within a couple of feet of the water, this not being very far from the keel, as we were nearly upon our beam-ends. To these spikes we now lashed our provisions, as being more secure than their former position beneath the chains. Suffered great agony from thirst during the whole day—no chance of bathing on account of the sharks, which never left us for a moment. Found it impossible to sleep.

August 4. A little before daybreak we perceived that the hulk was heeling over, and aroused ourselves to prevent being thrown off by the movement. At first the roll was slow and gradual, and we contrived to clamber over to windward very well, having taken the precaution to leave ropes hanging from the spikes we had driven in for the provision. But we had not calculated sufficiently upon the acceleration of the impetus; for, presently the heel became too violent to allow of our keeping pace with it; and, before either of us knew what was to happen, we found ourselves hurled furiously into the sea, and struggling several fathoms beneath the surface, with the huge hull immediately above us.

In going under the water I had been obliged to let go my hold upon the rope; and finding that I was completely beneath the vessel, and my strength nearly exhausted, I scarcely made a struggle for life, and resigned myself, in a few seconds, to die. But here again I was deceived, not having taken into consideration the natural rebound of the hull to windward. The whirl of the water upward, which the vessel occasioned in rolling partially back, brought me to the surface still more violently than I had been plunged beneath. Upon coming up I found myself about twenty yards from the hulk, as near as I could judge. She was lying keel up, rocking furiously from side to side, and the sea in all directions around was much agitated, and full of strong whirlpools. I could see nothing of Peters. An oil-cask was floating within a few feet of me, and various other articles from the brig were scattered about.

My principal terror was now on account of the sharks, which I knew to be in my vicinity. In order to deter these, if possible, from approaching me, I splashed the water vigorously with both hands and feet as I swam toward the hulk, creating a body of foam. I have no doubt that to this expedient, simple as it was, I was indebted for my preservation; for the sea all round the brig, just before her rolling over, was so crowded with these monsters, that I must have been, and really was, in actual contact with some of them during my progress. By great good fortune, however, I reached the side of the vessel in safety, although so utterly weakened by the violent exertion I had used that I should never have been able to get upon it but for the timely assistance of Peters, who, now, to my great joy, made his appearance (having scrambled up to the keel from the opposite side of the hull), and threw me the end of a rope—one of those which had been attached to the spikes.

Having barely escaped this danger, our attention was now directed to the dreadful imminency of another—that of absolute starvation. Our whole stock of provision had been swept overboard in spite of all our care in securing it; and seeing no longer the remotest possibility of obtaining more, we gave way both of us to despair, weeping aloud like children, and neither of us attempting to offer consolation to the other. Such weakness can scarcely be conceived, and to those who have never been similarly situated will, no doubt, appear unnatural; but it must be remembered that our intellects were so entirely disordered by the long course of privation and terror to which we had been subjected, that we could not justly be considered, at that period, in the light of rational beings. In subsequent perils, nearly as great, if not greater, I bore up with fortitude against all the evils of my situation, and Peters, it will be seen, evinced a stoical philosophy nearly as incredible as his present childlike supineness and imbecility—the mental condition made the difference.

The overturning of the brig, even with the consequent loss of the wine and turtle, would not, in fact, have rendered our situation more deplorable than before, except for the disappearance of the bedclothes by which we had been hitherto enabled to catch rainwater, and of the jug in which we had kept it when caught; for we found the whole bottom, from within two or three feet of the bends as far as the keel, together with the keel itself, *thickly covered with large barnacles, which proved to be excellent and highly nutritious food.* Thus, in two important respects, the accident we had so greatly dreaded proved to be a benefit rather than an injury; it had opened to us a supply of provisions which we could not have exhausted, using it moderately, in a month; and it had greatly contributed to our comfort as regards position, we being much more at ease, and in infinitely less danger, than before.

The difficulty, however, of now obtaining water blinded us to all the benefits of the change in our condition. That we might be ready to avail ourselves, as far as possible, of any shower which might fall we took off our shirts, to make use of them as we had of the sheets—not hoping, of course, to get more in this way, even under the most favorable circumstances, than half a gill at a time. No signs of a cloud appeared during the day, and the agonies of our thirst were nearly intolerable. At night, Peters obtained about an hour's disturbed sleep, but my intense sufferings would not permit me to close my eyes for a single moment.

August 5. To-day, a gentle breeze springing up carried us through a vast quantity of seaweed, among which we were so fortunate as to find eleven small crabs, which afforded us several delicious meals. Their shells being quite soft, we ate them entire, and found that they irritated our thirst far less than the barnacles. Seeing no trace of sharks among the seaweed, we also ventured to bathe, and remained in the water for four or five hours, during which we experienced a very sensible diminution of our thirst. Were greatly refreshed, and spent the night somewhat more comfortably than before, both of us snatching a little sleep.

August 6. This day we were blessed by a brisk and continual rain, lasting from about noon until after dark. Bitterly did we now regret the loss of our jug and carboy; for, in spite of the little means we had of catching the water, we might have filled one, if not both of them. As it was, we contrived to satisfy the cravings of thirst by suffering the shirts to become saturated, and then wringing them so as to let the grateful fluid trickle into our mouths. In this occupation we passed the entire day.

August 7. Just at daybreak we both at the same instant descried a sail to the eastward, and *evidently coming toward us*! We hailed the glorious sight with a long, although feeble shout of rapture; and began instantly to make every signal in our power, by flaring the shirts in the air, leaping as high as our weak condition would permit, and even by hallooing with all the strength of our lungs, although the vessel could not have been less than fifteen miles distant. However, she still continued to near our hulk, and we felt that, if she but held her present course, she must eventually come so close as to perceive us. In about an hour after we first discovered her, we could clearly see the people on her decks. She was a long, low, and rakish-looking topsail schooner, with a black ball in her foretopsail, and had, apparently, a full crew. We now became alarmed, for we could hardly imagine it possible that she did not observe us, and were apprehensive that she meant to leave us to perish as we were—an act of fiendish barbarity, which, however incredible it may appear, has been repeatedly perpetuated at sea, under circumstances very nearly similar, and by beings who were regarded as belonging to the human species.[1] In this instance, however, by the mercy of God, we were destined to be most happily deceived; for, presently we were aware of a sudden commotion on the deck of the stranger, who immediately afterward ran up a British flag, and, hauling her wind, bore up directly upon us. In half an hour more we found ourselves in her cabin. She proved to be the *Jane Guy*, of Liverpool, Captain Guy, bound on a sealing and trading voyage to the South Seas and Pacific.

1 The case of the brig *Polly*, of Boston, is one so much in point, and her fate, in many respects, so remarkably similar to our own, that I cannot forbear alluding to it here. This vessel, of one hundred and thirty tons burden, sailed from Boston, with a cargo of lumber and provisions, for Santa Croix, on the twelfth of December, 1811, under the command of Captain Casneau. There were eight souls on board besides the captain—the mate, four seamen, and the cook, together with a Mr. Hunt, and a negro girl belonging to him. On the fifteenth, having cleared the shoal of Georges, she sprung a leak in a gale of wind from the southeast, and was finally capsized; but, the mast going by the board, she afterward righted. They remained in this situation, without fire, and with very little provision, for the period of *one hundred and ninety-one days* (from December the fifteenth to June the twentieth) when Captain Casneau and Samuel Badger, the only survivers, were taken off the wreck by the *Fame*, of Hull, Captain Featherstone, bound home from Rio Janeiro. When picked up they were in latitude 28 *N.*, *longitude* 13 *W.*, *having drifted above two thousand miles*. On the ninth of July the *Fame* fell in with the brig *Dromero*, Captain Perkins, who landed the two sufferers in Kennebeck. The narrative from which we gather these details ends in the following words:

"It is natural to inquire how they could float such a vast distance, upon the most frequented part of the Atlantic, and not be discovered all this time. *They were passed by more than a dozen sail, one of which came so nigh them that they could distinctly see the people on deck and on the rigging looking at them; but, to the inexpressible disappointment of the starving and freezing men, they stifled the dictates of compassion, hoisted sail, and cruelly abandoned them to their fate.*"

CHAPTER 14

THE *JANE GUY* was a fine-looking topsail schooner of a hundred and eighty tons burden. She was unusually sharp in the bows, and on a wind, in moderate weather, the fastest sailer I have ever seen. Her qualities, however, as a rough sea-boat, were not so good, and her draft of water was by far too great for the trade to which she was destined. For this peculiar service, a larger vessel, and one of a light proportionate draft, is desirable—say a vessel of from three hundred to three hundred and fifty tons. She should be bark-rigged, and in other respects of a different construction from the usual South Sea ships. It is absolutely necessary that she should be well armed. She should have, say ten or twelve twelve-pound carronades, and two or three long twelves, with brass blunderbusses, and water-tight arm-chests for each top. Her anchors and cables should be of far greater strength than is required for any other species of trade, and, above all, her crew should be numerous and efficient—not less, for such a vessel as I have described, than fifty or sixty able-bodied men. The *Jane Guy* had a crew of thirty-five, all able seamen, besides the captain and mate, but she was not altogether as well armed or otherwise equipped, as a navigator acquainted with the difficulties and dangers of the trade could have desired.

Captain Guy was a gentleman of great urbanity of manner, and of considerable experience in the southern traffic, to which he had devoted a great portion of his life. He was deficient, however, in energy, and, consequently, in that spirit of enterprise which is here so absolutely requisite. He was part owner of the vessel in which he sailed, and was invested with discretionary powers to cruise in the South Seas for any cargo which might come most readily to hand. He had on board, as usual in such voyages, beads, looking-glasses, tinder-works, axes, hatchets, saws, adzes, planes, chisels, gouges, gimlets, files, spokeshaves, rasps, hammers, nails, knives, scissors, razors, needles, thread, crockery-ware, calico, trinkets, and other similar articles.

The schooner sailed from Liverpool on the tenth of July, crossed the Tropic of Cancer on the twenty-fifth, in longitude 20° west, and reached Sal, one of the Cape Verd islands, on the twenty-ninth, where she took in salt and other necessaries for the voyage. On the third of August, she left the Cape Verds and steered southwest, stretching over toward the coast of Brazil, so as to cross the equator between the meridians of twenty-eight and thirty degrees west longitude. This is the course usually taken by vessels bound from Europe to the Cape of Good Hope, or by that route to the East Indies. By proceeding thus they avoid the calms and strong contrary currents which continually prevail on the coast of Guinea, while, in the end, it is found to be the shortest track, as westerly winds are never wanting afterward by which to reach the Cape. It was Captain Guy's intention to make his first stoppage at Kerguelen's Land—I hardly know for what reason. On the day we were picked up the schooner was off Cape St. Roque, in longitude 31° west; so that, when found, we had drifted probably, from north to south, *not less than five-and-twenty degrees*!

On board the *Jane Guy* we were treated with all the kindness our distressed situation demanded. In about a fortnight, during which time we continued steering to the southeast, with gentle breezes and fine weather, both Peters and myself recovered entirely from the effects of our late privation and dreadful sufferings, and we began to remember what had passed rather as a frightful dream from which we had been happily awakened, than as events which had taken place in sober and naked reality. I have since found that this species of partial oblivion is usually brought about by sudden transition, whether from joy to sorrow or from sorrow to joy—the degree of forgetfulness being proportioned to the degree of difference in the exchange. Thus, in my own case, I now feel it impossible to realize the full extent of the misery which I endured during the days spent upon the hulk. The incidents are remembered, but not the feelings which the incidents elicited at the time of their occurrence. I only know, that when they did occur, I *then* thought human nature could sustain nothing more of agony.

We continued our voyage for some weeks without any incidents of greater moment than the occasional meeting with whaling-ships, and more frequently with the black or right whale, so called in contradistinction to the spermaceti. These, however, were chiefly found south of the twenty-fifth parallel. On the sixteenth of September, being in the vicinity of the Cape of Good Hope, the schooner encountered her first gale of any violence since leaving Liverpool. In this neighborhood, but more frequently to the south and east of the promontory (we were to the westward), navigators have often to contend with storms from the northward, which rage with great fury. They always bring with them a heavy sea, and one of their most dangerous features is the instantaneous chopping round of the wind, an occurrence almost certain to take place during the greatest force of the gale. A perfect hurricane will be blowing at one moment from the northward or northeast, and in the next not a breath of wind will be felt in that direction, while from the southwest it will come out all at once with a violence almost inconceivable. A bright spot to the southward is the sure forerunner of the change, and vessels are thus enabled to take the proper precautions.

It was about six in the morning when the blow came on with a white squall, and, as usual, from the northward. By eight it had increased very much, and brought down upon us one of the most tremendous seas I had then ever beheld. Every thing had been made as snug as possible, but the schooner labored excessively, and gave evidence of her bad qualities as a seaboat, pitching her forecastle under at every plunge and with the greatest difficulty struggling up from one wave before she was buried in another. just before sunset the bright spot for which we had been on the look-out made its appearance in the southwest, and in an hour afterward we perceived the little headsail we carried flapping listlessly against the mast. In two minutes more, in spite of every preparation, we were hurled on our beam-ends, as if by magic, and a perfect wilderness of foam made a clear breach over us as we lay. The blow from the southwest, however, luckily proved to be nothing more than a squall, and we had the good fortune to right the vessel without the loss of a spar. A heavy cross sea gave us great trouble for a few hours after this, but toward morning we found ourselves in nearly as good condition as before the gale. Captain Guy considered that he had made an escape little less than miraculous.

On the thirteenth of October we came in sight of Prince Edward's Island, in latitude 46° 53' S., longitude 37° 46' E. Two days afterward we found ourselves near Possession Island, and presently passed the islands of Crozet, in latitude 42° 59' S., longitude 48° E. On the eighteenth we made Kerguelen's or Desolation Island, in the Southern Indian Ocean, and came to anchor in Christmas Harbour, having four fathoms of water.

This island, or rather group of islands, bears southeast from the Cape of Good Hope, and is distant therefrom nearly eight hundred leagues.

It was first discovered in 1772, by the Baron de Kergulen, or Kerguelen, a Frenchman, who, thinking the land to form a portion of an extensive southern continent carried home information to that effect, which produced much excitement at the time. The government, taking the matter up, sent the baron back in the following year for the purpose of giving his new discovery a critical examination, when the mistake was discovered. In 1777, Captain Cook fell in with the same group, and gave to the principal one the name of Desolation Island, a title which it certainly well deserves. Upon approaching the land, however, the navigator might be induced to suppose otherwise, as the sides of most of the hills, from September to March, are clothed with very brilliant verdure. This deceitful appearance is caused by a small plant resembling saxifrage, which is abundant, growing in large patches on a species of crumbling moss. Besides this plant there is scarcely a sign of vegetation on the island, if we except some coarse rank grass near the harbor, some lichen, and a shrub which bears resemblance to a cabbage shooting into seed, and which has a bitter and acrid taste.

The face of the country is hilly, although none of the hills can be called lofty. Their tops are perpetually covered with snow. There are several harbors, of which Christmas Harbour is the most convenient. It is the first to be met with on the northeast side of the island after passing Cape Francois, which forms the northern shore, and, by its peculiar shape, serves to distinguish the harbour. Its projecting point terminates in a high rock, through which is a large hole, forming a natural arch. The entrance is in latitude 48° 40' S., longitude 69° 6' E. Passing in here, good anchorage may be found under the shelter of several small islands, which form a sufficient protection from all easterly winds. Proceeding on eastwardly from this anchorage you come to Wasp Bay, at the head of the harbour. This is a small basin, completely landlocked, into which you can go with four fathoms, and find anchorage in from ten to three, hard clay bottom. A ship might lie here with her best bower ahead all the year round without risk. To the westward, at the head of Wasp Bay, is a small stream of excellent water, easily procured.

Some seal of the fur and hair species are still to be found on Kerguelen's Island, and sea elephants abound. The feathered tribes are discovered in great numbers. Penguins are very plenty, and of these there are four different kinds. The royal penguin, so called from its size and beautiful plumage, is the largest. The upper part of the body is usually gray, sometimes of a lilac tint; the under portion of the purest white imaginable. The head is of a glossy and most brilliant black, the feet also. The chief beauty of plumage, however, consists in two broad stripes of a gold color, which pass along from the head to the breast. The bill is long, and either pink or bright scarlet. These birds walk erect; with a stately carriage. They carry their heads high with their wings drooping like two arms, and, as their tails project from their body in a line with the legs, the resemblance to a human figure is very striking, and would be apt to deceive the spectator at a casual glance or in the gloom of the evening. The royal penguins which we met with on Kerguelen's Land were rather larger than a goose. The other kinds are the macaroni, the jackass, and the rookery penguin. These are much smaller, less beautiful in plumage, and different in other respects.

Besides the penguin many other birds are here to be found, among which may be mentioned sea-hens, blue peterels, teal, ducks, Port Egmont hens, shags, Cape pigeons, the nelly, sea swallows, terns, sea gulls, Mother Carey's chickens, Mother Carey's geese, or the great peterel, and, lastly, the albatross.

The great peterel is as large as the common albatross, and is carnivorous. It is frequently called the break-bones, or osprey peterel. They are not at all shy, and, when properly cooked, are palatable food. In flying they sometimes sail very close to the surface of the water, with the wings expanded, without appearing to move them in the least degree, or make any exertion with them whatever.

The albatross is one of the largest and fiercest of the South Sea birds. It is of the gull species, and takes its prey on the wing, never coming on land except for the purpose of breeding. Between this bird and the penguin the most singular friendship exists. Their nests are constructed with great uniformity upon a plan concerted between the two species—that of the albatross being placed in the center of a little square formed by the nests of four penguins. Navigators have agreed in calling an assemblage of such encampments a rookery. These rookeries have been often described, but as my readers may not all have seen these descriptions, and as I shall have occasion hereafter to speak of the penguin and albatross, it will not be amiss to say something here of their mode of building and living.

When the season for incubation arrives, the birds assemble in vast numbers, and for some days appear to be deliberating upon the proper course to be pursued. At length they proceed to action. A level piece of ground is selected, of suitable extent, usually comprising three or four acres, and situated as near the sea as possible, being still beyond its reach. The spot is chosen with reference to its evenness of surface, and that is preferred which is the least encumbered with stones. This matter being arranged, the birds proceed, with one accord, and actuated apparently by one mind, to trace out, with mathematical accuracy, either a square or other parallelogram, as may best suit the nature of the ground, and of just sufficient size to accommodate easily all the birds assembled, and no more—in this particular seeming determined upon preventing the access of future stragglers who have not participated in the labor of the encampment. One side of the place thus marked out runs parallel with the water's edge, and is left open for ingress or egress.

Having defined the limits of the rookery, the colony now begin to clear it of every species of rubbish, picking up stone by stone, and carrying them outside of the lines, and close by them, so as to form a wall on the three inland sides. Just within this wall a perfectly level and smooth walk is formed, from six to eight feet wide, and extending around the encampment—thus serving the purpose of a general promenade.

The next process is to partition out the whole area into small squares exactly equal in size. This is done by forming narrow paths, very smooth, and crossing each other at right angles throughout the entire extent of the rookery. At each intersection of these paths the nest of an albatross is constructed, and a penguin's nest in the center of each square—thus every penguin is surrounded by four albatrosses, and each albatross by a like number of penguins. The penguin's nest consists of a hole in the earth, very shallow, being only just of sufficient depth to keep her single egg from rolling. The albatross is somewhat less simple in her arrangements, erecting a hillock about a foot high and two in diameter. This is made of earth, seaweed, and shells. On its summit she builds her nest.

The birds take especial care never to leave their nests unoccupied for an instant during the period of incubation, or, indeed, until the young progeny are sufficiently strong to take care of themselves. While the male is absent at sea in search of food, the female remains on duty, and it is only upon the return of her partner that she ventures abroad.

The eggs are never left uncovered at all—while one bird leaves the nest the other nestling in by its side. This precaution is rendered necessary by the thieving propensities prevalent in the rookery, the inhabitants making no scruple to purloin each other's eggs at every good opportunity.

Although there are some rookeries in which the penguin and albatross are the sole population, yet in most of them a variety of oceanic birds are to be met with, enjoying all the privileges of citizenship, and scattering their nests here and there, wherever they can find room, never interfering, however, with the stations of the larger species. The appearance of such encampments, when seen from a distance, is exceedingly singular. The whole atmosphere just above the settlement is darkened with the immense number of the albatross (mingled with the smaller tribes) which are continually hovering over it, either going to the ocean or returning home. At the same time a crowd of penguins are to be observed, some passing to and fro in the narrow alleys, and some marching with the military strut so peculiar to them, around the general promenade ground which encircles the rookery. In short, survey it as we will, nothing can be more astonishing than the spirit of reflection evinced by these feathered beings, and nothing surely can be better calculated to elicit reflection in every well-regulated human intellect.

On the morning after our arrival in Christmas Harbour the chief mate, Mr. Patterson, took the boats, and (although it was somewhat early in the season) went in search of seal, leaving the captain and a young relation of his on a point of barren land to the westward, they having some business, whose nature I could not ascertain, to transact in the interior of the island. Captain Guy took with him a bottle, in which was a sealed letter, and made his way from the point on which he was set on shore toward one of the highest peaks in the place. It is probable that his design was to leave the letter on that height for some vessel which he expected to come after him. As soon as we lost sight of him we proceeded (Peters and myself being in the mate's boat) on our cruise around the coast, looking for seal. In this business we were occupied about three weeks, examining with great care every nook and corner, not only of Kerguelen's Land, but of the several small islands in the vicinity. Our labors, however, were not crowned with any important success. We saw a great many fur seal, but they were exceedingly shy, and with the greatest exertions, we could only procure three hundred and fifty skins in all. Sea elephants were abundant, especially on the western coast of the mainland, but of these we killed only twenty, and this with great difficulty. On the smaller islands we discovered a good many of the hair seal, but did not molest them. We returned to the schooner: on the eleventh, where we found Captain Guy and his nephew, who gave a very bad account of the interior, representing it as one of the most dreary and utterly barren countries in the world. They had remained two nights on the island, owing to some misunderstanding, on the part of the second mate, in regard to the sending a jollyboat from the schooner to take them off.

CHAPTER 15

ON THE TWELFTH we made sail from Christmas Harbour retracing our way to the westward, and leaving Marion's Island, one of Crozet's group, on the larboard. We afterward passed Prince Edward's Island, leaving it also on our left, then, steering more to the northward, made, in fifteen days, the islands of Tristan d'Acunha, in latitude 37° 8' S, longitude 12° 8' W.

This group, now so well known, and which consists of three circular islands, was first discovered by the Portuguese, and was visited afterward by the Dutch in 1643, and by the French in 1767. The three islands together form a triangle, and are distant from each other about ten miles, there being fine open passages between. The land in all of them is very high, especially in Tristan d'Acunha, properly so called. This is the largest of the group, being fifteen miles in circumference, and so elevated that it can be seen in clear weather at the distance of eighty or ninety miles. A part of the land toward the north rises more than a thousand feet perpendicularly from the sea. A tableland at this height extends back nearly to the center of the island, and from this tableland arises a lofty cone like that of Teneriffe. The lower half of this cone is clothed with trees of good size, but the upper region is barren rock, usually hidden among the clouds, and covered with snow during the greater part of the year. There are no shoals or other dangers about the island, the shores being remarkably bold and the water deep. On the northwestern coast is a bay, with a beach of black sand where a landing with boats can be easily effected, provided there be a southerly wind. Plenty of excellent water may here be readily procured; also cod and other fish may be taken with hook and line.

The next island in point of size, and the most westwardly of the group, is that called the Inaccessible. Its precise situation is 37° 17' S. latitude, longitude 12° 24' W. It is seven or eight miles in circumference, and on all sides presents a forbidding and precipitous aspect. Its top is perfectly flat, and the whole region is sterile, nothing growing upon it except a few stunted shrubs.

Nightingale Island, the smallest and most southerly, is in latitude 37° 26' S., longitude 12° 12' W. Off its southern extremity is a high ledge of rocky islets; a few also of a similar appearance are seen to the northeast. The ground is irregular and sterile, and a deep valley partially separates it.

The shores of these islands abound, in the proper season, with sea lions, sea elephants, the hair and fur seal, together with a great variety of oceanic birds. Whales are also plenty in their vicinity. Owing to the ease with which these various animals were here formerly taken, the group has been much visited since its discovery. The Dutch and French frequented it at a very early period. In 1790, Captain Patten, of the ship *Industry*, of Philadelphia, made Tristan d'Acunha, where he remained seven months (from August, 1790, to April, 1791) for the purpose of collecting sealskins. In this time he gathered no less than five thousand six hundred, and says that he would have had no difficulty in loading a large ship with oil in three weeks. Upon his arrival he found no quadrupeds, with the exception of a few wild goats; the island now abounds with all our most valuable domestic animals, which have been introduced by subsequent navigators.

I believe it was not long after Captain Patten's visit that Captain Colquhoun, of the American brig *Betsey*, touched at the largest of the islands for the purpose of refreshment. He planted onions, potatoes, cabbages, and a great many other vegetables, an abundance of all which is now to be met with.

In 1811, a Captain Haywood, in the *Nereus*, visited Tristan. He found there three Americans, who were residing upon the island to prepare sealskins and oil. One of these men was named Jonathan Lambert, and he called himself the sovereign of the country. He had cleared and cultivated about sixty acres of land, and turned his attention to raising the coffee-plant and sugar-cane, with which he had been furnished by the American Minister at Rio Janeiro. This settlement, however, was finally abandoned, and in 1817 the islands were taken possession of by the British Government, who sent a detachment for that purpose from the Cape of Good Hope. They did not, however, retain them long; but, upon the evacuation of the country as a British possession, two or three English families took up their residence there independently of the Government. On the twenty-fifth of March, 1824, the *Berwick*, Captain Jeffrey, from London to Van Diemen's Land, arrived at the place, where they found an Englishman of the name of Glass, formerly a corporal in the British artillery. He claimed to be supreme governor of the islands, and had under his control twenty-one men and three women. He gave a very favorable account of the salubrity of the climate and of the productiveness of the soil. The population occupied themselves chiefly in collecting sealskins and sea elephant oil, with which they traded to the Cape of Good Hope, Glass owning a small schooner. At the period of our arrival the governor was still a resident, but his little community had multiplied, there being fifty-six persons upon Tristan, besides a smaller settlement of seven on Nightingale Island. We had no difficulty in procuring almost every kind of refreshment which we required—sheep, hogs, bullocks, rabbits, poultry, goats, fish in great variety, and vegetables were abundant. Having come to anchor close in with the large island, in eighteen fathoms, we took all we wanted on board very conveniently. Captain Guy also purchased of Glass five hundred sealskins and some ivory. We remained here a week, during which the prevailing winds were from the northward and westward, and the weather somewhat hazy. On the fifth of November we made sail to the southward and westward, with the intention of having a thorough search for a group of islands called the Auroras, respecting whose existence a great diversity of opinion has existed.

These islands are said to have been discovered as early as 1762, by the commander of the ship *Aurora*. In 1790, Captain Manuel de Oyarvido, in the ship *Princess*, belonging to the Royal Philippine Company, sailed, as he asserts, directly among them. In 1794, the Spanish corvette *Atrevida* went with the determination of ascertaining their precise situation, and, in a paper published by the Royal Hydrographical Society of Madrid in the year 1809, the following language is used respecting this expedition: "The corvette *Atrevida* practised, in their immediate vicinity, from the twenty-first to the twenty-seventh of January, all the necessary observations, and measured by chronometers the difference of longitude between these islands and the port of Soledad in the Manillas. The islands are three, they are very nearly in the same meridian; the centre one is rather low, and the other two may be seen at nine leagues' distance." The observations made on board the *Atrevida* give the following results as the precise situation of each island. The most northern is in latitude 52° 37' 24" S., longitude 47°, 43' 15" W.; the middle one in latitude 53° 2' 40" S., longitude 47° 55' 15" W.; and the most southern in latitude 53° 15' 22" S., longitude 47° 57' 15" W.

On the twenty-seventh of January, 1820, Captain James Weddel, of the British navy, sailed from Staten Land also in search of the Auroras. He reports that, having made the most diligent search and passed not only immediately over the spots indicated by the commander of the *Atrevida*, but in every direction throughout the vicinity of these spots, he could discover no indication of land. These conflicting statements have induced other navigators to look out for the islands; and, strange to say, while some have sailed through every inch of sea where they are supposed to lie without finding them, there have been not a few who declare positively that they have seen them; and even been close in with their shores. It was Captain Guy's intention to make every exertion within his power to settle the question so oddly in dispute.[1]

We kept on our course, between the south and west, with variable weather, until the twentieth of the month, when we found ourselves on the debated ground, being in latitude 53° 15' S., longitude 47° 58' W.—that is to say, very nearly upon the spot indicated as the situation of the most southern of the group. Not perceiving any sip of land, we continued to the westward of the parallel of 53° south, as far as the meridian of 50° west. We then stood to the north as far as the parallel of 52° south, when we turned to the eastward, and kept our parallel by double altitudes, morning and evening, and meridian altitudes of the planets and moon. Having thus gone eastwardly to the meridian of the western coast of Georgia, we kept that meridian until we were in the latitude from which we set out. We then took diagonal courses throughout the entire extent of sea circumscribed, keeping a lookout constantly at the masthead, and repeating our examination with the greatest care for a period of three weeks, during which the weather was remarkably pleasant and fair, with no haze whatsoever. Of course we were thoroughly satisfied that, whatever islands might have existed in this vicinity at any former period, no vestige of them remained at the present day. Since my return home I find that the same ground

1 Among the vessels which at various times have professed to meet with the Auroras may be mentioned the ship San Miguel, in 1769; the ship *Aurora*, in 1774; the brig *Pearl*, in 1779; and the ship *Dolores*, in 1790. They all agree in giving the mean latitude 53° south.

was traced over, with equal care, in 1822, by Captain Johnson, of the American schooner *Henry*, and by Captain Morrell in the American schooner *Wasp*—in both cases with the same result as in our own.

CHAPTER 16

IT HAD BEEN Captain Guy's original intention, after satisfying himself about the Auroras, to proceed through the Strait of Magellan, and up along the western coast of Patagonia; but information received at Tristan d'Acunha induced him to steer to the southward, in the hope of falling in with some small islands said to lie about the parallel of 60° S., longitude 41° 20' W. In the event of his not discovering these lands, he designed, should the season prove favorable, to push on toward the pole. Accordingly, on the twelfth of December, we made sail in that direction. On the eighteenth we found ourselves about the station indicated by Glass, and cruised for three days in that neighborhood without finding any traces of the islands he had mentioned. On the twenty-first, the weather being unusually pleasant, we again made sail to the southward, with the resolution of penetrating in that course as far as possible. Before entering upon this portion of my narrative, it may be as well, for the information of those readers who have paid little attention to the progress of discovery in these regions, to give some brief account of the very few attempts at reaching the southern pole which have hitherto been made.

That of Captain Cook was the first of which we have any distinct account. In 1772 he sailed to the south in the Resolution, accompanied by Lieutenant Furneaux in the Adventure. In December he found himself as far as the fifty-eighth parallel of south latitude, and in longitude 26° 57' E. Here he met with narrow fields of ice, about eight or ten inches thick, and running northwest and southeast. This ice was in large cakes, and usually it was packed so closely that the vessel had great difficulty in forcing a passage. At this period Captain Cook supposed, from the vast number of birds to be seen, and from other indications, that he was in the near vicinity of land. He kept on to the southward, the weather being exceedingly cold, until he reached the sixty-fourth parallel, in longitude 38° 14' W. Here he had mild weather, with gentle breezes, for five days, the thermometer being at thirty-six. In January, 1773, the vessels crossed the Antarctic circle, but did not succeed in penetrating much farther; for upon reaching latitude 67° 15' they found all farther progress impeded by an immense body of ice, extending all along the southern horizon as far as the eye could reach. This ice was of every variety—and some large floes of it, miles in extent, formed a compact mass, rising eighteen or twenty feet above the water. It being late in the season, and no hope entertained of rounding these obstructions, Captain Cook now reluctantly turned to the northward.

In the November following he renewed his search in the Antarctic. In latitude 59° 40' he met with a strong current setting to the southward. In December, when the vessels were in latitude 67° 31', longitude 142° 54' W., the cold was excessive, with heavy gales and fog. Here also birds were abundant; the albatross, the penguin, and the peterel especially. In latitude 70° 23' some large islands of ice were encountered, and shortly afterward the clouds to the southward were observed to be of a snowy whiteness, indicating the vicinity of field ice. In latitude 71° 10', longitude 106° 54' W., the navigators were stopped, as before, by an immense frozen expanse, which filled the whole area of the southern horizon. The northern edge of this expanse was ragged and broken, so firmly wedged together as to be utterly impassible, and extending about a mile to the southward. Behind it the frozen surface was comparatively smooth for some distance, until terminated in the extreme background by gigantic ranges of ice mountains, the one towering above the other. Captain Cook concluded that this vast field reached the southern pole or was joined to a continent. Mr. J. N. Reynolds, whose great exertions and perseverance have at length succeeded in getting set on foot a national expedition, partly for the purpose of exploring these regions, thus speaks of the attempt of the Resolution. "We are not surprised that Captain Cook was unable to go beyond 71° 10', but we are astonished that he did attain that point on the meridian of 106° 54' west longitude. Palmer's Land lies south of the Shetland, latitude 64°, and tends to the southward and westward farther than any navigator has yet penetrated. Cook was standing for this land when his progress was arrested by the ice; which, we apprehend, must always be the case in that point, and so early in the season as the sixth of January—and we should not be surprised if a portion of the icy mountains described was attached to the main body of Palmer's Land, or to some other portions of land lying farther to the southward and westward."

In 1803, Captains Kreutzenstern and Lisiausky were dispatched by Alexander of Russia for the purpose of circumnavigating the globe. In endeavoring to get south, they made no farther than 59° 58', in longitude 70° 15' W. They here met with strong currents setting eastwardly. Whales were abundant, but they saw no ice. In regard to this voyage, Mr. Reynolds observes that, if Kreutzenstern had arrived where he did earlier in the season, he must have encountered ice—it was March when he reached the latitude specified. The winds, prevailing, as they do, from the southward and westward, had carried the floes, aided by currents, into that icy region bounded on the north by Georgia, east by Sandwich Land and the South Orkneys, and west by the South Shetland islands.

In 1822, Captain James Weddell, of the British navy, with two very small vessels, penetrated farther to the south than any previous navigator, and this, too, without encountering extraordinary difficulties. He states that although he was frequently hemmed in by ice *before* reaching the seventy-second parallel, yet, upon attaining it, not a particle was to be discovered, and that, upon arriving at the latitude of 74° 15', no fields, and only three islands of ice were visible. It is somewhat remarkable that, although vast flocks of birds were seen, and other usual indications of land, and although, south of the Shetlands, unknown coasts were observed from the masthead tending southwardly, Weddell discourages the idea of land existing in the polar regions of the south.

On the 11th of January, 1823, Captain Benjamin Morrell, of the American schooner Wasp, sailed from Kerguelen's Land with a view of penetrating as far south as possible. On the first of February he found himself in latitude 64° 52' S., longitude 118° 27' E. The following passage is extracted from his journal of that date. "The wind soon freshened to an eleven-knot breeze, and we embraced this opportunity of making to the west,; being however convinced that the farther we went south beyond latitude 64°, the less ice was to be apprehended, we steered a little to the southward, until we crossed the Antarctic circle, and were in latitude 69° 15' E. In this latitude there was *no field ice*, and very few ice islands in sight.

Under the date of March fourteenth I find also this entry. The sea was now entirely free of field ice, and there were not more than a dozen ice islands in sight. At the same time the temperature of the air and water was at least thirteen degrees higher (more mild) than we had ever found it between the parallels of sixty and sixty-two south. We were now in latitude 70° 14' S., and the temperature of the air was forty-seven, and that of the water forty-four. In this situation I found the variation to be 14° 27' easterly, per azimuth...I have several times passed within the Antarctic circle, on different meridians, and have uniformly found the temperature, both of the air and the water, to become more and more mild the farther I advanced beyond the sixty-fifth degree of south latitude, and that the variation decreases in the same proportion. While north of this latitude, say between sixty and sixty-five south, we frequently had great difficulty in finding a passage for the vessel between the immense and almost innumerable ice islands, some of which were from one to two miles in circumference, and more than five hundred feet above the surface of the water."

Being nearly destitute of fuel and water, and without proper instruments, it being also late in the season, Captain Morrell was now obliged to put back, without attempting any further progress to the westward, although an entirely open, sea lay before him. He expresses the opinion that, had not these overruling considerations obliged him to retreat, he could have penetrated, if not to the pole itself, at least to the eighty-fifth parallel. I have given his ideas respecting these matters somewhat at length, that the reader may have an opportunity of seeing how far they were borne out by my own subsequent experience.

In 1831, Captain Briscoe, in the employ of the Messieurs Enderby, whale-ship owners of London, sailed in the brig Lively for the South Seas, accompanied by the cutter Tula. On the twenty-eighth of February, being in latitude 66° 30' S., longitude 47° 31' E., he descried land, and "clearly discovered through the snow the black peaks of a range of mountains running E. S. E." He remained in this neighborhood during the whole of the following month, but was unable to approach the coast nearer than within ten leagues, owing to the boisterous state of the weather. Finding it impossible to make further discovery during this season, he returned northward to winter in Van Diemen's Land.

In the beginning of 1832 he again proceeded southwardly, and on the fourth of February was seen to the southeast in latitude 67° 15' longitude 69° 29' W. This was soon found to be an island near the headland of the country he had first discovered. On the twenty-first of the month he succeeded in landing on the latter, and took possession of it in the name of William IV, calling it Adelaide's Island, in honor of the English queen. These particulars being made known to the Royal

Geographical Society of London, the conclusion was drawn by that body "that there is a continuous tract of land extending from 47° 30' E. to 69° 29' W. longitude, running the parallel of from sixty-six to sixty-seven degrees south latitude." In respect to this conclusion Mr. Reynolds observes: "In the correctness of it we by no means concur; nor do the discoveries of Briscoe warrant any such indifference. It was within these limits that Weddel proceeded south on a meridian to the east of Georgia, Sandwich Land, and the South Orkney and Shetland islands." My own experience will be found to testify most directly to the falsity of the conclusion arrived at by the society.

These are the principal attempts which have been made at penetrating to a high southern latitude, and it will now be seen that there remained, previous to the voyage of the *Jane*, nearly three hundred degrees of longitude in which the Antarctic circle had not been crossed at all. Of course a wide field lay before us for discovery, and it was with feelings of most intense interest that I heard Captain Guy express his resolution of pushing boldly to the southward.

CHAPTER 17

WE KEPT OUR course southwardly for four days after giving up the search for Glass's islands, without meeting with any ice at all. On the twenty-sixth, at noon, we were in latitude 63° 23' S., longitude 41° 25' W. We now saw several large ice islands, and a floe of field ice, not, however, of any great extent. The winds generally blew from the southeast, or the northeast, but were very light. Whenever we had a westerly wind, which was seldom, it was invariably attended with a rain squall. Every day we had more or less snow. The thermometer, on the twenty-seventh stood at thirty-five.

January 1, 1828.—This day we found ourselves completely hemmed in by the ice, and our prospects looked cheerless indeed. A strong gale blew, during the whole forenoon, from the northeast, and drove large cakes of the drift against the rudder and counter with such violence that we all trembled for the consequences. Toward evening, the gale still blowing with fury, a large field in front separated, and we were enabled, by carrying a press of sail to force a passage through the smaller flakes into some open water beyond. As we approached this space we took in sail by degrees, and having at length got clear, lay-to under a single. reefed foresail.

January 2.—We had now tolerably pleasant weather. At noon we found ourselves in latitude 69° 10' S, longitude 42° 20' W, having crossed the Antarctic circle. Very little ice was to be seen to the southward, although large fields of it lay behind us. This day we rigged some sounding gear, using a large iron pot capable of holding twenty gallons, and a line of two hundred fathoms. We found the current setting to the north, about a quarter of a mile per hour. The temperature of the air was now about thirty-three. Here we found the variation to be 14° 28' easterly, per azimuth.

January 5.—We had still held on to the southward without any very great impediments. On this morning, however, being in latitude 73° 15' E., longitude 42° 10' W, we were again brought to a stand by an immense expanse of firm ice. We saw, nevertheless, much open water to the southward, and felt no doubt of being able to reach it eventually. Standing to the eastward along the edge of the floe, we at length came to a passage of about a mile in width, through which we warped our way by sundown. The sea in which we now were was thickly covered with ice islands, but had no field ice, and we pushed on boldly as before. The cold did not seem to increase, although we had snow very frequently, and now and then hail squalls of great violence. Immense flocks of the albatross flew over the schooner this day, going from southeast to northwest.

January 7.—The sea still remained pretty well open, so that we had no difficulty in holding on our course. To the westward we saw some icebergs of incredible size, and in the afternoon passed very near one whose summit could not have been less than four hundred fathoms from the surface of the ocean. Its girth was probably, at the base, three-quarters of a league, and several streams of water were running from crevices in its sides. We remained in sight of this island two days, and then only lost it in a fog.

January 10.—Early this morning we had the misfortune to lose a man overboard. He was an American named Peter Vredenburgh, a native of New York, and was one of the most valuable hands on board the schooner. In going over the bows his foot slipped, and he fell between two cakes of ice, never rising again. At noon of this day we were in latitude 78° 30', longitude 40° 15' W. The cold was now excessive, and we had hail squalls continually from the northward and eastward. In this direction also we saw several more immense icebergs, and the whole horizon to the eastward appeared to be blocked up with field ice, rising in tiers, one mass above the other. Some driftwood floated by during the evening, and a great quantity of birds flew over, among which were nellies, peterels, albatrosses, and a large bird of a brilliant blue plumage. The variation here, per azimuth, was less than it had been previously to our passing the Antarctic circle.

January 12.—Our passage to the south again looked doubtful, as nothing was to be seen in the direction of the pole but one apparently limitless floe, backed by absolute mountains of ragged ice, one precipice of which arose frowningly above the other. We stood to the westward until the fourteenth, in the hope of finding an entrance.

January 14.—This morning we reached the western extremity of the field which had impeded us, and, weathering it, came to an open sea, without a particle of ice. Upon sounding with two hundred fathoms, we here found a current setting southwardly at the rate of half a mile per hour. The temperature of the air was forty-seven, that of the water thirty-four. We now sailed to the southward without meeting any interruption of moment until the sixteenth, when, at noon, we were in latitude 81° 21', longitude 42° W. We here again sounded, and found a current setting still southwardly, and at the rate of three quarters of a mile per hour. The variation per azimuth had diminished, and the temperature of the air was mild and pleasant, the thermometer being as high as fifty-one. At this period not a particle of ice was to be discovered. All hands on board now felt certain of attaining the pole.

January 17.—This day was full of incident. Innumerable flights of birds flew over us from the southward, and several were shot from the deck, one of them, a species of pelican, proved to be excellent eating. About midday a small floe of ice was seen from the masthead off the larboard bow, and upon it there appeared to be some large animal. As the weather was good and nearly calm, Captain Guy ordered out two of the boats to see what it was. Dirk Peters and myself accompanied the mate in the larger boat. Upon coming up with the floe, we perceived that it was in the possession of a gigantic creature of the race of the Arctic bear, but far exceeding in size the largest of these animals. Being well armed, we made no scruple of attacking it at once. Several shots were fired in quick succession, the most of which took effect, apparently, in the head and body. Nothing discouraged, however, the monster threw himself from the ice, and swam with open jaws, to the boat in which were Peters and myself. Owing to the confusion which ensued among us at this unexpected turn of the adventure, no person was ready immediately with a second shot, and the bear had actually succeeded in getting half his vast bulk across our gunwale, and seizing one of the men by the small of his back, before any efficient means were taken to repel him. In this extremity nothing but the promptness and agility of Peters saved us from destruction. Leaping upon the back of the huge beast, he plunged the blade of a knife behind the neck, reaching the spinal marrow at a blow. The brute tumbled into the sea lifeless, and without a struggle, rolling over Peters as he fell. The latter soon recovered himself, and a rope being thrown him, returned in triumph to the schooner, towing our trophy behind us. This bear, upon admeasurement, proved to be full fifteen feet in his greatest length. His wool was perfectly white, and very coarse, curling tightly. The eyes were of a blood red, and larger than those of the Arctic bear, the snout also more rounded, rather resembling the snout of the bulldog. The meat was tender, but excessively rank and fishy, although the men devoured it with avidity, and declared it excellent eating.

Scarcely had we got our prize alongside, when the man at the mast-head gave the joyful shout of "*land on the starboard bow!*" All hands were now upon the alert, and, a breeze springing up very opportunely from the northward and eastward, we were soon close in with the coast. It proved to be a low rocky islet, of about a league in circumference, and altogether destitute of vegetation, if we except a species of prickly pear. In approaching it from the northward, a singular ledge of rock is seen projecting into the sea, and bearing a strong resemblance to corded bales of cotton. Around this ledge to the westward is a small bay, at the bottom of which our boats effected a convenient landing.

It did not take us long to explore every portion of the island, but, with one exception, we found nothing worthy of our observation. In the southern extremity, we picked up near the shore, half buried in a pile of loose stones, a piece of wood, which seemed to have formed the prow of a canoe. There had been evidently some attempt at carving upon it, and Captain Guy fancied that he made out the figure of a tortoise, but the resemblance did not strike me very forcibly. Besides this prow, if such it were, we found no other token that any living creature had ever been here before. Around the coast we discovered occasional small floes of ice—but these were very few. The exact situation of the islet (to which Captain Guy gave the name of Bennet's Islet, in honor of his partner in the ownership of the schooner) is 82° 50' S. latitude, 42° 20' W. longitude.

We had now advanced to the southward more than eight degrees farther than any previous navigators, and the sea still lay perfectly open before us. We found, too, that the variation uniformly decreased as we proceeded, and, what was still more surprising, that the temperature of the air, and latterly of the water, became milder. The weather might even be called pleasant, and we had a steady but very gentle breeze always from some northern point of the compass. The sky was usually clear, with now and then a slight appearance of thin vapor in the southern horizon—this, however, was invariably of brief duration. Two difficulties alone presented themselves to our view; we were getting short of fuel, and symptoms of scurvy had occurred among several of the crew. These considerations began to impress upon Captain Guy the necessity of returning, and he spoke of it frequently. For my own part, confident as I was of soon arriving at land of some description upon the course we were pursuing, and having every reason to believe, from present appearances, that we should not find it the sterile soil met with in the higher Arctic latitudes, I warmly pressed upon him the expediency of persevering, at least for a few days longer, in the direction we were now holding. So tempting an opportunity of solving the great problem in regard to an Antarctic continent had never yet been afforded to man, and I confess that I felt myself bursting with indignation at the timid and ill-timed suggestions of our commander. I believe, indeed, that what I could not refrain from saying to him on this head had the effect of inducing him to push on. While, therefore, I cannot but lament the most unfortunate and bloody events which immediately arose from my advice, I must still be allowed to feel some degree of gratification at having been instrumental, however remotely, in opening to the eye of science one of the most intensely exciting secrets which has ever engrossed its attention.

CHAPTER 18

JANUARY 18.—THIS MORNING[1] we continued to the southward, with the same pleasant weather as before. The sea was entirely smooth, the air tolerably warm and from the northeast, the temperature of the water fifty-three. We now again got our sounding-gear in order, and, with a hundred and fifty fathoms of line, found the current setting toward the pole at the rate of a mile an hour. This constant tendency to the southward, both in the wind and current, caused some degree of speculation, and even of alarm, in different quarters of the schooner, and I saw distinctly that no little impression had been made upon the mind of Captain Guy. He was exceedingly sensitive to ridicule, however, and I finally succeeded in laughing him out of his apprehensions. The variation was now very trivial. In the course of the day we saw several large whales of the right species, and innumerable flights of the albatross passed over the vessel. We also picked up a bush, full of red berries, like those of the hawthorn, and the carcass of a singular-looking land-animal. It was three feet in length, and but six inches in height, with four very short legs, the feet armed with long claws of a brilliant scarlet, and resembling coral in substance. The body was covered with a straight silky hair, perfectly white. The tail was peaked like that of a rat, and about a foot and a half long. The head resembled a cat's, with the exception of the ears—these were flopped like the ears of a dog. The *teeth* were of the same brilliant scarlet as the claws.

January 19.—To-day, being in latitude 83° 20', longitude 43° 5' W. (the sea being of an extraordinarily dark color), we again saw land from the masthead, and, upon a closer scrutiny, found it to be one of a group of very large islands. The shore was precipitous, and the interior seemed to be well wooded, a circumstance which occasioned us great joy. In about four hours from our first discovering the land we came

1 The terms *morning* and *evening*, which I have made use of to avoid confusion in my narrative, as far as possible, must not, of course, be taken in their ordinary sense. For a long time past we had had no night at all, the daylight being continual. The dates throughout are according to nautical time, and the bearings must be understood asper compass. I would also remark in this place, that I cannot, in the first portion of what is here written, pretend to strict accuracy in respect to dates, or latitudes and longitudes, having kept no regular journal until after the period of which this first portion treats. In many instances I have relied altogether upon memory.

to anchor in ten fathoms, sandy bottom, a league from the coast, as a high surf, with strong ripples here and there, rendered a nearer approach of doubtful expediency. The two largest boats were now ordered out, and a party, well armed (among whom were Peters and myself), proceeded to look for an opening in the reef which appeared to encircle the island. After searching about for some time, we discovered an inlet, which we were entering, when we saw four large canoes put off from the shore, filled with men who seemed to be well armed. We waited for them to come up, and, as they moved with great rapidity, they were soon within hail. Captain Guy now held up a white handkerchief on the blade of an oar, when the strangers made a full stop, and commenced a loud jabbering all at once, intermingled with occasional shouts, in which we could distinguish the words *Anamoo-moo!* and *Lama-Lama!* They continued this for at least half an hour, during which we had a good opportunity of observing their appearance.

In the four canoes, which might have been fifty feet long and five broad, there were a hundred and ten savages in all. They were about the ordinary stature of Europeans, but of a more muscular and brawny frame. Their complexion a jet black, with thick and long woolly hair. They were clothed in skins of an unknown black animal, shaggy and silky, and made to fit the body with some degree of skill, the hair being inside, except where turned out about the neck, wrists, and ankles. Their arms consisted principally of clubs, of a dark, and apparently very heavy wood. Some spears, however, were observed among them, headed with flint, and a few slings. The bottoms of the canoes were full of black stones about the size of a large egg.

When they had concluded their harangue (for it was clear they intended their jabbering for such), one of them who seemed to be the chief stood up in the prow of his canoe, and made signs for us to bring our boats alongside of him. This hint we pretended not to understand, thinking it the wiser plan to maintain, if possible, the interval between us, as their number more than quadrupled our own. Finding this to be the case, the chief ordered the three other canoes to hold back, while he advanced toward us with his own. As soon as he came up with us he leaped on board the largest of our boats, and seated himself by the side of Captain Guy, pointing at the same time to the schooner, and repeating the word *Anamoo-moo!* and *Lama-Lama!*

We now put back to the vessel, the four canoes following at a little distance.

Upon getting alongside, the chief evinced symptoms of extreme surprise and delight, clapping his hands, slapping his thighs and breast, and laughing obstreperously. His followers behind joined in his merriment, and for some minutes the din was so excessive as to be absolutely deafening. Quiet being at length restored, Captain Guy ordered the boats to be hoisted up, as a necessary precaution, and gave the chief (whose name we soon found to be *Too-wit*) to understand that we could admit no more than twenty of his men on deck at one time. With this arrangement he appeared perfectly satisfied, and gave some directions to the canoes, when one of them approached, the rest remaining about fifty yards off. Twenty of the savages now got on board, and proceeded to ramble over every part of the deck, and scramble about among the rigging, making themselves much at home, and examining every article with great inquisitiveness.

It was quite evident that they had never before seen any of the white race—from whose complexion, indeed, they appeared to recoil. They believed the *Jane* to be a living creature, and seemed to be afraid of hurting it with the points of their spears, carefully turning them up. Our crew were much amused with the conduct of Too-wit in one instance. The cook was splitting some wood near the galley, and, by accident, struck his ax into the deck, making a gash of considerable depth. The chief immediately ran up, and pushing the cook on one side rather roughly, commenced a half whine, half howl, strongly indicative of sympathy in what he considered the sufferings of the schooner, patting and smoothing the gash with his hand, and washing it from a bucket of seawater which stood by. This was a degree of ignorance for which we were not prepared, and for my part I could not help thinking some of it affected.

When the visitors had satisfied, as well as they could, their curiosity in regard to our upper works, they were admitted below, when their amazement exceeded all bounds. Their astonishment now appeared to be far too deep for words, for they roamed about in silence, broken only by low ejaculations. The arms afforded them much food for speculation, and they were suffered to handle and examine them at leisure. I do not believe that they had the least suspicion of their actual use, but rather took them for idols, seeing the care we had of them, and the attention with which we watched their movements while handling them. At the great guns their wonder was redoubled. They approached them with every mark of the profoundest reverence and awe, but forbore to examine them minutely. There were two large mirrors in the cabin, and here was the acme of their amazement. Too-wit was the first to approach them, and he had got in the middle of the cabin, with his face to one and his back to the other, before he fairly perceived them. Upon raising his eyes and seeing his reflected self in the glass, I thought the savage would go mad; but, upon turning short round to make a retreat, and beholding himself a second time in the opposite direction, I was afraid he would expire upon the spot. No persuasion could prevail upon him to take another look; throwing himself upon the floor, with his face buried in his hands, he remained thus until we were obliged to drag him upon deck.

The whole of the savages were admitted on board in this manner, twenty at a time, Too-wit being suffered to remain during the entire period. We saw no disposition to thievery among them, nor did we miss a single article after their departure. Throughout the whole of their visit they evinced the most friendly manner. There were, however, some points in their demeanor which we found it impossible to understand; for example, we could not get them to approach several very harmless objects—such as the schooner's sails, an egg, an open book, or a pan of flour. We endeavored to ascertain if they had among them any articles which might be turned to account in the way of traffic, but found great difficulty in being comprehended. We made out, nevertheless, what greatly astonished us, that the islands abounded in the large tortoise of the Gallipagos, one of which we saw in the canoe of Too-wit. We saw also some *biche de mer* in the hands of one of the savages, who was greedily devouring it in its natural state. These anomalies—for they were such when considered in regard to the latitude—induced Captain Guy to wish for a thorough investigation of the country, in the hope of making a profitable speculation in his discovery. For my own part, anxious as I was to know something more of these islands, I was still more earnestly bent on prosecuting the voyage to the southward without delay. We had now fine weather, but there was no telling how long it would last; and being already in the eighty-fourth parallel, with an open sea before us, a current setting strongly to the southward, and the wind fair, I could not listen with any patience to a proposition of stopping longer than was absolutely necessary for the health of the crew and the taking on board a proper supply of fuel and fresh provisions. I represented to the captain that we might easily make this group on our return, and winter here in the event of being blocked up by the ice. He at length came into my views (for in some way, hardly known to myself, I had acquired much influence over him), and it was finally resolved that, even in the event of our finding *biche de mer*, we should only stay here a week to recruit, and then push on to the southward while we might. Accordingly we made every necessary preparation, and, under the guidance of Too-wit, got the *Jane* through the reef in safety, coming to anchor about a mile from the shore, in an excellent bay, completely landlocked, on the southeastern coast of the main island, and in ten fathoms of water, black sandy bottom. At the head of this bay there were three fine springs (we were told) of good water, and we saw abundance of wood in the vicinity. The four canoes followed us in, keeping, however, at a respectful distance. Too-wit himself remained on board, and, upon our dropping anchor, invited us to accompany him on shore, and visit his village in the interior. To this Captain Guy consented; and ten savages being left on board as hostages, a party of us, twelve in all, got in readiness to attend the chief. We took care to be well armed, yet without evincing any distrust. The schooner had her guns run out, her boarding-nettings up, and every other proper precaution was taken to guard against surprise. Directions were left with the chief mate to admit no person on board during our absence, and, in the event of our not appearing in twelve hours, to send the cutter, with a swivel, around the island in search of us.

At every step we took inland the conviction forced itself upon us that we were in a country differing essentially from any hitherto visited by civilized men. We saw nothing with which we had been formerly conversant. The trees resembled no growth of either the torrid, the temperate, of the northern frigid zones, and were altogether unlike those of the lower southern latitudes we had already traversed. The very rocks were novel in their mass, their color, and their stratification; and the streams themselves, utterly incredible as it may appear, had so little in common with those of other climates, that we were scrupulous of tasting them, and, indeed, had difficulty in bringing ourselves to believe that their qualities were purely those of nature. At a small brook which crossed our path (the first we had reached) Too-wit and his attendants halted to drink. On account of the singular character of the water, we refused to taste it, supposing it to be polluted; and it was not until some time afterward we came to understand that such was the appearance of the streams throughout the whole group. I am at a loss to give a distinct idea of the nature of this liquid, and cannot do so without many words. Although it flowed with rapidity in all declivities where common water would do so, yet never, except when falling in a cascade, had it the customary appearance of *limpidity*. It was, nevertheless, in point of fact, as perfectly limpid as any limestone water in existence, the difference being only in appearance. At first sight, and especially in cases where little declivity was found, it bore resemblance, as regards consistency, to a thick infusion of gum arabic in common water. But this was only the least remarkable of its extraordinary qualities. It was *not* colorless, nor was it of any one uniform color—presenting to the eye, as it flowed, every possible shade of purple; like the hues of a changeable silk. This variation in shade was produced in a manner which excited as profound astonishment in the minds of our party as the mirror had done in the case of Too-wit. Upon collecting a basinful, and allowing it to settle thoroughly, we perceived that the whole mass of liquid was made up of a number of distinct veins, each of a distinct hue; that these veins did not commingle; and that their cohesion was perfect in regard to their own particles among themselves, and imperfect in regard to neighboring veins. Upon passing the blade of a knife athwart the veins, the water closed over it immediately, as with us, and also, in withdrawing it, all traces of the passage of the knife were instantly obliterated. If, however, the blade was passed down accurately between the two veins, a perfect separation was effected, which the power of cohesion did not immediately rectify. The phenomena of this water formed the first definite link in that vast chain of apparent miracles with which I was destined to be at length encircled.

CHAPTER 19

WE WERE NEARLY three hours in reaching the village, it being more than nine miles in the interior, and the path lying through a rugged country. As we passed along, the party of Too-wit (the whole hundred and ten savages of the canoes) was momentarily strengthened by smaller detachments, of from two to six or seven, which joined us, as if by accident, at different turns of the road. There appeared so much of system in this that I could not help feeling distrust, and I spoke to Captain Guy of my apprehensions. It was now too late, however, to recede, and we concluded that our best security lay in evincing a perfect confidence in the good faith of Too-wit. We accordingly went on, keeping a wary eye upon the maneuvers of the savages, and not permitting them to divide our numbers by pushing in between. In this way, passing through a precipitous ravine, we at length reached what we were told was the only collection of habitations upon the island. As we came in sight of them, the chief set up a shout, and frequently repeated the word *Klock-klock*, which we supposed to be the name of the village, or perhaps the generic name for villages.

The dwellings were of the most miserable description imaginable, and, unlike those of even the lowest of the savage races with which mankind are acquainted, were of no uniform plan. Some of them (and these we found belonged to the *Wampoos* or *Yampoos*, the great men of the land) consisted of a tree cut down at about four feet from the root, with a large black skin thrown over it, and hanging in loose folds upon the ground. Under this the savage nestled. Others were formed by means of rough limbs of trees, with the withered foliage upon them, made to recline, at an angle of forty-five degrees, against a bank of clay, heaped up, without regular form, to the height of five or six feet. Others, again, were mere holes dug in the earth perpendicularly, and covered over with similar branches, these being removed when the tenant was about to enter, and pulled on again when he had entered. A few were built among the forked limbs of trees as they stood, the upper limbs being partially cut through, so as to bend over upon the lower, thus forming thicker shelter from the weather. The greater number, however, consisted of small shallow caverns, apparently scratched in the face of a precipitous ledge of dark stone, resembling fuller's earth, with which three sides of the village were bounded. At the door of each of these primitive caverns was a small rock, which the tenant carefully placed before the entrance upon leaving his residence, for what purpose I could not ascertain, as the stone itself was never of sufficient size to close up more than a third of the opening.

This village, if it were worthy of the name, lay in a valley of some depth, and could only be approached from the southward, the precipitous ledge of which I have already spoken cutting off all access in other directions. Through the middle of the valley ran a brawling stream of the same magical-looking water which has been described. We saw several strange animals about the dwellings, all appearing to be thoroughly domesticated. The largest of these creatures resembled our common hog in the structure of the body and snout; the tail, however, was bushy, and the legs slender as those of the antelope. Its motion was exceedingly awkward and indecisive, and we never saw it attempt to run. We noticed also several animals very similar in appearance, but of a greater length of body, and covered with a black wool. There were a great variety of tame fowls running about, and these seemed to constitute the chief food of the natives. To our astonishment we saw black albatross among these birds in a state of entire domestication, going to sea periodically for food, but always returning to the village as a home, and using the southern shore in the vicinity as a place of incubation. There they were joined by their friends the pelicans as usual, but these latter never followed them to the dwellings of the savages. Among the other kinds of tame fowls were ducks, differing very little from the canvass-back of our own country, black gannets, and a large bird not unlike the buzzard in appearance, but not carnivorous. Of fish there seemed to be a great abundance. We saw, during our visit, a quantity of dried salmon, rock cod, blue dolphins, mackerel, blackfish, skate, conger eels, elephantfish, mullets, soles, parrot-fish, leather-jackets, gurnards, hake, flounders, paracutas, and innumerable other varieties. We noticed, too, that most of them were similar to the fish about the group of Lord Auckland Islands, in a latitude as low as 51° south. The Gallipago tortoise was also very plentiful. We saw but few wild animals, and none of a large size, or of a species with which we were familiar. One or two serpents of a formidable aspect crossed our path, but the natives paid them little attention, and we concluded that they were not venomous.

As we approached the village with Too-wit and his party, a vast crowd of the people rushed out to meet us, with loud shouts, among which we could only distinguish the everlasting *Anamoo-moo!* and *Lama-Lama!* We were much surprised at perceiving that, with one or two exceptions, these new comers were entirely naked, and skins being used only by the men of the canoes. All the weapons of the country seemed also to be in the possession of the latter, for there was no appearance of any among the villagers. There were a great many women and children, the former not altogether wanting in what might be termed personal beauty. They were straight, tall, and well formed, with a grace and freedom of carriage not to be found in civilized society. Their lips, however, like those of the men, were thick and clumsy, so that, even when laughing, the teeth were never disclosed. Their hair was of a finer texture than that of the males. Among these naked villagers there might have been ten or twelve who were clothed, like the party of Too-wit, in dresses of black skin, and armed with lances and heavy clubs. These appeared to have great influence among the rest, and were always addressed by the title *Wampoo*. These, too, were the tenants of the black skin palaces. That of Too-wit was situated in the center of the village, and was much larger and somewhat better constructed than others of its kind. The tree which formed its support was cut off at a distance of twelve feet or thereabouts from the root, and there were several branches left just below the cut, these serving to extend the covering, and in this way prevent its flapping about the trunk. The covering, too, which consisted of four very large skins fastened together with wooden skewers, was secured at the bottom with pegs driven through it and into the ground. The floor was strewed with a quantity of dry leaves by way of carpet.

To this hut we were conducted with great solemnity, and as many of the natives crowded in after us as possible. Too-wit seated himself on the leaves, and made signs that we should follow his example. This we did, and presently found ourselves in a situation peculiarly uncomfortable, if not indeed critical. We were on the ground, twelve in number, with the savages, as many as forty, sitting on their hams so closely around us that, if any disturbance had arisen, we should have found it impossible to make use of our arms, or indeed to have risen to our feet. The pressure was not only inside the tent, but outside, where probably was every individual on the whole island, the crowd being prevented from trampling us to death only by the incessant exertions and vociferations of Too-wit. Our chief security lay, however, in the presence of Too-wit himself among us, and we resolved to stick by him closely, as the best chance of extricating ourselves from the dilemma, sacrificing him immediately upon the first appearance of hostile design.

After some trouble a certain degree of quiet was restored, when the chief addressed us in a speech of great length, and very nearly resembling the one delivered in the canoes, with the exception that the *Anamoo-moos!* were now somewhat more strenuously insisted upon than the *Lama-Lamas!* We listened in profound silence until the conclusion of this harangue, when Captain Guy replied by assuring the chief of his eternal friendship and goodwill, concluding what he had to say be a present of several strings of blue beads and a knife. At the former the monarch, much to our surprise, turned up his nose with some expression of contempt, but the knife gave him the most unlimited satisfaction, and he immediately ordered dinner. This was handed into the tent over the heads of the attendants, and consisted of the palpitating entrails of a specials of unknown animal, probably one of the slim-legged hogs which we had observed in our approach to the village. Seeing us at a loss how to proceed, he began, by way of setting us an example, to devour yard after yard of the enticing food, until we could positively stand it no longer, and evinced such manifest symptoms of rebellion of stomach as inspired his majesty with a degree of astonishment only inferior to that brought about by the looking-glasses. We declined, however, partaking of the delicacies before us, and endeavored to make him understand that we had no appetite whatever, having just finished a hearty *déjeuner*.

When the monarch had made an end of his meal, we commenced a series of cross-questioning in every ingenious manner we could devise, with a view of discovering what were the chief productions of the country, and whether any of them might be turned to profit. At length he seemed to have some idea of our meaning, and offered to accompany us to a part of coast where he assured us the *biche de mer* (pointing to a specimen of that animal) was to be found in great abundance. We were glad of this early opportunity of escaping from the oppression of the crowd, and signified our eagerness to proceed. We now left the tent, and, accompanied by the whole population of the village, followed the chief to the southeastern extremity of the island, nor far from the bay where our vessel lay at anchor. We waited here for about an hour, until the four canoes were brought around by some of the savages to our station. the whole of our party then getting into one of them, we were paddled along the edge of the reef before mentioned, and of another still farther out, where we saw a far greater quantity of *biche de mer* than the oldest seamen among us had ever seen in those groups of the lower latitudes most celebrated for this article of commerce. We stayed near these reefs only long enough to satisfy ourselves that we could easily load a dozen vessels with the animal if necessary, when we were taken alongside the schooner, and parted with Too-wit, after obtaining from him a promise that he would bring us, in the course of twenty-four hours, as many of the canvass-back ducks and Gallipago tortoises as his canoes would hold. In the whole of this adventure we saw nothing in the demeanor of the natives calculated to create suspicion, with the single exception of the systematic manner in which their party was strengthened during our route from the schooner to the village.

CHAPTER 20

THE CHIEF WAS as good as his word, and we were soon plentifully supplied with fresh provisions. We found the tortoises as fine as we had ever seen, and the ducks surpassed our best species of wild fowl, being exceedingly tender, juicy, and well-flavored. Besides these, the savages brought us, upon our making them comprehend our wishes, a vast quantity of brown celery and scurvy grass, with a canoe-load of fresh fish and some dried. The celery was a treat indeed, and the scurvy grass proved of incalculable benefit in restoring those of our men who had shown symptoms of disease. In a very short time we had not a single person on the sick-list. We had also plenty of other kinds of fresh provisions, among which may be mentioned a species of shellfish resembling the mussel in shape, but with the taste of an oyster. Shrimps, too, and prawns were abundant, and albatross and other birds' eggs with dark shells. We took in, too, a plentiful stock of the flesh of the hog which I have mentioned before. Most of the men found it a palatable food, but I thought it fishy and otherwise disagreeable. In return for these good things we presented the natives with blue beads, brass trinkets, nails, knives, and pieces of red cloth, they being fully delighted in the exchange. We established a regular market on shore, just under the guns of the schooner, where our barterings were carried on with every appearance of good faith, and a degree of order which their conduct at the village of *Klock-klock* had not led us to expect from the savages.

Matters went on thus very amicably for several days, during which parties of the natives were frequently on board the schooner, and parties of our men frequently on shore, making long excursions into the interior, and receiving no molestation whatever. Finding the ease with which the vessel might be loaded with *biche de mer*, owing to the friendly disposition of the islanders, and the readiness with which they would render us assistance in collecting it, Captain Guy resolved to enter into negotiations with Too-wit for the erection of suitable houses in which to cure the article, and for the services of himself and tribe in gathering as much as possible, while he himself took advantage of the fine weather to prosecute his voyage to the southward. Upon mentioning this project to the chief he seemed very willing to enter into an agreement. A bargain was accordingly struck, perfectly satisfactory to both parties, by which it was arranged that, after making the necessary preparations, such as laying off the proper grounds, erecting a portion of the buildings, and doing some other work in which the whole of our crew would be required, the schooner should proceed on her route, leaving three of her men on the island to superintend the fulfillment of the project, and instruct the natives in drying the *biche de mer*. In regard to terms, these were made to depend upon the exertions of the savages in our absence. They were to receive a stipulated quantity of blue beads, knives, red cloth, and so forth, for every certain number of piculs of the *biche de mer* which should be ready on our return.

A description of the nature of this important article of commerce, and the method of preparing it, may prove of some interest to my readers, and I can find no more suitable place than this for introducing an account of it. The following comprehensive notice of the substance is taken from a modern history of a voyage to the South Seas.

"It is that *mollusca* from the Indian Seas which is known to commerce by the French name *bouche de mer* (a nice morsel from the sea). If I am not much mistaken, the celebrated Cuvier calls it *gasteropeda pulmonifera*. It is abundantly gathered in the coasts of the Pacific islands, and gathered especially for the Chinese market, where it commands a great price, perhaps as much as their much-talked-of edible birds' nests, which are properly made up of the gelatinous matter picked up by a species of swallow from the body of these molluscae. They have no shell, no legs, nor any prominent part, except an *absorbing* and an *excretory*, opposite organs; but, by their elastic wings, like caterpillars or worms, they creep in shallow waters, in which, when low, they can be seen by a kind of swallow, the sharp bill of which, inserted in the soft animal, draws a gummy and filamentous substance, which, by drying, can be wrought into the solid walls of their nest. Hence the name of *gasteropeda pulmonifera*.

"This *mollusca* is oblong, and of different sizes, from three to eighteen inches in length; and I have seen a few that were not less than two feet long. They were nearly round, a little flattish on one side, which lies next to the bottom of the sea; and they are from one to eight inches thick. They crawl up into shallow water at particular seasons of the year, probably for the purpose of gendering, as we often find them in pairs. It is when the sun has the most power on the water, rendering it tepid, that they approach the shore; and they often go up into places so shallow that, on the tide's receding, they are left dry, exposed to the beat of the sun. But they do not bring forth their young in shallow water, as we never see any of their progeny, and full-grown ones are always observed coming in from deep water. They feed principally on that class of zoophytes which produce the coral.

"The *biche de mer* is generally taken in three or four feet of water; after which they are brought on shore, and split at one end with a knife, the incision being one inch or more, according to the size of the *mollusca*. Through this opening the entrails are forced out by pressure, and they are much like those of any other small tenant of the deep. The article is then washed, and afterward boiled to a certain degree, which must not be too much or too little. They are then buried in the ground for four hours, then boiled again for a short time, after which they are dried, either by the fire or the sun. Those cured by the sun are worth the most; but where one picul (133 1/3 lbs.) can be cured that way, I can cure thirty piculs by the fire. When once properly cured, they can be kept in a dry place for two or three years without any risk; but they should be examined once in every few months, say four times a year, to see if any dampness is likely to affect them.

"The Chinese, as before stated, consider *biche de mer* a very great luxury, believing that it wonderfully strengthens and nourishes the system, and renews the exhausted system of the immoderate voluptuary. The first quality commands a high price in Canton, being worth ninety dollars a picul; the second quality, seventy-five dollars; the third, fifty dollars; the fourth, thirty dollars; the fifth, twenty dollars; the sixth, twelve dollars; the seventh, eight dollars; and the eighth, four dollars; small cargoes, however, will often bring more in Manilla, Singapore, and Batavia."

An agreement having been thus entered into, we proceeded immediately to land everything necessary for preparing the buildings and clearing the ground. A large flat space near the eastern shore of the bay was selected, where there was plenty of both wood and water, and within a convenient distance of the principal reefs on which the *biche de mer* was to be procured. We now all set to work in good earnest, and soon, to the great astonishment of the savages, had felled a sufficient number of trees for our purpose, getting them quickly in order for the framework of the houses, which in two or three days were so far under way that we could safely trust the rest of the work to the three men whom we intended to leave behind. These were John Carson, Alfred Harris, and Peterson (all natives of London, I believe), who volunteered their services in this respect.

By the last of the month we had everything in readiness for departure. We had agreed, however, to pay a formal visit of leave-taking to the village, and Too-Wit insisted so pertinaciously upon our keeping the promise that we did not think it advisable to run the risk of offending him by a final refusal. I believe that not one of us had at this time the slightest suspicion of the good faith of the savages. They had uniformly behaved with the greatest decorum, aiding us with alacrity in our work, offering us their commodities, frequently without price, and never, in any instance, pilfering a single article, although the high value they set upon the goods we had with us was evident by the extravagant demonstrations of joy always manifested upon our making them a present. The women especially were most obliging in every respect, and, upon the whole, we should have been the most suspicious of human beings had we entertained a single thought of perfidy on the part of a people who treated us so well. A very short while sufficed to prove that this apparent kindness of disposition was only the result of a deeply laid plan for our destruction, and that the islanders for whom we entertained such inordinate feelings of esteem, were among the most barbarous, subtle, and bloodthirsty wretches that ever contaminated the face of the globe.

It was on the first of February that we went on shore for the purpose of visiting the village. Although, as said before, we entertained not the slightest suspicion, still no proper precaution was neglected. Six men were left in the schooner, with instructions to permit none of the savages to approach the vessel during our absence, under any pretence whatever, and to remain constantly on deck. The boarding-nettings were up, the guns double-shotted with grape and canister, and the swivels loaded with canisters of musket-balls. She lay, with her anchor apeak, about a mile from the shore, and no canoe could approach her in any direction without being distinctly seen and exposed to the full fire of our swivels immediately.

The six men being left on board, our shore-party consisted of thirty-two persons in all. We were armed to the teeth, having with us muskets, pistols, and cutlasses; besides, each had a long kind of seaman's knife, somewhat resembling the bowie knife now so much used throughout our western and southern country. A hundred of the black skin warriors met us at the landing for the purpose of accompanying us on our way. We noticed, however, with some surprise, that they were now entirely without arms; and, upon questioning Too-wit in relation to this circumstance, he merely answered that *Mattee non we pa pa si*—meaning that there was no need of arms where all were brothers. We took this in good part, and proceeded.

We had passed the spring and rivulet of which I before spoke, and were now entering upon a narrow gorge leading through the chain of soapstone hills among which the village was situated. This gorge was very rocky and uneven, so much so that it was with no little difficulty we scrambled through it on our first visit to Klock-klock. The whole length of the ravine might have been a mile and a half, or probably two miles. It wound in every possible direction through the hills (having apparently formed, at some remote period, the bed of a torrent), in no instance proceeding more than twenty yards without an abrupt turn. The sides of this dell would have averaged, I am sure, seventy or eighty feet in perpendicular altitude throughout the whole of their extent, and in some portions they arose to an astonishing height, overshadowing the pass so completely that but little of the light of day could penetrate. The general width was about forty feet, and occasionally it diminished so as not to allow the passage of more than five or six persons abreast. In short, there could be no place in the world better adapted for the consummation of an ambuscade, and it was no more than natural that we should look carefully to our arms as we entered upon it. When I now think of our egregious folly, the chief subject of astonishment seems to be, that we should have ever ventured, under any circumstances, so completely into the power of unknown savages as to permit them to march both before and behind us in our progress through this ravine. Yet such was the order we blindly took up, trusting foolishly to the force of our party, the unarmed condition of Too-wit and his men, the certain efficacy of our firearms (whose effect was yet a secret to the natives), and, more than all, to the long-sustained pretension of friendship kept up by these infamous wretches. Five or six of them went on before, as if to lead the way, ostentatiously busying themselves in removing the larger stones and rubbish from the path. Next came our own party. We walked closely together, taking care only to prevent separation. Behind followed the main body of the savages, observing unusual order and decorum.

Dirk Peters, a man named Wilson Allen, and myself were on the right of our companions, examining, as we went along, the singular stratification of the precipice which overhung us. A fissure in the soft rock attracted our attention. It was about wide enough for one person to enter without squeezing, and extended back into the hill some eighteen or twenty feet in a straight course, sloping afterward to the left. The height of the opening, is far as we could see into it from the main gorge, was perhaps sixty or seventy feet. There were one or two stunted shrubs growing from the crevices, bearing a species of filbert which I felt some curiosity to examine, and pushed in briskly for that purpose, gathering five or six of the nuts at a grasp, and then hastily retreating. As I turned, I found that Peters and Allen had followed me. I desired them to go back, as there was not room for two persons to pass, saying they should have some of my nuts. They accordingly turned, and were scrambling back, Allen being close to the mouth of the fissure, when I was suddenly aware of a concussion resembling nothing I had ever before experienced, and which impressed me with a vague conception, if indeed I then thought of anything, that the whole foundations of the solid globe were suddenly rent asunder, and that the day of universal dissolution was at hand.

CHAPTER 21

AS SOON AS I could collect my scattered senses, I found myself nearly suffocated, and grovelling in utter darkness among a quantity of loose earth, which was also falling upon me heavily in every direction, threatening to bury me entirely. Horribly alarmed at this idea, I struggled to gain my feet, and at last succeeded. I then remained motionless for some moments, endeavoring to conceive what had happened to me, and where I was. Presently I heard a deep groan just at my ear, and afterward the smothered voice of Peters calling to me for aid in the name of God. I scrambled one or two paces forward, when I fell directly over the head and shoulders of my companion, who, I soon discovered, was buried in a loose mass of earth as far as his middle, and struggling desperately to free himself from the pressure. I tore the dirt from around him with all the energy I could command, and at length succeeded in getting him out.

As soon as we sufficiently recovered from our fright and surprise to be capable of conversing rationally, we both came to the conclusion that the walls of the fissure in which we had ventured had, by some convulsion of nature, or probably from their own weight, caved in overhead, and that we were consequently lost for ever, being thus entombed alive. For a long time we gave up supinely to the most intense agony and despair, such as cannot be adequately imagined by those who have never been in a similar position. I firmly believed that no incident ever occurring in the course of human events is more adapted to inspire the supremeness of mental and bodily distress than a case like our own, of living inhumation. The blackness of darkness which envelops the victim, the terrific oppression of lungs, the stifling fumes from the damp earth, unite with the ghastly considerations that we are beyond the remotest confines of hope, and that such is the allotted portion of *the dead*, to carry into the human heart a degree of appalling awe and horror not to be tolerated—never to be conceived.

At length Peters proposed that we should endeavor to ascertain precisely the extent of our calamity, and grope about our prison; it being barely possible, he observed, that some opening might yet be left us for escape. I caught eagerly at this hope, and, arousing myself to exertion, attempted to force my way through the loose earth. Hardly had I advanced a single step before a glimmer of light became perceptible, enough to convince me that, at all events, we should not immediately perish for want of air. We now took some degree of heart, and encouraged each other to hope for the best. Having scrambled over a bank of rubbish which impeded our farther progress in the direction of the light, we found less difficulty in advancing and also experienced some relief from the excessive oppression of lungs which had tormented us. Presently we were enabled to obtain a glimpse of the objects around, and discovered that we were near the extremity of the straight portion of the fissure, where it made a turn to the left. A few struggles more, and we reached the bend, when to our inexpressible joy, there appeared a long seam or crack extending upward a vast distance, generally at an angle of about forty-five degrees, although sometimes much more precipitous. We could not see through the whole extent of this opening; but, as a good deal of light came down it, we had little doubt of finding at the top of it (if we could by any means reach the top) a clear passage into the open air.

I now called to mind that three of us had entered the fissure from the main gorge, and that our companion, Allen, was still missing; we determined at once to retrace our steps and look for him. After a long search, and much danger from the farther caving in of the earth above us, Peters at length cried out to me that he had hold of our companion's foot, and that his whole body was deeply buried beneath the rubbish beyond the possibility of extricating him. I soon found that what he said was too true, and that, of course, life had been long extinct. With sorrowful hearts, therefore, we left the corpse to its fate, and again made our way to the bend.

The breadth of the seam was barely sufficient to admit us, and, after one or two ineffectual efforts at getting up, we began once more to despair. I have before said that the chain of hills through which ran the main gorge was composed of a species of soft rock resembling soap. stone. The sides of the cleft we were now attempting to ascend were of the same material, and so excessively slippery, being wet, that we could get but little foothold upon them even in their least precipitous parts; in some places, where the ascent was nearly perpendicular, the difficulty was, of course, much aggravated; and, indeed, for some time we thought insurmountable. We took courage, however, from despair, and what, by dint of cutting steps in the soft stone with our bowie knives, and swinging at the risk of our lives, to small projecting points of a harder species of slaty rock which now and then protruded from the general mass, we at length reached a natural platform, from which was perceptible a patch of blue sky, at the extremity of a thickly-wooded ravine. Looking back now, with somewhat more leisure, at the passage through which we had thus far proceeded, we clearly saw from the appearance of its sides, that it was of late formation, and we concluded that the concussion, whatever it was, which had so unexpectedly overwhelmed us, had also, at the same moment, laid open this path for escape. Being quite exhausted with exertion, and indeed, so weak that we were scarcely able to stand or articulate, Peters now proposed that we should endeavor to bring our companions to the rescue by firing the pistols which still remained in our girdles—the muskets as well as cutlasses had been lost among the loose earth at the bottom of the chasm. Subsequent events proved that, had we fired, we should have sorely repented it, but luckily a half suspicion of foul play had by this time arisen in my mind, and we forbore to let the savages know of our whereabouts.

After having reposed for about an hour, we pushed on slowly up the ravine, and had gone no great way before we heard a succession of tremendous yells. At length we reached what might be called the surface of the ground; for our path hitherto, since leaving the platform, had lain beneath an archway of high rock and foliage, at a vast distance overhead. With great caution we stole to a narrow opening, through which we had a clear sight of the surrounding country, when the whole dreadful secret of the concussion broke upon us in one moment and at one view.

The spot from which we looked was not far from the summit of the highest peak in the range of the soapstone hills. The gorge in which our party of thirty-two had entered ran within fifty feet to the left of us. But, for at least one hundred yards, the channel or bed of this gorge was entirely filled up with the chaotic ruins of more than a million tons of earth and stone that had been artificially tumbled within it. The means by which the vast mass had been precipitated were not more simple than evident, for sure traces of the murderous work were yet remaining. In several spots along the top of the eastern side of the gorge (we were now on the western) might be seen stakes of wood driven into the earth. In these spots the earth had not given way, but throughout the whole extent of the face of the precipice from which the mass *had* fallen, it was clear, from marks left in the soil resembling those made by the drill of the rock blaster, that stakes similar to those we saw standing had been inserted, at not more than a yard apart, for the length of perhaps three hundred feet, and ranging at about ten feet back from the edge of the gulf. Strong cords of grape vine were attached to the stakes still remaining on the hill, and it was evident that such cords had also been attached to each of the other stakes. I have already spoken of the singular stratification of these soapstone hills; and the description just given of the narrow and deep fissure through which we effected our escape from inhumation will afford a further conception of its nature. This was such that almost every natural convulsion would be sure to split the soil into perpendicular layers or ridges running parallel with one another, and a very moderate exertion of art would be sufficient for effecting the same purpose. Of this stratification the savages had availed themselves to accomplish their treacherous ends. There can be no doubt that, by the continuous line of stakes, a partial rupture of the soil had been brought about probably to the depth of one or two feet, when by means of a savage pulling at the end of each of the cords (these cords being attached to the tops of the stakes, and extending back from the edge of the cliff), a vast leverage power was obtained, capable of hurling the whole face of the hill, upon a given signal, into the bosom of the abyss below. The fate of our poor companions was no longer a matter of uncertainty. We alone had escaped from the tempest of that overwhelming destruction. We were the only living white men upon the island.

CHAPTER 22

OUR SITUATION, AS it now appeared, was scarcely less dreadful than when we had conceived ourselves entombed forever. We saw before us no prospect but that of being put to death by the savages, or of dragging out a miserable existence in captivity among them. We might, to be sure, conceal ourselves for a time from their observation among the fastnesses of the hills, and, as a final resort, in the chasm from which we had just issued; but we must either perish in the long polar winter through cold and famine, or be ultimately discovered in our efforts to obtain relief.

The whole country around us seemed to be swarming with savages, crowds of whom, we now perceived, had come over from the islands to the southward on flat rafts, doubtless with a view of lending their aid in the capture and plunder of the *Jane*. The vessel still lay calmly at anchor in the bay, those on board being apparently quite unconscious of any danger awaiting them. How we longed at that moment to be with them! either to aid in effecting their escape, or to perish with them in attempting a defense. We saw no chance even of warning them of their danger without bringing immediate destruction upon our own heads, with but a remote hope of benefit to them. A pistol fired might suffice to apprise them that something wrong had occurred; but the report could not possibly inform them that their only prospect of safety lay in getting out of the harbour forthwith—nor tell them no principles of honor now bound them to remain, that their companions were no longer among the living. Upon hearing the discharge they could not be more thoroughly prepared to meet the foe, who were now getting ready to attack, than they already were, and always had been. No good, therefore, and infinite harm, would result from our firing, and after mature deliberation, we forbore.

Our next thought was to attempt to rush toward the vessel, to seize one of the four canoes which lay at the head of the bay, and endeavor to force a passage on board. But the utter impossibility of succeeding in this desperate task soon became evident. The country, as I said before, was literally swarming with the natives, skulking among the bushes and recesses of the hills, so as not to be observed from the schooner. In our immediate vicinity especially, and blockading the sole path by which we could hope to attain the shore at the proper point were stationed the whole party of the black skin warriors, with Too-wit at their head, and apparently only waiting for some re-enforcement to commence his onset upon the *Jane*. The canoes, too, which lay at the head of the bay, were manned with savages, unarmed, it is true, but who undoubtedly had arms within reach. We were forced, therefore, however unwillingly, to remain in our place of concealment, mere spectators of the conflict which presently ensued.

In about half an hour we saw some sixty or seventy rafts, or flatboats, with outriggers, filled with savages, and coming round the southern bight of the harbor. They appeared to have no arms except short clubs, and stones which lay in the bottom of the rafts. Immediately afterward another detachment, still larger, appeared in an opposite direction, and with similar weapons. The four canoes, too, were now quickly filled with natives, starting up from the bushes at the head of the bay, and put off swiftly to join the other parties. Thus, in less time than I have taken to tell it, and as if by magic, the *Jane* saw herself surrounded by an immense multitude of desperadoes evidently bent upon capturing her at all hazards.

That they would succeed in so doing could not be doubted for an instant. The six men left in the vessel, however resolutely they might engage in her defense, were altogether unequal to the proper management of the guns, or in any manner to sustain a contest at such odds. I could hardly imagine that they would make resistance at all, but in this was deceived; for presently I saw them get springs upon the cable, and bring the vessel's starboard broadside to bear upon the canoes, which by this time were within pistol range, the rafts being nearly a quarter of a mile to windward. Owing to some cause unknown, but most probably to the agitation of our poor friends at seeing themselves in so hopeless a situation, the discharge was an entire failure. Not a canoe was hit or a single savage injured, the shots striking short and *ricochêting* over their heads. The only effect produced upon them was astonishment at the unexpected report and smoke, which was so excessive that for some moments I almost thought they would abandon their design entirely, and return to the shore. And this they would most likely have done had our men followed up their broadside by a discharge of small arms, in which, as the canoes were now so near at hand, they could not have failed in doing some execution, sufficient, at least, to deter this party from a farther advance, until they could have given the rafts also a broadside. But, in place of this, they left the canoe party to recover from their panic, and, by looking about them, to see that no injury had been sustained, while they flew to the larboard to get ready for the rafts.

The discharge to larboard produced the most terrible effect. The star and double-headed shot of the large guns cut seven or eight of the rafts completely asunder, and killed, perhaps, thirty or forty of the savages outright, while a hundred of them, at least, were thrown into the water, the most of them dreadfully wounded. The remainder, frightened out of their senses, commenced at once a precipitate retreat, not even waiting to pick up their maimed companions, who were swimming about in every direction, screaming and yelling for aid. This great success, however, came too late for the salvation of our devoted people. The canoe party were already on board the schooner to the number of more than a hundred and fifty, the most of them having succeeded in scrambling up the chains and over the boarding-netting even before the matches had been applied to the larboard guns. Nothing now could withstand their brute rage. Our men were borne down at once, overwhelmed, trodden under foot, and absolutely torn to pieces in an instant.

Seeing this, the savages on the rafts got the better of their fears, and came up in shoals to the plunder. In five minutes the *Jane* was a pitiable scene indeed of havoc and tumultuous outrage. The decks were split open and ripped up; the cordage, sails, and everything movable on deck demolished as if by magic, while, by dint of pushing at the stern, towing with the canoes, and hauling at the sides, as they swam in thousands around the vessel, the wretches finally forced her on shore (the cable having been slipped), and delivered her over to the good offices of Too-wit, who, during the whole of the engagement, had maintained, like a skillful general, his post of security and reconnaissance among the hills, but, now that the victory was completed to his satisfaction, condescended to scamper down with his warriors of the black skin, and become a partaker in the spoils.

Too-wit's descent left us at liberty to quit our hiding place and reconnoitre the hill in the vicinity of the chasm. At about fifty yards from the mouth of it we saw a small spring of water, at which we slaked the burning thirst that now consumed us. Not far from the spring we discovered several of the filbert-bushes which I mentioned before. Upon tasting the nuts we found them palatable, and very nearly resembling in flavor the common English filbert. We collected our hats full immediately, deposited them within the ravine, and returned for more. While we were busily employed in gathering these, a rustling in the bushes alarmed us, and we were upon the point of stealing back to our covert, when a large black bird of the bittern species strugglingly and slowly arose above the shrubs. I was so much startled that I could do nothing, but Peters had sufficient presence of mind to run up to it before it could make its escape, and seize it by the neck. Its struggles and screams were tremendous, and we had thoughts of letting it go, lest the noise should alarm some of the savages who might be still lurking in the neighborhood. A stab with a bowie knife, however, at length brought it to the ground, and we dragged it into the ravine, congratulating ourselves that, at all events, we had thus obtained a supply of food enough to last us for a week.

We now went out again to look about us, and ventured a considerable distance down the southern declivity of the hill, but met with nothing else which could serve us for food. We therefore collected a quantity of dry wood and returned, seeing one or two large parties of the natives on their way to the village, laden with the plunder of the vessel, and who, we were apprehensive, might discover us in passing beneath the hill.

Our next care was to render our place of concealment as secure as possible, and with this object, we arranged some brushwood over the aperture which I have before spoken of as the one through which we saw the patch of blue sky, on reaching the platform from the interior of the chasm. We left only a very small opening just wide enough to admit of our seeing the, bay, without the risk of being discovered from below. Having done this, we congratulated ourselves upon the security of the position; for we were now completely excluded from observation, as long as we chose to remain within the ravine itself, and not venture out upon the hill, We could perceive no traces of the savages having ever been within this hollow; but, indeed, when we came to reflect upon the probability that the fissure through which we attained it had been only just now created by the fall of the cliff opposite, and that no other way of attaining it could be perceived, we were not so much rejoiced at the thought of being secure from molestation as fearful lest there should be absolutely no means left us for descent. We resolved to explore the summit of the hill thoroughly, when a good opportunity should offer. In the meantime we watched the motions of the savages through our loophole.

They had already made a complete wreck of the vessel, and were now preparing to set her on fire. In a little while we saw the smoke ascending in huge volumes from her main hatchway, and, shortly afterward, a dense mass of flame burst up from the forecastle. The rigging, masts and what remained of the sails caught immediately, and the fire spread rapidly along the decks. Still a great many of the savages retained their stations about her, hammering with large stones, axes, and cannon balls at the bolts and other iron and copper work. On the beach, and in canoes and rafts, there were not less, altogether, in the immediate vicinity of the schooner, than ten thousand natives, besides the shoals of them who, laden with booty, were making their way inland and over to the neighboring islands. We now anticipated a catastrophe, and were not disappointed. First of all there came a smart shock (which we felt as distinctly where we were as if we had been slightly galvanized), but unattended with any visible signs of an explosion. The savages were evidently startled, and paused for an instant from their labors and yellings. They were upon the point of recommencing, when suddenly a mass of smoke puffed up from the decks, resembling a black and heavy thundercloud—then, as if from its bowels, arose a tall stream of vivid fire to the height, apparently, of a quarter of a mile—then there came a sudden circular expansion of the flame—then the whole atmosphere was magically crowded, in a single instant, with a wild chaos of wood, and metal, and human limbs—and, lastly, came the concussion in its fullest fury, which hurled us impetuously from our feet, while the hills echoed and re-echoed the tumult, and a dense shower of the minutest fragments of the ruins tumbled headlong in every direction around us.

The havoc among the savages far exceeded our utmost expectation, and they had now, indeed, reaped the full and perfect fruits of their treachery. Perhaps a thousand perished by the explosion, while at least an equal number were desperately mangled. The whole surface of the bay was literally strewn with the struggling and drowning wretches, and on shore matters were even worse. They seemed utterly appalled by the suddenness and completeness of their discomfiture, and made no efforts at assisting one another. At length we observed a total change in their demeanor. From absolute stupor, they appeared to be, all at once, aroused to the highest pitch of excitement, and rushed wildly about, going to and from a certain point on the beach, with the strangest expressions of mingled horror, rage, and intense curiosity depicted on their countenances, and shouting, at the top of their voices, "*Tekeli-li! Tekeli-li!*"

Presently we saw a large body go off into the hills, whence they returned in a short time, carrying stakes of wood. These they brought to the station where the crowd was the thickest, which now separated so as to afford us a view of the object of all this excitement. We perceived something white lying upon the ground, but could not immediately make out what it was. At length we saw that it was the carcass of the strange animal with the scarlet teeth and claws which the schooner had picked up at sea on the eighteenth of January. Captain Guy had had the body preserved for the purpose of stuffing the skin and taking it to England. I remember he had given some directions about it just before our making the island, and it had been brought into the cabin and stowed away in one of the lockers. It had now been thrown on shore by the explosion; but why it had occasioned so much concern among the savages was more than we could comprehend. Although they crowded around the carcass at a little distance, none of them seemed willing to approach it closely. By-and-by the men with the stakes drove them in a circle around it, and no sooner was this arrangement completed, than the whole of the vast assemblage rushed into the interior of the island, with loud screams of "*Tekeli-li! Tekeli-li!*"

CHAPTER 23

DURING THE SIX or seven days immediately following we remained in our hiding-place upon the hill, going out only occasionally, and then with the greatest precaution, for water and filberts. We had made a kind of penthouse on the platform, furnishing it with a bed of dry leaves, and placing in it three large flat stones, which served us for both fireplace and table. We kindled a fire without difficulty by rubbing two pieces of dry wood together, the one soft, the other hard. The bird we had taken in such good season proved excellent eating, although somewhat tough. It was not an oceanic fowl, but a species of bittern, with jet black and grizzly plumage, and diminutive wings in proportion to its bulk. We afterward saw three of the same kind in the vicinity of the ravine, apparently seeking for the one we had captured; but, as they never alighted, we had no opportunity of catching them.

As long as this fowl lasted we suffered nothing from our situation, but it was now entirely consumed, and it became absolutely necessary that we should look out for provision. The filberts would not satisfy the cravings of hunger, afflicting us, too, with severe gripings of the bowels, and, if freely indulged in, with violent headache. We had seen several large tortoises near the seashore to the eastward of the hill, and perceived they might be easily taken, if we could get at them without the observation of the natives. It was resolved, therefore, to make an attempt at descending.

We commenced by going down the southern declivity, which seemed to offer the fewest difficulties, but had not proceeded a hundred yards before (as we had anticipated from appearances on the hilltop) our progress was entirely arrested by a branch of the gorge in which our companions had perished. We now passed along the edge of this for about a quarter of a mile, when we were again stopped by a precipice of immense depth, and, not being able to make our way along the brink of it, we were forced to retrace our steps by the main ravine.

We now pushed over to the eastward, but with precisely similar fortune. After an hour's scramble, at the risk of breaking our necks, we discovered that we had merely descended into a vast pit of black granite, with fine dust at the bottom, and whence the only egress was by the rugged path in which we had come down. Toiling again up this path, we now tried the northern edge of the hill. Here we were obliged to use the greatest possible caution in our maneuvers, as the least indiscretion would expose us to the full view of the savages in the village. We crawled along, therefore, on our hands and knees, and, occasionally, were even forced to throw ourselves at full length, dragging our bodies along by means of the shrubbery. In this careful manner we had proceeded but a little way, when we arrived at a chasm far deeper than any we had yet seen, and leading directly into the main gorge. Thus our fears were fully confirmed, and we found ourselves cut off entirely from access to the world below. Thoroughly exhausted by our exertions, we made the best of our way back to the platform, and throwing ourselves upon the bed of leaves, slept sweetly and soundly for some hours.

For several days after this fruitless search we were occupied in exploring every part of the summit of the hill, in order to inform ourselves of its actual resources. We found that it would afford us no food, with the exception of the unwholesome filberts, and a rank species of scurvy grass, which grew in a little patch of not more than four rods square, and would be soon exhausted. On the fifteenth of February, as near as I can remember, there was not a blade of this left, and the nuts were growing scarce; our situation, therefore, could hardly be more lamentable.[1] On the sixteenth we again went round the walls of our prison, in hope of finding some avenue of escape; but to no purpose. We also descended the chasm in which we had been overwhelmed, with the faint expectation of discovering, through this channel, some opening to the main ravine. Here, too, we were disappointed, although we found and brought up with us a musket.

On the seventeenth we set out with the determination of examining more thoroughly the chasm of black granite into which we had made our way in the first search. We remembered that one of the fissures in the sides of this pit had been but partially looked into, and we were anxious to explore it, although with no expectation of discovering here any opening.

We found no great difficulty in reaching the bottom of the hollow

1 This day was rendered remarkable by our observing in the south several huge wreaths of the grayish vapor I have spoken of.

as before, and were now sufficiently calm to survey it with some attention. It was, indeed, one of the most singular-looking places imaginable, and we could scarcely bring ourselves to believe it altogether the work of nature. The pit, from its eastern to its western extremity, was about five hundred yards in length, when all its windings were threaded; the distance from east to west in a straight line not being more (I should suppose, having no means of accurate examination) than forty or fifty yards. Upon first descending into the chasm, that is to say, for a hundred feet downward from the summit of the hill, the sides of the abyss bore little resemblance to each other, and, apparently, had at no time been connected, the one surface being of the soapstone, and the other of marl, granulated with some metallic matter. The average breadth or interval between the two cliffs was probably here sixty feet, but there seemed to be no regularity of formation. Passing down, however, beyond the limit spoken of, the interval rapidly contracted, and the sides began to run parallel, although, for some distance farther, they were still dissimilar in their material and form of surface. Upon arriving within fifty feet of the bottom, a perfect regularity commenced. The sides were now entirely uniform in substance, in color, and in lateral direction, the material being a very black and shining granite, and the distance between the two sides, at all points facing each other, exactly twenty yards. The precise formation of the chasm will be best understood by means of a delineation taken upon the spot; for I had luckily with me a pocketbook and pencil, which I preserved with great care through a long series of subsequent adventure, and to which I am indebted for memoranda of many subjects which would otherwise have been crowded from my remembrance.

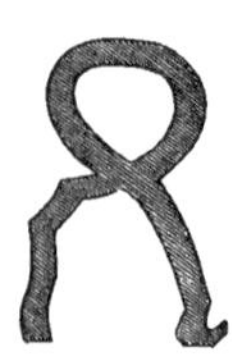

Figure 1

This figure (see figure 1) gives the general outlines of the chasm, without the minor cavities in the sides, of which there were several, each cavity having a corresponding protuberance opposite. The bottom of the gulf was covered to the depth of three or four inches with a powder almost impalpable, beneath which we found a continuation of the black granite. To the right, at the lower extremity, will be noticed the appearance of a small opening; this is the fissure alluded to above, and to examine which more minutely than before was the object of our second visit. We now pushed into it with vigor, cutting away a quantity of brambles which impeded us, and removing a vast heap of sharp flints somewhat resembling arrowheads in shape. We were encouraged to persevere, however, by perceiving some little light proceeding from the farther end. We at length squeezed our way for about thirty feet, and found that the aperture was a low and regularly formed arch, having a bottom of the same impalpable powder as that in the main chasm. A strong light now broke upon us, and, turning a short bend, we found ourselves in another lofty chamber, similar to the one we had left in every respect but longitudinal form. Its general figure is here given. (See figure 2.)

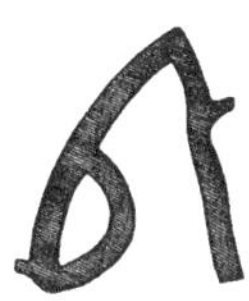

Figure 2

The total length of this chasm, commencing at the opening *a* and proceeding round the curve *b* to the extremity *d*, is five hundred and fifty yards. At *c* we discovered a small aperture similar to the one through which we had issued from the other chasm, and this was choked up in the same manner with brambles and a quantity of the white arrowhead flints. We forced our way through it, finding it about forty feet long, and emerged into a third chasm. This, too, was precisely like the first, except in its longitudinal shape, which was thus. (See figure 3.)

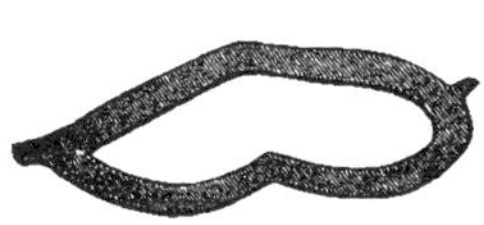

Figure 3

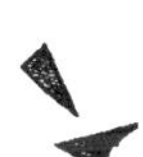

Figure 5

We found the entire length of the third chasm three hundred and twenty yards. At the point *a* was an opening about six feet wide, and extending fifteen feet into the rock, where it terminated in a bed of marl, there being no other chasm beyond, as we had expected. We were about leaving this fissure, into which very little light was admitted, when Peters called my attention to a range of singular-looking indentures in the surface of the marl forming the termination of the *cul-de-sac*. With a very slight exertion of the imagination, the left, or most northern of these indentures might have been taken for the intentional, although rude, representation of a human figure standing erect, with outstretched arm. The rest of them bore also some little resemblance to alphabetical characters, and Peters was willing, at all events, to adopt the idle opinion that they were really such. I convinced him of his error, finally, by directing his attention to the floor of the fissure, where, among the powder, we picked up, piece by piece, several large flakes of the marl, which had evidently been broken off by some convulsion from the surface where the indentures were found, and which had projecting points exactly fitting the indentures; thus proving them to have been the work of nature. Figure 4 presents an accurate copy of the whole.

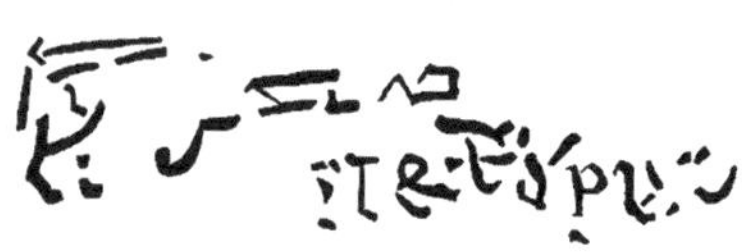

Figure 4

After satisfying ourselves that these singular caverns afforded us no means of escape from our prison, we made our way back, dejected and dispirited, to the summit of the hill. Nothing worth mentioning occurred during the next twenty-four hours, except that, in examining the ground to the eastward of the third chasm, we found two triangular holes of great depth, and also with black granite sides. Into these holes we did not think it worth while to attempt descending, as they had the appearance of mere natural wells, without outlet. They were each about twenty yards in circumference, and their shape, as well as relative position in regard to the third chasm, is shown in figure 5.

CHAPTER 24

ON THE TWENTIETH of the month, finding it altogether impossible to subsist any longer upon the filberts, the use of which occasioned us the most excruciating torment, we resolved to make a desperate attempt at descending the southern declivity of the hill. The face of the precipice was here of the softest species of soapstone, although nearly perpendicular throughout its whole extent (a depth of a hundred and fifty feet at the least), and in many places even overarching. After a long search we discovered a narrow ledge about twenty feet below the brink of the gulf; upon this Peters contrived to leap, with what assistance I could render him by means of our pocket-handkerchiefs tied together. With somewhat more difficulty I also got down; and we then saw the possibility of descending the whole way by the process in which we had clambered up from the chasm when we had been buried by the fall of the hill—that is, by cutting steps in the face of the soapstone with our knives. The extreme hazard of the attempt can scarcely be conceived; but, as there was no other resource, we determined to undertake it.

Upon the ledge where we stood there grew some filbert-bushes; and to one of these we made fast an end of our rope of handkerchiefs. The other end being tied round Peters' waist, I lowered him down over the edge of the precipice until the handkerchiefs were stretched tight. He now proceeded to dig a deep hole in the soapstone (as far in as eight or ten inches), sloping away the rock above to the height of a foot, or thereabout, so as to allow of his driving, with the butt of a pistol, a tolerably strong peg into the leveled surface. I then drew him up for about four feet, when he made a hole similar to the one below, driving in a peg as before, and having thus a resting-place for both feet and hands. I now unfastened the handkerchiefs from the bush, throwing him the end, which he tied to the peg in the uppermost hole, letting himself down gently to a station about three feet lower than he had yet been that is, to the full extent of the handkerchiefs. Here he dug another hole, and drove another peg. He then drew himself up, so as to rest his feet in the hole just cut, taking hold with his hands upon the peg in the one above. It was now necessary to untie the handkerchiefs from the topmost peg, with the view of fastening them to the second; and here he found that an error had been committed in cutting the holes at so great a distance apart. However, after one or two unsuccessful and dangerous attempts at reaching the knot (having to hold on with his left hand while he labored to undo the fastening with his right), he at length cut the string, leaving six inches of it affixed to the peg. Tying the handkerchiefs now to the second peg, he descended to a station below the third, taking care not to go too far down. By these means (means which I should never have conceived of myself, and for which we were indebted altogether to Peters' ingenuity and resolution) my companion finally succeeded, with the occasional aid of projections in the cliff, in reaching the bottom without accident.

It was some time before I could summon sufficient resolution to follow him; but I did at length attempt it. Peters had taken off his shirt before descending, and this, with my own, formed the rope necessary for the adventure. After throwing down the musket found in the chasm, I fastened this rope to the bushes, and let myself down rapidly, striving, by the vigor of my movements, to banish the trepidation which I could overcome in no other manner. This answered sufficiently well for the first four or five steps; but presently I found my imagination growing terribly excited by thoughts of the vast depths yet to be descended, and the precarious nature of the pegs and soapstone holes which were my only support. It was in vain I endeavored to banish these reflections, and to keep my eyes steadily bent upon the flat surface of the cliff before me. The more earnestly I struggled *not to think*, the more intensely vivid became my conceptions, and the more horribly distinct. At length arrived that crisis of fancy, so fearful in all similar cases, the crisis in which we began to anticipate the feelings with which we *shall* fall—to picture to ourselves the sickness, and dizziness, and the last struggle, and the half swoon, and the final bitterness of the rushing and headlong descent. And now I found these fancies creating their own realities, and all imagined horrors crowding upon me in fact. I felt my knees strike violently together, while my fingers were gradually but certainly relaxing their grasp. There was a ringing in my ears, and I said, "This is my knell of death!" And now I was consumed with the irrepressible desire of looking below. I could not, I would not, confine my glances to the cliff ; and, with a wild, indefinable emotion, half of horror, half of a relieved oppression, I threw my vision far down into the abyss. For one moment my fingers clutched convulsively upon their hold, while, with the movement, the faintest possible idea of ultimate escape wandered, like a shadow, through my mind—in the next my whole soul was pervaded with *a longing to fall*; a desire, a yearning, a passion utterly uncontrollable. I let go at once my grasp upon the peg, and, turning half round from the precipice, remained tottering for an instant against its naked face. But now there came a spinning of the brain; a shrill-sounding and phantom voice screamed within my ears; a dusky, fiendish, and filmy figure stood immediately beneath me; and, sighing, I sunk down with a bursting heart, and plunged within its arms.

I had swooned, and Peters had caught me as I fell. He had observed my proceedings from his station at the bottom of the cliff; and perceiving my imminent danger, had endeavored to inspire me with courage by every suggestion he could devise; although my confusion of mind had been so great as to prevent my hearing what he said, or being conscious that he had even spoken to me at all. At length, seeing me totter, he hastened to ascend to my rescue, and arrived just in time for my preservation. Had I fallen with my full weight, the rope of linen would inevitably have snapped, and I should have been precipitated into the abyss; as it was, he contrived to let me down gently, so as to remain suspended without danger until animation returned. This was in about fifteen minutes. On recovery, my trepidation had entirely vanished; I felt a new being, and, with some little further aid from my companion, reached the bottom also in safety.

We now found ourselves not far from the ravine which had proved the tomb of our friends, and to the southward of the spot where the hill had fallen. The place was one of singular wildness, and its aspect brought to my mind the descriptions given by travelers of those dreary regions marking the site of degraded Babylon. Not to speak of the ruins of the disrupted cliff, which formed a chaotic barrier in the vista to the northward, the surface of the ground in every other direction was strewn with huge tumuli, apparently the wreck of some gigantic structures of art; although, in detail, no semblance of art could be detected. Scoria were abundant, and large shapeless blocks of the black granite, intermingled with others of marl,[1] and both granulated with metal. Of

1 The marl was also black; indeed, we noticed no light-colored substances of any kind upon the island.

vegetation there were no traces whatsoever throughout the whole of the desolate area within sight. Several immense scorpions were seen, and various reptiles not elsewhere to be found in the high latitudes. As food was our most immediate object, we resolved to make our way to the seacoast, distant not more than half a mile, with a view of catching turtle, several of which we had observed from our place of concealment on the hill. We had proceeded some hundred yards, threading our route cautiously between the huge rocks and tumuli, when, upon turning a corner, five savages sprung upon us from a small cavern, felling Peters to the ground with a blow from a club. As he fell the whole party rushed upon him to secure their victim, leaving me time to recover from my astonishment. I still had the musket, but the barrel had received so much injury in being thrown from the precipice that I cast it aside as useless, preferring to trust my pistols, which had been carefully preserved in order. With these I advanced upon the assailants, firing one after the other in quick succession. Two savages fell, and one, who was in the act of thrusting a spear into Peters, sprung to his feet without accomplishing his purpose. My companion being thus released, we had no further difficulty. He had his pistols also, but prudently declined using them, confiding in his great personal strength, which far exceeded that of any person I have ever known. Seizing a club from one of the savages who had fallen, he dashed out the brains of the three who remained, killing each instantaneously with a single blow of the weapon, and leaving us completely masters of the field.

So rapidly bad these events passed, that we could scarcely believe in their reality, and were standing over the bodies of the dead in a species of stupid contemplation, when we were brought to recollection by the sound of shouts in the distance, It was clear that the savages had been alarmed by the firing, and that we had little chance of avoiding discovery. To regain the cliff, it would be necessary to proceed in the direction of the shouts, and even should we succeed in arriving at its base, we should never be able to ascend it without being seen. Our situation was one of the greatest peril, and we were hesitating in which path to commence a flight, when one of the savages whom I had shot, and supposed dead, sprang briskly to his feet, and attempted to make his escape. We overtook him, however, before he had advanced many paces, and were about to put him to death, when Peters suggested that we might derive some benefit from forcing him to accompany us in our attempt to escape. We therefore dragged him with us, making him understand that we would shoot him if he offered resistance. In a few minutes he was perfectly submissive, and ran by our sides as we pushed in among the rocks, making for the seashore.

So far, the irregularities of the ground we had been traversing hid the sea, except at intervals, from our sight, and, when we first had it fairly in view, it was perhaps two hundred yards distant. As we emerged into the open beach we saw, to our great dismay, an immense crowd of the natives pouring from the village, and from all visible quarters of the island, making toward us with gesticulations of extreme fury, and howling like wild beasts. We were upon the point of turning upon our steps, and trying to secure a retreat among the fastnesses of the rougher ground, when I discovered the bows of two canoes projecting from behind a large rock which ran out into the water. Toward these we now ran with all speed, and, reaching them, found them unguarded, and without any other freight than three of the large Gallipago turtles and the usual supply of paddles for sixty rowers. We instantly took possession of one of them, and, forcing our captive on board, pushed out to sea with all the strength we could command.

We had not made, however, more than fifty yards from the shore before we became sufficiently calm to perceive the great oversight of which we had been guilty in leaving the other canoe in the power of the savages, who, by this time, were not more than twice as far from the beach as ourselves, and were rapidly advancing to the pursuit. No time was now to be lost. Our hope was, at best, a forlorn one, but we had none other. It was very doubtful whether, with the utmost exertion, we could get back in time to anticipate them in taking possession of the canoe; but yet there was a chance that we could. We might save ourselves if we succeeded, while not to make the attempt was to resign ourselves to inevitable butchery.

The canoe was modeled with the bow and stern alike, and, in place of turning it around, we merely changed our position in paddling. As soon as the savages perceived this they redoubled their yells, as well as their speed, and approached with inconceivable rapidity. We pulled, however, with all the energy of desperation, and arrived at the contested point before more than one of the natives had attained it. This man paid dearly for his superior agility, Peters shooting him through the head with a pistol as he approached the shore. The foremost among the rest of his party were probably some twenty or thirty paces distant as we seized upon the canoe. We at first endeavored to pull her into the deep water, beyond the reach of the savages, but, finding her too firmly aground, and there being no time to spare, Peters, with one or two heavy strokes from the butt of the musket, succeeded in dashing out a large portion of the bow and of one side. We then pushed off. Two of the natives by this time had got hold of our boat, obstinately refusing to let go, until we were forced to despatch them with our knives. We were now clear off, and making great way out to sea. The main body of the savages, upon reaching the broken canoe, set up the most tremendous yell of rage and disappointment conceivable. In truth, from everything I could see of these wretches, they appeared to be the most wicked, hypocritical, vindictive, bloodthirsty, and altogether fiendish race of men upon the face of the globe. It is clear we should have had no mercy had we fallen into their hands. They made a mad attempt at following us in the fractured canoe, but, finding it useless, again vented their rage in a series of hideous vociferations, and rushed up into the hills.

We were thus relieved from immediate danger, but our situation was still sufficiently gloomy. We knew that four canoes of the kind we had were at one time in the possession of the savages, and were not aware of the fact (afterward ascertained from our captive) that two of these had been blown to pieces in the explosion of the *Jane Guy*. We calculated, therefore, upon being yet pursued, as soon as our enemies could get round to the bay (distant about three miles) where the boats were usually laid up. Fearing this, we made every exertion to leave the island behind us, and went rapidly through the water, forcing the prisoner to take a paddle. In about half an hour, when we had gained probably five or six miles to the southward, a large fleet of the flat-bottomed canoes or rafts were seen to emerge from the bay evidently with the design of pursuit. Presently they put back, despairing to overtake us.

CHAPTER 25

WE NOW FOUND ourselves in the wide and desolate Antarctic Ocean, in a latitude exceeding 84°, in a frail canoe, and with no provision but the three turtles. The long polar winter, too, could not be considered as far distant, and it became necessary that we should deliberate well upon the course to be pursued. There were six or seven islands in sight belonging to the same group, and distant from each other about five or six leagues; but upon neither of these had we any intention to venture. In coming from the northward in the *Jane Guy* we bad been gradually leaving behind us the severest regions of ice—this, however little it maybe in accordance with the generally received notions respecting the Antarctic, was a fact—experience would not permit us to deny. To attempt, therefore, getting back would be folly—especially at so late a period of the season. Only one course seemed to be left open for hope. We resolved to steer boldly to the southward, where there was at least a probability of discovering other lands, and more than a probability of finding a still milder climate.

So far we had found the Antarctic, like the Arctic Ocean, peculiarly free from violent storms or immoderately rough water; but our canoe was, at best, of frail structure, although large, and we set busily to work with a view of rendering her as safe as the limited means in our possession would admit. The body of the boat was of no better material than bark—the bark of a tree unknown. The ribs were of a tough osier, well adapted to the purpose for which it was used. We had fifty feet room from stem to stern, from four to six in breadth, and in depth throughout four feet and a half—the boats thus differing vastly in shape from those of any other inhabitants of the Southern Ocean with whom civilized nations are acquainted. We never did believe them the workmanship of the ignorant islanders who owned them; and some days after this period discovered, by questioning our captive, that they were in fact made by the natives of a group to the southwest of the country where we found them, having fallen accidentally into the hands of our barbarians. What we could do for the security of our boat was very little indeed. Several wide rents were discovered near both ends, and these we contrived to patch up with pieces of woolen jacket. With the help of the superfluous paddles, of which there were a great many, we erected a kind of framework about the bow, so as to break the force of any seas which might threaten to fill us in that quarter. We also set up two paddle-blades for masts, placing them opposite each other, one by each gunwale, thus saving the necessity of a yard. To these masts we attached a sail made of our shirts—doing this with some difficulty, as here we could get no assistance from our prisoner whatever, although he bad been willing enough to labor in all the other operations. The sight of the linen seemed to affect him in a very singular manner. He could not be prevailed upon to touch it or go near it, shuddering when we attempted to force him, and shrieking out, "*Tekeli-li!*"

Having completed our arrangements in regard to the security of the canoe, we now set sail to the south-southeast for the present, with the view of weathering the most southerly of the group in sight. This being done, we turned the bow full to the southward. The weather could by no means be considered disagreeable. We had a prevailing and very gentle wind from the northward, a smooth sea, and continual daylight. No ice whatever was to be seen; *nor did I ever see one particle of this after leaving the parallel of Bennet's Islet.* Indeed, the temperature of the water was here far too warm for its existence in any quantity. Having killed the largest of our tortoises, and obtained from him not only food but a copious supply of water, we continued on our course, without any incident of moment, for perhaps seven or eight days, during which period we must have proceeded a vast distance to the southward, as the wind blew constantly with us, and a very strong current set continually in the direction we were pursuing.

March 1st.[1] Many unusual phenomena now indicated that we were entering upon a region of novelty and wonder. A high range of light gray vapor appeared constantly in the southern horizon, flaring up occasionally in lofty streaks, now darting from cast to west, now from west to east, and again presenting a level and uniform summit—in short, having all the wild variations of the Aurora Borealis. The average height of this vapor, as apparent from our station, was about twenty-five degrees. The temperature of the sea seemed to be increasing momentarily, and there was a very perceptible alteration in its color.

1 For obvious reasons I cannot pretend to strict accuracy in these dates. They are given principally with a view to perspicuity of narration, and as set down in my pencil memorandum.

March 2nd. To-day by repeated questioning of our captive, we came to the knowledge of many particulars in regard to the island of the massacre, its inhabitants, and customs-but with these how can I *now* detain the reader? I may say, however, that we learned there were eight islands in the group-that they were governed by a common king, named *Tsalemon* or *Psalemoun*, who resided in one of the smallest of the islands; that the black skins forming the dress of the warriors came from an animal of huge size to be found only in a valley near the court of the king-that the inhabitants of the group fabricated no other boats than the flat-bottomed rafts; the four canoes being all of the kind in their possession, and, these having been obtained, by mere accident, from some large island in the southwest—that his own name was Nu-Nu-that he had no knowledge of Bennet's Islet—and that the appellation of the island he had left was *Tsalal*. The commencement of the words *Tsalemon* and *Tsalal* was given with a prolonged hissing sound, which we found it impossible to imitate, even after repeated endeavors, and which was precisely the same with the note of the black bittern we had eaten up on the summit of the hill.

March 3rd. The heat of the water was now truly remarkable, and in color was undergoing a rapid change, being no longer transparent, but of a milky consistency and hue. In our immediate vicinity it was usually smooth, never so rough as to endanger the canoe—but we were frequently surprised at perceiving, to our right and left, at different distances, sudden and extensive agitations of the surface these, we at length noticed, were always preceded by wild flickerings in the region of vapor to the southward.

March 4th. To-day, with the view of widening our sail, the breeze from the northward dying away perceptibly, I took from my coat-pocket a white handkerchief. Nu-Nu was seated at my elbow, and the linen accidentally flaring in his face, he became violently affected with convulsions. These were succeeded by drowsiness and stupor, and low murmurings of "*Tekeli-li! Tekeli-li!*"

March 5th. The wind had entirely ceased, but it was evident that we were still hurrying on to the southward, under the influence of a powerful current. And now, indeed, it would seem reasonable that we should experience some alarm at the turn events were taking—but we felt none. The countenance of Peters indicated nothing of this nature, although it wore at times an expression I could not fathom. The polar winter appeared to be coming on—but coming without its terrors. I felt a *numbness* of body and mind—a dreaminess of sensation but this was all.

March 6th. The gray vapor had now arisen many more degrees above the horizon, and was gradually losing its grayness of tint. The heat of the water was extreme, even unpleasant to the touch, and its milky hue was more evident than ever. Today a violent agitation of the water occurred very close to the canoe. It was attended, as usual, with a wild flaring up of the vapor at its summit, and a momentary division at its base. A fine white powder, resembling ashes—but certainly not such—fell over the canoe and over a large surface of the water, as the flickering died away among the vapor and the commotion subsided in the sea. Nu-Nu now threw himself on his face in the bottom of the boat, and no persuasions could induce him to arise.

March 7th. This day we questioned Nu-Nu concerning the motives of his countrymen in destroying our companions; but he appeared to be too utterly overcome by terror to afford us any rational reply. He still obstinately lay in the bottom of the boat; and, upon reiterating the questions as to the motive, made use only of idiotic gesticulations, such as raising with his forefinger the upper lip, and displaying the teeth which lay beneath it. These were black. We had never before seen the teeth of an inhabitant of Tsalal.

March 8th. To-day there floated by us one of the white animals whose appearance upon the beach at Tsalal had occasioned so wild a commotion among the savages. I would have picked it up, but there came over me a sudden listlessness, and I forbore. The heat of the water still increased, and the hand could no longer be endured within it. Peters spoke little, and I knew not what to think of his apathy. Nu-Nu breathed, and no more.

March 9th. The whole ashy material fell now continually around us, and in vast quantities. The range of vapor to the southward had arisen prodigiously in the horizon, and began to assume more distinctness of form. I can liken it to nothing but a limitless cataract, rolling silently into the sea from some immense and far-distant rampart in the heaven. The gigantic curtain ranged along the whole extent of the southern horizon. It emitted no sound.

March 21st. A sullen darkness now hovered above us—but from out the milky depths of the ocean a luminous glare arose, and stole up along the bulwarks of the boat. We were nearly overwhelmed by the white ashy shower which settled upon us and upon the canoe, but melted into the water as it fell. The summit of the cataract was utterly lost in the dimness and the distance. Yet we were evidently approaching it with a hideous velocity. At intervals there were visible in it wide, yawning, but momentary rents, and from out these rents, within which was a chaos of flitting and indistinct images, there came rushing and mighty. but soundless winds, tearing up the enkindled ocean in their course.

March 22nd. The darkness had materially increased, relieved only by the glare of the water thrown back from the white curtain before us. Many gigantic and pallidly white birds flew continuously now from beyond the veil, and their scream was the eternal *Tekeli-li!* as they retreated from our vision. Hereupon Nu-Nu stirred in the bottom of the boat; but upon touching him we found his spirit departed. And now we rushed into the embraces of the cataract, where a chasm threw itself open to receive us. But there arose in our pathway a shrouded human figure, very far larger in its proportions than any dweller among men. And the hue of the skin of the figure was of the perfect whiteness of the snow.

NOTE

THE CIRCUMSTANCES CONNECTED with the late sudden and distressing death of Mr. Pym are already well known to the public through the medium of the daily press. It is feared that the few remaining chapters which were to have completed his narrative, and which were retained by him, while the above were in type, for the purpose of revision, have been irrecoverably lost through the accident by which he perished himself. This, however, may prove not to be the case, and the papers, if ultimately found, will be given to the public.

No means have been left untried to remedy the deficiency. The gentleman whose name is mentioned in the preface, and who, from the statement there made, might be supposed able to fill the vacuum, has declined the task—this for satisfactory reasons connected with the general inaccuracy of the details afforded him, and his disbelief in the entire truth of the latter portions of the narration. Peters, from whom some information might be expected, is still alive, and a resident of Illinois, but cannot be met with at present. He may hereafter be found, and will, no doubt, afford material for a conclusion of Mr. Pym's account.

The loss of the two or three final chapters (for there were but two or three) is the more deeply to be regretted, as, it cannot be doubted, they contained matter relative to the Pole itself, or at least to regions in its very near proximity; and as, too, the statements of the author in relation to these regions may shortly be verified or contradicted by means of the governmental expedition now preparing for the Southern Ocean.

On one point in the Narrative some remarks may be well offered; and it would afford the writer of this appendix much pleasure if what he may here observe should have a tendency to throw credit, in any degree, upon the very singular pages now published. We allude to the chasms found in the island of Tsalal, and to the whole of the figures upon pages 182, 183, 184, 185.

Mr. Pym has given the figures of the chasm without comment, and speaks decidedly of the *indentures* found at the extremity of the most easterly of these chasms as having but a fanciful resemblance to alphabetical characters, and, in short, as being positively *not such*. This assertion is made in a manner so simple, and sustained by a species of demonstration so conclusive (viz., the fitting of the projections of the fragments found among the dust into the indentures upon the wall), that we are forced to believe the writer in earnest; and no reasonable reader should suppose otherwise. But as the facts in relation to *all* the figures are most singular (especially when taken in connexion with statements made in the body of the narrative), it may be as well to say a word or two concerning them all—this, too, the more especially as the facts in question have, beyond doubt, escaped the attention of Mr. Poe.

Figure 1, then figure 2, figure 3, and figure 5, when conjoined with one another in the precise order which the chasms themselves presented, and when deprived of the small lateral branches or arches (which, it will be remembered, served only as means of communication between the main chambers, and were of totally distinct character), constitute an Ethiopian verbal root—the root ጸለመ፡ "To be shady"—whence all the inflections of shadow or darkness.

In regard to the "left or most northwardly" of the indentures in figure 4, it is more than probable that the opinion of Peters was correct, and that the hieroglyphical appearance was really the work of art, and intended as the representation of a human form. The delineation is before the reader, and he may, or may not, perceive the resemblance suggested; but the rest of the indentures afford strong confirmation of Peters's idea. The upper range is evidently the Arabic verbal root ابيض "To be white," whence all the inflections of brilliancy and whiteness. The lower range is not so immediately perspicuous. The characters are somewhat broken and disjointed; nevertheless, it cannot be doubted that, in their perfect state, they formed the full Egyptian word ⲠⲀϢⲨⲢⲎⲤ, "The region of the south." It should be observed that these interpretations confirm the opinion of Peters in regard to the "most northwardly" of the figures. The arm is outstretched toward the south.

Conclusions such as these open a wide field for speculation and exciting conjecture. They should be regarded, perhaps, in connexion with some of the most faintly-detailed incidents of the narrative; although in no visible manner is this chain of connexion complete. *Tekeli-li!* was the cry of the affrighted natives of Tsalal upon discovering the carcass of the *white* animal picked up at sea. This also was the shuddering exclamation of the captive Tsalalian upon encountering the *white* materials in possession of Mr. Pym. This also was the shriek of the swift-flying, *white*, and gigantic birds which issued from the vapory *white* curtain of the South. Nothing *white* was to be found at Tsalal, and nothing otherwise in the subsequent voyage to the region beyond. It is not impossible that "Tsalal," the appellation of the island of the chasms, may be found, upon minute philological scrutiny, to betray either some alliance with the chasms themselves, or some reference to the Ethiopian characters so mysteriously written in their windings.

"*I have graven it within the hills, and my vengeance upon the dust within the rock.*"

THE END

THE JOURNAL OF JULIUS RODMAN

THE JOURNAL OF Julius Rodman. Being an account of the first passage across the Rocky Mountains of North America ever achieved by civilized man.

CONTENTS

CHAPTER I—INTRODUCTORY

WHAT WE MUST consider an unusual piece of good fortune has enabled us to present our readers, under this head, with a narrative of very remarkable character, and certainly of very deep interest. The Journal which follows not embodies a relation of the first successful attempt to cross the gigantic barriers of that immense chain of mountains which stretches from the Polar Sea in the north, to the Isthmus of Darien in the south, forming a craggy and snow-capped rampart throughout its whole course, but, what is of still greater importance, gives the particulars of a tour, beyond these mountains, through an immense extent of territory, which, *at this day*, is looked upon as totally untraveled and unknown, and which, in every map of the country to which we can obtain access, is marked as "*an unexplored region.*" It is, moreover, the only unexplored region within the limits of the continent of North America. Such being the case, our friends will know how to pardon us for the slight amount of unction with which we have urged this Journal upon the public attention. For our own parts, we have found, in its perusal, a degree, and a species of interest such as no similar narrative ever inspired. Nor do we think that our relation to these papers, as the channel through which they will be first made known, has had more than a moderate influence in begetting this interest. We feel assured that all our readers will unite with us in thinking the adventures here recorded unusually entertaining and important. The peculiar character of the gentleman who was the leader and soul of the expedition, as well as its historian, has imbued what he has written with a vast deal of romantic fervor, very different from the luke-warm and statistical air which pervades most records of the kind. Mr. James E. Rodman, from whom we obtained the MS., is well known to many of the readers of this Magazine; and partakes, in some degree, of that temperament which embittered the earlier portion of the life of his grandfather, Mr. Julius Rodman, the writer of the narrative. We allude to an hereditary hypochondria. It was the instigation of this disease which, more than any thing else, led him to attempt the extraordinary journey here detailed. The hunting and trapping designs, of which he speaks himself, in the beginning of his Journal, were, as far as we can perceive, but excuses made to his own reason, for the audacity and novelty of his attempt. There can be no doubt, we think (and our readers will think with us,) that he was urged solely by a desire to seek, in the bosom of the wilderness, that peace which his peculiar disposition would not suffer him to enjoy among men. He fled to the desert as to a friend. In no other view of the case can we reconcile many points of his record with our ordinary notions of human action.

As we have thought proper to omit two pages of the MS., in which Mr. R. gives some account of his life previous to his departure up the Missouri, it may be as well to state here that he was a native of England, where his relatives were of excellent standing, where he had received a good education, and from which country he emigrated to this, in 1784, (being then about eighteen years of age), with his father, and two maiden sisters. The family first settled in New York; but afterward made their way to Kentucky, and established themselves, almost in hermit fashion, on the banks of the Mississippi, near where Mills' Point now makes into the river. Here old Mr. Rodman died, in the fall of 1790; and, in the ensuing winter, both his daughters perished of the small-pox, within a few weeks of each other. Shortly afterward, (in the spring of 1791), Mr. Julius Rodman, the son, set out upon the expedition which forms the subject of the following pages. Returning from this in 1794, as hereinafter stated, he took up his abode near Abingdon, in Virginia, where he married, and had three children, and where most of his descendants now live.

We are informed by Mr. James Rodman, that his grandfather had merely kept an outline diary of his tour, during the many difficulties of its progress; and that the MS. with which we have been furnished were not written out in detail, from that diary, until many years afterward, when the tourist was induced to undertake the task, at the instigation of *M. Andre Michau*, the botanist, and author of the *Flora Boreali-Americana*, and of the *Histoire des Chenes d'Amerique. M. Michau*, it will be remembered, had made an offer of his services to Mr. Jefferson, when that statesman first contemplated sending an expedition across the Rocky Mountains. He was engaged to prosecute the journey, and had even proceeded on his way as far as Kentucky, when he was overtaken by an order from the French minister, then at Philadelphia, rcquiring him to relinquish the design, and to pursue elsewhere the botanical inquiries on which he was employed by his government. The contemplated undertaking then fell into the hands of Messieurs Lewis and Clarke, by whom it was successfully accomplished.

The MS. when completed, however, never reached M. Michau, for whose inspection it had been drawn up; and was always supposed to have been lost on the road by the young man to whom it was entrusted for delivery at M. M.'s temporary residence, near Monticello. Scarcely any attempt was made to recover the papers; Mr. Rodman's peculiar disposition leading him to take but little interest in the search. Indeed, strange as it may appear, we doubt, from what we are told of him, whether he would have ever taken any steps *to make public* the results of his most extraordinary tour; we think that his only object in retouching his original Diary was to oblige M. Michau. Even Mr. Jefferson's exploring project, a project which, at the time it was broached, excited almost universal comment, and was considered a perfect *novelty*, drew from the hero of our narrative, only a few general observations, addressed to the members of his family. He never made his own journey a subject of conversation; seeming, rather, to avoid the topic. He died before the return of Lewis and Clarke; and the Diary, *which had been given into the hands of the messenger for delivery to M. Michau*, was found, about three months ago, in a secret drawer of a bureau which had belonged to Mr. Julius R. We do not learn by whom it was placed there—Mr. R.'s relatives all exonerate *him* from the suspicion of having secreted it; but, without intending any disrespect to the memory of that gentleman, or to Mr. James Rodman, (to whom we feel under especial obligation), we cannot help thinking that the supposition of the narrator's having, by some means, reprocured the package from the messenger, and concealed it where it was discovered, is very reasonable, and not at all out of keeping with the character of that morbid sensibility which distinguished the individual.

We did not wish, by any means, to alter the manner of Mr. Rodman's narration, and have, therefore, taken very few liberties with the MS., and these few only in the way of abridgment. The style, indeed, could scarcely be improved—it is simple and very effective; giving evidence of the deep delight with which the traveler reveled in the majestic novelties through which he passed, day after day. There is a species of *affectionateness* which pervades his account, even of the severest hardships and dangers, which lets us at once into the man's whole idiosyncrasy.

He was possessed with a burning love of Nature; and worshiped her, perhaps, more in her dreary and savage aspects, than in her manifestations of placidity and joy. He stalked through that immense and often terrible wilderness with an evident rapture at his heart which we envy him as we read. He was, indeed, the man to journey amid all that solemn desolation which he, plainly, so loved to depict. His was the proper spirit to perceive; his the true ability to feel. We look, therefore, upon his MS. as a rich treasure—in its way absolutely unsurpassed—indeed, never equaled.

That the events of this narrative have hitherto lain *perdus*; that even the *fact* of the Rocky Mountains having been crossed by Mr. Rodman prior to the expedition of Lewis and Clarke, has never been made public, or at all alluded to in the works of any writer on American geography, (for it certainly never has been thus alluded to, as far as we can ascertain,) must be regarded as very remarkable—indeed, as exceedingly strange. The only reference to the joumey at all, of which we can hear in any direction, is said to be contained in an unpublished letter of M. Michau's, in the possession of Mr. W. Wyatt, of Charlottesville, Virginia. It is there spoken of in a casual way, and collaterally, as "a gigantic idea wonderfully carried out." If there has been any farther allusion to the journey, we know nothing of it.

Before entering upon Mr. Rodman's own relation, it will not be improper to glance at what has been done by others, in the way of discovery, upon the North-Western portion of our continent. If the reader will turn to a map of North America, he will be better enabled to follow us in our observations.

It will be seen that the continent extends from the Arctic ocean, or from about the 70th parallel of north latitude, to the 9th; and from the 56th meridian west of Greenwich, to the 168th. The whole of this immense extent of territory has been visited by civilized man, in a greater or less degree; and indeed a very large portion of it has been permanently settled. But there is an exceedingly wide tract which is still marked upon all our maps as *unexplored*, and which, until this day, has always been so considered. This tract lies within the 60th parallel on the south, the Arctic Ocean on the north, the Rocky Mountains on the west, and the possessions of Russia on the east. *To Mr. Rodman, however, belongs the honor of having traversed this singularly wild region in many directions; and the most interesting particulars of the narrative now published have reference to his adventures and discoveries therein.*

Perhaps the earliest travels of any extent made in North America by white people, were those of Hennepin and his friends, in 1698—but as his researches were mostly in the south, we do not feel called upon to speak of them more fully.

Mr. Irving, in his *Astoria*, mentions the attempt of Captain Jonathan Carver, as being the first ever made to cross the continent from the Atlantic to the Pacific Ocean; but in this he appears to be mistaken; for we find, in one of the journals of Sir Alexander Mackenzie, that two different enterprises were set on foot, with that especial object in view, by the Hudson Bay Fur Company, the one in 1758, the other as early as 1749; both of which are supposed to have entirely failed, as no accounts of the actual expeditions are extant. It was in 1763, shortly after the acquisition of the Canadas by Great Britain, that Captain Carver undertook the journey. His intention was to cross the country, between the forty-third and forty-sixth degrees of north latitude, to the shores of the Pacific. His object was to ascertain the breadth of the continent at its broadest part, and to determine upon some place, on the western coast, where government might establish a post to facilitate the discovery of a northwest passage, or a communication between Hudson's bay, and the Pacific ocean. He had supposed that the Columbia, then termed the Oregon, disembogued itself somewhere about the straits of Annian; and it was here that he expected the post to be formed. He thought, also, that a settlement in this neighborhood would disclose new sources of trade, and open a more direct cornmunication with China, and the British possessions in the East Indies, than the old route afforded, by the Cape of Good Hope. He was baffled, however, in his attempt to cross the mountains.

In point of time, the next important expedition, in the northern portion of America, was that of Samuel Hearne, who, with the object of discovering copper mines, pushed northwestwardly during the years 1769, '70, '71, and'72, from the Prince of Wales' Fort, in Hudson's bay, as far as the shores of the Arctic ocean.

We have, after this, to record a second attempt of Captain Carver's, which was set on foot in 1774, and in which he was joined by Richard Whitworth, a member of Parliament, and a man of wealth. We only notice this enterprise on account of the extensive scale on which it was projected; for in fact it was never carried into execution. The gentlemen were to take with them fifty or sixty men, artificers and mariners, and, with these, make their way up one of the branches of the Missouri, explore the mountains for the source of the Oregon, and sail down that river to its supposed mouth, near the straits of Annian. Here a fort was to be built, as well as vessels for the purpose of farther discovery. The undertaking was stopped by the breaking out of the American revolution.

As early as 1775, the fur trade had been carried by the Canadian missionaries, north and west to the banks of the Saskatchawine river, in 53 north latitude, 102 west longitude; and, in the beginning of 1776, Mr. Joseph Frobisher proceeded, in this direction, as far as 55, N. and 103, W.

In 1778, Mr. Peter Bond, with four canoes, pushed on to the Elk river, about thirty miles south of its junction with the Lake of the Hills.

We have now to mention another attempt, which was baffled at its very outset, to cross the broadest portion of the continent from ocean to ocean. This attempt is scarcely known by the public to have been made at all, and is mentioned by Mr. Jefferson alone, and by him only in a cursory way. Mr. J. relates that Ledyard called upon him in Paris, panting for some new enterprise, after his successful voyage with Captain Cook; and that he (Mr. J.) proposed to him that he should go by land to Kamschatka, cross in some of the Russian vessels to Nootka Sound, fall down into the latitude of the Missouri, and then, striking through the country, pass down that river to the United States. Ledyard agreed to the proposal provided the permission of the Russian government could be obtained. Mr. Jefferson succeeded in obtaining this; and the traveler, setting out from Paris, arrived at St. Petersburgh after the Empress had left that place to pass the winter at Moscow. His finances not permitting him to make unnecessary stay at St. P., he continued on his route with a passport from one of the ministers, and, at two hundred miles from Kamschatka, was arrested by an officer of the Empress, who had changed her mind, and now forbade his proceeding. He was put into a close carriage, and driven day and night, without stopping, till he reached Poland, where he was set down and dismissed. Mr. Jefferson, in speaking of Ledyard's undertaking, erroneously calls it "the first attempt to explore the western part of our northern continent."

The next enterprise of moment was the remarkable one of Sir Alexander Mackenzie, which was prosecuted in 1789. He started from Montreal, pushed through the Utawas river, Lake Nipissing, Lake Huron, around the northern shore of Lake Superior, through what is called the Grand Portage, thence along Rain River, the Lake of the Woods, Bonnet Lake, the upper part of Dog-Head Lake, the south coast of Lake Winnipeg, through Cedar Lake and past the mouth of the Saskatchawine, to Sturgeon Lake; thence again, by portage, to the Missinipi, and through Black Bear, Primo's and Buffalo Lakes, to a range of high mountains running N. E. and S. W.—then taking Elk river to the Lake of the Hills—then passing through Slave river to Slave Lake—around the northern shore of this latter to Mackenzie's river, and down this, lastly, to the Polar Sea—an immense journey, during which he encountered dangers innumerable, and hardships of the severest kind. In the whole of his course down Mackenzie's river to its embouchure, he passed along the bottom of the eastern declivity of the Rocky Mountains, but never crossed these barriers. In the spring of 1793, however, starting from Montreal and pursuing the route of his first journey as far as the mouth of the Unjigah or Peace River, he then turned off to the westward, up this stream, pushed through the Mountains in latitude 56, then proceeded to the south until he struck a river which he called the Salmon (now Frazer's) and following this, finally reached the Pacific in about the 40th parallel of N. L.

The memorable expedition of captains Lewis and Clarke was in progress during the years 1804, '5, and '6. In 1803, the act for establishing trading houses with the Indian tribes being about to expire, some modifications of it (with an extension of its views to the Indians on the Missouri) were recommended to Congress by a confidential Message from Mr. Jefferson, of January 18th. In order to prepare the way, it was proposed to send a party to trace the Missouri to its source, cross the Rocky Mountains, and follow the best water communication which offered itself thence to the Pacific ocean. This design was fully carried out; captain Lewis exploring (but not first "discovering" as Mr. Irving relates) the upper waters of the Columbia river, and following the course of that stream to its embouchure. The head waters of the Columbia were visited by Mackenzie as early as 1793.

Coincident with the exploring tour of Lewis and Clarke up the Missouri, was that of Major Zebulon M. Pike up the Mississippi, which he succeeded in tracing to its source in Itasca Lake. Upon his return from this voyage he penetrated, by the orders of government, from the Mississippi westwardly, during the years 1805, '6, and '7, to the head waters of the Arkansas (beyond the Rocky Mountains in latitude 40 N.) passing along the Osage and Kanzas rivers, and to the source of the Platte.

In 1810, Mr. David Thompson, a partner of the North West Fur Company, set out from Montreal, with a strong party, to cross the continent to the Pacific. The first part of the route was that of Mackenzie in 1793. The object was to anticipate a design of Mr. John Jacob Astor's—to wit, the establishment of a trading post at the mouth of the Columbia. Most of his people deserted him on the eastern side of the mountains; but he finally succeeded in crossing the chain, with only eight followers, when he struck the northern branch of the Columbia, and descended that river from a point much nearer its source than any white man had done before.

In 1811, Mr. Astor's own remarkable enterprise was carried into effect—at least so far as the joumey across the country is concerned. As Mr. Irving has already made all readers well acquainted with the particulars of this journey, we need only mention it in brief. The design we have just spoken of. The track of the party (under command of Mr. Wilson Price Hunt) was from Montreal, up the Utawas, through Lake Nipissing, and a succession of small lakes and rivers, to Michilimackinac, or Mackinaw—thence by Green Bay, Fox and Wisconsin rivers, to the Prairie du Chien—thence down the Mississippi to St. Louis—thence up the Missouri, to the village of the Arickara Indians, between the 46th and 47th parallels of N. latitude, and fourteen hundred and thirty miles above the mouth of the river—thence, bending to the southwest across the desert, over the mountains about where the head waters of the Platte and Yellowstone take rise, and, along the south branch of the Columbia, to the sea. Two small return parties from this expedition made most perilous and eventful passages across the country.

The travels of major Stephen H. Long are the next important ones in point of time. This gentleman, in 1823, proceeded to the source of St. Peter's river, to Lake Winnipeg, to the Lake of the Woods, etc., etc. Of the more recent journeys of Captain Bonneville and others it is scarcely necessary to speak, as they still dwell in the public memory. Captain B.'s adventures have been well related by Mr. Irving. In 1832, he passed from Fort Osage across the Rocky Mountains, and spent nearly three years in the regions beyond. Within the limits of the United States there is very little ground which has not, of late years, been traversed by the man of science, or the adventurer. But in those wide and desolate regions which lie north of our territory, and to the westward of Mackenzie's river, the foot of no civilized man, with the exception of Mr. Rodman and his very small party, has ever been known to tread. In regard to the question of the *first* passage across the Rocky Mountains, it will be seen, from what we have already said, that the credit of the enterprize should never have been given to Lewis and Clarke, since Mackenzie succeeded in it, in the year 1793; and that in point of fact, Mr. Rodman was the first who overcame those gigantic barriers; crossing them as he did in 1792. Thus it is not without good reason that we claim public attention for the extraordinary narrative which ensues.

CHAPTER II

AFTER THE DEATH of my father, and both sisters, I took no farther interest in our plantation at the Point, and sold it, at a complete sacrifice, to M. Junôt. I had often thought of trapping up the Missouri, and resolved now to go on an expedition up that river, and try to procure peltries, which I was sure of being able to sell at *Petite Côte* to the private agents of the Northwest Fur Company. I believed that much more property might be acquired in this way, with a little enterprise and courage, than I could make by any other means. I had always been fond, too, of hunting and trapping, although I had never made a business of either, and I had a great desire to explore some portion of our western country, about which Pierre Junôt had often spoken to me. He was the eldest son of the neighbor who bought me out, and was a man of strange manners and somewhat eccentric turn of mind, but still one of the best-hearted fellows in the world, and certainly as courageous a man as ever drew breath, although of no great bodily strength. He was of Canadian descent, and having gone, once or twice, on short excursions for the Fur Company, in which he had acted as *voyageur*, was fond of calling himself one, and of talking about his trips. My father had been very fond of Pierre, and I thought a good deal of him myself; he was a great favorite, too, with my younger sister, Jane, and I believe they would have been married had it been God's will to have spared her.

When Pierre discovered that I had not entirely made up my mind what course to pursue after my father's death, he urged me to fit out a small expedition for the river, in which he would accompany me; and he had no difficulty in bringing me over to his wishes. We agreed to push up the Missouri as long as we found it possible, hunting and trapping as we went, and not to return until we had secured as many peltries as would be a fortune for us both. His father made no objection, and gave him about three hundred dollars; when we proceeded to *Petite Côte* for the purpose of getting our equipments, and raising as many men as we could for the voyage.

Petite Côte[1] is a small place on the north bank of the Missouri, about twenty miles from its junction with the Mississippi. It lies at the foot of

1 Now St. Charles—Eds. G. M.

a range of low hills, and upon a sort of ledge, high enough above the river to be out of reach of the June freshets. There are not more than five or six houses, and these of wood, in the upper part of the place; but, nearer to the east, there is a chapel and twelve or fifteen good dwellings, running parrallel with the river. There are about a hundred inhabitants, mostly Creoles of Canadian descent. They are extremely indolent, and make no attempt at cultivating the country around them, which is a rich soil; except now and then when a little is done in the way of gardening. They live principally by hunting, and trading with the Indians for peltries, which they sell again to the North-West Company's agents. We expected to meet with no difficulty here in getting recruits for our journey, or equipments, but were disappointed in both particulars; for the place was too poor in every respect to furnish all that we wanted, so as to render our voyage safe and efficient.

We designed to pass through the heart of a country infested with Indian tribes, of whom we knew nothing except by vague report, and whom we had every reason to believe ferocious and treacherous. It was therefore particularly necessary that we should go well provided with arms and ammunition, as well as in some force as regards numbers; and if our voyage was to be a source of profit, we must take with us canoes of sufficient capacity to bring home what peltries we might collect. It was the middle of March when we first reached Petite Côte, and we did not succeed in getting ready until the last of May. We had to send twice down the river to the Point for men and supplies, and neither could be obtained except at great cost. We should have failed at last in getting many things absolutely requisite, if it had not so happened that Pierre met with a party on its return from a trip up the Mississippi, and engaged six of its best men, besides a canoe or piroque; purchasing, at the same time, most of the surplus stores and ammunition.

This seasonable aid enabled us to get fairly ready for the voyage before the first of June. On the third of this month (1791) we bid *adieu* to our friends at *Petite Côte*, and started on our expedition. Our party consisted in all of fifteen persons. Of these, five were Canadians from *Petite Côte*, and had all been on short excursions up the river. They were good boatmen, and excellent companions, as far as singing French songs went, and drinking, at which they were pre-eminent; although, in truth, it was a rare thing to see any of them so far the worse for liquor, as to be incapable of attending to duty. They were always in a good humor, and always ready to work; but as hunters I did not think them worth much, and as fighting men I soon discovered they were not to be depended upon. There were two of these five Canadians who engaged to act as interpreters for the first five or six hundred miles up the river (should we proceed so far) and then we hoped to procure an Indian occasionally to interpret, should it be necessary; but we had resolved to avoid, as far as possible, any meetings with the Indians, and rather to trap ourselves, than run the great risk of trading, with so small a party as we numbered. It was our policy to proceed with the greatest caution, and expose ourselves to notice only when we could not avoid it.

The six men whom Pierre had engaged from aboard the return Mississippi boat were as different a set from the Canadians as could well be imagined. Five of them were brothers, by the name of Greely (John, Robert, Meredith, Frank, and Poindexter) and bolder or finer looking persons it would have been difficult to find. John Greely was the eldest and stoutest of the five, and had the reputation of being the strongest man, as well as best shot in Kentucky—from which State they all came. He was full six feet in height, and of most extraordinary breadth across the shoulders, with large strongly-knit limbs. Like most men of great physical strength, he was exceedingly good-tempered, and on this account was greatly beloved by us all. The other four brothers were all strong well-built men, too, although not to be compared with John. Poindexter was as tall, but very gaunt, and of a singularly fierce appearance; but, like his elder brother, he was of peaceable demeanor. All of them were experienced hunters and capital shots. They had gladly accepted Pierre's offer to go with us, and we made an arrangement with them which ensured them an equal share with Pierre and myself in the profits of the enterprise—that is to say, we divided the proceeds into three parts; one of which was to be mine, one Pierre's, and one shared among the five brothers.

The sixth man whom we enlisted from the return boat was, also, a good recruit. His name was Alexander Wormley, a Virginian, and a very strange character. He had originally been a preacher of the gospel, and had afterward fancied himself a prophet, going about the country with a long beard and hair, and in his bare feet, haranguing every one he met. This hallucination was now diverted into another channel, and he thought of nothing else than of finding gold mines in some of the fastnesses of the country. Upon this subject he was as entirely mad as any man could well be; but upon all others was remarkably sensible and even acute. He was a good boatman and a good hunter, and as brave a fellow as ever stepped, besides being of great bodily strength and swiftness of foot. I counted much upon this recruit, on account of his enthusiastic character, and in the end I was not deceived, as will appear.

Our other two recruits were a negro belonging to Pierre Junôt, named Toby, and a stranger whom we had picked up in the woods near Mills' Point, and who joined our expedition upon the instant as soon as we mentioned our design. His name was Andrew Thornton, also a Virginian, and I believe of excellent family, belonging to the Thorntons of the northern part of the State. He had been from Virginia about three years; during the whole of which time he had been rambling about the western country, with no other companion than a large dog of the Newfoundland species. He had collected no peltries, and did not seem to have any object in view, more than the gratification of a roving and adventurous propensity. He frequently amused us, when sitting around our camp fires at night, with the relation of his adventures and hardships in the wilderness—recounting them with a strait-forward earnestness which left us no room to doubt their truth; although indeed, many of them had a marvelous air. Experience afterward taught us that the dangers and difficulties of the solitary hunter can scarcely be exaggerated, and that the real task is to depict them to the hearer in sufficiently distinct colors. I took a great liking to Thornton, from the first hour in which I saw him.

I have only said a few words respecting Toby; but he was not the least important personage of our party. He had been in old M. Junôt's family for a great number of years, and had proved himself a faithful negro. He was rather too old to accompany such an expedition as ours; but Pierre was not willing to leave him. He was an able-bodied man, however, and still capable of enduring great fatigue. Pierre himself was probably the feeblest of our whole company, as regards bodily strength, but he possessed great sagacity, and a courage which nothing could daunt. His manners were sometimes extravagant and boisterous, which led him to get into frequent quarrels, and had once or twice seriously endangered the success of our expedition; but he was a true friend, and in that one point I considered him invaluable.

I have now given a brief account of all our party, as it was when we left *Petite Côte*.[1] To carry ourselves and accoutrements, as well as to bring home what peltries might be obtained, we had two large boats. The smallest of these was a piroque made of birch bark, sewed together with the fibres of the roots of the spruce tree, the seams payed with pine resin, and the whole so light that six men could carry it with case. It was twenty feet long, and could be rowed with from four to twelve oars; drawing about eighteen inches water when loaded to the gunwale, and, when empty, not more than ten. The other was a keelboat which we had made at *Petite Côte* (the canoe having been purchased by Pierre from the Mississippi party.) It was thirty feet long, and, when loaded to the gunwale, drew two feet water. It had a deck for twenty feet of its length forward, forming a cuddy-cabin, with a strong door, and of sufficient dimensions to contain our whole party with close crowding, as the boat was very broad. This part of it was bulletproof, being wadded with oakum between two coatings of oak-plank; and in several positions we had small holes bored, through which we could have fired upon an enemy in case of attack, as well as observe their movements; these holes, at the same time, gave us air and light, when we closed the door; and we had secure plugs to fit them when necessary. The remaining ten feet of the length was open, and here we could use as many as six oars—but our main dependance was upon poles which we employed by walking along the deck. We had also a short mast, easily shipped and unshipped, which was stepped about seven feet from the bow, and upon which we set a large square sail when the wind was fair, taking in mast and all when it was ahead.

In a division made in the bow, under deck, we deposited ten kegs of good powder, and as much lead as we considered proportionate, one tenth ready molded in rifle bullets. We had also stowed away here, a small brass cannon and carriage, dismounted and taken to pieces, so as to lie in little compass, thinking that such a means of defense might

1 Mr. Rodman has not given any description of himself; and the account of his party is by no means complete without a portraiture of its leader. "He was about twenty-five years of age," says Mr. James Rodman in a memorandum now before us, "when he started up the river. He was a remarkably vigorous and active man, but short in stature, not being more than five feet three or four inches high—strongly built, with legs somewhat bowed. His physiognomy was of a Jewish cast, his lips thin, and his complexion saturnine."—Eds. G. M.

possibly come into play at some period of our expedition. This cannon was one of three which had been brought down the Missouri by the Spaniards two years previously, and lost overboard from a piroque, some miles above *Petite Côte*. A sand-bar had so far altered the channel at the place where the canoe capsized, that an Indian discovered one of the guns, and procured assistance to carry it down to the settlement, where he sold it for a gallon of whiskey. The people at Petite Côte then went up and procured the other two. They were very small guns, but of good metal, and beautifiil workmanship, being carved and ornamented with serpents like some of the French field pieces. Fifty iron balls were found with the guns, and these we procured. I mention the way in which we obtained this cannon, because it performed an important part in some of our operations, as will be found hereafter. Besides it, we had fifteen spare rifles, boxed up, and deposited forward with the other heavy goods. We put the weight here, to sink our bows well in the water, which is the best method, on account of the snags and sawyers in the river.

In the way of other arms we were sufficiently provided; each man having a stout hatchet, and knife, besides his ordinary rifle and ammunition. Each boat was provided with a camp kettle, three large axes, a towing-line, two oil-cloths to cover the goods when necessary, and two large sponges for bailing. The piroque had also a small mast and sail, (which I omitted to mention,) and carried a quantity of gum, birchbark and watape, to make repairs with. She, also, had in charge all the Indian goods which we had thought necessary to bring with us, and which we purchased from the Missisippi boat. It was not our design to trade with the Indians; but these goods were offered us at a low rate, and we thought it better to take them, as they might prove of service. They consisted of silk and cotton handkerchiefs; thread, lines and twine; hats, shoes, and hose; small cutlery and ironmongery; calicoes and printed cottons; Manchester goods; twist and carrot tobacco; milled blankets; and glass toys, beads, etc., etc. All these were done up in small packages, three of which were a man's load. The provisions were also put up so as to be easily handled; and a part was deposited in each boat. We had, altogether, two hundred weight of pork, six hundred weight of biscuit, and six hundred weight of pemmican. This we had made at *Petite Côte*, by the Canadians, who told us that it was used by the Northwest Fur Company in all their long voyages, when it is feared that game may not prove abundant. It is manufactured in a singular manner. The lean parts of the flesh of the larger animals is cut into thin slices, and placed on a wooden grate over a slow fire, or exposed to the sun (as ours was) or sometimes to the frost. When it was sufficiently dried in this way, it is pounded between two heavy stones, and will then keep for years. If, however, much of it is kept together, it ferments upon the breaking up of the frost in the spring, and, if not well exposed to the air, soon decays. The inside fat, with that of the rump, is melted down and mixed, in a boiling state, with the pounded meat, half and half; it is then squeezed into bags, and is ready to eat without any farther cooking, being very palatable without salt, or vegetables. The best pemmican is made with the addition of marrow and dried berries, and is a capital article of food.[1] Our whiskey was in carboys, of five gallons each, and we had twenty of these, a hundred gallons in all.

When every thing was well on board, with our whole company, including Thornton's dog, we found that there was but little room to spare, except in the big cabin, which we wished to preserve free of goods, as a sleeping place in bad weather; we had nothing in here except arms and ammunition, with some beaver-traps and a carpet of bear-skins. Our crowded state suggested an expedient which ought to have been adopted at all events; that of detaching four hunters from the party, to course along the river banks, and keep us in game, as well as to act in capacity of scouts, to warn us of the approach of Indians. With this object we procured two good horses, giving one of them in charge of Robert and Meredith Greely, who were to keep upon the south bank; and the other in charge of Frank and Poindexter (Greely) who were to course along the north side. By means of the horses they could bring in what game was shot.

1 The *pemmican* here described by Mr. Rodman is altogether new to us, and is very different from that with which our readers have no doubt been familiarised in the journals of Parry, Ross, Back, and other northern voyagers. This, if we remember, was prepared by long continued boiling of the lean meat (carefully excluding fat) until the soup was reduced to a very small proportion of its original bulk, and assumed a pulpy consistency. To this residue, many spices and much salt were added, and great nutriment was supposed to be contained in little bulk. The positive experience of an American surgeon, however, who had an opportunity of witnessing, and experimenting upon, the digestive process through an open wound in the stomach of a patient, has demonstrated that bulk is, in itself, an essential in this process, and that consequently the condensation of the nutritive property of food, involves, in a great measure, a paradox.—Eds. G. M.

This arrangement relieved our boats very considerably, lessening our number to eleven. In the small boat were two of the men from *Petite Côte*, with Toby and Pierre Junôt. In the large one were the Prophet (as we called him) or Alexander Wormley, John Greely, Andrew Thornton, three of the *Petite Côte* men, and myself, with Thomton's dog.

Our mode of proceeding was sometimes with oars, but not generally; we most frequently pulled ourselves along by the limbs of trees on shore; or, where the ground permitted it, we used a tow-line, which is the easiest way; some of us being on shore to haul, while some remained on board, to set the boat off shore with poles. Very often we poled altogether. In this method, (which is a good one when the bottom is not too muddy, or full of quicksands, and when the depth of water is not too great) the Canadians are very expert, as well as at rowing. They use long, stiff, and light poles, pointed with iron; with these they proceed to the bow of the boat, an equal number of men at each side; the face is then turned to the stern, and the pole inserted in the river, reaching the bottom; a firm hold being thus taken, the boatmen apply the heads of the poles to the shoulder, which is protected by a cushion, and, pushing in this manner, while they walk along the gunwale, the boat is urged forward with great force. There is no necessity for any steersman, while using the pole; for the poles direct the vessel with wonderful accuracy.

In these various modes of getting along, now and then varied with the necessity of wading, and dragging our vessels by hand, in rapid currents, or through shallow water, we commenced our eventful voyage up the Missouri river. The skins which were considered as the leading objects of the expedition were to be obtained, principally, by hunting and trapping, as privately as possible, and without direct trade with the Indians, whom we had long learned to know as, in the main, a treacherous race, not to be dealt with safely in so small a party as ours. The furs usually collected by previous adventurers upon our contemplated route, included beaver, otter, marten, lynx, mink, musquash, bear, fox, kitt-fox, wolverine, racoon, fisher, wolf, buffalo, deer, and elk; but we proposed to confine ourselves to the more costly kinds.

The morning on which we set out from *Petite Côte* was one of the most inspiring, and delicious; and nothing could exceed the hilarity of our whole party. The summer had hardly yet commenced, and the wind, which blew a strong breeze against us, at first starting, had all the voluptuous softness of spring. The sun shone clearly, but with no great heat. The ice had disappeared from the river, and the current, which was pretty full, concealed all those marshy, and ragged alluvia which disfigure the borders of the Missouri at low water. It had now the most majestic appearance, washing up among the willows and cotton-wood on one side, and rushing, with a bold volume, by the sharp cliffs on the other. As I looked up the stream (which here stretched away to the westward, until the waters apparently met the sky in the great distance) and reflected on the immensity of territory through which those waters had probably passed, a territory as yet altogether unknown to white people, and perhaps abounding in the magnificent works of God, I felt an excitement of soul such as I had never before experienced, and secretly resolved that it should be no slight obstacle which should prevent my pushing up this noble river farther than any previous adventurer had done. At that moment I seemed possessed of an energy more than human; and my animal spirits rose to so high a degree that I could with difficulty content myself in the narrow limits of the boat. I longed to be with the Greelys on the bank, that I might give full vent to the feelings which inspired me, by leaping and running in the prairie. In these feelings Thornton participated strongly, evincing a deep interest in our expedition, and an admiration of the beautiful scenery around us, which rendered him from that moment a particular favorite with myself. I never, at any period of my life, felt so keenly as I then did, the want of some friend to whom I could converse freely, and without danger of being misunderstood. The sudden loss of all my relatives by death, had saddened, but not depressed my spirits, which appeared to seek relief in a contemplation of the wild scenes of Nature; and these scenes and the reflections which they encouraged, could not, I found, be thoroughly enjoyed, without the society of some one person of reciprocal sentiments. Thornton was precisely the kind of individual to whom I could unburthen my full heart, and unburthen it of all its extravagant emotion, without fear of incurring a shadow of ridicule, and even in the certainty of finding a listener as impassioned as myself. I never, before or since, met with any one who so fully entered into my own notions respecting natural scenery; and this circumstance alone was sufficient to bind him to me in a firm friendship. We were as intimate, during our whole expedition, as brothers could possibly be, and I took no steps without consulting him. Pierre and myself were also friends, but there was not the tie of reciprocal thought between us—that strongest of all mortal bonds. His nature, although sensitive, was too volatile, to comprehend all the devotional fervor of my own.

The incidents of the first day of our voyage had nothing remarkable in them; except that we had some difficulty in forcing our way, toward nightfall, by the mouth of a large cave on the south side of the river. This cave had a very dismal appearance as we passed it, being situated at the foot of a lofty bluff, full two hundred feet high, and jutting somewhat over the stream. We could not distinctly perceive the depth of the cavern, but it was about sixteen or seventeen feet high, and at least fifty in width.[1] The current ran past it with great velocity, and, as from the nature of the cliff, we could not tow, it required the utmost exertion to make our way by it; which we at length effected by getting all of us, with the exception of one man, into the large boat. This one remained in the piroque, and anchored it below the cave. By uniting our force, then, in rowing, we brought the large boat up beyond the difficult pass, paying out a line to the piroque as we proceeded, and by this line hauling it up after us, when we had fairly ascended. We passed, during the day, Bonhomme, and Osage Femme Rivers, with two small creeks, and several islands of little extent. We made about twenty-five miles, notwithstanding

1 The cave here mentioned is that called the "Tavern" by the traders and boatmen. Some grotesque images are painted on the cliffs, and commanded, at one period, great respect from the Indians. In speaking of this cavern, Captain Lewis says that it is a hundred and twenty feet wide, twenty feet high, and forty deep, and that the bluffs overhanging it are nearly three hundred feet high. We wish to call attention to the circumstance that, in every point, Mr. R.'s account *falls short* of Captain Lewis's. With all his evident enthusiasm, our traveler is never prone to the exaggeration of facts. In a great variety of instances like the present, it will be found that his statements respecting *quantity* (in the full sense of the term) always fall *within* the truth, as this truth is since ascertained. We regard this as a remarkable trait in his mind; and it is assuredly one which should entitle his observations to the highest credit, when they concern regions about which we know nothing beyond these observations. In all points which relate to *effects*, on the contrary, Mr. Rodman's peculiar temperament leads him into *excess*. For example, he speaks of the cavem now in question, as of a *dismal appearance*, and the coloring of his narrative respecting it is derived principally from the somber hue of his own spirit, at the time of passing the rock. It will be as well to bear these distinctions in mind, as we read his journal. His facts are never heightened; his impressions from these facts must have, to ordinary perceptions, a tone of exaggeration. Yet there is no falsity in this exaggeration, except in view of a general sentiment upon the thing seen and described. As regards his own mind, the apparent gaudiness of color is the absolute and only true tint.—Eds. G. M.

the head wind, and encamped at night on the north bank, and at the foot of a rapid called Diable.

June the fourth. Early this morning, Frank and Poindexter Greely came into our camp with a fat buck, upon which we all breakfasted in high glee, and afterward pushed on with spirit. At the Diable rapid, the current sets with much force against some rocks which jut out from the south, and render the navigation difficult. A short distance above this we met with several quicksand bars, which put us to trouble; the banks of the river here fall in continually, and, in the process of time, must greatly alter the bed. At eight o'clock we had a fine fresh wind from the eastward, and, with its assistance, made rapid progress, so that by night we had gone perhaps thirty miles, or more. We passed, on the north, the river Du Bois, a creek called Charité,[1] and several small islands. The river was rising fast as we came to, at night, under a group of cotton-wood trees, there being no ground near at hand upon which we were disposed to encamp. It was beautifiil weather, and I felt too much excited to sleep; so, asking Thornton to accompany me, I took a stroll into the country, and did not return until nearly daylight. The rest of our crew occupied the cabin, for the first time, and found it quite roomy enough for five or six more persons. They had been disturbed, in the night, by a strange noise overhead, on deck, the origin of which they had not been able to ascertain; as, when some of the party rushed out to see, the disturber had disappeared. From the account given of the noise, I concluded that it must have proceeded from an Indian dog, who had scented our fresh provisions (the buck of yesterday) and was endeavoring to make off with a portion. In this view I felt perfectly satisfied; but the occurrence suggested the great risk we ran in not posting a regular watch at night, and it was agreed to do so for the future.

[Having thus given, in Mr. Rodman's own words, the incidents of the two first days of the voyage, we forbear to follow him minutely in his passage up the Missouri to the mouth of the Platte, at which he arrived on the tenth of August. The character of the river throughout this extent is so well known, and has been so frequently described, that any farther account of it is unnecessary; and the Journal takes note of little else, at this portion of the tour, than the natural features of the

1 *La Charette? Du Bois* is no doubt *Wood* river.—Eds. G. M.

country—together with the ordinary boating and hunting occurrences. The party made three several halts for the purpose of trapping, but met with no great success; and finally concluded to push farther into the heart of the country, before making any regular attempts at collecting peltries. Only two events, of moment, are recorded, for the two months which we omit. One of these was the death of a Canadian, Jacques Lauzanne, by the bite of a rattle-snake; the other was the encountering a Spanish commission sent to intercept and turn the party back, by order of the commandant of the province. The officer in charge of the detachment, however, was so much interested in the expedition, and took so great a fancy to Mr. Rodman, that our travelers were permitted to proceed. Many small bodies of Osage and Kanzas Indians hovered occasionally about the boats, but evinced nothing of hostility. We leave the voyagers for the present, therefore, at the mouth of the river Platte, on the tenth of August, 1791—their number having been reduced to fourteen.]

CHAPTER III

HAVING REACHED THE mouth of the river Platte, our voyagers encamped for three days, during which they were busily occupied in drying and airing their goods and provisions, making new oars and poles, and repairing the birch canoe, which had sustained material injury. The hunters brought in an abundance of game, with which the boats were loaded to repletion. Deer was had for the asking, and turkeys and fat grouse were met with in great plenty. The party, moreover, regaled on several species of fish, and, at a short distance from the river banks, found an exquisite kind of wild grape. No Indians had been seen for better than a fortnight, as this was the hunting season, and they were doubtless engaged in the prairies, taking buffalo. After perfectly recruiting, the voyagers broke up their encampment, and pushed on up the Missouri. We resume the words of the Journal.

August 14. We started with a delightful breeze from the S. E., and kept along by the Southern shore, taking advantage of the eddy, and going at a great rate, notwithstanding the current, which, in the middle, was unusually full and strong. At noon, we stopped to examine some remarkable mounds on the southwestern shore, at a spot where the ground seems to have sunk considerably to an extent of three hundred acres, or more. A large pond is in the vicinity, and appears to have drained the low tract. This is covered with mounds of various sizes, and shapes, all formed of sand and mud, the highest being nearest the river. I could not make up my mind whether these hillocks were of natural or artificial construction. I should have supposed them made by the Indians, but for the general appearance of the soil, which had apparently been subjected to the violent action of water.[1] We staid at this spot the rest of the day, having made altogether twenty miles.

August 15. To-day we had a heavy, disagreeable head wind, and made only fifteen miles, with great labor; encamping at night beneath a bluff on the north shore, this being the first bluff on that side which we had seen since leaving the Nodaway river. In the night it came on to rain

1 These mounds are now well understood to indicate the position of the ancient city of the Ottoes, who were once a very powerful tribe. Being reduced by continual hostilities, they sought protection of the Pawnees, and migrated to the south of the Platte, about thirty miles from its mouth.—Eds. G. M.

in torrents, and the Greelys brought in their horses, and ensconced themselves in the cabin. Robert swam the river with his horse from the South shore, and then took the canoe across for Meredith. He appeared to think nothing of either of these feats, although the night was one of the darkest and most boisterous I ever saw, and the river was much swollen. We all sat in the cabin very comfortably, for the weather was quite cool, and were kept awake for a long time by the anecdotes of Thornton, who told story after story of his adventures with the Indians on the Mississippi. His huge dog appeared to listen with profound attention to every word that was said. Whenever any particularly incredible circumstance was related, Thornton would gravely refer to him as a witness. "Nep," he would say, "don't you remember that time?"—or "Nep can swear to the truth of that—can't you, Nep?"—when the animal would roll up his eyes immediately, loll out his monstrous tongue, and wag his great head up and down, as much as to say—"Oh it's every bit as true as the Bible." Although we all knew that this trick had been taught the dog, yet for our lives we could not forbear shouting with laughter, whenever Thornton would appeal to him.

August 16. Early this morning passed an island, and a creek about fifteen yards wide, and, at a farther distance of twelve miles, a large island in the middle of the river. We had now, generally, high prairie, and timbered hills on the north, with low ground on the south, covered with cotton-wood. The river was excessively crooked, but not so rapid as before we passed the Platte. Altogether there is less timber than formerly; what there is, is mostly elm, cotton-wood, hickory, and walnut, with some oak. Had a strong wind nearly all day, and by means of the eddy and this, we made twenty-five miles before night. Our encampment was on the south, upon a large plain, covered with high grass, and bearing a great number of plum-trees and currant-bushes. In our rear was a steep woody ridge, ascending which we found another prairie extending back for about a mile, and stopped again by a similar woody ridge, followed by another vast prairie, going off into the distance as far as the eye can reach. From the cliffs just above us we had one of the most beautiful prospects in the world.[1]

August 17. We remained at the encampment all day, and occupied

1 The Council Bluffs.—Eds. G. M.

ourselves in various employments. Getting Thornton, with his dog, to accompany me, I strolled to some distance to the southward, and was enchanted with the voluptuous beauty of the country. The prairies exceeded in beauty any thing told in the tales of the Arabian Nights. On the edges of the creeks there was a wild mass of flowers which looked more like Art than Nature, so profusely and fantastically were their vivid colors blended together. Their rich odor was almost oppressive. Every now and then we came to a kind of green island of trees, placed amid an ocean of purple, blue, orange, and crimson blossoms, all waving to and fro in the wind. These islands consisted of the most majestic forest oaks, and, beneath them, the grass resembled a robe of the softest green velvet, while up their huge stems there clambered, generally, a profusion of grape vines, laden with delicious ripe fruit. The Missouri, in the distance, presented the most majestic appearance; and many of the real islands with which it was studded were entirely covered with plum bushes, or other shrubbery, except where crossed in various directions by narrow, mazy paths, like the alleys in an English flowergarden; and in these alleys we could always see either elks or antelopes, who had no doubt made them. We returned, at sun-set, to the encampment, delighted with our excursion. The night was warm, and we were excessively annoyed by mosquitoes.

August 18. To-day passed through a narrow part of the river, not more than two hundred yards wide, with a rapid channel, much obstructed with logs and drift wood. Ran the large boat on a sawyer, and half filled her with water before we could extricate her from the difficulty. We were obliged to halt, in consequence, and overhaul our things. Some of the biscuit was injured, but none of the powder. Remained all day—having only made five miles.

August 19. We started early this morning and made great headway. The weather was cool and cloudy, and at noon we had a drenching shower. Passed a creek on the south, the mouth of which is nearly concealed by a large sand-island of singular appearance. Went about fifteen miles beyond this. The highlands now recede from the river, and are probably from ten to twenty miles apart. On the north is a good deal of fine timber, but on the south very little. Near the river are beautiful prairies, and along the banks we procured four or five different species of grape, all of good flavor and quite ripe; one is a large purple grape of excellent quality. The hunters came into camp, at night, from both sides of the river, and brought us more game than we well knew what to do with—grouse, turkies, two deer, an antelope, and a quantity of yellow birds with black-striped wings—these latter proved delicious eating. We made about twenty miles during the day.

August 20. The river, this morning, was full of sand-bars and other obstructions; but we proceeded with spirit, and reached the mouth of a pretty large creek, before night, at a distance of twenty miles from our last encampment. The creek comes in from the north, and has a large island opposite its mouth. Here we made our camp, with the resolution of remaining four or five days to trap beaver, as we saw great signs of them in the neighborhood. This island was one of the most fairy-looking situations in the world, and filled my mind with the most delightful and novel emotions. The whole scenery rather resembled what I had dreamed of when a boy, than an actual reality. The banks sloped down very gradually into the water, and were carpeted with a short soft grass of a brilliant green hue, which was visible under the surface of the stream for some distance from the shore; especially on the north side, where the clear creek fell into the river. All round the island, which was probably about twenty acres in extent, was a complete fringe of cotton-wood; the trunks loaded with grape vines in full fruit, and so closely-interlocking with each other, that we could scarcely get a glimpse of the river between the leaves. Within this circle the grass was somewhat higher, and of a coarser texture, with a pale yellow or white streak down the middle of each blade, and giving out a remarkably delicious perfume, resembling that of the Vanilla bean, but much stronger, so that the whole atmosphere was loaded with it. The common English sweet grass is no doubt of the same genus, but greatly inferior in beauty, and fragrance. Interspersed among it in every direction, were myriads of the most brilliant flowers, in full bloom, and most of them of fine odor—blue, pure white, bright yellow, purple, crimson, gaudy scarlet, and some with streaked leaves like tulips. Little knots of cherry trees and plum bushes grew in various directions about, and there were many narrow winding paths which circled the island, and which had been made by elk or antelopes. Nearly in the center, was a spring of sweet and clear water, which bubbled up from among a cluster of steep rocks, covered from head to foot with moss and flowering vines. The whole bore a wonderful resemblance to an artificial flower garden, but was infinitely more beautiful—looking rather like some of those scenes of enchantment which we read of in old books. We were all in extacy with the spot, and prepared our camp in the highest glee, amid its wilderness of sweets.

[The party remained here a week, during which time, the neighboring country to the north was explored in many directions, and some peltries obtained, especially upon the creek mentioned. The weather was fine, and the enjoyment of the voyagers suffered no alloy, in their terrestrial Paradise. Mr. Rodman, however, omitted no necessary precautions, and sentries were regularly posted every night, when all hands assembled at camp, and made merry. Such feasting and drinking were never before known; the Canadians proving themselves the very best fellows in the world at a song, or over a flagon. They did nothing but eat, and cook, and dance, and shout French carols at the top of their voice. During the day they were chiefly entrusted with the charge of the encampment, while the steadier members of the party were absent upon hunting or trapping expeditions. In one of these Mr. Rodman enjoyed an excellent opportunity of observing the habits of the beaver; and his account of this singular animal is highly interesting—the more so as it differs materially, in some points, from the ordinary descriptions.

He was attended, as usual, by Thornton and his dog, and had traced up a small creek to its source in the highlands about ten miles from the river. The party came at length to a place where a large swamp had been made by the beavers, in damming up the creek. A thick grove of willows occupied one extremity of the swamp, some of them overhanging the water at a spot where several of the animals were observed. Our adventurers crept stealthily round to these willows, and making Neptune lie down at a little distance, succeeded in climbing, unobserved, into a large and thick tree, where they could look immediately down upon all that was going on.

The beavers were repairing a portion of their dam, and every step of their progress was distinctly seen. One by one the architects were perceived to approach the edge of the swamp, each with a small branch in his mouth. With this he proceeded to the dam, and placed it carefully, and longitudinally, on the part which had given way. Having done this, he dived immediately, and in a few seconds reappeared above the surface with a quantity of stiff mud, which he first squeezed so as to drain it of its moisture in a great degree, and then applied with its feet and tail (using the latter as a trowel) to the branch which he had just laid upon the breach. He then made off among the trees, and was quickly succeeded by another of the community, who went through precisely the same operation.

In this way the damage sustained by the dam was in a fair way of being soon repaired. Messieurs Rodman and Thornton observed the progress of the work for more than two hours, and bear testimony to the exquisite skill of the artizans. But as soon as a beaver left the edge of the swamp in search of a branch, he was lost sight of among the willows, much to the chagrin of the observers, who were anxious to watch his farther operations. By clambering a little higher up in the tree, however, they discovered every thing. A small sycamore had been felled, apparently, and was now nearly denuded of all its fine branches, a few beavers still nibbling off some that remained, and proceeding with them to the dam. In the mean time a great number of the animals surrounded a much older and larger tree, which they were busily occupied in cutting down. There were as many as fifty or sixty of the creatures around the trunk, of which number six or seven would work at once, leaving off one by one, as each became weary; a fresh one stepping in to the vacated place. When our travelers first observed the sycamore, it had been already cut through to a great extent, but only on the side nearest the swamp, upon the edge of which it grew. The incision was nearly a foot wide, and as cleanly made as if done with an ax; and the ground at the bottom of the tree was covered with fine longitudinal slips, like straws, which had been nibbled out, and not eaten; as it appears that these animals only use the bark for food. When at work some sat upon the hind legs, in the posture so conunon with squirrels, and gnawed at the wood; their fore feet resting upon the edge of the cut, and their heads thrust far into the aperture. Two of them, however, were entirely within the incision; lying at length, and working with great eagerness for a short time, when they were relieved by their companions.

Although the position of our voyagers was any thing but comfortable, so great was their curiosity to witness the felling of the sycamore, that they resolutely maintained their post until sunset, an interval of eight hours from the time of ascending. Their chief embarrassment was on

Neptune's account, who could with difficulty be kept from plunging in the swamp after the plasterers who were repairing the dam. The noise he made had several times disturbed the nibblers at the tree, who would every now and then start, as if all actuated by one mind, and listen attentively for many minutes. As evening approached, however, the dog gave over his freaks, and lay quiet; while the beavers went on uninterruptedly with their labor.

Just as the sun began to set, a sudden commotion was observed among the wood-cutters, who all started from the tree, and flew round to the side which was untouched. In an instant afterward it was seen to settle down gradually on the gnawed side, till the lips of the incision met; but still it did not fall, being sustained partially by the unsundered bark. This was now attacked with zeal by as many nibblers as could find room to work at it, and very quickly severed; when the huge tree, to which the proper inclination had already been so ingeniously given, fell with a tremendous crash, and spread a great portion of its topmost branches over the surface of the swamp. This matter accomplished, the whole community seemed to think a holiday was deserved, and, ceasing work at once, began to chase each other about in the water, diving, and slapping the surface with their tails.

The account here given of the method employed by the beaver in its wood-cutting operations, is more circumstantial than any we have yet seen, and seems to be conclusive in regard to the question of *design* on the animal's part. The intention of making the tree fall toward the water appears here to be obvious. Captain Bonneville, it will be remembered, discredits the alleged sagacity of the animal in this respect, and thinks it has no farther aim than to get the tree down, without any subtle calculation in respect to its mode of descent. This attribute, he thinks, has been ascribed to it from the circumstance that trees in general, which grow near the margin of water, either lean bodily toward the stream, or stretch their most ponderous limbs in that direction, in search of the light, space, and air, which are there usually found. The beaver, he says, attacks, of course, those trees which are nearest at hand, and on the banks of the stream or pond, and these, when cut through, naturally preponderate toward the water. This suggestion is well-timed; but by no means conclusive against the design of the beaver; whose sagacity, at best, is far beneath that which is positively ascertained in respect to many classes of inferior animals—infinitely below that of the lion-ant, of the bee, and of the corralliferi. The probability is that, were two trees offered to the choice of the beaver, one of which preponderated to the water, and the other did not, he would, in felling the first, omit, as unnecessary, the precautions just described, but observe them in felling the second.

In a subsequent portion of the Journal other particulars are given respecting the habits of the singular animal in question, and of the mode of trapping it employed by the party, and we give them here for the sake of continuity. The principal food of the beavers is bark, and of this they put by regularly a large store for winter provision, selecting the proper kind with care and deliberation. A whole tribe, consisting sometimes of two or three hundred, will set out together upon a foraging expedition, and pass through groves of trees all apparently similar, until a particular one suits their fancy. This they cut down, and, breaking off its most tender branches, divide them into short slips of equal length and divest these slips of their bark, which they carry to the nearest stream leading to their village, thence floating it home. Occasionally the slips are stored away for the winter without being stripped of the bark; and, in this event, they are careful to remove the refuse wood from their dwellings, as soon as they have eaten the rind, taking the sticks to some distance. During the spring ot the year the males are never found with the tribe at home, but always by themselves, either singly, or in parties of two or threc, when they appear to lose their usual habits of sagacity, and fall an easy prey to the arts of the trapper. In sununer they return home, and busy themselves, with the females, in making provision for winter. They are described as exceedingly ferocious animals when irritated.

Now and then they may be caught upon shore; especially the males in spring, who are then fond of roving to some distance from the water in search of food. When thus caught, they are easily killed with a blow from a stick; but the most certain and efficacious mode of taking them is by means of the trap. This is simply constructed to catch the foot of the animal. The trapper places it usually in some position near the shore, and just below the surface of the water, fastening it by a small chain to a pole stuck in the mud. In the mouth of the machine is placed one end of a small branch; the other end rising above the surface, and well soaked in the liquid bait whose odor is found to be attractive to the beaver. As soon as the animal scents it, he rubs his nose against the twig, and, in so doing, steps upon the trap, springs it, and is caught. The trap is made very light, for the convenience of portage, and the prey would easily swim off with it but for its being fastened to the pole by a chain—no other species of fastening could resist his teeth. The experienced trapper readily detects the presence of beaver in any pond or stream; discovering them by a thousand appearances which would afford no indication to the unpracticed observer.

Many of the identical woodcutters whom the two voyagers had watched so narrowly from the tree-top, fell afterward a victim to trap, and their fine furs became a prey to the spoilers, who made sad havoc in the lodge at the swamp. Other waters in the neighborhood also afforded the travelers much sport; and they long remembered the island at the creek's mouth, by the name of Beaver Island, in consequence. They left this little Paradise in high spirits on the twenty-seventh of the month, and, pursuing their hitherto somewhat uneventful voyage up the river, arrived, by the first of September, without any incident of note, at the mouth of a large river on the south, to which they gave the name of Currant River, from some berries abounding upon its margin, but which was, beyond doubt, the Quicourre. The principal objects of which the Journal takes notice in this interval, are the numerous herds of buffalo which darkened the prairies in every direction, and the remains of a fortification on the south shore of the river, nearly opposite the upper extremity of what has been since called Bonhomme Island. Of these remains a minute description is given, which tallies in every important particular with that of Captains Lewis and Clarke. The travelers had passed the Little Sioux, Floyd's, the Great Sioux, White-Stone, and Jacques rivers on the North; with Wawandyscnche creek, and White-Paint river on the south, but at neither of these streams did they stop to trap for any long period. They had also passed the great village of the Omahas, of which the Journal takes no notice whatever. This village, at the time, consisted of full three hundred houses, and was inhabited by a numerous and powerful tribe; but it is not immediately upon the banks of the Missouri, and the boats probably went by it during the night—for the party had begun to adopt this mode of progress, through fear of the Sioux. We resume the narrative of Mr. Rodman, with the second of September.]

September 2. We had now reached a part of the river where, according to all report, a great deal of danger was to be apprehended from the Indians, and we became extremely cautious in our movements. This was the region inhabited by the Sioux, a warlike and ferocious tribe, who had, upon several occasions, evinced hostility to the whites, and were known to be constantly at war with all the neighboring tribes. The Canadians had many incidents to relate respecting their savage propensities, and I had much apprehension lest these cowardly creatures should take an opportunity of deserting, and retracing their way to the Mississippi. To lessen the chances of this, I removed one of them from the piroque, and supplied his place by Poindexter Greely. All the Greelys came in from the shore, turning loose the horses. Our arrangement was now as follows:—In the piroque, Poindexter Greely, Pierre Junôt, Toby, and one Canadian—in the large boat, myself; Thornton; Wormley; John, Frank, Robert, and Meredith Greely; and three Canadians, with the dog. We set sail about dusk, and, having a brisk wind from the south, made good head-way, although, as night came on, we were greatly embarrassed by the shoals. We continued our course without interruption, however, until a short time before day-break, when we ran into the mouth of a creek, and concealed the boats among the underwood.

September 3 and 4. During both of these days it rained and blew with excessive violence, so that we did not leave our retreat at all. The weather depressed our spirits very much, and the narratives of the Canadians about the terrible Sioux did not serve to raise them. We all congregated in the cabin of the large boat, and held a council in regard to our future movements. The Greelys were for a bold push through the dangerous country, maintaining that the stories of the voyagers were mere exaggerations, and that the Sioux would only be a little troublesome, without proceeding to hostility. Wormley and Thornton, however, as well as Pierre (all of whom had much experience in the Indian character) thought that our present policy was the best, although it would necessarily detain us much longer on our voyage than would otherwise be the case. My own opinion coincided with theirs—in our present course we might escape any collision with the Sioux—and I did not regard the delay as a matter of consequence.

September 5. We set off at night, and proceeded for about ten miles, when the day began to appear, and we hid the boats as before, in a narrow creek, which was well adapted to the purpose, as its mouth was almost blocked up by a thickly-wooded island. It again came on to rain furiously, and we were all drenched to the skin before we could arrange matters for turning in, in the cabin. Our spirits were much depressed by the bad weather, and the Canadians especially were in a miserable state of dejection. We had now come to a narrow part of the river where the current was strong, and the cliffs on both sides overhung the water, and were thickly wooded with lynn, oak, black-walnut, ash, and chesnut. Through such a gorge we knew it would be exceedingly difficult to pass without observation, even at night, and our apprehensions of attack were greatly increased. We resolved not to recommence our journey until late, and then to proceed with the most stealthy caution. In the meantime we posted a sentry on shore, and one in the piroque, while the rest of us busied ourselves in overhauling the arms and ammunition, and preparing for the worst.

About ten o'clock we were getting ready to start, when the dog gave a low growl, which made us all fly to our rifles; but the cause of the disturbance proved to be a single Indian of the Ponca tribe, who came up frankly to our sentry on shore, and extended his hand. We brought him on board, and gave him whiskey, when he became very communicative, and told us that his tribe, who lived some miles lower down the river, had been watching our movements for several days past, but that the Poncas were friends and would not molest the whites, and would trade with us upon our return. They had sent him now to caution the whites against the Sioux, who were great robbers, and who were lying in wait for the party at a bend of the river, twenty miles farther up. There were three bands of them, he said, and it was their intention to kill us all, in revenge for an insult sustained by one of their chiefs, many years previously, at the hands of a French trapper.

CHAPTER IV

[WE LEFT OUR travelers, on the fifth of September, apprehending a present attack from the Sioux. Exaggerated accounts of the ferocity of this tribe had inspired the party with an earnest wish to avoid them; but the tale told by the friendly Ponca made it evident that a collision must take place. The night voyages were therefore abandoned as impolitic, and it was resolved to put a bold face upon the matter, and try what could be effccted by blustering. The remainder of the night of the fifth was spent in warlike demonstration. The large boat was cleared for action as well as possible, and the fiercest aspect assumed which the nature of the case would permit. Among other preparations for defense, the cannon was got out from below, and placed forward upon the cuddy deck, with a load of bullets, by way of cannister shot. Just before sunrise the adventurers started up the river in high bravado, aided by a heavv wind. That the enemy might perceive no semblance of fear or mistrust, the whole party joined the Canadians in an uproarious boat song at the top of their voices, making the woods reverberate, and the buffaloes stare.

The Sioux, indeed, appear to have been Mr. Rodman's bugbears *par excellence*, and he dwells upon them and their exploits with peculiar emphasis. The narrative embodies a detailed account of the tribe—an account which we can only follow in such portions as appear to possess novelty, or other important interest. *Sioux* is the French term for the Indians in question—the English have corrupted it into *Sues*. Their primitive name is said to be Darcotas. Their original seats were on the Mississippi, but they had gradually extended their dominions, and, at the date of the Journal, occupied almost the whole of that vast territory circumscribed by the Mississippi, the Saskatchawine, the Missouri, and the Red River of Lake Winnipeg. They were sub-divided into numerous clans. The Darcotas proper were the Winowacants, called the Gens du Lac by the French—consisting of about five hundred warriors, and living on both sides of the Mississippi, in the vicinity of the Falls of St. Anthony. Neighbors of the Winowacants, and residing north of them on the river St. Peters', were the Wappatomies, about two hundred men. Still farther up the St. Peters' lived a band of one hundred, called the Wappytooties, among themselves, and by the French the Gens des

Feuilles. Higher up the river yet, and near its source, resided the Sissytoonies, in number two hundred or thereabouts. On the Missouri dwelt the Yanktons and the Tetons. Of the first tribe there were two branches, the northern and southern, of which the former led an Arab life in the plains at the sources of the Red, Sioux, and Jacques rivers, being in number about five hundred. The southern branch kept possession of the tract lying between the river Des Moines on the one hand, and the rivers Jacques and Sioux on the other. But the Sioux most renowned for deeds of violence are the Tetons; and of these there were four tribes—the Saonies, the Minnakenozzies, the Okydandies, and the Bois-Brulés. These last, a body of whom were now lying in wait to intercept the voyagers, were the most savage and formidable of the whole race, numbering about two hundred men, and residing on both sides of the Missouri near the rivers called by Captains Lewis and Clarke, The White and Teton. Just below the Chayenne river were the Okydandies, one hundred and fifty. The Minnackennozzies—two hundred and fifty—occupied a tract between the Chayenne and the Watarhoo; and the Saonies, the largest of the Teton bands, counting as many as three hundred warriors, were found in the vicinity of the Warreconne.

Besides these four divisions—the regular Sioux—there were five tribes of seceders called Assiniboins; the Menatopæ Assiniboins, two hundred, on Mouse river, between the Assiniboin and the Missouri; the Gens de Feuilles Assiniboins, two hundred and fifty, occupying both sides of White river; the Big Devils, four hundred and fifty, wandering about the heads of Porcupine and Milk rivers; with two other bands whose names are not mentioned, but who roved on the Saskatchawine, and numbered together, about seven hundred men. These seceders were often at war with the parent or original Sioux.

In person, the Sioux generally are an ugly ill-made race, their limbs being much too small for the trunk, according to our ideas of the human form—their cheek bones are high, and their eyes protruding and dull. The heads of the men are shaved, with the exception of a small spot on the crown, whence a long tuft is permitted to fall in plaits upon the shoulders; this tuft is an object of scrupulous care, but is now and then cut off, upon an occasion of grief or solemnity. A full dressed Sioux chief presents a striking appearance. The whole surface of the body is painted with grease and coal. A shirt of skins is worn as far down as the waist, while round the middle is a girdle of the same material, and sometimes of cloth, about an inch in width; this supports a piece of blanket or fur passing between the thighs. Over the shoulders is a white-dressed buffalo mantle, the hair of which is worn next the skin in fair weather, but turned outward in wet. This robe is large enough to envelope the whole body, and is frequently ornamented with porcupine quills (which make a rattling noise as the warrior moves) as well as with a great variety of rudely painted figures, emblematical of the wearer's military character. Fastened to the top of the head is worn a hawk's feather, adorned with porcupine quills. Leggings of dressed antelope skin serve the purpose of pantaloons, and have seams at the sides, about two inches wide, and bespotted here and there with small tufts of human hair, the trophies of some scalping excursion. The moccasins are of elk or buffalo skin, the hair worn inward; on great occasions the chief is seen with the skin of a polecat dangling at the heel of each boot. The Sioux are indeed partial to this noisome animal; whose fur is in high favor for tobacco-pouches and other appendages.

The dress of a chieftain's squaw is also remarkable. Her hair is suffered to grow long, is parted across the forehead, and hangs loosely behind, or is collected into a kind of net. Her moccasins do not differ from her husband's; but her leggings extend upward only as far as the knee, where they are met by an awkward shirt of elk-skin depending to the ancles, and supported above by a string going over the shoulders. This shirt is usually confined to the waist by a girdle, and over all is thrown a buffalo mantle like that of the men. The tents of the Teton Sioux are described as of neat construction, being formed of white-dressed buffalo hide, well secured and supported by poles.

The region infested by the tribe in question extends along the banks of the Missouri for some hundred and fifty miles or more, and is chiefly prairie land, but is occasionally diversified by hills. These latter are always deeply cut by gorges or ravines, which in the middle of summer are dry, but form the channels of muddy and impetuous torrents during the season of rain. Their edges are fringed with thick woods, as well at top, as at bottom; but the prevalent aspect of the country is that of a bleak low land, with rank herbage, and without trees. The soil is strongly impregnated with mineral substances in great variety—among others with glauber salts, copperas, sulfur, and alum, which tinge the water of the river and impart to it a nauseous odor and taste. The wild animals most usual are the buffalo, deer, elk, and antelope. We again resume the words of the Journal.]

September 6. The country was open, and the day remarkably pleasant: so that we were all in pretty good spirits notwithstanding the expectation of attack. So far, we had not caught even a glimpse of an Indian, and we were making rapid way through their dreaded territory. I was too well aware, however, of the savage tactics to suppose that we were not narrowly watched, and had made up my mind that we should hear something of the Tetons at the first gorge which would afford them a convenient lurking-place.

About noon a Canadian bawled out "The Sioux!—the Sioux"—and directed attention to a long narrow ravine, which intersected the prairie on our left, extending from the banks of the Missouri as far as the eye could reach, in a southwardly course. This gully was the bed of a creek, but its waters were now low, and the sides rose up like huge regular walls on each side. By the aid of a spy glass I perceived at once the cause of the alarm given by the voyageur. A large party of mounted savages were coming down the gorge in Indian file, with the evident intention of taking us unawares. Their calumet feathers had been the means of their detection; for every now and then we could see some of these bobbing up above the edge of the gulley, as the bed of the ravine forced the wearer to rise higher than usual. We could tell that they were on horseback by the motion of these feathers. The party was coming upon us with great rapidity; and I gave the word to pull on with all haste so as to pass the mouth of the creek before they reached it. As soon as the Indians perceived by our increased speed that they were discovered, they immediately raised a yell, scrambled out of the gorge, and galloped down upon us, to the number of about one hundred.

Our situation was now somewhat alarming. At almost any other part of the Missouri which we had passed during the day, I should not have cared so much for these freebooters; but, just here, the banks were remarkably steep and high, partaking of the character of the creek banks, and the savages were enabled to overlook us completely, while the cannon, upon which we had placed so much reliance, could not be brought to bear upon them at all. What added to our difficulty was that the current in the middle of the river was so turbulent and strong that we could make no headway against it except by dropping arms, and employing our whole force at the oars. The water near the northern shore was too shallow even for the piroque, and our only mode of proceeding, if we designed to proceed at all, was by pushing in within a moderate stone's throw of the left or southern bank, where we were completely at the mercy of the Sioux, but where we could make good headway by means of our poles and the wind, aided by the eddy. Had the savages attacked us at this juncture I cannot see how we could have escaped them. They were all well provided with bows and arrows, and small round shields, presenting a very noble and picturesque appearance. Some of the chiefs had spears, with fanciful flags attached, and were really gallant-looking men. The portrait here annexed is that of the commander-in-chief of the party which now interrupted us, and was sketched by Thornton, at a subsequent period.

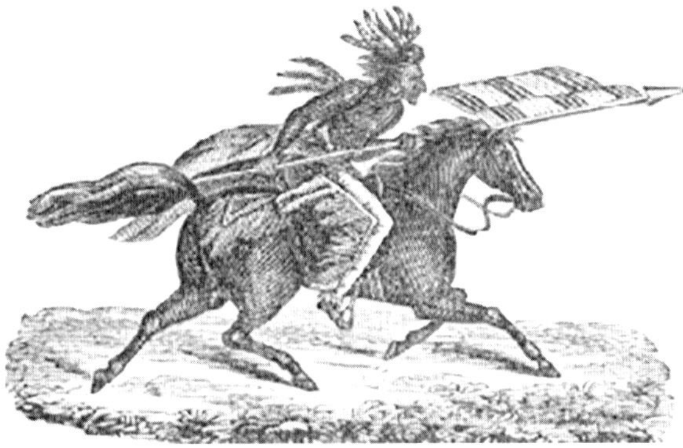

Either good luck upon our own parts, or great stupidity on the parts of the Indians, relieved us very unexpectedly from the dilemma. The savages, having galloped up to the edge of the cliff just above us, set up another yell, and commenced a variety of gesticulations, whose meaning we at once knew to be that we should stop and come on shore. I had expected this demand, and had made up my mind that it would be most prudent to pay no attention to it at all, but proceed on our course. My refusal to stop had at least one good effect, for it appeared to mystify the Indians most wonderfully, who could not be brought to understand the measure in the least, and stared at us, as we kept on our way without answering them, in the most ludicrous amazement. Presently they commenced an agitated conversation among themselves, and at last finding that nothing could be made of us, fairly turned their horses' heads to the southward and galloped out of sight, leaving us as much surprised as rejoiced at their departure.

In the meantime we made the most of the opportunity, and pushed on with might and main, in order to get out of the region of steep banks before the anticipated return of our foes. In about two hours we again saw them in the south, at a great distance, and their number much augmented. They came on at full gallop, and were soon at the river; but our position was now much more advantageous, for the banks were sloping, and there were no trees to shelter the savages from our shot. The current, moreover, was not so rapid as before, and we were enabled to keep in mid-channel. The party, it seems, had only retreated to procure an interpreter, who now appeared upon a large gray horse, and, coming into the river as far as he could without swimming, called out to us in bad French to stop, and come on shore. To this I made one of the Canadians reply that, to oblige our friends the Sioux, we would willingly stop, for a short time, and converse, but that it was inconvenient for us to come on shore, as we could not do so without incommoding our great medicine (here the Canadian pointed to the cannon) who was anxious to proceed on his voyage, and whom we were afraid to disobey.

At this they began again their agitated whisperings and gesticulations among themselves, and seemed quite at a loss what to do. In the meantime the boats had been brought to anchor in a favorable position, and I was resolved to fight now, if necessary, and endeavor to give the freebooters so warm a reception as would inspire them with wholesome dread for the future. I reflected that it was nearly impossible to keep on good terms with these Sioux, who were our enemies at heart, and who could only be restrained from pillaging and murdering us by a conviction of our prowess. Should we comply with their present demands, go on shore, and even succeed in purchasing a temporary safety by concessions and donations, such conduct would not avail us in the end, and would be rather a palliation than a radical cure of the evil. They would be sure to glut their vengeance sooner or later, and, if they suffered us to go on our way now, might hereafter attack us at a disadvantage, when it might be as much as we could do to repel them, to say nothing of inspiring them with awe. Situated as we were here, it was in our power to give them a lesson they would be apt to remember; and we might never be in so good a situation again. Thinking thus, and all except the Canadians agreeing with me in opinion, I determined to assume a bold stand, and rather provoke hostilities than avoid them. This was our true policy. The savages had no fire arms which we could discover, except an old carabine carried by one of the chiefs; and their arrows would not prove very effective weapons when employed at so great a distance as that now between us. In regard to their number, we did not care much for that. Their position was one which would expose them to the full sweep of our cannon.

When Jules (the Canadian) had finished his speech about incommoding our great medicine, and when the consequent agitation had somewhat subsided among the savages, the interpreter spoke again and propounded three queries. He wished to know, first, whether we had any tobacco, or whiskey, or fire-guns—secondly, whether we did not wish the aid of the Sioux in rowing our large boat up the Missouri as far as the country of the Ricarees, who were great rascals—and, thirdly, whether our great medicine was not a very large and strong green grass-hopper.

To these questions, propounded with profound gravity, Jules replied, by my directions, as follows. First, that we had plenty of whiskey, as well as tobacco, with an inexhaustible supply of fire-guns and powder—but that our great medicine had just told us that the Tetons were greater rascals than the Ricarees—that they were our enemies—that they had been lying in wait to intercept and kill us for many days past—that we must give them nothing at all, and hold no intercourse with them whatever; we should therefore be afraid to give them anything, even if so disposed, for fear of the anger of the great medicine, who was not to be trifled with. Secondly, that, after the character just given the Sioux Tetons, we could not think of employing them to row our boat—and, thirdly, that it was a good thing for them (the Sioux) that our great medicine had not overheard their last query, respecting the "large green grasshopper;" for, in that case, it might have gone very hard with them (the Sioux). Our great medicine was anything but a large green grasshopper, and that they should soon see, to their cost, if they did not immediately go, the whole of them, about their business.

Notwithstanding the imminent danger in which we were all placed, we could scarcely keep our countenances in beholding the air of profound admiration and astonishment with which the savages listened to these replies; and I believe that they would have immediately dispersed, and left us to proceed on our voyage, had it not been for the unfortunate words in which I informed them that they were greater rascals than the Ricarees. This was, apparently, an insult of the last atrocity, and excited them to an incontrollable degree of fury. We heard the words "Ricaree! Ricaree!" repeated, every now and then, with the utmost emphasis and excitement; and the whole band, as well as we could judge, seemed to be divided into two factions; the one urging the immense power of the great medicine, and the other the outrageous insult of being called greater rascals than the Ricarees. While matters stood thus, we retained our position in the middle of the stream, firmly resolved to give the villains a dose of our cannister shot, upon the first indignity which should be offered us.

Presently, the interpreter on the gray horse came again into the river, and said that he believed we were no better than we should be—that all the pale faces who had previously gone up the river had been friends of the Sioux, and had made them large presents—that they, the Tetons, were determined not to let us proceed another step unless we came on shore and gave up all our fire-guns and whiskey, with half of our tobacco—that it was plain we were allies of the Ricarees, (who were now at war with the Sioux,) and that our design was to carry them supplies, which we should not do—lastly, that they did not think very much of our great medicine, for he had told us a lie in relation to the designs of the Tetons, and was positively nothing but a great green grasshopper, in spite of all that we thought to the contrary. These latter words, about the great green grasshopper, were taken up by the whole assemblage as the interpreter uttered them, and shouted out at the top of the voice, that the great medicine himself might be sure to hear the taunt. At the same time, they all broke into wild disorder, galloping their horses furiously in short circles, using contemptuous and indecent gesticulations, brandishing their spears, and drawing their arrows to the head.

I knew that the next thing would be an attack, and so determined to anticipate it at once, before any of our party were wounded by the discharge of their weapons—there was nothing to be gained by delay, and every thing by prompt and resolute action. As soon as a good opportunity presented itself, the word was given to fire, and instantly obeyed. The effect of the discharge was very severe, and answered all our purposes to the full. Six of the Indians were killed, and perhaps three times as many badly wounded. The rest were thrown into the greatest terror and confusion, and made off into the prairie at full speed, as we drew up our anchors, after reloading the gun, and pulled boldly in for the shore. By the time we had reached it, there was not an unwounded Teton within sight.

I now left John Greely, with three Canadians, in charge of the boats, landed with the rest of the men, and, approaching a savage who was severely but not dangerously wounded, held a conversation with him, by means of Jules. I told him that the whites were well disposed to the Sioux, and to all the Indian nations; that our sole object in visiting his country was to trap beaver, and see the beautiful region which had been given the red men by the Great Spirit; that when we had procured as many furs as we wished, and seen all we came to see, we should return home; that we had heard that the Sioux, and especially the Tetons, were a quarrelsome race, and that therefore we had brought with us our great medicine for protection; that he was now much exasperated with the Tetons on account of their intolerable insult in calling him a green grasshopper (which he was not); that I had had great difficulty in restraining him from a pursuit of the warriors who had fled, and from sacrificing the wounded who now lay around us; and that I had only succeeded in pacifying him by becoming personally responsible for the future good behavior of the savages. At this portion of my discourse the poor fellow appeared much relieved, and extended his hand in token of amity. I took it, and assured him and his friends of my protection as long as we were unmolested, following up this promise by a present of twenty carrots of tobacco, some small hardware, beads, and red flannel, for himself and the rest of the wounded.

While all this was going on, we kept a sharp look out for the fugitive Sioux. As I concluded making the presents, several gangs of these were observable in the distance, and were evidently seen by the disabled savage; but I thought it best to pretend not to perceive them, and shortly afterward returned to the boats. The whole interruption had detained us full three hours, and it was after three o'clock when we once more started on our route. We made extraordinary haste, as I was anxious to get as far as possible from the scene of action before night. We had a strong wind at our back, and the current diminished in strength as we proceeded, owing to the widening of the stream. We therefore made great way, and by nine o'clock, had reached a large and thickly wooded island, near the northern bank, and close by the mouth of a creek. Here we resolved to encamp, and had scarcely set foot on shore, when one of the Greelys shot and secured a fine buffalo, many of which were upon the place. After posting our sentries for the night, we had the hump for supper, with as much whiskey as was good for us. Our exploit of the day was then freely discussed, and by most of the men was treated as an excellent joke; but I could by no means enter into any merriment upon the subject. Human blood had never, before this epoch, been shed at my hands; and although reason urged that I had taken the wisest, and what would no doubt prove in the end the most merciful course, still conscience, refusing to hearken even to reason herself, whispered pertinaciously within my ear—"it is human blood which thou hast shed." The hours wore away slowly—I found it impossible to sleep. At length the morning dawned, and with its fresh dews, its fresher breezes, and smiling flowers, there came a new courage, and a bolder tone of thought, which enabled me to look more steadily upon what had been done, and to regard in its only proper point of view the urgent necessity of the deed.

September 7. Started early, and made great way, with a strong cold wind from the east. Arrived about noon at the upper gorge of what is called the Great Bend, a place where the river performs a circuit of full thirty miles, while by land the direct distance is not more than fifteen hundred yards. Six miles beyond this is a creek about thirty-five yards wide, coming in from the south. The country here is of peculiar character; on each side of the river the shore is strewed thickly with round stones washed from the bluffs, and presenting a remarkable appearance for miles. The channel is very shallow, and much interrupted with sand-bars. Cedar is here met with more frequently than any other species of timber, and the prairies are covered with a stiff kind of prickly pear, over which our men found it no easy matter to walk in their moccasins.

About sunset, in endeavoring to avoid a rapid channel, we had the misfortune to run the larboard side of the large boat on the edge of a sand-bar, which so heeled us over that we were very near getting filled with water, in spite of the greatest exertion. As it was, much damage was done to the loose powder, and the Indian goods were all more or less injured. As soon as we found the boat careering, we all jumped into the water, which was here up to our arm-pits, and by main force held the sinking side up. But we were still in a dilemma, for all our exertions were barely sufficient to keep from capsizing, and we could not spare a man to do any thing toward pushing off. We were relieved, very unexpectedly, by the sinking of the whole sand-bar from under the boat, just as we were upon the point of despair. The bed of the river in this neighborhood is much obstructed by these shifting sands, which frequently change situations with great rapidity, and without apparent cause. The material of the bars is a fine hard yellow sand, which, when dry, is of a brilliant glass-like appearance, and almost impalpable.

September 8. We were still in the heart of the Teton country, and kept a sharp look-out, stopping as seldom as possible, and then only upon the islands, which abounded with game in great variety—buffaloes, elk, deer, goats, black-tailed deer, and antelopes, with plover and brant of many kinds. The goats are uncommonly tame, and have no beard. Fish is not so abundant here as lower down the river. A white wolf was killed by John Greely in a ravine upon one of the smaller islands. Owing to the difficult navigation, and the frequent necessity of employing the tow-line, we did not make great progress this day.

September 9. Weather growing sensibly colder, which made us all anxious of pushing our way through the Sioux country, as it would be highly dangerous to form our winter encampment in their vicinity. We aroused ourselves to exertion, and proceeded rapidly, the Canadians singing and shouting as we went. Now and then we saw, in the extreme distance, a solitary Teton, but no attempt was made to molest us, and we began to gather courage from this circumstance. Made twenty-eight miles during the day, and encamped at night, in high glee, on a large island well stocked with game, and thickly covered with cotton-wood.

[We omit the adventures of Mr. Rodman from this period until the tenth of April. By the last of October, nothing of importance happening in the interval, the party made their way to a small creek which they designated as Otter creek, and, proceeding up this about a mile to an island well adapted for their purpose, built a log fort and took up their quarters for the winter. The location is just above the old Ricara villages. Several parties of these Indians visited the voyagers, and behaved with perfect friendliness—they had heard of the skirmish with the Tetons, the result of which hugely pleased them. No farther trouble was experienced from any of the Sioux. The winter wore away pleasantly, and without accident of note. On the tenth of April the party resumed their voyage.]

CHAPTER V

APRIL 10, 1792. The weather was now again most delicious, and revived our spirits exceedingly. The sun began to have power, and the river was quite free of ice, so the Indians assured us, for a hundred miles ahead. We bade *adieu* to Little Snake [a chief of the Ricarees who had shown the voyagers many evidences of friendship during the winter] and his band, with unfeigned regret, and set out, after breakfast, on our voyage. Perrine [an agent of the Hudson Bay fur company on his way to Petite Côte] accompanied us with three Indians for the first ten miles, when he took leave of us and made his way back to the village, where (as we afterward heard) he met with a violent death from the hands of a squaw, to whom he offered some insult. Upon parting with the agent, we pushed on vigorously up the river, and made great way, notwithstanding a rapid current. In the afternoon, Thornton, who had been complaining for some days past, was taken seriously ill; so much so that I urged the return of the whole party to the hut, there to wait until he should get better; but he resisted this offer so strongly that I was forced to yield. We made him a comfortable bed in the cabin, and paid him every attention; but he had a raging fever, with occasional delirium, and I was much afraid that we should lose him. In the meantime we still pushed ahead with resolution, and by night had made twenty miles—an excellent day's work.

April 11. Still beautiful weather. We started early, and had a good wind, which aided us greatly; so that, but for Thornton's illness, we should all have been in fine spirits. He seemed to grow much worse, and I scarcely knew how to act. Every thing was done for his comfort which could be done; Jules, the Canadian, made him some tea, from prairie herbs, which had the effect of inducing perspiration, and allayed the fever very sensibly. We stopped at night on the main land to the north, and three hunters went out into the prairie by moonlight, returning at one in the morning, without their rifles, and with a fat antelope.

They related that, having proceeded many miles across the country, they reached the banks of a beautiful rivulet, where they were much surprised and alarmed at discovering a large war-party of the Saonie Sioux, who immediately took them prisoners, and carried them a mile on the other side of the stream to a kind of park, or enclosure, walled with mud and sticks, in which was a large herd of antelopes. These animals were still coming into the park, the gates of which were so contrived as to prevent escape. This was an annual practice of the Indians. In the autumn, the antelopes retire for food and shelter from the prairie to the mountainous regions on the south of the river. In the spring they recross it in great numbers, and are then easily taken by being enticed into a strong enclosure as above described.

The hunters (John Greely, the Prophet, and a Canadian) had scarcely any hope of escape from the clutches of the Indians (who numbered as many as fifty), and had well nigh made up their minds to die. Greely and the Prophet were disarmed and tied hand and foot; the Canadian, however, was suffered, for some reason not perfectly understood, to remain unbound, and was only deprived of his rifle, the savages leaving him in possession of his hunter's knife (which, possibly they did not perceive, as it was worn in a sort of sheath in the side of his legging) and treating him otherwise with a marked difference from their demeanor to the others. This circumstance proved the source of the party's deliverance.

It was, perhaps, nine o'clock at night when they were first taken. The moon was bright, but, as the air was unusually cool for the season, the savages had kindled two large fires at a sufficient distance from the park not to frighten the antelopes, who were still pouring into it continually. At these fires they were occupied in cooking their game when the hunters so unexpectedly came upon them from round a clump of trees. Greely and the Prophet, after being disarmed and bound with strong thongs of buffalo hide, were thrown down under a tree at some distance from the blaze; while the Canadian was permitted to seat himself, in charge of two savages, by one of the fires, the rest of the Indians forming a circle round the other and larger one. In this arrangement, the time wore away slowly, and the hunters were in momentary expectation of death; the cords of the two who were bound caused them, also, infinite pain, from the tightness with which they were fastened. The Canadian had endeavored to hold a conversation with his guards, in the hope of bribing them to release him, but could not make himself understood. About midnight, the congregation around the large fire were suddenly disturbed by the dash of several large antelopes in succession through the midst of the blaze. These animals had burst through a portion of the mud wall which confined them, and, mad with rage and affright, had made for the light of the fire, as is the habit of insects at night in like circumstances. It seems, however, that the Saonies had never heard of any similar feat of these usually timid creatures, for they were in great terror at the unexpected interruption, and their alarm increased to perfect dismay, as the whole captured herd came rushing and bounding upon them, after the lapse of a minute or so from the outbreak of the first few. The hunters described the scene as one of the most singular nature. The beasts were apparently frantic, and the velocity and impetuosity with which they flew, rather than leaped, through the flames, and through the midst of the terrified savages, was said by Greely (a man not in the least prone to exaggerate) to have been not only an imposing but even a terrible spectacle. They carried every thing before them in their first plunges; but, having cleared the large fire, they immediately dashed at the small one, scattering the brands and blazing wood about; then returned, as if bewildered, to the large one, and so backward and forward until the decline of the fires, when, in small parties, they scampered off like lightning to the woods.

Many of the Indians were knocked down in this furious *mêlée*, and there is no doubt that some of them were seriously, if not mortally, wounded by the sharp hoofs of the agile antelopes. Some threw themselves flat on the ground, and so avoided injury. The Prophet and Greely, not being near the fires, were in no danger. The Canadian was prostrated at the first onset by a kick which rendered him senseless for some minutes. When he came to himself he was nearly in darkness; for the moon had gone behind a heavy thundercloud, and the fires were almost out, or only existed in brands scattered hither and thither. He saw no Indians near him, and instantly arousing himself to escape, made, as well as he could, for the tree where his two comrades were lying. Their thongs were soon cut, and the three set off at full speed in the direction of the river, without stopping to think of their rifles, or of any thing beyond present security. Having run for some miles, and finding no one in pursuit, they slackened their pace, and made their way to a spring for a draft of water. Here it was they met with the antelope which, as I mentioned before, they brought with them to the boats. The poor creature lay panting, and unable to move, by the border of the spring.

One of its legs was broken, and it bore evident traces of fire. It was no doubt one of the herd which had been the means of deliverance. Had there been even a chance of its recovery the hunters would have spared it in token of their gratitude, but it was miserably injured, so they put it at once out of its misery, and brought it home to the boats, where we made an excellent breakfast upon it next morning.

April 12, *13*, *14*, and *15*. During these four days we kept on our course without any adventure of note. The weather was very pleasant during the middle of the day, but the nights and mornings were exceedingly cold, and we had sharp frosts. Game was abundant. Thornton still continued ill, and his sickness perplexed and grieved me beyond measure. I missed his society very much, and now found that he was almost the only member of our party in whom I could strictly confide. By this I merely mean that he was almost the only one to whom I could, or would, freely unburthen my heart, with all its wild hopes, and fantastic wishes—not that any individual among us was unworthy of implicit faith. On the contrary, we were all like brothers, and a dispute, of any importance, never occurred. One interest seemed to bind all; or rather we appeared to be a band of voyagers without interest in view—mere travelers for pleasure. What ideas the Canadians might have held upon this subject I cannot, indeed, exactly say. These fellows talked a great deal, to be sure, about the profits of the enterprise, and especially about their expected share of it; yet I can scarcely think they cared much for these points, for they were the most simple-minded, and certainly the most obliging set of beings upon the face of the earth. As for the rest of the crew, I have no doubt in the world that the pecuniary benefit to be afforded by the expedition was the last thing upon which they speculated. Some singular evidences of the feeling which more or less pervaded us all occurred during the prosecution of the voyage. Interests, which, in the settlements, would have been looked upon as of the highest importance, were here treated as matters unworthy of a serious word, and neglected, or totally discarded upon the most frivolous pretext. Men who had traveled thousands of miles through a howling wilderness, beset by horrible dangers, and enduring the most heart-rending privations for the ostensible purpose of collecting peltries, would seldom take the trouble to secure them when obtained, and would leave behind them without a sigh an entire cache of fine beaver skin rather than forego the pleasure of pushing up some romantic-looking river, or penetrating into some craggy and dangerous cavern, for minerals whose use they knew nothing about, and which they threw aside as lumber at the first decent opportunity.

In all this my own heart was very much with the rest of the party; and I am free to say that, as we proceeded on our journey, I found myself less and less interested in the main business of the expedition, and more and more willing to turn aside in pursuit of idle amusement—if indeed I am right in calling by so feeble a name as amusement that deep and most intense excitement with which I surveyed the wonders and majestic beauties of the wilderness. No sooner had I examined one region than I was possessed with an irresistible desire to push forward and explore another. As yet, however, I felt as if in too close proximity to the settlements for the full enjoyment of my burning love of Nature, and of *the unknown*. I could not help being aware that some civilized footsteps, although few, had preceded me in my journey—that *some* eyes before mine own had been enraptured with the scenes around me. But for this sentiment, ever obtruding itself, I should no doubt have loitered more frequently on the way, turning aside to survey the features of the region bordering upon the river, and perhaps penetrating deeply, at times, into the heart of the country to the north and south of our route. But I was anxious to *go on*—to get, if possible, beyond the extreme bounds of civilization—to gaze, if I could, upon those gigantic mountains of which the existence had been made known to us only by the vague accounts of the Indians. These ulterior hopes and views I communicated fully to no one of our party save Thornton. He participated in all my most visionary projects, and entered completely into the spirit of romantic enterprise which pervaded my soul. I therefore felt his illness as a bitter evil. He grew worse daily, while it was out of our power to render him any effectual assistance.

April 16. To-day we had a cold rain with a high wind from the north, obliging us to come to anchor until late in the afternoon. At four o'clock, P. M., we proceeded, and made five miles by night. Thornton was much worse.

April 17, and *18*. During both these days we had a continuance of raw unpleasant weather, with the same cold wind from the north. We observed many large masses of ice in the river, which was much swollen and very muddy. The time passed unpleasantly, and we made no way.

Thornton appeared to be dying, and I now resolved to encamp at the first convenient spot, and remain until his illness should terminate. We accordingly, at noon this day, drew the boats up a large creek coming in from the south, and formed an encampment on the main land.

April 25. We remained at the creek until this morning, when, to the great joy of us all, Thornton was sufficiently recovered to go on. The weather was fine, and we proceeded gaily through a most lovely portion of the country, without encountering a single Indian, or meeting with any adventure out of the usual course until the last of the month, when we reached the country of the Mandans, or rather of the Mandans, the Minnetarees, and the Ahnahaways; for these three tribes all live in the near vicinity of each other, occupying five villages. Not a great many years ago the Mandans were settled in nine villages, about eighty miles below, the ruins of which we passed without knowing what they were—seven on the west and two on the east of the river; but they were thinned off by the small-pox and their old enemies the Sioux, until reduced to a mere handful, when they ascended to their present position. [Mr. R. gives here a tolerably full account of the Minnetarees and Ahnahaways or Wassatoons; but we omit it, as differing in no important particular from the ordinary statements respecting these nations.] The Mandans received us with perfect friendliness, and we remained in their neighborhood three days, during which we overhauled and repaired the piroque, and otherwise refitted. We also obtained a good supply of a hard corn, of a mixed color, which the savages had preserved through the winter in holes, near the front of their lodges. While with the Mandans we were visited by a Minnetaree chief, called Waukerassah, who behaved with much civility, and was of service to us in many respects. The son of this chief we engaged to accompany us as interpreter as far as the great fork. We made the father several presents, with which he was greatly pleased.[1] On the first of May we bade adieu to the Mandans, and went on our way.

May 1. The weather was mild, and the surrounding country began to assume a lovely appearance with the opening vegetation, which was now much advanced. The cotton-wood leaves were quite as large as a crown, and many flowers were full blown. The low grounds began to

1 The chief Waukerassah is mentioned by Captains Lewis and Clarke, whom he also visited..

spread out here more than usual, and were well supplied with timber. The cotton-wood and common willow, as well as red willow, abounded; with rose-bushes in great plenty. Beyond the low grounds on the river, the country extended in one immense plain without wood of any kind. The soil was remarkably rich. The game was more abundant than we had ever yet seen it. We kept a hunter ahead of us on each bank, and to-day they brought in an elk, a goat, five beavers, and a great number of plovers. The beavers were very tame and easily taken. This animal is quite a *bonne bouche* as an article of food; especially the tail, which is of a somewhat glutinous nature, like the fins of the halibut. A beaver tall will suffice for a plentiful dinner for three men. We made twenty miles before night.

May 2. We had a fine wind this morning, and used our sails until noon, when it became rather too much for us, and we stopped for the day. Our hunters went out and shortly returned with an immense elk, whom Neptune had pulled down after a long chase, the animal having been only slightly wounded by a buck shot. He measured six feet in height. An antelope was also caught about dusk. As soon as the creature saw our men, it flew off with the greatest velocity, but after a few minutes stopped, and returned on its steps, apparently through curiosity—then bounded away again. This conduct was repeated frequently, each time the game coming nearer and nearer, until at length it ventured within rifle distance, when a shot from the Prophet brought it down. It was lean and with young. These animals, although of incredible swiftness of foot, are still bad swimmers, and thus frequently fall a victim to the wolves, in their attempts to cross a stream. Today made twelve miles.

May 3. This morning we made great headway, and by night had accomplished full thirty miles. The game continued to be abundant. Buffaloes, in vast numbers, lay dead along the shore, and we saw many wolves devouring the carcases. They fled always at our approach. We were much at a loss to account for the death of the buffaloes, but some weeks afterward the mystery was cleared up. Arriving at a pass of the river where the bluffs were steep and the water deep at their base, we observed a large herd of the huge beasts swimming across, and stopped to watch their motions. They came in a sidelong manner down the current, and had apparently entered the water from a gorge, about half a mile above, where the bank sloped into the stream. Upon reaching the land on the west side of the river they found it impossible to ascend the cliffs, and the water was beyond their depth. After struggling for some time, and endeavoring in vain to get a foothold in the steep and slippery clay, they turned and swam to the eastern shore, where the same kind of inaccessible precipices presented themselves, and where the ineffectual struggle to ascend was repeated. They now turned a second time, a third, a fourth, and a fifth—always making the shore at very nearly the same places. Instead of suffering themselves to go down with the current in search of a more favorable landing, (which might have been found a quarter of a mile below), they seemed bent upon maintaining their position, and, for this purpose, swam with their breasts at an acute angle to the stream and used violent exertions to prevent being borne down. At the fifth time of crossing, the poor beasts were so entirely exhausted that it was evident they could do no more. They now struggled fearfully to scramble up the bank, and one or two of them had nearly succeeded, when, to our great distress (for we could not witness their noble efforts without commisseration) the whole mass of loose earth above caved in, and buried several of them in its fall, without leaving the cliff in better condition for ascent. Upon this the rest of the herd commenced a lamentable kind of lowing or moaning—a sound conveying more of a dismal sorrow and despair than any thing which it is possible to imagine—I shall never get it out of my head. Some of the beasts made another attempt to swim the river, struggled a few minutes, and sank—the waves above them being dyed with the red blood that gushed from their nostrils in the death agony. But the greater part, after the moaning described, seemed to yield supinely to their fate, rolled over on their backs, and disappeared. The whole herd were drowned—not a buffalo escaped. Their carcases were thrown up in half an hour afterward upon the flat grounds a short distance below, where, but for their ignorant obstinacy, they might so easily have landed in safety.

May 4. The weather was delightful, and, with a fair warm wind from the south, we made twenty-five miles before night. To-day Thornton was sufficiently recovered to assist in the duties of the boat. In the afternoon he went out with me into the prairie on the west, where we saw a great number of early spring flowers of a kind never seen in the settlements. Many of them were of a rare beauty and delicious perfume. We saw also game in great variety, but shot none, as we were sure the hunters would bring in more than was wanted for use, and I was averse to the wanton destruction of life. On our way home we came upon two Indians of the Assiniboin nation, who accompanied us to the boats. They had evinced nothing like distrust on the way, but, on the contrary, had been frank and bold in demeanor; we were therefore much surprised to see them, upon coming within a stone's throw of the piroque, turn, both of them, suddenly round, and make off into the prairie at full speed. Upon getting a good distance from us, they stopped and ascended a knoll which commanded a view of the river. Here they lay on their bellies, and, resting their chins on their hands, seemed to regard us with the deepest astonishment. By the aid of a spy-glass I could minutely observe their countenances, which bore evidence of both amazement and terror. They continued watching us for a long time. At length, as if struck with a sudden thought, they arose hurriedly and commenced a rapid flight in the direction from which we had seen them issue at first.

May 5. As we were getting under way very early this morning, a large party of Assiniboins suddenly rushed upon the boats, and succeeded in taking possession of the piroque before we could make any effectual resistance. No one was in it at the time except Jules, who escaped by throwing himself into the river, and swimming to the large boat, which we had pushed out into the stream. These Indians had been brought upon us by the two who had visited us the day before, and the party must have approached us in the most stealthy manner imaginable, as we had our sentries regularly posted, and even Neptune failed to give any token of their vicinity.

We were preparing to fire upon the enemy when Misquash (the new interpreter—son of Waukerassah) gave us to understand that the Assiniboins were friends and were now making signals of amity. Although we could not help thinking that the highway robbery of our boat was but an indifferent way of evincing friendship, still we were willing to see what these people had to say, and desired Misquash to ask them why they had behaved as they did. They replied with many protestations of regard; and we at length found that they really had no intention of molesting us any farther than to satisfy an ardent curiosity which consumed them, and which they now entreated us to appease. It appeared that the two Indians of the day before, whose singular conduct had so surprised us, had been struck with sudden amazement at the sooty appearance of our negro, Toby. They had never before seen or heard of a blackamoor, and it must therefore be confessed that their astonishment was not altogether causeless. Toby, moreover, was as ugly an old gentleman as ever spoke—having all the peculiar features of his race; the swollen lips, large white protruding eyes, flat nose, long ears, double head, pot-belly, and bow legs. Upon relating their adventure to their companions, the two savages could obtain no credit for the wonderful story, and were about losing caste for ever, as liars and double-dealers, when they proposed to conduct the whole band to the boats by way of vindicating their veracity. The sudden attack seemed to have been the mere result of impatience on the part of the still incredulous Assiniboins; for they never afterward evinced the slightest hostility, and yielded up the piroque as soon as we made them understand that we would let them have a good look at old Toby. The latter personage took the matter as a very good joke, and went ashore at once, *in naturalibus*, that the inquisitive savages might observe the whole extent of the question. Their astonishment and satisfaction were profound and complete. At first they doubted the evidence of their own eyes, spitting upon their fingers and rubbing the skin of the negro to be sure that it was not painted. The wool on the head elicited repeated shouts of applause, and the bandy legs were the subject of unqualified admiration. A jig dance on the part of our ugly friend brought matters to a climax. Wonder was now at its height. Approbation could go no farther. Had Toby but possessed a single spark of ambition he might then have made his fortune for ever by ascending the throne of the Assiniboins, and reigning as King Toby the First.

This incident detained us until late in the day. After interchanging some civilities and presents with the savages, we accepted the aid of six of the band in rowing us about five miles on our route—a very acceptable assistance, and one for which we did not fail to thank Toby. We made, to-day, only twelve miles, and encamped at night on a beautiful island which we long remembered for the delicious fish and fowl which its vicinity afforded us. We staid at this pleasant spot two days, during which we feasted and made merry, with very little care for the morrow, and with very little regard to the numerous beaver which disported around us. We might have taken at this island one or two hundred skins without difficulty. As it was, we collected about twenty. The island is at the mouth of a tolerably large river coming in from the south, and at a point where the Missouri strikes off in a due westerly direction. The latitude is about 48.

May 8. We proceeded with fair winds and fine weather, and after making twenty or twenty-five miles, reached a large river coming in from the north. Where it *debouches*, however, it is very narrow—not more than a dozen yards wide, and appears to be quite choked up with mud. Upon ascending it a short distance, a fine bold stream is seen, seventy or eighty yards wide, and very deep, passing through a beautiful valley, abounding in game. Our new guide told us the name of this river, but I have no memorandum of it.[1] Robert Greely shot here some geese which build their nests upon trees.

May 9. In many places a little distant from the river banks, to-day, we observed the ground encrusted with a white substance which proved to be a strong salt. We made only fifteen miles, owing to several petty hindrances, and encamped at night on the main land, among some clumps of cotton-wood and rabbit-berry bushes.

May 10. To-day the weather was cold, and the wind strong, but fair. We made great headway. The hills in this vicinity are rough and jagged, showing irregular broken masses of rock, some of which tower to a great height, and appear to have been subject to the action of water. We picked up several pieces of petrified wood and bone; and coal was scattered about in every direction. The river gets very crooked.

May 11. Detained the greater part of the day by squalls and rain. Toward evening it cleared up beautifully with a fair wind, of which we took advantage, making ten miles before encamping. Several fat beavers were caught, and a wolf was shot upon the bank. He seemed to have strayed from a large herd which were prowling about us.

May 12. Landed to-day at noon, after making ten miles, upon a small steep island, for the purpose of overhauling some of our things. As we were about taking our departure, one of the Canadians, who led the van of the party and was several yards in advance, suddenly disappeared from our view with a loud scream. We all ran forward immediately, and laughed heartily upon finding that our man had only tumbled into an

1 Probably White-earth River.—Eds. G. M.

empty *cache*, from which we soon extricated him. Had he been alone, however, there is much room for question if he would have got out at all. We examined the hole carefully but found nothing in it beyond a few empty bottles; we did not even see any thing serving to show whether French, British, or Americans had concealed their goods here; and we felt some curiosity upon this point.

May 13. Arrived at the junction of the Yellowstone with the Missouri, after making twenty-five miles during the day. Misquash here left us, and returned home.

CHAPTER VI

THE CHARACTER OF the country through which we had passed for the last two or three days was cheerless in comparison with that to which we had been accustomed. In general it was more level; the timber being more abundant on the skirts of the stream, with little or none at all in the distance. Wherever bluffs appeared upon the margin we descried indications of coal, and we saw one extensive bed of a thick bituminous nature which very much discolored the water for some hundred yards below it. The current is more gentle than hitherto, the water clearer, and the rocky points and shoals fewer, although such as we had to pass were as difficult as ever. We had rain incessantly, which rendered the banks so slippery that the men who had the towing lines could scarcely walk. The air too was disagreeably chilly, and upon ascending some low hills near the river we observed no small quantity of snow lying in the clefts and ridges. In the extreme distance on our right we had perceived several Indian encampments which had the appearance of being temporary, and had been only lately abandoned. This region gives no indication of any permanent settlement, but appears to be a favorite hunting ground with the tribes in the vicinity—a fact rendered evident by the frequent traces of the hunt, which we came across in every direction. The Minnetarees of the Missouri, it is well known, extend their excursions in pursuit of game as high as the great fork, on the south side; while the Assiniboins go up still higher. Misquash informed us that between our present encampment and the Rocky Mountains we should meet with no lodges except those of the Minnetarees that reside on the lower or south side of the Saskatchawine.

The game had been exceedingly abundant, and in great variety—elk, buffalo, big-horn, mule-deer, bears, foxes, beaver, etc., etc., with wild fowl innumerable. Fish was also plentiful. The width of the stream varied considerably from two hundred and fifty yards to passes where the current rushed between bluffs not more than a hundred feet apart. The face of these bluffs generally was composed of a light yellowish freestone, intermingled with burnt earth, pumice-stone, and mineral salts. At one point the aspect of the country underwent a remarkable change, the hills retiring on both sides to a great distance from the river, which was thickly interspersed with small and beautiful islands, covered with cotton-wood. The low grounds appeared to be very fertile; those on the north wide and low, and opening into three extensive valleys. Here seemed to be the extreme northern termination of the range of mountains through which the Missouri had been passing for so long a time, and which are called the Black Hills by the savages. The change from the mountainous region to the level was indicated by the atmosphere, which now became dry and pure; so much so indeed that we perceived its effects upon the seams of our boats, and our few mathematical instruments.

As we made immediate approach to the forks it came on to rain very hard, and the obstructions in the river were harassing in the extreme. The banks in some places were so slippery, and the clay so soft and stiff that the men were obliged to go barefooted, as they could not keep on their moccasins. The shores also were full of pools of stagnant water, through which we were obliged to wade, sometimes up to our armpits. Then again we had to scramble over enormous shoals of sharp-pointed flints, which appeared to be the wreck of cliffs that had fallen down *en masse*. Occasionally we came to a precipitous gorge or gully, which it would put us to the greatest labor to pass, and in attempting to push by one of these the rope of the large boat (being old and much worn) gave way and permitted her to be swung round by the current upon a ledge of rock in the middle of the stream, where the water was so deep that we could only work in getting her off by the aid of the piroque, and so were full six hours in effecting it.

At one period we arrived at a high wall of black rock on the south, towering above the ordinary cliffs for about a quarter of a mile along the stream; after which there was an open plain, and about three miles beyond this again, another wall of a light color on the same side, fully two hundred feet high; then another plain or valley, and then still another wall of the most singular appearance arises on the north, soaring in height probably two hundred and fifty feet, and being in thickness about twelve, with a very regular artificial character. These cliffs present indeed the most extraordinary aspect, rising perpendicularly from the water. The last mentioned are composed of very white soft sandstone, which readily receives the impression of the water. In the upper portion of them appears a sort of frieze or cornice formed by the intervention of several thin horizontal strata of a white freestone, hard, and unaffected by the rains. Above them is a dark rich soil, sloping gradually back from the water to the extent of a mile or thereabouts, when other hills spring up abruptly to the height of full five hundred feet more.

The face of these remarkable cliffs, as might be supposed, is checkered with a variety of lines formed by the trickling of the rains upon the soft material, so that a fertile fancy might easily imagine them to be gigantic monuments reared by human art, and carved over with hieroglyphical devices. Sometimes there are complete niches (like those we see for statues in common temples) formed by the dropping out bodily of large fragments of the sandstone; and there are several points where staircases and long corridors appear, as accidental fractures in the freestone cornice happen to let the rain trickle down uniformly upon the softer material below. We passed these singular bluffs in a bright moonlight and their effect upon my imagination I shall never forget. They had all the air of enchanted structures, (such as I have dreamed of), and the twittering of myriads of martins, which have built their nests in the holes that every where perforate the mass, aided this conception not a little. Besides the main walls there are, at intervals, inferior ones, of from twenty to a hundred feet high, and from one to twelve or fifteen feet thick, perfectly regular in shape, and perpendicular. These are formed of a succession of large black-looking stones, apparently made up of loam, sand, and quartz, and absolutely symmetrical in figure, although of various sizes. They are usually square, but sometimes oblong (always parrallelepipedal) and are lying one above the other as exactly and with as perfect regularity as if placed there by some mortal mason; each upper stone covering and securing the point of junction between two lower ones, just as bricks are laid in a wall. Sometimes these singular erections run in parallel lines, as many as four abreast; sometimes they leave the river and go back until lost amid the hills; sometimes they cross each other at right angles, seeming to enclose large artificial gardens, the vegetation within which is often of a character to preserve the illusion. Where the walls are thinnest, there the bricks are less in size, and the converse. We regarded the scenery presented to our view at this portion of the Missouri as altogether the most surprising, if not the most beautiful which we had yet seen. It left upon my own mind an impression of novelty—of singularity, which can never be effaced.

Shortly before reaching the fork we came to a pretty large island on the northern side, one mile and a quarter from which is a low ground on the south very thickly covered with fine timber. After this there were several small islands, at each of which we touched for a few minutes as we passed. Then we came to a very black-looking bluff on the north, and then to two other small islands, about which we observed nothing remarkable. Going a few miles farther we reached a tolerably large island situated near the point of a steep promontory; afterward passing two others, smaller. All these islands are well timbered. It was at night on the 13th of May, that we were shown by

Misquash the mouth of the large river, which in the settlements goes by the name of the Yellow Stone, but by the Indians is called the Ahmateaza.[1] We made our camp on the south shore in a beautiful plain covered with cotton-wood.

May 14. This morning we were all awake and stirring at an early hour, as the point we had now reached was one of great importance, and it was requisite that, before proceeding any farther, we should make some survey by way of ascertaining which of the two large streams in view would afford us the best passage onward. It seemed to be the general wish of the party to push up one of these rivers as far as practicable, with a view of reaching the Rocky Mountains, when we might perhaps hit upon the head waters of the large stream Aregan, described by all the Indians with whom we had conversed upon the subject, as running into the great Pacific Ocean. I was also anxious to attain this object, which opened to my fancy a world of exciting adventure, but I foresaw many difficulties which we must necessarily encounter if we made the attempt with our present limited information in respect to the region we should have to traverse, and the savages who occupied it; about which latter we only knew indeed that they were generally the most ferocious of the North American Indians. I was afraid, too, that we might get into the wrong stream, and involve ourselves in an endless labyrinth of troubles which would dishearten the men. These thoughts, however, did not give me any long uneasiness, and I set to work at once to explore the neighborhood; sending some of the party up the banks of each stream to estimate the comparative volume of water in each, while I myself, with Thornton and John Greely, proceeded to ascend the high grounds in the fork, whence an extensive prospect of the surrounding region might be attained. We saw here an immense and magnificent country spreading out on every side into a vast plain, waving with glorious verdure, and alive with countless herds of buffaloes and wolves, intermingled with occasional elk and antelope. To the south the prospect was interrupted by a range of high, snow-capped mountains, stretching from south east to north west, and terminating abruptly. Behind these again was a higher range, extending to the very horizon in the north west. The two rivers presented the most enchanting appearance as they wound

1 There appears to be some discrepancy here which we have not thought it worth while to alter, as, after all, Mr. Rodman may not be in the wrong. The Amateaza (according to the Narrative of Lewis and Clarke) is the name given by the Minnetarees, not to the Yellow Stone, but to the Missouri itself.

away their long snake-like lengths in the distance, growing thinner and thinner until they looked like mere faint threads of silver as they vanished in the shadowy mists of the sky. We could glean nothing, from their direction so far, as regards their ultimate course, and so descended from our position much at a loss what to do.

The examination of the two currents gave us but little more satisfaction. The north stream was found to be the deeper, but the south was the wider, and the volume of water differed but little. The first had all the color of the Missouri, but the latter had the peculiar round gravelly bed which distinguishes a river that issues from a mountainous region. We were finally determined by the easier navigation of the north branch to pursue this course, although from the rapidly increasing shallowness we found that in a few days, at farthest, we should have to dispense with the large boat. We spent three days at our encampment, during which we collected a great many fine skins, and deposited them with our whole stock on hand, in a well constructed *cache* on a small island in the river a mile below the junction.[1] We also brought in a great quantity of game, and especially of deer, some haunches of which we pickled or corned for future use. We found great abundance of the prickly pear in this vicinity, as well as chokeberries in great plenty upon the low grounds and ravines. There were also many yellow and red currants (not ripe) with gooseberries. Wild roses were just beginning to open their buds in the most wonderful profusion. We left our encampment in fine spirits on the morning of

May 18. The day was pleasant, and we proceeded merrily, notwithstanding the consistent interruptions occasioned by the shoals and jutting points with which the stream abounds. The men, one and all, were enthusiastic in their determination to persevere, and the Rocky Mountains were the sole theme

1 Caches are holes very frequently dug by the trappers and fur traders, in which to deposit their furs or other goods during a temporary absence. A dry and retired situation is first selected. A circle about two feet in diameter is then described—the sod within this carefully removed and laid by. A hole is now sunk perpendicularly to the depth of a foot, and afterward gradually widened until the excavation becomes eight or ten feet deep, and six or seven feet wide. As the earth is dug up, it is cautiously placed on a skin, so as to prevent any traces upon the grass, and, when all is completed, is thrown into the nearest river, or otherwise effectually concealed. This *cache* is lined throughout with dried sticks and hay, or with skins, and within it almost any species of backwoods property may be safely and soundly kept for years. When the goods are in, and well covered with buffalo hide, earth is thrown upon the whole, and stamped firmly down. Afterward the sod is replaced, and a private mark made upon the neighboring trees, or elsewhere, indicating the precise location of the depôt.—Eds. G. M.

of conversation. In leaving our peltries behind us, we had considerably lightened the boats, and we found much less difficulty in getting them forward through the rapid currents than would otherwise have been the case. The river was crowded with islands, at nearly all of which we touched. At night we reached a deserted Indian encampment, near bluffs of a blackish clay. Rattlesnakes disturbed us very much, and before morning we had a heavy rain.

May 19. We had not proceeded far before we found the character of the stream materially altered, and very much obstructed by sand bars, or rather ridges of small stones, so that it was with the greatest difficulty we could force a passage for the larger boat. Sending two men ahead to reconnoitre, they returned with an account of a wider and deeper channel above, and once again we felt encouraged to persevere. We pushed on for ten miles and encamped on a small island for the night. We observed a peculiar mountain in the distance to the south, of a conical form, isolated, and entirely covered with snow.

May 20. We now entered into a better channel, and pursued our course with little interruption for sixteen miles, through a clayey country of peculiar character, and nearly destitute of vegetation. At night we encamped on a very large island, covered with tall trees, many of which were new to us. We remained at this spot for five days to make some repairs in the piroque.

During our sojourn here an incident of note occurred. The banks of the Missouri in this neighborhood are precipitous, and formed of a peculiar blue clay, which becomes excessively slippery after rain. The cliffs, from the bed of the stream back to the distance of a hundred yards, or thereabouts, form a succession of steep terraces of this clay, intersected in numerous directions by deep and narrow ravines, so sharply worn by the action of water at some remote period of time as to have the appearance of artificial channels. The mouths of these ravines, where they *debouche* upon the river, have a very remarkable appearance, and look from the opposite bank, by moonlight, like gigantic columns standing erect upon the shore. To an observer from the uppermost terrace the whole descent toward the stream has an indescribably chaotic and dreary air. No vegetation of any kind is seen.

John Greely, the Prophet, the interpreter Jules, and myself started out after breakfast one morning to ascend to the topmost terrace on the south shore for the purpose of looking around us; in short to see what could be seen. With great labor, and by using scrupulous caution, we succeeded in reaching the level grounds at the summit opposite our encampment. The prairie here differs from the general character of that kind of land in being thickly overgrown for many miles back with cotton-wood, rose-bushes, red willow, and broad-leaved willow; the soil being unsteady, and at times swampy, like that of the ordinary low grounds—it consists of a black-looking loam, one-third sand, and when a handful of it is thrown into water, it dissolves in the manner of sugar, with strong bubbles. In several spots we observed deep incrustations of common salt, some of which we collected and used.

Upon reaching these level grounds we all sat down to rest, and had scarcely done so when we were alarmed by a loud growl immediately in our rear, proceeding from the thick underwood. We started to our feet at once in great terror, for we had left our rifles at the island, that we might be unincumbered in the scramble up the cliffs, and the only arms we had were pistols and knives. We had scarcely time to say a word to each other before two enormous brown bears (the first we had yet encountered during the voyage) came rushing at us open-mouthed from a clump of rose-bushes. These animals are much dreaded by the Indians, and with reason, for they are indeed formidable creatures, possessing prodigious strength, with untameable ferocity, and the most wonderful tenacity of life. There is scarcely any way of killing them by a bullet, unless the shot be through the brains, and these are defended by two large muscles covering the side of the forehead, as well as by a projection of a thick frontal bone. They have been known to live for days with half a dozen balls through the lungs, and even with very severe injuries in the heart. So far we had never met with a brown bear, although often with its tracks in the mud or sand, and these we had seen nearly a foot in length, exclusive of the claws, and full eight inches in width.

What to do was now the question. To stand and fight, with such weapons as we possessed, was madness; and it was folly to think of escape by flight in the direction of the prairie; for not only were the bears running toward us from that quarter, but, at a very short distance back from the cliffs, the underwood of briar-bushes, dwarf willow, etc., was so thick that we could not have made our way through it at all, and if we kept our course along the river between the underwood and the top of the cliff, the animals would catch us in an instant; for as the ground was boggy we could make no progress upon it, while the large flat foot of the bear would enable him to travel with ease. It seemed as if these reflections (which it takes some time to embody in words) flashed all of them through the minds of all of us in an instant—for every man sprang at once to the cliffs, without sufficiently thinking of the hazard that lay there.

The first descent was some thirty or forty feet, and not very precipitous; the clay here also partook in a slight degree of the loam of the upper soil; so that we scrambled down with no great difficulty to the first terrace, the bears plunging after us with headlong fury. Arrived here, we had not a moment for hesitation. There was nothing left for us now but to encounter the enraged beasts upon the narrow platform where we stood, or to go over the second precipice. This was nearly perpendicular, sixty or seventy feet deep, and composed entirely of the blue clay which was now saturated with late rains, and as slippery as glass itself. The Canadian, frightened out of his senses, leaped to the edge at once, slid with the greatest velocity down the cliff, and was hurled over the third descent by the impetus of his course. We then lost sight of him, and of course supposed him killed; for we could have no doubt that his terrific slide would be continued from precipice to precipice until it terminated with a plunge over the last into the river—a fall of more than a hundred and fifty feet.

Had Jules not gone in this way it is more than probable that we should all have decided, in our extremity, upon attempting the descent; but his fate caused us to waver, and in the meantime the monsters were upon us. This was the first time in all my life I had ever been brought to close quarters with a wild animal of any strength or ferocity, and I have no scruple to acknowledge that my nerves were completely unstrung. For some moments I felt as if about to swoon, but a loud scream from Greely, who had been seized by the foremost bear, had the effect of arousing me to exertion, and when once fairly aroused I experienced a kind of wild and savage pleasure from the conflict.

One of the beasts, upon reaching the narrow ledge where we stood, had made an immediate rush at Greely, and had borne him to the earth, where he stood over him, holding him with his huge teeth lodged in the breast of his overcoat—which, by the greatest good fortune, he had worn, the wind being chilly. The other, rolling rather than scrambling down the cliff, was under so much headway when he reached our station that he could not stop himself until the one-half of his body hung over the precipice; he staggered in a sidelong manner, and his right legs went over while he held on in an awkward way with his two left. While thus situated he seized Wormley by the heel with his mouth, and for an instant I feared the worst, for in his efforts to free himself from the grasp the terrified struggler aided the bear to regain his footing. While I stood helpless, as above described, through terror, and watching the event without ability to render the slightest aid, the shoe and moccasin of W. were torn off in the grasp of the animal, who now tumbled headlong down to the next terrace, but stopped himself, by means of his huge claws, from sliding farther. It was now that Greely screamed for aid, and the Prophet and myself rushed to his assistance. We both fired our pistols at the bear's head; and my own ball, I am sure, must have gone through some portion of his skull, for I held the weapon close to his ear. He seemed more angry, however, than hurt; the only good effect of the discharge was in his quitting his hold of Greely (who had sustained no injury) and making at us. We had nothing but our knives to depend upon, and even the refuge of the terrace below was cut off from us by the presence of another bear there. We had our backs to the cliff, and were preparing for a deadly contest, not dreaming of help from Greely (whom we supposed mortally injured) when we heard a shot, and the huge beast fell at our feet, just when we felt his hot and horribly fetid breath in our faces. Our deliverer, who had fought many a bear in his life-time, had put his pistol deliberately to the eye of the monster, and the contents had entered the brain.

Looking now downward, we discovered the fallen bruin making ineffectual efforts to scramble up to us—the soft clay yielded to his claws, and he fell repeatedly and heavily. We tried him with several shots, but did no harm, and resolved to leave him where he was for the crows. I do not see how he could ever have made his escape from the spot. We crawled along the ledge on which we stood for nearly half a mile before we found a practicable path to the prairie above us, and did not get to camp until late in the night. Jules was there all alive, but cruelly bruised—so much so indeed that he had been unable to give any intelligible account of his accident or of our whereabouts. He had lodged in one of the ravines upon the third terrace, and had made his way down its bed to the river shore.

POETRY

CONTENTS

THE RAVEN

Once upon a midnight dreary, while I pondered, weak and weary,
Over many a quaint and curious volume of forgotten lore—
While I nodded, nearly napping, suddenly there came a tapping,
As of some one gently rapping, rapping at my chamber door.
"'Tis some visitor," I muttered, "tapping at my chamber door—
Only this and nothing more."

Ah, distinctly I remember, it was in the bleak December,
And each separate dying ember wrought its ghost upon the floor.
Eagerly I wished the morrow; —vainly I had sought to borrow
From my books surcease of sorrow—sorrow for the lost Lenore—
For the rare and radiant maiden whom the angels name Lenore—
Nameless here for evermore.

And the silken, sad, uncertain rustling of each purple curtain
Thrilled me—filled me with fantastic terrors never felt before;
So that now, to still the beating of my heart, I stood repeating
"'Tis some visitor entreating entrance at my chamber door—
Some late visitor entrcating entrance at my chamber door;—
This it is, and nothing more."

Presently my soul grew stronger; hesitating then no longer,
"Sir," said I, "or Madam, truly your forgiveness I implore;
But the fact is I was napping, and so gently you came rapping,
And so faintly you came tapping, tapping at my chamber door,
That I scarce was sure I heard you"—here I opened wide the door;—
Darkness there and nothing more.

Deep into that darkness peering, long I stood there wondering, fearing,
Doubting, dreaming dreams no mortal ever dared to dream before;
But the silence was unbroken, and the stillness gave no token,

And the only word there spoken was the whispered word, "Lenore!"
This I whispered, and an echo murmured back the word,
"Lenore!"—
Merely this and nothing more.

Back into the chamber turning, all my soul within me burning,
Soon again I heard a tapping somewhat louder than before.
"Surely," said I, "surely that is something at my window lattice;
Let me see, then, what thereat is, and this mystery explore—
Let my heart be still a moment and this mystery explore;—
'Tis the wind and nothing more!"

Open here I flung the shutter, when, with many a flirt and flutter,
In there stepped a stately Raven of the saintly days of yore.
Not the least obeisance made he; not a minute stopped or stayed he;
But, with mien of lord or lady, perched above my chamber door—
Perched upon a bust of Pallas just above my chamber door—
Perched, and sat, and nothing more.

Then this ebony bird beguiling my sad fancy into smiling,
By the grave and stern decorum of the countenance it wore,
"Though thy crest be shorn and shaven, thou," I said, "art sure
no craven,
Ghastly grim and ancient Raven wandering from the Nightly
shore—
Tell me what thy lordly name is on the Night's Plutonian shore!"
Quoth the Raven, "Nevermore."

Much I marveled this ungainly fowl to hear discourse so plainly,
Though its answer little meaning—little relevancy bore;
For we cannot help agreeing that no living human being
Ever yet was blessed with seeing bird above his chamber door—
Bird or beast upon the sculptured bust above his chamber door,
With such name as "Nevermore."

But the Raven, sitting lonely on the placid bust, spoke only
That one word, as if his soul in that one word he did outpour.

Nothing further then he uttered—not a feather then he fluttered—
Till I scarcely more than muttered, "Other friends have flown
before—
On the morrow he will leave me, as my Hopes have flown before."
Then the bird said, "Nevermore."

Startled at the stillness broken by reply so aptly spoken,
"Doubtless," said I, "what it utters is its only stock and store
Caught from some unhappy master whom unmerciful Disaster
Followed fast and followed faster till his songs one burden bore—
Till the dirges of his Hope that melancholy burden bore
Of 'Never—nevermore.'"

But the Raven still beguiling all my sad soul into smiling,
Straight I wheeled a cushioned seat in front of bird, and bust
and door;
Then, upon the velvet sinking, I betook myself to linking
Fancy unto fancy, thinking what this ominous bird of yore—
What this grim, ungainly, ghastly, gaunt and ominous bird of yore
Meant in croaking "Nevermore."

This I sat engaged in guessing, but no syllable expressing
To the fowl whose fiery eyes now burned into my bosom's core;
This and more I sat divining, with my head at ease reclining
On the cushion's velvet lining that the lamp-light gloated o'er,
But whose velvet violet lining with the lamp-light gloating o'er,
She shall press, ah, nevermore!

Then, methought, the air grew denser, perfumed from an unseen
censer
Swung by angels whose faint foot-falls tinkled on the tufted floor.
"Wretch," I cried, "thy God hath lent thee—by these angels he
hath sent thee
Respite—respite and nepenthe from thy memories of Lenore!
Quaff, oh quaff this kind nepenthe and forget this lost Lenore!"
Quoth the Raven, "Nevermore."

"Prophet!" said I, "thing of evil!—prophet still, if bird or devil!—
Whether Tempter sent, or whether tempest tossed thee here
ashore,
Desolate yet all undaunted, on this desert land enchanted—
On this home by Horror haunted—tell me truly, I implore—
Is there – is there balm in Gilead?—tell me—tell me, I implore!"
Quoth the Raven, "Nevermore."

"Prophet!" said I, "thing of evil!—prophet still, if bird or devil!
By that Heaven that bends above us—by that God we both
adore—
Tell this soul with sorrow laden if, within the distant Aidenn,
It shall clasp a sainted maiden whom the angels name Lenore—
Clasp a rare and radiant maiden whom the angels name Lenore."
Quoth the Raven, "Nevermore."

"Be that word our sign of parting, bird or fiend!" I shrieked,
upstarting—
"Get thee back into the tempest and the Night's Plutonian shore!
Leave no black plume as a token of that lie thy soul hath spoken!
Leave my loneliness unbroken!—quit the bust above my door!
Take thy beak from out my heart, and take thy form from off
my door!"
Quoth the Raven, "Nevermore."

And the Raven, never flitting, still is sitting, still is sitting
On the pallid bust of Pallas just above my chamber door;
And his eyes have all the seeming of a demon's that is dreaming,
And the lamp-light o'er him streaming throws his shadow on
the floor;
And my soul from out that shadow that lies floating on the floor
Shall be lifted—nevermore!

LENORE

Ah, broken is the golden bowl! the spirit flown forever!
Let the bell toll!—a saintly soul floats on the Stygian river;
And, Guy De Vere, hast thou no tear?—weep now or never more!
See! on yon drear and rigid bier low lies thy love, Lenore!
Come! let the burial rite be read—the funeral song be sung!—
An anthem for the queenliest dead that ever died so young—
A dirge for her the doubly dead in that she died so young.

"Wretches! ye loved her for her wealth and hated her for her pride,
And when she fell in feeble health, ye blessed her—that she died!
How shall the ritual, then, be read?—the requiem how be sung
By you—by yours, the evil eye,—by yours, the slanderous tongue
That did to death the innocence that died, and died so young?"

Peccavimus; but rave not thus! and let a Sabbath song
Go up to God so solemnly the dead may feel no wrong!
The sweet Lenore hath "gone before," with Hope, that flew beside,
Leaving thee wild for the dear child that should have been thy bride—
For her, the fair and *debonnaire*, that now so lowly lies,
The life upon her yellow hair but not within her eyes—
The life still there, upon her hair—the death upon her eyes.

"Avaunt! to-night my heart is light. No dirge will I upraise,
But waft the angel on her flight with a Pæan of old days!
Let *no* bell toll!—lest her sweet soul, amid its hallowed mirth,
Should catch the note, as it doth float—up from the damnéd Earth.
To friends above, from fiends below, the indignant ghost is riven—
From Hell unto a high estate far up within the Heaven—
From grief and groan, to a golden throne, beside the King of Heaven."

TO THE LAKE

In spring of youth it was my lot
To haunt of the wide earth a spot
The which I could not love the less—
So lovely was the loneliness
Of a wild lake, with black rock bound,
And the tall pines that towered around.

But when the Night had thrown her pall
Upon that spot, as upon all,
And the mystic wind went by
Murmuring in melody—
Then—ah then I would awake
To the terror of the lone lake.

Yet that terror was not fright,
But a tremulous delight—
A feeling not the jeweled mine
Could teach or bribe me to define—
Nor Love—although the Love were thine.

Death was in that poisonous wave,
And in its gulf a fitting grave
For him who thence could solace bring
To his lone imagining—
Whose solitary soul could make
An Eden of that dim lake.

THE SLEEPER

At midnight, in the month of June,
I stand beneath the mystic moon.
An opiate vapor, dewy, dim,
Exhales from out her golden rim,
And, softly dripping, drop by drop,
Upon the quiet mountain top,
Steals drowsily and musically
Into the universal valley.
The rosemary nods upon the grave;
The lily lolls upon the wave;
Wrapping the fog about its breast,
The ruin molders into rest;
Looking like Lethe, see! the lake
A conscious slumber seems to take,
And would not, for the world, awake.
All Beauty sleeps!—and lo! where lies
(Her casement open to the skies)
Irene, with her Destinies!

Oh, lady bright! can it be right—
This window open to the night?
The wanton airs, from the tree-top,
Laughingly through the lattice drop—
The bodiless airs, a wizard rout,
Flit through thy chamber in and out,
And wave the curtain canopy
So fitfully—so fearfully—
Above the closed and fringed lid
'Neath which thy slumb'ring soul lies hid,
That, o'er the floor and down the wall,
Like ghosts the shadows rise and fall!
Oh, lady dear, hast thou no fear?
Why and what art thou dreaming here?

Sure thou art come o'er far-off seas,
A wonder to these garden trees!
Strange is thy pallor! strange thy dress!
Strange, above all, thy length of tress,
And this all solemn silentness!

The lady sleeps! Oh, may her sleep,
Which is enduring, so be deep!
Heaven have her in its sacred keep!
This chamber changed for one more holy,
This bed for one more melancholy,
I pray to God that she may lie
Forever with unopened eye,
While the dim sheeted ghosts go by!

My love, she sleeps! Oh, may her sleep,
As it is lasting, so be deep!
Soft may the worms about her creep!
Far in the forest, dim and old,
For her may some tall vault unfold—
Some vault that oft hath flung its black
And winged panels fluttering back,
Triumphant, o'er the crested palls,
Of her grand family funerals—
Some sepulchre, remote, alone,
Against whose portal she hath thrown,
In childhood, many an idle stone—
Some tomb from out whose sounding door
She ne'er shall force an echo more,
Thrilling to think, poor child of sin!
It was the dead who groaned within.

FAIRYLAND

Dim vales—and shadowy floods—
And cloudy-looking woods,
Whose forms we can't discover
For the tears that drip all over
Huge moons there wax and wane—
Again—again—again—
Every moment of the night—
Forever changing places—
And they put out the star-light
With the breath from their pale faces.
About twelve by the moon-dial
One more filmy than the rest
(A kind which, upon trial,
They have found to be the best)
Comes down—still down—and down
With its center on the crown
Of a mountain's eminence,
While its wide circumference
In easy drapery falls
Over hamlets, over halls,
Wherever they may be—
O'er the strange woods—o'er the sea—
Over spirits on the wing—
Over every drowsy thing—
And buries them up quite
In a labyrinth of light—
And then, how deep!—O, deep!
Is the passion of their sleep.
In the morning they arise,
And their moony covering
Is soaring in the skies,
With the tempests as they toss,
Like——almost any thing—

Or a yellow Albatross.
They use that moon no more
For the same end as before—
Videlicet a tent—
Which I think extravagant:
Its atomies, however,
Into a shower dissever,
Of which those butterflies,
Of Earth, who seek the skies,
And so come down again
(Never-contented things!)
Have brought a specimen
Upon their quivering wings

THE VALLEY OF UNREST

Once it smiled a silent dell
Where the people did not dwell;
They had gone unto the wars,
Trusting to the mild-eyed stars,
Nightly, from their azure towers,
To keep watch above the flowers,
In the midst of which all day
The red sun-light lazily lay.
Now each visitor shall confess
The sad valley's restlessness.
Nothing there is motionless—
Nothing save the airs that brood
Over the magic solitude.
Ah, by no wind are stirred those trees
That palpitate like the chill seas
Around the misty Hebrides!
Ah, by no wind those clouds are driven
That rustle through the unquiet Heaven
Uneasily, from morn till even,
Over the violets there that lie
In myriad types of the human eye—
Over the lilies there that wave
And weep above a nameless grave!
They wave:—from out their fragrant tops
Eternal dews come down in drops.
They weep:—from off their delicate stems
Perennial tears descend in gems.

DREAMLAND

By a route obscure and lonely,
Haunted by ill angels only,
Where an Eidolon, named Night,
On a black throne reigns upright,
I have reached these lands but newly
From an ultimate dim Thule—
From a wild weird clime that lieth, sublime,
        Out of Space—out of Time.

Bottomless vales and boundless floods,
And chasms, and caves, and Titan woods,
With forms that no man can discover
For the dews that drip all over;
Mountains toppling evermore
Into seas without a shore;
Seas that restlessly aspire,
Surging, unto skies of fire;
Lakes that endlessly outspread
Their lone waters—lone and dead,—
Their still waters—still and chilly
With the snows of the lolling lily.

By the lakes that thus outspread
Their lone waters, lone and dead,—
Their sad waters, sad and chilly
With the snows of the lolling lily,—
By the mountains—near the river
Murmuring lowly, murmuring ever,—
By the gray woods,—by the swamp
Where the toad and the newt encamp,—
By the dismal tarns and pools
        Where dwell the Ghouls,—
By each spot the most unholy—

In each nook most melancholy,—
There the traveler meets aghast
Sheeted Memories of the Past—
Shrouded forms that start and sigh
As they pass the wanderer by—
White-robed forms of friends long given,
In agony, to the Earth—and Heaven.

For the heart whose woes are legion
'Tis a peaceful, soothing region—
For the spirit that walks in shadow
'Tis—oh 'tis an Eldorado!
But the traveler, traveling through it,
May not—dare not openly view it;
Never its mysteries are exposed
To the weak human eye unclosed;
So wills its King, who hath forbid
The uplifting of the fringed lid;
And thus the sad Soul that here passes
Beholds it but through darkened glasses.

By a route obscure and lonely,
Haunted by ill angels only,
Where an Eidolon, named Night,
On a black throne reigns upright,
I have wandered home but newly
From this ultimate dim Thule.

TO HELEN

Helen, thy beauty is to me
    Like those Nicean barks of yore,
That gently, o'er a perfumed sea,
    The weary way-worn wanderer bore
    To his own native shore.

On desperate seas long wont to roam,
    Thy hyacinth hair, thy classic face,
Thy Naiad airs have brought me home
    To the glory that was Greece,
And the grandeur that was Rome.

Lo! in yon brilliant window-niche
    How statue-like I see thee stand,
    The agate lamp within thy hand!
Ah, Psyche, from the regions which
    Are Holy-land!

TO ONE IN PARADISE

Thou wast all that to me, love,
For which my soul did pine—
A green isle in the sea, love,
A fountain and a shrine,
All wreathed with fairy fruits and flowers,
And all the flowers were mine.

Ah, dream too bright to last!
Ah, starry Hope! that didst arise
But to be overcast!
A voice from out the Future cries,
"On! on!"—but o'er the Past
(Dim gulf!) my spirit hovering lies
Mute, motionless, aghast!

For, alas! alas! with me
The light of Life is o'er!
No more—no more—no more—
(Such language holds the solemn sea
To the sands upon the shore)
Shall bloom the thunder-blasted tree,
Or the stricken eagle soar!

And all my days are trances,
And all my nightly dreams
Are where thy dark eye glances,
And where thy footstep gleams—
In what ethereal dances,
By what eternal streams.

ISRAFEL

In Heaven a spirit doth dwell
  "Whose heart-strings are a lute;"
None sing so wildly well
As the angel Israfel,
And the giddy stars (so legends tell)
Ceasing their hymns, attend the spell
  Of his voice, all mute.

Tottering above
  In her highest noon,
  The enamored moon
Blushes with love,
  While, to listen, the red levin
  (With the rapid Pleiads, even,
  Which were seven,)
  Pauses in Heaven.

And they say (the starry choir
  And the other listening things)
That Israfel's fire
Is owing to that lyre
  By which he sits and sings—
The trembling living wire
Of those unusual strings.

But the skies that angel trod,
  Where deep thoughts are a duty—
Where Love's a grown-up God—
  Where the Houri glances are
Imbued with all the beauty
  Which we worship in a star.

Therefore, thou art not wrong,
  Israfel, who despisest
An unimpassioned song;
To thee the laurels belong,
  Best bard, because the wisest!
Merrily live, and long!

The ecstasies above
  With thy burning measures suit—
Thy grief, thy joy, thy hate, thy love,
  With the fervor of thy lute—
  Well may the stars be mute!

Yes, Heaven is thine; but this
  Is a world of sweets and sours;
  Our flowers are merely—flowers,
And the shadow of thy perfect bliss
  Is the sunshine of ours.

If I could dwell
Where Israfel
  Hath dwelt, and he where I,
He might not sing so wildly well
  A mortal melody,
While a bolder note than this might swell
  From my lyre within the sky.

ROMANCE

Romance, who loves to nod and sing,
With drowsy head and folded wing,
Among the green leaves as they shake
Far down within some shadowy lake,
To me a painted paroquet
Hath been—a most familiar bird—
Taught me my alphabet to say—
To lisp my very earliest word
While in the wild wood I did lie,
A child—with a most knowing eye.

Of late, eternal Condor years
So shake the very Heaven on high
With tumult as they thunder by,
I have no time for idle cares
Through gazing on the unquiet sky.
And when an hour with calmer wings
Its down upon my spirit flings—
That little time with lyre and rhyme
To while away—forbidden things!
My heart would feel to be a crime
Unless it trembled with the strings.

THE CITY IN THE SEA

Lo! Death has reared himself a throne
In a strange city lying alone
Far down within the dim West
Where the good and the bad and the worst and the best
Have gone to their eternal rest.
There shrines and palaces and towers
(Time-eaten towers that tremble not!)
Resemble nothing that is ours.
Around, by lifting winds forgot,
Resignedly beneath the sky
The melancholy waters lie.

No rays from the holy Heaven come down
On the long night-time of that town;
But light from out the lurid sea
Streams up the turrets silently—
Gleams up the pinnacles far and free—
Up domes—up spires—up kingly halls—
Up fanes—up Babylon-like walls—
Up shadowy long-forgotten bowers
Of sculptured ivy and stone flowers—
Up many and many a marvelous shrine
Whose wreathed friezes intertwine
The viol, the violet, and the vine.
Resignedly beneath the sky
The melancholy waters lie.
So blend the turrets and shadows there
That all seem pendulous in air,
While from a proud tower in the town
Death looks gigantically down.

There open fanes and gaping graves
Yawn level with the luminous waves;

But not the riches there that lie
In each idol's diamond eye—
Not the gaily-jeweled dead
Tempt the waters from their bed;
For no ripples curl, alas!
Along that wilderness of glass—
No swellings tell that winds may be
Upon some far-off happier sea—
No heavings hint that winds have been
On seas less hideously serene.

But lo, a stir is in the air!
The wave—there is a movement there!
As if the towers had thrown aside,
In slightly sinking, the dull tide—
As if their tops had feebly given
A void within the filmy Heaven.
The waves have now a redder glow—
The hours are breathing faint and low—
And when, amid no earthly moans,
Down, down that town shall settle hence,
Hell, rising from a thousand thrones,
Shall do it reverence.

THE CONQUEROR WORM

Lo! 'tis a gala night
Within the lonesome latter years!
An angel throng, bewinged, bedight
In veils, and drowned in tears,
Sit in a theater, to see
A play of hopes and fears,
While the orchestra breathes fitfully
The music of the spheres.

Mimes, in the form of God on high,
Mutter and mumble low,
And hither and thither fly—
Mere puppets they, who come and go
At bidding of vast formless things
That shift the scenery to and fro,
Flapping from out their Condor wings
Invisible Woe!

That motley drama—oh, be sure
It shall not be forgot!
With its Phantom chased for evermore,
By a crowd that seize it not,
Through a circle that ever returneth in
To the self-same spot,
And much of Madness, and more of Sin,
And Horror the soul of the plot.

But see, amid the mimic rout
A crawling shape intrude!
A blood-red thing that writhes from out
The scenic solitude!
It writhes!—it writhes!—with mortal pangs
The mimes become its food,

And the angels sob at vermin fangs
    In human gore imbued.

Out—out are the lights—out all!
    And, over each quivering form,
The curtain, a funeral pall,
    Comes down with the rush of a storm,
And the angels, all pallid and wan,
    Uprising, unveiling, affirm
That the play is the tragedy, "Man,"
    And its hero the Conqueror Worm.

THE HAUNTED PALACE

In the greenest of our valleys
By good angels tenanted,
Once a fair and stately palace—
Radiant palace—reared its head.
In the monarch Thought's dominion—
It stood there!
Never seraph spread a pinion
Over fabric half so fair!

Banners yellow, glorious, golden,
On its roof did float and flow,
(This—all this—was in the olden
Time long ago)
And every gentle air that dallied,
In that sweet day,
Along the ramparts plumed and pallid,
A wingéd odor went away.

Wanderers in that happy valley,
Through two luminous windows, saw
Spirits moving musically,
To a lute's well-tunéd law,
Round about a throne where, sitting
(Porphyrogene!)
In state his glory well befitting,
The ruler of the realm was seen.

And all with pearl and ruby glowing
Was the fair palace door,
Through which came flowing, flowing, flowing,
And sparkling evermore,
A troop of Echoes, whose sweet duty
Was but to sing,

In voices of surpassing beauty,
  The wit and wisdom of their king.

But evil things, in robes of sorrow,
  Assailed the monarch's high estate.
(Ah, let us mourn!—for never morrow
  Shall dawn upon him desolate!)
And round about his home the glory
  That blushed and bloomed,
Is but a dim-remembered story
  Of the old time entombed.

And travelers, now, within that valley,
  Through the red-litten windows see
Vast forms, that move fantastically
  To a discordant melody,
While, like a ghastly rapid river,
  Through the pale door
A hideous throng rush out forever
  And laugh—but smile no more.

SONNET—TO SILENCE

There are some qualities—some incorporate things,
　That have a double life, which thus is made
A type of that twin entity which springs
　From matter and light, evinced in solid and shade.
There is a two-fold *Silence*—sea and shore—
　Body and soul. One dwells in lonely places,
　Newly with grass o'ergrown; some solemn graces,
Some human memories and tearful lore,
Render him terrorless: his name's "No More."
He is the corporate Silence: dread him not!
　No power hath he of evil in himself;
But should some urgent fate (untimely lot!)
　Bring thee to meet his shadow (nameless elf,
That haunteth the lone regions where hath trod
No foot of man,) commend thyself to God!

TAMERLANE

Kind solace in a dying hour!
Such, father, is not (now) my theme—
I will not madly deem that power
Of Earth may shrive me of the sin
Unearthly pride hath revel'd in—
I have no time to dote or dream:
You call it hope—that fire of fire!
It is but agony of desire:
If I *can* hope—Oh God! I can—
Its fount is holier—more divine—
I would not call thee fool, old man,
But such is not a gift of thine.

Know thou the secret of a spirit
Bow'd from its wild pride into shame.
O yearning heart! I did inherit
Thy withering portion with the fame,
The searing glory which hath shone
Amid the jewels of my throne,
Halo of Hell! and with a pain
Not Hell shall make me fear again—
O craving heart, for the lost flowers
And sunshine of my summer hours!
Th' undying voice of that dead time,
With its interminable chime,
Rings, in the spirit of a spell,
Upon thy emptiness—a knell.

I have not always been as now:
The fever'd diadem on my brow
I claim'd and won usurpingly—
Hath not the same fierce heirdom given
Rome to the Cæsar—this to me?

The heritage of a kingly mind,
And a proud spirit which hath striven
Triumphantly with human kind.

On mountain soil I first drew life:
The mists of the Taglay have shed
Nightly their dews upon my head,
And, I believe, the winged strife
And tumult of the headlong air
Have nestled in my very hair.

So late from Heaven—that dew—it fell
('Mid dreams of an unholy night)
Upon me with the touch of Hell,
While the red flashing of the light
From clouds that hung, like banners, o'er,
Appeared to my half-closing eye
The pageantry of monarchy,
And the deep trumpet-thunder's roar
Came hurriedly upon me, telling
Of human battle, where my voice,
My own voice, silly child!—was swelling
(O! how my spirit would rejoice,
And leap within me at the cry)
The battle-cry of Victory!

The rain came down upon my head
Unshelter'd—and the heavy wind
Rendered me mad and deaf and blind.
It was but man, I thought, who shed
Laurels upon me: and the rush—
The torrent of the chilly air
Gurgled within my ear the crush
Of empires—with the captive's prayer—
The hum of suitors—and the tone
Of flattery 'round a sovereign's throne.

My passions, from that hapless hour,
Usurp'd a tyranny which men
Have deem'd, since I have reach'd to power;
My innate nature—be it so:
But, father, there liv'd one who, then,
Then—in my boyhood—when their fire
Burn'd with a still intenser glow,
(For passion must, with youth, expire)
E'en *then* who knew this iron heart
In woman's weakness had a part.

I have no words—alas!—to tell
The loveliness of loving well!
Nor would I now attempt to trace
The more than beauty of a face
Whose lineaments, upon my mind,
Are——shadows on th' unstable wind:
Thus I remember having dwelt
Some page of early lore upon,
With loitering eye, till I have felt
The letters—with their meaning—melt
To fantasies—with none.

O, she was worthy of all love!
Love—as in infancy was mine—
'Twas such as angel minds above
Might envy; her young heart the shrine
On which my every hope and thought
Were incense—then a goodly gift,
For they were childish and upright—
Pure——as her young example taught:
Why did I leave it, and, adrift,
Trust to the fire within, for light?

We grew in age—and love—together—
Roaming the forest, and the wild;
My breast her shield in wintry weather—

And, when the friendly sunshine smil'd,
And she would mark the opening skies,
I saw no Heaven—but in her eyes.

Young Love's first lesson is——the heart:
For 'mid that sunshine, and those smiles,
When, from our little cares apart,
And laughing at her girlish wiles,
I'd throw me on her throbbing breast,
And pour my spirit out in tears—
There was no need to speak the rest—
No need to quiet any fears
Of her—who ask'd no reason why,
But turn'd on me her quiet eye!

Yet *more* than worthy of the love
My spirit struggled with, and strove,
When, on the mountain peak, alone,
Ambition lent it a new tone—
I had no being—but in thee:
The world, and all it did contain
In the earth—the air—the sea—
Its joy—its little lot of pain
That was new pleasure——the ideal,
Dim, vanities of dreams by night—
And dimmer nothings which were real—
(Shadows—and a more shadowy light!)
Parted upon their misty wings,
And, so, confusedly, became
Thine image, and—a name—a name!
Two separate—yet most intimate things.

I was ambitious—have you known
The passion, father? You have not:
A cottager, I mark'd a throne
Of half the world as all my own,
And murmur'd at such lowly lot—

But, just like any other dream,
        Upon the vapor of the dew
My own had past, did not the beam
        Of beauty which did while it thro'
The minute—the hour—the day—oppress
My mind with double loveliness.

We walk'd together on the crown
Of a high mountain which look'd down
Afar from its proud natural towers
    Of rock and forest, on the hills—
The dwindled hills! begirt with bowers
    And shouting with a thousand rills.

I spoke to her of power and pride,
    But mystically—in such guise
That she might deem it nought beside
    The moment's converse; in her eyes
I read, perhaps too carelessly—
    A mingled feeling with my own—
The flush on her bright cheek, to me
    Seem'd to become a queenly throne
Too well that I should let it be
    Light in the wilderness alone.

I wrapp'd myself in grandeur then,
    And donn'd a visionary crown——
        Yet it was not that Fantasy
        Had thrown her mantle over me—
But that, among the rabble—men,
        Lion ambition is chain'd down—
And crouches to a keeper's hand—
Not so in deserts where the grand—
The wild—the terrible conspire
With their own breath to fan his fire.

Look 'round thee now on Samarcand!—

Is not she queen of Earth? her pride
Above all cities? in her hand
Their destinies? in all beside
Of glory which the world hath known
Stands she not nobly and alone?
Falling—her veriest stepping-stone
Shall form the pedestal of a throne—
And who her sovereign? Timour—he
Whom the astonished people saw
Striding o'er empires haughtily
A diadem'd outlaw!

O, human love! thou spirit given,
On Earth, of all we hope in Heaven!
Which fall'st into the soul like rain
Upon the Siroc-wither'd plain,
And, failing in thy power to bless,
But leav'st the heart a wilderness!
Idea! which bindest life around
With music of so strange a sound
And beauty of so wild a birth—
Farewell! for I have won the Earth!

When Hope, the eagle that tower'd, could see
No cliff beyond him in the sky,
His pinions were bent droopingly—
And homeward turn'd his soften'd eye.
'Twas sunset: when the sun will part
There comes a sullenness of heart
To him who still would look upon
The glory of the summer sun.
That soul will hate the ev'ning mist
So often lovely, and will list
To the sound of the coming darkness (known
To those whose spirits hearken) as one
Who, in a dream of night, *would* fly
But *cannot* from a danger nigh.

What tho' the moon—the white moon
Shed all the splendor of her noon,
Her smile is chilly—and *her* beam,
In that time of dreariness, will seem
(So like you gather in your breath)
A portrait taken after death.
And boyhood is a summer sun
Whose waning is the dreariest one—
For all we live to know is known
And all we seek to keep hath flown—
Let life, then, as the day-flower, fall
With the noon-day beauty—which is all.
I reach'd my home—my home no more—
    For all had flown who made it so.
I pass'd from out its mossy door,
    And, tho' my tread was soft and low,
A voice came from the threshold stone
Of one whom I had earlier known—
    O, I defy thee, Hell, to show
    On beds of fire that burn below,
    An humbler heart—a deeper woe.

Father, I firmly do believe—
    I *know*—for Death who comes for me
        From regions of the blest afar,
Where there is nothing to deceive,
        Hath left his iron gate ajar,
    And rays of truth you cannot see
    Are flashing thro' Eternity—
I do believe that Eblis hath
A snare in every human path—
Else how, when in the holy grove
I wandered of the idol, Love,
Who daily scents his snowy wings
With incense of burnt offerings
From the most unpolluted things,
Whose pleasant bowers are yet so riven

Above with trellis'd rays from Heaven
No mote may shun—no tiniest fly
The light'ning of his eagle eye—
How was it that Ambition crept,
    Unseen, amid the revels there,
Till growing bold, he laughed and leapt
    In the tangles of Love's very hair?

ELDORADO

Gaily bedight,
A gallant knight,
In sunshine and in shadow,
Had journeyed long,
Singing a song,
In search of Eldorado.

But he grew old—
This knight so bold—
And o'er his heart a shadow
Fell as he found
No spot of ground
That looked like Eldorado.

And, as his strength
Failed him at length,
He met a pilgrim shadow—
"Shadow," said he,
"Where can it be—
This land of Eldorado?"

"Over the Mountains
Of the Moon,
Down the Valley of the Shadow,
Ride, boldly ride,"
The shade replied,—
"If you seek for Eldorado!"

THE BELLS

I

HEAR the sledges with the bells—
Silver bells!
What a world of merriment their melody foretells!
How they tinkle, tinkle, tinkle,
In the icy air of night!
While the stars that oversprinkle
All the heavens, seem to twinkle
With a crystalline delight;
Keeping time, time, time,
In a sort of Runic rhyme,
To the tintinabulation that so musically wells
From the bells, bells, bells, bells,
Bells, bells, bells—
From the jingling and the tinkling of the bells.

II

Hear the mellow wedding bells,
Golden bells!
What a world of happiness their harmony foretells!
Through the balmy air of night
How they ring out their delight!
From the molten-golden notes,
And all in tune,
What a liquid ditty floats
To the turtle-dove that listens, while she gloats
On the moon!
Oh, from out the sounding cells,
What a gush of euphony voluminously wells!
How it swells!
How it dwells
On the Future! how it tells

Of the rapture that impels
To the swinging and the ringing
Of the bells, bells, bells,
Of the bells, bells, bells, bells,
Bells, bells, bells—
To the rhyming and the chiming of the bells!

III

Hear the loud alarum bells—
Brazen bells!
What a tale of terror, now, their turbulency tells!
In the startled ear of night
How they scream out their affright!
Too much horrified to speak,
They can only shriek, shriek,
Out of tune,
In a clamorous appealing to the mercy of the fire,
In a mad expostulation with the deaf and frantic fire,
Leaping higher, higher, higher,
With a desperate desire,
And a resolute endeavor
Now—now to sit or never,
By the side of the pale-faced moon.
Oh, the bells, bells, bells!
What a tale their terror tells
Of Despair!
How they clang, and clash, and roar!
What a horror they outpour
On the bosom of the palpitating air!
Yet the ear it fully knows,
By the twanging,
And the clanging,
How the danger ebbs and flows;
Yet the ear distinctly tells,
In the jangling,
And the wrangling,

How the danger sinks and swells,
By the sinking or the swelling in the anger of the bells—
Of the bells—
Of the bells, bells, bells, bells,
Bells, bells, bells—
In the clamor and the clangor of the bells!

IV

Hear the tolling of the bells—
Iron bells!
What a world of solemn thought their monody compels!
In the silence of the night,
How we shiver with affright
At the melancholy menace of their tone!
For every sound that floats
From the rust within their throats
Is a groan.
And the people—ah, the people—
They that dwell up in the steeple,
All alone,
And who tolling, tolling, tolling,
In that muffled monotone,
Feel a glory in so rolling
On the human heart a stone—
They are neither man nor woman—
They are neither brute nor human—
They are Ghouls:
And their king it is who tolls;
And he rolls, rolls, rolls,
Rolls
A pæan from the bells!
And his merry bosom swells
With the pæan of the bells!
And he dances, and he yells;
Keeping time, time, time,
In a sort of Runic rhyme,

To the pæan of the bells—
Of the bells:
Keeping time, time, time,
In a sort of Runic rhyme,
To the throbbing of the bells—
Of the bells, bells, bells—
To the sobbing of the bells;
Keeping time, time, time,
As he knells, knells, knells,
In a happy Runic rhyme,
To the rolling of the bells—
Of the bells, bells, bells—
To the tolling of the bells,
Of the bells, bells, bells, bells—
Bells, bells, bells—
To the moaning and the groaning of the bells.

ALONE

From childhood's hour I have not been
As others were—I have not seen
As others saw—I could not bring
My passions from a common spring—
From the same source I have not taken
My sorrow—I could not awaken
My heart to joy at the same tone—
And all I lov'd—*I* lov>d alone—
Then—in my childhood—in the dawn
Of a most stormy life—was drawn
From ev'ry depth of good and ill
The mystery which binds me still—
From the torrent, or the fountain—
From the red cliff of the mountain—
From the sun that 'round me roll'd
In its autumn tint of gold—
From the lightning in the sky
As it pass'd me flying by—
From the thunder, and the storm—
And the cloud that took the form
(When the rest of Heaven was blue)
Of a daemon in my view—

A DREAM WITHIN A DREAM

TAKE this kiss upon the brow!
And, in parting from you now,
Thus much let me avow—
You are not wrong, who deem
That my days have been a dream;
Yet if hope has flown away
In a night, or in a day,
In a vision, or in none,
s it therefore the less *gone?*
All that we see or seem
Is but a dream within a dream.

I stand amid the roar
Of a surf-tormented shore,
And I hold within my hand
Grains of the golden sand—
How few! yet how they creep
hrough my fingers to the deep,
While I weep—while I weep!
O God! can I not grasp
Them with a tighter clasp?
O God! can I not save
One from the pitiless wave?
Is *all* that we see or seem
But a dream within a dream?

ANNABEL LEE

It was many and many a year ago,
In a kingdom by the sea,
That a maiden there lived whom you may know
By the name of Annabel Lee;
And this maiden she lived with no other thought
Than to love and be loved by me.

I was a child and *she* was a child,
In this kingdom by the sea:
But we loved with a love that was more than love—
I and my Annabel Lee;
With a love that the winged seraphs of heaven
Coveted her and me.

And this was the reason that, long ago,
In this kingdom by the sea,
A wind blew out of a cloud,
Chilling my beautiful Annabel Lee;
So that her highborn kinsman came
And bore her away from me,
To shut her up in a sepulchre
In this kingdom by the sea.

The angels, not half so happy in heaven,
 Went envying her and me—
Yes!—that was the reason (as all men know,
 In this kingdom by the sea)
That the wind came out of the cloud by night, chilling
 And killing my ANNABEL LEE.

But our love it was stronger by far than the love
 Of those who were older than we—
 Of many far wiser than we—
And neither the angels in heaven above,
 Nor the demons down under the sea,
Can ever dissever my soul from the soul
 Of the beautiful ANNABEL LEE:

For the moon never beams, without bringing me dreams
 Of the beautiful ANNABEL LEE;
And the stars never rise, but I feel the bright eyes
 Of the beautiful ANNABEL LEE;
And so, all the night-tide, I lie down by the side
Of my darling—my darling—my life and my bride,
 In the sepulchre there by the sea,
 In her tomb by the sounding sea.

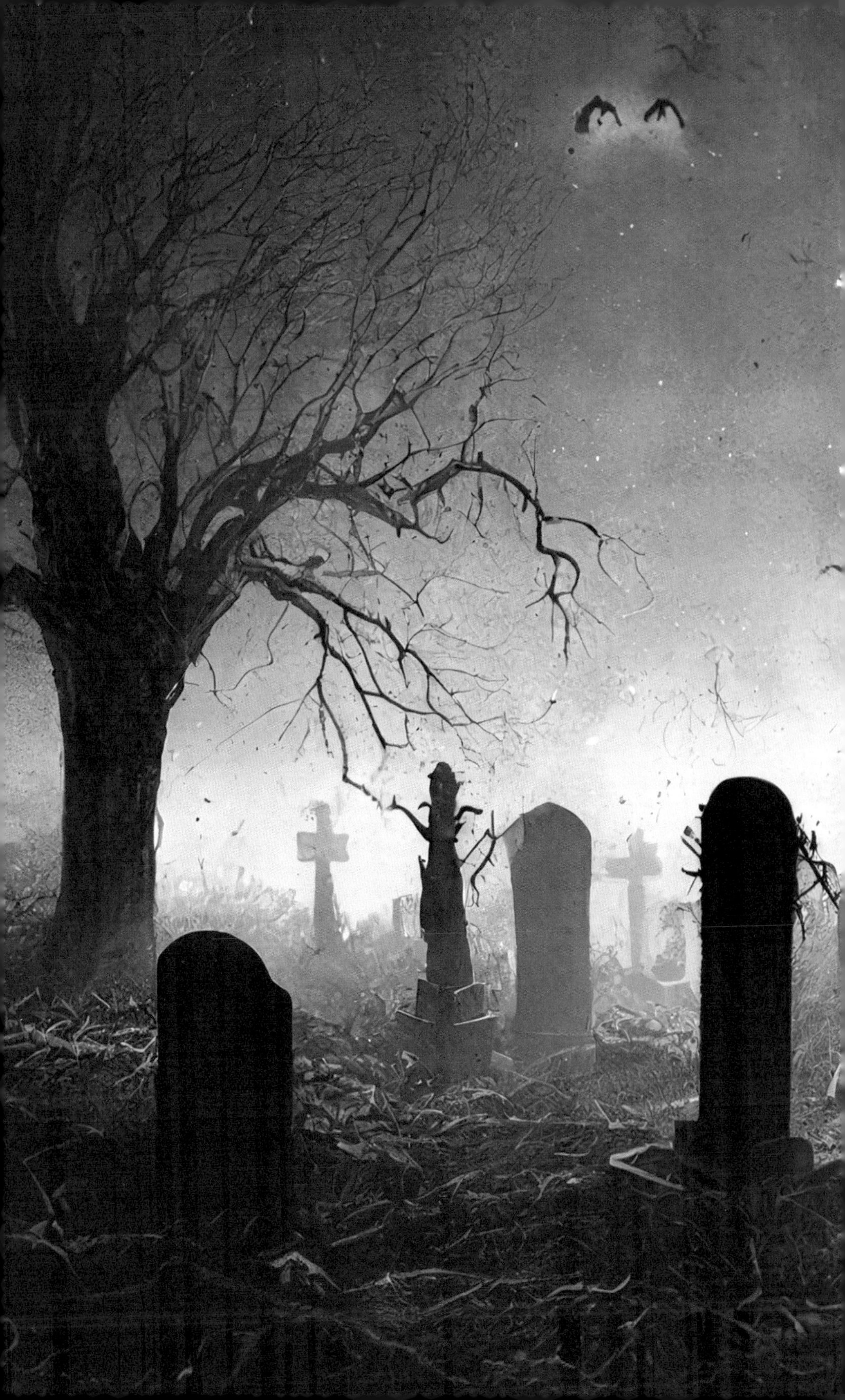